LASHER

ANNE RICE

arrow books

Published by Arrow Books in 2004

20

First published in Great Britain in 1993 by
Chatto & Windus

Arrow Books
Random House, 20 Vauxhall Bridge Road,
London SW1V 2SA

www.randomhouse.co.uk

Addresses for companies within The Random House Group Limited
can be found at: www.randomhouse.co.uk/offices.htm

The Random House Group Limited Reg. No. 954009

A CIP catalogue record for this book
is available from the British Library

ISBN 9780099471431

Penguin Random House is committed to a sustainable future for
our business, our readers and our planet. This book is made from
Forest Stewardship Council® certified paper.

Printed and bound in Great Britain by Clays Ltd, Elcograf S.p.A.

The sow came in with the saddle.
The little pig rocked the cradle.
The dish jumped over the table
To see the pot swallow the ladle.
The spit that stood behind the door
Threw the pudding-stick on the floor.
'Odsplut!' said the gridiron,
'Can't you agree?
I'm the head constable,
Bring them to me!'

MOTHER GOOSE

ONE

In the beginning was the voice of Father.

'Emaleth!' whispering close to her mother's belly while her mother slept. And then singing to her, the long songs of the past. Songs of the Glen of Donnelaith and of the castle, and of where they would sometime come together, and how she would be born knowing all that Father knew. It is our way, he said to her in the fast language, which others could not understand.

To others it sounded like humming, or whistling. It was their secret tongue, for they could hear syllables which ran too fast for the others to grasp. They could sing out to each other. Emaleth could almost do it, almost speak –

'Emaleth, my darling, Emaleth, my daughter, Emaleth, my mate.' Father was waiting for her. She had to grow fast and grow strong for Father. When the time came, Mother had to help her. She had to drink Mother's milk.

Mother slept. Mother cried. Mother dreamed. Mother was sick. And when Father and Mother quarreled, the world trembled. Emaleth knew dread.

But Father always came after, singing to her, reminding her that the words of his song were too rapid for Mother to comprehend. The melody made Emaleth feel as if the tiny round world in which she lived had expanded and she was floating in a place without limits, pushed hither and thither by Father's song.

Father said poetry which was beautiful, especially words that rhyme. Rhymes made a thrill pass through Emaleth. She stretched her legs and her arms, and turned her head this way and that, it felt so good, the rhymes.

Mother didn't talk to Emaleth. Mother wasn't supposed to know that Emaleth was there. Emaleth was tiny, said Father, but perfectly formed. Emaleth already had her long hair.

But when Mother talked, Emaleth understood her; when Mother wrote, Emaleth saw the words. Emaleth heard Mother's frequent whisper. She knew that Mother was afraid. Sometimes she saw Mother's dreams. She saw the face of Michael. She saw fighting. She saw Father's face as Mother saw it and it made Mother sad.

Father loved Mother, but Mother made him fiercely angry, and when he struck Mother, Mother suffered, even falling, and Emaleth screamed, or tried to scream. But Father always came after, while Mother slept, and said Emaleth must not fear. That they would come together in the circle of stones at Donnelaith, and then he told stories to her of the old days, when all the beautiful ones had lived on an island, and it was Paradise, before the others and the little people had come.

Sad and sorrowful the weakness of humans and the tragedy of the little people, and is it not better that all be driven from the Earth?

'I tell you the things I know now. And things that were told to me,' he said. And Emaleth saw the circle of stones, and the tall figure of Father as he was now, strumming the strings of the harp. Everyone was dancing. She saw the little people hiding in the shadows, spiteful and angry. She did not like them, she did not want them to steal down into the town. They loathe us instinctively, said Father, of the little people. How can they not? But they do not matter now. They are only a lingering from dreams which failed to come true.

Now is the hour. The hour for Emaleth and Father.

She saw Father in the old days, with his arms out stretched. This was Christmas and the glen was filled with snow. The Scots pines were close. Hymns rose from the people. Emaleth loved the rise and fall of the voices. There was so much she must see and learn later on.

'If we are separated, my beloved, come to the glen at Donnelaith. You can find it. You can do this. People are searching for Mother, people who would divide us. But remember, you will be born into this world knowing all you need to know. Now can you answer me?'

Emaleth tried but she could not.

'Taltos,' he said, and kissed Mother's belly, 'I hear you, darling, I love you.' And while Mother slept Emaleth was happy, because when Mother woke, Mother would cry.

'You think I wouldn't kill him in an instant?' Father said to Mother. They were fighting about Michael. 'I would kill him just like that. You leave me, and what makes you think that won't happen?'

Emaleth saw this person, Michael, whom Mother loved and Father did not. Michael lived in New Orleans in a great house. Father wanted to go back to the great house. He wanted to possess it, it was his house, and it made him deeply angry that Michael was there. But he knew he must bide his time. Emaleth had to come to him, tall and strong. There had to be the Beginning. He wanted them to come together in the Glen of Donnelaith. Beginning was everything. There was nothing if there was no beginning.

Prosper, my daughter.

Taltos.

No one lived in Donnelaith anymore. But they would live there – Father and Emaleth and their children. Hundreds of children. It would become the shrine of the Beginning. 'Our Bethlehem,' he whispered to her. And that would be the beginning of all time.

It was dark. Mother cried against the pillow, Michael, Michael, Michael.

Emaleth knew when the sun rose.

The color of everything brightened, and she saw Mother's hand high above her, dark and thin and immense, covering the whole world.

TWO

The house was all dark now. The cars were gone, and only one light burned in Michael Curry's window, in the old room where Cousin Deirdre had died. Mona understood exactly what had happened tonight and had to admit she was glad. She had almost planned it, almost . . .

She'd told her father she would go back to Metairie with Uncle Ryan and Cousin Jenn and Clancy, but then she hadn't told Uncle Ryan. And Uncle Ryan was long gone, assuming as everyone would that Mona had gone home to Amelia Street with her father, which of course she had not.

She'd been in the cemetery losing her bet that David wouldn't do it with her, right there on Mardi Gras Night in front of the Mayfair tomb. David had done it. Not so very great, actually, but for a fifteen-year-old not bad. And Mona had loved it – sneaking away with him, his fear and her excitement, their climbing the whitewashed wall of the cemetery together and creeping through the alleyways of high marble tombs. To lie right down on the gravel path in the dampness and cold, that had been no small part of the dare, but she'd done it, smoothing her skirt under her, so that she could pull down her panties without getting dirty. 'Now do it!' she'd said to David, who hadn't needed any more encouragement, or direct orders, by that time at all. She'd stared past him at the cold cloudy sky, at a single visible star, and then let her eyes move up the wall of little rectangular tombstones to the name: Deirdre Mayfair.

Then David had finished. Just like that.

'You're not afraid of anything,' he had said after.

'Like I'm supposed to be afraid of you?' She'd sat up, cheated, having not even pretended to enjoy it, overheated and really not much liking her cousin David, but still satisfied that it had been done.

Mission accomplished, she would write in her computer later, in the secret directory \WS\MONA\ AGENDA, where she deposited all her confessions of the triumphs she could not share with anyone in the world. No one could crack her computer system, not even Uncle Ryan or Cousin Pierce, each of whom she had caught, at various times, firing up her system, and searching through various directories – 'Some setup, Mona.' All it was, was the fastest 386 IBM clone on the market, with max memory and max hard drive. Ah, what people didn't know about computers. It always amazed Mona. She herself learned more about them every day.

Yes, this was a moment that only the computer would witness. Maybe they would start to be a regular occurrence now that her father and mother were truly drinking themselves to death. And there were so many Mayfairs to be conquered. In fact, her agenda did not even include non-Mayfairs at this point, except, of course, for Michael Curry, but he was a Mayfair now, most definitely. The whole family had him in its grip.

Michael Curry in that house alone. Take stock. It

was Mardi Gras Night, 10 p.m., three hours after Comus, and Mona Mayfair was on her own, and on the corner of First and Chestnut, light as a ghost, looking at *the* house, with the whole soft dark night to do as she pleased.

Her father was surely passed out by now; in fact somebody had probably driven him home. If he'd walked the thirteen blocks up to Amelia and St Charles, that was a miracle. He'd been so drunk before Comus even passed that he'd sat right down on the neutral ground on St Charles, knees up, hands on a naked bottle of Southern Comfort, drinking right in front of Uncle Ryan and Aunt Bea and whoever else cared to look at him, and telling Mona in no uncertain terms to leave him alone.

Fine with Mona. Michael Curry had picked her up just like she weighed nothing and put her on his shoulders for the entire parade. How good it had felt to be riding that strong man, with one hand in his soft curly black hair. She'd loved the feeling of his face against her thighs, and she'd hugged him just a little, much as she dared, and let her left hand rest against his cheek.

Some man, Michael Curry. And her father much too drunk to notice anything that she did.

As for Mona's mother, she'd passed out Mardi Gras afternoon. If she ever woke up to see Comus pass St Charles and Amelia, that was a miracle too. Ancient Evelyn was there of course, her usual silent self, but she was awake. She knew what went on. If Alicia set the bed on fire, Ancient Evelyn could call for help. And you really couldn't leave Alicia alone anymore.

The point was, everything was covered. Even Michael's Aunt Vivian was not at home at First Street.

She'd gone uptown for the night with Aunt Cecilia. Mona had seen them leave right after the parade. And Aaron Lightner, that mysterious scholar, he'd taken off with Aunt Bea. Mona had heard them planning it. Her car? His? It made Mona happy to think of Beatrice Mayfair and Aaron Lightner together. Aaron Lightner sloughed off ten years when he was around Beatrice, and she was that kind of gray-haired woman who can make men look at her anywhere and everywhere she goes. If she went into Walgreen's, the men came out of the stock room to help her. Or some gentleman asked her opinion on a good dandruff shampoo. It was almost a joke, the way Aunt Bea attracted men, but Aaron Lightner was a man she wanted, and that was new.

If that old maid, Eugenia, was there, that was OK because she was tucked away in the farthest back bedroom and they said, once she drank her nightly glass of port, nothing could wake her up.

Nobody in that house – practically speaking – but her man. And now that Mona knew the history of the Mayfair Witches – now that she had finally got her hands on Aaron Lightner's long document – there was no keeping her out of First Street any longer. Of course she had her questions about what she'd read; thirteen witches descended from a Scottish village called Donnelaith where the first, a poor cunning woman, had been burnt at the stake in 1659. It was just the kind of juicy history you dreamed about having. Well, she did anyway.

But there had been things in that long family tale that had special meaning for her, and the long account of Oncle Julien's life had been the most intriguing part of all.

Even Mona's very own Aunt Gifford was far away from New Orleans tonight, in her house in Destin, Florida, hiding from everyone and everything, and worrying about the entire clan. Gifford had begged the family not to go up to the house for Mardi Gras. Poor Aunt Gifford. She had banned the Talamasca History of the Mayfair Witches from her house and from her consciousness. 'I don't believe those things!'

Aunt Gifford lived and breathed fear. She shut her ears to the tales of the old days. Poor Aunt Gifford could be around her grandmother, Ancient Evelyn, only now because Ancient Evelyn said almost nothing anymore. Aunt Gifford didn't even like to say that she was Julien's granddaughter.

Sometimes Mona felt so deeply and hopelessly sad for Aunt Gifford, she almost burst into tears. Aunt Gifford seemed to suffer for the whole family, and no one was more distraught over Rowan Mayfair's disappearance than Gifford. Not even Ryan. Aunt Gifford was at heart a tender and loving soul, and there was no one better when you needed to talk the practical things of life – clothes for a school dance; whether or not to shave one's legs yet; which perfume was best for a girl of thirteen? (Laura Ashley No. 1.) And these were the dumb things Mona actually did not know, half the time.

Well, what was Mona going to do now that she was out on Mardi Gras Night, free, and nobody knew it, or might ever know it? Of course she knew. She was ready. First Street was hers! It was as if the great dark house with its white columns were whispering to her, saying, Mona, Mona, Come in. This is where Oncle Julien lived and died. This is the house of the witches, and you are a witch, Mona, as surely as any of them! You belong here.

Maybe it was Oncle Julien himself speaking to her. No, just a fancy. With an imagination like Mona's you could make yourself see and hear whatever you liked.

But who knew? Once she got inside, maybe she'd actually see the ghost of Oncle Julien! Ah, that would be absolutely wonderful. Especially if it was the same debonair and playful Oncle Julien about whom she incessantly dreamed.

She walked across the intersection under the heavy dark roof of the oak branches, and quickly climbed the old wrought-iron fence. She came down heavily in the thick shrubbery and elephant ears, feeling the cold and the wet foliage against her face and not liking it. Pushing her pink skirt down, she tiptoed out of the dampish earth and onto the flagstone path.

Lamps burned dim on either side of the big keyhole doorway. The porch lay in darkness, its rocking chairs barely visible, painted black as they were to match the shutters. The garden seemed to gather round and press in.

The house itself looked to her as it always had, beautiful, mysterious, and inviting, though she had to admit in her heart of hearts she had liked it better when it was a spidery ruin, before Michael came with his hammer and nails. She had liked it when Aunt Deirdre sat forever on the side porch in a rocker, and the vines threatened to swallow the whole place.

Of course Michael saved it, but oh, if only she'd gotten into it once while it was still ruined. She'd known all about that body they found in the attic. She'd heard her mother and Aunt Gifford arguing about it for years and years. Mona's mother had been only thirteen when Mona was born, and Gifford had been there from the time of Mona's earliest memories.

In fact there had actually been a time when Mona wasn't sure which one was her mother – Gifford or Alicia. And then there had been Ancient Evelyn always holding Mona on her lap, and even though Ancient Evelyn wouldn't talk very much she still sang those old melancholy songs. Gifford had seemed the logical choice for a mother, because Alicia by that time was already a prodigious drunk, but Mona had it right and had for years. Mona was the woman of the house at Amelia Street.

They'd talked a lot in those days about that body upstairs. They'd talked about Cousin Deirdre, the heiress, who wasted away in her catatonia. They'd talked about all the mysteries of First Street.

The first time Mona had ever come into First Street – right before Rowan's marriage to Michael – she had fancied she could smell that body still. She'd wanted to go up and lay her hands on the spot. Michael Curry had been restoring the house, and workmen were up there painting away. Aunt Gifford had said for Mona to 'Stay put!' and given her a stern look every time Mona tried to wander.

It had been a miracle to watch Michael Curry's work. Mona dreamed such a thing would someday happen to the house on St Charles and Amelia.

Well, Mona would get to that third-floor room now. And thanks to the history she knew who the dead man had been, a young investigator from the Talamasca called Stuart Townsend. Still wasn't clear who had poisoned the man. But Mona's bet was it had been her

Uncle Cortland, who really wasn't her uncle at all, but actually her great-great-grandfather, which was really one of the most fun puzzles in the family history to figure out.

Smells. She wanted to investigate that other smell – the scent that lingered in the hallway and the living room of First Street. Nothing to do with a dead body, that one. The smell that had come with disaster at Christmas. The smell which no one else could smell, it seemed, unless Aunt Gifford had been lying when Mona asked her.

Aunt Gifford did that. She wouldn't admit to 'seeing things' or picking up strange scents. 'I don't smell anything!' she'd said with annoyance. Well, maybe that was true. Mayfairs could read other people's minds a lot of the time, but they were good at blocking out each other.

Mona wanted to touch everything. She wanted to look for the Victrola. She did not care about the pearls. She wanted the Victrola. And she wanted to know THE BIG FAMILY SECRET – what had happened to Rowan Mayfair on Christmas Day. Why had Rowan left her new husband, Michael? And why had they found him drowned in the ice-cold swimming pool? Just nearly dead. Everybody had thought he was going to die after that, except Mona.

Of course Mona could conjecture what happened like everyone else. But she wanted more than that. She wanted the Michael Curry version. And to date, there was no such version. If he'd told anyone what happened on Christmas Day, it was his friend Aaron Lightner, from the Talamasca, who would not tell anyone else. But people felt too sorry for Michael to press it. They'd thought he was going to die from what happened to him.

Mona had managed to get into his room in Intensive Care on Christmas Night and hold his hand. He wasn't going to die. There was hurt to his heart, yes, because he'd stopped breathing for a long time in the cold water, and he had to rest to heal that hurt, but he was nowhere near dying, she knew that as soon as she felt his pulse. And touching him had been rather like touching a Mayfair. He had something extra to him which Mayfairs always had. He could see ghosts, she knew. The History of the Mayfair Witches had not included him and Rowan, but she knew. She wondered if he'd tell the truth about it. Fact, she'd even heard some maddening whispers to the effect that he had.

Oh, so much to learn, so much to uncover. And being thirteen was kind of like a bad joke on her. She was no more thirteen than Joan of Arc had ever been thirteen. the way she saw it. Or Catherine of Siena. Of course they were saints but only by a hair. They were almost witches.

And what about the Children's Crusade? If Mona had been there, they would have gotten back the Holy Land, she figured. What if she started a nationwide revolt of genius thirteen-year-olds right now – demand for the power to vote based on intelligence, a driver's license as soon as you could qualify and see over the dashboard. Well, a lot of this would have to wait.

The point was, she'd known tonight as they walked back from the Comus parade that Michael was quite strong enough to go to bed with her, if only she could get him to do it, which was not going to be an easy thing.

Men Michael's age had the best combination of conscience and self-control. An old man, like her Great-uncle Randall, that had been easy, and young boys, like her cousin David, were nothing at all.

But a thirteen-year-old going after Michael Curry? It was like scaling Everest, Mona thought with a smile. *I'm going to do it if it kills me.* And maybe then, when she had him, she'd know what he knew about Rowan, why Rowan and he had fought on Christmas Day, and why Rowan had disappeared. After all, this wasn't really a betrayal of Rowan. Rowan had gone off with someone, that was almost for sure, and everybody in the family, whether they would talk about it or not, was terrified for Rowan.

It wasn't like Rowan was dead; it was like she'd gone off and left the barn door open. And here was Mona coming along, mad for Michael Curry, this big woolly mammoth of a man.

Mona stared up at the huge keyhole doorway for one moment, thinking of all the pictures she'd seen of family members in that doorway, over the years. Great-oncle Julien's portrait still hung at Amelia Street, though Mona's mother had to take it down every time Aunt Gifford came, even though it was a dreadful insult to Ancient Evelyn. Ancient Evelyn rarely said a word – only drawn out of her reverie by her terrible worry for Mona and Mona's mother, that Alicia was really dying finally from the drink, and Patrick was so far gone he didn't know for sure who he even was.

Staring at the keyhole doorway, Mona felt almost as if she could see Oncle Julien now with his white hair and blue eyes. And to think he had once danced up there with Ancient Evelyn. The Talamasca hadn't known about that. The history had passed over Ancient Evelyn and her granddaughters Gifford and Alicia, and Alicia's only child, Mona.

But this was a game she was playing, making visions. Oncle Julien wasn't in the door. Had to be careful. Those visions were not the real thing. But the real thing was coming.

Mona walked along the flagstone path to the side of the house, and then back the flags, past the side porch where Aunt Deirdre had sat in her rocker for so many years. Poor Aunt Deirdre. Mona had seen her from the fence many a time, but she'd never managed to get inside the gate. And now to know the awful story of the way they'd drugged her.

The porch was all clean and pretty these days, with no screen on it anymore, though Uncle Michael had put back Deirdre's rocking chair and did use it, as if he had become as crazy as she had been, sitting there for hours in the cold. The windows to the living room were hung with lace curtains and fancy silk drapes. Ah, such riches.

And here, where the path turned and widened, this was where Aunt Antha had fallen and died, years and years ago, as doomed a witch as her daughter, Deirdre, would become, Antha's skull broken and blood flowing out of her head and her heart.

No one was here now to stop Mona from dropping down to her knees and laying her hands on the very stones. For one flashing instant, she thought she saw Antha, a girl of eighteen, with big dead eyes, and an emerald necklace tangled with blood and hair.

But again, this was making pictures. You couldn't be sure they were any more than imagination, especially

15

when you'd heard the stories all your life as Mona had, and dreamed so many strange dreams. Gifford sobbing at the kitchen table at Amelia Street. 'That house is evil, evil, I tell you. Don't let Mona go up there.'

'Oh, nonsense, Gifford, she wants to be the flower girl in Rowan Mayfair's wedding. It's an honor.'

It certainly had been an honor. The greatest family wedding ever. And Mona had loved it. If it hadn't been for Aunt Gifford watching her, Mona would have made a sneaky search of the whole First Street house that very afternoon, while everyone else swilled champagne and talked about the wholesome side of things, and speculated about Mr Lightner, who had not yet revealed his history to them.

But Mona would not have been in the wedding at all if Ancient Evelyn had not risen from her chair to overrule Gifford. 'Let the child walk up the aisle,' she had said in her dry whisper. She was ninety-one years old now. And the great virtue of almost never speaking was that when Ancient Evelyn did, everybody stopped to listen. If she wasn't mumbling, that is.

There were times when Mona hated Aunt Gifford for her fears and her worry, the constant look of dread on her face. But nobody could really hate Aunt Gifford. She was too good to everybody around her, especially to her sister, Alicia, Mona's mother, whom everyone regarded as hopeless now that she'd been hospitalized three times for her drinking and it hadn't done any good. And every Sunday without fail, Gifford came to Amelia Street, to clean up a bit, sweep the walk, and sit with Ancient Evelyn. She brought dresses for Mona, who hated to go shopping.

'You know you ought to dress more like a teenager

these days,' Gifford had volunteered only a few weeks ago.

'I like my little-girl dresses, thanks,' said Mona, 'they're my disguise. Besides if you ask me, most teenagers look tacky. I wouldn't mind looking corporate, but I'm a bit short for that.'

'Well, your bra cup is giving you away! It's hard to find you sweet cotton frocks with enough room in them, you know.'

'One minute you want me to grow up; the next minute you want me to behave. What am I to you, a little girl or a sociological problem? I don't like to conform. Aunt Gif, did it ever occur to you that conformity can be destructive? Take a look at men today on the news. Never in history have all the men in a nation's capital dressed exactly alike. Ties, shirts, coats of gray. It's appalling.'

'Responsibility, that's what I'm talking about. To dress your age and behave your age. You don't do either, and we're talking about two contrary directions of course. The Whore of Babylon with a ribbon in her hair just isn't your garden-variety teenage experience.'

Then Gifford had stopped, shocked that she'd said that word, *whore*, her cheeks flaming, and her hands clasped, her bobbed black hair falling down around her face. 'Oh, Mona, darling, I love you.'

'I know that, Aunt Gif, but please for the love of God and all we hold sacred, never refer to me as garden-variety anything, ever again!'

Mona knelt on the flagstones for a long time, until the cold started to bother her knees.

'Poor Antha,' Mona whispered. She stood up, and once again smoothed her pink dress. She brushed her hair back off her shoulders, and made sure that her satin bow was still properly pinned to the back of her head. Uncle Michael loved her satin bow, he had told her that.

'As long as Mona has her bow,' he'd said this evening, on the way to see Comus, 'everything is going to be all right.'

'I turned thirteen in November,' she'd told him in a whisper, drawing near to hold his hand. 'They're telling me to turn in my ribbon.'

'You? Thirteen?' His eyes had moved over her, lingering just for a split second on her breasts, and then he had actually blushed. 'Well, Mona, I didn't realize. But no, don't you dare stop wearing that ribbon. I see that red hair and the ribbon in my dreams.'

Of course he meant all this poetically and playfully. He was an innocent and wholesome man, just really nice. Anyone could see that. But then again, there had been a bit of blush to his cheeks, hadn't there? After all, there were some men his age who did see a thirteen-year-old with large breasts as just one species of uninteresting baby, but Michael didn't happen to be one of those.

Well, she'd think a little bit more about strategy when she got inside the house, and close to him. For now, she wanted to walk around the pool. She went up the steps and out along the broad flagstone terrace. The lights were on beneath the surface of the water, making it a shining blue, and a faint bit of steam rose from the surface, though why it was heated, Mona didn't know. Michael wouldn't swim in it ever again. He'd said so. Well, come St Patrick's Day, whatever the temperature, there would probably be a hundred Mayfair kids in there. So best to leave the heat on.

She followed the terrace to the far end, near the cabana, where they'd found the blood in the snow, which meant that a fight had taken place. All clean now and swept, with only a little sprinkling of leaves. The garden was still down a bit from the snows of this mad winter, so unusual for New Orleans, but due to the warmth of the last week, the four-o'clocks had come back and she could smell them, and see their tiny little blooms in the dark. Hard to imagine all this covered with snow and blood, and Michael Curry floating under the surface of the water, face bleeding and bruised, heart stopped.

Then another scent caught her – that same strange smell she'd picked up earlier in the hallway of the house and in the front parlor where the Chinese rug used to be. It was faint but it was here all right. When she drew near the balustrade she smelled it. All mingled with the cold four-o'clocks. A very seductive smell. Sort of, well, delicious, she thought. Like caramel or butterscotch could be delicious, only it wasn't a food smell.

A little rage kindled in her suddenly for whoever had hurt Michael Curry. She'd liked him from the moment she laid eyes on him. She'd liked Rowan Mayfair too. She'd longed for moments alone with them to ask them things and tell them things, and especially to ask them to give her the Victrola, if they could find it. But those opportunities had never come.

She knelt down on the flags now as she had done before. She touched the cold stone that hurt her bare knees. The smell was here all right. But she saw nothing. She looked up at the dark servants' porch of the main house. Not a light anywhere. Then she looked beyond the iron fence to the carriage house behind Deirdre's oak.

One light. That meant Henri was still awake. Well, what about it? She could handle Henri. She had figured out tonight at the supper after Comus that Henri was already scared of this house, and didn't like working in it, and probably wouldn't stay long. He couldn't quite figure how to make Michael happy, Michael who kept saying, 'I'm what's called a high prole, Henri. If you fix red beans and rice, I'll be fine.'

A high prole. Mona had gone up to Uncle Michael after supper, just as he was trying to get away from everyone and take his nightly constitutional, as he called it, and said, 'What the hell is a high prole, Uncle Michael?'

'Such language,' he'd whispered with mock surprise. Then before he could stop himself, he'd stroked the ribbon in her hair

'Oh, sorry,' she'd said, 'but for an uptown girl, it's sort of, you know, *de rigueur* to have a large vocabulary.'

He'd laughed, a little fascinated maybe. 'A high prole is a person who doesn't have to worry about making the middle class happy,' he said. 'Would an uptown girl understand that?'

'Sure would. It's extremely logical, what you're saying, and I want you to know I loathe conformity in any form.'

Again his gentle beguiling laughter.

'How did you get to be a high prole?' She'd pushed it. 'Where do I go to sign on?'

'You can't sign on, Mona,' he'd answered. 'A high prole is born a prole. He is a fire-fighter's son who has made plenty of money. A high prole can mow his own grass any time he likes. He can wash his own car. Or he can drive a van when everybody keeps telling him he ought to drive a Mercedes. A high prole is a free man.' What a smile he had given her. Of course he was laughing at himself a little, in a weary sort of way. But he liked to look at her, that she could see. Yes, indeed, he did like to look at her. Only some weariness and some sense of propriety held him in check.

'Sounds good to me,' she'd said. 'Do you take off your shirt when you mow the grass?'

'How old are you, Mona?' he'd asked her playfully, cocking his head to one side. But the eyes were completely innocent.

'I told you, thirteen,' she'd answered. She'd stood on tiptoe and kissed him quickly on the cheek, and there had come that blush again. Yes, he saw her, saw her breasts and the contour of her waist and hips under the loose pink cotton dress. Yet he'd seemed moved by her show of affection, an emotion quite entirely separate. His eyes had glassed over for a minute, and then he'd said he had to go walk outside. He'd said something about Mardi Gras Night, about passing this house once when he'd been a boy, on Mardi Gras Night, when they'd been on their way to see Comus.

No, nothing really wrong with his heart now at all, except that the doctors kept scaring him, and giving him much too much medicine, though he did now and then have those little pains, he'd told Ryan, which reminded him of what he could and couldn't do. Well, Mona would find out what he could or couldn't do.

She stood by the pool for a long moment, thinking of all the bits and pieces of the story – Rowan run off, some kind of miscarriage in the front hall, blood everywhere, and Michael bruised and knocked unconscious in the pool. Could the miscarriage account for the smell? She'd asked Pierce earlier if he could smell it. No. She'd asked Bea. No. She'd asked Ryan. Of course not. Stop going around looking for mysterious things! She thought of Aunt Gifford's drawn face as she stood in the hospital corridor on Christmas Night, when they'd thought Michael was dying, and the way she had looked at Uncle Ryan.

'You know what's happened!' she had said.

'That's superstition and madness,' Ryan had answered. 'I won't listen to it. I won't let you speak of it in front of the children.'

'I don't want to talk about it in front of the children,' Aunt Gifford had said, her jaw trembling. 'I don't want the children to know! Keep them away from that house, I'm begging you. I've been begging you all along.'

'Like it's my fault!' Uncle Ryan had whispered. Poor Uncle Ryan, the family lawyer, the family protector. Now that was a fine example of what conformity could do to one, because Uncle Ryan was in every respect a super-looking male animal, of the basically heroic type, with square jaw, and blue eyes, and good strong shoulders and a flat belly and a musician's hands. But you never noticed it. All you saw when you looked at Uncle Ryan was his suit, and his oxford-cloth shirt, and the shine on his Church's shoes. Every male at Mayfair and Mayfair dressed in exactly this fashion. It's a wonder the women didn't, that they had evolved a style which included pearls and pastel colors, and heels of varying height. Real wingdings, thought Mona. When she was a multimillionaire mogul, she would cut her own style.

But during that argument in the hallway, Uncle Ryan had showed how desperate he was, and how worried for

Michael Curry; he hadn't meant to hurt Aunt Gifford. He never did.

Then Aunt Bea had come and quieted them both. Mona would have told Aunt Gifford then and there that Michael Curry wasn't going to die, but if she had she would have frightened Gifford all the more. You couldn't talk to Aunt Gifford about anything.

And now that Mona's mother was pretty much drunk all the time, you couldn't talk to her either, and Ancient Evelyn often did not answer at all when Mona spoke to her. Of course when she did, her mind was all there. 'Mentation perfect,' said her doctor.

Mona would never forget the time she'd asked to visit the house when it was still ruined and dirty, when Deirdre sat in her rocker. 'I had a dream last night,' she'd explained to her mother and to Aunt Gifford. 'Oncle Julien was in it, and he told me to climb the fence, whether Aunt Carlotta was there or not, and to sit in Deirdre's lap.'

This was all true. Aunt Gifford had gotten hysterical. 'Don't you ever go near Cousin Deirdre.' And Alicia had laughed and laughed and laughed. Ancient Evelyn had merely watched them.

'Ever see anybody with your Aunt Deirdre when you pass there?' Alicia had asked.

'CeeCee, how could you!' Gifford had demanded.

'Only that young man who's always with her.'

That had put Aunt Gifford over the edge. After that Mona was technically sworn to stay away from First and Chestnut, to never set eyes on the house again. Of course she didn't pay much attention. She walked by whenever she could. Two of her friends from Sacred Heart lived pretty close to First and Chestnut. Sometimes she went home with them after school, just to have the excuse. They loved to have her help with their homework, and she was glad to do it. And they told her things about the house.

'The man's a ghost,' her mother had whispered to her right in front of Gifford. 'Don't ever tell the others that you've seen him. But you can tell me. What did he look like?' And then Alicia had gone into shrieking laughter again until Gifford had actually begun to cry. Ancient Evelyn had said nothing, but she'd been listening to all of this. You could tell when she listened by the alert look in her small blue eyes. What in God's name did she think of her two granddaughters?

Gifford had taken Mona aside later, as they walked to Gifford's car (Jaguar sedan, very Gifford, very Metairie). 'Please believe me when I tell you to stay away from there,' she'd said. 'Nothing but evil comes out of that house.'

Mona had tried to promise. But it hadn't interested her much at all; indeed, the die was cast for her. She had to know all about that place even then. And now, after the quarrel of Rowan and Michael, it was top priority: get inside and find out.

Finding the Talamasca document on Ryan's desk downtown had only tripled her curiosity. The File on the Mayfair Witches. She'd scooped it up and hurried out to a lunch counter to read the whole thing, there had been no stopping her, before anybody caught on to what she'd done. Donnelaith, Scotland. Didn't the family own property there still? Oh, what a history. The details about Antha and Deirdre of course were the real scandal. And it was perfectly clear to her that this document, in its original form, had gone on to include Michael and Rowan Mayfair. But it didn't anymore.

Aaron Lightner had broken off 'the narrative', as he referred to it in those pages, before the birth of 'the present designee'. This was not to violate the privacy of the living, though the Order feels that the family has every right to know its history, insofar as such a history is known by anyone and recorded anywhere.

Hmmmm. These Talamasca people were amazing. 'And Aunt Bea is about to marry one of them,' thought Mona. That was like hearing that a juicy big fly had just been snared in one's sticky web.

That Rowan Mayfair had slipped through Mona's clutches, that Mona had never had five minutes alone with Rowan, that was a tragedy to be filed under \WS\ MONA\DEFEAT.

But Mona had caught the very strong impression that Rowan was afraid of whatever power she had, just as the others were afraid.

Well, these powers didn't scare Mona. More and more Mona felt like a dancer just coming into a time of perfect strength. So she was only five feet one inch tall, and not likely to grow much taller. Her body was maturing with every passing day.

She liked being strong and unusual. She liked reading people's thoughts and seeing things that other people couldn't see. The fact that the man she'd seen was a ghost thrilled her. And she hadn't really been surprised to hear it. If only she had gotten into the house in those days.

Well, those days were gone, weren't they? And now was now. And now was really quite terrific. The disappearance of Rowan Mayfair had stirred up the family; people were revealing things. And here was this great house, empty except for Michael Curry, and for her.

The smell by the pool had dissipated somewhat, or she'd gotten used to it. But it was still there.

And the moment was all hers.

She proceeded to the back screen porch and checked one by one the locks of the many kitchen doors. If only one door had been forgotten ... but no, that stiff-necked Henri had locked up the place like a fort. Well, no problem. Mona knew how to get in this house.

She crept around to the very back of the house, to the end of the old kitchen, which was now a bathroom, and she looked up at the bathroom window. Who would lock a window that high? And how would she get to it? Pull up one of the big plastic garbage cans which weighed almost nothing at all. She went down the alley, caught the can by its handle, and what do you know, it rolled. How efficient! And then she climbed on top of it, knees first, then feet crushing down the flexible black plastic lid, and she pried open the green shutters, and pushed at the sash.

Up it went, just that easy. It didn't jam until there was an opening quite big enough for her to get in. She was going to get her dress dirty on the dusty sill, but it didn't matter. She gave herself a boost with both hands, and slipped through the window, and all but tumbled to the carpeted floor.

Inside First Street! And it had been a slam dunk! For one second she stood there in the little bathroom, staring at the glimmering white porcelain of the old toilet and the marble top of the washstand, and remembering that last dream of Oncle Julien where he had taken her to this house and together they had climbed the stairs.

It was hazy now, as dreams always get, but she had written it in her computer diary under \WS\

26

DREAMS\JULIEN as she did all the dreams in which he came to her. She could remember now the file, which she had reread many times, though not the dream.

Oncle Julien had been playing the Victrola, the one that Mona was supposed to have, and he had been dancing about, in his long quilted satin robe. He'd said that Michael was too good. Angels have their limits. 'Pure goodness has rarely defeated me, you understand, Mona,' he had said with his charming French accent, speaking English for her as he always did in her dreams, though she spoke French perfectly, 'but it is invariably a nuisance to everyone else but the person who is so perfectly good.'

Perfectly good. Mona had typed in 'Perfectly Scrumptious, Perfectly Delectable, Perfectly a hunk!' Then she'd gone and made those entries in the file marked 'Michael'.

'Thoughts on Michael Curry: he is even more attractive now that he has had the heart attack, like a great beast with a wounded paw, a knight with a broken limb, Lord Byron with his club foot.'

She had always found Michael 'to die for', as the expression went. She hadn't needed her dreams to tell her, though they did embolden her somewhat, all that drama of Oncle Julien suggesting it to her, that Michael was a splendid conquest, and telling her how when Ancient Evelyn was only thirteen – Mona's age – Oncle Julien had bedded her in the attic at First Street, and from that illicit union had been born poor Laura Lee, the mother of Gifford and Alicia. Oncle Julien had given Ancient Evelyn the Victrola then and said, 'Take it out of the house before they come. Take it away and keep it . . .'

'. . . It was a mad scheme. I never believed in witch-craft, you must understand, Mona. But I had to try something. Mary Beth had started to burn my books even before the end. She burnt them on the lawn outside, as if I were a child without rights or dignity. The Victrola was a little voodoo, magic, a focus of my will.'

All that had been very clear and understandable when she dreamed it but even by the next day the 'mad scheme' was largely lost. OK. The Victrola. Oncle Julien wants me to have it. Witchcraft, my favorite thing.

And look what had happened to the damned Victrola, so far.

He'd gone to all that trouble in 1914 to get it out of the house – assuming that sleeping with thirteen-year-old Ancient Evelyn had been trouble – and when Ancient Evelyn tried to pass on that Victrola to Mona, Gifford and Alicia had had a terrible quarrel. Oh, that was the worst of days.

Mona had never seen such a fight as happened then between Alicia and Gifford. 'You're not giving her that Victrola,' Gifford had screamed. She'd run at Alicia and slapped her over and over, and tried to push her out of the bedroom where she had taken the Victrola.

'You can't do this, she's my daughter, and Ancient Evelyn said it is to be hers!' Alicia had screamed.

They had fought all the time like that as girls, think nothing of it, Ancient Evelyn had said. She had remained in the parlor. 'Gifford will not destroy the Victrola. The time will come when you may have the Victrola. No Mayfair would destroy Oncle Julien's Victrola. As for the pearls, Gifford can keep them for now.'

Mona didn't care about the pearls.

That had pretty much been Ancient Evelyn's quota of speech for the next three or four weeks.

Gifford had been sick after that, sick for months. Strife exhausted Gifford, which was only logical. Uncle Ryan had had to take her to Destin, Florida, to rest at the beach house. Same thing had happened after Deirdre's funeral; Aunt Gifford had been so sick that Ryan had taken her up to Destin. Aunt Gifford always fled to Destin, to the white beach and the clean water of the Gulf, to the peace and quiet of a little modern house with no cobwebs and no stories.

But the truly awful part for Mona was that Aunt Gifford had never given her the Victrola! When Mona had finally cornered her and demanded to know where it was, Aunt Gifford had said, 'I took it up to First Street. I took the pearls there too. I put them back in a safe place. There's where all Oncle Julien's things belong, in that house, along with his memory.' And Alicia had screamed and they'd started fighting again.

In one of the dreams, Oncle Julien had said, dancing to the record on the Victrola: 'The waltz is from *La Traviata*, my child, good music for a courtesan.' Julien danced, and the pinched little soprano voice sang on and on.

She had heard the melody so distinctly. Rare to be able to hum a song that you hear in a dream. Lovely scratchy sound to the Victrola. Ancient Evelyn had later recognized the song Mona was humming. It was from Verdi – Violetta's waltz.

'That was Julien's record,' she'd said.

'Yes, but how am I going to get the Victrola?' Mona had asked in the dream.

'Can't anyone in this family figure out anything for

herself!' Oncle Julien had almost wept. 'I'm so tired. Don't you see? I'm getting weaker and weaker. *Chérie*, please wear a violet ribbon. I don't care for pink ribbons, though it is very shocking with red hair. Wear violet for your Oncle Julien. I am so weary –'

'Why?' she'd asked. But he had already disappeared.

That had been last spring, that dream. She had bought some violet ribbon, but Alicia swore it was bad luck and took it all away. Mona's bow tonight was pink, like her cotton and lace dress.

Seems poor Cousin Deirdre had died last May right after Mona had had that dream, and First Street had come into the hands of Rowan and Michael, and the great restoration had begun. Every time she'd passed she'd seen Michael up there on the roof, or just climbing a ladder, or climbing over a high iron railing, or walking right on the parapet with his hammer in hand.

'Thor!' she'd called out to him once. He hadn't heard her, but he'd waved and smiled. Yes, to die for, all right.

She wasn't so sure about the times of all the dreams. When they'd started, she hadn't known there would be so many of them. Her dreams floated in space. She hadn't been smart enough in the beginning to date them, and to make a chronology of Mayfair events. She had that now in \WS\MAYFAIR\CHRONO. Every month she learned more tricks in her computer system, more ways of keeping track of all her thoughts and feelings, and plans.

She opened the bathroom door and stepped into the kitchen. Beyond the glass doors the swimming pool positively glittered for an instant as if a vagrant wind had touched its surface. As if it were alive. As she stepped forward, a tiny red light flashed on the motion detector, but she could see immediately by the control panel on the kitchen counter that the alarm wasn't set. That was why it hadn't gone off when she opened the window. What luck! She'd forgotten about that damned alarm, and it had been the alarm that had saved Michael's life. He'd have drowned if the firemen had not come and found him – men from his father's own firehouse, though Michael's father had died a long long time ago.

Michael. Yes, it was fatal attraction from the moment she'd first met him. And the sheer size of the man had a lot to do with it – things like the perfect width of his neck. Mona had a keen appreciation of men's necks. She could watch a whole movie just to get a load of Tom Berenger's neck.

Then there was that constant good humor. When had she ever not gotten a smile from Uncle Michael, and often she'd gotten winks. She loved those immense and amazingly innocent blue eyes. Downright flashy, Bea had said once, but she'd meant it as a compliment. 'The man's just sort of too vivid!' Even Gifford had understood that.

Usually when a man was that well-built, he was an idiot. Intelligent Mayfair men were always perfectly proportioned. If Brooks Brothers or Burberry's couldn't fit you, you were illegitimate. They'd put poison in your tea. And they behaved like wind-up toys once they came home from Harvard, always combed and tanned, and shaking people's hands.

Even Cousin Pierce, Ryan's pride and joy, was turning out that way – a shining replica of his father, down to the Princeton cut of the blond hair, and loving Cousin

Clancy was perfect for Pierce. She was a small clone of Aunt Gifford – only without the pain. They looked like they were made of vinyl, Pierce and Ryan, and Clancy. Corporation lawyers; their whole goal in life was to see how much they could leave undisturbed.

Mayfair and Mayfair was a law firm full of vinyl people.

'Never mind,' her mother had said once to her criticism. 'They take care of all the money so that you and I don't have to worry about a thing.'

'I wonder if that's such a good idea,' Mona had said, watching her mother miss her mouth with the cigarette, and then grope for the glass of wine on the table. Mona had pushed it towards her, disliking herself for doing it, disliking that she did it because it was torture to watch her mother not be able to find it on her own.

But Michael Curry was a different sort from the Mayfair men altogether – husky and relaxed, more beautifully hirsute, altogether lacking in the perpetual preppie gleam perfected by men like Ryan, yet very adorable in a beastly way when he wore his dark-rimmed glasses and read Dickens the way he'd been doing it this very afternoon when she'd gone up to his room. He hadn't cared a thing about Mardi Gras. He hadn't wanted to come down. He was still reeling from Rowan's defection. Time just didn't mean anything to him, because if he had started to think about it, he would have had to think on how long Rowan had been gone.

'What are you reading?' she'd asked.

'Oh, *Great Expectations*,' he'd said. 'I read it over and over. I'm reading the part about Joe's wife, Mrs Joe. The way she kept making the *T* on the chalkboard.

Ever read it? I like to read things I've read before. It's like listening over and over to your favorite song.'

A brilliant Neanderthal slumbered in his body waiting to drag you into the cave by your hair. Yes, a Neanderthal with the brain of a Cro-Magnon, who could be all smiles and a gentleman and as well-bred as anybody in this family could possibly want. He had a great vocabulary, when he chose to use it. Mona admired his vocabulary. Mona's vocabulary was ranked equal to that of a senior in college. In fact, someone at school had once said, she had the biggest words coming out of the littlest body in the world.

Michael could sound like a New Orleans policeman one moment and a headmaster at another. 'Unbeatable combination of elements,' Mona had written in her computer diary. Then remembered Oncle Julien's admonition. 'The man is simply too good.'

'Am I evil?' she whispered aloud in the dark. 'Doesn't compute.' She really hadn't the slightest doubt that she wasn't evil. Such thoughts were old-fashioned to her, and typical of Oncle Julien, especially the way he was in her dreams. She hadn't known the words for it when she was little, but she knew them now: 'Self-deprecating, self-mocking.' That is what she'd written into the computer in the subdirectory \WS\JULIEN\CHARAC-TER in the file DREAM13.

She walked across the kitchen and slowly through the narrow butler's pantry, a lovely white light falling on the floorboards from the porch outside. Such a grand dining room. Michael thought the hardwood floor had been laid in the thirties, but Julien had told Mona it was 1890s, a flooring they called wooden carpet, and it had come in a roll. What was Mona supposed to do with all the things Julien had told her in these dreams?

The dense murky murals were surprisingly visible to her in the darkness – Riverbend Plantation, where Julien had been born – and its quaint world of sugar mill, slave cabins, stables and carriages moving along the old river road. But then she had cat's eyes, didn't she? Always had. She loved the darkness. She felt safe and at home in it. It made her want to sing. Impossible to explain to people how good she felt when she roamed alone in the darkness.

She walked around the long table, now all cleared and stripped and polished, though only hours ago it had held the last Mardi Gras banquet complete with frosted King cakes, and a silver punch bowl full of champagne. Boy, the Mayfairs sure ate themselves sick when they came to First Street, she thought. Everybody was just so happy that Michael was willing to keep the place going though Rowan had flat-out disappeared, and under suspicious circumstances. Did Michael know where she was?

Aunt Bea had said, with tears in her eyes, 'His heart is broken!'

Well, here comes the kid with the wonder glue for broken hearts! Stand back, world, it's little Mona.

She passed through the high keyhole doorway into the front hall, and then she stopped and put her hands on the frame, as Oncle Julien had done in so many old pictures, in this door or the other, and she just felt the silence and bigness of the house around her, and smelled its wood.

That other smell. There it was again, making her . . . what? Almost hungry. It was delicious, whatever it was. Not butterscotch, no, not caramel, not chocolate, but something thick like that, a flavor that seemed a hundred flavors compressed into one. Like the first time you bit into a chocolate-covered cherry cordial. Or a Cadbury Easter egg.

No, she needed a better comparison. Something you didn't eat. What about the smell of hot tar? That tantalized her, too, and then there was the smell of gasoline that she just couldn't tear herself away from. Well, this was more like that.

She moved down the hall, noting the winking lights of other alarm devices, none of them armed, all of them waiting, and the smell became strongest when she stood at the foot of the stairs.

She knew Uncle Ryan had investigated this entire area, that even after all the blood had been washed away, and the Chinese rug in the living room had been taken out, he had come with a chemical that made lots of other blood glow in the dark. Well, it was all gone now. Just gone. He'd seen to that before Michael came home from the hospital. And he'd sworn he detected no smell.

Mona took a deep breath of it. Yes, it made you feel a kind of craving. Like the time she was riding the bus downtown on one of her escapades, all alone and reckless and loaded with dough, and she'd smelled that delicious barbecue from the bus and actually gotten off to find the place from which it was coming, a little French Quarter restaurant in a ramshackle building on Esplanade. Hadn't tasted half as good as it smelled.

But we're back to food again and this isn't food.

She looked into the living room, startled again, as she'd been earlier, to see how Michael had changed things after Rowan left. Of course the Chinese carpet had been taken out. It was all bloody. But he didn't have to abolish the old scheme of double parlors, did he? Well, he had. Mayfair Blasphemy.

It was one vast room now, with a giant soft sofa beneath the arch against the inside wall. A nice scattering of French chairs – all Oncle Julien's to hear him tell it, now tricked out in new gold damask or a striped fabric, wickedly rich looking, and a glass table through which you could see the dark amber colors of the enormous old rug. It must have been twenty-five feet, that rug, to stretch through both rooms as it did, embracing the floor before both of the hearths. And how old it looked, like something out of the attic upstairs, most likely. Maybe Michael had brought it down with the gilded chairs.

They'd said the only orders he'd given after he came home were to change that double parlor. Put Julien's things down there. Make it look entirely different.

Made sense. He'd obviously wanted to erase all traces of Rowan; he had wanted to obliterate the rooms in which they spent their happiest moments Some of the chairs were faded, wood chipped here and there. And the carpet rested right on the heart-pine floor, thin and silky looking.

Maybe there had been blood all over that other furniture. Nobody would tell Mona exactly what had gone on. No one would tell her anything much except Oncle Julien. And in her dreams, she seldom had the presence of dreammind to ask a question. Oncle Julien just talked and talked or danced and danced.

No Victrola in this room now. What a stroke of luck it would have been, if they'd brought it down too with all this other stuff. But they hadn't. She hadn't heard anybody say a thing about finding a Victrola.

She'd checked out the first floor every time she'd

come. Michael listened to a little tape machine in the library. This room lay in stillness, and its great Bösendorfer piano, at an angle before the second fireplace, seemed more a piece of furniture than a thing which could sing.

The room was still beautiful. It had been nice earlier to flop on the big soft sofa, from which you could see all the mirrors, the two white marble fireplaces, one to your left, one to your right, across from you, and the two doors directly opposite to Deirdre's old porch. Yes, Mona had thought, a good vantage point, and still an enchanting room. Sometimes she danced on the bare floors of the double parlor at Amelia, dreaming of mirrors, dreaming of making a killing in mutual funds with money she'd borrow from Mayfair and Mayfair

Just give me another year, she thought, I'll crack the market, then if I can find but one gambler in that whole stodgy law firm – ! It was no use asking them now to fix up Amelia Street. Ancient Evelyn had always sent carpenters and workmen away. She cherished her 'quiet'. And then what good was it to fix up a house in which Patrick and Alicia were simply drunk all the time, and Ancient Evelyn like a fixture?

Mona had her own space, as they say, the big bedroom upstairs on the Avenue. And there she kept her computer equipment, all her disks and files, and books. Her day would come. And until then she had plenty of time after school to study stocks, bonds, money instruments, and the like.

Her dream really was the management of her own mutual fund, called Mona One. She'd invite Mayfairs only to buy in, and she'd handpick every company in which the fund invested, on the basis of its environmental worthiness.

Mona knew from the *Wall Street Journal* and from *The New York Times* what was going on. Environmentally sensitive companies were making big bucks. Somebody had invented a microbe that ate oil spills and could even clean up your oven for you, if you turned it loose inside. This was the wave of the future. Mona One would be a legend among mutual funds, like Fidelity Magellan, or Nicholas II. Mona could have begun now, if anybody would take a chance on her. If only the Realm of Adults would open, just one tiny little bit, and let her in!

Uncle Ryan was interested, yes, and amused and amazed and confused, but not about to take a chance. 'Keep studying,' he'd said. 'But I must say I'm impressed with your knowledge of the market. How do you know all this stuff?'

'You kidding me? Same way you know it,' she had said. 'From the *Journal* and from *Barron's* and from going online any time night or day for the latest statistics.' She'd been speaking of the modem in her computer, and of the many bulletin boards she could call. 'You want to know something about stocks in the middle of the night? Don't call the office. Call me.'

How Pierce had laughed. 'Just call Mona!'

Uncle Ryan had been intrigued, Mardi Gras fatigue or no, but not enough not to back away with another lame comment: 'Well, I'm pleased that you're taking an interest in all this.'

'An interest!' Mona had replied. 'I'm ready to take over! What makes you such a wimp, Uncle Ryan, when it comes to aggressive growth funds? And what about Japan? Don't you know the simple principle that if you balance your United States stock market investments abroad then you've got global –'

'Hold it,' he'd said. 'Who's going to invest in a fund called Mona One?'

Mona had been quick on the reply. 'Everyone!'

The best part was Uncle Ryan had finally laughed and promised again to buy her a black Porsche Carrera for her fifteenth birthday. She had never let him forget that from the moment she'd become obsessed with the car. She didn't see why all the Mayfair money couldn't buy her a fake driver's license, too, so she could slam the pedal to the floor right now. She knew all about cars. The Porsche was her car, and every time she saw a parked Carrera she crawled all over it, hoping the owner would come. She'd hitched rides three times that way with perfect strangers. But never tell anyone that! They'll die.

As if a witch couldn't protect herself.

'Yes, yes,' he'd said this evening, 'I haven't forgotten the black Porsche, but you haven't forgotten your promise to me, have you, that you'll never drive it over fifty-five miles an hour?'

'There you go kidding again,' she said. 'Why the hell would I want to drive a Porsche over fifty-five miles an hour?'

Pierce had nearly choked on his gin and tonic.

'You're not buying that child a coffin on wheels!' Aunt Bea had declared. Always interfering. No doubt she'd be calling Gifford about the whole idea.

'What child? I don't see any child around here, do you?' Pierce had said.

Mona would have kept things going on the mutual funds, but it was Mardi Gras, people were tired, and Uncle Ryan had been drawn into a bottomless pit of polite conversation with Uncle Randall. Uncle Randall had turned his back to her, to shut her out. He'd been doing this sort of thing ever since Mona had gotten him into bed. She didn't care. That had been an experiment, nothing more, to compare a man in his eighties with young boys.

Now, Michael was her goal. To hell with Uncle Randall. Uncle Randall had been interesting because he was so old, and there is a way a really old man looks at a young girl which she found very exciting. But Uncle Randall wasn't a kind man. And Michael was. And Mona liked kindness. She'd isolated that trait in herself a long time ago. Sometimes she divided the world between kind and unkind – fundamentally speaking.

Well, tomorrow she would get to the stocks.

Tomorrow, or the next day, maybe she'd work up the actual portfolio for Mona One, based on the top stock performers for the last five years. It was so easy for her to be carried away, with visions of Mona One becoming so large she had to clone it with a second mutual fund called Mona Two and then Mona Three, and traveling all over the world in her own plane to meet the CEOs of the companies in which she invested.

She'd check out factories in Mainland China, offices in Hong Kong, scientific research in Paris. She pictured herself wearing a cowboy hat when she did this. She didn't actually have a cowboy hat right now. Her bow was her thing. But somehow or other she always had the hat on as she stepped off the imaginary plane. And all this was coming. She knew it.

Maybe it was time she showed Uncle Ryan the print-out of the stocks she'd tracked last year. If she'd really had money in them, she'd have her own fortune. Yes, got to boot that file and print that out.

Ah, but she was wasting the moment.

Tonight she was here, with her most important goal in mind. The conquest of the hunk known as Michael. And the finding of the mysterious Victrola.

The gilt *fauteuils* gleamed in the shadows, graceful straight-backed chairs. Tapestried pillows lay higgledy-piggledy in the deep damask sofa. A veil of stillness lay over all, as if the world beyond had gone up in smoke. Dust on the piano. That poor old Eugenia, she wasn't much good, was she? And Henri was probably *too* good to dust or mop or sweep. And in their midst was Michael, too sick and indifferent to care what they did.

She left the double parlor, and moved to the foot of the stairs. Very dark up there, as it ought to be, like a ladder to a heaven of shadows. She touched the newel post, and then began her ascent. In the house, in it, wandering, free and in the dark alone! 'Oncle Julien, I'm here,' she sang in a tiny whisper. When she reached the top she saw that Aunt Viv's room stood empty, just as she had expected.

'Poor Michael, you're all mine,' she said softly. And when she turned she saw that the door of the master bedroom was open, and the weak illumination of a little night-lamp poured out into the high narrow hall.

So you're alone in there, big boy, she thought. Not scared to be in the very room where Deirdre died. And let's not forget Great-aunt Mary Beth and all the people who saw the ghosts around her when she lay in that very same bed, and who knows what went on before that?

Gifford had thought it a deplorable decision for Michael to move back into that accursed room. But Mona understood. Why would he want to stay in the bridal chamber after Rowan had left him? Besides, it was the prettiest and fanciest room in the house, the north master bedroom. He himself had restored the plaster ceiling and the medallion. He had polished the enormous half tester bed.

Oh, she understood Michael. Michael liked darkness too, in his own way. Why else would anyone have married into this family? she thought. Something in him was seduced by darkness. He felt good in the twilight and good in the dark, just like she did. She knew that when she watched him walk in the nighttime garden. His thing. If he liked the early morning at all, which she doubted, it was only because it was dim and distorting.

'He is simply too good.' Oncle Julien's words came back to her. Well, we'll see.

She crept to the doorframe and saw the tiny night-light, plugged directly into the outlet over on the far wall. The light of the street lamps filtered softly through the lace curtains, and there lay Michael, his head turned away from her, in his immaculate white cotton pajamas, pressed so carefully by Henri that they had a perfect seam down the arm. Michael's hand lay half open on the top of the comforter as though ready to accept a gift. She heard him take a long, raw and uneasy breath.

But he hadn't heard her. He was dreaming. He turned on his side away from her, and sank deeper into a murmuring sleep.

She slipped into the room.

His diary was on the bedside table.

She knew it by the cover; she had seen him writing in it this very night. Oh, it was unconscionable to look into it. She couldn't do it, but how she wanted just to glimpse a few words.

What if she just took a little peek?

Rowan, come back to me. I'm waiting.

With a silent sigh she let it close.

Look at all the bottles of pills. They were bombing him with this stuff. She knew most of the names because they were common and other old Mayfairs had taken them often enough. Blood pressure medicines mostly, and then Lasix, that evil diuretic which probably pulled all the potassium out of him the way it had out of Alicia, when she'd straightened up and tried to lose weight, and three other dangerous-sounding potions that were probably what made him look all the time like he was trying to wake up.

Ought to do you a big favor and throw this junk in the garbage for you, she thought. What you need is Mayfair Witches' Brew. When she got home, she'd look up all these drugs in one of the big pharmaceutical books she had in her library. Ah, look, Xanax. That could make anyone into a zombie. Why give him that four times a day? They'd taken Xanax away from her mother, because Alicia took it in handfuls with her wine and her beer.

Hmmm, this did feel like a very unlucky room. She liked the fancy decorative work above the windows, and the chandelier, but it was an unlucky room. And that smell was in here too.

Very faint, but it was here, the delicious smell, the smell that didn't belong in the house, and had something to do with Christmas.

She came close to the bed, which was very high like so many old-fashioned beds, and she looked at Uncle Michael lying there, his profile deep in the snow-white cotton cover of the down pillow, dark lashes and eyebrows surprisingly distinct. Very much a man, just a smidgen more testosterone and you would have had a barrel-chested ape with bushy eyebrows. But there had not been the smidgen. Perfection had been the result.

"'O brave new world,'" she whispered, "'that has such people in't!'"

He was drugged, all right. Totally out of it.

That was probably why he'd lost that gift with his hands. He'd worn gloves most of the time up till Christmas, telling people his hands were very sensitive. Oh, Mona had tried hard to get to talk to him about that! And tonight, he'd remarked several times he didn't need the gloves anymore at all. Well, of course not if you were taking two milligrams of Xanax every four hours on top of all this other crap! That's how they'd shut down Deirdre's powers, drugging her. Oh, so many opportunities had passed by. Well, this opportunity wouldn't.

And what was this cute little bottle, Elavil? That had a sedative effect too, didn't it? And wow, what a dose. It's a wonder Michael had been able to come downstairs tonight. And to think he'd held her on his shoulders for Comus. Poor guy. This was damn near sadistic.

She touched his cheek lightly. Very clean-shaven. He didn't wake. Another long deep breath came out of him, almost a yawn, sounding very male.

She knew she could wake him, however, he wasn't in a coma after all, and then the most disturbing thought came to her! She'd been with David already tonight! Damn! It had been safe, sanitary but still messy. She couldn't wake Michael, not till she'd sunk down into a nice warm bath.

Hmmm. And she hadn't even thought of that till

now. Her clothes were still soiled. That was the whole trouble with being thirteen. Your brilliance was uneven. You forgot enormous things! Even Alicia had told her that.

'One minute, dear, you are a little computer whiz, and the next moment, you're screaming 'cause you can't find your dolls. I told you your dolls are in the cabinet. Nobody took your damned dolls! Oh, I'm so glad I don't ever have to be thirteen again! You know I was thirteen when you were born!'

Tell me about it. And you were sixteen when I was three and you left me downtown in Maison Blanche and I was lost there for two hours! 'I forgot, OK! Like I don't take her downtown that much!' Who else but a sixteen-year-old mother would give an excuse like that? It wasn't so bad. Mona had ridden the escalators up and down to her heart's content.

'Take me in your arms,' she prayed, looking down at Michael. 'I've had a terrible childhood!' But on he slept as if he'd been touched by the witch's wand.

Maybe this wasn't the night for getting him into bed. No, she'd rather everything be perfect for the assault. And not only had she been with David, she was soiled from the ground in the cemetery. Why, there were even a few dead leaves snarled in her hair, very Ophelia, but probably not very sexy.

Maybe it was the night for searching the attics. For finding the Victrola, and cranking it up. Maybe there were old records with it, that record that Ancient Evelyn used to play? Maybe it was time to meet Oncle Julien here in the shadows, and not time to be with Michael at all?

But he was so luscious there, gorgeously imperfect,

her high prole Endymion, with the slight bump to his nose, and the soft creases in his forehead, very Spencer Tracy, yes, the man of her dreams. And a man in the hand is worth two ghosts in a dream.

And speaking of hands, look at it, his large, soft hand! Now that was a man's hand. Nobody would say to him, 'You have the fingers of a violinist.' And she used to find men like that sexy, the delicate kind, like Cousin David, with hairless chins, with eyes full of soul. Ah, her whole appreciation of masculinity was taking a turn for the rough and the deep and the better.

She touched Michael's jaw, and the edge of his ear, his neck. She felt his curly black hair. Oh, nothing softer and finer than curly black hair. Her mother and Gifford had such fine black hair. But Mona's red hair would never be soft, and then she caught the fragrance of his skin, very subtle and nice and warm, and she bent down and kissed his cheek.

His eyes opened, but it seemed he couldn't see anything. She sank down beside him – just couldn't stop herself, even though she knew this was an invasion of his privacy – and he turned over. What *was* her plan? Hmmm . . . She felt such a craving for him suddenly. It wasn't even erotic. It was all a kind of swoony romance. She wanted to feel his arms around her; she wanted him to pick her up; she wanted him to kiss her; common things like that. A man's arms, not a boy's. They should dance. In fact, it was plain wonderful that there was no boy in him, that he was all wild beast in a way some men never would be, very jagged and roughened and overgrown, with skin-colored lips and slightly wild eyebrows.

She realized he was looking at her, and in the even light from the street, his face was pale yet clear.

46

'Mona!' he whispered.

'Yes, Uncle Michael. I got forgotten. It was a mix-up. Can I spend the night?'

'Well, honey, we have to call your father and mother.'

He started to sit up, deliciously rumpled, black hair tumbling over his eyes. He really was drugged, though, no doubt of it.

'Wrong, Uncle Michael!' she said quickly but gently. She put her hand on his chest. Ah, terrific. 'My dad and mom are asleep. They think I'm with Uncle Ryan out in Metairie. And Uncle Ryan thinks I'm home with them. Don't call anybody. You'll just get everybody all excited, and I'll have to take a cab home all alone and I don't want to. I want to spend the night.'

'But they'll realize . . .'

'My parents? You have it on good authority from me that they will not realize anything. Did you see my dad tonight, Uncle Michael?'

'Yeah, I did, honey.' He tried to stifle a yawn and failed. He looked very concerned for her suddenly, as if it wasn't appropriate to yawn while discussing her alcoholic father.

'He's not going to live very long,' she said in a bored voice. She didn't want to talk about him either. 'I can't stand Amelia Street when they're both drunk. Nobody there but Ancient Evelyn, and she never sleeps anymore. She's watching them.'

'Ancient Evelyn,' he mused. 'Such a lovely name. Do I know Ancient Evelyn?'

'Nope. She never leaves the house. She told them once to bring you up home, but they never did. She's my great-grandmother.'

'Ah, yes, the Mayfairs of Amelia Street,' he said. 'The

47

big pink house.' He gave a little yawn again, and forced himself into a more truly upright position. 'Bea pointed out the house. Nice house. Italianate. Bea said Gifford grew up there.'

Italianate. Architectural term, late nineteenth century. 'Yeah, well, it's a New Orleans bracketed style, as we call it,' she said. 'Built 1882, remodeled once by an architect named Sully. Full of all kinds of junk from a plantation called Fontevrault.'

He was intrigued. But she didn't want to talk history and plaster. She wanted him.

'So will you please let me stay here?' she asked. 'I really really have to stay here now, Uncle Michael. I mean, like, there's not really any other possibility now, logically, I mean. I should stay.'

He sat against the pillows, struggling to keep his eyes open.

She took his wrist suddenly. He didn't seem to know what she was doing – that she was feeling the pulse the same way a doctor would do it. His hand was heavy and slightly cold, too cold. But the heartbeat was steady. It was OK. He wasn't nearly as sick as her own father. Her own father wasn't going to live six months. But it wasn't his heart, it was his liver.

If she closed her eyes she could see the chambers of Michael's heart. She could see things so brilliant and unnameable and complex as to be like modern painting – a sprawl of daring colors and clots and lines and swelling shapes! Ah. He was OK, this man. If she did get him into bed tonight, she wouldn't kill him.

'You know your problem right now?' she asked. 'It's those bottles of medicine. Throw them in the trash. That much medicine will make anyone sick.'

'You think so?'

'You're talking to Mona Mayfair, a twentyfold member of the Mayfair family, who knows things that others don't know. Oncle Julien was my great-great-grandfather three times. You know what that means?'

'Three lines of descent, from Julien?'

'Yep, and then the other tangled lines from everybody else. Without a computer, no one could even put it all together. But I have a computer and I figured it all out. I've got more Mayfair blood in me than just about anybody in the whole family. It's all 'cause my father and mother were too close as cousins to get married, but my father got my mother pregnant, and that was it. And besides, we're all so inter-married it doesn't make much difference . . .'

She stopped, she was doing her chattering number. Too much talk for a man his age who was this sleepy. Play it with more craft. 'You're OK, big boy,' she said. 'Throw out the drugs.'

He smiled. 'You mean I'm going to live? I will climb ladders and hammer nails once again?'

'You'll wield your hammer like Thor,' she said. 'But you do have to get off all these sedatives. I don't know why they're drugging you like this, probably scared if they don't that you'll worry yourself to death about Aunt Rowan.'

He laughed softly, and took her hand now with obvious affection. But there was a dark shadow in his face, in his eyes, and for a second it was in his voice. 'But you have more faith in me, right, Mona?'

'Absolutely. But then I'm in love with you.'

'Oh no!' He scoffed.

She held fast to his hand as he tried to pull away. No,

there was nothing wrong with his heart now. The drugs were doing him in.

'I am in love with you but you don't have to do anything about it, Uncle Michael. Just be worthy of it.'

'Right. Be worthy of it, just what I was thinking. A nice little Sacred Heart Academy girl like you.'

'Uncle Michael, pa . . . leeze!' she said. 'I began my erotic adventures when I was eight. I didn't lose my virginity. I eradicated all traces of it. I am a full-grown woman only pretending to be this little girl sitting on the side of your bed. When you are thirteen, and you cannot disprove it, because all your relatives know, being a little girl becomes simply a political decision. Logical. But believe me, I am not what I seem.'

He gave the most knowing laugh, the most ironic laugh.

'And what if my wife, Rowan, comes home and finds you here with me, talking about sex and politics?'

'Your wife, Rowan, isn't coming home,' she said, and then instantly regretted it. She hadn't meant to say something so ominous, so depressing. And his face told her that he believed her. 'I mean . . . she's . . .'

'She's what, Mona? Tell me.' He was quietly and deadly serious. 'What do you know? Tell me what's inside your little Mayfair heart? Where is my wife? Give me some witchcraft.'

Mona gave a sigh. She tried to make her voice as hushed and quiet as his voice. 'Nobody knows,' she said. 'They're plenty scared, but nobody knows. And the feeling I get is . . . she's not dead, but . . . well, it might not ever be the same again.' She looked at him. 'Do you know what I mean?'

'You don't have a good feeling about her, that she's coming back? That's what you're saying.'

'Yeah, kind of. But then I don't know what happened here on Christmas Day, not that I'm asking you to tell me. I can tell this, however. I'm holding your wrist, right? We're talking all about it, and you're worried about her, and your pulse is just fine. You aren't that sick. They've doped you. They overreacted. They got illogical. Detox is what you need.'

He sighed, and looked defeated.

She leant forward and kissed him on the mouth. Immediate connection. In fact, it startled her a little, and even startled him. But there wasn't much follow-up. The drugs took care of that, like folding up the kiss in a blanket.

Age made such a difference. Kissing a man who'd been to bed a thousand times was nothing like kissing a boy who'd done it twice, maybe. All the machinery was here. She just needed a stronger jolt to turn it on.

'Hold on, honey, hold on,' he said gently, taking her by the left shoulder, and forcing her back.

She found it almost painful suddenly that this man was right there, and she probably couldn't get him to do what she wanted, and maybe never would.

'I know, Uncle Michael. But you have to understand that we have our family traditions.'

'Is that so?'

'Oncle Julien slept with my great-grandmother in this house when she was thirteen. That's how come I'm so clever.'

'And pretty,' he said. 'But I inherited something from my ancestors too. It's called moral fiber.' He raised his eyebrows, smiling at her slowly, taking her hand now and patting it as if she really were a little kitten or a child.

51

Best to step back. He looked groggier now than when they'd started. It seemed wrong, really, to try to draw him to her. Yet she ached for him. She really did; she ached for intimacy with him and the entire world of adults which he embodied for her. Stranded in childhood, she suddenly felt freakish and confused. She might have cried.

'Why don't I put you in the front bedroom?' he said. 'It's all clean and neat in there, has been since Rowan left. You want to sleep in there? That's a nice room.' His voice was thick. His eyes were closed as he talked. He stroked her hand affectionately.

'Front bedroom's fine,' she said.

'There are some flannel nightgowns in there. They were Rowan's. I gave them to her. They'll be too long. But wait a minute, maybe Aunt Viv is still awake. Maybe I should tell her you're here.'

'Aunt Viv is uptown, with Aunt Cecilia,' she said, venturing to squeeze his hand one more time. It was beginning to feel a little warm. 'They've become famous friends, Aunt Viv and Aunt Cecilia. I think Aunt Viv is now an honorary Mayfair.'

'Aaron. Aaron is in the second bedroom,' he said, as though thinking aloud.

'Aaron's with Aunt Bea. He and Bea have a thing together. They went back to his suite at the Pontchartrain, because she is far too proper to take him home.'

'Is that true? Bea and Aaron. Gee, I never noticed.'

'Well, you wouldn't. I'll bet Aaron will be an honorary Mayfair soon too.'

'Wouldn't that be something? Beatrice is perfect. You need a woman for Aaron who appreciates a gentleman, don't you think?' His eyes closed again, as if he couldn't prevent it.

'Uncle Michael, there's no such thing as a woman who doesn't appreciate a gentleman,' said Mona.

He opened his eyes. 'Do you know everything?'

'Nope. Wish I did, but then again, who would want to know everything? God must be bored. What do you think?'

'I can't figure it out,' he said, smiling again. 'You're a firecracker, Mona.'

'Wait till you see me in a flannel nightgown.'

'I won't. I expect you to lock your door, and go to sleep. Aaron might come home, Eugenia could get up and start her ceaseless walking . . .'

'Ceaseless walking?'

'You know old people. I'm so sleepy, Mona. Are you sleepy?'

'What if I get scared all alone in that front bedroom?'

'Doesn't compute.'

'What did you say?'

'Just means you're not scared of anything. And you know it, and you know I know it.'

'You want to sleep with me, don't you?'

'No.'

'You're lying.'

'Doesn't matter. I won't do what I'm not supposed to do. Honey, I think I should call somebody.'

'Trust me,' she said. 'I'm going to go to bed now. We'll have breakfast in the morning. Henri says he makes perfect Eggs Benedict.'

He smiled at her vaguely, too tired to argue, too tired perhaps to even remember the phone numbers he ought to call. What evil things drugs were. They made him grope for the simplest verbal constructions. She hated them. She never touched alcohol, or drugs in any form.

She wanted her mind like a scythe.

He laughed suddenly. 'Like a scythe!' he whispered.

Ah, so he'd caught it. She had to stop herself from acknowledging this, because he didn't realize that she hadn't spoken. She smiled. She wanted to kiss him again, but didn't think it would do any good. Probably do harm. He'd be dead asleep again in a few minutes. Then maybe, after a nice long bath, she'd search for the Victrola upstairs.

He surprised her by throwing back the covers and climbing out of the bed. He walked ahead of her, unsteady, but obviously chivalric.

'Come on, I'll show you where everything is,' he said. Another yawn and a deep breath as he led her out the door.

The front bedroom was as beautiful as it had been on the day of the wedding. There was even a bouquet of yellow and white roses on the marble mantel, somewhat like the bouquet which had been there on that day. And Rowan's white silk robe was laid out, as if she really were coming home again, on the pale damask coverlet of the four-poster bed.

He stopped for a moment, looking about as if he had forgotten what he meant to do. He wasn't remembering. She would have felt it if he'd been remembering. He was struggling for the context. That's what drugs did to you, they took the context of familiar things away.

'The nightgowns,' he said. He made a halfhearted little gesture towards the open bathroom door.

'I'll find them, Uncle Michael. Go back to bed.'

'You're not really scared, are you, honey?' Too innocent.

'No, Uncle Michael,' she said, 'you go back to sleep.'

He stared at her for a long moment, as if he could not even concentrate on the words she spoke. But he was determined to be protective, determined to worry appropriately. 'If you get scared . . .' he said.

'I won't, Uncle Michael. I was teasing you.' She couldn't help smiling. 'I'm the thing to be afraid of, most of the time.'

He couldn't repress a smile at that either. He shook his head and went out, throwing her one last very blue-eyed and adorable glance in which fire burned up the drugs for a moment, and then he closed the door.

The bathroom had a small pretty gas heater. She turned it on immediately. There were dozens of thick white towels on the wicker shelf. Then she found the flannel nightgowns, in rows on the top shelf of the closet – thick, old-fashioned gowns, in gay flowered patterns. She chose the most outrageous – a pink gown, with red roses on it, and she turned on the water in the long deep tub.

Carefully she removed the pink taffeta bow from the back of her hair, and laid it on the dressing table beside the brush and comb.

Ah, what a dream house, she thought. So unlike Amelia Street with its claw-foot tubs, and damp rotted floorboards; where the few remaining towels were chewed and worn, and would be until Aunt Bea brought by a new load of hand-me-downs. Mona was the only one who ever laundered them; she was the only one who ever laundered anything, though Ancient Evelyn swept the banquette, as she called the sidewalk, every day.

This house showed you what could be done with love. Old white tile, yes, but new and thick plum-colored carpet. Brass fixtures that really worked, and parchment shades over the sconces beside the mirror. A chair with a pink cushion; a small chandelier descending from the tiny medallion above, with four candle-shaped bulbs of pink glass.

'And money, don't forget money,' Alicia had said to her not long ago, when she had wished aloud that Amelia could be beautiful again.

'Why don't we ask Uncle Ryan for the money? We're Mayfairs. There's the legacy! Hell, I'm old enough to hire a contractor, to bring in a plumber. Why is everything always falling apart?'

Alicia had waved that away with disgust. Asking people for money meant inviting them to interfere. Nobody at Amelia Street wanted the Mayfair Police on the premises, did they? Ancient Evelyn did not like noise, or strange men. Mona's father didn't want anybody asking him questions. On and on it went. The excuses.

So things rusted, and rotted and broke, and no one did anything about them. And two of the rear bathrooms hadn't worked now in years. Window sashes were broken, or painted shut. Ah, the list was endless.

An evil little thought crept into Mona's head. It had almost crept into her head before, when Michael had said her house was Italianate. What would he think of the present state of affairs at Amelia Street? Maybe he could suggest a few things, like whether or not the plaster in her room would start falling again? At least he would know. That was his thing, of course, restoring houses. So bring him home to see the house, she thought.

But then the inevitable would happen. He was bound

to see Alicia and Patrick drinking all the time, and then to call Uncle Ryan, the way everybody did sooner or later. There would be the usual row. Aunt Bea might come again and once more suggest a hospital.

But what nobody understood was that these hospitalizations did more harm than good. Alicia came back crazier, more eager to drown her misery. The tirade last time had been the worst ever. She'd tried to smash everything in Mona's room. Mona had stood with her back to the computer.

'Lock your own mother up? You did that! You and Gifford, you lying little witch, you did that to me, your own mother! You think I would have done such a thing to my mother? You are a witch, Ancient Evelyn's right, you're a witch, take that bow out of your hair.' And then they'd fought, Mona holding Alicia's wrists, forcing her back.

'Come on, Mom! Stop it!'

And then Alicia went limp as she always did, just a sack of potatoes on the floor, sobbing and pounding her fist. And the shock of seeing Ancient Evelyn in the doorway, which meant that she had made the long trek up the stairs by herself, not very good, and her dour words.

'Do not hurt that child! Alicia, you are a common drunkard. Your husband is a common drunkard.'

'That child hurts me!' Alicia had wailed.

No, Mona would never put her in a hospital again. But the others might. You never knew. Best not to drag Michael into it, even if he wanted to help her fix up the place. Scrap that plan. Go on to the next one.

By the time she'd peeled off her clothes, the room was filled with delicious warm steam. She turned off the lights, so the only illumination came from the orange flames of the gas heater, and then she sank down into the tub of hot water, letting her hair stream out as if she were Ophelia again, or so she always imagined, floating to her death in the famous stream.

She turned her head this way and that to stir her long hair in the water, seeing the swirl of red around her, to get it really clean. She pulled at the bits and pieces of dead leaf. God! One of these could have been a roach! How ghastly. It was this swirling back and forth that made her hair so thick and shining after, the long soak and the turning. A shower would just beat it flat. She loved her hair to be as big and thick as possible.

Perfumed soap. Wouldn't you know it? And a bottle of pearly thick shampoo. These people knew how to live. This was like a fine hotel.

She washed her hair and body slowly, enjoying every minute of it, lathering gently all over and then sinking down to rinse the soap and shampoo away. Maybe she could somehow restore Amelia Street without inviting in all the new brooms of the family. Maybe she could explain to Uncle Michael that things had to be done cautiously and quietly, that he mustn't talk about Patrick and Alicia, that everybody knew anyway. But then what would they do when Ancient Evelyn started to tell the workmen to go home, or that they could not use noisy equipment?

It was comforting to be clean. She thought again of Michael, the sleeping giant, in there in the witch's bed.

She stood up and reached for the towel. She dried her hair roughly, tossing it forward and then backward, loving the freedom of being naked, and then she stepped out of the tub. The soft clean flannel gown felt snug and safe to her, though it was too long of course. So she'd pick it up like a little girl in an old-fashioned picture. That's how it made her feel. That's how her bow made her feel. Little old-fashioned girl was her favorite disguise, to the point where it wasn't a disguise at all.

She rubbed her hair fiercely one more time, and then picked up the brush off the dressing table, stared at herself for a moment in the mirror, and then began brushing her hair firmly back away from her forehead and behind her shoulders, so that it would dry neatly as it should.

The gas heat seemed to curl and breathe around her, to tap on her forehead with fingers. She picked up her bow of ribbon, and pinned it in place on the back of her head. She could just see two little bits of it sticking up. Like devil's horns.

'Oncle Julien, the hour has come,' she whispered, shutting her eyes tight. 'Give me a clue. Where do I look for the Victrola?' She rocked from side to side, Ray Charles style, trying to recapture one vivid moment from all those ever fading dreams.

A thin distant sound came to her, under the gentle roar of the gas heater, a song she could barely hear. Violins? Too thin a sound to tell what the instruments were, except there were many, and it was ... it was ... She opened the bathroom door. Far far away, but it was the waltz from *La Traviata* playing. It was ... the soprano singing. She started to hum it, irresistibly, but then she couldn't hear it! My God, what if the Victrola was down there in the living room!

She padded barefoot, towel over her shoulders like a shawl, into the hallway and peered down over the balusters. Very distinctly came the song of the waltz, louder than it had ever been in her dreams. The woman sang gaily in Italian, and now came the chorus behind her, sounding on the whole scratchy record like so many birds.

Her heart was pounding suddenly. She reached up and touched her bow to make sure it was securely clipped to her hair. Then she dropped the towel in a little careless heap and went to the head of the stairs. At that very instant, light softly leapt out of the doorways of the double parlor, and grew soundlessly brighter as she went down the steps. The wool carpet felt slightly rough to her bare feet, and when she incidentally saw her toes they looked very babyfied beneath the flannel, which she had to lift now, just like a picture-book kid.

She stopped. As she looked down, she saw that the carpet was no longer the red wool carpet. It was an oriental runner, very worn, very thin. She felt the change of texture. Or rather she became aware of standing on something more threadbare, and she followed the cascade of Persian blue and pink roses down the stairs. The walls had changed around her. The wallpaper was a deep dusty gold, and far below an unfamiliar chandelier hung from the oval cluster of plaster leaves on the hallway ceiling – something frothy and Venetian that she could never recall having seen before. And it had real lighted candles in it, this little chandelier.

She could smell the wax. The song of the soprano went on with its reliable and swinging rhythm, making her want to sing with it again. Her heart was brimming.

'Oncle Julien!' she whispered, almost bursting into tears. Oh, this was the grandest vision she had ever beheld!

She looked down into the hallway. More lovely patterns that she'd never seen before. And through the first of the high parlor doorways, the very doorway through which a long-ago cousin had been shot from this very stairway, she saw that the room was no longer the room of the present, and that tiny flames danced in the graceful crystal gasoliers.

Ah, but the rug was the same rug! And there were Julien's gold damask chairs.

She hurried down, glancing to right and left as the details caught her – the old gas sconces with their fluted crystal saucers of light, and the leaded glass around the huge front door, which had not been there before.

The music was as loud perhaps as a Victrola could get. And ah, behold the whatnot shelf all crowded with tiny ceramic figures, and the brass clock on the front mantel, and the Greek statues on the rear mantel, and the draperies of a mellow old velvet, burnished and fringed, and puddling on the polished floor.

The doorframes were painted to look like marble! So were the baseboards. It was that old kind of graining, so popular at the end of the century, and the gaslight flickered steadily against the darkly papered ceiling as if the little jets were dancing to the rhythm of the waltz.

What flaw could there be in this fabric? The rug was the very same rug she'd seen earlier, but that made perfect sense, didn't it, it had been Julien's, and there were his lovely *fauteuils* grouped together for conversation in the very center of the rooms.

She lifted her arms, and found herself dancing on the balls of her feet, in a circle, round and round, till the narrow nightgown flared around her, making a perfect narrow bell. She sang with the soprano, understanding the Italian effortlessly, though that was the most recent of all the languages she'd learned, and enchanted with the simple rhythm, and then swaying wildly back and forth, bending from the waist and letting her hair whip out and all over her face and tossing it again, so it tumbled down her back. Her eyes swept the veined and yellowed paper of the ceiling, and then in a blur, she saw the big sofa, Michael's new sofa, only it didn't have the beige damask on it now, but rather a worn gold velvet like the draperies which hung from the windows, gorgeous and warm in the flickering light.

Michael was sitting motionless on the couch looking at her. She stopped in mid-step, her arms curved downward like those of a ballerina, and felt her hair shift and tumble again off her shoulders. He was afraid. He sat in the middle of the couch in his cotton pajamas staring at her, as if she were something utterly terrifying or grotesque. The music went on and on, and slowly she took a deep breath, getting her pulse under control again and then coming near to him, thinking that if she had ever seen anything truly scary in her life, it was the sight of him sitting there in this room, staring at her, as if he were about to go out of his mind.

He wasn't trembling. He was like her. He feared nothing. He was just all anxious and upset and horrified by the vision, and he was seeing it, he had to be, and he was hearing the music, and as she drew closer, and sank down on the sofa beside him, he turned, looking at her, eyes wide with gentle amazement, and then she locked her mouth on his, pulled him down to her, and slam, bang, it connected, the chain reaction snapping through her. She had him. He was hers.

He pulled back for one instant as if to look at her again, as if to make sure that she was there. His eyes were still cloudy from the drugs. Maybe they were helping now – putting his sublime Catholic conscience to sleep. She kissed him again hurriedly and a little sloppily and then reached between his legs. Ah, he was ready!

His arms locked around her, and he gave some soft complaining sound that was very like him, like it's just too late now, or something, or God forgive me. She could all but hear the words.

She pulled him down on top of her, sinking deep into the sofa, smelling dust, as the waltz surged and the soprano sang on. She stretched out beneath him as he rose up, protectively, and then she felt his hand, trembling slightly in a beguiling fashion, as it ripped up the flannel and felt her naked belly and then her naked thigh.

'You know what else is there,' she whispered, and she pulled him down hard again. But his hand went before him, pushing gently into her, awakening her, rather like setting off a burglar alarm, and she felt her own juices slipping between her legs.

'Come on, I can't hold back,' she said, feeling the heat flood her face. 'Give it to me.' It probably sounded savage, but she couldn't play little girl a moment more. He went into her, hurting her deliciously, and then began the piston motion that made her throw back her head and almost scream. 'Yes, yes, yes.'

'OK, Molly Bloom!' he cried out in a hoarse whisper, and then she came and came and came – gritting her teeth, scarce able to stand it, moaning, and then screaming with her lips shut – and so did he.

She lay to one side, out of breath, wet all over as if she were Ophelia and they had just found her in the flower-strewn stream. Her hand was caught in his hair, pulling it too hard maybe. And then a shrieking sound shocked her and she opened her eyes.

Someone had torn the needle from the Victrola record. She turned, just as he did, and she stared at the bent little figure of Eugenia, the black maid, standing grimly beside the table, her arms folded, her chin jutting.

And quite suddenly there was no Victrola. The sofa was damask. The dim lights were electric.

And Eugenia was standing by nothing, having merely taken a righteous position, dead opposite to them, as they lay tangled on the sofa, and she said:

'Mr Mike, what do you think you are doing with that child!'

He was baffled, distressed, ashamed, confused, probably ready to commit suicide. He climbed up off her, tightening the string of his cotton pajamas, and staring at Eugenia and then at her.

It was time to be a Mayfair. Time to be Julien's great-great-granddaughter. She stood up and went towards the old woman.

'You want to keep your job in this house, Eugenia? Then go back up to your room now and shut the door.'

The old woman's dark wrinkled face froze for an instant in conscious outrage, and then softened as Mona looked right into her eyes. 'Do as I tell you. There's nothing here to worry about. Mona is doing what Mona wants. And Mona is good for Uncle Michael and you know it! Now go!'

Was she spellbound, or merely overwhelmed? It didn't matter. Witch power was witch power. The woman gave in. They always gave in. It was almost a cowardly thing, to make them do her bidding, staring them down this way. But she had to do it.

Eugenia lowered her gaze uncertainly and hurried from the room, with a crazy, twisted neurotic gait, and went rustling up the stairs. What a surprise that she could do it so fast.

And there was Michael sitting back on the sofa, staring at her with his eyes narrow now, and very calm, as though trying to recall what happened, blinking a little to show his confusion. 'Christ, Mona,' he whispered.

'It's done, Uncle Michael,' she said. And suddenly her voice failed her! Her strength was failing her. She heard the catch as she spoke again, she felt the quaver. 'Now, let me go up to bed with you,' she said, almost breaking down. 'Because I am really really sort of scared.'

They lay in the big bed in the dark. She was staring at the pleated satin of the half tester, wondering what pattern Mary Beth had once looked at. He was quiet beside her, druggy and worn out. The door was locked.

'You awake?' she whispered. She wanted so badly to ask him what he had seen. But she didn't dare. She held the picture of the double parlor in her mind, like a sacred sepia photograph – hadn't she seen such pictures, with the gasoliers, and those very chairs?

'Can't happen again, honey,' he said groggily. 'Never, never again.' He nestled her close to him, but he was very sleepy, and his heart was laboring just a little now, just a little but it was OK.

'If you say so, Uncle Michael,' she whispered. 'But I wish I had something to say about it.' *In Mary Beth's bed, in Deirdre's bed.* She snuggled close, feeling the warmth of his hand now, lying idly on her breast.

'Honey,' he whispered. 'What was that waltz? Was that Verdi? *La Traviata?* It sounded like it was but . . .' and then he was gone.

She lay there smiling in the darkness. He'd heard it! He'd been there with her. She turned to him and kissed his cheek, carefully so he didn't waken, and then she slept against his chest, one arm slipped beneath his shirt against his warm skin.

THREE

A dreary endless winter rain poured down on San Francisco, gently flooding the steep-sloped streets of Nob Hill and veiling in mist its curious mixture of buildings – the gray ghostlike Gothic façade of Grace Cathedral, the heavy imposing stucco apartment houses, the lofty modern towers rising from the old structure of the Fairmont Hotel. The sky was darkening heavily and quickly, and the five o'clock traffic was about as unpleasant as it could get.

Dr Samuel Larkin drove slowly past the Mark Hopkins, though whatever they called that hotel now he didn't know, and down California Street, crawling patiently behind a noisy crowded cable car, wondering vaguely at the perseverance of the tourists who clung to it, in the dark and in the cold, their clothes soaked. He was careful not to skid on the car tracks – the bane of out-of-town drivers – and he gave the cable car a head start as the light changed.

Then he made his descent towards Market Street, block after block, past the pretty exotic wooden entrance to Chinatown, a route which he always found slightly frightening and very beautiful, and which often reminded him of his first years in this city, when one could ride the cable car to work with ease, and the Top of the Mark had indeed been the highest point in the city, and none of these Manhattan skyscrapers were here at all.

How could Rowan Mayfair have ever left this place? he thought. But then Lark had only been to New Orleans a couple of times. Nevertheless, it had been like turning your back on Paris for the provinces, and it was only one part of Rowan's story that he did not understand.

He almost went by the unobtrusive gates of the Keplinger Institute. He made a sharp turn, plunged a little too fast down the driveway and into the dry darkness of the underground garage. It was now five-ten. And his plane for New Orleans left at eight-thirty. He did not have a moment to waste.

He flashed his identification card for the guard, who at once called up to verify the information, and then let him through with a nod.

Once again, in front of the elevator, he had to identify himself – this time to a woman's voice strangled by a tiny speaker beneath a video camera. Lark hated it, being seen but unable to see who saw.

The elevator carried him soundlessly and quickly up the fifteen floors to Mitchell Flanagan's laboratory. And within seconds, he had found the door, seen the light behind the smoked glass and knocked hard.

'Lark here, Mitchell,' he said in answer to a murmur on the other side.

Mitchell Flanagan looked the way he always did, half blind and utterly incompetent, peering at Lark through thick wire-rimmed glasses, his thatch of yellow hair the perfect wig for a scarecrow, his lab coat dusty but miraculously unstained.

Rowan's favorite genius, thought Lark. Well, I was

her favorite surgeon. So why am I so jealous? His crush on Rowan Mayfair was dying hard. So what if she'd gone south, gotten married and was now embroiled in some frightening medical mayhem? He'd really wanted to get her into bed, and he never had.

'Come inside,' said Mitch, apparently resisting the urge to pull Lark right into the carpeted corridor, where strings of tiny white lights softly outlined both the ceiling and the floor.

This place could drive me mad, Lark thought. You really expect to open a door and find human beings in antiseptic cages.

Mitch led the way – past the numerous steel doors with their small lighted windows, behind which various electronic noises could be heard.

Lark knew better than to ask to be admitted to these inner sanctums. Genetic research was entirely secret at Keplinger, even to most of the medical community. This private interview with Mitchell Flanagan had been bought and paid for by Rowan Mayfair – or the Mayfair family at any rate – at an exorbitant price.

Mitchell led Lark into a large office, with huge glass windows open to the crowded buildings of Lower California Street and a sudden dramatic view of the Bay Bridge. Sheer drapery, rather like mosquito netting, was fixed to the long chrome poles over the windows, masking and softening the night, and making it seem to Lark even more close and rather terrible. His memories of San Francisco before the era of the high-rise were simply too clear. The bridge looked totally out of proportion, and surely misplaced.

A wall of computer screens rose on one side of the large mahogany desk. Mitchell took the high-backed chair facing Lark and gestured for him to be seated in the more comfortable upholstered chair before the desk. The fabric was the color of claret, a heavy silk probably, and the style of the furnishings was vaguely oriental. Either that, or there was no style at all.

Beneath the windows, and their spectacle of the frightening night, stood rows and rows of file drawers, each with its own digital coded lock. The rug was the same deep claret as the chair in which Lark had made himself comfortable. Other chairs here and there were done up in the same color so that they all but vanished into the floor or into the darkly paneled walls.

The top of the desk was blank. Behind Mitchell's head of scarecrow hair was a great abstract painting that resembled nothing so much as a spermatozoon swimming like mad to a fertilized egg. It was wonderfully colored, however – full of cobalt and burning orange and neon green – as if painted by a Haitian artist who, having stumbled upon a drawing of sperm and egg in a scientific journal, had chosen it for a model, never guessing or caring what it was.

The office reeked of wealth. The Keplinger Institute reeked of wealth. It was reassuring that Mitch looked sloppy, incapable and even a little dirty – a mad scientist who made no concessions to corporate or scientific tyranny. He had not shaved in at least two days.

'God, am I glad you finally got here,' said Mitch. 'I was about to go out of my mind. Two weeks ago you dump this on me, with no explanation except that Rowan Mayfair sent it to you ... and that I have to find out everything that I can.'

'So did you?' asked Lark. He started to unbutton his raincoat, then thought better of it. He eased his briefcase to the floor. There was a tape recorder inside but he didn't want to use it. It would inhibit him and possibly scare Mitchell to death.

'What do you expect in two weeks? It's going to take fifteen years to map the human genome, or haven't you heard?'

'What can you tell me? This isn't an interview with the science editor of *The New York Times*. Give me a picture. What are we dealing with here?'

'You want that sort of speculation?' Mitch gestured to the computer. 'You want to see something three-dimensional and in living color?'

'Talk first. I distrust computer simulations.'

'Look, before I say anything, I want more specimens. I want more blood, tissue, everything I can get. I've had my secretary calling your office every day about this. Why didn't you call me back?'

'Impossible to get anything more. What you've seen is what you get.'

'What do you mean?'

'You've got the only samples to which I have access. You have the only data which came to me. There is something else in New York ... but we'll get to that later. The point is, I can't give you any more blood, tissue, amniotic fluid or anything else. You have everything Rowan Mayfair sent to me.'

'Then I have to talk to Rowan Mayfair.'

'Impossible.'

'Why?'

'Can you turn off that blinking fluorescent light up there? It's driving me crazy. Do you have an incandescent lamp in this fancy room?'

Mitchell looked startled. He sat back as though he'd

been pushed. For a moment, he seemed not to understand the words, and then he said, 'Oh yes.' He touched a panel under the lip of his desk. The overhead light went out suddenly and finally, and a pair of small lamps on the desk were quickly illuminated, soft, yellow, pleasant. They made the deep green of the desk blotter come to life.

Lark hadn't noticed the perfect, markless blotter, or its leather corners. Or the still, odd-shaped black phone hunkering there with its numerous and mysterious buttons like a symbolic Chinese toad.

'That's better. I hate that kind of light,' said Lark. 'And tell me exactly what you know.'

'First tell me why I can't talk to Rowan Mayfair, why I can't get more data. Why didn't she send you photographs of this thing? I have to talk to her –'

'Nobody can find her. I've been trying for weeks. Her family has been trying since Christmas Day. That's when she disappeared. I'm on an eight-thirty plane tonight to see her family in New Orleans. I'm the last one to have heard from Rowan. Her phone call to me two weeks ago is the only current evidence that Rowan is even alive. One phone call, then the specimens. When I contacted her family for funds, which is what she asked me to do, they told me about her disappearance. She has been spotted once since Christmas Day ... maybe ... in a town in Scotland called Donnelaith.'

'What about the courier service which delivered the specimens? Where was the pickup? Trace it.'

'Done. Dead end. The service picked them up from a hotel concierge in Geneva, to which they were given by a female guest as she was checking out. The woman does fit Rowan's description, somewhat, but there's no proof that Rowan was ever a guest in this hotel, at least not under her own name.

'The whole thing was surreptitious. She'd given the concierge info as to the destination of the package several days before. Look, the family has investigated all this, believe me. They're more eager to find Rowan than anybody else. When I called to tell them about all this, they went nuts. That's why I'm going down there. They want to see me personally, and it's their nickel, and I'm happy to oblige. But these people have had detectives all over Geneva. No trace of Rowan. And believe you me, when this family can't find someone, that person cannot be found.'

'How come?'

'Money. Mayfair money. You couldn't have not heard of Rowan's plans last fall for Mayfair Medical. Now talk, Mitch, what are these samples? I have to make that plane. Count on my common sense. If you don't mind the expression, let yourself go!'

Mitchell Flanagan reflected quietly for a moment. He folded his arms, his lower lip jutting a little, and then absently he pulled off his glasses, stared into space, then put his glasses back on, as though he could not think except when he was behind them. He stared intently at Lark.

'OK. It's what you said,' said Mitch, 'or what you said Rowan said.'

Lark didn't respond. But he knew that he had registered his reaction before he could stop himself. He bit his tongue. He wanted Mitch to go on.

'This offspring isn't Homo sapiens,' Mitch continued. 'It's primate, it's mammalian, it's male, it's potent, it has a dynamite immune system, it appears in the final

73

tests to have reached maturity, but this is by no means certain, and it has a baffling way of using minerals and proteins. Something to do with its bones. Its brain is enormous. It may have profound weaknesses. Until I run more tests I don't know.'

'Draw me a picture in words.'

'Based on the X rays alone, I'd say it is one-hundred-fifty pounds in weight or less, and that when the final tests were done in late January, it was six and one-half feet tall. Its height changed remarkably between the first X rays taken on December twenty-eighth in Paris, and those taken in Berlin on January fifth. There was no change between January fifth and January twenty-seventh. No change in any measurement. Which is why I'm saying it may have reached maturity, but I don't know. The skull is not fully developed, but that may be as developed as it gets.'

'How much did it grow between December and January?'

'It grew three inches. Growth took place mostly in the thighs, with some growth in the forearms and a very slight lengthening of the fingers. Its hands, by the way, are very long. The head became slightly larger. Not enough to attract attention, probably. But it's larger than a normal head. Say the word and I'll show what I mean on the computer. I'll show you how it looks, moves . . .'

'No, just tell me. What else?'

'What else?' Mitch demanded.

'Yes, what else.'

'That's not enough? Lark, *you* have to explain all this to *me*. Where were these tests taken? This stuff is from clinics all over Europe. Who did these tests?'

'Rowan did the tests, we *think*. The family's been working on it. But the clinics never even knew what was going on. Apparently Rowan slipped in with this creature, had the X rays taken and slipped out, before anybody ever realized there was an unauthorized doctor on the premises, or that her male subject wasn't a patient. In fact, in Berlin, nobody remembers seeing her at all. It's only the computerized date and time on the X-ray film that confirms she was there. Same with the brain scans, the electrocardiogram and the thallium stress test. She entered the clinic in Geneva, directed the laboratory herself for the tests she wanted, wasn't questioned for obvious reasons – white coat, authority, speaks German – and then she took the results and left.'

'How incredibly simple that must have been.'

'It was. These were all public facilities, and you remember Rowan. Who would question Rowan?'

'Oh, absolutely.'

'The people in Paris who do remember her, by the way, remember her well. But they can't help us find her. They don't know where she came from or where she went. As for the male friend, he was "tall and thin and had long hair and wore a hat."'

'"Long hair"! You're sure of that.'

'As sure as the woman in Paris who told this to the family's detectives.' Lark shrugged. 'When Rowan was seen in Donnelaith it was also with a tall thin male companion who had long black hair.'

'And you haven't heard one word from her since the night before she sent you this stuff.'

'Correct. She said she'd get in touch as soon as she could.'

'What about the call? Any record? Did she call collect?'

'She told me she was in Geneva. She told me what I already told you. She was desperate to get this stuff to me. That she'd try to get it out before morning, that I was to bring it to you. She said that she gave birth to the subject in question. The amniotic fluid was in the pieces and bits of towel. Her own blood, sputum, and hair was included for analysis as well. I hope you did that analysis.'

'You bet I did.'

'How did she give birth to something that isn't a human being? I want everything you've discovered, no matter how random or contradictory. I have to explain all this to the family tomorrow! I have to explain it to myself.'

Mitch curled his right hand and pressed it to his mouth to cover a slight cough. He cleared his throat.

'As I said, it isn't Homo sapiens,' he began, looking directly at Lark. 'It may look like Homo sapiens, however. Its skin is much more plastic – in fact, you only find skin like that in human fetuses, and apparently the creature will retain this plasticity, though only time will tell. The skull appears to be malleable, like that of an infant, and that too may be permanent, but it's impossible to tell. It still had the soft spot, the fontanel, when it was last X-rayed; indeed there's some indication the fontanel is permanent.'

'Lord God,' said Lark. He couldn't resist touching his own head. The fontanels of babies always made him nervous! But then Lark didn't have any children; mothers seemed to get used to it, having little critters around with skin-covered holes in their skulls.

'This thing was never a conventional fetus, by the way,' said Mitch. 'The cells from the amniotic fluid indicate it was a fully developed diminutive male adult when it was born; it probably unwound itself with remarkable elasticity and walked away from its mother, the way a young colt or a young giraffe walks away after birth.'

'A total mutation,' said Lark.

'No, put that word out of your mind entirely. This is no mutation. This appears to be the product of a separate and complex evolutionary process. The end product of a whole different set of chance mutations and choices over some millions of years. If Rowan Mayfair hadn't given birth to this – and it is certain now to me from the specimens that she did – my guess is we would be dealing with some creature developed in full isolation on some unknown continent, something older than Homo erectus or Homo sapiens, much older in fact, and with an entire spectrum of genetic inheritance from other species, which human beings don't possess.'

'Other species.'

'Exactly. This thing climbed its own evolutionary ladder. It is not alien to us. It evolved from the same primal soup. But its DNA is much more complex. If you took its double helix and flattened it out, it would be twice the length of that of a human being. The creature seems – superficially at least – to have carried up the ladder with it all kinds of similarities to lower life forms which we as humans no longer have. I've only begun to break it down. That's the problem.'

'Can you work any faster? Can you find out more?'

'Lark, this isn't only a matter of speed. We're just beginning to understand the human genome – what's a junk gene and real gene. How can we break down the genotype of this thing? It has ninety-two chromosomes, by the way – that's double the number of a normal human being. The makeup of its cell membranes is obviously very different from ours, but how I can't tell you, since I can't tell you very much about our own cell membranes since nobody knows what they're made of, either. That's the dominant theme here. The limits of what I know about this being are the limits of what I know about us. But it is not us.'

'I still don't understand why it can't be a mutant.'

'Lark, it's far too much of a departure. It's way beyond the orbit of mutation. It's highly organized and complete in itself. It's no accident. And it's just too beautifully developed as it is. Think in terms of percentages of chromosomal similarity. Man and the chimpanzee are ninety-seven percent similar. This thing is no more than forty percent similar at most. I've already run simple immunological tests on its blood which prove this. That means it diverged off the human family tree millions of years ago, if it was ever part of the human family tree. I don't think it was. I think it was another tree altogether.'

'But how could Rowan be the mother? I mean you can't just –'

'The answer is as surprising as it is simple. Rowan also has ninety-two chromosomes. The exact same number of exons and introns. The blood, the amniotic fluid and the tissue samples she sent confirm it. I'm sure she'd figured out that much herself.'

'But what about Rowan's past records? Didn't anybody ever notice this woman had double the number of human chromosomes?'

'I've verified everything through blood samples on

file at University from her last physical. She has ninety-two chromosomes, though there is no evidence in the rest of the physical picture to indicate the additional chromosomes were anything but dormant in her case. Nobody ever noticed because nobody ever took a genetic blueprint of Rowan. Who would? For what? Rowan has never been sick a day in her life.'

'But someone . . .'

'Lark, DNA blueprinting is in its infancy. Some people are totally opposed to doing it on anyone. There are millions of doctors all over the world who have no idea what's in their own genes. Some of us don't want to know. I don't want to know. My grandfather died of Huntington's chorea. My brothers don't want to know if they carry the gene for it. Neither do I. Of course sooner or later I'll have myself tested. But the point is, genetic research has just begun. If this creature had surfaced twenty years ago, it would have passed for human. It would have appeared to be some kind of freak.'

'So you're telling me Rowan isn't a human being?'

'No, she is human. Absolutely. As I was trying to explain, every other test taken on her throughout her life has been normal; her pediatric records, all normal, growth rate normal. Which means that this entire set of extra chromosomes was never switched on during her development . . . until this child started to grow in her womb.'

'And what happened then?'

'I suspect its conception triggered several complex chemical responses in Rowan. That's why the amniotic fluid is full of all kinds of nutrients. The fluid was dense with proteins and amino acids. There is some evidence

79

that a substantial yolk remained with this developing creature long after the embryonic stage. And the breast milk. Did you know there was breast milk? It's not normal density or composition. It contains infinitely more protein than human breast milk. But again, it's going to take me months, maybe years, to break all this down. It's a whole new type of placental we are dealing with here. And I barely have what I need to begin.'

'Rowan was normal,' said Lark. 'Rowan carried a package of apparently useless genes. When conception occurred these genes were switched on to start certain processes.'

'Yes. The normal human genome functioned consistently and well in her, but she had these extra genes intertwined within the double helix, waiting for some sort of trigger to cause their DNA to begin its instructions.'

'Are you cloning this DNA successfully?'

'Absolutely. But even at the rate that these cells multiply it takes time. And by the way, there is another curious aspect to these cells. They're resistant to every virus I've hit them with; they're resistant to every strain of bacteria. But they are also extremely elastic. It's all in the membrane, as I said before. It's not human membrane. And when these cells die – in intense heat or intense cold – they tend to leave almost no residue at all.'

'They shrink? They disappear?'

'Let's say they contract, and there you have one of the most provocative aspects of this thing. If there are others like it on this earth, they have left no evidence in the fossil record for the simple reason that the remains tend to contract and disintegrate much more quickly than human remains.'

'Fossil record? Why are we suddenly talking about a fossil record? One minute we have a monster . . .'

'No, we never had a monster. We have a different sort of placental primate, one with enormous advantages. Its own enzymes dissolve it at the moment of death, apparently. And the bones, that is another whole question. The bones don't appear to have hardened. I don't know for sure. I wish I had a team of men working on this. I wish I had the entire Institute –'

'Is this stuff compatible with our own DNA? I mean can you split the strand and combine it with our –'

'No. God, you surgeons are geniuses. Forty percent similarity isn't enough. You can't breed rats to monkeys, Lark. And there's some other violent reaction going on. Maybe just too much conflicting genetic instruction being given by its DNA. Damned if I know. But they sure as hell don't combine. I haven't been able to culture it with any human cells. But that doesn't mean it can't be done. The thing might have come about because of very rapid repetitive mutations inside of nucleotides in a given gene.'

'Back up, I can't follow that. Like you just said, I'm a surgeon.'

'I always knew you guys didn't really know what you were doing.'

'Mitch, if we did know what we were doing, how could we do it? When you need us, and pray you never do, you'll bless us for our ignorance and our sense of humor and our sheer nerve. Now . . . this thing . . . it can't breed with humans?'

'Not unless they're like Rowan. They have to have the dormant forty-six chromosomes. Which is why we must reach Rowan, and test her in every way that we can.'

'But this thing could breed with Rowan, couldn't it?'

'With its mother? Yes. It probably could! But surely she's not crazy enough to try that.'

'She said it had already impregnated her and she'd lost the offspring. She suspected she had been impregnated again.'

'She told you this?'

'Yes. And I have to decide whether or not I can tell this to the family, the Mayfair family, the family that is about to build the largest single neurosurgery and research center in the entire United States.'

'Yes . . . Rowan's big dream. But to get back to this family. How many of them are there? Are we talking brothers and sisters who can be tested? What about Rowan's mother? Is she alive? Is her father alive?'

'There are no brothers and sisters. The father and the mother are dead. But there are many many cousins in this family, and inbreeding has been rampant. No, inbreeding has been almost calculated, and these people are not exactly proud of it. They don't want genetic testing. They've been approached in the past.'

'But there could be others carrying this extra chromosomal package. What about the father of the creature . . . the man who impregnated Rowan! He has to have the ninety-two chromosomes.'

'He does? The man was her husband. You're certain of that?'

'Yes, absolutely.'

'We'll get to him in a minute. There's lots of data on him. Talk to me about the creature's brain. What did you see in the CAT scans?'

'It's one and one-half the size of a human brain. Phenomenal growth took place in the frontal lobes between the scans done in Paris and those in Berlin. I would bet it has immense linguistic and verbal abilities. But that's just a guess. And there is something also extremely complex about its hearing. Superficially there is every indication it can hear sounds humans can't hear. Rather like bats, or sea creatures. In fact, that's a very important point. Its sense of smell is also highly developed, or at least there is room for it to be. One never knows. You know what's so marvelous about this thing? That its phenotype is so similar to others. It evolved in a wholly different way, requiring three times the protein of a normal human being, creating its own type of lactase which is far more acidic, and yet it ended up looking pretty much the way we do.'

'How do you sum it up?'

'I don't. Let's get back to the man who impregnated Rowan. What do we know about him?'

'Everything we could want to know. He lived in San Francisco. He was famous before he married Rowan. San Francisco General tested him in every conceivable way. He just suffered a severe heart attack in New Orleans. His latest records can be accessed immediately. We can do it without asking him, but we're going to ask him. If he has the ninety-two chromosomes . . . well, if he –'

'He has to have them.'

'But Rowan said something about an outside factor. She said the father was normal, she even said she loved the father. He was her husband. She started to get upset on the phone. That's about the time she ended the conversation. Told me to contact the family for money, and then rang off. I'm not sure to this day whether she and I were not cut off.'

'Oh, I know who this man is! Of course. Everyone was talking about this. This is the man Rowan rescued from the sea.'

'Exactly, Michael Curry.'

'Yeah, Curry. The guy who came back from death with the psychic power in his hands. Oh, how we wanted to run some tests with him. I even tried to call Rowan about it. I saw the articles on the guy in the papers.'

'Yes. That's the man all right.'

'He went back to New Orleans with Rowan.'

'More or less.'

'They got married.'

'Definitely.'

'Psychic ability. Don't you realize what that means?'

'Well, I know Rowan was supposed to have it. I always thought she was a great surgeon, but other people insisted she had a healing gift and a diagnostic gift and God knows what. No, what does psychic ability mean?'

'Forget the voodoo crap. I'm thinking genetic markers. This psychic ability could be such a marker. It could occur when the ninety-two chromosomes occur. Oh, this is a real chicken and egg question. God, if there were only records available on these people's parents! Look, you have to persuade this family to allow some testing.'

'Difficult. They're familiar with the genetic studies which have been done on the Amish. They've heard about studies of the Mormons in Salt Lake. They know what the Founders Effect is, and they aren't proud of all their inbreeding. On the contrary, it's sort of a big family joke and a huge family embarrassment. And they continue to inbreed. Cousins marry cousins constantly, just like the Wilkes family in *Gone with the Wind*.'

'They have to cooperate. This is too important. I'm wondering if this damned thing could skip a generation. I mean . . . the possibilities make me dizzy. As for the husband, we can get his records right now?'

'Let me ask him. It's always best to try to be polite. But they are at San Francisco General and there's nothing stopping your picking up the phone as soon as I walk out of here. Curry let them study him. He wanted to know what this gift in his hands was all about. He might have let you study him if you'd reached him in time. The press kind of drove him underground. He kept seeing images, knowing things about people. I think he ended up wearing gloves to stop the images from popping into his head.'

'Yes, yes, I filed the whole story,' said Mitch. He stopped, stymied for an instant, it seemed, then opened his desk drawer and drew out a huge yellow legal pad covered with scribbled messages and, taking a pen out of his pocket, began to scrawl some near-indecipherable message to himself. He started murmuring and then cleared his throat.

Lark waited, and when it was clear that he had lost Mitch totally, he drew him back.

'Rowan said something about interference at the birth of this thing. Possible chemical or thermal interference. She wouldn't explain what she was talking about.'

'Well,' said Mitch, scrawling still, and running his left fingers through his pile of straight dry hair. 'There was thermal activity, obviously, and the chemical activity was enormous. There's some other fluid on these rags. Lots of it. It's like colostrum, you know, what comes before women start nursing, only it's different, too. Much denser, more acidic, full of nutrients like the milk, but with a composition all its own. Much more lactase. But to get back to your question, yes, there was interference, but it's hard to say whence it came.'

'Could it have been psychic?'

'You're asking me? And this is a private conference? We aren't calling the *National Enquirer* when we get out of here? Of course it could have been psychic. You know as well as I do that we can measure heat coming from the hands of people who have a so-called healing gift. It could be psychic, yes. God, Lark, I have to find Rowan and this thing. I have to. I can't just sit here and . . .'

'That's exactly what you have to do. Sit here, with those specimens, see that nothing happens to them. Keep cloning the DNA and analyzing it from every standpoint. And I will call you tomorrow from New Orleans with permission from Michael Curry to test his blood.'

Lark rose, clasping the briefcase handle tightly.

'Wait a minute, you said something about New York. That there was some other material in New York.'

'Oh yes, New York. When Rowan gave birth to this thing, there was a great deal of blood involved. Then there was the question of her disappearance. It happened on Christmas Day. The coroner in New Orleans took all kinds of forensic evidence. This has found its way to International Genome in New York.'

'Good heavens. They must be going crazy.'

'I don't know that any one person has put it all together yet. So far, the family has had scattered reports that corroborate what you've found out – genetic abnormality in mother and child. Rampant amounts of human growth hormone; different enzymes. But you're one up on all of them. You have the X rays and bone scans.'

'The family is sharing all this with you.'

'Oh yes, once they realized I'd spoken directly to Rowan; she gave me some code word to tell them so they would finance your work here. Once they realized I was the last person to talk to Rowan, they became very cooperative. I don't think they grasp what's involved here, however, and they may cease to be cooperative after I begin to explain all this. But right now, they will do anything and everything to find Rowan. They are deeply concerned about her. They're going to meet my plane, and since it was on time when last I checked, I have to get out of here. I'm on my way.'

Mitch came round the desk hurriedly and followed Lark out of the office and into the dim corridor, with its long decorative horizontal strips of lights.

'But what do they have in New York? Do they have what I have?'

'They have less than you have, by far,' said Lark, 'except for one thing. They have some of the placenta.'

'I have to get it.'

'You will. The family will release it to you. And nobody in New York is putting all this together yet, as I told you. But there is another group involved.'

'What do you mean? Where?'

Lark stopped before the door to the outer corridor. He placed his hand on the knob. 'Rowan had some friends in an organization called the Talamasca. Historical research group. They too took samples at the site of the birth and the disappearance.'

'They did?'

87

'Yes. I don't know what's happened on that. I just know the organization is extremely interested in the history of the Mayfair family. They seem to feel they have a proprietary interest. They've been calling me night and day about this since I contacted the family. I'll see one of them – Aaron Lightner – tomorrow morning in New Orleans. I'll find out if they know anything else.'

Lark opened the door and walked towards the elevator, Mitch coming behind him hastily and awkwardly and then staring in his usual confused and unfocused way as Lark pressed the button and the elevator doors opened.

'Gotta go now, old boy,' said Lark. 'You want to come with me?'

'Not on your life. I'm going right back into the lab. If you don't call me tomorrow –'

'I'll call you. In the meantime, this is all –'

'– totally under wraps. I mean totally. Is there something in the Keplinger Institute that isn't under wraps? It's a secret buried in a forest of secrets. Don't worry about that part. No one has access to that computer in my office but me. No one could find the files if they did gain access. Don't worry. This is regular for Keplinger. Someday I'll tell you some of our stories . . . with names and dates changed of course.'

'Good man. I'll call you tomorrow.'

Lark took Mitch's hand.

'Don't leave me dangling, Lark. This thing could breed with Rowan! And if this thing did . . .'

'I'll call you.'

Lark caught one last glimpse of Mitch, standing there, staring, before the elevator doors closed. He remembered Rowan's words on the phone. 'There's one guy at the Keplinger Institute who can be trusted with this. You have to get him. Mitch Flanagan. Tell him I said this is worth his time.'

Rowan had been dead right on that one. Mitch was that man all right. Lark had no fears there.

But as he drove to the airport he had plenty of fears about Rowan. He'd thought she had gone insane when he first heard her voice long distance and her warnings that the call might abruptly be cut off.

The whole problem was, all this was very exciting to Lark. It had been from the start. Rowan's phone call, the samples themselves, the subsequent series of discoveries, even this bizarre New Orleans family. Lark had never experienced anything like this in his life. He wished he could feel more worry and less exhilaration. He was off on an adventure, taking an open-ended holiday from his life at University Hospital, and he couldn't wait to see these people in New Orleans – to see the house there that Rowan had inherited, and the man she had married – the family for whom Rowan had given up her entire medical career.

It was raining harder by the time he reached the airport. But Lark for years had traveled in all kinds of weather and this meant nothing to him, any more than snow in Chicago, or monsoons in Japan.

He hurried to the First Class counter to pick up his ticket and was on his way to the gate within minutes, timing it just exactly right. The flight to New Orleans was boarding now.

Of course there was the whole problem of this creature itself, he realized. He had not begun to separate out that mystery from the mystery of Rowan and her family.

89

And for the first time, he had to admit to himself, he wasn't sure he believed that this thing existed. He knew Rowan existed. But this offspring? Then he realized something else. Mitch Flanagan absolutely believed this being existed. And so did this Talamasca which kept calling him. And so did Rowan herself!

Of course this thing existed. There was as much proof of its existence as there is of bubonic plague.

Lark was the last one to reach the gate. Great timing, he thought again, no waiting, no standing.

Just as he handed his ticket to the young stewardess, someone took his arm.

'Dr Larkin.'

He saw a tall robust man, very young, blond with near-colorless eyes.

'Yes, I'm Dr Larkin,' he answered. What he wanted to say was *Not now*.

'Erich Stolov. I spoke to you on the phone.' The man flashed a little white card in front of Lark. Lark didn't have a free hand to take it. Then the stewardess took his ticket and he took the card.

'Talamasca, you told me.'

'Where are the samples?'

'What samples?'

'The ones Rowan sent you.

'Look, I can't . . .'

'Tell me where they are, please, now.'

'I beg your pardon. I'll do nothing of the sort. Now if you want to call me in New Orleans I'll be seeing your friend Aaron Lightner there tomorrow afternoon.'

'Where are the samples?' said the young man, and he suddenly slipped in front of Lark, blocking the entrance to the plane.

Lark dropped his voice to a whisper. 'Get out of my way.' He was instantly and irreparably furious. He wanted to shove this guy against the wall.

'Please, sir,' the stewardess very quietly said to Stolov. 'Unless you have a ticket for this flight, you'll have to leave the gate now.'

'That's right. Leave the gate,' said Lark, his temper cresting. 'How dare you approach me like this!' And then he pushed past the young man and stormed down the ramp, heart pounding, sweat pouring down under his clothes.

'Damned son of a bitch, how dare he?' he muttered aloud.

Five minutes after takeoff, he was on the portable phone. The connection was abominable and he could never hear a thing on airline phones anyway, but he managed to reach Mitch.

'Just don't tell anybody anything about any of it,' he said over and over.

'Got you,' said Mitch. 'No one knows anything, I assure you. I have fifty technicians working on fifty pieces of the puzzle. I am the only one who sees the picture. No one will get into this building, this office, or these files.'

'Tomorrow, Mitch, I'll call you.' Lark rang off. 'Arrogant bastard,' he whispered as he replaced the phone. And Lightner had been such a nice man. Very British, very Old World, very formal when they'd spoken on the phone. Who were these people, the Talamasca?

And were they really friends of Rowan Mayfair as they claimed? Just didn't seem so.

He sat back; he tried to think through his long conversation with Mitch, tried to relive his phone conversation with Rowan. Molecular evolution; DNA; cell membranes. All of it frightened and enthralled him.

The stewardess put a fresh drink in his hand; nice double martini for which he had not even had to ask. He drank a good icy swallow.

Then he remembered with a start that Mitch had told him he could produce a three-dimensional computer projection of what this creature looked like. Why the hell hadn't he taken a look, for god's sakes? Of course all he would have seen was some crazy neon drawing on the screen, an outline. What did Mitch know about the way the creature really looked? Was it ugly for instance? Or was it beautiful?

He found himself trying to picture it, this thin reed of a being with the large brain and the incredibly long hands.

FOUR

One hour until Ash Wednesday. All was quiet in the small house on the Gulf with its many doors open to the white beach. The stars hung low over the distant dark horizon, a mere stroke of light between heaven and sea. The soft wind swept through the small rooms of the house, beneath the low ceilings, bringing a tropical freshness to every nook and cranny, though the little house itself was cold.

Gifford didn't care. Bundled in a long huge Shetland wool turtle-neck, and legs snug in wool stockings, she enjoyed the chill of the breeze as much as the fierce and specific heat coming from the busy fire. The cold, the smell of the water, the smell of the fire – all of it was Florida in winter for Gifford, her hideaway, her refuge, her safe place to be.

She lay on the couch opposite the hearth, staring at the white ceiling, watching the play of the light on it, and wondering in a passive, uncurious sort of way, what it was about Destin that made her so happy – why it had always been such a perfect escape from the perpetual gloom of her life at home. She'd inherited this little beach house from her Great-grandmother Dorothy, on her father's side, and over the years, she had spent her most contented moments here.

Gifford wasn't happy now, however. She was only

less miserable than she would have been if she had stayed in New Orleans for Mardi Gras, and she knew it. She knew this misery. She knew this tension. And she knew that she could not have gone to the old First Street house on Mardi Gras, no matter how much she might have wanted to, or how guilty she felt for running away.

Mardi Gras in Destin, Florida. Might as well have been any day of the year. Clean and quiet, and removed from all the ugliness of the parades, the crowds, the garbage littering St Charles Avenue, the relatives drinking and arguing, and her beloved husband, Ryan, carrying on as if Rowan Mayfair had not run away and left her husband, Michael Curry, as if there had not been some sort of bloody struggle on Christmas Day at First Street, as if everything could be smoothed over and tightened up, and reinforced by a series of careful legal pronouncements and predictions, when in fact, everything was falling apart.

Michael Curry had nearly died on Christmas. No one knew what had happened to Rowan. It was all too awful, and everyone knew it, yet everyone wanted to gather on Mardi Gras Day at First Street. Well, they would have to tell Gifford how it went.

Of course the great Mayfair legacy itself was in no real danger. Gifford's mountainous trust funds were in no real danger. It was the Mayfair State of Mind that was threatened – the collective spirit of some six hundred local Mayfairs, some triple and quadruple cousins of each other, who had been lifted to the heights recently by the marriage of Rowan Mayfair, the new heiress of the legacy, and then dashed to the rocks of hell by her sudden defection, and the obvious sufferings of Michael

Curry, who was still recovering from the heart attack he'd suffered on December 25th. Poor Michael. He had aged ten years in the month of January, as far as Gifford was concerned.

Gathering this Mardi Gras Day at the house had been an act, not of faith, but of desperation – of trying to hold to an optimism and excitement which in one afternoon of horror had become impossible to maintain. And what a dreadful thing they had all done to Michael. Didn't anyone care what the man felt? Imagine. Surrounding him with Rowan's family as if it were just business as usual, when Rowan had gone. The whole thing was typical Mayfair – bad judgment, bad manners, bad morals – all disguised as some sort of lofty family activity or celebration.

I wasn't born a human being, I was born a Mayfair, Gifford thought. And I married a Mayfair, and I have given birth to Mayfairs; and I shall die a Mayfair death no doubt, and they will pile into the funeral parlor, weeping in Mayfair style, and what will my life have been? This was often Gifford's thought of late, but the disappearance of Rowan had driven her nearly to the brink. How much could she take? Why had she not warned Michael and Rowan not to marry, not to live in that house, not even to remain in New Orleans?

Also there was the whole question of Mayfair Medical – the giant neuro-research complex which Rowan had been masterminding before her departure, a venture which had elicited enthusiasm from hundreds of family members, especially Gifford's eldest and favorite son, Pierce, who was now heartbroken that the medical center along with everything else pertaining to Rowan was on indefinite hold. Shelby was also crushed, though being in law school still, she'd never been so involved; and even Lilia, Gifford's youngest and most estranged, at Oxford now, who had written home to say they must – at all costs – go on with the medical center.

Gifford felt a sudden tensing all over, as once again she put it all together, only to be frightened by the picture and convinced that something had to be discovered, revealed, done!

And then there was Michael's ultimate fate. What was it to be? He was recovering, so they said. But how could they tell Michael how bad things really were without causing him a setback? Michael could suffer another heart attack, one which might be fatal.

So the Mayfair legacy has destroyed another innocent male, Gifford thought bitterly. It's no wonder we all marry our cousins; we don't want to bring in the innocents. When you marry a Mayfair, you should be a Mayfair. You have lots of blood on your hands.

As for the idea that Rowan was in real danger, that Rowan had been forced somehow to leave on Christmas Day, that something might have happened to her – that was almost too terrible a thought for Gifford to bear. Yet Gifford was pretty sure something had happened to Rowan. Something really bad. They could all feel it. Mona could feel it, and when Gifford's niece, Mona, felt something you had to pay attention. Mona had never been a melodramatic, bragging Mayfair, claiming to see ghosts on the St Charles streetcar. Mona had said last week she didn't think anybody should bank on Rowan coming back, that if they wanted the medical center, they ought to go ahead without her.

And to think, Gifford smiled to herself, that the august firm of Mayfair and Mayfair, representing Mayfair *ad infinitum*, stops to listen when a thirteen-year-old speaks. But it was true.

Gifford's biggest secret regret was that she had not connected Rowan with Mona while there had been time. Maybe Mona would have sensed something and spoken up. But then Gifford had so many regrets. Sometimes it seemed to her that her entire life was a great sighing regret. Beneath the lovely surface of her picture-book Metairie home, her gorgeous children, her handsome husband, and her own subdued southern style, was nothing but regret, as if her life had been built atop a great and secret dungeon.

She was just waiting to hear the news. Rowan dead. And for the first time in hundreds of years, no designee for the legacy. Ah, the legacy, and now that she had read Aaron Lightner's long account, how would she ever feel the same way about the legacy? Where was the precious emerald, she wondered? Surely her efficient husband, Ryan, had stashed it in an appropriate vault. That was where he should have stashed that awful 'history'. She could never forgive him for letting it slip into Mona's hands, that long Talamasca discussion of generations of witchcraft.

Maybe Rowan had run away with the emerald. Oh, that made her realize something else, just one of those minor-league regrets –! She'd forgotten to send the medal to Michael.

She'd found the medal out by the pool only two days after Christmas, while the detectives and the coroner's office were making all their tests inside the house, and while Aaron Lightner and that strange colleague of his, Erich Somethingorother, were gathering specimens of the blood that stained the walls and the carpets.

'You realize they will write all this in that file?' Gifford had protested, but Ryan had let these men proceed. It was Lightner. Everyone trusted him. Indeed Beatrice was in love with him. Gifford wouldn't be surprised if Beatrice married him.

The medal was St Michael the Archangel. A gorgeous old silver medal on a broken chain. She'd slipped it into her purse, and meant a thousand times to send it to him – after he came home from the hospital of course, so as not to upset him. Well, she should have given it to Ryan before she left. But then again, who knew? Maybe he'd been wearing that medal on Christmas Day, when he'd nearly drowned in the pool. Poor Michael.

The logs in the fire shifted noisily and the mellow soothing light flared on the plain sloped ceiling. It made Gifford aware of how very quiet the surf was and had been all day. Sometimes the surf died to absolutely nothing on the Gulf of Mexico. She wondered if that could happen on the ocean. She loved the sound of the waves, actually. She wished they were roaring away out there in the dark, as if the Gulf were threatening to invade the land. As if nature were lashing back at the beach houses and the condominiums and the trailer parks, reminding them that they might be wiped off the smooth sandy face of the earth at any minute, should a hurricane or a tidal wave come. And certainly those things would inevitably come.

Gifford liked that idea. She could always sleep well when the waves were fierce and rapid. Her dreads and miseries didn't stem from the fear of anything natural. They came from legends, and secrets, and tales of the family's past. She loved her little house on account of its fragility, that a storm would most surely fold it up like a pack of cards.

This afternoon she had walked several miles south to inspect the house bought so recently by Michael and Rowan, a high contemporary structure built as it ought to be built – on pilings, and looking down upon a deserted sweep of beach. No sign of life there, but what had she expected?

She'd wandered back, heavily depressed by the mere sight of the place – how Rowan and Michael had loved it; they'd gone there on their honeymoon – and glad that her own little house was low and old and hidden behind a small and insignificant little dune, the way you couldn't and shouldn't build them today. She loved its privacy, its intimacy with the beach and the water. She loved that she could walk out her doors, and up three steps and along her boardwalk, and then down and out across the sand to the lip of the sea.

And the Gulf was the sea. Noisy or quiet, it was the sea. The great and endless open sea. The Gulf was the entire southern horizon. This might as well have been the end of the world.

One hour more and then it would be Ash Wednesday; she waited as if waiting for the witching hour, tense and resentful of Mardi Gras, a festival which had never made her particularly happy and always involved far more than she could endure.

She wanted to be awake when it was over; she wanted to feel Lent come on, as if the temperature itself would change. Earlier she'd built up the fire, and slumped down on the couch, merely to think away the hours, as if working on something, counting the minutes, feeling guilty naturally, for not going to First Street, for not having done all sorts of things to try to prevent this disaster, and then tensing with resentment against those who always tried to stop her from implementing her good intentions, those who seemed unable to distinguish between the real and imagined threat, and dismissed everything Gifford said out of hand.

Should have warned Michael Curry, she thought. Should have warned Rowan Mayfair. *But they had read that tale. They should have known!* Nobody could be happy in that First Street house. Fixing it up, that was sheer nonsense. The evil in that house lived in every brick and every bit of mortar; thirteen witches; and to think, all those old possessions of Julien's were up in the attic. The evil lived in those things; it lived in the plaster ceilings, and under the porches and eaves, like bees' nests hidden in the capitals of the Corinthian columns. That house had no hope, no future. And Gifford had known it all her life.

She hadn't needed these Talamasca scholars from Amsterdam to tell her. She knew.

She'd known it when she'd first gone to First Street – a little girl with her beloved grandmother Ancient Evelyn, who was even then called Ancient because she was already old, and there were several young Evelyns then – one married to Charles Mayfair and another to Bryce – though whatever became of them, she couldn't now remember.

She and Ancient Evelyn had gone to First Street, to visit Aunt Carl and poor doomed Deirdre Mayfair, the heiress in her rocking-chair throne. Gifford had seen the famous ghost of First Street – clearly and distinctly – a male figure standing behind Deirdre's chair. Ancient Evelyn had seen it too, no doubt in Gifford's mind. And Aunt Carlotta, that steely, cold and vicious Aunt Carlotta, had chatted with them in the dreary parlor as if there were no ghost there at all.

As for Deirdre, she had been already catatonic. 'Poor child,' Ancient Evelyn had said. 'Julien foresaw everything.' That was one of those statements Ancient Evelyn always refused to explain, though she often repeated it. And later, to her little granddaughter Gifford: 'Deirdre's known all the sorrow and never knew the fun of being one of us.'

'There was fun?' Gifford wondered about that now, as she had wondered then. What did Ancient Evelyn mean by fun? Gifford suspected she knew. It was all recorded in those old photographs of her with Oncle Julien. Julien and Evelyn in the Stutz Bearcat on a summer day, in white coats and goggles. Julien and Evelyn under the oaks at Audubon Park; Julien and Evelyn in Julien's third-floor room. And then there was the decade after Julien's death, when Evelyn had gone away with Stella to Europe, and they had had their 'affair', of which Evelyn spoke with great solemnity.

In Gifford's early years, before Ancient Evelyn had gone silent, Ancient Evelyn had always been willing to tell those tales in a whispered but steady voice – how Julien had bedded her when she was thirteen, of how he'd come up to Amelia Street, and cried from the sidewalk, 'Evelyn, come down, come down!' and forced Evelyn's grandfather Walker to let her loose from the attic bedroom where he had locked her up.

Bad bad blood between Julien and Evelyn's grandfather – going way back to a murder at Riverbend when Julien was a boy, and a gun had gone off by accident, killing his cousin Augustin. The grandson of Augustin swore hate for the man who had shot his ancestor, though all were ancestors of everyone involved in some way or another. Tangle, tangle. Family trees of the

Mayfair clan were like the thorny vines that choked off the windows and doors of Sleeping Beauty's castle.

And to think, Mona was working it all out on her computer, and had only recently made the proud announcement that she had more lines of descent from Julien, and from Angélique, than anyone. Not to mention the lines feeding in from the old Mayfairs of Saint-Domingue. It made Gifford dizzy and sad, and she wished Mona would go for boys her own age, and care a little about clothes, and stop this obsession with family, and computers, and race cars, and guns.

'Doesn't it teach you something about guns?' Gifford had demanded. 'This huge rift between us and the Mayfairs of First Street? All happened on account of a gun.'

But there was no stopping Mona's obsessions, large or small. She had dragged Gifford five times to a miserable little shooting gallery across the river just so they both could learn how to shoot their big noisy .38s. It was enough to make Gifford go mad. But better to be with Mona than to worry what Mona was doing on her own.

And to think, Ryan had approved of it. Made Gifford keep a gun after that in her glove compartment. Made her bring a gun to this house.

There was so much for Mona to learn. Had Ancient Evelyn ever told Mona those old tales? Now and then Ancient Evelyn emerged from her silence. And her voice was still her voice, and she could still begin her chant, like the elder of a tribe giving forth the oral history:

'I would have died in that attic had it not been for Julien – mad and mute, and white as a plant that has never seen sun. Julien got me with child and that was your mother, poor thing that she became.'

'But why, why did Oncle Julien do it with a girl so young?' Gifford had asked only once, so great was the thunder in response:

'Be proud of your Mayfair blood. Be proud. Julien foresaw everything. The legacy line was losing his strength. And I loved Julien. And Julien loved me. Don't seek to understand those people – Julien and Mary Beth and Cortland – for then there were giants in the earth which there are not now.'

Giants in the earth. Cortland, Julien's own son, had been Ancient Evelyn's father, though Ancient Evelyn would never admit it! And Laura Lee, Julien's child! Dear God, Gifford couldn't even keep track of the lines unless she took a pen and paper and traced them out, and that she frankly never wanted to do. Giants in the earth! More truly devils from hell.

'Oh, how perfectly delicious,' Alicia had said, listening gleefully and always ready to mock Gifford and her fears. 'Go on, Ancient Evelyn, what happened then? Tell us about Stella.'

Alicia had already been a drunk by the age of thirteen. She had looked old for her age, though thin and slight like Gifford. She'd gone into barrooms downtown and drunk with strange men, and then Granddaddy Fielding had 'fixed her up' with Patrick just to get some control of her. Patrick, of all the cousins. A horrid idea, though he hadn't seemed so bad in himself back then.

This is my blood, all these people, Gifford thought. This is my sister, married to her double or triple cousin, Patrick, whatever he is. Well, one thing can be said for sure. Mona is no idiot. Inbred, yes, child of an alcoholic, yes, but except for being rather 'petite', as they said of short girls in the South, she was on every count a winner.

Probably the prettiest of that entire generation of Mayfairs far and wide, and surely the most intelligent and the most reckless and belligerent, though Gifford could not stop loving Mona no matter what Mona did. She had to smile when she thought of Mona firing that gun in the shooting gallery and shouting to her over the earplugs: 'Come on, Aunt Gifford, you never know when you might have to use it. Come on, both hands.'

Even Mona's sexual maturity – this mad idea that she must know many men, which had Gifford frantic – was part of her precocity. And Gifford had to admit, protective though she was, she feared for the men who caught Mona's attention. Heartless Mona. Something hideous had happened with old Randall for instance, Mona seducing him almost certainly, and then losing interest in the entire venture, but Gifford could get no straight answers out of anyone. Certainly not Randall, who went into an apoplectic fit at the mention of Mona's name, denying that he would 'harm a fly', let alone a child, et cetera. As if they were going to send him to prison!

And to think the Talamasca with all their scholarship knew nothing about Mona; knew nothing about Ancient Evelyn and Oncle Julien. Knew nothing about the one little girl in this day and age who might be a real witch, no joke.

It gave Gifford a confusing, almost embarrassing, satisfaction to think of it. That the Talamasca did not know any more than the family did why Julien had shot Augustin, or what Julien was about and why he had left so many illegitimate children behind him?

Ah, but most of that Talamasca history had been quite impossible to accept. A ghost was one thing; a spirit that –. Ah, it was all too distasteful to Gifford. She had refused to let Ryan circulate the document. It was bad enough that he and Lauren and Randall had read the thing, and that Mona, of all people, Mona had snatched up the file off his desk and read it in its entirety before anyone knew what had happened.

But the thing about Mona was this: she did know reality from fantasy. Alicia didn't. That's why she drank. Most Mayfairs didn't. Ryan, Gifford's husband, didn't. In his refusal to believe in anything supernatural or inherently evil, he was as unrealistic as an old voodoo queen who sees spirits everywhere.

But Mona had a mind. Even when she called Gifford last year to announce that she, Mona Mayfair, was no longer a virgin, and that the actual moment of deflowering had been unimportant but the change in her outlook was the most important thing in the world, she had made it a point to add: 'I'm taking the pill, Aunt Gifford; and I have an agenda. It has to do with discovery, experience, drinking from the cup, you know, all the things Ancient Evelyn used to say. But I am very health-conscious.'

'Do you know right from wrong, Mona?' Gifford had asked, overwhelmed, and in her deep secret heart even a little envious. Gifford had already begun to cry.

'Yes, I do, Aunt Gifford, and you know I do. And for the record, I've made the Honor Roll again. I just cleaned up the house. And I managed to make Mom and Dad both eat dinner before they started their nightly party. Everything is nice and quiet up here. Ancient Evelyn spoke today. She said she wanted to sit on the porch and watch the streetcars pass. So don't worry. I've got everything covered.'

Everything covered! And then there was Mona's strange admission to Pierce, surely a calculated lie, 'Look, I like having them drunk all the time. I mean I wish they were living human beings and all, and that they weren't drinking themselves right into the grave before my eyes, but hell, I have plenty of freedom. I can't stand it when meddlesome cousins come over here and start asking me what my bedtime is, or if I've done my homework. I walk all over town. Nobody bugs me.'

Pierce had been so amused. Pierce adored Mona, which was a surprising thing, because in general Pierce liked innocent, cheerful people like his cousin and fiancée, Clancy Mayfair.

Mona wasn't innocent, except in the most serious sense of the word. That is, she didn't think she was bad, and she didn't mean to do bad. She was just sort of a ... pagan.

And freedom she had all right, for her pagan ways, and the confession of accelerated sexual activity had also been calculated. Within weeks of Mona's decision to go active, the phone had been ringing off the hook with stories of Mona's various liaisons. 'Do you know that child likes to do it in the cemetery!' Cecilia had cried.

But what could Gifford do? Alicia loathed the very sight of Gifford now. She would not let Gifford in the house, though Gifford went there all the time of course. Ancient Evelyn told no one what she saw or didn't see.

'I told you all about my boyfriends,' Mona had said. 'Don't choose to worry about this!'

At least Ancient Evelyn did not tell those tales night and day, of how she and Julien had danced together to the music of the Victrola. And it may not have ever reached Mona's tender ears that her great-grandmother had had an affair with Cousin Stella. After all, not even clever Mr Lightner had known about that! Not a word in his history about Stella's ladies!

'That was my grand time,' Ancient Evelyn had told Gifford and Alicia with relish. 'We were in Europe, and Stella and I were together in Rome when it happened. I don't know where Lionel was, and that horrid nurse, she was out with baby Antha. I never experienced such love as with Stella. Stella had been with many women, she told me that night. She couldn't even count them. She said the love of women was like the *crème de la crème*. I think it is. I would have done it again, if ever there had been anyone who stole my heart as Stella stole it. I remember when we came back from Europe, we went to the French Quarter together. Stella kept this little place, and we slept in the big bed and then ate oysters and shrimps and drank wine together. Oh, those weeks in Rome had been too brief. Oh . . .' And on and on it had gone, until they were back to the Victrola again; Julien had given it to her. Stella understood. Stella never asked for it back. It was Mary Beth who had come up to Amelia Street and said, 'Give me Julien's Victrola.' He had been dead six months, and she'd been tearing through his rooms.

'Of course I didn't give it to her.' Then Ancient Evelyn would take Gifford and Alicia into her room, and crank up the little Victrola. She would play so many old music-hall songs, and then the arias from *La Traviata*. 'I saw that opera with Stella in New York. How I loved Stella.'

'My dear,' she had once said to all of them – Alicia, Gifford and little Mona, who might have been too

107

young then to understand – 'sometime or other you must know the soft yielding and precious love of another woman. Don't be a fool. It's nothing abnormal. It's sugar with your coffee. It's strawberry ice cream. It's chocolate.'

No wonder Alicia had become what everyone called a perfect slut. She had never known what she was doing. She'd slept with the sailors off the ships, with the army men, with anyone and everyone, until Patrick had swept her off her feet. 'Alicia, I'm going to save you.'

Their first night had been one long drunk, until dawn, and then Patrick had announced he was taking Alicia in hand. She was a lost soul, little thing, he would care for her. He got her pregnant with Mona. But those had been the years of champagne and laughter. Now they were just plain drunks; there was nothing left of romance. Except Mona.

Gifford checked her watch – the tiny gold wristwatch that Ancient Evelyn had given her. Yes, less than one hour more of Mardi Gras, and then at the witching hour it would be Ash Wednesday, and she could go home – back to New Orleans.

She'd wait until morning, probably, maybe even noon. Then she'd drive into the city, cheerfully oblivious to the hideous stream of traffic exiting New Orleans in the other direction, and be home by four o'clock. She'd stop in Mobile at St Cecilia's to get the ashes on her forehead. Merely thinking of the little church, of her saints, and her angels, comforted her, and allowed her to close her eyes. Ashes to ashes. One hour more of Mardi Gras, and then I can go home.

What had been so scary about Mardi Gras, Ryan had wanted to know.

'That you would all gather there at First Street, just as if Rowan were opening the front door! That's what was so scary.'

She thought again of that medal. Must go make certain it was in her purse. Later.

'You have to realize what this house means to this family,' Ryan had said to her. Ryan! As if she had no idea growing up as she had only ten blocks away, with Ancient Evelyn reciting history to her daily. 'I'm not speaking of this Mayfair Witches tale now. I'm speaking of us, this family!'

She turned her head in against the back of the couch. Oh, if she could only stay in Destin forever. But that wasn't possible and never would be. Destin was for hiding out, not really living. Destin was just a beach and a house with a fireplace.

The small white phone nestled into the pillows beside her gave a sudden and jarring peal. For a moment she couldn't remember where it was. The receiver fell off the hook as she grappled for it, then put it to her ear.

'This is Gifford,' she said wearily. And thank God it was Ryan who answered:

'I didn't wake you up?'

'No,' she said with a sigh. 'When do I ever sleep anymore? I've been waiting. Tell me everything went all right up there, tell me Michael is better, tell me no one got hurt or . . .'

'Gifford, for heaven's sakes. What are you thinking when you say something like that, that a litany will change what may have already taken place? You're flinging charms at me. What good will it do? Do you want to hear the words that are scheduled to come out of my mouth? What am I supposed to do? Break it to you gently if someone got stomped to death by a mounted policeman or crushed by the wheels of a float?'

Ah, everything was fine. Nothing was wrong at all. Gifford could have hung up then, but that wouldn't have been very considerate of Ryan, who would now break it down for her into a series of small reports, the central theme of which was: 'Everything went fine, you fool, you should have stayed in town.'

'After twenty-six years, you don't know what I'm thinking,' she said halfheartedly, not really wanting to argue, or even to talk anymore. Her exhaustion was hitting her now, now that Mardi Gras was truly almost over.

'No, I sure as hell don't know what you're thinking,' he said evenly. 'I don't know why you're in Florida, instead of here with us.'

'Skip to the next subject,' said Gifford blandly.

'Michael is fine, just fine. Everybody is fine. Jean caught more beads than anybody else in the family; Little CeeCee won the costume award, and Pierce definitely wants to marry Clancy any minute! If you want your son to do things right and proper, you'd better get back here and start talking about the wedding to Clancy's mother. She's certainly not listening to me.'

'Did you tell her we'd pay for the wedding?'

'No, I didn't get to that.'

'Get to it. That's all she wants to hear. Talk about Michael again. What did you all tell him about Rowan?'

'As little as we could.'

'Thank God for that.'

'He's just not strong enough to hear the whole story.'

'Who knows the whole story?' asked Gifford, bitterly.

'But we are going to have to tell him, Gifford. We can't put it off much longer. He has to know. He is on the mend, physically. Mentally, I can't say. No one can say. He looks . . . so different.'

'Older, you mean,' she said dismally.

'No, just different. It isn't just his graying hair. It's the look in his eye, his way of behaving. He's so gentlemanly and placid, so patient with everyone.'

'You don't need to upset him,' said Gifford.

'Well, you leave it to me,' said Ryan, using one of his favorite phrases, which was always brought out with exquisite tenderness. 'Just take care of yourself up there. Don't go into the water alone.'

'Ryan, the water's freezing. I've had a fire going all day. It was clear, though, clear and blue and quiet. Sometimes I think I could stay here forever. Ryan, I'm sorry. I just couldn't go up to First Street, I just couldn't be in that house.'

'I know, Gifford, I know. But be assured, the kids thought it was the best Mardi Gras ever. Everybody loves being back at First Street. Just about everybody was there, too, at some time or other during the day. I mean at least six or seven hundred of the family trooped in and out. I frankly lost count. Remember the Mayfairs from Denton, Texas? Even they came. And the Gradys from New York. It was wonderful of Michael to let it all go on as usual. Gifford, I don't mean this reproachfully, but if you'd seen how well it went, you'd understand.'

'What about Alicia?' Gifford asked, meaning, Did Alicia make it through sober? 'Were she and Patrick all right?'

'Alicia never made it up to the house. She was completely drunk by 3 p.m. Patrick shouldn't have come. Patrick's sick. We have to get him some medical attention.'

Gifford sighed. She hoped that Patrick would die. She knew she did. Why kid herself? She had never liked or loved Patrick, and now he was the worst sort of burden to all those around him – a vicious drunk, who took special pleasure in being mean to his wife, and his daughter. Mona didn't give a damn. 'I have no respect for Dad,' she said coldly. But Alicia was forever at Patrick's mercy. 'Why are you looking at me like that? What have I done now? Did you drink the last beer? You knew it was the last beer and you deliberately drank it!'

'Well, how did Patrick do?' Gifford asked, hoping against hope that he'd fallen and broken his neck, and that Ryan just hadn't wanted to tell her.

'Had a fight with Beatrice. Something about Mona. I doubt he'll remember a thing. He stormed off home after the parade. You know Bea on the subject of Mona. She still wants to send Mona away to school. And do you realize what's happening between Aaron and Bea? Michael's Aunt Vivian said . . .'

'I know,' sighed Gifford. 'You'd think he would have learned something from his own research into our family.'

Ryan gave a polite laugh. 'Oh, forget about that nonsense. If you'd forget that foolishness, you'd stay here and be with us, and enjoy this time. God knows, things can only get worse when we do find Rowan.'

'Why do you say that?'

'We'll have problems to deal with then, real problems.

Look, I'm too tired now to take that on. Rowan's been missing sixty-seven days exactly. I'm worn out from talking to detectives in Zurich and Scotland and in France. Mardi Gras was fun. We all had fun. We were together. But Bea's right, you know, Mona should go away to school, don't you think? After all, she is some sort of bona fide genius.'

Gifford wanted to answer. She wanted to say again that Mona wouldn't go away to school, and that if they tried to force her, Mona would simply get right back on the plane, or the train, or the bus, and come directly home. You couldn't make Mona go away to school! If you sent Mona to Switzerland, she'd be home in forty-eight hours. If you sent her to China, she'd be back, perhaps in less time than that. Gifford said nothing now. She only felt the usual comfortable aching love for Mona, and the desperate faith that Mona somehow would be all right.

One time Gifford had asked Mona: 'What's the difference between men and women?'

Mona had said: 'Men don't know what can happen. They're happy. But women know everything that can happen. They worry all the time.'

Gifford had laughed at that. Her other precious memory was of six-year-old Mona on the day that Alicia had passed out on the porch of the Amelia Street house, right on top of her pocketbook, and Mona, unable to get the key out of it, had climbed up the trellis to the high second-story window, and carefully broken out only a small jagged hole in the glass with the heel of her Mary Jane so that she could reach the lock. Of course the entire glass had to be replaced, but Mona had been so neat about it, so sure of herself. Just little splinters of glass scattered in the garden and on the rug upstairs. 'Why don't you just tape wax paper to it?' she'd asked later, when Gifford called the man to fix the window. 'That's the way all the other holes in this place are fixed.'

Why had Gifford let that child go through these things? And Mona was still going through them. There was another carousel of grief and guilt that she could ride for hours and hours. Like the Michael and Rowan carousel. Why not? Did a month ever pass that Gifford didn't remember that incident, the image of six-year-old Mona dragging the unconscious Alicia through the front door. And Dr Blades calling from the clinic across the street:

'Gifford, your sister is really sick over there, you know, and that child and Ancient Evelyn really have their hands full!'

'Don't worry about Mona,' said Ryan now, as if he were reading her thoughts in this uneasy weary silence. 'Mona is the least of our worries. We have a conference scheduled for Tuesday regarding Rowan's disappearance. We will all sit down and decide what to do.'

'How can you decide what to do!' Gifford asked. 'You have no evidence that Rowan is being forced to stay away from Michael. You . . .'

'Well, honey, we do have evidence, rather strong evidence. That's the thing. We have to realize it. We are certain now that the last two checks cashed on Rowan's personal account were not signed by her. That is what we have to tell Michael.'

Silence. That was the first definitive thing that had happened. And it struck Gifford as hard as if someone had socked her in the chest. She caught her breath.

'We know for sure they were forgeries,' said Ryan. 'And honey, those are the last checks. Nothing, I mean nothing, has come into the bank since those were cashed in New York two weeks ago.'

'New York.'

'Yes. That's where the trail runs out, Gifford. We're not even sure that Rowan herself was ever in New York. Look, I've been on the phone three times today about all this. There is no Mardi Gras Day in the rest of the country. I came home to a machine full of messages. The doctor who spoke to Rowan by phone is on his way here from San Francisco. He has important things to say. But he doesn't know where Rowan is. Those checks are our last bit of –'

'I follow you,' said Gifford weakly.

'Look, Pierce is picking up the doctor tomorrow morning. I'm coming up to get you. I made up my mind earlier.'

'That's absurd. I have my car. We won't be able to drive back together. Ryan, go to bed and sleep. I'll be home tomorrow in time to see this doctor from San Francisco.'

'I want to come get you, Gif. I'll hire a car, and I'll drive your car home.'

'That's stupid, Ryan. I'll leave at noon. I've already planned it. Go meet the doctor. Go to the office. Do whatever you have to do. The point is, the family gathered and it was splendid, just the way it was supposed to be, Rowan or no Rowan. Michael was apparently a trouper. And two forged checks, well, what does that mean?'

Silence. Of course they both knew what it could mean.

'Did Mona shock anybody tonight?'

'Only her cousin David. I'd say she had a good day. Pierce is fine. He's gone out for a dip with Clancy. The pool is steaming. Barbara's asleep. Shelby called; sorry she didn't come home. Lilia called too. Mandrake called. Jenn's snuggled up with Elizabeth in the den. I'm about to collapse where I stand.'

Gifford gave a long sigh. 'Mona went home to that house with those two? All alone on Mardi Gras?'

'Mona is all right, you know she is. Ancient Evelyn would call me here if anything was wrong. She was sitting beside Alicia's bed this afternoon when I left them.'

'And so we lie to ourselves about that, as always, along with everything else.'

'Gifford.'

'Yes, Ryan?'

'I want to ask you a question. I've never asked you anything like this before, and I don't think I could ask you now, if we weren't . . .'

'Talking on the phone.'

'Yes. Talking on the phone.'

They had many times discussed this strange aspect of their long marriage, that their best conversations were on the phone, that somehow or other, they were patient with each other on the phone, and could avoid the battles they fought when together.

'This is the question,' said Ryan in his customary direct way. 'What do you think *happened* on Christmas Day at that house? What happened to Rowan? Do you have any suspicion, any inkling, any vibe of any kind?'

Gifford was speechless. It was more than true that Ryan had never asked her a question like this in all their lives. Most of Ryan's energy went to preventing Gifford from seeking answers to difficult questions. This was not only unprecedented, it was alarming. Because Gifford realized that she could not rise to the occasion. She didn't have a witch's answer to this question. She thought for a long moment, listening to the fire burn, and to the soft sigh of the water outside, so soft it might have been her own breath.

A number of thoughts passed vagrantly through her mind. She even almost said, 'Ask Mona.' But then she caught herself, protective and full of shame that she would encourage her niece in that sort of thing. And without preamble, or any sort of forethought, Gifford said:

'The man came through on Christmas Day. That thing, that spirit – I'm not going to say its name, you know its name – it got into the world and it did something to Rowan. That's what happened. The man's no longer at First Street. All of us know it. All of us who ever saw him know he's not there. The house is empty. The thing got into the world. It –' Her speech, rapid, high-pitched, faintly hysterical, broke off as abruptly as it had begun. She thought: Lasher. But she could not say it. Years and years ago Aunt Carlotta had shaken her and said, 'Never, never, never say that name, do you hear me?'

And even now, in this quiet safe place, she could not speak the name. Something stopped her, rather like a hand on her throat. Maybe it had to do with the peculiar blend of cruelty and protectiveness which Carlotta had always shown for her. The Talamasca history had said that Antha was pushed through the attic window, that the eye was torn from her head. Dear God! Carlotta couldn't have done such a thing.

She wasn't surprised that her husband hesitated before responding to her. In the silence she was full of surprise herself. It all loomed before her, and she also knew in these moments the terrible loneliness of her marriage.

'You really believe that, Gifford. In your heart of hearts, you, my beloved Gifford, believe that.'

She didn't answer. Couldn't. She felt too defeated. They had been arguing all of their lives, it seemed. Would it storm, would it shine? Would a stranger rape Mona on St Charles Avenue as she walked alone at night? Would income taxes go up again? Would Castro be overthrown? Were there ghosts? Were the Mayfairs witches? Could anyone really speak with the dead? Why did the dead behave so strangely? What the hell did the dead want? Butter is not unhealthy, and neither is red meat. Drink your milk. One cannot metabolize milk as an adult, and so forth and so on, forever.

'Yes, Ryan,' she said sadly and almost offhandedly. 'I believe it. But you see, Ryan, seeing is believing. And I always saw him. You never could.'

She had used the wrong word. Could. Real mistake, that. She could hear the little soft sighs with which he drew away from her, away from the possibility of belief or trust, into his well-constructed universe where ghosts did not exist, and Mayfair witchcraft was a family joke, as much fun as all the old houses, and quaint trust funds, and jewelry and gold coins in the vaults. As much fun as Clancy Mayfair marrying Pierce Mayfair, which really, really, really shouldn't happen, since both were – like Alicia and Patrick – descended from Julien, but what was the use of telling him? What was the use? There was no reason, there was no exchange of ideas, there was no genuine trust.

But there's love, she thought. There is love and there is a form of respect. She didn't depend on anyone in the world the way she did on Ryan. So she said what she always said at such times:

'I love you, my darling,' and it was wonderful to say an Ingrid Bergman line like that with so much heart and mean it so completely. 'I really do.' Lucky Gifford.

'Gifford . . .' Silence on the other end of the line. A lawyer thinking quietly, the man with the silver-white hair and blue eyes, who did the practical worrying with her for the whole family. Why should he believe in ghosts? Ghosts don't try to break wills, they don't sue you, they don't threaten you with Internal Revenue investigations, they don't bill you for the two-martini lunch.

'What is it, darling?' she asked softly.

'If you believe that,' he said. 'If you really believe what you just said to me . . . if this ghost got through . . . and the house is empty . . . then why wouldn't you go there, Gifford? Why wouldn't you come today?'

'The thing took Rowan away,' she said angrily. 'This isn't finished, Ryan!' Suddenly she was sitting up. Every bit of goodwill she felt for her husband had done its usual evaporation act. He was the same tiresome and impossible man who had wrecked her life. That was true. It was true that she loved him. It was true that the ghost had come through. 'Ryan, don't you feel things in that house? Don't you sense things? It isn't over, it's just begun! We have to find Rowan!'

'I'm going to come get you in the morning,' he said. He was furious. Her anger had drawn out his anger. But he was struggling. 'I want to come up there and drive you back home.'

'OK, Ryan,' she said. 'I wish you would.' She heard the plea in her own voice, the plea that meant surrender.

She was only glad that she'd had the courage to say the little bit she had about 'the man', that for the record, she had spoken her piece, and he could argue with her, and beat her down, and criticize her to death later on, perhaps. Tomorrow.

'Gifford, Gifford, Gifford . . .' he sang softly. 'I'm going to drive up. I'll be there before you wake up.'

And she felt so weak suddenly, so irrationally incapable of moving until he came there, until she saw him come through the door.

'Now, lock up the house tight, please,' he said, 'and go to sleep. I'll bet you're sacked out on the couch and everything's open . . .'

'This is Destin, Ryan.'

'Lock up, make sure the gun is in the chest by the bed, and please, please, please set the alarm.'

The gun, good Lord! 'As if I'd use it with you not here.'

'That's when you need it, darling, when I'm not there.'

She smiled again, remembering Mona. Bang, bang, bang.

Kisses.

They still blew kisses to each other before they rang off.

The first time she had kissed him, she was fifteen, and they were 'in love', and later Alicia said, when Mona was born: 'You're lucky. You love your Mayfair. I married mine 'cause of this!'

Gifford wished she had taken Mona, then and there.

Probably Alicia would have let her do it. Alicia was already a full-time drunk. It's a wonder Mona had been born at all, let alone robust and healthy. But Gifford hadn't really thought of taking Alicia's baby from her; she could still remember when Ellie Mayfair, whom Gifford never knew, had taken Deirdre's baby, Rowan, all the way to California, to save her from the family curse, and everyone had hated her for it. That had been the same terrible year that Oncle Cortland had died, after falling down the steps at First Street. So terrible for Ryan.

Gifford had been fifteen and already they were very much in love. No, you simply did not take a baby away from a mother, no matter what you thought. They'd driven Deirdre mad, and Oncle Cortland had tried to stop it.

Of course Gifford could have taken better care of Mona. Hell, anybody could have taken better care of Mona than Alicia and Patrick. And in her own way, Gifford always had taken care of Mona, as surely as she took care of her own children.

The fire had died away. She was getting just a little uncomfortably cold. Best to build it up again. She didn't need much sleep anymore. If she dozed off sometime around two, she'd be fine when Ryan got here. That was one thing about being forty-six. She didn't need sleep anymore.

She went down on her knees in front of the broad stone hearth and, lifting another small oak log from the neat stack beside the fireplace, threw it into the weak little fire. A bunch of newspaper, crumpled, with kindling, and off it went, curling and flaring against the soot-blackened bricks. The bright warmth came out all over her hands and her face, until she was driven back by it, and there was a sudden moment of remembering something unpleasant, something to do with fire and the family history, but then she deliberately and carefully forgot.

She stood in the living room looking out over the white beach. Now she could not hear the waves at all. The breeze covered everything in a heavy drape of silence. The stars shone as brightly as if they were tumbling on the Final Day. And the sheer cleanness of the breeze delighted her and made her want to cry.

She wished she could stay until all this seemed too much. Until she longed for the oaks of home again. But that had never happened. She'd always left before she truly wanted to. Duty, family, something – always compelled her home from Destin before she was ready.

That was not to say that she didn't love the cobwebs and old oaks, that she didn't love the crumbling walls, and listing town houses, and broken pavements; and the lovely endless embrace of her good cousins and cousins and cousins. Yes, she loved it, but sometimes she only wanted to be away.

This was away.

She shuddered. 'I wish I could die,' she whispered, her voice trembling and fading away on the breeze. She went into the open kitchen – no more than a section of the giant main room – and filled a glass with water, and drank the water down. Then she went out through the open glass doors, through the yard, and up the steps and out the boardwalk over the little dune and down on the clean-swept sand.

Now you could hear the Gulf. The sound filled you. There was nothing else in the world. The breeze broke you loose from everything, and all sensation. When she glanced back, the house looked deceptively small and insignificant, more of a bunker than the handsome little cottage it was, behind its levee of sand.

The law couldn't make you change something which had been built in 1955. And that is when Great-grand-mother Dorothy had built it for her children and her grandchildren, and Destin was no more than a sleepy little fishing village, or so everyone said. No condo-minium towers in those days. No Goofy Golf. Just this.

And the Mayfairs still had their bits and pieces of it, tucked away every few miles from Pensacola all the way down to Seaside – old bungalows of various size and age built before the thundering hordes – and the building codes – had come.

Gifford felt chilled, pummeled by the breeze suddenly, as if it had doubled its fist and tried to push her rudely to one side. She walked against it, down to the water, eyes fixed on the soft waves that barely lapped on the glittering beach. She wanted to lie down here and sleep. She had done that when she was a girl. What safer beach was there than this unknown sweep of Destin, where no dune buggies or vehicles of any kind could ever come to hurt you with their wheels or their hideous-ness, or their noise?

Who was that poet who had been killed long ago on the beach at Fire Island? Run over in his sleep, they thought, though no one ever knew? Horrible thing, horrible. She couldn't remember his name. Only his poems. College days; beer; Ryan kissing her on the deck of the dancing boat, and promising her he would take her away from New Orleans. What lies! They were going to live in China! Or was it Brazil? Ryan had gone right into Mayfair and Mayfair. It had swallowed him whole before his twenty-first birthday. She wondered if he could remember now their favorite poets – how they loved D. H. Lawrence's poem about blue gentians, or Wallace Stevens's 'Sunday Morning'.

But she couldn't blame him for what had happened. She had been unable to say no to Ancient Evelyn, and Granddaddy Fielding and all the old ones who cared so much, even though her own father and mother were dead; it was as if Gifford and Alicia both had always belonged to the older ones. Ryan's mother never would have forgiven them had they not gone through with the white-dress wedding. And Gifford could not have left Alicia then, who was still so young and already mad and getting into constant trouble. Gifford hadn't even gone away to school; when she'd asked to go, Ancient Evelyn had said:

'And what is wrong with Tulane? You can ride the streetcar.' And Gifford had. To Sophie Newcomb College. That they'd let her go to the Sorbonne in her sophomore year had been a minor miracle.

'And you a tenfold Mayfair,' Ancient Evelyn had declared when the wedding was being discussed. 'Even your mother would be shocked, God rest her soul, and to think how she suffered.'

No, there had been no real question of Gifford getting away, of a life up north or in Europe or anywhere else on the planet. The biggest fight had been over the church. Would Gifford and Ryan marry at Holy Name or go back in the Irish Channel to St Alphonsus?

Gifford and Alicia had gone to Holy Name School; on Sundays they went to Mass at Holy Name, uptown across from Audubon Park, a world away from old St

Alphonsus. The church had been white still in those days, before they painted the nave, and the statues were exquisitely made of pure marble.

In that church on the Avenue, Gifford had made her Communion and her Confirmation, and walked in procession her senior year, with bouquet in hand, in white ankle-length dress and high heels, a ritual worthy of a debutante.

Marry at Holy Name. It seemed so natural. What was St Alphonsus to her, the old Mayfair church? And Deirdre Mayfair would never know. She was by that time, already, hopelessly crazy. It was Granddaddy Fielding who made the fuss. 'St Alphonsus is our church and you a tenfold Mayfair!'

Tenfold Mayfair. 'I hate that expression. It doesn't mean anything,' Gifford had said often enough. 'It makes me think of folded napkins.'

'Nonsense,' Ancient Evelyn had said. 'It means you are ten times from within the fold. Ten different lines of descent. That's what it means. You ought to be proud of it.'

Evenings, Ancient Evelyn sat on the porch of Amelia Street, knitting until it got too dark for her to see. Enjoying as she always had the drowsy twilight on St Charles Avenue with so many people out strolling, and the streetcars with their yellow lights on inside, crashing along the curving track. Dust, those were the days of noise and dust – before air-conditioning and wall-to-wall carpets, the days of helping take laundry stiff as paper off the back line. You could make people out of the little old clothespins – little wooden men wearing tiny hats.

Yes, we had belonged to the old ones, Gifford

thought. All Gifford's life, her mother had been ill, a recluse, suffering, and pacing the floor behind closed doors, and then dying when Gifford and Alicia were so young.

But Gifford had a lingering fondness for that old way of life, or walking on the Avenue with Ancient Evelyn, who always had her Irish cane. Or reading to Granddaddy Fielding.

No, I never really wanted to leave, she thought. She had never stayed long in any modern American city. Dallas, Houston, Los Angeles, they weren't to her taste, even though their initial cleanliness and efficiency might prove very attractive. She remembered the first time she'd seen Los Angeles as a child. What a city of wonders! But she tired of those other places quickly. And maybe the charm of Destin was that it was so very close to home. You gave up nothing to come here. She could push the pedal to the floor and see those oaks by sunset. New Orleans, city of roaches, city of decay, city of our family, and of happy, happy people.

She remembered that quote from Hilaire Belloc that she'd found in her father's papers, after his death:

> Where e'er the Catholic sun does shine
> There's music, laughter, and good red wine
> At least I've always found it so.
> Benedicamus Domino!

'Let me tell you a little secret,' her mother, Laura Lee, had said to her once. 'If you're a tenfold Mayfair, which you are, you'll never be happy outside New Orleans. Don't bother.' Well, she'd probably been right. Tenfold, fifteenfold. But had Laura Lee been happy? Gifford could still remember her laugh, the crack in her deep voice. 'I'm too sick to think about happiness, daughter dear. Bring me the *Times-Picayune* and a cup of hot tea.'

And to think Mona had more Mayfair blood than anyone in the clan. What was she? Twentyfold? Now, Gifford had to see this computerized family exploration for herself, this endless chart that traced all those many lines, of double cousins and triple cousins marrying one another. What she had wanted to know was this: was there any fresh blood at all during the last four or five generations?

It was becoming ridiculous now, Mayfair marrying Mayfair. They didn't bother to try to explain it to others. And now Michael Curry, all alone in that house, and Rowan gone, heaven only knew where, the child once stolen away for her own good, come right back home to be cursed somehow . . .

Ryan had said once, in a very reckless moment, 'You know, Gifford, there are only two things in life that matter – family and money, that's really it. Being very very rich, like we are, and having your family around you.'

How she had laughed. It must have been April 15th, and he had only just filed his income tax. But she'd known what he meant. She was no painter, no singer, no dancer, no musician. Neither was Ryan. And family and money were their entire world. Same with all the Mayfairs she knew. The family was not just the family to them; it was the clan; the nation; the religion; the obsession.

I could never have lived a life without them, she thought, mouthing the words as she liked to do out here, where the wind off the water devoured everything, where the featureless roar of the waves made her feel lightheaded and as if she could in fact sing. Ought to sing.

And Mona will have a good life! Mona will go to whatever college she wants! Mona can stay or go. She will have choices. There wasn't a fit cousin for Mona to marry, now, was there? Of course there was. She could think of twenty if she tried, but she didn't. The point was Mona would have a freedom that Gifford never had. Mona was strong. Gifford had dreams in which Mona was always very strong, and doing things that nobody else could do, like walking on top of a high wall, and saying, 'Hurry up, Aunt Gifford.' Once in a dream, Mona had been sitting on the wing of a plane, smoking a cigarette as they flew through the clouds, and Gifford, terrified, had been clinging to a rope ladder.

She stopped very still on the beach and tipped her head to the side, letting the wind bring her hair tight around her face, covering her eyes. She floated, the wind holding her steady. Ah, the loveliness of it all, she thought, the sheer loveliness. And Ryan coming to take her home. Ryan would be here. Maybe by some miracle Rowan was alive! Rowan would come home! All would be explained and the great shining miracle of Rowan's first return would begin to give forth its light again.

Yes, sink down and sleep in the sand. Dream of it. Think about Clancy's dress. You have to help her with her dress. Her mother doesn't know a thing about clothes.

Was it now Ash Wednesday?

She couldn't see her watch by the light of the clear heavens. Even the moon did not help, shining so brightly down upon the water. But she felt in her bones that it was the beginning of Lent. That far away in New Orleans, Rex and Comus had opened their ballrooms to one another, and the courts had taken their final Mardi Gras bows. Shrove Tuesday was over.

But she had to go in. Ryan had said to go in, to lock everything up, to turn on the alarm. She knew she would do it because he had said so. Some night when she was really angry with him, she'd sleep in the sand, safe, and free, beneath the stars, like a wanderer. On this beach, you were all alone with the oldest part of the known world – the sand, the sea. You could have been in any time. You could have been in any book, in biblical lands, in Atlantis of legend. But for now, do what Ryan says. Don't for the love of God be asleep out here when he comes! He'll be so furious!

Ah, she wished he was here now.

The night last year that Deirdre Mayfair had died, Gifford had wakened with a scream, and Ryan had taken hold of her. 'Somebody's dead,' she'd cried, and he'd held her. Only the phone ringing had taken him away. 'Deirdre. It's Deirdre.'

Would she have such a feeling when something finally happened to Rowan? Or was Rowan too far away from the fold? Had she died already in some horrid and shabby way, perhaps only hours after her departure? No, there had been letters and messages from her in the beginning. All the codes are correct, Ryan had said. And then Rowan had actually called that doctor in California long distance on the phone.

Ah, tomorrow we'll know something from this doctor, and round her thoughts came again to the same place, and she turned her back on the sea, and walked towards the dark dune and the soft seam of light above it.

Low houses to one side and the other, seemingly forever, and then the great threatening mass of a high-rise, studded with tiny lights to warn the low-flying planes, and far far away, in the curve of the land, the lights of the town, and out to sea the clouds curling in the moonlight.

Time to lock up and sleep, yes. But by the fire. Time to sleep that thin vigilant sleep she always enjoyed when she was alone and the fire was still burning. She'd hear the coffeepot click on at five-thirty; she'd hear the first boat that came near the shore.

Ash Wednesday. A lovely consolation came over her; something like piety and faith combined. Ashes to ashes. Stop for the ashes. And when the time comes cut the blessed palm for Palm Sunday. And take Mona with you and Pierce and Clancy and Jenn to church on Good Friday, 'to kiss the cross' like in the old days. Maybe make the nine churches like they used to do. She and Ancient Evelyn and Alicia walking to nine churches, all of them uptown in those days, when the city was dense with Catholics, true believing Catholics – Holy Name, Holy Ghost, St Stephen's, St Henry's, Our Lady of Good Counsel, Mother of Perpetual Help Chapel, St Mary's, St Alphonsus, St Teresa's. Wasn't that nine?

They hadn't always bothered to go as far as St Patrick's or stop into the church of the coloured on Louisiana Avenue, though they certainly would have, segregation not existing really in Catholic churches, and Holy Ghost being a fine church. The saddest part was Ancient Evelyn always remembering St Michael's and how they had torn it down. Cousin Marianne had been a Sister of Mercy at St Michael's, and it was sad when a church was torn down, and a convent, sad when all those memories were sold to the salvage company. And to think Marianne too had been Julien's spawn, or so it had been said.

How many of those churches were left? thought Gifford. Well, this year on Good Friday, she'd drive up to Amelia and St Charles and challenge Mona to find them with her. Mona loved walking in dangerous neighborhoods. That's how Gifford would lure her out. 'Come on, I want to find Grandmother's nine churches. I think they're all still there!' What if they could get Ancient Evelyn herself to come? Hercules could drive her along as they walked. She certainly couldn't walk now, she was far too old. That would have been foolish.

Mona would go for it, only Mona would start asking about that Victrola again. She had it in her head that now that First Street was refurbished, somebody would find that Victrola in the attic and give it to her. She didn't know that the Victrola really wasn't in the attic at all, but once again hidden with the pearls where no one –

The thought left Gifford. It went right out of her mind. She had just reached the top of the boardwalk and was looking down into her own house, into the warm rectangle of the living room, with its steady flickering fire, and the sprawling cream-colored leather couches on the caramel-colored tile floor.

There was someone in Gifford's house. There was someone standing right by the couch where Gifford had napped all evening, standing right by the fire. Indeed, the man had his foot on the hearth, just the way Gifford liked to put hers, especially when her feet were bare, to feel the inevitable cold that lingered in the stone.

This man was not barefoot or in any form of casual attire. This man looked dapper to her in the firelight, very tall, and 'imperially thin' like Richard Cory in the old Edwin Arlington Robinson poem.

She moved a little slowly along the boardwalk, and then stepped down out of the wind into the relative quiet and warmth of the rear yard. Through the glass doors, her house looked like a picture. Only this man was wrong. And the truly wrong part of him was not his dark tweed jacket, or wool sweater; it was his hair; his long, shining black hair.

It hung over his shoulders, rather Christlike she thought. Indeed as he turned and looked at her, it was a dime-store Christ that came to mind – one of those blinding color pictures of Jesus with eyes that open and close when you tilt it, full of lurid color and immediately accessible prettiness – Jesus of soft curls and soft garments, and a tender smile with no mystery and no pain. The man even had the mustache and neatly groomed beard of the familiar Christ. They made his face seem grand and saintly.

Yes, he looked like that, sort of – this man. Who the hell was this man? Some neighbor who had wandered in the front door to beg a twenty-five-amp fuse or a flashlight? Dressed in Harris tweed?

He stood in her living room, looking down at the fire, with the long flowing profile of Jesus, and gradually he turned and looked at her, as if he had heard her all along, moving through the windy dark, and knew that she had come into earshot and stood now silently questioning him with her hand on the steel frame of the door.

Full face. It was suddenly a bright redeeming beauty

that impressed her; something that bore the weight of the extravagant hair and the precious clothes; and another element struck her, other than the seductiveness of his face. It was a fragrance, almost a perfume.

It wasn't sweet, however, this perfume. It wasn't flowers, and it wasn't candy and it wasn't spice. No. But it was so inviting. It made her want to take a deep breath. And she'd caught this scent somewhere else, only recently. Yes, known this same strange craving before. But could not now remember it. In fact, hadn't she remarked on it then, the strange scent . . . Something to do with the medal of St Michael. Ah, the medal. Make sure the medal is in your purse. But she was thinking foolishly. There was a strange person here!

She knew she ought to be wary of him. She ought to find out who he was and what he wanted immediately, perhaps before she stepped inside. But every time in her life that something like this had frightened her, she had always come through it, half embarrassed to have made such a fuss. Nothing really bad had ever happened directly to Gifford.

Probably was a neighbor, or someone whose car had stalled. Someone who saw the light of her fire, or even the sparks flying from the chimney along this lonely stretch of sleeping beach.

It didn't greatly concern her, not half as much as it intrigued her, that this strange being should be standing there watching her in her own house, by her own fire. There was no menace in this man's face or manner; indeed, he seemed to be experiencing the very same curiosity and warmth of interest towards her.

He watched her come into the room. She started to close the glass door behind her, but then thought better of it.

'Yes? What can I do for you?' she asked. Once again the Gulf had fallen back into a whisper near silence. Her back was to the edge of the world, and the edge of the world was quiet.

The fragrance was suddenly overpowering. It seemed to fill the entire room. It mingled with the burning oak logs in the fireplace, and the charred smell of the bricks, and with the cold fresh air.

'Come to me, Gifford,' he answered with a smooth astonishing simplicity. 'Come into my arms.'

'I didn't quite hear you,' she answered, the forced and uneasy smile flashing before she could stop it, the words falling from her lips as she drew closer and felt the heat of the fire. The fragrance was so delicious, made her want to do nothing suddenly but breathe. 'Who are you?' She tried to make it sound polite. Casual. Normal. 'Do we know each other, you and I?'

'Yes, Gifford. You know me. You know who I am,' he said. His voice was lyrical as if he were reciting something that rhymed, but it didn't rhyme. He seemed to cherish the simple syllables he spoke. 'You saw me when you were a little girl,' he said, making the last word very beautiful. 'I know you did. I can't really remember the moment now. You can remember for both of us. Gifford, think back, think back to the dusty porch, the overgrown garden.' He looked sad, thoughtful.

'I don't know you,' she said, but her voice had no conviction.

He came closer to her. The bones of his face were gracefully sculptured but the skin, how fine and flawless was the skin. He was better than the dime-store Christ, certainly. Oh, more truly like the famous self-portrait of

Dürer. '*Salvator Mundi*,' she whispered. Wasn't that the painting's name?

'I've lost those recent centuries,' he said, 'if ever I possessed them, struggling as I did then to see the simplest of solid things. But I claim older truths and memories now, before the time of my Mayfair beauties and their fragile nurture. And must rely as men do upon my chronicles – those words I wrote in haste, as the veil thickened, as the flesh tightened, robbing me of a ghost's perspective which might have seen me triumph all the quicker and all the easier than I shall do.

'Gifford. I myself recorded the name Gifford. Gifford Mayfair – Gifford, the granddaughter of Julien. Gifford came to First Street. Gifford is one who saw Lasher, don't I speak the truth?'

At the sound of the name, she stiffened. And the rest of his words, going on and on like a song, were barely intelligible to her.

'Yes, I paid the price of every mewling babe, but only to recover a more precious destiny, and for you a more precious and tragic love.'

He looked Christlike as he spoke, as Dürer had in the painting, deliberately perhaps, nodding just a little for emphasis, fingers pressed together in a steeple for a fleeting moment and then released to appeal to the open air. The Christ who doesn't know how to make change and has to ask one of the Twelve Apostles, but knows he is going to die on the cross.

Her mind was utterly blank, unable to proceed, to frame a response or a plan. *Lasher*. Her body told her suddenly how frightened of this strange man she was. She had lifted her own hands and was almost wringing them, a characteristic gesture with her, and she saw her own fingers like blurred wings in the corner of her vision.

In a rush of rampant pulse and heat, she could not see anything distinct about him suddenly, only the beauty itself, like a reflection marring the view through a window. Her fear surged, paralyzing her, while at the same instant forcing from her another gesture. She raised her hand to her forehead; and in a dark obliterating flash, his hand came out and locked itself around her wrist. Hot, hurtful.

Her eyes closed. She was so very frightened that she was not really there for a moment. She was not really alive. She was disconnected and out of time and out of any place; then the fear subsided and rose again, whipping her once again into terror. She felt the tightness and the pressure of his fingers; she smelled the deep warm inviting fragrance. She said willfully, in terror and in rage:

'Let me go.'

'What did you mean to do, Gifford?' The voice was almost timid; mellow; lilting as before.

He stood now very close to her. He was nearly monstrously tall, a man of six and half feet perhaps. She couldn't calculate; just the right side of monstrous perhaps, a being of slender parts, the bones of the forehead very prominent beneath the smooth skin.

'What did you mean to do?' he asked her. Childlike, not petulant, simply very innocent and young.

'Make the Sign of the Cross!' she said in a hoarse whisper. And she did it, convulsively, tearing loose from him, and beginning again, In the Name of the Father, and of the Son, and of the Holy Ghost. The words were spoken inside her. Then she steadied herself, and looked him full in the face. 'You're not Lasher,' she said, the word almost dying on her lips. 'You're just a man. You're a man standing here.'

'I am Lasher,' he said gently as if trying to protect her from the coarseness of his words. 'I am Lasher and I am in the flesh, and have come again, my beautiful one, my Mayfair Witch.' Lovely enunciation, careful yet so rapid. 'Flesh and blood now, yes, a man, yes, again, and needing you, my beauty, my Gifford Mayfair. Cut me and I bleed. Kiss me and you quicken my passion. Learn for yourself.'

Again there was that disconnection. The terror couldn't become old, or tedious, or even manageable. Surely a person this frightened ought to mercifully lose consciousness, and for one second she thought indeed she might do that. But she knew that if she did, she was lost. This man was standing there before her; the aroma that flooded her was coming from him. He was only a foot or two away from her now as he looked down at her, eyes radiant and fixed and imploring, face smooth as a baby's and lips almost rosy as a child's lips.

He seemed unaware of his beauty, or rather not to be consciously using it to dazzle her, or distract her, to comfort or quiet her. He seemed to see not himself in her eyes, but only her. 'Gifford,' he whispered. 'Granddaughter of Julien.'

It was as terrible suddenly, as dismal and as endless as any fear in childhood, any moment of disconsolate gloom when she had hugged her knees and cried and cried, afraid to even open her eyes, afraid of the creaking house, afraid of the sound of her mother's moans, afraid of darkness itself, and the endless vistas of horror that lay in it.

She forced herself to look down, to feel the moment, to feel the tile beneath her feet, and the fire's annoying and persistent flickering, to see his hands, so very white and heavily veined like those of an elderly person, and then to look up at the smooth, serene Christlike forehead with its flowing dark hair. Sculpted ridges for his sleek black eyebrows, fine bones framing his eyes, making them all the more vivid as they peered out at her. A man's jaw, giving force and shape to the lustrous close-cropped beard.

'I want you to leave now,' she said. It sounded so nonsensical, so helpless. She pictured the gun in the closet. She had always secretly longed for a reason to use it, she knew it now. She smelled the cordite in her memory, and the dirt of the cement-walled shooting gallery in Gretna. Heard Mona cheering her on. She could feel that big heavy thing dance upwards as she pulled the trigger. Oh, how she wanted it now.

'I want you to come back in the morning,' she said, nodding emphatically as she said it. 'You must leave my house now.' She even thought of the medal. Oh, God, why hadn't she put the medal on! She had wanted to. St Michael the Archangel, defend us in battle.

'Go away from here.'

'I can't do that, my precious one, my Gifford,' he said as if singing to a slow-paced melody.

'You're saying crazy things to me. I don't know you. I'm asking you again to leave.' But when she went to step back, she did not dare. Some bit of charm or compassion had left his face abruptly. He was staring at her warily, maybe even bitterly. This was like the face of a child, all right, mobile and seductive, and endearing in its quick and abandoned flashes of feeling. How smooth and perfect the forehead; such proportion. Had Dürer been born so perfect?

'Remember me, Gifford. I wish I could remember you. I stood beneath the trees when you saw me. Surely I did. Tell me what you saw. Help me remember, Gifford. Help me weave the whole into one great picture. I'm lost in this heat, and full of ancient hates and ancient grudges! Full of ancient ignorance and pain. Surely I had wisdom when I was invisible. Surely I was nearer the angels of the air, than the devils of the earth. But, oh, the flesh is so inviting. And I will not lose again, I will not be destroyed. My flesh shall live on. You know me. Say you do.'

'I don't know you!' she declared. She had backed away, but only a step. There was so little space between them. If she had turned to run, he could have caught her by the neck. The terror rose in her again, the absolute irrational terror that he would put his long fingers on her neck. That he could, that no one could stop him, that people did such things, that she was alone with him, all of this collided silently inside her. Yet she spoke again. 'Get out of here, do you hear what I'm telling you?'

'Can't do it, beautiful one,' he answered, one eyebrow arched slightly. 'Speak to me, tell me what did you see when you came to that house so long ago?'

'Why do you want me?' She dared to take one more step, very tentative. The beach lay behind. What if she were to run, across the yard over the boardwalk? And the long beach seemed the empty deserted landscapes of horrid dreams. Had she not dreamed this very thing long ago? *Never, never say that name!*

'I'm clumsy now,' he said with sudden heartfelt

sincerity. 'I think when I was a spirit I had more grace, did I not? I came and went at the perfect moment. Now I blunder through life, as do we all. I need my Mayfairs. I need you all. Would that I were singing in some still and beautiful valley; in the glen, under the moon. And I could bring you all together, back to the circle. Oh, but we will never have such luck now, Gifford. Love me, Gifford.'

He turned away as if in pain. It wasn't that he wanted her sympathy or expected it. He didn't care. He was anguished and silent for a long moment, staring dully and insignificantly towards the kitchen. There was something utterly compelling in his face, his attitude. 'Gifford,' he said. 'Gifford, tell me, what do you see in me? Am I beautiful to you?' He turned back. 'Look at me.'

He bent down to kiss her like a bird coming to the edge of a pool, that swift, with the heady beat of wings, and the inundation of that fragrance as if it were an animal smell, a warm scent like the good scent of a dog, or a bird when you take it from its cage; his lips covered hers, and his long fingers slipped up around her neck, thumbs gently touching her jaw and then her cheeks, and as she tried to flee deep into herself, alone and locked away from all pain. She felt a swift delicious sensation spread out in her loins. She wanted to say, This will not happen, but she was caught so off guard by it that she realized he was holding her upright; he was cradling her in his fingers, by her neck, tenderly, and perhaps his thumbs were pressed right against her throat. The chills ran over her, up her back, down the backs of her arms. Lord, she was swooning. Swooning.

'No, no, darling, I wouldn't hurt you. Gifford, what is my victory without this?'

Just like a song. She could almost hear a beat to it and a melody, the way the words flowed out of him in the darkness. He kissed her again, and again, and his thumbs did not crush her throat. Her arms were tingling. She did not know where her own hands were. Then she realized she had placed them against his chest. Of course she could not move him. He was a man all right, stronger than she without question, and it was vain to try to move. Then the deep thrilling sensation engulfed her, rather like the fragrance, and a lovely spasm passed through her, almost a consummation, except that it promised a great rolling succession of consummations to follow, and when you had that many consummations, it wasn't a consummation. It was only a continuous surrender.

'Yes, give in to me,' he said, again with childlike simplicity. 'You are for me. You must be.'

He released her, and then put his hands on her arms and lifted her tenderly off the floor. Next she knew she was lying on it, on the cold tile, and her eyes were open and she could feel and hear him ripping her wool stockings, and she wondered if the sweater wasn't scratchy and rough. What was it like to embrace someone in a sweater that was so thick and rough? She tried to speak, but the fragrance was actually sickening her, or disorienting her, maybe that was more truly it. His hair fell down on her face with delicious silkiness.

'I won't do this,' she said, but her voice sounded distant and without authority, or any power at all to speak to her own self. 'Get away from me, Lasher, get away from me. I'm telling you. And Stella told Mother . . .' The thought was gone, just gone. An image flashed into her mind, an image from long ago of the teenaged

Deirdre, her older cousin, high in the oak, leaning back, lids shut, hips thrust forward beneath her little flowered dress, the look of Bad Thoughts and Evil Touches, the look of ecstasy! And she, Gifford, had been standing beneath the tree, and she had seen the dim outline of the man, the flash of the man, and the man had been with Deirdre.

'Deliver us from evil,' she whispered.

In all her forty-six years, only one man had ever touched Gifford like that, or like this – only one man had ever torn off her clothing, in jest or clumsiness, ever forced his organ inside her, and kissed her throat. And this was flesh, no ghost, yes, flesh. Came through. I can't. God help me.

'Angel of God, my guardian dear . . .' Her own words fell away from her. She had not consented, and then the horrible realization came to her that she had not fought. They would say she had not fought. There was only this hideous passivity, this confusion, and her trying to get a grip, and to push against his shoulder, with the palm of her hand sliding against the smooth wool of his coat, and his coming inside her violently as she herself felt the climax sweep over her, carrying her near to darkness and near to silence and near to peace.

But not quite.

'Why? Why are you doing this?' Had she spoken aloud? She was drifting and dizzy and full of sweet and powerful sensations, sensations like the scent and the powerful stride of his organ inside her, the pumping against her that felt so natural, so thorough, so good! She thought it had stopped and that she was turning over on her side, but then she realized she hadn't moved at all. He was entering her again.

'Lovely Gifford,' he sang. 'Fit to be my bride in the glen, in the circle, my bride.'

'I think, I think you're hurting me . . .' she said. 'Oh God! Oh Mother. Help me. God. Somebody.'

He covered her mouth again as once more the hot flood of semen came into her, spilling over and out and leaking down beneath her, and the sweet soft enchanting sensations lifted her and tossed her from one side to the other.

'Help me, somebody.'

'There isn't anybody, darling. That's the secret of the universe,' he said. 'That is my theme, that is my cry. That is my message. And it feels so good, doesn't it? All your life you've told yourself it wasn't important . . .'

'Yes . . .'

'That there were loftier things, and now you know, you know why people risk hell for this, this flesh, this ecstasy.'

'Yes.'

'You know that whatever you have been forever or before, you are now alive, and with me, and I am inside you, and you are this body, no matter what else you are. My precious Gifford.'

'Yes.'

'Make my baby. See it, Gifford. See it. See its tiny limbs; see it swim to consciousness; see it; pick it out of the dark. Be the witch of my dreams, Gifford, be the mother of my child.'

The sun shone down on her, making her hot and uncomfortable in the heavy sweater, and the pain inside her woke her suddenly, pushing her all the way up through the mist until she squinted not into mist at all but into the glaring sky.

The pain twisted, pulsed. These were cramps, these pains. These were contractions! She willed her hand to slip down between her legs. She felt the wetness and held up her hand to see the blood. She brought it close to her face and the blood dripped down on her. She felt it. Even the glare could not stop her from seeing how very red it was.

The water struck her suddenly; big waves washed right up against her, ice-cold, immensely powerful and then dying away all at once as if sucked back by the wind. She was lying in the surf! And the sun rose beyond the high stack of glowing clouds in the east, and gradually spread across the blue sky.

'Ah, do you see it?' she whispered.

'I'm sorry, my darling,' he said to her. He stood way way far away, a wraith against the brightness, so dark himself that she could make out nothing, except his long hair blowing. And then it came back to her, how silky his hair was, how very fine and black, and how good it smelled. But he was just a distant figure now. There was the fragrance, naturally; and there was the voice; that was all.

'I'm sorry, my precious. I wanted for it to live. And I know that you tried. I'm sorry, my darling dear, my beloved Gifford. I didn't mean to hurt you. And we both tried. Lord. God, forgive me! What am I to do, Gifford?'

Silence. Again came the waves.

Was he gone? Her willowy Christ with his soft hair, who'd been talking to her for so long? The water washed over her face. It felt so good. What had he told her, something about going down into the little town, and seeing the crèche there, with the little plaster Christ Child in the hay, and all the brothers in their brown robes. He had not asked to be a priest, only one of the brothers. 'But you are meant for better things.'

It cut right through the pain for a moment, that sense of lost hours, lost words and images, she too had been to Assisi, she had told him. St Francis was her saint. Would he get the medal for her? Out of her purse? It was St Michael, but she wanted it. He'd understand. If you understood about St Francis you understood about St Michael. You understood about all saints. She had meant to ask, but he had been talking on and on about the songs he used to sing, songs in Italian, and the Latin hymn, naturally, about the sunny hills of Italy and then that dark cold mist hanging over Donnelaith.

She felt nausea and tasted salt on her lips. And her hands were painfully cold. The water stung her! It came again, rolling her to the left, so that the sand hurt her cheek, and the pain in her belly was unbearable. Oh, God, you cannot feel pain like this and not ... what? Help me.

She fell again to the right; she looked out into the glare of the Gulf; she looked into the full blaze of the morning. Lord God, it had all been true and she had failed to stop it, and now it had reached out through the great tangled mass of whispered secrets and threats and it had killed her.

But what will Ryan do without me? What will happen to Pierce if I'm not there? Clancy needs me. They can't have the wedding if this happens to me! It will ruin everything for them! Where in the name of God is

Rowan? And which church would they use? They shouldn't go back to St Alphonsus. Rowan!

How busy she was suddenly, making lists and charts, and drifting, and meaning to call Shelby and Lilia, and when the water came again, she didn't mind the salt so much or the numbing chill of it. Alicia didn't know where the Victrola was! Nobody did but Gifford. And the napkins for the wedding. There were hundreds of linen napkins in the attic at First Street, and they could be used for the wedding, if only Rowan would come home and say that – Good heavens, the only one she didn't have to worry about was Mona. Mona would be fine. Mona didn't really need her. Mona . . .!

Ah, the water felt good. No, she didn't mind it, not a bit, as they say. Where was the emerald? *Did you take it with you, Rowan?* He'd given her the medal. She had it around her neck, but getting her hand up there to clasp the chain was now out of the question. What was required now was an entire inventory, including the Victrola and the pearls and the emerald and those records of Oncle Julien's, all those old Victrola songs, and the dress in the attic in the box which had belonged to Ancient Evelyn. She turned her face this time into the water, thinking that it was probably washing the blood away from her, and off her hand.

No, didn't mind the cold water. Never had. She just minded the pain, the awful sharpening and grinding pain. You think life is worth it? I don't know. What do you think? This pain, it's not particularly unusual, you know, to feel pain like this, to feel this suffering, it's nothing special, you know, it's just. I don't know if it's worth it. I really really don't.

FIVE

Mother was miserable now. She could not free herself from the tape that bound her arms. She struggled. And Emaleth tossed in misery, listening to Mother cry. Mother was sickened by the soiled bed in which she lay; she turned her head to the side and sickness came out of her mouth. The world of Emaleth trembled.

Emaleth ached for Mother. If only Mother knew that she was there, but Mother did not. Mother had screamed and screamed. But no one had come. Mother had gone into a rage and torn at the tape, but it had not come loose. Mother slept for long periods and dreamed strange dreams, and then woke and cried again.

When Mother looked out the distant windows, Emaleth saw the city of towers and lights. She heard what Mother heard – the airplanes above, and the cars far below – and she saw the clouds, and when Mother knew the names of these things, so did Emaleth. Mother cursed this place, she cursed herself, she said prayers to humans who were dead. Father had told Emaleth who these humans were and that they could never help Mother.

The dead lie beyond, Father said. He had been with the dead, and he did not want to be with them again, until his time came. It would come but by that time he and Emaleth would have multiplied and subdued the Earth. The Earth would be for their children.

'We have come again at the perfect moment. Never has the world been so prepared. In the distant past survival was too difficult for us. But not so now; we are the meek; we shall inherit the Earth.'

Emaleth prayed Father would come back. Father would free Mother from the bed; and Mother would not cry anymore. Father loved Mother. He had said, 'Remember I love her. We need her. She has the milk, and without the milk you cannot grow to full height.'

Emaleth waited to rise out of this dark place and stretch her limbs and grow and walk and smile and be in Father's arms. Poor Mother. Mother was in pain. More and more Mother slept.

It was lonely and still in the room when Mother slept. Deeper and deeper Mother slept. Emaleth was frightened Mother would not wake. She rolled over and reached out to touch the edges of the world. She saw the light dying all around her. Ah, but it was only twilight again, and the buildings came on, full of light. Soon Emaleth would see light for what it really was, see it distinctly, Father had said. And it was glorious.

The dead don't know light, Father had said. The dead know confusion.

Emaleth opened her mouth and tried to make words. She pressed on the roof of the world. She pushed and turned inside Mother. But Mother slept, tired and hungry and all alone. Maybe it was for the best that she dreamed now and knew no fear. Poor Mother.

SIX

Yuri had to go to Aaron Lightner, it was as simple as that. He had to leave the Talamasca now, no matter what orders he had been given, and he had to seek out Aaron in the city of New Orleans and find out what had happened in recent months to so distress his beloved mentor and friend.

As the car pulled away from the gates of the Motherhouse, Yuri knew he might never be inside those walls again. The Talamasca was unforgiving to those who disobeyed orders. And Yuri could not plead ignorance of the Talamasca's rules.

Yet it was so simple, this departure – driving away in the muffled gray solitude of the cold morning, leaving behind this blessed place outside London where Yuri had spent so much of his life.

Yuri pondered this and he pondered his remarkable lack of conflict or doubt. Indeed he tried to assume a responsible man's uncertainty, and to review his actions from a moral and logical standpoint as a good man should do.

But Yuri had made his decision. Or rather the Elders had made it for him, when they had ordered him to cease all contact with Aaron, when they had told him that the File on the Mayfair Witches was now closed.

Something bad had happened with the Mayfair

Witches, something bad that had hurt and discouraged Aaron. And Yuri was going to Aaron. In a way, it was the simplest thing Yuri had ever done.

Yuri was a Serbian gypsy, tall, dark-skinned, with very dark eyelashes and large jet-black eyes. His hair was slightly wavy, but cut too short for one to notice. Slender and spry in appearance, he presented a rather narrow figure in his usual careless wool jacket, soft-collared knit shirt and wrinkled khaki pants.

His eyes had a slight upward tilt to them at the outside edges, and his face was squarish with a pleasant, often smiling mouth. In many a country from India to Mexico, he passed for a native. Even in Cambodia and in Thailand, he went unnoticed. There was that bit of Asia in his features and his smooth golden complexion, and perhaps even in his quiet manner. His bosses in the Talamasca called him 'The Invisible Man'.

Yuri was the premier investigator for the Talamasca. He had belonged to this secret order of 'psychic detectives' since he was a child. Though he himself possessed no unusual mental powers, he worked unfailingly well with the Talamasca's exorcists, mediums, seers, and sorcerers on their various cases worldwide. He was a most effective tracer of missing persons, a tireless and accurate gatherer of information, a spy in the normal world, a natural and infallible private eye. He loved the Talamasca. There was nothing he would not do for the Order, no risk that he would not take.

Seldom if ever did he ask questions about his assignments. He did not seek to understand the full scope of what he did. He worked only for Aaron Lightner, or David Talbot, very high placed in the Order, and it pleased him that they sometimes quarreled over Yuri, so well did he do his work.

In a smooth, unhurried voice Yuri spoke a score of languages with scarcely a trace of an accent. He'd learnt English, Russian and Italian with his mother – and her men – before he was eight years old.

When a child learns that much language very early he has a great advantage, not only in the realm of linguistics but in the realm of logic and imagistic thought. Yuri's mind was inherently agile, and not secretive by nature, though much of his life he had repressed his natural talkativeness and only now and then let it come forth.

Yuri had many other advantages from the time of his mother – that she'd been clever, effortlessly beautiful, and a bit devil-may-care. She had always earned plenty from her male companions, yet was a social being, chatting with the employees in the hotels where she entertained her men, and having other women friends with whom to spend an afternoon at a café talking rapidly over coffee or English tea.

Her men had never been mean to Yuri. Many never saw Yuri at all. And those who were longtime companions were always nice to him, otherwise Yuri's mother would never have had them around. He had flourished in this atmosphere of kindness and general indulgent disorganization, learning to read early almost entirely from magazines and newspapers, and loving to roam the streets.

When the gypsies got Yuri, that was when his bitterness and his silence began. And he never forgot that they had been his own kinsmen, his cousins, this band of thieves who bought children and dragged them to

Paris and to Rome to steal. They had got their hands on Yuri after his mother's death in her native village in Serbia, a miserable place to which she had retreated as soon as she realized she was going to die.

Years later Yuri tried to find the little village and what was left of that family; but he could not retrace that journey, northward through Italy and into Serbia. His memory of those traveling days had been maimed by suffering – the knowledge that his mother was in great pain, and laboring for every breath, that he was in a strange land, and that he might soon be alone.

Why had he stayed with the gypsies for so long? Why had he been such a good little pickpocket, dancing and clambering around the tourists, and snatching the wallets from them, as he'd been taught to do? What was wrong in his head that he did that?

The question would probably torment him till the day he died. Of course they had beaten him, starved him, taunted and threatened him, caught him twice when he'd tried to run away, and finally convinced him they would kill him if he tried again. They had also been tender at times, and persuasive, full of promises – all that was true too.

But at nine years old, Yuri should have known better. That's what he figured. His mother, even in childhood, would not have been such a fool. No pimp had ever enslaved Yuri's mother. No man had ever intimidated her, though she had fallen in love now and then . . . at least for a little while.

As for Yuri's father, Yuri never knew that man, but he knew of him – an American from Los Angeles, and rich. Before Yuri and his mother had left Rome on that last journey together, she had hidden in a safe-deposit box the passport of Yuri's father, along with some money, some photographs and a fine Japanese watch. That was all they had left of Yuri's father, who had died when Yuri was only two.

Yuri was ten before he managed to reclaim those old treasures.

The gypsies had had him stealing in Paris for months, and then in Venice, and in Florence, and only as winter came on had they gone to Rome.

When he beheld the Eternal City, the city he had known with his mother, Yuri seized his opportunity. He knew where to go. In the middle of a Sunday morning, while the gypsy thieves worked the crowds of Vatican Square, he made his bid for freedom, diving right into a taxi with a wallet of newly stolen money, and soon was making his way through the crowded tourist cafés of the Via Veneto, looking for rich company as his mother had always so gracefully done.

It was no mystery to Yuri that there were men who preferred little boys to women. And he had learnt much from example, having watched his mother often through the keyhole or the crack in the door. It was quite obvious to him that to be an initiator can be easier than to be passive; and that if intimacy with strangers occurs in an atmosphere of graciousness, it is not so hard to bear.

Another advantage perhaps was that he was by nature as affectionate as his mother, and now he would call upon that, for he needed it, and it had always worked so well for her.

He was lean from the miserable diet allowed him by his captors, but his teeth were very straight and he had managed to keep them very white. That his voice was beautiful he had no doubt. Practicing his smile before the mirror of a public lavatory, he then struck out to try it upon the companions of his choice.

He proved an excellent judge of character.

Except for a couple of little mistakes, he was soon back in his mother's element, among the familiar accoutrements of fine hotel rooms, quietly grateful for the delicious hot showers, and the scrumptious room service suppers, rattling off with convincing ease – and a little bitter laughter – whatever story was necessary to satisfy the questions of his bed partners and release from the constraints of conscience their obvious and predictable and entirely manageable desires.

To one he said he was Hindu, to another Portuguese, and even once that he was American. His parents were tourists on vacation, he said, who left him to shop and to wander. Yes, if the nice gentleman wanted to buy him clothes in the lobby shops, he was delighted to accept this. His parents would never notice, don't even think about it. As for books and magazines, yes, indeed, and chocolate, he loved it. His smiles and expressions of thanks were a mixture of art and truth.

He translated for his customers when they required it. He carried their bundles for them. He took them by taxi to the Villa Borghese – one of his favorite places – and showed them all the murals and statues, and special things he liked. He did not even count the money they paid him, slipping it into his pocket with a bright smile and a little knowing wink.

But he lived in terror that the gypsies would spot him and reclaim him. He was so afraid of it that it took the breath out of him. He stayed indoors as much as he could. Sometimes he stood shivering with fear in alleyways, smoking a cigarette, and cursing to himself, and wondering if he dared leave Rome. The gypsies had been headed to Naples. Maybe they were gone.

Sometimes he hung about the hotel corridors, eating what he could from the leftovers on the room service trays set outside the doors.

But things became easier and easier. He learnt to ask about sleeping the night through in a clean bed before he made his little deals.

One sweet gray-haired American man bought him a camera simply because he inquired about such things, and a Frenchman gave him a portable radio, saying he was tired of carrying it around. Two young Arabs bought him a heavy sweater in an English import shop.

By the tenth day of his new freedom, his paper wealth was becoming too cumbersome for him. His pockets were bulging. He had even worked up his nerve to go into a fine restaurant at noon and order a meal for himself alone. 'Mamma says I'm to eat my spinach,' he said to the waiter in his best Italian. 'You have spinach?' – knowing full well that the spinach is one of the nicest things in a Roman restaurant, barely cooked as it is so that it is not bitter. The tender veal piccata was excellent! He left a large tip near his plate as he went out.

But how long could this go on?

On the fifteenth day of his adventure – perhaps – it might have been slightly later – he came upon the man who was to change the course of his life.

It was November now and just getting cold. Yuri was in the Via Condotti, where he had bought himself a new cashmere scarf in one of the fashionable shops not too far from the Spanish Steps. His camera was hanging from his shoulder; his radio was in his shirt pocket under his sweater. He was loaded with cash, smoking a cigarette and munching on popcorn from a small cellophane bag, as he strolled along, enjoying the early evening with the cafés full of lights and noisy Americans, not thinking too much about the gypsies now, as he had not seen them since his flight.

The narrow street was for pedestrians only, and the pretty young girls were going home from work, walking arm in arm as was their custom in Rome, or guiding their brightly painted Vespa scooters through the crowds to reach the nearby thoroughfares. Yuri was getting hungry. Popcorn wasn't enough. Maybe he would go into one of these restaurants. He'd ask for a table for him and his mother, wait an appropriate amount of time, and then order, being careful to display his money so that the waiter would think he was rich.

As he tried to make up his mind on this matter, licking the salt from the popcorn off his lips and crushing out his cigarette, he saw a man at a café table, hunched over a half-empty glass and a carafe of wine. A man in his twenties, it was, with shoulder-length shaggy hair, but fine tailored clothes. This indicated a young American, not a penniless hippie, and yes, there was a very expensive Japanese camera on the table beside the man, and a notebook and a valise. Indeed, the man was apparently trying to write in the leather-covered notebook, but each time he would take pen in hand and jot a few words, he would begin to cough painfully, just the way that Yuri's mother had coughed on that last journey, each shudder sending a flash of pain through his features, so that his eyes squinched shut and then opened as if in disbelief that something so simple could hurt so much.

Yuri watched him. Not only was this person sick, he was cold. He was shivering. He was also drunk. This repelled Yuri slightly because it made him think of his gypsy masters who were always drunk; and Yuri by nature hated to be muddled, and so had his mother, whose only addiction was coffee as far as he could ever recall.

But in spite of this drunkenness, everything else about the man drew Yuri. His helplessness, his obvious youth, his clear despair. The man tried to write a little more; then he looked about as if he knew he must seek some warm place now that the evening had come down full upon him, and then he lifted his glass of dark red wine and drained it slowly and sat back, giving another one of those agonizing coughs which shook his narrow shoulders and left him sagging against the back of the iron chair.

About twenty-five perhaps was this man; his shaggy hair was clean. He wore a wool vest under his blue jacket and over his white shirt and silk tie. And surely if he had not been so drunk and so sick, this man would have been fair game. Good game.

Only he was sick. And it ripped at Yuri's heart the way he sat there, so obviously miserable, and seemingly incapable of moving, though he wanted to move. Yuri cast an eye around. He saw no gypsies, nor anyone who might be a gypsy. He saw no police. It would be no problem at all to help this poor man get off the streets and into someplace warm.

He went up to the table. He said in English, 'You're cold. Let me help you to a taxi. You can get a taxi up there by the Piazza di Spagna. You can go to your hotel.'

The man gazed at him as if he could not understand the English. Yuri bent down and put his hand on the man's shoulder. The man was feverish. The man's eyes were bloodshot. But what an interesting face he had. The bones of his face were very large, especially the cheekbones, and the high lobes of the forehead. And how very fair was this man. Perhaps Yuri had been wrong, and this was a Swede or a Norwegian who did not understand English.

But then the man said, 'Little man,' softly and smiled. 'My little man.'

'I *am* a little man,' said Yuri, squaring his shoulders. He gave a smile and a wink with his right eye. But in fact, a thrill of pain passed through him, because this was exactly the phrase his mother had always used to him. And this stranger had said it in the very same way. 'Let me help you,' said Yuri. He took the man's right hand, which lay lifeless and wet on the table. 'You're so cold.'

The man tried to speak again but he began to cough. Yuri stiffened. He feared suddenly that the man would cough blood. The man took out a handkerchief, awkwardly as if he could scarce manage the gesture, and covered his face with it. He shuddered in perfect silence as if swallowing everything – blood, noise, pain. Then in a curiously awkward and lopsided fashion, he tried to get to his feet.

Yuri took command. He slung his arm around the man's narrow waist and pulled him gently up and off through the crowd of iron tables with the chattering tourists, and then he helped him slowly and patiently along the beautiful clean Via Condotti, past the bright flower stands, and the open shops.

It was now dark.

When they reached the traffic rushing before the Spanish Steps, the man whispered that there was a hotel just at the top. He did not know if he could make that climb. Yuri debated. A taxi ride round and about would take a long time. But that was best for this man, for the climb might really hurt him. Yuri flagged a taxi, he gave quick directions.

'Yes, the Hassler,' said the man with great relief, sinking down against the seat, his eyes rolling up in his head suddenly as if he were going to die then and there.

But when they reached the familiar lobby, where Yuri had played often as a child, but not enough to be remembered by the aloof and critical-looking employees, it seemed the man had no room there – only a great wad of Italian money, and an impressive packet of international credit cards. In smooth and easy Italian – broken only by a few coughs – the man explained that he wanted a suite, his right arm all the while heavily draped over Yuri's shoulder, no explanation for Yuri's presence as he leaned upon Yuri, as if, if it weren't for Yuri, he would fall.

On the bed, he collapsed and lay silent for a long time. A faint warm stagnant odor rose from him, and his eyes slowly opened and closed.

Yuri ordered soup from room service, bread and butter, wine. He didn't know what else to do for this man. The man lay there smiling at him, as if he found something in Yuri's manner endearing. Yuri knew that expression. His mother had often looked at him in that way.

Yuri went into the bathroom to smoke a cigarette, so the smoke would not bother the man.

When the soup came he fed the man spoon by spoon. The room was nice and warm. And he did not mind lifting the wineglass to the man's lips. It made him feel good to see the man eat. His own hunger in recent months among the gypsies had been a terrible, terrible thing to him, something he'd never known as a little child.

Only when some of the wine trickled down the man's badly shaven chin did Yuri realize that part of this man's body was paralyzed. The man tried to move his right arm and hand but couldn't. Indeed, it had been with his left hand that he'd been trying to write in the café, Yuri realized, and with his left hand that he had taken his money from his pocket downstairs; and that was why he had dropped it. The arm placed around Yuri had been useless, almost impossible to control. Half the man's face was paralyzed as well.

'What can I do for you?' Yuri asked in Italian. 'Shall I call a doctor? You must have a doctor. What about your family? Can you tell me how to call them?'

'Talk to me,' said the man in Italian. 'Stay with me. Don't go away.'

'Talk? But why? What should I say?'

'Tell me stories,' said the man softly in Italian. 'Tell me who you are and where you come from. Tell me your name.'

Yuri made up a story. This time he was from India, the son of a maharaja. His mother had run away with him. They had been kidnapped by murderous men in Paris. Yuri had only just escaped. He said all these things rapidly and lightly, with little or no feeling, and he realized the man was smiling at him; the man knew he was making it up; and as the man smiled, and even laughed a little, Yuri began to embellish, making the tale all the more fantastic and slightly silly and as surprising as possible, loving to see the flash of good humor in the man's eyes.

Yuri's make-believe mother had had a fabulous jewel in her possession. A giant ruby which the maharaja must have back. But his mother had hid it in a safe-deposit box in Rome, and when the murderers strangled her and threw her body in the Tiber, she shouted with her last gasp of breath to Yuri that he must never tell where it was. He had then hopped into a little Fiat automobile and made a spectacular escape from his captors. And when he got the jewel, he had discovered the most amazing thing. It was no jewel at all but a tiny box, with a spring lock and little hinges, and inside lay a vial of fluid which gave one eternal health and youth.

Yuri stopped suddenly. A great sinking feeling came over him. Indeed he thought he was going to be sick. In a panic, he continued, speaking in the same voice. 'Of course it was too late for my mother; she was dead and gone into the Tiber. But the fluid can save the whole world.'

He looked down. The man was smiling at him from the pillow, his hair matted and damp on his forehead and on his neck, his shirt soiled around the collar from this dampness, his tie loose.

'Could it save me?' asked the man.

'Oh, yes!' said Yuri. 'Yes, but . . .'

'Your captors took it,' said the man.

'Yes, they crept up behind me right in the lobby of the bank! They snatched it from my fingers. I ran to the bank guard. I seized his pistol. I shot two of them dead on the floor. But the other ran with the jewel. And the tragedy, the horror, yes, the horror is that he does not know what is in it. He will probably sell it to some peddler. He does not know! The maharaja never told the evil men why he wanted my mother brought back.'

Yuri stopped. How could he have said such a thing . . . a fluid that would give one eternal youth? And here this young man was sick unto death, maybe even dying, unable to move his right arm, though he tried again and again to lift it. How could Yuri have said it? And he thought of his own mother, dead on the little bed in Serbia, and the gypsies coming in and saying they were his cousins and uncles! Liars! And the filth there, the filth.

Surely she would never never have left him there if she had dreamed of what was going to happen. A cold fury filled him.

'Tell me about the maharaja's palace,' said the man softly.

'Oh, yes, the palace. Well, it's made entirely of white marble . . .' With a great soft relief Yuri pictured it. He talked of the floors, the carpets, the furniture . . .

And after that he told many stories about India, and Paris, and fabulous places he had been.

When he woke it was early morning. He was seated at the window with his arms folded on the sill. He had been sleeping that way, his head on his arms. The great sprawling city of Rome lay under a gray hazy light. Noises rose from the narrow streets below. He could hear the thunder of all those tiny motorcars rushing to and fro.

He looked at the man. The man was staring at him. For a moment he thought the man was dead. Then the man said softly, 'Yuri, you must make a call for me now.'

Yuri nodded. He noted silently that he had not told this man his name. Well, perhaps he'd used it in the stories. It didn't matter. He brought the phone from the bedside table, and, climbing on the bed, beside the man, he repeated the name and number to the operator. The call was to a man in London. When he answered, it was in English, what Yuri knew to be an educated voice.

Yuri relayed the message as the sick man lay there speaking softly and spiritlessly in Italian.

'I am calling for your son, Andrew. He is very sick. Very. He is in the Hotel Hassler in Rome. He asks that you come to him. He says he can no longer come to you.'

The man on the other end switched quickly into Italian and the conversation went on for some time.

'No, sir,' Yuri argued, obeying Andrew's instructions. 'He says he will not see a doctor. Yes, sir, he will remain here.' Yuri gave the room number. 'I will see that he eats, sir.' Yuri described the man's condition as best he could with the man listening to him. He described the apparent paralysis. He knew the father was frantic with worry. The father would take the next plane for Rome.

'I'll try to persuade him to see a doctor. Yes, sir.'

'Thank you, Yuri,' said the man on the other end of the line. And once again, Yuri realized he had not told this man his name. 'Please do stay with him,' said the man. 'And I shall be there as soon as I possibly can.'

'Don't worry,' said Yuri. 'I won't leave.'

As soon as he'd rung off, he put forth the argument again.

'No doctors,' said Andrew. 'If you pick up that phone and call for a doctor, I'll jump from this window. Do you hear? No doctors. It's much too late for that.'

Yuri was speechless. He felt that he might burst into tears. He remembered his mother coughing as they sat together on the train going into Serbia. Why had he not forced her to see a doctor? Why?

'Talk to me, Yuri,' said the man. 'Make up stories. Or you can tell me about her, if you wish. Tell me about your mother. I see her. I see her beautiful black hair. The doctor wouldn't have helped her, Yuri. She knew it. Talk to me, please.'

A faint chill passed over Yuri as he looked into the man's eyes. He knew the man was reading his thoughts. Yuri's mother had told him of gypsies who could do this. Yuri did not have this talent himself. His mother had claimed to have it, but Yuri had not believed it. He had never seen any real evidence of it. He felt a deep hurt, thinking of her on the train, and he wanted to believe that it had been too late for a doctor, but he would never know for sure. The knowledge numbed him and made him feel utterly silent and black inside and cold.

'I'll tell you stories if you will eat some breakfast,' said Yuri. 'I'll order something hot for you.'

The man stared again listlessly and then he smiled. 'All right, little man,' he said, 'anything you say. But no doctor. Call for the food from right here. And Yuri, if I don't speak again, remember this. Don't let the gypsies get you again. Ask my father to help you . . . when he comes.'

The father did not arrive until evening.

Yuri was in the bathroom with the man, and the man was vomiting into the toilet, and clinging to Yuri's neck so that he did not fall. The vomit had blood in it. Yuri had a time of it holding him, the wretched smell of the vomit sickening him, but he held tight to the man. Then he looked up and saw the figure of the father, white-haired, though not so very old, and plainly rich. Beside him stood a bellhop of the hotel.

Ah, so this is the father, thought Yuri, and a quiet burst of anger heated him for a moment, and then left him feeling oddly listless, and unable to move.

How well-groomed was this man with his thick wavy white hair, and what fine clothes he had. He came forward and took his son by the shoulders, and Yuri stepped back. The young bellhop also gave his assistance. They placed Andrew on the bed.

Andrew reached out frantically for Yuri. He called Yuri's name.

'I'm here, Andrew,' said Yuri. 'I won't leave you. You mustn't worry. Now let your father call the doctor, please, Andrew. Do as your father says.'

He sat beside the sick man, one knee bent, holding the man's hand and looking into his face. The sick man's stubbly beard was thicker now, coarse, and brownish, and his hair gave off the smell of sweat and grease. Yuri struggled not to cry.

Would the father blame him that he had not called a doctor? He did not know. The father was talking to the bellhop. Then the bellhop went away and the father sat in a chair and merely looked at his son. The father didn't seem sad or alarmed so much as merely worried in a mild sort of way. He had kindly blue eyes, and hands with large knuckles, and heavy blue veins. Old hands.

Andrew dozed for a long time. Then he asked again for Yuri to tell him the story about the maharaja's palace. Yuri was distressed by the father's presence. But he blotted out the presence of the father. This man was dying. And the father was not calling a doctor! He was not insisting upon it. What in the name of God was wrong with this father that he did not take care of his son? But if Andrew wanted to hear the story again, fine.

He remembered once his mother had been with a very old German man in the Hotel Danieli for many days. When one of her women friends had asked how she could stand such an old man, she'd said, 'He's kind to me and he's dying. I would do anything to make it easy for him.' And Yuri remembered the expression in her eyes when they had come at last to that miserable village and the gypsies told her that her own mother was already dead.

Yuri told all about the maharaja. He told about his elephants, and their beautiful saddles of red velvet trimmed in gold. He told about his harem, of which Yuri's mother had been the queen. He told about a game of chess that he and his mother played for five long years with nobody winning as they sat at a richly draped table beneath a mangrove tree. He told about his little brothers and sisters. He told about a pet tiger on a golden chain.

Andrew was sweating terribly. Yuri went for a washcloth from the bathroom, but the man opened his eyes and cried out for him. He hurried back, and wiped the man's forehead and then all of his face. The father never moved. What the hell was wrong with this father!

Andrew tried to touch Yuri with his left hand but it seemed he could not move that hand either now. Yuri felt a sudden panic. Firmly, he lifted the man's hand and stroked his own face with the man's fingers, and he saw the man smile.

About a half hour after that, the man lapsed into sleep. And then died. Yuri was watching him. He saw it happen. The chest ceased to move. The eyelids opened a fraction. Then nothing more.

He glanced at the father. The father sat there with his eyes riveted upon the son. Yuri dared not move.

Then at last the father came over to the bed, and stood looking down upon Andrew, and then he bent and kissed Andrew's forehead. Yuri was amazed. No doctor, and now he kisses him, he thought angrily. He could feel his own face twisting up, he knew he was going to cry, and he couldn't stop it. And suddenly he was crying.

He went into the bathroom, blew his nose with toilet tissue, and took out a cigarette, packing it on the back of his hand, shoving it in his mouth and lighting it, even though his lips were quivering, and he began to smoke in hasty but delicious gulps as the tears clouded up his eyes.

In the room, beyond the door, there was much noise. People came and went. Yuri leaned against the white tile, smoking cigarette after cigarette. He soon stopped crying. He drank a glass of water, and stood there, arms folded, thinking, I ought to slip away.

The hell he would ask this man for help against the gypsies. The hell he would ask him for anything. He'd wait until they had finished all their commotion in there, and then slip out. If anyone questioned him, he would give some clever little excuse, and then be off. No problem. No problem at all. Maybe he'd leave Rome.

'Don't forget the safe-deposit box,' said the father.

Yuri jumped. The white-haired man was standing in the door. Behind him, the room appeared to be empty. The body of Andrew had been taken away.

'What do you mean?' demanded Yuri in Italian. 'What are you saying to me?'

'Your mother left it for you, with your father's passport, and money. She wanted you to have it.'

'I no longer have the key.'

'We'll go to the bank. We'll explain.'

'I don't want anything from you!' said Yuri furiously. 'I can do well on my own.' He made to move past the man, but the man caught his shoulder, and the man's hand was surprisingly strong for such an old hand.

'Yuri, please. Andrew wanted me to help you.'

'You let him die. Some father you are! You sat there and you let him die!' Yuri shoved the man off balance, and was about to make his getaway when the man caught him around the waist.

'I'm not really his father, Yuri,' he said, as he set Yuri down and pushed him gently against the wall. The man collected himself somewhat. He straightened the lapels of his coat, and he gave a long sigh. He looked calmly at Yuri. 'We belong to an organization. In that organization, he thought of me as his father, but I wasn't really his father. And he came to Rome in order to die. It was his wish to die here. I did what he wanted. If he had wanted anything else done he would have told me. But all he asked of me was that I take care of you.'

Again, mind reading. So clever, these men! What were they? A bunch of rich gypsies? Yuri sneered. He folded his arms, and dug his heel into the carpet and looked at the man suspiciously.

'I want to help you,' the man said. 'You're better than the gypsies who stole you.'

'I know,' said Yuri. He thought of his mother. 'Some people are better than others. Much better.'

'Exactly.'

Bolt now, he thought. And he tried it, but once again the man tackled him and held him tight. Yuri was strong for ten and this was an old man. But it was no good.

'Give up just for a moment, Yuri,' said the man. 'Give up long enough for us to go to the bank and open the deposit box. Then we can decide what to do.'

And Yuri was soon crying, and letting the man lead him out of the hotel and into the waiting car, a fine German sedan. The bank was vaguely familiar to Yuri, but the people inside it were perfect strangers. Yuri watched in keen amazement as the white-haired Englishman explained everything, and soon the deposit box was opened, and Yuri was presented with the contents – several passports, the Japanese watch of his father, a thick envelope of lire and American dollars, and a packet of letters, one of which at least was addressed to his mother at a Rome address.

Yuri found himself powerfully excited to see these things, to touch them, to be close again in his mind to the moment when he and his mother had come here and she had placed everything in the box. After the bank men put all these articles into brown envelopes for him, he held these envelopes to his chest.

The Englishman led him back out and into the car, and within minutes they were making another stop. It was a small office, where the Englishman greeted a person familiar to him. Yuri saw a camera on a tripod. The man gestured for Yuri to stand in front of it.

'For what?' he asked sharply. He was still holding the brown envelopes. He stared angrily at the white-haired man and his friendly companion, who laughed now at Yuri as if Yuri were cute.

'For another passport,' said the Englishman in Italian. 'None of those you have is exactly right.'

'This is no passport office,' said Yuri contemptuously.

'We arrange our own passports,' said the man. 'We like it better that way. What name do you want to have? Or will you leave this to me? I would like you to cooperate, and then you can come to Amsterdam with me and see if you like it.'

'No,' said Yuri. He remembered Andrew saying no doctors. 'No police,' said Yuri. 'No orphanages, no convents, no authorities. No!' He rattled off several other terms he knew for such persons in Italian and Romanian and Russian. It all meant the same thing. 'No jail!' he said.

'No, none of that,' said the man patiently. 'You can come with me to our house in Amsterdam, and go and come as you like. This is a safe place, our house in Amsterdam. You will have a room of your own.'

A safe place. A room of his own.

'But who are you?' asked Yuri.

'Our name is the Talamasca,' the man said. 'We are scholars, students if you please. We accumulate records; we are responsible for bearing witness to things. That is, we feel we are responsible. It's what we do. I'll explain all to you on the plane.'

'Mind readers,' said Yuri.

'Yes,' said the man. 'And outcasts, and lonely ones, and ones sometimes who have no one else. And people who are better sometimes than others, much better sometimes. Like you. My name is Aaron Lightner. I wish you would come with me.'

In the Motherhouse in Amsterdam, Yuri made certain

that he could escape any time he wanted. He checked and rechecked the many unlocked doors. The room was small, immaculate, with a window over the canal and the cobblestoned quais. He loved it. He missed the bright light of Italy. This was a dimmer place, northern, like Paris, but that was all right. Inside were warm fires, and soft couches and chairs for dozing; firm beds, and lots of good food. The streets of Amsterdam pleased him, because the many old houses of the 1600s were built right against each other, making long stretches of solid and beautiful façades. He liked the steep gables of the houses. He liked the elm trees. He liked the clean-smelling clothing he was given, and he came to even like the cold.

People with cheerful faces came and went from the Motherhouse. There was steady day-to-day talk of the Elders, though who these people were, Yuri didn't know.

'You want to a ride a bike, Yuri?' asked Aaron. Yuri tried it. Taking his cue from the other riders young and old, he rode the bike like a demon through the streets.

Still Yuri wouldn't talk. Then, after constant prodding, he told the story of the maharaja.

'No. Tell me what really happened,' asked Aaron.

'Why should I tell you anything?' Yuri demanded. 'I don't know why I came here with you.' It had been a year since he had spoken real truth about himself to anyone. He had not even told Andrew the real truth. Why tell this man? And suddenly, denying that he had any need of telling the truth, or confiding, or explaining, he began to do both. He told all about his mother, about the gypsies, about everything ... He talked and talked. The night wore on and became the morning, and still Aaron Lightner sat across from him at the table listening, and Yuri talked and talked and talked.

And when he finished he knew Aaron Lightner and Aaron Lightner knew him. It was decided that Yuri would not leave the Talamasca, at least not right then.

For six years, Yuri went to school in Amsterdam.

He lived in the Talamasca house, spent most of his time on his studies, and worked after school and on weekends for Aaron Lightner, entering records into the computer, looking up obscure references in the library, sometimes merely running errands – deliver this to the post office, pick up this important box.

He came to realize that the Elders were in fact all around him, rank and file members of the Order, but nobody knew who they were. It worked like this. Once you became an Elder, you didn't tell anybody that you were. And it was forbidden to ask a person, 'Are you an Elder?' or, 'Do you know whether or not Aaron is an Elder?' It was forbidden to speculate on such matters in one's mind.

The Elders knew who the Elders were. The Elders communicated with everyone via the computers and the fax machines in the Motherhouse. Indeed, any member, even an unofficial member like Yuri, could talk to the Elders whenever he chose. In the dead of night, he could boot up his computer, write a long letter to the Elders, and sometime later that very morning an answer would come to him through the computer printer, flowing out page after page.

This meant of course that there were many Elders, and that some of them were always 'on call'. The Elders had no real personality as far as Yuri could detect, no real voice in their communications, except that they were kindly and attentive and they knew everything, and often they revealed that they knew all about Yuri, maybe even about things of which he himself was unsure.

It fascinated Yuri, this silent communication with the Elders. He began to ask them about many things. They never failed to answer.

In the morning, when Yuri went down to breakfast in the refectory, he looked around him and wondered who was an Elder, who here in this room had answered his letter this very night. Of course, his communication might have gone to Rome, for all he knew. Indeed, Elders were everywhere in every Motherhouse, and all you knew was that they were the old ones, the experienced ones, the ones who really ran the Order, though the Superior General, appointed by them, and answerable only to them, was the official head.

When Aaron relocated to London, it was a sad day for Yuri, because the house in Amsterdam had been his only permanent home. But he would not be separated from Aaron, and so they left the Amsterdam Motherhouse together, and went to live in the big house outside London which was also beautiful and warm and safe.

Yuri came to love London. When he learnt that he was to go to school at Oxford, he was delighted by this decision, and he spent six years there, coming home often on weekends, wallowing as it were in the life of the mind.

By the age of twenty-six, Yuri was ready to become a serious member of the Order. There was not the slightest doubt in his mind. He welcomed the travel assignments given him by Aaron and David. Soon he was receiving travel instructions directly from the Elders. And he was making out his reports to them on the computer when he returned.

'Assignment from the Elders,' he would say to Aaron on leaving. Aaron never questioned it. And never seemed particularly surprised.

Always, wherever he went and whatever he did, Yuri talked on the phone long distance to Aaron. Yuri was also devoted to David Talbot, but it was no secret that David Talbot was old and tired of the Order and might soon step down as Superior General, or even be politely asked by the Elders to resign the post.

Aaron was the one to whom Yuri responded, Aaron was the one about whom Yuri cared.

Yuri knew that between him and Aaron there was a special bond. For Yuri, it was the powerful irrational love that forms its roots in childhood, in loneliness, in ineradicable memories of tenderness and rescue, a love that no one but the recipient can destroy. Aaron is my father, Yuri thought, just as Aaron must have been a father to Andrew, who had died in the hotel in Rome.

As Yuri grew older he was away more of the time. He loved to wander on his own. He was most comfortable when anonymous. He needed to hear different languages around him, to submerge himself in giant cities teeming with people of all ranks and ages; when he was so immersed – with his individuality an entirely private and unrecognized matter – he felt most alive.

But almost every day of his life – wherever he was – Yuri spoke to Aaron by phone. Aaron never chided Yuri for this dependence. Indeed, Aaron was always open and ready for Yuri, and as the years passed, Aaron began to confide to Yuri more of his own feelings, his own little disappointments and hopes.

Sometimes they talked in a guarded way about the Elders, and Yuri could not discern from the conversation whether Aaron was an Elder or not. Of course Yuri wasn't supposed to know if Aaron was an Elder. But Yuri was almost certain Aaron was. If Aaron wasn't an Elder, then who were the Elders, for Aaron was one of the wisest and oldest men in the entire Talamasca worldwide?

When Aaron stayed month after month in the United States investigating the Mayfair Witches, Yuri was disappointed. He'd never known Aaron to be away from the Motherhouse so long.

When Christmas came near, a lonely time for Yuri as it is for so many, Yuri went into the computer and accessed the File on the Mayfair Witches, printing it out in its entirety and studying it very carefully to get a grasp of what was keeping Aaron in New Orleans for so much time.

Yuri enjoyed the story of the Mayfair Witches, but it aroused no special feeling in him any more than any other Talamasca file. He looked for a role to play – could he perhaps gather information on Donnelaith for Aaron? Otherwise, the totality of the story did not impress itself on his mind. The Talamasca files were filled with strange stories, some far stranger than this.

The Talamasca itself held many mysteries. They had never been Yuri's concern.

The week before Christmas, the Elders announced the resignation of David Talbot as Superior General, and that a man of German-Italian background, Anton Marcus, would take his place. No one in London knew Anton Marcus.

Yuri didn't know Anton. Yuri's main concern was

that he had never had the chance to tell David good-bye. There was some mystery surrounding David's disappearance, and, as often happens in the Talamasca, the members spoke of the Elders, and the remarks were made reflecting puzzlement and resentment, and confusion as to how the Order was organized and run. People wanted to know – would David remain an Elder, assuming he had always been one, now that he was retired? Were Elders made up of retired members as well as active ones? It seemed a bit medieval at times that no one knew.

Yuri had heard all this before. It only lasted a few days. Anton Marcus arrived the day after the announcement and at once won everyone over with his charming manner and intimate knowledge of each member's history and background, and the London Motherhouse was immediately at peace.

Anton Marcus spoke after supper in the grand dining room to all members. A man of large frame with smooth silver hair and thick gold-rimmed glasses, he had a clean corporate appearance to him, and a smooth British accent of the kind which the Talamasca seemed to favor. An accent which Yuri now possessed himself.

Anton Marcus reminded everyone of the importance of secrecy and discretion regarding the Elders. The Elders are all around us. The Elders cannot govern effectively if confronted and questioned. The Elders perform best as an anonymous body in whom we all place our trust.

Yuri shrugged.

When Yuri went to his room one morning at 2 a.m. he found a communiqué from the Elders in his printer. 'We are pleased that you have gone out of your way to welcome Anton. We feel that Anton will be a superb Superior General. If this adjustment is difficult for you, we are here.' There was also an assignment for Yuri. He was to go to Dubrovnik to pick up several important packages and take them to Amsterdam, then come home. Routine. Fun.

Yuri would have gone to spend Christmas with Aaron in New Orleans, but Aaron told him long distance that this was not possible, and that the investigation was at this point very discouraging, the most discouraging of his career.

'What's happened with the Mayfair Witches?' asked Yuri. He explained to Aaron that he had read the entire file. He asked if he might perform some small task in connection with the investigation. Aaron said no.

'Keep the faith, Yuri,' said Aaron. 'I'll see you when God wills.'

It was not like Aaron to make such a statement. It was the first decisive signal to Yuri that something was really wrong.

Early on Christmas Eve in New Orleans, Aaron called Yuri in London. He said, 'This is my most difficult time. There are things I want to do and the Order will not allow it. I have to remain here in the country, and I want to be in the town. What have I always taught you, Yuri? That obeying the rules is of absolute importance. Would you repeat those words of advice to me?'

'But what would you do if you could, Aaron?' asked Yuri.

Aaron said terrible trouble was about to happen to Rowan Mayfair, and that Rowan needed him, and he ought to go to her and do what he could. But the Elders had forbidden it. The Elders had told him to keep to the Motherhouse of Oak Haven and that he couldn't 'intervene'.

'Aaron,' said Yuri, 'all through the story of the Mayfair Witches we have tried – and failed – to intervene. Surely it's not safe for you to be close to these people, any more than it was for Stuart Townsend or Arthur Langtry – both of whom died as the result of their contact. What can you do?'

Aaron reluctantly agreed. Indeed, it had been a conversation of reconciling himself to the state of things. He mentioned that David and Anton were probably right to keep him out of the action, that Anton had inherited his position from David, and David had known the whole story. Nevertheless it was hard.

'I'm not sure about the merits of a life of watching from the sidelines,' Aaron said. 'I'm not sure at all. Perhaps I have always been waiting for a moment, and now the moment is at hand.'

This was strange, strange talk from Aaron. Yuri was deeply disturbed by it. But he had two new assignments from Anton, and off he went to India and then to Bali to photograph certain places and persons, and he was busy all the while, enjoying his wanderings as he always had.

It was not till mid-January that Yuri heard from Aaron again. Aaron wanted Yuri to go to Donnelaith in Scotland, to discover whether or not a mysterious couple had been seen by anyone there. Yuri took down the notes hastily: 'You are looking for Rowan Mayfair and a male companion, very tall, slender, dark hair.'

Yuri quietly realized what had happened – the ghost of the Mayfair family, the spirit which had haunted it for generations, had achieved some sort of passage into the visible world. Yuri didn't question this, but he was secretly excited by it. It seemed momentous as well as terrible, and he wanted to find this being.

'That's what you want, isn't it? To find them? Are you sure the best place to begin is Donnelaith?'

'It's the only place I know to begin right now,' said Aaron. 'These two individuals could be anywhere in Europe. They might even have returned to the United States.'

Yuri left for Donnelaith that night.

There was that tone of deep discouragement to Aaron's words.

Yuri typed out his notification of this assignment for the Elders in the customary form – on the computer to be sent by fax instantly to Amsterdam. He told them what he had been asked to do, and that he was doing it, and off he went.

Yuri had a good time in Donnelaith. Many people had seen the mysterious couple. Many people described the male companion. Yuri was even able to make a sketch. He was able to sleep in the same room which had been occupied by the couple, and he gathered fingerprints from all over it, though whose they were, he could not possibly tell.

That was all right, said the Elders to him in a special fax message from London to his hotel in Edinburgh. Top Priority. That meant no expense was to be spared. If the mysterious couple had left behind any articles, Yuri was to find them. Meantime he must be absolutely discreet. No one in Donnelaith was to know about this investigation. Yuri was slightly insulted. Yuri had always done things in such a way that people didn't know about it. He told the Elders this.

'We apologize,' they said in their next fax. 'Keep up the good work.'

As for Donnelaith, the place captured Yuri's imagination. For the first time the Mayfair Witches seemed real to him; as a matter of fact, the entire investigation acquired a luminescence for him which no investigation had ever had in the past.

Yuri picked up the books and brochures sold for tourists. He photographed the ruins of the Donnelaith Cathedral and the new chapel only recently uncovered, with the sarcophagus of an unknown saint. He spent his last afternoon in Donnelaith exploring the ruins until sunset, and that night, he eagerly called Aaron from Edinburgh and told him all these feelings, and tried to draw from Aaron some statement about the mysterious couple and who they were.

Could the male companion be the spirit Lasher, come into the world in some human guise?

Aaron said that he was eager to explain everything, but now was not the time. Michael Curry, Rowan Mayfair's husband, had been nearly killed on Christmas Day in New Orleans, and Aaron wanted to stay close to him, no matter what else was going on.

When Yuri got back to London, he turned the fingerprints and photographs over to the laboratory for processing and classification, and he wrote up his full report to Aaron and sent it by fax to a number in the United States. He sent the customary full copy to the Elders, via fax to Amsterdam. He filed the hard copy – the actual printed pages – and went to sleep.

That morning, when he tried to boot up the primary source material on the Mayfair Witches, he realized the investigation had changed.

All the primary sources – unedited testimony, inventories of items stored, photographs, pictures, et cetera – were closed. Indeed the File on the Mayfair Witches was closed. Yuri could find nothing by means of cross-reference.

When Yuri finally reached Aaron, to ask why this had happened, something curious occurred. Aaron clearly had not known the files had been marked confidential. But he did not want to reveal his surprise to Yuri. Aaron was angry, and disconcerted. Yuri realized he had alarmed Aaron.

That night Yuri wrote to the Elders. 'I request permission to join Aaron in this investigation, to go to New Orleans. I do not profess to understand the full scope of what has happened, nor do I need to understand it. But I feel the pressing need to be with Aaron.'

The Elders said no.

Within days, Yuri was pulled off the investigation. He was told that Erich Stolov would take over, a seasoned expert in the field of 'these things', and that Yuri should take a little vacation in Paris for a while, as he would soon be going to Russia, where it was very dreary and cold.

'Sending me to Siberia?' asked Yuri ironically, typing his questions into the computer. 'What's happening with the Mayfair Witches?'

The answer came from Amsterdam that Erich would take care of all European activity on the Mayfair Witches. And once again Yuri was advised to get some rest. He was also told that anything he knew about the Mayfair Witches was confidential, and he must not discuss this matter even with Aaron. It was a standard admonition, advised the Elders, where 'this sort' of investigation was involved.

'You know our nature,' read the communiqué. 'We do not intervene in things. We are cautious. We are watchers. Yet we have our principles. Now there is danger in this situation of an unprecedented sort. You must leave it to more experienced men like Erich. Aaron knows the Elders have closed the records. You will not hear from him again.'

That was the disturbing sentence, the chain of words which had thrown everything off.

You will not hear from him again.

In the middle of the night, while the Motherhouse slept in the sharp cold of winter, Yuri typed a message on the computer to the Elders.

'I find I cannot leave this investigation without mixed feelings. I am concerned about Aaron Lightner. He has not called me for weeks. I would like to contact Aaron. Please advise.'

Around 4 a.m., the fax awakened Yuri. The reply had come back from Amsterdam. 'Yuri, let this matter alone. Aaron is in good hands. There are no better investigators than Erich Stolov and Clement Norgan, both of whom are now assigned full-time to this case. This investigation is proceeding very rapidly, and someday you will hear the whole tale. Until then, all is secret. Do not ask to speak to Aaron again.'

Do not ask to speak to Aaron again?

Yuri couldn't sleep after that. He went down into the kitchen. The kitchen was made up of several huge, cavernous rooms and full of the smell of baking bread. Only the night cooks worked, preparing this bread and pushing it into the huge ovens, and they took no notice of Yuri as he poured himself some coffee, with cream, and sat on a wooden bench by the fire.

Yuri realized that he could not abide by this directive from the Elders! He realized very simply that he loved Aaron, indeed that he was so dependent upon Aaron that he could not think of life without him.

It is a terrible thing to realize that you depend so much upon another; that your entire sense of well-being is connected to that one – that you need him, love him, that he is the chief witness of your life. Yuri was disappointed in himself and leery. But this was the realization.

He went upstairs and quietly placed a long-distance call to Aaron.

'The Elders have told me not to talk to you directly any longer,' he said.

Aaron was astounded.

'I'm coming,' said Yuri.

'This might mean expulsion,' said Aaron.

'We'll see. I will be in New Orleans as soon as I can.'

Yuri made his plane arrangements, packed his bags and went down to wait for the car. Anton Marcus came down to see him, disheveled, in his dark blue robe and leather slippers, obviously just awakened from sleep.

'You can't go, Yuri,' he said. 'This investigation is becoming more dangerous by the moment. Aaron doesn't understand it.'

He took Yuri into his office.

'Our world has its own timekeeper,' said Anton gently. 'We are like the Vatican if you will. A century or two – that is not long to us. We have watched the Mayfair Witches for many centuries.'

'I know.'

'Now something has happened which we feared and could not prevent. It presents immense danger to us and to others. We need you to remain here, to wait for orders, to do as you are told.'

'No, I'm sorry. I'm going to Aaron,' said Yuri. He got up and walked out. He did not think about this. He did not look back. He had no particular interest in Anton's emotional reaction.

He did take a long farewell look at the Motherhouse itself, but as the car went on towards Heathrow, there was really only one theme which played itself out in his mind, rather like a fugue. He saw Andrew dying in the hotel room in Rome. He saw Aaron sitting opposite him, Yuri, at the table, saying, 'I am your friend.' He saw his mother, too, dying in the village in Serbia.

There was no conflict in him.

He was going to Aaron. He knew that was what he had to do.

SEVEN

Lark was sound asleep when the plane landed in New Orleans. It startled him to discover that they were already at the gate. Indeed, people were disembarking. The stewardess was beaming down at him, his raincoat dangling from her graceful arm. He felt a little embarrassed for a moment, as though he had lost some precious advantage; then he was on his feet.

He had a terrible headache, and he was hungry, and then the searing excitement of this mystery, this Rowan Mayfair offspring mystery, came back to him in the shape of a great burden. How could a rational man be expected to explain such a thing? What time was it? Eight a.m. in New Orleans. That meant it was only 6 a.m. back on the coast.

Immediately he saw the white-haired man waiting for him and realized it was Lightner before the man clasped his hand and said his own name. Very personable old guy; gray suit and all.

'Dr Larkin. There's been a family emergency. Neither Ryan nor Pierce Mayfair could be here. Let me take you to your hotel. Ryan will be in touch with us as soon as he can.' Same British polish that Lark had admired so much over the phone.

'Glad to see you, Mr Lightner, but I have to tell you,

I had a run-in with one of your colleagues in San Francisco. Not so good.'

Lightner was clearly surprised. They walked up the concourse together, Lightner's profile rather grave for a moment and distant. 'Who was this, I wonder,' he said with unconcealed annoyance. He looked tired, as if he had not slept all night.

Lark was feeling better now. The headache was dissipating. He was fantasizing about coffee and sweet rolls, and a dinner reservation at Commander's Palace, and maybe an afternoon nap. And then he thought of the specimens. He thought of Rowan. That embarrassing excitement overcame him, and with it, an ugly feeling of being involved in something unwholesome, something all wrong.

'Our hotel is only a few blocks from Commander's Palace,' said Lightner easily. 'We can take you there this evening. Maybe we can persuade Michael to go with us. There has been ... an emergency. Something to do with Ryan's family. Otherwise Ryan would have been here himself. But this colleague of mine? Can you tell me what happened? Do you have luggage?'

'No, just my valise here, loaded for a one-night stand.' Like most surgeons, Lark liked being up at this hour. If he were back in San Francisco, he'd be in surgery right now. He was feeling better with every step he took.

They proceeded towards the bright warm daylight, and the busy gathering of cabs and limousines beyond the glass doors. It wasn't terribly cold here. No, not as bitingly cold as San Francisco, not at all. But the light was the real difference. There was more of it. And the air stood motionless around you. Kind of nice.

'This colleague,' said Lark, 'said his name was Erich

Stolov. He demanded to know where the specimens were.'

'Is that so?' said Lightner with a slight frown. He gestured to the left, and one of the many limousines, a great sleek gray Lincoln, crawled out and towards them, its windows black and secretive. Lightner didn't wait for the driver to come round. He opened the back door himself.

Gratefully, Lark climbed into the soft velvet gray interior, shifting over to the far seat, faintly disturbed by the smell of cigarette smoke lingering in the upholstery and stretching out his legs comfortably in the luxuriant space. Lightner sat beside him, and away the car sped instantly, in its own realm of darkness thanks to the tinted windows, suddenly shut off from all the airport traffic and the pure brilliance of the morning sun.

But it was comfortable, this car. And it was fast.

'What did Erich say to you?' asked Lightner, with deliberate concealing evenness.

Lark wasn't fooled by it. 'Stood right in front of me, demanding to know where the specimens were. Rude. Downright aggressive and rude. I can't figure it. Was he trying to intimidate me?'

'You didn't tell him what he wanted to know,' said Lightner softly and conclusively and looked out the darkened glass. They were on the highway, turning onto the freeway, and this place looked a little like any place – squat suburban buildings with names blaring from them, empty space, uncut grass, motels.

'Well, no, of course not. I didn't tell him anything,' said Lark. 'I didn't like it. I didn't like it at all. I told you Rowan Mayfair asked me to handle this confidentially. I'm here because of information you volunteered and because the family asked me to come. I'm not in a position really to turn over these specimens to anyone. In fact, I don't think I could successfully retrieve them from the people who have them at this point. Rowan was specific. She wanted them tested in secret at a certain place.'

'The Keplinger Institute,' said Lightner gently and politely, as if reading this off a cue card on Lark's forehead, his pale eyes calm. 'Mitch Flanagan, the genetic genius, the man who worked with Rowan there before she decided not to stay in research.'

Lark didn't say anything. The car floated soundlessly along the skyway. The buildings grew denser and the grass more unkempt.

'If you know, then why did this guy ask me?' Lark demanded. 'Why did he stand in my path and try to force me to tell him all this? How did you find out, by the way? I'd like to know. Who are you? I would like to know that too.'

Lightner was looking away, weary, saddened.

'I told you there was a family emergency this morning, did I not?'

'Yes, I'm sorry to hear it. I didn't mean to be insensitive on that account. I was mad about your friend.'

'I know,' said Lightner affably. 'I understand. He should not have behaved that way. I'll call the Motherhouse in London. I'll try to find out why that happened. Or more truly, I'll make certain that nothing like that ever happens again.' There was a little blaze of temper in the man's eyes for an instant, and then something sour and fearful in his gaze. Very transitory. He smiled pleasantly. 'I'll take care of it.'

'Appreciate it,' said Lark. 'How did you know about Mitch Flanagan and the Keplinger Institute?'

'You could call it a guess,' said Lightner. He was deeply disturbed by all this; that was plain even though his face was now a carefully painted picture of serenity, and his voice betrayed nothing but his tiredness, and a general low frame of mind.

'What is this emergency? What happened?'

'I don't know all the details yet. Only that Pierce and Ryan Mayfair had to go to Destin, Florida, early this morning. They asked me to meet you. Seems something has happened to Ryan's wife, Gifford. Again I'm not sure. I don't know.'

'This Erich Stolov. You work with him?'

'Not directly. He was here two months ago. He's a new generation of Talamasca. It's the old story. I'll find out why he behaved the way he did. The Motherhouse does not know the specimens are at the Keplinger Institute. If the younger members showed as much zeal at reading the files as they do for fieldwork, they could have figured it out.'

'What files, what do you mean?'

'Oh, it's a long story. And never a particularly easy one to tell. I understand your reluctance to tell anyone about these specimens. I wouldn't tell anyone else if I were you.'

'Is there any news on Rowan's whereabouts?'

'Not a word. Except the old report's been confirmed. That she and her companion were in Scotland, in Donnelaith.'

'What is all that about? Where is Donnelaith, Scotland? I've been all over the Highlands, hunting, fishing. I never heard of Donnelaith.'

'It's a ruined village. At the moment it's swarming with archaeologists. There is an inn there principally for tourists and people from universities. Rowan was seen there about four weeks ago.'

'Well, that's old news. That's no good. Nothing new is what I meant.'

'Nothing new.'

'This companion of hers, what did he look like?' Lark asked.

Lightner's expression darkened slightly. Was this weariness or bitterness? Lark was baffled.

'Oh, you know more about him now than I do, don't you?' asked Lightner. 'Rowan sent you X-ray film, printouts of electroencephalograms, all of that sort of thing. Didn't she send a picture?'

'No, she didn't,' Lark said. 'Who are you people, really?'

'You know, Dr Larkin, I don't honestly know the answer to that question. I suppose I never have. I'm just more frank with myself about it these days. Things happen. New Orleans works its spell on people. So do the Mayfairs. I was guessing on the tests; you might say I was trying to read your mind.'

Lark laughed. All this had been said so agreeably, and so philosophically. Lark sympathized with this man suddenly. In the dim light of the car, he also noticed things about him. That Lightner suffered from mild emphysema and that he had never smoked, and probably never been a drinker, and was fairly hale in a decade of programmed fragility – his eighties.

Lightner smiled, and looked out the window. The driver of the car was a mere dark shape behind the blackened glass.

Lark realized the car was loaded with all the standard amenities – the little television set, and the soft drinks tucked into ice in pockets on the middle doors.

What about coffee? When would they have coffee?

'There in the carafe,' said Lightner.

'Ah, you read my mind,' Lark said with a little laugh.

'It's that time of morning, isn't it?' said Lightner, and for the first time there was a little smile on his lips. He watched Lark open the carafe and discover the plastic cup in the side pocket. Lark poured the steaming coffee.

'You want some, Lightner?'

'No, thank you. Do you want to tell me what your friend Mitch Flanagan has found out?'

'Not particularly. I don't want to tell anyone but Rowan. I called Ryan Mayfair for the money. That's what Rowan instructed me to do. But she didn't say anything about giving anybody the test results. She said she'd contact me when she could. And Ryan Mayfair says that Rowan may be hurt. Maybe even dead.'

'That's true,' said Lightner. 'It was good of you to come.'

'Hell, I'm worried about Rowan. I wasn't too happy when Rowan left University. I wasn't too happy that she up and got married. I wasn't too happy that she left medicine. In fact, I was as astonished as if somebody had said, "The world ends today at three o'clock." I didn't believe it all, until Rowan herself told me over and over.'

'I remember. She called you often last fall. She was very concerned about your disapproval.' It was said mildly like everything else. 'She wanted your advice on the creation of Mayfair Medical. She was sure that when you realized she was serious about the center you would understand why she was no longer practicing, that there was a great deal involved.'

'Then you are a friend of hers, aren't you? I mean not this Talamasca necessarily, but you.'

'I think I was her friend. I may have failed her. I don't know. Maybe she failed me.' There was a hint of bitterness to it, maybe even anger. Then the man smiled pleasantly again.

'I have to confess something to you, Mr Lightner,' said Lark, 'I thought this Mayfair Medical was a pipe dream. Rowan caught me off guard. But I've since done a little investigating of my own. Obviously this family has the resources to create Mayfair Medical. I just didn't know. I should have known, I suppose. Everybody was talking about it. Rowan is the smartest and best surgeon I ever trained.'

'I'm sure she is. Did she tell you anything about the specimens when she talked to you? You said she called from Geneva and that was February twelfth.'

'Again, I want to talk to Ryan, next of kin. Talk to the husband, see what is the right thing to do.'

'The specimens ought to have everyone at the Keplinger Institute quite astonished,' said Lightner. 'I wish you would tell me the full extent of what Rowan sent. Let me explain my interest. Was Rowan herself in ill health when she spoke to you? Did she send any sort of medical material that pertained to her?'

'Yes, she did send samples of her own blood and tissue, but there's no evidence she was sick.'

'Just different.'

'Yeah, I dare say. Different. You are right on that.'

Lightner nodded. He looked off again, out over what appeared to be a great sprawling cemetery, full of little marble houses with pointed roofs. The car sped on in the sparse traffic. There seemed so much space here. So much quiet. There was a seedy look to things, even a botched look. But Lark liked the openness, the sense of not being hampered by a moving traffic jam as he was always at home.

'Lightner, my position on this is really difficult,' he said. 'Whether you are her friend or not.'

They were turning off already, gliding down past an old brick church steeple that seemed perilously close to the descending ramp. Lark felt relief when they reached the street, shabby though it was. Again, he liked the spacious feeling of things here, though all was a bit forlorn. Things moved slowly here. The South. A town.

'I know all that, Dr Larkin,' said Lightner. 'I understand. I know all about confidentiality and medical ethics. I know about manners and decency. People here know all about them. It's rather nice, being here. We don't have to talk about Rowan now if you don't want to. Let's have breakfast at the hotel, shall we? Perhaps you want to take a nap. We can meet at the First Street house later. It's just a few blocks away. The family has arranged everything for you.'

'You know this is really very very serious,' said Lark suddenly. The car had come to a halt. They were in front of a little hotel with smart blue awnings. A doorman stood ready to open the limousine door.

'Of course it is,' said Aaron Lightner. 'But it's also very simple. Rowan gave birth to this strange child. Indeed, as we both know, he is not a child. He is the male companion seen with her in Scotland. What we want to know now is can he reproduce? Can he breed with his mother or with other human beings? Reproduction is the only real concern of evolution, isn't it? If he was a simple one-and-only mutation, something created by external forces – radiation say, or some sort of telekinetic ability – well, we wouldn't be all that concerned, would we? We might just catch up with him and ascertain whether or not Rowan is remaining with him of her own free will, and then ... shoot him. Perhaps.'

'You know all about it, don't you?'

'No, not all about it. That's the disturbing thing. But I know this. If Rowan sent you those samples, it was because Rowan was afraid this thing could breed. Let's go inside, shall we? I'd like to call the family about this incident in Destin. I'd also like to call the Talamasca about Stolov. I have rooms here too, you see. You might call it my New Orleans headquarters. I rather like the place.'

'Sure, let's go.'

Before they reached the desk, Lark had regretted the small valise and the one change of clothes. He wasn't going to be leaving here so soon. He knew it. The dim feeling of something unwholesome and menacing warred in him with a new surge of excitement. He liked this little lobby, the amiable southern voices surrounding him, the tall, elegant black man in the elevator.

Yes, he would have to do some shopping. But that was fine. Lightner had the key in hand. The suite was ready for Lark. And Lark was ready for breakfast.

Yeah, she was afraid of that all right, Lark thought, as they went up in the elevator. She had even said something like, If this thing can breed ...

Of course he hadn't known then what the hell she was talking about. But she'd known. Anyone else, you might think this was a hoax or something. But not Rowan Mayfair.

Well, he was too hungry just now to think about it anymore.

EIGHT

It was not her custom to speak into the phone when she answered it. She would pick up the receiver, hold it to her ear; then if someone spoke, someone she knew, perhaps she would answer.

Ryan knew this. And he said immediately into the silence: 'Ancient Evelyn, something dreadful has happened.'

'What is it, son?' she asked, identifying herself with an uncommon warmth. Her voice sounded frail and small to her, not the voice of herself which she had always known.

'They've found Gifford on the beach at Destin. They said –' Ryan's voice broke and he could not continue. Then Ryan's son, Pierce, came on the line and he said that he and his father were driving up together. Ryan came back on the phone. Ryan told her she must stay with Alicia, that Alicia would go mad when she 'heard'.

'I understand,' said Ancient Evelyn. And she did. Gifford wasn't merely hurt. Gifford was dead. 'I will find Mona,' she said softly. She did not know if they even heard.

Ryan said something vague and confused and rushed, that they would call her later, that Lauren was calling 'the family'. And then the conversation was finished, and Ancient Evelyn put down the phone and went to the closet for her walking stick.

Ancient Evelyn did not much like Lauren Mayfair. Lauren Mayfair was a brittle, arrogant lawyer in Ancient Evelyn's book, a sterile, frosty businesswoman of the worst sort who had always preferred legal documents to people. But she would be fine for calling everyone. Except for Mona. And Mona was not here, and Mona had to be told.

Mona was up at the First Street house. Ancient Evelyn knew it. Perhaps Mona was searching for that Victrola and the beautiful pearls.

Ancient Evelyn had known all night that Mona was out. But she never really had to worry about Mona. Mona would do all the things in life that everyone wanted to do. She would do them for her grandmother Laura Lee and for her mother, CeeCee, and for Ancient Evelyn herself. She would do them for Gifford . . .

Gifford dead. No, that did not seem possible, or likely. *Why did I not feel it when it happened? Why didn't I hear her voice?*

Back to the practical things. Ancient Evelyn stood in the hallway, thinking whether she ought to go on her own in search of Mona, to go out on the bumpy streets, the sidewalks of brick and flag on which she might fall, but never had, and then she thought with her new eyes she could do it. Yes, and who knew? It might be her last time to really see.

A year ago, she could not have seen to walk downtown. But young Dr Rhodes had taken the cataracts from her eyes. And now she saw so well it astonished people. That is, when she told them what she saw, which she didn't often do.

Ancient Evelyn knew perfectly well that talking made

little difference. Ancient Evelyn didn't talk for years on end. People took it in stride. People did what they wanted. No one would let Ancient Evelyn tell Mona her stories anyway, and Ancient Evelyn had deepened into her memories of the early times, and she did not always need anymore to examine or explain them.

What good had it done besides to tell Alicia and Gifford her tales? What had their lives been? And Gifford's life was over!

It seemed astonishing again that Gifford could be dead. Completely dead. Yes, Alicia will go mad, she thought, but then so will Mona. And so will I when I really know.

Ancient Evelyn went into Alicia's room. Alicia slept, curled up like a child. In the night, she'd gotten up and drunk half a flask of whiskey down as if it were medicine. That sort of drinking could kill you. Alicia should have died, thought Ancient Evelyn. That is what was meant to be. The horse passed the wrong gate.

She laid the knitted cover over Alicia's shoulders and went out.

Slowly, she went down the stairway, very very slowly, carefully examining each tread with the rubber tip of her cane, pushing and poking at the carpet to make sure there was nothing lurking there that would trip her and make her fall. On her eightieth birthday she had fallen. It had been the worst time of her old age, lying in bed as the hip mended. But it had done her heart good, Dr Rhodes had told her. 'You will live to be one hundred.'

Dr Rhodes had fought the others when they said she was too old for the cataract operation. 'She is going blind, don't you understand? I can make her see again. And her mentation is perfect.'

Mentation – she had liked that word, she had told him so.

'Why don't you talk to them more?' he'd asked her in the hospital. 'You know they think you're a feeble-minded old woman.'

She had laughed and laughed. 'But I am,' she had said, 'and the ones I loved to talk to are all gone. Now there's only Mona. And most of the time, Mona talks to me.'

How he had laughed at that.

Ancient Evelyn had grown up speaking as little as possible. The truth was Ancient Evelyn might never have spoken much to a soul if it hadn't been for Julien.

And the one thing she did want to do was tell Mona someday all about Julien. Maybe today should be that day. It struck her with a shimmering power! Tell Mona. The Victrola and the pearls are in that house. Mona can have them now.

She stopped before the mirrored hat rack in the alcove. She was satisfied; yes, ready to go out. She had slept all night in her warm gabardine dress and it would be fine in this mild spring weather. She was not rumpled at all. It was so easy to sleep sitting up perfectly straight, with her hands crossed on her knee. She put a handkerchief against the tapestried back of the chair, by her cheek as she turned her head, in case anything came out of her mouth as she slept. But there was rarely a stain upon the cloth. She could use the same handkerchief over and over.

She did not have a hat. But it had been years since she had gone out – except for Rowan Mayfair's wedding – and she did not know what Alicia had done with her hats. Surely there had been one for the wedding, and if she tried she might recollect what it looked like, probably gray with an old-fashioned little veil. Probably had pink flowers. But maybe she was dreaming. The wedding itself hadn't seemed very real.

Surely she could not climb the stairs again to look for a hat now, and there were none in her little back room down here. Besides, her hair was done. It was the same soft bouffant she had made of it for years, and she could feel that the coil on the back of her head was firm, pins in place. It made a grand white frame for her face, her hair. She had never regretted its turning white. No, she did not require a hat. As for gloves, there were none now and no one would buy them for her.

At Rowan Mayfair's wedding, that horrid Lauren Mayfair had even said, 'Nobody wears gloves anymore,' as if it didn't matter. Perhaps Lauren was right.

Ancient Evelyn didn't mind so terribly about the gloves. She had her brooches and her pins. Her stockings were not wrinkled at all. Her shoes were tied. Mona had tied them yesterday very tight. She was ready to go. She did not look at her face; she never did anymore because it wasn't her face, it was someone else's old and wrinkled face, with deep vertical lines, very solemn and cold, and drooping lids, and the skin was too large for the bones underneath, and her eyebrows and her chin had lost their contour.

She would prefer to think about the walk ahead. It made her happy merely to think of it, and that Gifford was gone, and if Ancient Evelyn fell, or was struck down, or became lost, there was no more grand-daughter Gifford to become hysterical. It felt wonderful to her suddenly to be free of Gifford's love – as if a gate had opened wide once more on the world. And Mona would eventually know this too, this relief, this release. But not immediately.

She went down the long, high hall, and opened the front door. It had been a year since she'd gone down the front steps, except for the wedding, and someone had carried her then. There was no rail now to hold to. The banisters had just rotted away years ago and Alicia and Patrick had done nothing about it, except tear them off and throw them under the house.

'My great-grandfather built this house!' she had declared. 'He ordered those balusters himself, picked them from the catalogue. And look what you have allowed to happen.' Damn them all.

And damn him too, when she thought about it. How she had hated him, the giant shadow over her childhood, raving Tobias, hissing at her when he snatched up her hand and held it: 'Witch, witch's mark, look at it.' Pinching that tiny sixth finger. She had never answered him, only loathed him in silence. She had never spoken one word to him all of his life.

But a house falling to ruin, that was something more important than whether you hated the person who built it. Why, building this house was maybe the only good thing Tobias Mayfair had ever done. Fontevrault, their once beautiful plantation, had died out in the swampland, or so she had been told every time she asked to be taken to see it. 'That old house? The Bayou flooded it!' But then maybe they were lying. What if she could walk all the way to Fontevrault, and find the house standing there.

That was a dream surely. But Amelia Street stood mighty and beautiful on its corner on the Avenue. And something ought to be done, be done, be done . . .

Banister or no banister, she could manage perfectly well with her cane, especially now that she could see so clearly. She took the steps easily. And went directly down the path and opened the iron picket gate. Imagine. She was walking away from the house for the first time in all these years.

Squinting at the glimmer of traffic in the distance, she crossed the lakeside of the Avenue at once. She had to wait a moment on the riverside, but soon her chance came.

She had always liked the riverside as they called it. And she knew that Patrick was in the restaurant on the corner, drinking and eating his breakfast as he always did.

She crossed Amelia Street and the tiny street called Antonine which came in there only a few feet from Amelia, and she stood on the corner and looked through the glass windows of the restaurant. There was Patrick – scrawny and pale – at the end table, as always, with his beer and his eggs, and the newspaper. He did not even see her. He would stay there, drinking beer and reading the paper for half the day, and then go downtown for a little while perhaps and drink some more in a bar he liked in the Quarter. In the late afternoon, Alicia might wake up and call Patrick at the bar and begin to scream for him to come home.

So he was there, and he did not see her. How could he? Would he ever have expected Ancient Evelyn to leave the house of her own accord?

That was perfectly fine, exactly what she wanted. And on she walked down the block, unseen, unstopped, towards downtown.

How clear were the black-barked oaks, and the beaten

down grass of the tree parks. She saw the clutter and trash of Mardi Gras still piled everywhere in the gutters, and in the trash cans which were never enough to contain it.

She walked on, past the drab shabby portable bathrooms they brought out now for Mardi Gras Day, catching the wretched smell of all that filth, and on and on to Louisiana Avenue. Litter everywhere she looked, and from the high branches of the trees hung Mardi Gras necklaces of plastic beads, the kind they threw now, glittering in the sunlight. There was nothing so sorry in the world ever, she thought, as St Charles Avenue after Mardi Gras Day.

She waited for the stoplight to change. An old colored woman, very properly dressed, waited there also. 'Good morning, Patricia,' she said to the woman, and the woman gave a start beneath her black straw hat.

'Why, Miss Ancient Evelyn. What are you doing all the way down here?'

'I'm walking down to the Garden District. I will be fine, Patricia. I have my cane. I wish I had my gloves and my hat, but I do not.'

'That's a shame, Miss Ancient Evelyn,' said the old woman, very proper, her voice soft and mellow. She was a sweet old thing, Patricia, came by all the time with her little grandchild, who could have passed for white, but didn't, obviously, or maybe had yet to figure it all out.

Something terribly exciting had happened.

'Oh, I'll be all right,' Ancient Evelyn said. 'My niece is up there, in the Garden District. I have to give her the Victrola.' And then she realized that Patricia knew nothing about these things! That Patricia had stopped many a time at the gate to speak, but she did not know the whole story. How could she? Ancient Evelyn had thought for a moment she was speaking to someone who knew.

Patricia was still talking, but Ancient Evelyn didn't hear the words. The light was green. She had to cross.

And off she went as rapidly as she could, skirting the raised strip of concrete that divided the street, because stepping up and stepping down would be needlessly hard for her.

She was too slow for the light of course, that had been true twenty years ago, when she still made this walk all the time to pass the First Street house and look at poor Deirdre.

All the young ones of that generation doomed, she thought – sacrificed, as it were, to the viciousness and stupidity of Carlotta Mayfair. Carlotta Mayfair drugged and killed her niece Deirdre. But why think of it now?

It seemed Ancient Evelyn was plagued with a thousand confusing thoughts.

Cortland, Julien's beloved son, dead from a fall down the steps – that was all Carlotta's fault, too, wasn't it? They'd brought him into Touro only two blocks away. Ancient Evelyn had been sitting on the porch. She could see the top of the brick walls of the hospital from her very chair, and what a shock it had been to learn that Cortland had died there, only two blocks away, talking to strangers in the emergency room.

And to think that Cortland had been Ancient Evelyn's father. Ah, well, that had never mattered, not really. Julien had mattered, yes, and Stella, but fathers and mothers, no.

Barbara Ann had died giving birth to Ancient Evelyn.

That was no mother, really. Only a cameo, a silhouette, a portrait in oils. 'See? That's your mother.' A trunk full of old clothes, and a rosary and some unfinished embroidery that might have been for a sachet.

How Ancient Evelyn's mind wandered. But she had been counting murders, hadn't she? The murders committed by Carlotta Mayfair who was now dead, thank God, and gone.

The murder of Stella, that had been the worst of them all. That Carlotta had most definitely done. Surely that had to be laid on Carlotta's conscience. And in the rosy days of 1914, Evelyn and Julien had known such terrible things were coming, but there had been nothing either of them could do.

For one brief instant, Ancient Evelyn saw the words of the poem again, same way she had seen them on that long-ago day when she had recited them aloud to Julien in his attic bedroom. 'I see it. I do not know what it means.'

> Pain and suffering as they stumble
> Blood and fear before they learn.
> Woe betide this Springtime Eden
> Now the vale of those who mourn.

Ah, what a day this was. So much was coming back to her, and yet the present itself was so fresh and sweet. The breeze so good to her.

On and on, Ancient Evelyn walked.

Here was the vacant lot at Toledano. Would they never build anything else there, and look at these apartment buildings, so plain, so ugly, where once glorious mansions had stood, houses grander than her own. Oh, to think of all those people gone since the days when she took Gifford and Alicia downtown, or the other way to the park, walking between them. But the Avenue did keep its beauty. The streetcar rattled into view even as she spoke, and then roared round the bend – the Avenue was one endless curve, just as it had been all of Ancient Evelyn's life from the time she rode it to go up to First Street. Of course she could not step up on the streetcar now. That was out of the question.

She could not now remember when she stopped riding the car, except that it was decades ago. She'd nearly fallen one night when she was coming home, and dropped her sacks from Marks Isaacs and Maison Blanche and the conductor himself had had to come and help her up. Very embarrassing and upsetting to her it had been. Silent as usual, she had given the conductor her special nod, and touched his hand.

Then the car had rushed away, in a sweep of wind, and she'd been left alone on the neutral ground, and the oncoming traffic had seemed endless and impossible to defeat – the big house in another world on the other side of the street.

'And would you have believed it then if they'd told you you'd live to see another twenty years, to see Deirdre buried and dead, to see poor Gifford dead?'

She had thought sure she'd die the year that Stella died. And then when Laura Lee died it was the same way. Her only daughter. She thought if she stopped talking, death could come and take her.

But it hadn't happened. Alicia and Gifford had needed her. Then Alicia had married. And Mona needed her. Mona's birth had given Ancient Evelyn a new voice.

Oh, she didn't want to be considering things in such a

perspective. Not on such a lovely morning. She did try to speak to people. It was simply so unnatural a thing for her to do.

She'd hear the others speaking to her, or more truly she saw their lips move and she knew they wanted her attention. But she could stay in her dreams, walking through the streets of Rome with her arm around Stella's waist, or lying with her in the little room at the hotel, and kissing so gently and endlessly in the shadows, just woman and woman, her breasts pressed softly against Stella's.

Oh, that had been the richest time. Thank God she had not known how pale it would all be ... after. She would only know the wide world once, really, and with Stella, and when Stella died, the world did too.

Which had been the greatest love of her prime? Julien in the locked room or Stella of the great adventures? She could not make up her mind.

One thing was true. It was Julien who haunted her, Julien she saw in her waking dreams, Julien's voice she heard. There was a time when she was sure Julien was going to come right up the front steps the way he had when she was thirteen, pushing her great-grandfather out of the way. 'Let that girl out, you bloody fool!' And she in the attic had shivered in fear. Julien come to take me away. It would make sense, wouldn't it? Julien hovering about her still. 'Crank the Victrola, Evelyn. Say my name.'

Stella was more abruptly and totally gone with her tragic death, vanished into a sweet and agonizing grief, as though she had with her last breath truly ascended into heaven. Surely Stella went to heaven. How could anyone who made so many people happy go to hell?

Poor Stella. She had never been a real witch, only a child. Maybe gentle souls like Stella did not want to haunt you; maybe they found the light quickly and far better things to do. Stella was memories, yes, but never a ghost.

In the hotel room in Rome, Stella had put her hand between Evelyn's legs, and said, 'No, don't be frightened. Let me touch you. Yes, let me see you.' Parting Evelyn's legs. 'Don't be ashamed. Don't be afraid, with a woman there is never any cause to be afraid. You should know that. Besides, wasn't Oncle Julien gentle?'

'If only we could shut the blinds,' Evelyn had pleaded. 'It's the light, it's the noise from the piazza. I don't know.' But in fact, her body had been stirring and she wanted Stella. It had only just struck her that she could touch Stella all over with her own hands, that she could suckle Stella's breasts and let Stella's weight fall down on her. How she loved Stella. She could have drowned in Stella.

And in a true and deep way Ancient Evelyn's life had ended on that night when Stella was shot in 1929.

She had seen Stella fall on the living room floor and that man from the Talamasca, that Arthur Langtry, run to take the gun from Lionel Mayfair's hand. That man from the Talamasca had died at sea only a little while after. Poor fool, she thought. And Stella had hoped to escape with him, to run off to Europe and leave Lasher with her child. Oh, Stella, to think that such a thing could be done, how foolish and terrible. Ancient Evelyn had tried to warn Stella about those men from Europe who kept their secret books and charts; she'd tried to explain that Stella must not talk to them. Carlotta knew, Evelyn had to give her that, though for all the wrong reasons.

And now there was one of those men about again, and nobody suspected anything. Aaron Lightner was his name; they talked about him as though he were a saint because he had the records of the clan all the way back to Donnelaith. What did any of them know about Donnelaith? Julien had hinted of terrible things in a hushed voice as they lay together, with the music playing in the background. Julien had gone to that place in Scotland. The others had not.

Ancient Evelyn might have died even with his passing, if it hadn't been for little Laura Lee. She wasn't going to leave her daughter. Some baby was always catching hold of her, and drawing her back in. Laura Lee. Now Mona. And would she live to see Mona's child?

Stella had come with a dress for Laura Lee, and to take her to school. Suddenly she'd said, 'My darling, forget about all this rubbish, sending her to school. Poor little creature. I always hated school. You two come with us to Europe. Come with me and Lionel. You can't spend your life on one single corner of the world.'

Evelyn would have never seen Rome or Paris or London or any of those marvelous places to which Stella took her, Stella her beloved, Stella who was not faithful but devoted, teaching her that the latter was the thing.

Evelyn had worn a gray silk dress the night of Stella's death, with ropes of pearls, Stella's pearls, and she had gone out onto the grass and sunk down weeping as they took Lionel away. The dress had been utterly ruined. Glass broken all around the house. And Stella a little heap on the waxed floor, with flashbulbs exploding all around her. Stella lying where they had all danced, and that Talamasca man so horrified, rushing away. Horrified . . .

Julien, did you foresee this? Has the poem been fulfilled? Evelyn had cried and cried, and later when no one was about, when they had taken Stella's body away, when all was quiet, and the First Street house was plunged into darkness and the random glitter of the broken glass, Evelyn had crept to the library and pulled out the books and opened Stella's secret hiding place in the library wall.

Here Stella had hidden all their pictures, their letters, all the things she meant to keep from Carlotta. 'We don't want her knowing about us, ducky, but I'll be damned if I'll burn our pictures.'

Evelyn had taken off the long ropes of pearls that were Stella's and put them there in the dark cavity, with the little keepsakes of their soft and shining romance.

'Why can't we love each other always, Stella?' She had cried on the boat home.

'Oh, my darling, the real world will never accept,' Stella had said. She'd been already having an affair with a man on board. 'But we shall meet. I shall arrange a little place downtown for us together.'

Stella had been true to her word, and what an enchanting little courtyard apartment it had been, and only for them.

Laura Lee had been back in school all day, no trouble. Laura Lee had never suspected a thing.

It had rather amused Evelyn – she and Stella making love in that little cluttered place, with its bare brick walls, and the noise of the restaurant beyond, and none of the Mayfair clan knowing a thing about it. *Love you, my darling*.

It was only to Stella that Evelyn had ever shown Julien's Victrola. Only Stella knew that Evelyn had taken it from the First Street house at Julien's command. Julien the ghost who was ever close to her, whenever she imagined him, the feel of his hair, the touch of his skin.

For years after his death, Evelyn had crept up to her room, and wound the Victrola. She'd put on the records and played the waltz; she'd closed her eyes and imagined she danced with Julien – so sprightly and graceful in his old age, so ready to laugh at the ironies of it all, so patient with the weaknesses and deceptions of others. She'd played the waltz for little Laura Lee.

'Your father gave me this record,' she had told her daughter. The child's face was so sad, it could make her cry just to look at Laura Lee's face. Had Laura Lee ever known happiness? She'd known peace and perhaps that was just as good.

Could Julien hear the Victrola? Was he really bound to the earth by his own will? 'There are dark times ahead, Evie. But I will not give up. I will not go quietly into hell and let him triumph. I will overreach death if I can, same as he has done. I will thrive in the shadows. Play the song for me so that I might hear it, so that it might call me back.'

Stella had been so puzzled to hear about it, years after, when they ate spaghetti and drank wine, and listened to the Dixieland in the little place in the Quarter – Evelyn's old tales of Julien.

'So you were the one who took that little Victrola! Ah, yes, I remember, but Evie, I think you're all mixed up about the rest. He was always so gay around us, Evelyn, are you sure he was so frightened?

'Of course I do remember the day Mother burnt his books. He was so angry! So angry. And then we went to get you. Do you remember? I think I told him you were in the attic up there at Amelia, a prisoner, just so he would get angry enough not to die on the couch that very afternoon. All those books. I wonder what was in them. But he was happy after that, Evie, especially after you started coming. Happy till the end.'

'Yes, happy,' Evelyn had declared. 'He was right in his head till the day he died.'

In her mind's eye, she was in that time once more. She grabbed the tangled, thorny vines, climbing higher and higher up the stucco wall. Oh, to be that strong again, even for a moment, to step up to one bar of the trellis after another, fingers tugging on the vines, pushing through the wet flowers, until she had reached the roof of the second floor porch, all the way above those flagstones, and saw Julien, through the window, in his brass bed.

'Evalynn!' he'd said peering through the glass to welcome her, reaching out for her. She'd never told Stella about all that.

Evelyn had been thirteen when Julien first brought her to that room.

In a way, that day had been the first of her true life. To Julien she could talk the way she couldn't to other people. How powerless she had been in her silence, only now and then breaking it when her grandfather beat her, or the others begged her and then mostly to speak in rhymes. Why, she wasn't speaking them at all really, she was reading the words from the air.

Julien had asked to hear her strange poetry, her prophecy. Julien had been afraid. He had known of the dark times to come.

But oh, they had been so carefree in their own way, the old man and the mute child. In the afternoon, he'd made love to her very slowly, a little heavier and clumsier than Stella later on, yes, but then, he'd been an old man, hadn't he? He'd apologized that it had taken him so long to finish, but what delights he'd given her with his nether kisses and embraces, with his skilled fingers, and the secret little erotic words he spoke into her ear as he touched her. That was the thing about them both, they knew how to touch you and kiss you.

They made of love a soft and luxurious thing. And when the violence came you were ready. You wanted it.

'Dark times,' he said. 'I can't tell you all, my pretty girl. I don't dare to explain it. She's burnt my books, you know, right out there on the grass. She burnt what was mine. She burnt my life when she did that. But I want you to do this for me, believe in this for me. Take the Victrola out of this house. You must keep it, in memory of me. It's mine, this thing, I have loved it, touched it, imbued it with my spirit as surely as any stumbling mortal can imbue an object with spirit. Keep it safe, Eve, play the waltz for me.

'Pass it on to those who would cherish it after Mary Beth is gone. Mary Beth can't live forever any more than I can. Never let Carlotta get it. A time will come . . .'

And then he'd sunk into sadness again. Better to make love.

'I cannot help it,' he had said. 'I see but I can do nothing. I do not know any more than any man what is really possible. What if hell is utterly solitary? What if there is no one there to hate? What if it's like the dark night over Donnelaith, Scotland? Then Lasher comes from hell.'

'Did he really say all that, now?' asked Stella, years later, and only a month after that very conversation, Stella herself had been shot and killed. Stella whose eyes closed forever in the year 1929.

So much life since the death of Stella. So many generations. So much world.

Sometimes it was a downright consolation to hear her beloved red-haired Mona Mayfair railing against modernism.

'We've had nearly an entire century, you realize, and the most coherent and successful styles were developed in those first twenty years. Stella saw it. If she saw art deco, if she heard jazz, if she saw a Kandinsky, she saw the twentieth century. What have we had since? Look at these ads for this hotel in Miami. Might as well have been done in 1923 when you were running around with Stella.'

Yes, Mona was a consolation in more ways than one.

'Well, ducky, you know, I might run off to England with this man from the Talamasca,' Stella had said in those last weeks of her life. She'd stopped eating her spaghetti as if this were something to be decided then and there, with fork in hand. To run from First Street, run from Lasher, seek help from these strange scholars.

'But Julien warned against those men. Stella, he said they were the alchemists in my poem. He said they would only hurt us in the long run. Stella, he used that word, he said not to speak with them ever at all!'

'You know, this Talamasca man or whatever he is, he's going to find out about that other one, that the body's in the attic. When you're a Mayfair you can kill anyone you want, and nobody does anything about it. Nobody can think what to do.' She'd shrugged, and a month later her brother Lionel killed her. No more Stella.

No more anyone who knew about the Victrola or Julien with Evelyn in Julien's bedroom. Evelyn's only living witness gone to the grave.

It had not been a simple thing, during Julien's last illness, to get the Victrola out of the house. He'd waited for a time when Mary Beth and Carlotta were not at home, and then sent the boys down to fetch another 'music box', as he stubbornly called it, from the dining room.

And only when he had a record ready to play full blast on the big one, did he tell her to take the little Victrola and run away. He'd told her to sing as she walked with it, sing as if it were playing, just sing and sing aloud until she reached her house uptown.

'People will think I am crazy,' she had said softly. She had looked at her hands, her left hand with the extra finger – witches' marks.

'Do you care what they think?' His smile had always been so beautiful. Only in sleep did he look his age. He had cranked the big music box. 'You take these records of my opera – I have others – take them under your arm, you can do it. Take it uptown, my darling. If I could be a gentleman and carry the whole load for you up to your attic, you can be sure I would. Now, here, when you get to the Avenue, flag a taxi. Give him this. Let him carry the thing inside.'

And there she was singing that song, singing along with the big music box, while carrying the little one out of the house.

Out she had walked, like an altar boy in a procession, carrying the precious thing.

She'd carried it until her arms ached so much she

couldn't go any further. Had to set down the burden on the corner of Prytania and Fourth Street, and sit there on the curb with her elbows on her knees and rest for a while. Traffic whizzing by. Finally she had stopped a taxi, though she had never done such a thing before, and when she got home, the man had brought the Victrola all the way up to the attic for the five dollars Julien had given her. 'Thank you, ma'am!'

The darkest of days had been right after his death, when Mary Beth had come to ask if she had 'anything of Julien's', if she had taken anything from his room. She had shaken her head, refusing as always to answer. Mary Beth had known she was lying. 'What did Julien give you?' she asked.

Evelyn had sat on the floor of her attic room, her back to the armoire, which was locked, with the Victrola inside, refusing to answer. Julien is dead, that was all she could think, Julien is dead.

She hadn't even known then about the child inside her, about Laura Lee, poor doomed Laura Lee. At night, she walked the streets in silence, burning for Julien, and dared not play the Victrola while any light burned in the big Amelia Street house at all.

Years later, when Stella died, it was as if the old wound opened, and they became one – the loss of her two brilliant loves, the loss of the only warm light which had ever penetrated her life's mysteries, the loss of the music, the loss of all fire.

'Don't try to make her talk,' her great-grandfather had said to Mary Beth. 'You go out of here. You go back up to your house. You leave us alone. We don't want you here. If there is anything of that abominable man in this house, I'll destroy it.'

Oh, such a cruel cruel man. He would have killed Laura Lee if he could have. 'Witches!' Once he'd taken a kitchen knife and threatened to cut the little extra finger off Evelyn's hand. How she'd screamed. The others had to stop him – Pearl, and Aurora, and all the old ones from Fontevrault who'd still been there.

But Tobias had been the worst of them, as well as the eldest. How he hated Julien, and all over the gunshot in 1843, when Julien had shot his father, Augustin, at Riverbend, Julien no more than a boy, Augustin a young man, and Tobias, the terrified witness, only a baby still in dresses. That's the way they dressed boys then, in dresses. 'I saw my father fall over dead at my feet!'

'I never meant to kill him,' Julien had told Evelyn as they lay in bed. 'I never meant for one whole branch of the family to veer off in bitterness and rage, and everyone else has been trying to get them back ever since, but somehow there are two camps. There is here, and there is Amelia Street. I feel so sorry when I think of all that. I was just a boy, and the fool didn't know how to run the plantation. I have no compunction about shooting people, you understand, only that time I didn't plan it, honestly I did not. I did not mean to kill your great-great-grandfather. It was all just the most blundering mistake.'

She had not cared. She hated Tobias. She hated all of them. Old men.

Yet it was with an old man that love had first touched her, in Julien's attic.

And then there were those nights when she had walked downtown in the dark to that house, climbed the wall, and gone up, hand over hand on the trellis. So easy to climb so high, to swing out and stare down at the flags.

The flags on which poor Antha died. But that had been yet to come, all that, those horrible deaths – Stella, Antha.

It would always be pleasant to remember the thick green vine and the softness of it under her slipper as she climbed.

'Ah, *Chérie*,' he said. 'My delight, my wild thing,' and he raised the window to receive her, to bring her inside. '*Mon Dieu*, child, you could have fallen.'

'Never,' she whispered. Safe in his arms.

Even Richard Llewellyn, that boy he kept, didn't come between them. Richard knew to knock on Julien's door, and one was never sure what Richard Llewellyn knew, really. Years ago Richard Llewellyn had talked to that last Talamasca man, though Evelyn had warned him not to. Richard had come up to see her the next day.

'Well, you didn't tell him about me, did you?' Ancient Evelyn had demanded. Richard was so old. He didn't have very long.

'No, I didn't tell him that story. I didn't want him to think –'

'What? That Julien would bed a girl my age?' She had laughed. 'You shouldn't have talked to that man at all.' Richard hadn't lasted out the year, and when he died, they gave her his old records. He must have known about the Victrola, why else would he have left those old records to her?

Evelyn should have given Mona the little Victrola a long time ago, and not with such ceremony in front of the other two, her idiot granddaughters, Alicia and

Gifford. Leave it to Gifford to confiscate everything – the music box itself and the beautiful necklace.

'You dare!'

Leave it to Gifford to have made the very wrong choice, leave it to Gifford to misunderstand. To gasp in horror when Ancient Evelyn had said the poem. 'Why would he want you to have this? What did he think it could do? He was a witch and you know it. A witch as surely as the others.'

And then the terrible confession from Gifford, that she had gone and taken those things and hidden them back up at First Street, in that house whence they'd come.

'You little fool, how could you do such a thing?' Ancient Evelyn had asked. 'Mona should have had it! Mona is his great-granddaughter! Gifford, not back to that house where Carlotta will find it, where it will be destroyed.'

She remembered suddenly. Gifford had died this morning!

She was walking on St Charles Avenue, going up to First Street, and her aggravating, annoying, grating, nerve-wracking grandchild was dead!

'Why didn't I know it? Julien, why didn't you come to tell me!'

Well over half a century ago, she'd heard Julien's voice an hour before his death. She'd heard him calling from beneath her window. She'd sprung up and opened it wide to the rain, and there was Julien down there, only at once she knew it wasn't really Julien. She'd been terrified he was already dead. He had waved at her, so cheerful and gay, with a big dark mare beside him. '*Au revoir, ma Chérie,*' he had called out.

And then she had gone to him, running all the way those ten blocks downtown, and climbed the trellis, and for those precious moments seen his eyes – the life still in them – fixed on her. Oh, Julien, I heard you calling me. I saw you. I saw the embodiment of your love. She had raised the window. She had lifted him.

'Eve,' he had whispered. 'Evie, I want to sit up. Evie, help me, I'm dying, Evie! It's happening, it's come!'

They had never known she was there.

She'd crouched outside on the porch roof in the fury of the storm, listening to them. They'd never thought to even look outside as they closed the window and laid him out, and sent for everyone. And there she'd been huddled against the chimney, watching the lightning and thinking, Why don't you strike me? Why don't I die? Julien is dead.

'What did he give you?' Mary Beth had asked her every time she saw her. Year after year she came.

Mary Beth had stared at little Laura Lee, such a weak, thin baby, never a baby that people wanted to hold. Mary Beth had always known that Julien had been Laura Lee's father.

And how the others had hated her. 'Julien's spawn, look at her, with the witch's mark on her hand, look, like you!'

It wasn't so bad, just a tiny extra finger. Why, most people had never noticed it, though Laura Lee had been so self-conscious, and no one at Sacred Heart knew what it meant.

'The mark of the witch,' Tobias used to say. 'There are many. Red hair is the worst, and a sixth finger the second, and a monster's height, the third. And you with the sixth finger. Go live up at First Street, live with the damned who gave you your talents. Get out of my house.'

Of course she had never gone, not with Carlotta there! Better to ignore the old men as she and her little daughter went about their business. Laura Lee had been too sickly ever to finish high school. Poor Laura Lee, who spent her life taking in stray cats, and talking to them, and going round the block to find them and feed them, until the neighbors complained. She'd been too old by the time she married; and to be left with those two girls!

Were we the powerful witches, those of us who bore the mark of the sixth finger? What about Mona with her red hair?

As the years passed the great Mayfair legacy had gone to Stella and then to Antha and then to Deirdre . . .

All of them lost, who had lived in the times of shadows. Even the bright blaze of Stella pinched out, like that!

'But there will come another time. A time of battle and catastrophe.' That Julien had promised her the last night she had really spoken with him. 'That's the meaning of your poem, Evelyn. I shall try to be here.'

The music whined and thumped. He was always playing it.

'You see, *Chérie*, I have a secret about *him* and music. He cannot hear us so well when we play music. It's an old secret, my grandmère Marie Claudette told me herself.

'The evil daemon is actually drawn to the music. Music can distract him. He can hear music when he can hear nothing else. Rhythm and rhyme can also entrap him. All ghosts find such things irresistible, as they do visible patterns. In their gloom, they pine for order, for symmetry. I use the music to draw him and confuse him. Mary Beth knows this too. Why do you think there are music boxes in every room? Why do you think she loves her many Victrolas? They give her privacy from this being, which she would have now and then, just as anyone would.

'And when I am gone, child, play the Victrola. Play it and think of me. Perhaps I can hear it, perhaps I can come to you, perhaps the waltz will penetrate the darkness, and bring me back to myself and to you.'

'Julien, why do you call *him* evil? They always said at home that the spirit in this house was yours to command. Tobias said it to Walker. They said it to me when they told me Cortland was my father. Lasher was the magic slave of Julien and Mary Beth, they said, which will grant their every wish.'

He'd shaken his head, talking under cover of a Neapolitan song. 'He's evil, mark my word, and the worst kind of evil, but he does not know it himself. Recite the poem again. Tell it to me.'

Ancient Evelyn had hated to say the poem. The poem came from her as if she were the Victrola and someone had touched her with an invisible needle, and out came the words, and she did not know what they meant. Words that frightened Julien, and had frightened his niece Carlotta beforehand, words that Julien said over and over again as the months passed.

How vigorous he had looked, his white curly hair still very thick, his eyes very clever and focused upon her. He'd never suffered the blindness and deafness of old age, had he? Was it his many loves that kept him young? Perhaps so. He'd laid his soft dry hand over hers, and kissed her cheek.

'Soon I shall die like everyone else, and there's nothing I can do about it.'

Oh, that precious year, those precious few months.

And to think of him coming to her, young in that vision. That she'd heard his voice all the way up at her window. And there he'd stood in the rain, all chipper and handsome and beaming at her as he held the bridle of his horse. '*Au revoir, ma Chérie.*'

Afterwards little visions of him came so fast they were like the pop of flashbulbs. Julien on the streetcar passing by. Julien in a car. Julien in the cemetery at Antha's funeral. All make-believe perhaps. Why, she could have sworn she glimpsed him for one precious second at Stella's funeral.

Is that why she'd spoken so to Carlotta, accusing her outright, as they stood together amongst the graves?

'It was the music, wasn't it?' Evelyn had said, trembling as she made her verbal assault, fired with hatred and grief. 'You had to have the music. When the band was playing loud and wild, Lionel could come up on Stella and shoot her with the gun. And "the man" didn't even know, did he? You used the music to distract "the man". You knew the trick. Julien told me the trick. You tricked "the man" with music. You killed your sister, you were the one.'

'Witch, get away from me,' Carlotta had said, seething with anger. 'You and all your kind.'

'Ah, but I know, and your brother's in the straitjacket, yes, but you're the killer! You put him up to it. You used the music, you knew the trick.'

It had taken all her strength to say those words, but

her love for Stella had demanded it. Stella. Evelyn had lain alone in the bed in the little French Quarter apartment, holding Stella's dress in her hands, crying against it. And the pearls, they would never find Stella's pearls. She had turned inward after Stella, she had never dared to want again.

'I'd give them to you, ducky,' Stella had said of the pearls, 'you know, I really would, but Carlotta will raise hell! She's read me the riot act, ducky, I cannot give away the heirlooms and things! If she ever knew about that Victrola – that Julien let you take it – she'd get it away from you. She's an inventory taker that one. That's what she ought to do in hell, make sure nobody's gotten out to purgatory by mistake, or is not suffering his fair share of fire and brimstone. She's a beast. You may not see me again so soon, ducky dear, I may run away with that Talamasca person from England.'

'No good can come of that!' she said. 'I feel afraid.'

'Dance tonight. Have fun. Come on. You cannot wear my pearls if you won't dance.'

And never again had they even spoken together, she and Stella. Oh, to see the blood oozing on the waxed floor.

Well, yes, Evelyn had answered Carlotta later, she did have the pearls but she'd left them there at the house that night, and after that she would never answer another question about them.

Over the decades, others asked. Even Lauren came in time and asked. 'They were priceless pearls. You don't remember what happened to them?'

And young Ryan, Gifford's beloved, and her beloved, even he had been forced to bring up the unpleasant subject.

'Ancient Evelyn, Aunt Carlotta will not drop the question of these pearls.' At least Gifford had kept her counsel then, thank heaven, and Gifford had looked so miserable. Never should have showed the pearls to Gifford. But Gifford had said not a word.

Well, if it hadn't been for Gifford, the priceless pearls would have stayed in the wall forever. Gifford, Gifford, Gifford, Miss Goody-two-shoes, Miss Meddler! But then they were in the wall again, weren't they? That was the lovely part. They were in the wall right now.

All the more reason to walk straight, to walk slow, to walk sure. The pearls too are up there, and surely they must be given to Mona, for Rowan Mayfair was gone and might never return.

My, so many houses on this long avenue had vanished. It was too sad, really. Whatever made up for a magnificent house, full of ornament and gay shutters and rounded windows? Not these, these mock buildings of stucco and glue, these dreary little tenements all got up for the middle class as if people were fools after all.

You had to hand it to Mona, she knew. She said quite flatly that modern architecture had been a failure. You had only to look around to see, and that was why people loved the old houses now. 'You know, I figure, Ancient Evelyn, that probably more houses were built and torn down between 1860 and 1960 than ever before in human history. Think about the cities of Europe. The houses of Amsterdam go back to the 1600s. And then think about New York. Almost every structure on Fifth Avenue is new; there is hardly a house left standing on the whole street from the turn of the century. I believe there is the Frick mansion, and I can't think of another one. Of course I've never been to New York, except with Gifford, and it wasn't Gifford's thing to go examining old buildings. I think she thought we went there to go shopping, and shop we did.'

Evelyn had agreed, though she hadn't said so. On all accounts, Evelyn always agreed with Mona. Though Aunt Evelyn never said.

But that was the great thing about Mona; before her computer had drawn off all her love, Mona had used Ancient Evelyn as her sounding board, and it had never been necessary to say anything to Mona. Mona could make a long conversation all on her own, proceeding with manic fire from one topic to another. Mona was her treasure, and now that Gifford was gone, why, she would talk to Mona and they could sit alone, and they could play the Victrola. And the pearls. Yes, she would wrap them around Mona's neck.

Again came that wicked and terrible relief. No more Gifford of the haggard face, and frightened eyes, speaking of conscience and right in a hushed voice, no more Gifford to witness Alicia's decay and death with horror in her face, no more Gifford standing watch over all of them.

Was the Avenue still the Avenue? Surely she would come to the corner of Washington soon, but there were so many of these new buildings that she had lost her bearings.

Life had become so noisy. Life had become crude. Garbage trucks roared as they devoured the trash. Trucks clattered in the street. The banana man was gone, the ice cream man was gone. The chimney sweeps came no more. The old woman no longer came with the blackberries. Laura Lee died in pain. Deirdre went mad, and then Deirdre's daughter, Rowan, came home, only one day too late to see her mother alive, and a horror happened on Christmas Day and no one wanted to speak of it. And Rowan Mayfair was gone.

What if Rowan Mayfair and her new man had found the Victrola and the records? But no, Gifford said they had not. Gifford kept watch. Gifford would have snatched them away again, if she had to do it.

And Gifford's hiding place had been Stella's own, known only to Gifford because Evelyn had revealed it to her. Stupid thing to have done, to have ever wasted a tale or a song or a verse upon Gifford or Alicia. They were mere links in a chain and the jewel was Mona.

'They won't find them, Ancient Evelyn, I put the pearls back in the very same secret place in the library. The Victrola with them. The whole kit and caboodle will be safe there forever.'

And Gifford, the country club Mayfair, had gone up to that dark house and hidden those things away on her own. Had she seen the man on that dark journey?

'They'll never be found. They'll rot with that house,' Gifford had said. 'You know. You showed me the place yourself the day we were in the library.'

'You mock me, you evil child.' But she had shown little Gifford the secret niche on the very afternoon of Laura Lee's funeral. That must have been the last time Carlotta opened the house.

It was 1960, and Deirdre was already very sick, and having lost her baby, Rowan, Deirdre had gone back for a long time in the hospital. Cortland had been dead a year.

But Carlotta had always pitied Laura Lee, always pitied her that she had Evelyn for a mother. And then there were Millie Dear and Belle, both saying, Carlotta, can't we bring them all back here? And Carlotta looking sadly at Evelyn, trying to hate her, yet feeling so sorry for her that she had buried her daughter. And perhaps that she, Evelyn, had been buried alive, herself, since the day of Stella's death.

'You can bring the family here,' Millie Dear had said, and Carlotta had not dared to contradict her. 'Yes, indeed,' said Belle, for Belle had always known that Laura Lee was Julien's child. Everyone had known. 'Yes, indeed,' said Belle, sweet Belle. 'Come back to the house with us, all of you.'

Why had she gone? She did not really know! Maybe to see Julien's house again. Maybe she had intended all along to slip into the library and see if the pearls were still there, if anyone had ever found them.

And as the others gathered, as they whispered of Laura Lee's suffering and poor little Gifford and poor little Alicia, and all the sad things that had befallen them all, Evelyn had taken Gifford by the hand and led her into the library.

'Stop your crying for your mother,' Evelyn had said. 'Laura Lee's gone to heaven. Now come here, and I'll show you a secret place. I'll show you something beautiful. I have a necklace for you.'

Gifford had wiped her eyes. She had been in a daze since her mother's death, and that daze wouldn't break until she married Ryan many years later on. But with Gifford there had always been hope. On the afternoon of Laura Lee's funeral, there had been plenty of hope.

Indeed, Gifford had had a good life, one had to admit, fretting it away as she did, but still she had her love of Ryan, she had her beautiful children, she had heart enough to love Mona and leave her alone, though Mona frightened the life out of her.

Life. Gifford dead. Not possible. Should have been Alicia. All a mix-up. Horse stopped at the wrong gate. Did Julien foresee this?

It was like just a moment ago – Laura Lee's funeral. Think again about the library – dusty, neglected. Women talking in the other room.

Evelyn had taken little Gifford to the bookcase, and pushed the books aside. She'd drawn out the long string of pearls. 'We're taking this home now. I hid it thirty years ago, the day that Stella died here in the parlor. Carlotta never found it. And these, these are pictures of Stella and me too. I'm taking them too. Someday I will give these things to you and your sister.'

Gifford, leaning back on her heels, had looked at the long necklace in amazement.

It made Evelyn feel so good to have beaten Carlotta, to have kept the pearls when all else seemed lost. The necklace and the music box, her treasures.

'What do you mean, the love of another woman?' Gifford had asked her many nights after that, when they sat on the porch talking over the cheerful noise of the Avenue traffic.

'I mean the love of a woman, that's what I mean, that I kissed her mouth, that I sucked her breasts, that I went down and put my tongue between her legs and tasted her taste, that I loved her, that I drowned in her!'

Gifford had been shocked and afraid. Had she married with her hair down? Very very likely. A horrid thing, a virgin girl. Though if anyone could make the best of such a thing, it had probably been Gifford.

Ah, this was Washington Avenue. It was. No doubt of it. And behold, the florist shop was still here, and that meant that Ancient Evelyn could go carefully up these few little steps and order the flowers herself for her precious girl.

'What did you do with my treasures?'

'Don't tell those things to Mona!'

Ancient Evelyn stared in bafflement at the florist blossoms crowding against the glass, like flowers in prison, wondering where to send the flowers for Gifford. Gifford was the one who had died.

Oh, my darling . . .

She knew what flowers she wanted to send. She knew what flowers Gifford liked.

They wouldn't bring her home for the wake. Of course not. Not the Metairie Mayfairs. They would never never do such a thing. Why, her body was probably already being painted in some refrigerated funeral home.

'Don't try to put me on ice in such a place,' Evelyn had said after Deirdre's funeral last year, when Mona stood describing the whole thing, how Rowan Mayfair had come from California to lean over the coffin and kiss her dead mother. How Carlotta had keeled over dead that very night into Deirdre's rocker, like she wanted to be dead with Deirdre, leaving that poor Rowan Mayfair from California all alone in that spooky house.

'Oh, life, oh, time!' Mona had said, stretching out her thin pale arms, and swinging her long red hair to the left and the right. 'It was worse than the death of Ophelia.'

'Probably not,' Ancient Evelyn had said. For Deirdre had lost her mind years before, and if this California doctor, Rowan Mayfair, had had any gumption at all, she would have come home long before now, demanding answers of those who drugged and hurt her mother. No good could come of that California girl, Ancient Evelyn knew, and that was why they'd never brought her up to Amelia Street, and Ancient Evelyn had therefore seen her only once, at the woman's wedding, when she wasn't a woman at all, but a sacrificial creature for the family, decked out in white with the emerald burning on her neck.

She'd gone to that wedding not because Rowan Mayfair, the designee of the legacy, was marrying a young man named Michael Curry in St Mary's church, but because Mona would be the flower girl, and it had made Mona happy for Ancient Evelyn to come, to sit in the pew and see, and nod as Mona passed.

So hard it had been to enter the house after all those years, and see it beautiful once more the way it had been in those times when she had been with Julien. To see the happiness of Dr Rowan Mayfair and her innocent husband, Michael Curry. Like one of Mary Beth's Irish boys, he was big and muscular, and very frank and kind in his brusque and ignorant way, though he was educated they said, and affected the common air, so to speak, because he'd come from the back streets, and his father had been a fireman.

Oh, so like the boys of Mary Beth, Ancient Evelyn had thought, but that was all she remembered of that wedding, all she remembered of Deirdre's daughter. They'd taken Ancient Evelyn home early when Alicia had been too drunk to stay. She hadn't minded. She'd sat by Alicia's bed as always, saying her beads, and dreaming, and humming the songs that Julien used to play in the upstairs room.

And the bride and groom of last year had danced in

that double parlor. And the Victrola was hidden in the library wall, and no one would ever find it. She herself did not think of it, or maybe she would have gone to it, as all the others sang and drank and laughed together. Maybe under that roof, she would have wound it again and said 'Julien,' and to the wedding he would have come, an unexpected guest!

Hadn't even thought of it then. Too afraid Alicia would stumble.

That night, late, Gifford had come upstairs to Alicia's room at Amelia Street. She'd put her hand on Ancient Evelyn's shoulder. 'I'm glad you came to the wedding,' she'd said so kindly. 'I wish you would come out again, more often.' And then she had asked. 'You didn't go to the secret place? You didn't tell them?'

Ancient Evelyn had not bothered to answer.

'Rowan and Michael will be happy!' Gifford had kissed her cheek and gone off. The room stank of drink. Alicia moaned as her mother had moaned, determined to die at all costs, be with Mother.

Washington Avenue. Yes, indeed this was it. Over there, the white-shingled Queen Anne house same as always. It was the only one left on any of the four corners, of course, but it was the same, very same.

And here the florist. Yes, she had been about to buy the flowers, hadn't she? For her darling girl, her darling . . .

And look, the strangest thing was happening. A little bespectacled young man had appeared in the doorway of the florist, and he was speaking to her, was he not? Time to listen over the rumble of the traffic.

'Ancient Evelyn. That's you. I hardly recognized you. What are you doing so far from home, Ancient Evelyn, come inside. Let me call your granddaughter.'

'My granddaughter's dead,' she said. 'You can't call her.'

'Yes, ma'am, I'm sorry, I know.' He came to the edge of the little porch. He wasn't so young, really, she could see that now, and she did know this young man, didn't she?

'I'm so sorry about Miss Gifford, ma'am. I've been taking orders for flowers all morning long. I meant I'd like to call Miss Alicia to come and get you and take you home.'

'You think Alicia could come to pick me up, shows what you know, poor boy.' But why speak? Why speak at all? She had given up this sort of feisty foolishness long ago. She would wear herself crazy today going back to this sort of chatter.

But what was this man's name? What on earth was he saying now? Oh, she'd remember if she tried, who he was, and where she'd seen him last, or most, and that he'd come with a delivery or two, or that he'd waved to her in the evening as he walked along, but was it worth it to remember such things? Like following the string back through the labyrinth. Oh bother! Oh stupid bother!

The young man came down the steps.

'Ancient Evelyn, won't you let me help you inside? How pretty you look today, with that lovely pin on your dress.'

I'm sure I do, she thought dreamily. Hiding in the body of this old woman. But why say such things to hurt the feelings of an innocent man, an unimportant man, even if he was hairless and anemic? He didn't know how *long* she'd been an old woman! Why it had started not long after Laura Lee was born, in a way, her walking the wicker baby carriage all the way up here and round and back around the cemetery. Might as well have been old.

'How did you know my granddaughter died! Who told you?' It was astonishing. She wasn't certain now how she herself knew.

'Mr Fielding called. He said to fill that room with flowers. He was crying when he called. It's oh, so sad. I'm sorry, Ancient Evelyn, truly I am. I don't know what to say at such times.'

'Well, you ought to, you sell people flowers. Flowers for the dead more often probably than flowers for the living. You ought to learn and memorize some nice things to say. People expect you to talk, don't they?'

'What was that, ma'am?'

'Listen, young man, whoever you are. You send flowers for me for my grandchild Gifford.'

He'd heard that right enough but it was a dollars and cents order.

'You make it a standing spray of white gladiolus and red roses and lilies, and you put a ribbon on it. You write *Grandchild* on the ribbon, do you hear? That's all. Make sure it's big and beautiful and they put it beside her coffin. And where is that coffin to be, by the way, did my cousin Fielding have the decency to say, or are you supposed to call funeral parlors on your own until you discover it?'

'Metairie, ma'am. I already know. Others are calling.'

What was in Metairie? What? What was he saying? A huge truck had bounced and rattled across the intersection and down towards Carondolet. Nuisance. And look at those town houses over there! Good lord, so they had torn down that beautiful house too, idiots. I am surrounded by idiots.

She pushed at her hair. The young man was pulling at her arm. 'Get away from me,' she said, or tried to say. What had she been discussing with this young man? Indeed, she did not know. And what was she doing here of all places? Had he just asked her that very question?

'Let me put you in a cab for home, or I'll take you there myself.'

'You will not,' she said, and as she looked at the flowers behind the glass she remembered. She walked on, past him, turning off the Avenue and going into the Garden District and towards the cemetery. Always been one of her favorite walks this way to see the Mayfair tomb when she passed the gates, and lo and behold, Commander's Palace was still there. She could see the awnings all the way from here. How many a year had it been since she dined inside! Of course Gifford was always begging to take her.

Lunch with Gifford at Commander's, and Ryan such a proper shiny-faced boy. Hard to believe a child like that was a Mayfair, a great-grandson of Julien. But more and more the Mayfairs had taken on that shiny look. Gifford always ordered the Shrimp Remoulade, and never spilt a drop of the sauce on her scarf or her blouse.

Gifford. Nothing really could have happened to Gifford.

'Young man,' she said.

He walked beside her holding her arm, perplexed, superior, confused, proud.

'What happened to my grandchild? Tell me. What did Fielding Mayfair tell you? I am so distraught. Don't think me a forgetful old woman, and let go of my arm.

I don't need you. What happened to Gifford Mayfair, I'm asking you now.'

'I don't know for sure, ma'am,' he said. 'They found her in the sand. She'd lost a lot of blood, some kind of hemorrhage they said. But I don't know any more than that. She was dead by the time they got her to the hospital. That's all I know, and her husband is on his way there now to find out everything.'

'Well, of course he is on his way,' she said. She jerked her arm free. 'I thought I told you to let me go.'

'I'm afraid you'll fall, Ancient Evelyn. I've never seen you so far from home.'

'What are we talking about, son? Eight blocks? I used to make this walk all the time. Used to be a little drugstore there on the corner of Prytania and Washington. Used to stop for ice cream. Feed Laura Lee ice cream. Please, do let go of my arm!'

He looked so crushed, so hurt, so frozen and sorry. Poor thing. But when you were old and weak, your authority was all you had left, and it could crumble in an instant. If she fell now, if her leg went out from under her – But no, she would not let that happen!

'Well, bless your soul, you are a sweet boy. I didn't mean to hurt your feelings, but please don't talk to me as if I were addle-brained, for I am not. Walk me across Prytania Street. It's too wide. Then you go back and fix the flowers for my darling girl, won't you, and how do you know who I am, may I ask?'

'I bring your flowers on your birthday, ma'am, lots and lots of flowers every year. You know my name. My name is Hanky. Don't you remember me? I wave when I pass the gate.'

It wasn't said with reproach, but he was highly

suspicious now and very likely to take action, to force her into a cab, or worse, to go call someone to head her off, for it was perfectly obvious that she ought not to be able to make this trek alone.

'Ah, yes, Hanky, I do remember you of course, and your father was Harry who went in the Vietnam War. And then there was your mother, who moved back to Virginia.'

'Yes, ma'am, you've got it all right. You've got it perfect.' How delighted he was. That was the most maddening and annoying aspect of old age. If you could add two and two people clapped for you! They clapped. It was true. It was pathetic. Of course she remembered Harry. He'd delivered flowers to them for years and years. Or was that old Harry? Oh, Lord, Julien, why have I lived this long? For what? What am I doing?

There was the white wall of the cemetery.

'Come on, young Hanky, be a nice boy and cross me over. I have to go,' she said.

'Ancient Evelyn, please let me drive you home. Let me call your grandson-in-law.'

'That sot, you twit!' She turned on him full face. 'I'm going to hit you with this walking stick.' She laughed in spite of herself at the idea of it, and he laughed too.

'But ma'am, aren't you tired? Don't you want to rest? Come back into the florist shop and rest.'

She felt too weary suddenly to say another word. Why speak? They never listened.

She planted her feet on the corner and held tight to her cane with both hands and stared down the leafy corridor of Washington Avenue. The best oaks in the city, she often thought, all the way to the river. Should she give up? Something was terribly wrong, terribly terribly wrong, and her mission, what had it been? Good God, she could not recollect.

An old white-haired gentleman stood opposite, was he as old as she? And he smiled at her. He smiled and he waved for her to come on. What a dandy he was! And at his age. It made her laugh to see such colorful clothes, the yellow silk waistcoat! By God, that was Julien. Julien Mayfair! It gave her such a great and pleasurable shock, she felt it all over her face, as if someone had touched her with a cool cloth and wakened her. Look at him. Julien! Waving to her to come on, hurry it up.

And then he was gone, simply gone, yellow waistcoat and all, the way he always did it, the stubborn dead, the crazy dead, the puzzling dead! But she had remembered everything. Mona was up at that house. Gifford had suffered a fatal loss of blood, and Ancient Evelyn had to go to First Street. Julien knew she must go on. That was good enough for her.

'You let him touch you!' Gifford had asked her, in amazement, CeeCee laughing in that snide, silly way.

'My dears, I adored it.'

If only she could have said such a thing to Tobias and to Walker. Nights before Laura Lee's birth she'd unlocked the attic door and she had walked on her own to the hospital. The old men had not been told until the child was safe in her arms.

'Don't you see what that bastard has done?' Walker had cried. 'It's to plant the witches' seeds! This is a witch too!'

How frail was Laura Lee. Was that a witch's seed? If it was, then only the cats had known it. Think of the way they had crowded about Laura Lee, arching their backs and rubbing themselves on her thin little legs. Laura Lee with the witch's finger which she had not passed on to Alicia or Gifford, thank God!

The light turned green.

Ancient Evelyn began to walk across the street. The young man talked and talked, but she paid him no mind. She walked on, beside the whitewashed walls, next to the quiet and invisible dead, the properly buried dead, and by the time she reached the gates in the middle of the block, young Hanky-of-the-flowers was nowhere about, and she was not going to look back to see what he had done or where he'd gone or if he was rushing back to his flower shop to call the patrol for her. She stopped at the gates. She could just see the edge of the Mayfair tomb down there in the middle of the block, jutting out ever so slightly into the path. She knew everyone inside, she could knock on every rectangle of stone. 'Hello in there, my darlings.'

Gifford wouldn't be buried there, oh, no. Gifford would be buried out in Metairie. Country club Mayfairs, she thought. They had always called them that, even in Cortland's time, or was it Cortland who started that expression to describe his own children? Cortland who had whispered in her ear once, 'Daughter, I love you,' so quick the country club Mayfairs couldn't hear.

Gifford, my darling Gifford.

She imagined Gifford in her lovely red wool suit, and white blouse with a soft silk bow at the neck. Gifford wore gloves, but only to drive. She had been putting them on, very carefully, caramel leather gloves. She looked younger than Alicia now, though she was not. She cared for herself, groomed herself, loved other people.

'I can't stay for Mardi Gras this year,' she'd said. 'I just can't.' She'd come to tell them she was driving to Destin.

'Well, I hope you don't expect me to receive everybody here!' Alicia had cried. Utter panic. She'd dropped the magazine on the porch. 'I can't do all that. I can't get the ham and the bread. I can't. I won't. I'll lock up the house. I'm not well. And Aunt Evelyn just sits there and sits there. Where is Patrick? You should stay here and help me. Why don't you do something about Patrick? Do you know Patrick drinks in the morning now? He drinks all morning. Where is Mona? Goddamnit, Mona went out without telling me. Mona is always going out without telling me. Somebody should put a leash on Mona. I need Mona! Board up the damned windows, will you, before you leave?'

Gifford had remained so calm.

'They're all going to First Street this year, CeeCee,' Gifford had said. 'You don't have to do anything except what you always do, no matter how you plan to do otherwise.'

'Oh, you are so mean to me. Did you come uptown just to say this to me? And what about Michael Curry? They say he almost died on Christmas Day, may I ask why he is giving a party on Shrove Tuesday?' Alicia was by that time trembling with indignation and rage at the sheer madness of life, at the utter lack of logic to things, that anything could expect anything of her. After all, had she not practically killed herself just to secure that from all responsibility she would be forever exempt? How much more liquor did it take?

'This Michael Curry nearly drowns and so what does he do? He gives a party? Doesn't he know his wife is

239

missing! His wife could be dead! What kind of man is he, this crazy Michael Curry! And who the hell said he could live in that house! What are they going to do about the legacy! What if Rowan Mayfair never comes back! Go on, go to Destin. Why should you care? Leave me here. It doesn't matter! Go to hell.'

Wasted anger, wasted words, beside the point, always beside the point. Had Alicia said anything straightforward or honest in twenty years? Most likely not.

'They want to gather at First Street, CeeCee, it's not my idea. I'm going away.' Gifford's voice had been so soft that Alicia probably had not even heard, and those had been the last words her sister would ever speak to her. Oh, my darling, my darling dear, bend to kiss me again, kiss my cheek, now, hold my hand, even with your soft leather glove, I loved you my sweetheart, my grandbaby, no matter what I said. I did, I loved you.

Gifford.

Gifford's car had driven away, as Alicia stood on the porch and swore. Barefoot and cold. She'd kicked the magazine. 'So she just leaves. She just leaves. I can't believe it. She just leaves. What am I supposed to do?'

Ancient Evelyn had spoken not a word. Words spoken to drunkards were truly words written in water. They vanished into the endless void in which the drunkard languished. Could a ghost be any worse off?

Gifford had tried and tried. Gifford was Mayfair through and through. Gifford had loved; fretted, yes, but loved.

Little girl with a conscience, on the floor of the library, 'But should we just take these pearls?'

All doomed, that generation, the Mayfair children of the time of science and psychology. Better to have lived

240

in the time of crinolines and carriages and voodooiennes. We are past our time. Julien knew.

But Mona wasn't doomed, was she? Now that was a
witch for this day and time. Mona at her computer,
chewing gum and typing faster than any person in the
universe. 'If there was an Olympic race for typing, I'd
win it.' And on the screen, all those charts and graphs.
'See this? This is a Mayfair family tree. Know what I
figured out?'

Art and magic will triumph in the end, Julien had
said. I know it. Was the computer art and magic? Even
the way the screen glowed in the dark, and that little
voice box inside that Mona had programmed to say in
an eerie flat way:

'Good morning, Mona. This is your computer talking
to you. Don't forget to brush your teeth.' It was perfectly frightening to see Mona's room come alive at
eight o'clock, what with the computer talking like that
as the coffeepot gurgled and hissed, and the microwave
oven went on to heat the rolls with a tiny beep, and
CNN Headline News came alive and talking on the
TV. 'I like to wake up connected,' said Mona. The
paperboy had learned to throw the *Wall Street Journal*
up to the second floor porch outside her window.

Mona, to find Mona.

To find Mona, she was going to Chestnut Street. She
had come so far.

Time to cross big Washington Avenue. She should
have crossed it at the light back there, but then she
might not have seen Julien. Everything works out. The
morning was still and empty, and quiet. And the oaks
made a church of the street. And there stood the old
firehouse so deserted. Had the firemen gone away? But

that was way off her course. She had to go down Chestnut Street now, and here would come the slippery sidewalks, the bricks and the stones, and it was best perhaps that she walked in the street itself, just along the parked cars, as she'd done years ago, rather than slip and fall. The cars came slow through these streets.

Soft and leafy as Paradise, the Garden District.

The traffic waited until she reached the curb, and then with a loud swoosh it moved on behind her. Yes, take to the street. And even here was the litter of Mardi Gras. What a shame, for shame.

Why doesn't everyone come out and sweep the banquette? She felt sad suddenly that she had not done this herself this morning as was her plan. She had meant to go out. She liked to sweep. It took her forever. And Alicia would call down to her, 'Come inside!' but she swept and swept.

'Miss Ancient Evelyn, you've been sweeping out here for hours,' Patricia would say.

But of course, why not? Will the leaves ever stop falling? Why, whenever she thought of Mardi Gras coming, all that entered her mind was that it was going to be fun to sweep the banquette after. So much rubble and trash. Sweep and sweep.

Only something this morning had come between her and the broom. What was it?

The Garden District was dead quiet. It really was as if no one had lived here. The noise of the Avenue was so much better. On the Avenue, you were never alone; even late at night the headlamps shone through windows, and threw a cheery yellow glow into the mirrors. You could go outside in the very cool of the darkest morning, and stand on the corner and see the streetcar drift by, or a man strolling past, or a car creeping along with young men inside laughing and talking to each other, furtive yet happy.

On and on she walked. But they had destroyed the old houses here too, some of them. It was probably true, Mona's observation, whatever it had been, something to do with architecture. A stunning lack of vision. A clash between science and imagination. 'A misunderstanding,' Mona had said, 'of the relationship of form and function.' Some forms succeed and some fail. Everything is form. Mona had said that. Mona would have loved Julien.

She came to Third Street now. Halfway there. It was nothing to cross these little streets. There was no traffic at all. No one was awake yet. On she walked, sure of herself on the asphalt that gleamed in the sun, with no evil cracks or crevices to trip her.

Julien, why don't you come back? Why don't you help me? Why are you always such a tease? Good God, Julien. I can play the Victrola now in the library. There is no one to stop me, just Michael Curry, that sweet man, and Mona. I can play the Victrola and say your name.

Ah, what a lovely perfume, the ligustrum in bloom. She had forgotten all about it. And there was the house, my Lord, look at the color of it. She had never known it to have much of a color at all, and now it was all bright and grayish violet, with shutters painted in green, and the fence very black against it.

Oh, it *was* restored! What a good thing Michael Curry had done.

And there, there on the upstairs porch he stood looking down at her. Michael Curry. Yes, that was the man.

He was in his pajamas and very rumpled, robe open in front and he was smoking a cigarette. Like Spencer Tracy he looked, that chunky and Irish and rough, though his hair was black. Nice good-looking man with lots of black hair. And weren't his eyes blue? Certainly seemed so.

'Hello there, Michael Curry,' she said. 'I've come to see you. I've come to talk to Mona Mayfair.'

Good Lord, what a shock that gave him. How alarmed he was. But she sang it out loud and clear.

'I know Mona's inside. You tell her to come out.'

And then there was her sleepy girl, in a white gown, all frazzled and yawning the way children do, as if no one is holding them accountable.

Up in the treetops they stood behind the black railing, and it struck her suddenly what had happened, where they had been together. Oh, good Lord, and Gifford had warned her about this, that Mona was 'on the path' so to speak, and must be watched, and that child hadn't been looking for the Victrola at all, she'd been looking for Mary Beth's style of Irish boy, Rowan Mayfair's husband: Michael Curry.

Ancient Evelyn felt a lovely desire to laugh and laugh.

As Stella would have said, 'What a scream!'

But Ancient Evelyn was tired and her fingers curled over the black wire of the fence and she was relieved as she bowed her head to hear the big front door open, to hear naked feet slap across the porch, that intimate unmistakable patter, and to see Mona standing there, until she realized what she had to tell Mona.

'What is it, Ancient Evelyn?' she asked. 'What's happened?'

'You didn't see anything, child? She didn't call your name? Think, my precious girl, before I tell you. No, it's not your mother.'

And then Mona's little-girl face crumpled and became wet with tears, and, opening the gate, she wiped at her eye with the back of her hand.

'Aunt Gifford,' she cried in a wee voice, so fragile and young and so unlike Mona the Strong, and Mona the Genius. 'Aunt Gifford! And I had been so glad that she wasn't here.'

'You didn't do it, darling child,' she said. 'Blood in the sand. Happened this morning. Maybe she didn't suffer. Maybe she's in heaven this very minute looking down on us and wondering why we are sad.'

Michael Curry stood at the top of the marble steps, robe properly closed, with slippers on his feet, hands in his pockets, hair even combed.

'Why, that young man isn't sick,' she said.

Mona broke into sobs, staring helplessly from Ancient Evelyn to the ruddy dark-haired man on the porch.

'Who said he was dying of a bad heart?' asked Ancient Evelyn as she watched him come down the steps. She reached out and clasped the young man's hand. 'There's nothing wrong with this strapping young man at all!'

NINE

He had asked them to gather in the library. The little brown portable gramophone was in the corner and that splendid necklace of long pearls, and the little packet of pictures of Stella and Ancient Evelyn when they had been young together. But he didn't want to talk about that now. He had to talk about Rowan.

It made Mona happy that these things had been found, very happy, in the middle of her grief for the death of Gifford, but Mona was not his concern. He was suffering agonies over his indiscretion with Mona; well, one minute he was, and the next he had other things to think about. Like that two months had passed, and he had lived in this house like one of its ghosts, and that was over, and he had to search for his wife.

They had just come back from Ryan's house, from the two hours of drinking and talking after Gifford's funeral. They had come back to the house – come for this conference, and some merely to be with each other a little longer, crying for Gifford as it was the family custom to do.

All during last night's wake and the funeral today he had seen the looks of amazement on their faces as they shook his hand, as they told him he looked 'so much better', as they whispered about him to one another. 'Look at Michael! Michael's come back from the dead.'

There was the awful raucous shock of Gifford's untimely death on the one hand – a perfect wife and mother removed from life, leaving behind a brilliant and beloved lawyer husband and three exquisite children. And then there was the shock that Michael was OK, that the legendary abandoned husband, the latest male victim of the Mayfair legacy, was not actually wasting away. Michael was fine. He was up and dressed and driving his own car in the funeral procession. And he wasn't short of breath, or dizzy or sick to his stomach.

And he and Dr Rhodes had fought it out about the drugs in the foyer of the funeral home, and Michael had won. He wasn't experiencing any bad withdrawal. He had emptied the bottles, and then put them away. Later he would check the labels. He would discover what he had been taking, but not now. The sickness was over. He had work to do.

And there was Mona always in the corner of his eyes, staring at him, and now and then whispering, 'I told you so.' Mona with her slightly chubby cheeks and pale pale freckles, and her long rich red hair. No one ever called that kind of redhead a carrot top. People always turned to stare.

And then there was the house. How explain about the house? That the house felt alive again. That the moment he'd wakened in Mona's arms, he'd known the old awareness – of something unseen, and present, and watching. The house creaked as it had before. It looked as it had before. Then of course there was the entire mystery of the music in the parlor and what he had done with Mona. Had his powers to see the invisible actually returned?

He and Mona had never talked for one moment about what had happened. Nor had Eugenia ever said a word. Poor old soul. Undoubtedly she thought him a rapist and a monster. And technically he was both, and he had apparently gotten away with it. But he would never forget the sight of her, so real, so familiar, standing before a small portable gramophone that had not been there, a gramophone that looked exactly like the one later found in the library wall.

No, they had talked about none of it yet. The death of Gifford had swept everything in its path.

Ancient Evelyn had held Mona in her arms all yesterday morning as Mona cried over Gifford, struggling to remember a dream in which she felt she had struck down her aunt, deliberately and hatefully. Of course it was all irrational. She knew that. They all knew that. Finally he had taken Mona's hand, and said, 'Whatever happened here, it was my fault, and you didn't kill your aunt. It wasn't you. It was a coincidence. How could what you were doing here kill her?'

And Mona, indeed, had seemed to snap back with the fierce exuberance of the very young – and something else too, a steadiness he had sensed in her from the beginning, the cold self-sufficiency of a drunkard's child, of which he knew a great deal on his own account. She was no ordinary little girl, Mona. But it still had been wrong, a man of his age with a girl of thirteen. How could he have done it? But the strange thing was this – the house did not despise him for it, and it seemed that the house knew.

For the moment, however, the sin had been lost in the shuffle. Just lost. Last night, before the wake, Mona and Ancient Evelyn had taken out the books from the shelf and discovered the pearls and the gramophone and Violetta's waltz on a shiny old RCA Victor record. The same gramophone. He had wanted to ask – but they had talked in rushed, excited voices. And Gifford had been waiting for them.

'We cannot play it now,' said Ancient Evelyn, 'not with Gifford dead. Close the piano. Drape the mirrors. Gifford would have wanted it that way.'

Henri had driven Mona and Ancient Evelyn home to change for the wake, and then out to the funeral parlor. Michael had gone with Bea, Aaron, his Aunt Vivian and several others. The world had baffled him and confronted him and shamed him in its vivid beauty, the night alive with new flowers, trees laden with new leaves. The gentle nighttime of spring.

Gifford looked all wrong in the coffin. Short hair too black, face too thin, lips too red, too sharply pointed all over, even to the tips of her folded fingers, and her small breasts beneath the austere wool of her suit. One of those mannequins upon which they have skimped that does not wear clothes well in its stiffness, but makes even fashion look like junk. Frozen. You would have thought it was a deep-freeze, the coffin. And the Metairie funeral home was just like any one anywhere in the nation, carpeted in gray, with grand plaster ornament beneath a low ceiling, and packed with flowers and middling Queen Anne chairs.

But it had been a Mayfair wake for sure, with lots of wine and talk and crying, and several Catholic dignitaries come to pay their respects, and flocks of nuns like birds in their blue and white, and dozens of business friends and lawyer friends, and Metairie neighbors, who might as well have been bluebirds in their blue suits, also.

Shock, misery, nightmare. With faces of wax the

immediate family had received each grieving relative or friend. And the world outside shone in spring splendor, whenever in the course of things he had stepped out the doors.

Even the simplest things blazed in Michael's eyes, after his long illness, his long housebound depression, as if they'd just been invented – the foolish gold curlicues on the plaster, the moist and perfect flowers beneath the outside fluorescent light. Never had Michael seen so many children cry at a funeral, so many children brought to witness, to pray by the coffin, and to kiss the departed, laid out in Betty Crocker perfection, her peculiarities lost to clichés in this final public gesture, as she slept on her white satin bed.

He'd come home alone at eleven o'clock and gone through his clothes, packed up his suitcase and made his plans. He'd walked through the whole house. It was then that he fully sensed the difference, that it was inhabited again by something he could almost feel and see. No, that was not it. The house itself talked to him; the house itself responded.

Madness, perhaps, to think the house was alive, but he had known it before in mingled happiness and misery, and he knew it again, and it was better than the two wretched months of aloneness, of sickness, and drug fog, of being 'half in love with easeful death' and the house in silence and without personality, witnessing nothing, having no use for him at all.

He'd stared a long time at the gramophone and the pearls that lay as carelessly as Mardi Gras beads on the carpet. Priceless pearls. He could still hear Ancient Evelyn's strange voice, both deep and soft, and pretty all at once, talking on and on to Mona.

Nobody else seemed to know or care about these treasures from the compartment beneath the bookcase wall; they lay in the shadowy corner near the heap of books, like so much junk. Nobody touched them or noticed them.

Now was the conference after the funeral. Had to be done.

He would have had it at Ryan's house if that had been easier for him. But Ryan and Pierce said they had to go to the office, they had no choice. They confessed they were tired of visiting now, and they'd come up to First Street on the way, they didn't mind. They were very concerned about Rowan. He must not think they had forgotten about Rowan for one single moment. Poor wretched father and son.

In the sharp glare of attention, they looked no less perfect – Ryan with his tanned skin and smooth white hair and eyes that were so opaque and blue. Pierce, the son whom anyone in the world would want, brilliant, well-mannered, and so obviously shattered by the fact of his mother's death. Didn't seem it ought to happen this way; they should have had insurance against it. What was death to the country club Mayfairs, as Bea had put it? It had been more than kind of them to agree to come.

But Michael could not put this meeting off. He really couldn't. He'd wasted so much time. He'd lived in this house like a spook since he'd come home from the hospital. Was it the death of Gifford, random and terrible and irrelevant, which had wakened him from his stupor? He knew it was not. It was Mona.

Well, they would gather now, and he would explain that he must take action regarding Rowan, he was packed and ready to go.

That is what they had to understand. He had been lying here under a curse, a man in a dream, hurt in his heart that Rowan had left. He had failed.

And then there had been the medal. The Archangel medal. It had been in Gifford's purse in Destin. And when Ryan had put that in his hand, at graveside, no less, as they embraced, he had known. I must find Rowan. I must do what I was sent here to do. I must do what I want to do. I have to move. I have to be strong again.

The medal. Gifford had found it out by the pool some time ago, maybe even Christmas Day, Ryan wasn't sure; she kept meaning to give it to Michael. But she was afraid to upset him with the medal. She'd been sure the medal was his. There had been blood on the medal. And here it was, all cleaned up and shiny. It had fallen out of her purse while Ryan was going through it. Little graveside chat, no more than a few seconds in the cool marble mausoleum with the noonday sun streaming in, and hundreds waiting to shake Ryan's hand. 'Gifford would want me to give you this without further delay.'

So what time was there to feel appropriately guilty about the little redhead who'd slept in his arms, who'd said, 'Throw out those drugs. You don't need them.'

He held the door open for them as they entered the library.

'Come in,' he said, feeling a little strange as he always did, being the master of this, their house, and gestured for Ryan and Pierce and Aaron Lightner to sit before the desk. He took his customary place behind it. He saw Pierce look at the little phonograph, and those long pearls, but they would get to that later on.

'Now, I know how bad this is,' he said to Ryan.

Someone had to start things. 'You buried your wife today. And my heart goes out to you. I wish I could let this wait. Everything should be made to wait. But I have to talk about Rowan.'

'Of course you do,' said Ryan immediately. 'And we're here to tell you what we know. We don't know much, however.'

'I see. I can't get a word out of Randall or Lauren. They say, Talk to Ryan, Ryan knows everything, and so I've asked you to come and tell me what has been going on. I've been like a man in a coma. I have to find Rowan. I'm packed and ready to go.'

Ryan looked amazingly composed, as if he'd thrown an inner switch to Business Mode; there was nothing bitter or resentful in his attitude. Pierce on the other hand was still crushed; he wore a look of inconsolable grief. It was doubtful he was hearing Michael's words, or should even be here.

Aaron too had been devastated by Gifford's death. He had taken Bea under his wing, and comforted her throughout the ordeal of the Metairie funeral parlor, and cemetery and mausoleum. He was worn and tired, and fairly miserable, and no amount of British decorum could hide it any longer. Then there had been Alicia, hysterical and hospitalized at last; Aaron had helped with that too, side by side with Ryan as he broke the news to Patrick that Alicia was malnourished and sick and must be cared for. Patrick had tried to hit Ryan. And Bea had made no secret anymore of her developing affection for Aaron; she had found a man she could depend upon, she said quietly to Michael as they drove home.

But now it all fell on this man, Ryan Mayfair, this

lawyer who managed every little detail for everyone –
and he didn't have Gifford at his side anymore, to
argue with him, to believe in him, to help him. And he
was already back at work. It was too soon to know how
bad it was going to be, Michael reasoned. It was too
soon for this man to be really afraid.

'I gotta go,' Michael said. 'It's that simple. What
should I know? Where am I headed? What's the latest
info we have on Rowan? What are our best leads?'

A silence fell. Mona came into the room, a white bow
drooping appropriately over her locks, and dressed in a
simple white cotton frock, the proper thing for children
at a time of death. She shut the door to the hall behind
her. She did not speak to anyone, and no one looked at
her, and no one seemed to notice or care that she took
the leather chair against the far wall, and that she
looked across the dusty span of the room at Michael.
Michael could not stop for this, and really, it didn't
matter. There was nothing going on that Mona didn't
know, or couldn't hear. And for that matter, there was
this secret between them that was a bond. The child
fascinated him as much as she made him feel guilty; she
was part and parcel of the excitement of his recovery
and what he had to do now.

He had not woken up the morning after with the
feeling 'Who is the strange child in my bed?' Quite to
the contrary. He sort of knew who she was, and knew
that she knew him.

'You can't go,' said Aaron.

The firmness of his voice caught Michael off guard.
He realized he'd been drifting, back to Mona, and
Mona's caresses and the dreamy appearance of Ancient
Evelyn in the street.

254

'You don't know the full picture,' said Aaron.

'What full picture?'

'We didn't feel we should tell you everything,' said Ryan, 'but before we proceed, let me explain. We don't really know where Rowan is, and we don't know what's happened to her. I'm not saying that anything bad has happened to her. That's what I want you to understand.'

'Have you spoken to your doctor?' asked Pierce, suddenly coming alert and joining in, as if he meant to do business. 'Does he say your convalescence is over?'

'Gentlemen, it's over. I'm going to find my wife. Now tell me who's heading the investigation to find Rowan. Who has the File on Rowan Mayfair?'

Aaron cleared his throat in eloquent British style, a soft traditional preamble to a speech, and then began.

'The Talamasca and the Mayfair family have been unable to find her,' said Aaron. 'That is to say, a considerable amount of investigation and expense has resulted in frustration.'

'I see.'

'This is what we know. Rowan left here with a tall dark-haired man. As we told you, she was seen with him on the plane to New York. She was definitely in Zurich at the end of the year, and from there she went to Paris, and from Paris to Scotland. Later on she was in Geneva. From Geneva, she might have gone back to New York. We are not certain.'

'You mean she could be in this country again.'

'She could,' said Ryan. 'We don't know.' Ryan paused as though this was all he had to say, or simply to gather his thoughts.

'She and this man,' said Aaron, 'were seen in

Donnelaith, Scotland. There seems no doubt of that. In Geneva, eyewitness testimony isn't as conclusive. We know she was in Zurich only because of the banking transactions she performed; in Paris, because she ran certain medical tests there which she later sent to Dr Samuel Larkin in California. Geneva, because that is the city from which she called the doctor on the phone and from which she sent him the medical information. She ran tests at a clinic there, and those too were forwarded to Dr Larkin.'

'She called this doctor? He actually spoke to her?'

This should have given him hope; this should have been something other than the sting it was. But he knew that his face was reddening. She called, but she did not call me. She called her old doctor friend in San Francisco. He tried to look tranquil, appreciative, open-minded.

'Yes,' said Aaron, 'she called Dr Larkin on February twelfth. She was brief. She told him she was sending a shipment of medical tests, specimens, samples, et cetera, that he was to take them to the Keplinger Institute for analysis. She told him she would contact him. That this was confidential. She indicated she might be interrupted at any time. She sounded as if she was in danger.'

Michael sat quiet, trying simply to process this, to realize what it meant. One moment his beloved wife had been making phone calls to another man. Now the picture was entirely different.

'This is what you didn't want to tell me,' he said.

'Yes,' said Aaron. 'And that the people we interviewed in Geneva and in Donnelaith indicated she might have been under coercion. Ryan's detectives drew the same inference from these witnesses, though none of the people themselves actually used the word *coercion*.'

'I see. But she was alive and well when she spoke to Samuel Larkin. And that was February twelfth!' said Michael.

'Yes . . .'

'OK, what did these people see? What did the people at these medical clinics see?'

'No one at any of the clinics noticed anything. But we are talking about enormous institutions, you must realize. There seems little doubt that Rowan and Lasher slipped in, with Rowan impersonating a staff doctor or a technician as the situation required. She completed various tests and left before anyone in any of these places was the wiser.'

'And this you know from the material she sent this Dr Larkin?'

'Yes.'

'Amazing, but a doctor could do that, couldn't she?' Michael said. He tried to keep his voice steady. He didn't want anyone taking his pulse. 'Last proof that she was alive was February twelfth,' he said again. He was trying to calculate the date, the number of days. His mind went blank.

'There has been one other small bit of intelligence,' said Ryan. 'And one which we do not like.'

'So tell me.'

'Rowan made huge bank transfers while she was in Europe. Huge transfers through banks in France and in Switzerland. But the transfers stopped at the end of January, and thereafter, only two simple checks were cashed in New York, on February fourteenth. We know now the signatures on these checks were forgeries.'

'Ah.' Michael sat back. 'He's keeping her prisoner. He forged the checks.'

Aaron sighed. 'We don't know . . . for certain. She was described by those in Donnelaith – and those in Geneva – as being pale, sickly. Her companion was said to have been very attentive; indeed, she was never seen when not in his company.'

'I see,' Michael whispered. 'What else did they say? Tell me everything.'

'Donnelaith is an archaeological site now,' said Aaron.

'Yes, I knew that, I believe,' said Michael. He looked at Ryan. 'You've read the Mayfair History?'

'If you mean the file from the Talamasca, yes, I did examine it but I think our concern here is simply this: where is Rowan and how can we reach her?'

'Go on about Donnelaith,' said Michael to Aaron.

'Apparently Rowan and Lasher had a suite in the inn there for four days. They spent considerable time exploring the ruins of the castle, the Cathedral and the village. Lasher talked to many, many people.'

'Must you call him by that name?' asked Ryan 'The legal name he used was different.'

'The legal name has nothing to do with it,' said Pierce. 'Dad, please, let's just get this information out. This Donnelaith, it's an archaeological project apparently funded entirely by our family. I'd never heard of it till I read the Talamasca file. Neither had Dad. It was all administered by . . .'

'Lauren,' said Ryan, with a faint tone of distaste. 'But that's all beside the point. They haven't been seen there since January.'

'Get on with it,' said Michael as gently as he could. 'What did people see when they looked at them?'

'They are described as a woman five foot seven in

height, very pale and in ill health, and an extremely tall man, possibly six and a half feet in height with luxuriant long black hair – both American.'

Michael wanted to say something, but his heart was rushing on him, no doubt of it. He felt the increased rate, and a little pain in his chest. He didn't want anyone to know this. He took out his handkerchief, folded it and patted his upper lip. 'She's alive, she's in danger, the thing is holding her prisoner,' he whispered.

'This is anecdotal material,' said Ryan. 'It would not stand up in a court of law. We are conjecturing. The forged checks are another matter altogether. They make it incumbent upon the legacy to do something immediately.'

'The forensic statements are quite a puzzle,' Aaron said.

'Yes, that is a maddening kettle of soup,' said Pierce. 'We sent forensic samples of the blood we found here to two different genetic institutes and neither will give us a straight answer.'

'They are giving us an answer,' said Aaron. 'They are saying that the specimens must have been contaminated or tampered with because they pertain to a nonhuman species of primate which they cannot identify.'

Michael smiled bitterly.

'But what does this Dr Larkin say? Rowan sent him the stuff direct. What does he know? What did she say to him on the phone? I have to know everything.'

'Rowan was agitated,' said Pierce. 'She was afraid she might be cut off. She was desperate that Larkin receive the medical material and take it to Keplinger. The whole thing alarmed Larkin. That's why he is cooperating with us. He is devoted to Rowan, doesn't want to break her confidence, but he shares our concern for her.'

'This Dr Larkin is here,' said Michael. 'I saw him at the wake.'

'Yes, he's here,' said Ryan. 'But he's reluctant to discuss the medical materials taken to the Keplinger Institute.'

'One can infer,' said Aaron quietly, 'from what the doctor is willing to say that he has extensive test material on this creature.'

'Creature,' said Ryan. 'And there we go off into fantasy land again.' He was angry. 'We don't know that this man is a creature or a ... subhuman type, or anything else. And we don't know what the man's name is. We do know he is genial, educated, intelligent, and speaks rapidly with an American voice, and that the people who spoke to him at Donnelaith found him interesting.'

'What in the world has that got to do with it all?' demanded Pierce. 'Dad, for the love of ...'

Michael interrupted. 'What did Rowan send to Dr Larkin? What has the Keplinger Institute found out?'

'Well, that's it,' said Aaron. 'He won't give us a complete report. But he might give it to you. He wants to talk to you. He wants to do genetic testing on you.'

Michael smiled. 'Does he, now?'

'You're right to be very suspicious of this,' said Ryan. He seemed to be vacillating between angry impatience and exhaustion. 'People have approached us with genetic proposals in the past. We are perceived as a closed group. Consent to nothing.'

'Like the Mormons, or the Amish,' said Michael.

'Exactly,' said Ryan, 'and there are many excellent

legal reasons not to allow this sort of testing. And what does it have to do with the Curry family anyway?'

'I think we are straying from the point,' said Aaron. He looked meaningfully at Michael. 'Whatever we call this companion of Rowan's, he's flesh and blood, and obviously passes for human.'

'Are you listening to your own words!' Ryan demanded, plainly furious.

'Of course I am,' said Aaron.

'I want to see the medical evidence myself,' said Ryan.

'How will you know how to interpret it?' Pierce asked.

'Just hold on,' said Ryan.

'Dad, we have to talk this out.'

Michael raised his hand for calm. 'Listen, the medical tests aren't going to determine anything. *I saw him. I spoke to him.*'

The room was silent.

He realized this was the first time he had uttered such a thing to the family since the entire incident had happened. He had never, never admitted to Ryan or to Pierce, and certainly never to any other Mayfair, what had happened on Christmas Day. He found himself glancing now at Mona. And then his eyes fixed on the man to whom he had told the whole tale – Aaron.

The others stared at him in clear and unembarrassed anticipation.

'I didn't think he was six and a half feet tall,' said Michael, trying again to steady his voice. He ran his hand back through his hair, and stopped himself in the act of reaching for a pen he didn't need. He closed his right hand into a fist, then opened it, splaying the fingers. 'But then I was having a pitched battle with him when he was here. I'd say he was my height, six foot two at most. His hair was short. It was black, like mine. He had blue eyes.'

'Are you telling me,' Ryan asked with deceptive calm, 'that you saw the man who went off with Rowan!'

'You said you actually did speak to him?' Pierce asked.

Ryan was clearly pale with anger. 'You can describe or identify this person?' he asked.

'Let's get on with what we have to do,' said Aaron. 'We almost lost Michael on Christmas Day. Michael was unable to tell us anything for weeks. Michael was . . .'

'It's OK, Aaron,' said Michael. 'It's OK. Ryan, what do you want to know? She left with a man. He was six feet two, he was thin, he was wearing my clothes. He had black hair. I don't think he looks the same now. His hair wasn't long. He wasn't so tall. Do you believe me? Do you believe anything anybody's told you? Ryan, I know who he is. So does the Talamasca.'

Ryan seemed incapable of responding. Pierce was also obviously stunned.

'Uncle Ryan, it was "the man",' said Mona flatly. 'For Chrissakes, get off Michael's case. He didn't let "the man" through. It was Rowan.'

'Stay out of this, Mona!' Ryan flashed. It seemed he would lose control completely. Pierce laid his hand on his father's hand. 'What are you doing in here!' Ryan demanded. 'Go on, out.'

Mona didn't move.

Pierce gestured for her to be quiet.

'This thing,' said Michael, 'our "man", our Lasher. Does he appear normal to other people?'

'An unusual man,' said Ryan. 'That is the testimony we have. An unusual man, well-mannered, rather gregarious.' He paused as if he had to force himself to go on. 'I have all the statements for you. And by the way, we combed Paris, Geneva, Zurich, New York. Tall as he is, he does not attract that much attention. The archaeologists at Donnelaith had the most contact. They said he was fascinating, a little peculiar, that he spoke very fast. That he had strange notions about the town and the ruins.'

'OK, I see what's happened. She didn't run away with him; he took her. He forced her to take him there. He forced her to get the money. She persuaded him to have these medical tests, then she got the stuff out when she could to this Dr Larkin.'

'Not certain,' said Ryan. 'Not certain at all. But the forgery gives us something legal to go on. Also the money deposited for Rowan in banks abroad has now disappeared. We have to act. We have no choice. We have to protect the legacy.'

Aaron interrupted with a little gesture. 'Dr Larkin said that Rowan said she knew the creature wasn't human. She wanted him to study the genetic blueprint. She wanted to know specifically whether or not the creature could breed with humans, and with her in particular. She sent some of her own blood for analysis.'

There was an uneasy silence.

For the space of a second, Ryan looked almost panic-stricken. Then he drew himself up, crossed his legs, and laid his left hand on the edge of Michael's desk.

'I don't know what I believe about this strange man,' Ryan said. 'I honestly don't. All this Talamasca history, this chain of thirteen witches, all this. I don't believe it. That's the frank truth. I don't. And I don't think most of the family believes in all this either.' He looked directly at Michael. 'But this is clear. There is no place for you to go now to search for Rowan. Going to Geneva is a waste of time. We have covered Geneva. The Talamasca has covered Geneva. In Donnelaith we have a private detective on twenty-four-hour duty. So does the Talamasca, who are, by the way, very good at this sort of thing. New York? We've turned up no real leads, other than the forged checks. They weren't large. They aroused no suspicion.'

'I see,' Michael said. 'Where would I go? What would I do? Those are really valid questions here.'

'Absolutely,' said Ryan. 'We didn't want to tell you all we'd found out for obvious reasons. But you know now, and you know that the best thing is for you to stay here, to follow Dr Rhodes's advice, and to wait. It makes sense from absolutely every standpoint.'

'There's one other thing,' Pierce said.

His father looked plainly annoyed, and then again too fatigued to protest. He raised his hand to cover his eyes, elbow resting on the edge of the desk.

But Pierce went on.

'You have to tell us exactly what did happen here on Christmas Day,' said Pierce. 'I want to know. I've been helping with this all along. Mayfair Medical has been left in my hands. I want to continue with Mayfair Medical. Lots of the others want to continue. But everybody has to talk to everybody else. What happened, Michael? Who is this man? What is he?'

Michael knew he ought to say something, but for the moment it seemed impossible. He sat back, staring past them at the rows and rows of books, unable to see at this moment the stack heaped on the floor or the mysterious gramophone. His eyes moved almost furtively to Mona.

Mona had slumped back in the chair and slung one knee over the arm of it. She looked too old for the white funeral dress, which she had demurely crumpled between her legs. She was watching him with that level and somewhat ironic gaze – her old self, before the news of the death of Gifford.

'She left with the man,' Mona said very quietly and distinctly. 'The man came through.'

It was her teenaged flat voice, bored with the stupidity of others and making no concession to the marvelous. She went on:

'She left with him. This long-haired guy, this is the man. This thin mutant guy, that's who he is. The ghost, the Devil, Lasher. Michael had a fight with him out by the pool, and he knocked Michael into the water. There's a smell out there that comes from him. And the smell is in the living room where he was born.'

'You're imagining things,' said Ryan, so wrathfully that it was almost a whisper. 'I told you to stay out of this.'

'When he and Rowan left,' said Mona, 'she turned the alarm on so help would come for Michael. Or he did it himself, the man. Any moron can see now from all this – that that is what happened.'

'Mona, I am telling you to leave this room now,' said Ryan.

'No,' she answered.

Michael said nothing. He had heard all these words, but he could think of no way to respond to them. He wanted to say that Rowan had tried to stop the man from throwing him in the pool. But what was the purpose? Rowan had left him drowning in the pool, or had she? *Rowan was being coerced!*

Ryan made a small sound of exasperation.

'Allow me to say,' said Aaron with patience, 'that Dr Larkin has a great deal of information which we do not have. He has X rays of hands, feet, spinal cord, pelvis, as well as PET scans of the brain, and other such tests. The creature's not human. It has a confusing genetic makeup. It is a mammal. It is a primate. It is warm-blooded. It looks like us. But it isn't human.'

Pierce was staring at his father, as if afraid his father would come unglued at any moment. Ryan merely shook his head. 'I'll believe this when I see it, when that Dr Larkin tells me himself.'

'Dad,' said Pierce, 'if you look at the forensic reports, it's the same picture. They said, contaminated, or tampered with, or spoiled, because otherwise it's the blood and tissue of something with a nonhuman genetic makeup.'

'It's what Mona said,' said Michael. His voice had dropped very low. He roused himself a little and looked at Ryan and then at Mona.

Something in Aaron's manner was disturbing him, had been all along, but he didn't know what it was, and he hadn't known he was disturbed until he failed to look at Aaron.

'I came home,' said Michael, 'and he was here. He looked like her. He looked like me. He might have come from . . . our child. Our baby. Rowan had been pregnant.'

He stopped. He let out a long slow breath, shaking his head a little and then realizing he ought to go on.

266

'This man-thing was newborn,' he said. 'He was very strong. He taunted me. He . . . he was moving like the straw man in *The Wizard of Oz* . . . clumsily, falling down, laughing, climbing back up. I should have been able to wring his neck. I wasn't. He was much much stronger than he looked. I connected more than once. Should have pulverized a few facial bones. No damage except a cut. Rowan did try to stop the fight, but it wasn't clear to me then . . . and it isn't now . . . whom Rowan was trying to protect. Me? Or him.'

He hated hearing these words from his own mouth. But it was time to get it all out, for everything to be shared, the pain and the defeat included.

'Did she help him knock you in the pool?' Mona asked.

'Mona, shut up,' said Ryan. Mona ignored him utterly. She was looking at Michael.

'No, she didn't,' said Michael. 'And he shouldn't have been able to do it alone. I've been decked once or twice in my life. It took big men and lucky punches to do it. He was thin, delicate, he was sliding on the ice out there; but he shoved me and into the pool I went. I remember him looking at me as I went down. He has blue eyes. He has very black hair. I told you that already. His skin is very pale, and kind of beautiful. At least it was then.'

'Like the skin of an infant,' said Aaron softly.

'And all of you are trying to tell me,' said Ryan nervously, anxiously, 'that this is not a human being?'

'We're talking science, man,' said Aaron, 'not voodoo. This is a creature, so to speak, of flesh and blood. But its genetic blueprint is not human.'

'Larkin told you that.'

'Well, more or less,' said Aaron. 'Let's say I picked up the message from him.'

'Ghosts, spirits and creatures,' Ryan said. It was as though the wax he was made of was beginning to melt altogether.

'Come on, Dad, take it easy,' said Pierce, and for the moment sounded like the elder.

'Gifford told me that she thought the man had come through,' Ryan said. 'It was the last conversation I ever had with my wife and she said . . .' He stopped.

Silence.

'I think we are resolved on one point, Michael,' said Aaron, with a touch of impatience. 'That you remain here.'

'Yeah, I got that,' said Michael. 'I'm staying. But I want to see all the reports. I want to become involved on every level. I want to talk to this Dr Larkin.'

'There is one other very important matter,' said Aaron. 'Ryan, for obvious reasons, did not consent to an autopsy being performed on Gifford.'

Ryan glared at him. Michael had never seen Ryan so full of blatant hostility. Aaron caught it as well, and he hesitated, very obviously at a loss for a moment, before he continued:

'But there is bloodstained clothing which can be tested.'

'For what?' demanded Ryan. 'What has my wife to do with you? With any of this?'

Aaron couldn't answer. He looked distraught suddenly. He fell quiet.

'Are you trying to tell me my wife had some doings with this thing? That he killed her?'

Aaron didn't answer.

'Dad, she had a miscarriage up there,' said Pierce, 'and you and I both know –' The young man stopped himself but the blow was struck. 'My mother was highstrung,' he said. 'She and my father . . .'

Ryan didn't reply. His rage had hardened into something worse. Michael shook his head before he could stop himself. Mona's face was impassive as ever.

'There was evidence of a miscarriage?' Aaron asked.

'Well, she suffered a uterine hemorrhage,' said Pierce. 'That's what the local doctor said, some kind of miscarriage.'

'He doesn't know,' said Ryan. 'The local doctors said she died from loss of blood. That's all they knew. Loss of blood. She started to hemorrhage and she didn't or couldn't call for help. She died on the sand. My wife was an affectionate and normal woman. But she was forty-six years old. It is highly unlikely she had a miscarriage. Indeed, it is almost a preposterous idea. She suffered from fibroid tumors.'

'Dad, let them test what they have, please. I want to know why Mother died. If it was the tumors, I want to know. Please. All of us want to know. Why did she have the hemorrhage?'

'All right,' said Ryan, in a seething rage. 'You want these tests run on your mother's clothes?' He threw up his hands.

'Yes,' said Pierce calmly.

'All right. For you then this will be done, for you and your sisters. We'll run the tests. We'll find out what triggered the hemorrhage.'

Pierce was satisfied, but clearly worried about his father.

Ryan had more to say. But he gestured for them to

wait. He held his right hand in the air, and gestured again, tentatively, and then he began to speak.

'I will do what I can do under these circumstances. I will continue the search for Rowan. I will have the bloodstained clothes tested. I will do the sane and proper thing. I will do the honorable thing. The legal thing. The necessary thing. But I do not believe in this man! I do not believe in this ghost. I never have! And I have no reason to believe in it now. And whatever the truth of it all, it has nothing to do with the death of my wife!

'But let us take up the matter of Rowan again. Gifford is in God's hands. Rowan may still be in ours. Now, Aaron, how can we get this scientific data, or whatever it is, from the Keplinger Institute? That will be my first order of business. To find out how we can subpoena the material Rowan sent to Larkin. I'm going to the office now. I'm going to lay hands on that material. The designee of the legacy has disappeared, there may have been foul play, legal actions have already been taken regarding funds, accounts, signatures et al. –' He stopped as though he had gone as far as he could, staring forward, like a machine that had run out of electricity.

'I understand your feelings, Ryan,' said Aaron softly. 'Even the most conservative witness can say that there is a mystery here revolving around this male creature.'

'You and the Talamasca,' Ryan whispered. 'You infer. You observe, you witness. You look at all these puzzling things and you throw out an interpretation which fits with your beliefs, your superstitions, your dogmatic insistence that the world of ghosts and spirits is real. I don't buy it. I think your history of our family is some sort of . . . some sort of dazzling hoax, if you want the truth. I don't . . . I'm having an investigation of my own done, of you, if you want to know.'

Aaron's eyes narrowed. There was a touch of bitterness, sourness, in his voice when he spoke.

'I don't blame you,' he said.

There was something very cross and bitter in his face suddenly. Repression of temper. Repression of confusion or ambivalence. Michael sensed it more strongly now than before. Aaron wasn't himself, as they say.

'Do you have the clothing, Ryan?' Aaron asked, pushing on with this unpleasant request, as if he resented very deeply having to do it. He was taking out that resentment on Ryan. 'Gifford's clothes. What she was wearing when she died?'

'Goddamnit,' Ryan whispered. He picked up the phone. He reached his secretary downtown within seconds. 'Carla,' he said, 'Ryan here. Call the coroner in Walton County, Florida. Call the funeral parlor. What happened to Gifford's clothes? I have to have them.'

He put down the phone. 'Is there anything else?' he asked. 'I'd like to go to the office. I have work to do. I have to go home early. My children need me. Alicia has been hospitalized. She needs me. I need to be alone for a while. I need to . . . I need to grieve for my wife. Pierce, I'd like it if we left now. If you came with me.' All this was too hurried.

'Yes, Dad, but I want to know about Mother's clothes.'

'What in God's name has this to do with Gifford!' Ryan demanded. 'God, have you all lost your minds?'

'Just want to know,' said Pierce. 'You know . . . you know Mom was scared to come here on Mardi Gras, she was . . .'

'No, don't go on. Don't do it,' said Ryan. 'Let's stick

271

to what we have here. What we know. We'll do whatever anybody wants us to do for any reason! And Michael, tomorrow I'll make available to you everything we have on Rowan. Hell, I'll make it available now. I'll send you the records of the entire investigation.'

Once again, he picked up the phone and punched in the office numbers at the speed of light. He did not bother to say his name. He told the person on the other end, 'Messenger over a copy of all the papers pertaining to Rowan. Yes, all that. The detectives, the Xeroxes of the checks, every scrap of paper we have on her. Her husband wants it. He has a right to see it. He's her husband. He has . . . a right.'

Silence. He was listening.

'What do you mean?' he asked.

His face went blank and then it began to color, to redden, and as he hung up the phone, he turned his gaze on Aaron. 'Your investigators picked up my wife's clothes? They took them from the Walton County coroner's office and from the funeral parlor? Who told you you could do such a thing?'

Aaron didn't answer. But Michael could read the surprise and the confusion in his face. Aaron hadn't known. He was shocked as well as humiliated. He seemed to be thinking it all over, and then he gave a little careful shrug.

'I'm sorry,' Aaron said at last. 'I did not authorize anyone to do this. I apologize to you. I'll see that everything is returned, immediately.'

Now Michael understood why Aaron was not himself. Something was happening within the ranks, something between Aaron and the Order. He had sensed it earlier but he hadn't known how to interpret it.

'You damn well better!' said Ryan. 'I've had enough of scholars and secrets and people spying on one another.' He stood up. Pierce stood also.

'Come on, Dad,' Pierce said, once again taking charge. 'Let's go home. I'll go back to the office this afternoon. Let's go.'

Aaron did not rise to his feet. He did not look up at Ryan. He was gazing off, and then he seemed to drift away from them, into his own thoughts. He was disgruntled, but it was worse than that.

Michael rose and took Ryan's hand. He shook hands also, as he always did, with Pierce. 'Thank you both.'

'It's the least you could expect,' said Ryan disgustedly. 'We'll meet tomorrow, you and I, and Lauren and Randall. We'll find Rowan if Rowan . . .'

'. . . can be found,' said Mona.

'I told you to shut up,' said Ryan. 'I want you to go home,' Ryan said. 'Ancient Evelyn is there alone.'

'Oh, yeah, somebody's always there alone and they need me, don't they?' Mona said. She brought her leg round and stood up, straightening the girlish cotton dress. The two loops of her white ribbon poked up behind her head: 'I'll go on home. Don't worry.'

Ryan stood staring at her as if he could not endure any of this a moment longer. And then he moved towards her and took her in his arms and crushed her to his chest. There was an awful silence and then the more awful sound of his crying – the deep, choked, repressed sob of a man, full of shame as well as misery, a sound a woman seldom made, almost unnatural.

Pierce put his arm around his father's shoulder. Ryan pulled Mona back, gave her a fierce kiss on the cheek, and then, squeezing her shoulder, let her go. She had gone all soft towards him, and squeezed him, and kissed his cheek, too.

He followed Pierce out of the library.

As the door opened and closed, Michael heard a chorus of voices from the hall – the hushed voice of Beatrice, and the deeper voice of Randall, and others he could not distinguish in the hubbub that followed.

He realized he was alone with Aaron and with Mona. And Aaron had not moved. Aaron had about him that listless look. Aaron seemed gravely disabled as Michael himself had been only days ago.

Mona had slunk into the corner, glowing like a little candle with her flaming hair, arms folded, not about to leave, obviously.

'Tell me your thoughts,' said Michael to Aaron. 'This is the first time I've really asked you since . . . it happened. What do you think? Talk to me.'

'You mean you want my scholarly opinion,' said Aaron, with that same touch of sourness, his eyes veering off.

'I want your unbiased opinion,' said Michael. 'Ryan's refusal to believe in this whole thing is almost a religious stance. What is there you've been keeping from me?'

He should ask Mona to go, he should escort her out, turn her over to Bea, take care of her. But he didn't do these things. He simply looked at Aaron.

Aaron's face had tightened, then relaxed again. 'I haven't been deliberately keeping back anything,' he said, but the voice was not typical of him. 'I'm embarrassed,' he said, looking Michael in the eye. 'I was heading this investigation until Rowan left. I thought I was heading it even afterwards. But there are strong indications now that the Elders themselves are in charge, that the investigation has broadened without my knowledge. I don't know who took Gifford's clothing. That's not the Talamasca style. You know it's not. After Rowan's disappearance, we asked Ryan's permission to come to this house, to take specimens from the bloodstained rug, the wallpaper. We would have asked you, but you were not . . .'

'I know, I know . . .'

'That's our manner. To go in the wake of disaster, to proceed with care, to observe, not to conclude.'

'You don't owe me any explanations. We're friends, you and me. You know that. But I think I can tell what's happened. This must be a momentous investigation to your Elders. We don't have a ghost now; we have a mutant being.' Michael laughed bitterly. 'And the being is holding my wife prisoner.'

'I could have told you that,' said Mona.

Aaron's utter lack of response was startling. Aaron was staring off, and deeply distressed and unable to confide about it because it was the business of the Order. Finally he looked again at Michael.

'You're all right, you're very well indeed. Dr Rhodes calls you his miracle. You're going to be all right. We'll meet tomorrow. You and I, even if I am not admitted to the meeting with Ryan.'

'This file they're sending over,' Michael said.

'I've seen it,' Aaron said. 'We were cooperating with each other. My reports are in the file. You'll see. I don't know what's happened now. But Beatrice and Vivian are waiting for me. Beatrice is greatly concerned about you, Mona. And then there is Dr Larkin. He wants to talk to you, Michael. I've asked him to wait until tomorrow. He's waiting for me now.'

'Yes, OK. I want to read the report. Don't let Larkin get away, however.'

'Oh, he's happy. He's hitting every good restaurant in town and has been partying all night with some young female surgeon from Tulane. He's not going to slip through our fingers.'

Mona volunteered nothing. She merely watched as Michael followed Aaron into the hallway. She remained in the door, and he was painfully conscious of her presence suddenly, of her perfume, of her red hair glowing in the shadows, of the rumpled white satin ribbon, of all of her and everything that had happened, and that people were leaving the house, and he might soon again be alone with her.

Ryan and Pierce were just getting out the front door. Mayfair farewells took so long. Beatrice was crying again, and assuring Ryan that everything would be all right. Randall sat in the living room, beside the first fireplace, looking like a great dark gray toad in the chair, his face baffled and pondering.

'Darlings, how are you both?' Bea asked, rushing to take Michael's hand and Mona's hand as well. She kissed Mona's cheek.

Aaron slipped past her.

'I'm OK now,' said Mona. 'What about Mom?'

'She's sedated. They're feeding her intravenously. She'll sleep the night. Don't you worry about her another moment. Your father is all right. He's keeping company with Ancient Evelyn. I believe Cecilia is there now. Anne Marie is with your mother.'

'That's what I figured,' said Mona disgustedly.

'What do you want to do, my darling? Shall I take you home? Will you come and stay with me for a while?

What can I do? You can bunk in with me for the night, or sleep in the room with the rose wallpaper.'

Mona shook her head. 'I'm fine.' She gave a careless disrespectful shrug. 'I'm really just fine. I'll walk up home in a little while.'

'And you!' Bea said to Michael. 'Just look at you. There's color in your cheeks! You're a new man.'

'Yeah, seems so. Listen. I gotta think about things. They're sending over the file on Rowan.'

'Oh, don't read all those reports. It's too depressing.' She turned to search out Aaron, who stood far away against the wall. 'Aaron, don't let him.'

'He should read them, my dear,' Aaron said. 'And now I must go back to the hotel. Dr Larkin is waiting for me.'

'Oh, you and that doctor.' She took Aaron's arm and kissed him on the cheek as they proceeded to the door. 'I'll wait for you.'

Randall had risen to go. Two young Mayfairs in the dining room drifted into the hall. The good-byes were protracted, full of heartfelt words, and sudden sobs of grief, and confessions of love for Gifford, poor beautiful Gifford, kind and generous Gifford. Bea turned back, and rushed to embrace Michael and Mona with both arms, kissed them both, and then went down the hall, tearing herself away obviously. There was an intimacy in the way she took Aaron's arm, in the way he guided her down the steps. Randall went out the gate before them.

Then they were all gone. Mona stood waving in the keyhole door, looking thoroughly incongruous now in the childish dress with its sash, though the white ribbon in her hair seemed an essential part of her.

She turned around, and looked at Michael. She banged the door shut behind her.

'Where's my Aunt Viv?' Michael asked.

'She can't save you, big boy,' Mona said. 'She's out in Metairie comforting Gifford's other kids, with Aunt Bernadette.'

'Where's Eugenia?'

'Would you believe I poisoned her?' Mona walked past him back the hall, and into the library.

He followed her, adamant and full of righteous speeches and declarations. 'This is not going to happen again,' he began, but she shut the library door as soon as he was inside, and she threw her arms around him.

He began to kiss her, his hands sliding over her breasts, and down suddenly to lift the cotton skirt. 'This cannot happen!' he said. 'I'm not going to let you. You're not even giving me a fifty-fifty –'

Her soft sweet young limbs overwhelmed him – the ripe, firm feel of her arms, of her back, of her hips beneath the cotton. She was fiercely aroused, aroused as any grown woman he'd ever made love to. He heard a small sound. She had reached over and snapped the lock of the library door.

'Comfort me, big man,' she said. 'My beloved aunt just died. I'm really a wreck. No kidding.' She stepped back. There was a glimmer of tears in her eyes. She sniffled, and looked as if she might break down.

She undid the buttons of the cotton dress, and then let it slip down around her. She stepped out of the circle of glowing fabric. And he saw her snow-white brassiere with its full cups of expensive lace, and the soft pale skin of midriff above the waistband of her half-slip. The tears spilt down again as they had before, her soundless crying. Then she rushed at him, and locked her arms around his neck, kissing him, and slipping her hand down between his legs.

It was a *fait accompli*, as they say. And then there was her faint whisper as they snuggled together on the carpet.

'Don't worry about it.'

He was sleepy; he listed; he didn't fall deep; he couldn't; there was too much right there before his mind's eye. He started humming. How could he not worry about everything? He could not close his eyes. He hummed and softly sang.

'Violetta's waltz,' she said. 'Just hold on to me for a little while, will you?'

It seems he slept, or sank into some sort of approximate peaceful state, his fingers on her sweaty adorable little neck, and his lips pressed to her forehead. But then the doorbell sounded, and he heard Eugenia in the hall, taking her time to answer, talking aloud as she always did, 'On my way, I'm comin'.'

The report had been delivered. He had to see it. How to get it without revealing the sleeping child on the rug, he didn't know. But he had to see it. It hadn't taken a half hour for that file to get here. He thought of Rowan and he felt such dread that he couldn't form words about it, or make decisions, or even reflect.

He sat up, trying to regain his strength, to shake off the languor of sex, and not see this naked girl on the carpet asleep, head cradled on a nest of her own red hair, her belly as smooth and perfect as her breasts, all of her luscious and inviting to him. Michael, you pig, that you could do this!

There was the dull vibration of the big front door

slamming shut. Eugenia passed again, steady tread, silence.

He put on his clothes, and then combed his hair. He was staring at the phonograph. Yes, that was exactly the one he had seen in the living room, the one which had played for him the ghost waltz. And there sat the black disk on which the ghost waltz had been recorded many decades ago!

He was confounded for a moment. Trying to keep his eyes off the gleaming child, pondering and wondering that for a moment he had gone calm in the midst of all of it. But you did this. You could not stay at top pitch every moment. And so he thought, My wife may be alive; she may be dead; but I have to believe she's alive! And she's with that thing. That thing must need her!

Mona turned over. Her back was flawless and white, her hips for all their smallness proportioned like those of a little woman. Nothing boyish about her in her youth; resolutely female.

Tear your eyes off her, man. Eugenia and Henri are both around somewhere. You are pushing your luck. You are asking to be bricked up in the cellar.

There is no cellar.

I know that. Well, then the attic.

He opened the door slowly. Silence in the big hall. Silence in the double parlor. But there was the envelope on the hall table – where all mail and deliveries were placed. He could see the familiar embossed name of Mayfair and Mayfair. He tiptoed out, took the envelope, fearful that any moment Eugenia or Henri would appear, and then he went into the dining room. He could sit at the head of the table and read the thing, and that way, if anybody went near that library door, he could stop them.

Sooner or later, she would wake up and get dressed. And then? He didn't know. He just hoped she didn't go home, that she didn't leave him here.

Rotten coward, he thought. Rowan, would you understand all this? Funny thing was, Rowan might. Rowan understood men, better than any woman he'd ever known, even Mona.

He switched on the floor lamp by the fireplace, then sat down at the head of the table and removed the packet of Xeroxes from the envelope.

It was pretty much what they'd told him.

The geneticists in New York and Europe had gotten a bit sarcastic about the specimens. 'This seems to be a calculated combination of genetic material from more than one primate species.'

It was the eyewitness material from Donnelaith that killed him. 'The woman was sick. She stayed in her room most of the time. But when he went out, she went with him. It was as if he insisted she go. She looked sick, very sick. I almost suggested that she see a physician.'

At one point, in Geneva, Rowan was described by a hotel clerk as being an emaciated woman of perhaps 120 pounds. He found that horrifying.

He stared at the Xeroxes of the forged checks. Forgery! It wasn't even good. It was a great old-fashioned Elizabethan hand, by God, like something out of a parchment document.

Payee: Oscar Aldrich Tamen.

Why had he chosen that name? When Michael looked on the back of the check he realized. Fake passport. The bank clerk had written down all the information.

Surely they were following up that lead. Then he saw

the law firm memorandum. Oscar Aldrich Tamen had last been seen in New York on February 13th. Wife reported him missing on February 16th. Whereabouts unknown. Conclusion? Stolen passport.

He slapped shut the manila folder. He put his hands up and leaned on them, and tried not to feel that little twinge in his heart, or to remind himself that it was very small, the pain, no more than a little nag, and he'd had it before, for years, hadn't he?

'Rowan,' he said aloud as if it were a prayer. His thoughts went back to Christmas Day, to that last glimpse of her when she had torn the chain off his neck, and the medal had fallen.

Why did you leave me? How could you!

And then a terrible shame came over him, a shame and a fear. He'd been glad in his selfish little heart when they told him that demon thing had forced her, glad the investigators thought she was coerced! Glad that this had been declared in front of proud Ryan Mayfair. Ah, this meant his wily bride had not cuckolded him with the devil! She loved him!

And what in God's name did this mean for her! For her safety, her fate, her fortune! Lord God, you selfish and despicable man, he thought. But the pain was so great, the pain of her going that day, the pain of the icy water of the pool, and the Mayfair Witches in his dream, and the hospital room, and the pain in his heart when he'd first climbed the stairs –

He folded his arms on the table in front of him, and, weeping silently, laid his head down against it.

He did not know how much time had passed. He knew everything, however. That the library door had not opened, and that Mona must still be asleep, and that his servants knew what he'd done, or else they would have been hovering around him. That twilight had come. That the house was waiting for something, or witnessing something.

Finally he sat back and saw that the light outside was that shining white of spring evenings, making all the leaves distinct, and that the golden light of the lamp gave a little cheer to the vast room with its old paintings.

A tiny voice reached his ears, singing, thin, distant. And gradually as he sat very still, he realized it was Violetta's song, on the gramophone. This meant his nymph had waked; she was about, winding the old toy. He must rouse himself. He must talk to her about these mortal sins.

He stood up and made his way slowly through the shadowy room, and to the library. The music came strongly through the door, the happy song of Violetta from *La Traviata*. The waltz they'd played when Violetta was strong and gay, before she began to die so wondrously in operatic fashion. Light came from beneath the door, golden and soft.

She sat on the floor, half risen more or less, resting back on her hands, naked as before, her breasts loose but high placed and the color of baby skin. The nipples the pink of baby's nipples.

There was no music. Had it been some trick of noise? She was staring at the window to the cast-iron porch outside. And Michael saw that it was open. It was what they called a pocket window, and the sash had been thrown up all the way to make a doorway out of it. The shutters, which he had kept closed all the time himself, rather liking to see slats of afternoon sun, were open, too. A loud noise sounded in the street, but it was only a passing car, jetting too fast through the narrow shadowy intersection.

She was startled; her hair was mussed, her face still smooth with lingering sleep.

'What is this?' he said. 'Someone came in that window?'

'Tried to come,' she said. Her voice was foggy with sleep. 'Do you smell that smell?' She turned and looked at him, and before he could make an answer, she started to dress.

Michael went to the window and cranked shut the green blinds immediately. The corner beyond stood deserted or so dark beneath the oaks that it might as well have been. The mercury street lamp was like a moon face snared in the branches above. Michael brought down the sash, and turned the lock. Should have been locked all the time! He was furious.

'Do you smell it?' she said. She was dressed when he turned around. The room was all shadows now that he had shut out the corner light. She came to him and turned her back for him to tie her cotton sash.

'Goddamnit, who was it?' The stiff starched cotton felt good to his fingers. He tied the sash as best he could, having never done this for a little girl before, trying to make the bow pretty when he was finished with it. She turned around, staring past him at the window.

'You don't catch that scent, do you?' She went past him and peered through the glass, through the slats. Then she shook her head.

'You didn't see who it was, did you?' He had half a mind to go out there, charging through the garden, and around the block, to accost whatever strangers he might find, to search up Chestnut Street and down First until he found some suspicious person. 'My hammer, I need it,' he said.

'Your hammer?'

'I don't use a gun, honey. My hammer's always been good enough.' He went to the hall closet.

'Michael, the person's long gone. He was gone when I woke up. I heard him running away. I don't think . . . I don't know that he knew there was anyone in here.'

He came back. Something white was shining on the dark carpet. Her ribbon. He picked it up and absently she took it from him and fixed it in her hair with no need of a mirror.

'I've got to go,' she said. 'I gotta go see my mother, CeeCee, I should have gone before now. She's probably scared to death that she's in a hospital.'

'You didn't see anything at all?' he said.

He followed her out and down the hall.

'I caught that scent,' she said. 'I think it was the scent that woke me up, and then I heard the noise of the window.'

How calm she was. He was in a blaze of protective fury.

He opened the front door, and went out first, to the edge of the porch. Anyone could have hidden anywhere out there, behind the oaks, across the street behind a wall, even low down among the big elephant ears and palms that crowded his own garden. *My own garden.*

'I'm going, Michael, I'll call you later,' she said.

'You must be nuts, you think I'm going to let you walk off home like this in the dark? Are you crazy?'

She stopped on the steps. She had been about to

protest, but then she too cast a wary eye on the shadows that surrounded them. She looked thoughtfully up into the branches and at the dark shadows of Chestnut Street. 'I've got an idea. You follow me. Then when he springs out, whoever he is, you kill him with your hammer. You have your hammer?'

'That's ridiculous. I'll drive you home,' he said. He pulled her in and shut the door.

Henri was in the kitchen, just as he ought to have been, in white shirt and suspenders and drinking his whiskey from a white china cup so no one would know it. He put down the newspaper, and stood up. He would take the child home, of course. Or to the hospital? Certainly. Whatever Miss Mona wanted. He reached for his coat, which was ever ready on the chair behind him.

Michael walked out with them to the drive, distrustful of the darkness, and saw them safely to the car. Mona waved, a smear of red hair at the window. He felt an ache for her as they drove away, that he had let her go without a parting embrace, and then he was ashamed of it.

He went back inside, locking the kitchen door behind him.

He went back to the hall closet. His old tool chest was here, on the first floor under the stairs. This house was so big you had to have a tool chest for every floor of it. But these were his old tools, his favorites, and this was the claw hammer with the chewed-up old wooden handle, the one he had owned all his years in San Francisco.

A strange awareness came over him and he clutched it tight, and went to peer through the library window again. This had been his dad's hammer. He'd taken it out to San Francisco when he was a boy, with all his dad's tools. Nice to have something of his dad's amid all the great carefully inventoried Mayfair wealth, just one simple tool or two. He lifted the hammer. Love to bash it through the burglar's skull, he thought. As if we don't have enough trouble in this house, and some bastard tries to break in the library window!

Unless . . .

He switched on the light nearest the corner and examined the little gramophone. Covered with dust. No one had touched it. He didn't know whether or not he could touch it. He knelt down, put his fingers on the soft felt turntable. The records of *La Traviata* were in their thick old faded album. The crank lay beside the thing. It looked impossibly old. Who had made the waltz play twice now in this house, when this thing itself lay inert and dust-covered?

There was a sound in the house, a creaking as if someone was walking. Perhaps Eugenia. Or perhaps not.

'Goddamnit,' he said. 'Son of a bitch is in this place?'

He set out at once to make a search. He covered the whole first floor room by room, listening, watching, studying the tiny lights in the control boxes of the alarm which told him if anything was moving in rooms beyond him. Then he went upstairs, and covered the second floor as well, poking into closets and bathrooms that he had not entered in all this time, and even into the front bedroom, where the bed was all made and a vase of yellow roses stood on the mantel.

Everything seemed all right. Eugenia was not here. But from the servants' porch he could see the distant guest house in back, all aglow as if there were a party going on. That was Eugenia. She always turned on all the lights. She and Henri swapped shifts now, and so this was her turn to be alone back there, with the radio playing in the kitchen *and* the television tuned to *Murder, She Wrote*.

The dark trees shifted in the wind. He could see the still lawn, the swimming pool, the flags. Nothing stirred but the trees themselves, making the lights of the distant guest house twinkle deceptively.

On to the third floor. He had to check every crevice and crack.

He found it still and dark. The little landing at the top of the stairs was empty. The street lamp shone through the window. The storage room lay with its door open, all empty shelves clean and white and waiting for something. He turned and opened the door of Julien's old room, his own workroom.

The first thing he saw was the two windows opposite, the window on the right, beneath which Julien had died in his narrow bed, and the window on the left, through which Antha had fled only to fall to her death from the edge of the porch roof. Like two eyes, these windows.

The shades were up; the soft light of early evening flooded in on the bare boards and on his drafting table.

Only those were not bare boards. On the contrary, a threadbare rug lay there, and where his drafting table should have been was the narrow brass bed, which had long ago been moved out of here.

He groped for the light.

'Please don't turn it on.' The voice was frayed and soft, French.

'Who the hell are you?'

'It's Julien,' came the whispered response. 'For the love of heaven. I am not the one who came to the library door! Come in now while there is still time, and let me talk to you.'

He shut the door behind him. His face was teeming with heat. He was sweating and his grip had tightened on the hammer. But he knew it was Julien's voice, because he had heard it before, high high above the sea, in another realm, the very same voice, speaking to him softly and rapidly, putting the case to him, so to speak, and telling him he could refuse.

It seemed the veil would lift; he would see the shining Pacific again, his own drowned body on the heaving waves, and he would remember everything. But no such thing occurred. What occurred was infinitely more frightening and exciting! He saw a dark figure by the fireplace, arm on the mantel, long thin legs. He saw the soft hair, white in the light from the windows.

'*Eh bien*, Michael, I am so tired. It is so hard for me.'

'Julien! Did they burn the book? Your life story.'

'*Oui, mon fils*,' he said. 'My beloved Mary Beth burnt every page of those books. All my writing . . .' His voice was soft with sad wonder, eyebrows rising slightly. 'Come in, come closer. Take the chair there. Please. You must listen to me.'

Michael obeyed, taking the leather chair, the one which he knew to be real, lost now among so many alien dusty objects. He touched the bed. Solid. He heard the creak of the springs! He touched the silken quilt. Real. He was dazed, and marveling.

On the mantelpiece stood a pair of silver candlesticks, and the figure had turned and, with the sharp sudden scratch of a match, was putting a light to the wicks. His shoulders were narrow but very straight; he seemed ageless, tall, graceful.

When he faced Michael again, the warm yellow light spread out behind him. Perfectly realized, he stood, his blue eyes rather cheerful and open, his face almost rapt.

'Yes, my boy,' he said. 'Look at me! Hear me. You must act now. But let me speak my piece. Ah, do you hear it? My voice is getting stronger.'

It was a beautiful voice, and not a syllable was lost on Michael, who all his life had loved beautiful voices. It was an old-fashioned voice, like the cultured voices of those long-ago film stars he so cherished, the actors who made an art of simple speech, and it occurred to him in his strange daze that perhaps this was all more of his own fancy.

'I don't know how long I have,' the ghost said. 'I don't know where I've been as I've waited for this moment. I am the earthbound dead.'

'I'm here, I'm listening to you. Don't go. Whatever you do, don't go!'

'If only you knew how hard it has been to come through, how I have tried, and your own soul has shut me out.'

'I'm afraid of ghosts,' Michael said. 'It's an Irish trait. But you know that now.'

Julien smiled and stood back against the mantel, folding his arms, and the tiny candle flames danced, as if he really were solid flesh and he had stirred the air. And solid enough he seemed in his black wool coat and silk shirt. He wore long trousers and old-fashioned button shoes, polished to a perfect luster. As he smiled, his gently lined face with its curling white hair and blue eyes seemed to grow ever more vivid.

'I'm going to tell my tale,' he said, as a gentle teacher might. 'Condemn me not. Take what I have to give.'

Michael was flooded by an inexplicable combination of trust and excitement. The thing he had feared all this time, the thing which had haunted him, was now here, and it was his friend, and he was with it. Only Julien had never really been the thing to fear.

'You are the angel, Michael,' said Julien. 'You are the one who still has a chance.'

'Then the battle isn't over.'

'No, *mon fils*, not at all.'

He seemed distracted suddenly, woefully sad, and searching, and for one second Michael was terrified the vision would fail. But it only grew stronger, more richly colored, as Julien gestured to the far corner, and smiled.

There the small wooden box of the gramophone stood on a table at the very foot of the brass bed!

'What is real in this room?' Michael demanded softly. 'And what is a phantom?'

'*Mon Dieu*, if I only knew. I *never* knew.' Julien's smile broadened, and once again he relaxed against the mantel shelf, eyes catching the light of the candles, as he looked from left to right, almost dreamily over the walls. 'Oh for a cigarette, for a glass of red wine!' he whispered. 'Michael, when you can't see me anymore, when we leave each other – Michael, play the waltz for me. I played it for *you*.' His eyes moved imploringly across the ceiling. 'Play it every day for fear that I am still here.'

'I'll do it, Julien.'

'Now listen well . . .'

TEN

New Orleans was very simply a fabulous place. Lark didn't care if he never left here. The Pontchartrain Hotel was small, but utterly comfortable. He had a spacious suite over the Avenue, with agreeable, traditional furnishings, and the food from the Caribbean Room kitchen was the best he'd ever tasted. They could keep San Francisco for a while. He'd slept till noon today, then eaten a fabulous southern breakfast. When he got home, he was going to learn how to make grits. And this coffee with chicory was a funny thing – tasted awful the first time, and then you couldn't do without it.

But these Mayfairs were driving him crazy. It was late afternoon of his second day in this town and he'd accomplished nothing. He sat on the long gold velvet couch, a very comfortable L-shaped affair, ankle on knee, scribbling away in his notebook, while Lightner made some call in the other room. Lightner had been really tired when he came back to the hotel. Lark figured he'd prefer to be upstairs asleep in his own room now. And a man that age ought to nap; he couldn't simply drive himself night and day as Lightner did.

Lark could hear Lightner's voice rising. Somebody on the other end of the line in London, or wherever it was, was exasperating him.

Of course it wasn't the family's fault that Gifford Mayfair had died unexpectedly in Destin, Florida, that the last two days had been entirely devoted to a wake and a funeral and a sustained pitch of grief which Lark had seldom witnessed in his lifetime. Lightner had been drawn away over and over again by the women of the family, sent on errands, called for consolation and advice. Lark had scarcely had two words with him.

Lark had gone to the wake last night out of prurient curiosity. He could not imagine Rowan Mayfair living with these strange garrulous southerners, who spoke of the living and the dead with equal enthusiasm. And what a handsome well-oiled crowd they were. Seems everybody drove a Beamer or Jag or Porsche. The jewels looked real. The genetic mix included good looks, whatever else came with it.

Then there was the husband; everybody was protecting this Michael Curry. The man looked ordinary enough; in fact, he looked as good as all the others. Well fed, well groomed. Certainly not like a man who'd just suffered a heart attack.

But Mitch Flanagan on the coast was breaking down Curry's DNA now and he'd said it was extremely strange, that he had as unusual a blueprint as Rowan. Flanagan had 'managed', as the Keplinger Institute always did, to get the records on Michael Curry without the man's knowledge or permission. But now Lark couldn't get Flanagan!

Flanagan hadn't answered last night or this morning. Some sort of machine kept giving Lark some minimal song and dance with the customary invitation to leave a number.

Lark didn't like this at all. Why was Flanagan stalling

him? Lark wanted to see Curry. He wanted to talk to him, ask him certain questions.

It was fun to party and all – he'd gotten much too drunk last night after the wake – and he was headed to Antoine's tonight for dinner with two doctor friends from Tulane, both of them roaring sots, but he had business to do here, and now that Mrs Ryan Mayfair was buried perhaps they could get on with it.

He stopped his scribbling as Lightner came back into the room.

'Bad news?' he asked.

Lightner took his usual seat in the morris chair, and pondered, finger curled beneath his lip, before he answered. He was a pale man with rather attractive white hair, and a very disarming personal manner. He was also really fatigued. Lark thought this was the one with the heart to worry about.

'Well,' said Lightner, 'I'm in an awkward position. It seems Erich Stolov was the one who signed for Gifford's clothes in Florida. He was here. He picked up her old clothes at the funeral parlor. And now he's gone, and he and I have not consulted on all this with each other.'

'But he's a member of your gang.'

'Yes,' Aaron answered with a slight sarcastic grimace. 'A member of my gang. And the advice from the Elders according to the new Superior General is that I am not to question "that part" of the investigation.'

'So what does all this mean?'

Lightner grew quiet before answering. Then he looked up.

'You said something earlier to me about genetic testing of this entire family. You want to try to broach that subject with Ryan? I think tomorrow morning would not be too early to do it.'

'Oh, I'm for it. But you do realize what they'd be getting into. I mean they are the ones taking the risk, essentially. If we turn up congenital diseases, if we turn up predispositions to certain conditions – well, this information might affect everything from insurance eligibility to qualifying for the military. Yes, I want to do it, but I'd much rather concentrate on Curry right now. And this woman Gifford. No way we can get records on Gifford? I mean, let's take our time with this. This Ryan Mayfair is a pretty smart lawyer, as I see it. He won't go for wholesale genetic testing of his entire family. He'd be a fool if he consented or encouraged it.'

'And I am not in his good graces just now. If it weren't for my friendship with Beatrice Mayfair, he'd be far more suspicious than he is, and with reason.'

Lark had seen the woman in question. She'd come to the hotel yesterday with the news of the tragic death in Destin – a comely small-waisted woman, with upswept gray hair, and one of the most successful face-lifts he'd seen in recent years, though he figured it was probably not her first one. Eyes bright, cheeks perfectly sculpted, only a little telltale indentation beneath the chin and neck smooth as a young woman's neck. So – it was she and Lightner. He should have figured from the wake; she had clung to Lightner desperately, and several times Lark had seen Lightner kiss her. Lark hoped he'd have that kind of luck when he reached eighty, assuming he would. If he didn't stop hitting the booze, he might not make it.

'Look,' he said now, 'if Gifford Mayfair has medical records in this city, I think I can access them through

Keplinger, confidentially, without disturbing or alerting anyone.'

Lightner frowned and shook his head as if he thought this most distasteful. 'Not again without consent,' he said.

'Ryan Mayfair will never know. You leave that to us, the Medical Secret Service or whatever you want to call it. But I want to see Curry.'

'I understand. We can arrange that tomorrow as well. Maybe even later this evening. I have to think.'

'About what?'

'All of this. Why the Elders would permit Stolov to come here and to interfere this way, to risk the displeasure of the family.' The man seemed to be thinking aloud, not really directing his comments to Lark for an answer. 'You know, I've spent all my life in psychic investigation. I've never become so involved with a family before. I feel increasing loyalty to them, and increasing concern. I'm rather ashamed I didn't interfere before Rowan left, but the Elders had given me a very specific directive.'

'Well, obviously they too think there is something genetically strange about this family,' said Lark. 'They too are looking for hereditary traits. Good Lord, at least six people at the wake last night told me Gifford was psychic. They said she'd seen "the man", some sort of family ghost. They said she was more powerful than she ever let on. I think your friends in the Talamasca are simply on the same track.'

Lightner wasn't quick to respond. Then he said, 'But that's just it. We *should* be on the same track, and I'm not sure we are. It's all rather . . . puzzling.'

The phone interrupted, a low pulsing ring from the

handset beside the couch, which looked rather crudely modern among all the mahogany and velvet furniture.

Lark picked it up. 'Dr Larkin,' he said, as he always had wherever he answered a phone, even one time a ringing pay phone in an airport, which had jerked him suddenly from his reverie.

'This is Ryan Mayfair,' said the man on the other end. 'You're the doctor from California?'

'Yes, glad to talk to you, Mr Mayfair, didn't want to bother you on this of all days. I can hang in here until tomorrow.'

'Is Aaron Lightner with you, Doctor?'

'Yes, as a matter of fact he is. Do you want to speak to him?'

'No. Please listen. Edith Mayfair died early today from a uterine hemorrhage. Edith Mayfair was Lauren Mayfair's granddaughter by Jacques Mayfair, my cousin and Gifford's cousin. And Rowan's cousin. Same exact thing which had happened to my wife. Edith apparently bled to death alone in her apartment on Esplanade Avenue. Her grandmother found her this afternoon after the funeral. I think we should talk about this question of genetic testing. There may be problems . . . coming to the surface in this family.'

'Good God,' Lark whispered.

The man's voice was so level, so cold.

'Can you come downtown to my office?' Ryan Mayfair asked. 'And ask Lightner to come with you?'

'Absolutely. We'll be there in –'

'Ten minutes,' Lightner said. He was already on his feet. He took the phone from Lark.

'Ryan,' he said. 'Get the word out to the women of the family. You don't want to alarm anyone, but none

297

of the women should be alone just now. If something does happen, there should be someone there to call for medical help. Obviously neither Edith nor Gifford was able to do this. I know what I'm asking ... Yes. Yes. All of them. Everyone. That's exactly the way to go. Yes, we'll see you in ten minutes.'

The two men left the suite, choosing the short flight of stairs to the street over the elegant little elevator.

'What the hell do you think is going on?' Lark asked. 'I mean what does this mean, another death exactly like that of Gifford Mayfair?'

Lightner didn't respond. He looked grim and impatient.

'And by the way, do you have super-hearing? How did you know what he'd told me on the phone?'

'Super-hearing,' murmured Lightner vaguely.

They slipped out the front door and right into a waiting cab. The air still had its coolness, but there was a bit of balmy warmth mixed up in it. Everywhere Lark looked he saw greenery, and some random, shabby bit of charm – an old-fashioned lamppost perhaps, or a bit of iron balcony on the upper façade of a house behind its stucco store-front.

'I think the question is,' Lightner said, once again talking to himself as much as to Lark, 'what are we going to tell them. You know perfectly well what's happening. You know this has nothing to do with genetic illness, except in the broadest interpretation of those words.'

The cab driver made a U-turn and tore down the Avenue, bouncing them uncomfortably together on the leather seat of the cab.

'I don't follow you,' said Larkin. 'I don't know what's

going on. This is some kind of syndrome, like toxic shock.'

'Oh, come on, man,' said Lightner. 'We both know. He's trying to mate with them. You told me yourself, did you not? Rowan said she wanted to know if the creature could mate with humans or with her. She wanted an entire genetic examination of all material.'

Lark was stunned. He had not in all seriousness thought of this, and he realized once more that he had not been sure really that he believed in this new species of being, this male creature who had been born to Rowan Mayfair. He was still assuming in the back of his mind that all this would have some 'natural' explanation.

'It's natural,' said Lightner. '*Natural* is a deceptive word. I wonder if I shall ever before my time is up lay eyes on him. I wonder if he really can reason, if he possesses human self-control, if there is any moral framework to his mind, assuming it is a mind as we know mind . . .'

'But are you seriously suggesting that he is preying upon these women?'

'Of course I am,' said Lightner. 'It's obvious. Why do you think the Talamasca took Gifford's bloodstained clothes? He impregnated her and she lost the child. Look, Dr Larkin, you'd better come clean on all this. I understand your scholarly interest and your loyalty to Rowan. But we may have no further contact with Rowan.'

'God.'

'The point is you'd better come clean about what you know. We have to tell this family that this creature is on the prowl. We don't have time for vague talk of genetic illness, and genetic testing. We don't have time to go about gathering data. The family is too vulnerable. You realize that woman died today? She died while the family was burying Gifford!'

'Did you know her?'

'No. But I know she was thirty-five, a recluse by nature, and something of a family nut, as they call them, of which there are a great many. Her grandmother Lauren Mayfair didn't approve of her very much. In fact, I'm fairly certain she went to see her this afternoon to condemn her roundly for not attending her cousin's funeral.'

'Well, she sure had a good excuse, didn't she?' said Lark. He was instantly sorry. 'God, if I had a single clue as to where Rowan was.'

'What an optimist you are,' said Lightner bitterly. 'We have a lot of clues, don't we, but they do not suggest that you or I will ever see or speak to Rowan Mayfair again.'

ELEVEN

The note was waiting for him when he picked up his ticket for New Orleans. Call London at once.

'Yuri, Anton wants to talk to you.' It was not a voice he knew. 'He wants you to stay in New York until Erich Stolov gets there. Erich can meet you in New York tomorrow afternoon.'

'Why is that, do you think?' asked Yuri. Who was this person? He had never heard this voice before, and yet this person spoke as if she knew him.

'He thinks you'll feel better if you talk to Stolov.'

'Better? Better than what?'

As far as he was concerned, there was nothing he would say to Stolov that he had not said to Anton Marcus. He could not understand this decision at all.

'We've arranged a room for you, Yuri,' said the woman. 'We have you booked at the St Regis. Erich will call you tomorrow afternoon. Shall we send a car for you? Or will you take a cab?'

Yuri thought about it. In less than twenty minutes the airline would call his plane. He looked at the ticket. He did not know what he was thinking or feeling. His eyes roved the long concourse, the motley drift of passersby. Luggage, children, round-shouldered staff in uniform. Newspapers in a darkened plastic box. Airports of the world. He could not have told from this place whether he was in Washington, DC, or Rome. No sparrows. That meant it couldn't be Cairo. But it could have been Frankfurt or L.A.

Hindus, Arabs, Japanese passed him. And the countless unclassifiable individuals who might have been Canadian, American, British, Australian, German, French, how could one know?

'Are you there, Yuri? Please go to the St Regis. Erich wants to talk to you, wants to bring you up to date on the investigation himself. Anton is very concerned.'

Ah, that is what it was – the conciliatory tone, the pretense that he had not disobeyed an order, not walked out of the house. The strange intimacy and politeness of one he did not even know.

'Anton himself is very anxious to speak to you,' she said. 'He will be distressed when he discovers you called while he was out. Let me tell him you are going to the St Regis. We can arrange a car. It's no trouble.'

As if he, Yuri, did not know? As if he had not taken a thousand planes and a thousand cars and stayed in a thousand hotel rooms booked by the Order? As if he were not a defector?

No, this was all wrong. They were never rude, never, but they did not speak this way to Yuri, who knew their ways perfectly. Was it the tone for lunatics who had left the Motherhouse without permission, people who had simply walked out after years of obedience and commitment, and support?

His eyes settled on one figure – that of a woman, standing against the far wall. Sneakers, jeans, a wool jacket. Nondescript, except for her short dark hair. Swept back, rather pretty. Small eyes. She smoked a cigarette, and she kept her hands in her pockets, so that the cigarette hung on her lip. She was looking at him.

Right at him. And he understood. It was only a partial understanding but it was plenty. He dropped his eyes, he murmured something about he would think about it, yes, he would probably go to the St Regis, he would call again from there.

'Oh, I'm so relieved to hear it,' came that warm ingratiating voice. 'Anton will be so pleased.'

'I'll bet.' He hung up, picked up his bag and walked down the concourse. He did not notice the numbers of the various gates, the names of the snack stands, the bookshops, the gift stores. He walked and he walked. At some point he turned to the left. And then on he went to a great gate that ended this arm of the terminal and then he pivoted and walked very fast back the way he'd come.

He almost ran into her, she was that close on him. He came face to face with her, and she – startled – stepped to the side. She almost tripped. Her face colored. She glanced back at him, and then she took off down a little corridor, disappeared through a service door, and was seen no more. He waited. She did not come back. She did not want him to see her again or be close to her. He felt the hairs stand up on the back of his head.

An instinct told him to turn in the ticket. To go to another airline, and proceed south by another, less obvious route. He would fly to Nashville, then to Atlanta and on to New Orleans. It would take longer, but he would be harder to find.

He stopped at a phone booth long enough to send a telegram to himself at the St Regis, to be held for him when he came, which of course he never would.

This was no fun to him. He had been followed before by policemen in various countries. He had been stalked once by an angry and malevolent young man. He had even been attacked a few times in barroom arguments, when his world had carried him down into the dregs of some slum or port. Once he'd been arrested by the police in Paris, but it had all been straightened out.

Those things he could handle.

What was this happening to him now?

There was a terrible feeling inside him, a mixture of distrust and anger, a feeling of betrayal and loss. He had to talk to Aaron. But there was no time to call him. Besides, how could he burden Aaron with this now? He wanted to go to Aaron, be of assistance, not confuse him with some mad story of being followed in an airport, of a voice on the phone from London which he did not know.

For one second he was tempted to blow the lid, to call back, demand to speak to Anton, ask what was happening, and who was this woman who was tailing him at the airport?

But then he felt no spirit for it, no trust that it would work.

That was the awful part. No trust at all that it would do any good. Something had happened. Something had changed.

The flight was leaving. He looked around, and he did not see her. But that didn't mean anything. Then he went to board the plane.

In Nashville, he found a desk with a fax machine, and he wrote out a long letter to the Elders directly, to the Amsterdam number, telling them all that had taken place. 'I will contact you again. I am loyal. I am

304

trustworthy. I do not understand what has happened. You must give me some explanation, personally, of why you told me not to talk to Aaron Lightner, of who this woman in London was, of why I am being followed. I do not mean to throw my life out a window. I am worried about Aaron. We are human beings. What do you expect me to do?'

He read it over. Very like him, very melodramatic, the manner that often prompted from them a little humor or a pat on the head. He felt sick suddenly.

He gave the letter to the clerk with a twenty. He said, 'Send it three hours from now, not before.' The man promised. By that time Yuri would have already left Atlanta.

He saw the woman again, the very same woman in the wool coat, with the cigarette on her lip, standing by the desk, and staring at him coldly as he boarded the Atlanta plane.

TWELVE

Have I done this to myself? Is this how it ends for me, because of my own selfishness, my own vanity? She closed her eyes again on the vast empty cube of a room. Sterile, white, it flashed against her eyelids. She thought, Michael. She said his name in the darkness, 'Michael,' and tried to picture him, to bring him up like an image on the computer of her mind. Michael, the archangel.

She lay still, trying not to fight, to struggle, to tense, to scream. Just lie as if it were her choice to be on the filthy bed, her hands chained with loops of plastic tape to the ends of the headboard. She had given up all deliberate efforts to break the tape, either with her own physical strength or with the power of her mind – a power she knew could work fatal results upon the soft tissue inside the human frame.

But late last night, she had managed to free her left ankle. She wasn't sure why. She'd managed to slip it loose from the encircling tape, which had become a thick ill-fitted cuff. And with that foot free she had, over the long hours of the night, managed to shift her position several times, and to slowly drag loose the top sheet of the bed, stiff with urine and vomit, and force it down and away.

Of course the sheets beneath were filthy too. Had she lain here three days or four? She didn't know and this was maddening her. If she even thought about the taste of water she would go mad.

This very well might have been the fourth day.

She was trying to remember how long a human being could survive without food and water. She ought to know that. Every neurosurgeon ought to know something as simple as that. But since most of us do not tie people to beds and leave them captive for days on end, we don't have need of that specific information.

She was casting back through her memory – of the heroic stories she'd read, wondrous tales of those who had not starved when others had starved around them, those who had walked miles through heavy snow when others would have died. She had will. That was true. But something else was very wrong with her. She'd been sick when he'd tied her here. She had been sick off and on since they'd left New Orleans together. Nausea, dizziness – even lying flat she sometimes felt she was falling – and an ache in her bones.

She turned, twisting, and then moved her arms the little bit that she could, up and down, up and down, and worked her free leg, and twisted the other one in the strap of tape. Would she be able to stand up when he returned?

And then the obvious thought came. What if he does not return? What if he chooses not to return; or what if something prevents him? He was blundering out there like a mad creature, intoxicated with everything he saw, and no doubt making his characteristic ludicrous errors in judgment. Well, there really wasn't much to think about if he didn't come back. She'd die.

Nobody would ever find her here.

This was a perfectly isolated place. A high empty

office tower, crowded among hundreds of others – an unrented and undeveloped 'medical building' which she had chosen herself for their hiding place, deep in the middle of this sprawling ugly southern metropolis – a city chock-full of hospitals and clinics and medical libraries, where they'd be hidden as they did their experiments, like two leaves on a tree.

She'd arranged the utilities for the entire building herself, and all of its fifty floors were probably still lighted as she had left them. This room was dark. He'd snapped off the lights. And that had proved a mercy as the days passed.

When darkness fell, she could see the dense, charmless skyscrapers through the broad windows. Sometimes the dying sun made the silvery glass buildings glow as if they were burning, and beyond against the ruby-red sky rose the high dense ever-rolling white clouds.

The light, that was the thing you could always watch, the light. But at full dark when the lights came on, silently, all around her, she felt a little better. People were near, whether they knew she was there or not. Someone might come. Someone ... Someone might stand at an office window with a pair of binoculars, but why?

She began to dream again, thank God, to feel the bottom of the cycle again – 'I don't care' – and imagine that she and Michael were together and walking through the field at Donnelaith and she was explaining everything to him, her favorite fancy, the one into which she could sink when she wanted to suffer, to measure, to deny all at the same time.

'It was one wrong judgment call after another. I had only certain choices. But the mistake was pride, to think

I could do this thing, to think I could handle it. It's always been pride. The History of the Mayfair Witches was pride. But this came to me wrapped in the mysteries of science. We have such a terrible, terrible misconception of science. We think it involves the definite, the precise, the known; it is a horrid series of gates to an unknown as vast as the universe; which means endless. And I knew this, I knew but I forgot. That was my mistake.'

She pictured the grass; conjured the ruins; saw the tall fragile gray arches of the Cathedral rising from the glen, and it seemed she was really there and free.

A sound jolted her.

It was the key in the lock.

She grew still and quiet. Yes, the key turning. The outer door was closed loudly and fearlessly, and then she heard his tread on the tile floor. She heard him whistling, humming.

Oh, God, thank you, God.

Another key. Another lock, and that fragrance, the soft good fragrance of him as he drew close to the bed.

She tried to feel hate, to grow rigid with it, to resist the compassionate expression on his face, his large glistening eyes, so very beautiful as only eyes can be, and filled with sorrow as he looked at her. His beard and mustache were now very black and thick and like those of saints in pictures. His forehead was exquisitely shaped where the hair grew back from it, parted in the center with the smallest widow's peak.

Yes, a beautiful being, undeniably beautiful. Maybe he wasn't there. Maybe she was dreaming. Maybe it was all imagined that he had finally come back.

'No, my darling dear, I love you,' he whispered. Or did he?

As he drew closer, she realized she was looking at his mouth. There had been a subtle change to his mouth. It was more a man's mouth, perhaps, pink and decisively molded. A mouth had to be that way to hold its own beneath the dark glossy mustache, above the curling close-cut locks of the beard.

She turned away as he bent down. His warm fingers wound around her upper arms, and his lips grazed her cheek. He touched her breasts with his large hand, rubbing the nipples, and the unwelcome sensation ran through her. No dream. His hands. She could have lost consciousness to shut it out. But she was there, helpless, and she couldn't stop it or get away.

It was as degrading as anything else to feel this sudden utter joy that he was here, to kindle beneath his fingers as if he were a lover, not a jailer, to rise out of her isolation towards any kindness or gentleness proffered by the captor in a swoon.

'My darling, my darling.' He rested his head on her belly, nuzzled his face into the skin, oblivious to the filth of the bed, humming, whispering, and then he gave off a loud cry, and drawing up began to dance, round and round, a jig with one leg lifted, singing and clapping his hands. He seemed to be in ecstasy! Oh, how many times had she seen him do it, but never with such gusto. And what a curious spectacle it was. So delicate were his long arms, his straight shoulders; his wrists seemed double the length of those of a normal man.

She shut her eyes, and against her darkened lids the figure continued to jig and to twirl, and she could hear his feet thudding on the carpet, and his peals of delighted laughter.

'God, why doesn't he kill me?' she whispered.

He went silent and bent over her again.

'I'm sorry, my darling dear. I'm sorry.' Oh, the pretty voice. The deep voice. The voice that could read Scripture over a radio in a car in the night as you drove endless miles all alone with it. 'I didn't mean to be gone so long,' he said. 'I was off on a bitter and heartbreaking adventure.' His words became more rapid. 'In sorrow, in discovery, witnessing death, and beset with miseries and frustrations . . .' Then he lapsed as always into the whispering and humming, rocking on his feet, humming and murmuring, or was it a whistling, a tiny whistling through his dry lips?

He knelt as if he had collapsed. He laid his head on her waist again, his warm hand dangling between her legs, on her sex, ignoring the filth of the bed once more, and he kissed the skin of her belly. 'My darling, my dear.'

She couldn't prevent herself from crying out.

'Let me loose, let me up. I'm lying here in filth. Look what you've done to me.' And then her anger clamped down on her voice, and she went motionless and soundless, paralyzed with rage. If she stung him, he might sulk for hours. He might stand at the window and cry. Be silent. Be clever.

He stood watching her.

Then he drew out his knife, small, flashing, like his teeth, a flash like that in the sterile twilight of this empty room.

He cut through the tape so quickly! Nothing to it, this spindly giant reaching over her, slice, slice, slice.

Her arms were free – numb and useless – and free. With all her might and main she tried to lift them. She couldn't lift her right leg.

She felt his arms sliding under her. He lifted her, and rose to his feet with her, tumbling her against his chest.

She cried. She sobbed. Free from the bed, free, if only she had the strength to put her hands around his neck and –

'I'll bathe you, my darling dear, my poor darling love,' he said. 'My poor beloved Rowan.' Were they dancing in circles? Or was it only that she was so dizzy? She smelled the bathroom – soap, shampoo, clean things.

He laid her down in the cold porcelain tub, and then she felt the first jet of warm water. 'Not too hot,' she whispered. The glaring white tile was moving, marching up the walls all around her. Flashing. Stop.

'No, not too hot,' he said. His eyes were bigger, brighter, the lids better defined when she had last looked at them, the eyelashes smaller yet still luxuriant and jet-black. She noted this as if jotting it down on a laptop computer. Finished? Who could guess? To whom would she ever give her findings? Dear God, if that package had not reached Larkin . . .

'Don't fret, my darling dear,' he said. 'We are going to be good to each other, we are going to love each other. You will trust me. You will love me again. There's no reason for you to die, Rowan, no reason at all for you to leave me. Rowan, love me.'

She lay like a cadaver, unable to work her parts. The water swirled round her. He unbuttoned her white shirt, pulled loose the pants. The water rushed and hissed and was so warm. And the dirt smell was being broken. He hurled the soiled clothes away.

She managed to lift her right hand, to tug at the panties, and rip at them, but she hadn't the strength to pull them off. He had gone into the other room. She could hear the sound of sheets being ripped from the bed; it was amazing all the sounds our minds registered; sheets being thrown in a heap. Who would have thought that such things even made a sound? And yet she knew it perfectly well, and remembered foolishly an afternoon at home in California when her mother had been changing the beds – that very sound.

A plastic package torn open; a fresh sheet let to fall open and then shaken out to loose its wrinkles and land on the bed.

She was slipping and the water was rising to her shoulders. Once again she tried to use her arms; she pushed and pushed against the tile and managed to sit forward.

He stood over her. He had taken off his heavy coat. He was dressed in a simple turtleneck sweater, and as always he looked alarmingly thin. But he was strong and stalwart in his thinness, with none of the twisted neurotic apology of the very lanky and the underfed and the overgrown. His hair was so long now it covered his shoulders. It was as black as Michael's hair, and the longer it became the looser its curl, so that it was now almost wavy. In the steam from the tub, the hair at his temples curled somewhat, and she could see a glistening sheen on his seemingly poreless skin as he bent down again to caress her.

He steadied her against the back of the tub. He lifted his little knife – Oh dare she try to get hold of it! – and he cut loose her soiled panties, and pulled them up out of the bubbling water and threw them aside. He knelt by the tub.

He was singing again, looking at her, singing or

humming, or whatever it was – this strange sound that almost reminded her of the cicadas at evening in New Orleans. He cocked his head to the side.

His face was narrower than it had been days ago, more manly perhaps, that was the secret, the last of the roundness had left his cheeks. His nose had become slightly narrower, too, more rounded at the tip, more fine. But his head was just about the same size, she figured, and his height was very nearly the same too, and as he took the washrag and squeezed it out, she tried to figure whether his fingers had grown any longer. It did not seem so.

His head. Was the soft spot still there in the top? How long would it take for the skull to close? She suspected the growth had slowed but not stopped.

'Where did you go?' she asked. 'Why did you leave me?'

'You made me leave,' he said with a sigh. 'You made me leave with hate. And I had to go back out in the world and learn things. I had to see the world. I had to wander. I had to build my dreams. I can't dream when you hate me. When you scream at me and torment me.'

'Why don't you kill me?'

A look of sadness came over him. He wiped her face with the warm, folded rag, and wiped her lips.

'I love you,' he said. 'I need you. Why can't you give yourself to me? Why have you not given yourself? What do you want that I can give? The world will soon be ours, my darling dear, and you my queen, my beauteous queen. If only you would help me.'

'Help you do what?' she asked.

She looked at him, and drew deep on her hatred, and her rage, and with all her might tried to send some invisible and lethal power against him. Shatter the cells; shatter the veins; shatter the heart. She tried and she tried, and then exhausted, lay back against the tub.

In her life she had accidentally with such hate killed several human beings, but she could not kill him. He was too strong; the membranes of the cells were too strong; the osteoblasts swarming at their accelerated rate, just as everything within him worked at that rate, defensively and aggressively. Oh, if only she had had more of a chance to analyze these cells! If only, if only . . .

'Is that all I am to you?' he said, his lip quivering. 'Oh, God, what am I? A mere experiment?'

'And what am I to you that you hold me prisoner here, and leave me for days on end like this? Don't ask love of me. You're a fool if you do. Oh, if only I had learned from the others, learned how to be a real witch! I could have done what they wanted of me.'

He was convulsed with silent hurt. The tears stood in his eyes, and his pliant glistening skin flamed with blood for an instant. He made his long hands into fists as if he would hit her again, as he had in the past, though he'd vowed he never would again.

She did not care. That was the horror. Her own limbs were failing her; tingling, aching; pains in her joints. Could she have escaped from here herself if she had managed to kill him? Perhaps not.

'What did you expect me to do?' he asked. He leant down and kissed her again. She turned away. Her hair was wet now. She wanted to slide down into the water, but she feared she might not be able to bring herself back up. He crushed the rag in his hands, and began again to bathe her. He bathed her all over. He squeezed the water into her hair, washing it back from her forehead.

She was so used to his scent that now she didn't really smell it; she felt only a warm sense of his nearness and a deep enervating desire for him. Of course, desire for him.

'Let me trust you again, tell me you love me again,' he implored, 'and I'm your slave, not your captor. I swear it, my love, my brilliant one, my Rowan. Mother of us all.'

No answer came from her. He'd risen to his feet.

'I'm going to clean everything for you,' he said proudly like a child. 'I'm going to clean it all and make it fresh and beautiful. I've brought things for you. New clothes. I've brought flowers. I'll make a bower of our secret place. Everything is waiting by the elevators. You will be so surprised.'

'You think so?'

'Oh yes, you will be pleased, you'll see. You're only tired and hungry. Yes, hungry. Oh, you must have food.'

'And when you leave me again, you'll tie me up with white satin ribbon?' How harsh her voice was, how filled with utter contempt. She shut her eyes. Without thinking, she raised her right hand and touched her face. Yes, muscles and joints were beginning to work again.

He went out, and she struggled to sit up and she caught the floating cloth and began to wash herself. The bath was polluted. Too much filth. Flakes of human excrement, her excrement, floated on the surface of the water. She felt nausea again, and lay back until it was gone. Then she bent forward, her back aching, and she pulled up the stopper, fingers still numb and weak and clumsy, and she turned on the flood again to wash away the tiny crusted curls of dirt.

She lay back, feeling the force of the water flowing all around her, bubbling at her feet, and she breathed deep, calling upon the right hand and then the left to flex, and then on the right foot and then the left; and then began these exercises over again. The water grew hotter, comfortably so. The rushing noise blotted out all sounds from the other room. She listed in moments of pure and thoughtless comfort, the last moments of comfort she might ever know.

It had gone like this:

Christmas Day and the sun coming in on the parlor floor, and she lying on the Chinese rug in a pool of her own blood, and he sitting there beside her – newborn, amazed, unfinished.

But then human infants are actually born unfinished, far more unfinished than he had been. That was the way to view it. He was simply more fully completed than a human baby. Not a monster, no.

She helped him walk, stand, marveling at his eruptions of speech, and ringing laughter. He was not so much weak as lacking in coordination. He seemed to recognize everything he saw, to be able to name it correctly, as soon as the initial shock had been experienced. The color red had baffled and almost horrified him.

She had dressed him in plain drab clothes, because he did not want the bright colors to touch him. He smelled like a newborn baby. He felt like a newborn baby, except that the musculature was there, all of it, and he was growing stronger with every passing minute.

Then Michael had come. The terrible battle.

During the battle with Michael she had watched him learn on his feet, so to speak, go from frantic dancing and seemingly drunken staggering to coordinated efforts to strike Michael, and finally to pitch Michael off balance, which he had done with remarkable ease, once he had decided, or realized, how it could be done.

She was sure that if she had not dragged him from the site, he would have killed Michael. She had half lured him, half bullied him into the car, the alarm screaming for help, taking advantage of his growing fear of the sound, and his general confusion. How he hated loud sounds.

He had talked all the way to the airport about how it all looked, the sharp contours, the absolutely paralyzing sense of being the same size as other human beings, of looking out the car window and seeing another human at eye level. In the other realm, he had seen from above, or even inside, but almost never from the human perspective. Only when he possessed beings did he know this and then it had always been torture. Except with Julien. Yes, Julien, but that was a long tale.

His voice was eloquent, very like her own or Michael's, accentless, and giving words a more lyrical dimension, perhaps, she wasn't certain. He jumped at sounds; he rubbed his hands on her jacket to feel its texture; he laughed continuously.

In the airport, she had to stop him from sniffing her hair and her skin and from trying to kiss her. But he walked perfectly by then. He ran, for the sheer fun of it, down the concourse. He leapt into the air. Under the

318

spell of a passing radio, he had rocked to and fro – a trance she would see again and again.

She took the plane to New York because it was leaving. She would have gone anywhere to get out of there. She felt a wild panic, a need to protect him from everyone in the world until she could get him quiet and see what he really was; she felt possessive and madly excited, and fearful, and wildly ambitious.

She had given birth to this thing; she had created it. They weren't going to get their hands on it, take it away, lock it up away from her. But even so, she knew she wasn't thinking straight. She was sick, weakened from the birth. Several times in the airport she had almost passed out. He was holding her when they got on the plane, and whispering rapidly in her ear, a sort of running commentary on all they passed and saw, filled with random explanations about things in the past.

'I recognize everything. I remember, don't you see, when Julien said this was the age of wonders, predicting that the very machines they then found so essential to life were going to be obsolete within the decade. Look at the steamboats, he would declare, and how fast they gave way to the railroad, and now people drive in these automobiles. He knew all of it, he would have loved this plane, you see. I understand how the engine works ... The highly combustible fuel is altered from a gelatinous liquid to a vapor and ...'

... On and on it had gone as she tried from time to time to quiet him, and finally she had encouraged him to try to write, because she was so exhausted, she could no longer make sense of what he was saying. He couldn't write. He couldn't control the pen. But he could read, and thereafter went through every piece of reading material he could acquire.

In New York, he demanded a tape recorder, and she fell asleep in a suite at the Helmsley Palace, as he walked back and forth, now and then bending his knees, or stretching his arm, talking into the recorder.

'Now there is in fact a real sense of time, of a ticking, as if there existed in the world even before the invention of clocks a pure ticking, a natural measurement, perhaps connected to the rhythm of our hearts, and our breath; and the smallest changes in temperature affect me. I do not like the cold. I do not know if I am hungry or not. But Rowan must eat, Rowan is weak, and sick-smelling . . .'

She'd awakened to the most erotic sensations, a mouth on her breast pulling so hard on the nipple it almost hurt. She'd screamed, opened her eyes, and felt his head there, and felt his fingers lying on her belly as he sucked and sucked. Her breast itself was hard and full; the left breast, free in her own hand, felt like marble.

She'd panicked for a moment. She had wanted to cry for help. She'd pushed him aside, assuring him she would order food for them both, and after she'd made the call, she'd started to make another.

'For what?' he'd demanded. His baby face had already elongated slightly, and his blue eyes seemed not so round anymore, as though the lids were lowering just a bit and becoming more natural.

He snatched the phone out of her hand. 'Don't call anyone else.'

'I want to know if Michael is all right.'

'It doesn't matter whether he is or not. Where shall we go? What do we do?'

She was so tired she could scarce keep her eyes open. He lifted her effortlessly and carried her into the bath and told her he had to wash the smell off her — of sickness and birth and of Michael. Especially the smell of Michael, his 'unwilling' father. Michael, the Irishman.

At one point, as they sat in the tub together, facing each other, a moment of consummate horror overtook her. It seemed he was the word made flesh in the absolute sense, staring at her, his face very round and pale in a healthy pinkish way like the face of an infant, eyes gazing at her with wonder, lips curling in an angelic smile. She almost began to scream again.

There was no hair on his chest. The food had come. He wanted her milk again. He held her in the bath sucking her, hurting her, until she cried out.

The waiters in the other room would hear her, she said, stop. He waited until the clatter of silver domes was over. Then he sucked hard at the other breast; it seemed a perfect balance between pain and pleasure, this zinging, thrilling sensation, radiating out from her nipples, and the hurt of the nipples themselves. She begged him to be gentle.

He rose up on all fours in the water over her, and his cock was thick and slightly curved. He covered her mouth and slipped his cock between her legs. She was sore from the birth, but she locked her arms around his neck, and it seemed the pleasure would kill her.

Dressed in terry-cloth robes, they lay on the floor together, doing it again and again. Then he rolled over on his back and he spoke about the endless darkness, the sense of being lost, the warm blaze of Mary Beth. The great fire of Marie Claudette. The radiance of

Angélique; the dazzling glow of Stella; his witches, his witches! He talked about how he would collect around Suzanne's body and feel her shiver, and know what she felt, but now he felt a distinct and separate sensation himself, which was infinitely more powerful, sweeter, richer. He said the flesh was worth the price of death.

'You think you'll die like anyone else?' she asked.

'Yes,' he said and fell silent but only for a moment. He began to sing, or hum, or make some strange combination of both, imitating bits of melody which seemed familiar to her. He ate everything on the table that was soft and liquid. 'Baby food,' he said with laughter. He ate the mashed potato, and the butter, and drank the mineral water, but he did not want the meat.

She examined his teeth. They were perfect, the same number as that of a mature human. No sign of wear or decay, obviously, and then his tongue was soft, but he couldn't bear this examination for long. He needed air! He told her she didn't know how much air he needed, and he threw open the windows.

'Tell me about the others,' she said.

The tape recorder was on; he had loaded whole shelves of cassette tape onto the counter at the airport store. He was prepared. He knew. He understood the inner workings and the outer workings. Very few creatures knew both.

'Talk about Suzanne and Donnelaith.'

'Donnelaith,' he said, and he began to weep, saying he could not remember what had come before, only it was pain, it was something, it was a crowd of faceless beings in an antechamber, and when Suzanne had called his name, it was just a word tossed out on the night: Lasher! Lasher! Perhaps a confluence of syllables never intended to be that word, but it had rung some recognition in him, in a core of himself that he had forgotten he possessed, and he had 'come together' for her and drawn close and sent the winds lashing down around her.

'I wanted her to go to the ruins of the Cathedral. I wanted her to see the stained glass. But I could not tell her. And there was no more stained glass.'

'Explain all this to me slowly.'

But he couldn't disentangle it. 'She said to make the woman sick. I made her sick. I found I could toss things into the air, strike the roof. It was like reaching for the light down a long long dark tunnel, and now, it's so sharp, I feel the sound, I smell it . . . say rhymes to me, tell me rhymes. I want to see something red again; how many shades of red are there in this room?'

He began to crawl about on all fours looking at the colors in the carpet, and then moving along the walls. He had long hard sturdy white thighs, and forearms of uncommon length. But when he was dressed it wasn't so noticeable.

Around three in the morning, she managed to escape to the bathroom alone; it seemed the greatest of dreams to have that moment of privacy. That was to be the pattern of the future. At times in Paris, she had dreamed only of finding a private bathroom, where he was not right outside the door, listening to every sound, calling out to her to make her confess she was still there and not trying to escape, whether or not there was a window through which she might have climbed.

He got the passport himself the next day. He said that he would find a man who resembled him. 'And what if he doesn't have a passport?' she asked.

'Well, we shall go to a place of traveling men, won't we? Where people go to get passports, and then we shall wait for a likely suspect, as they say, and take the passport from him. You are not so very bright as you think you are, hmmm? That is simple enough for a baby.'

They went to the bureau itself; they waited outside; they followed a tall man who had just received his passport; at last he stepped in the man's path. She watched, afraid, and then he struck the man and took the passport from him. No one seemed to notice, if anyone even saw. The streets were crowded and the noise of the traffic hurt her head. It was cold, very cold. He pulled the man by his coat into a doorway. It was that simple. She watched all this. He was not needlessly brutal. He disabled the man, as he said, and the passport was now his.

Frederick Lamarr, aged twenty-five, resident of Manhattan.

The picture was close enough, and by the time he trimmed off some of his hair, no casual eye would know the difference.

'But the man, he could be dead,' she said.

'I have no special feeling for human beings,' he said. And then he was surprised. 'Am I not a human being?' He clutched at his head, walking ahead of her on the pavement, pivoting every few seconds to make certain she was there, though he said he had her scent and he'd know if the crowds separated them. He said he was trying to remember about the Cathedral. That Suzanne would not go. She was scared of the ruins of the church, an ignorant girl, ignorant and sad. The glen had been empty! Charlotte could write. Charlotte had been so much stronger than Suzanne or Deborah.

'All my witches,' he said. 'I put gold in their hands. Once I knew how to get it, I gave them all that I could. Oh, God, but to be alive, to feel the ground beneath me, to reach up, and feel the earth pulling down upon my arms!'

Back in the hotel, they continued the more organized chronology. He recorded descriptions of each witch from Suzanne down through Rowan, and to her surprise he included Julien. That made fourteen. She did not point this out, because the number thirteen was something highly significant to him and mentioned by him over and over, thirteen witches to make one strong enough to have his child, he said, as if Michael had had nothing to do with it, as if he were his own father. He tossed in strange words – *maleficium, ergot, belladonna.* Once he even rattled along in Latin.

'What do you mean?' she asked. 'Why was I able to give birth to you?'

'I don't know,' he said.

By dark something was becoming obvious. There was not a sense of proportion to his tale-telling. He might describe for forty-five minutes all the colors which Charlotte had worn, and how vague they had looked and how he could imagine them now, those fragile, dyed silks, and then in two sentences describe the flight of the family from Saint-Domingue to America.

He wept when she asked about Deborah's death; he could not describe this.

'All my witches, I brought them ruin, one way or another, except for the very strongest ones, and they hurt me, and whipped me and made me obey,' he declared.

'Who?' she asked.

'Marguerite, Mary Beth, Julien! Damn him, Julien.'
And he began to laugh in an uncontrollable way and
then sprang to his feet to do a complete imitation of
Julien – proper gentleman tying a four-in-hand silk tie,
putting on his hat, then going out, cutting off the end of
a cigar, then putting it to his lip.

It was spectacular, this little performance, in which
he became another being, even to drawling a few words
in languid French.

'What is a four and hand?' she said.

'I don't know,' he confessed, 'but I knew a moment
ago. I walked in his body with him. He liked me to do
this. Not so the others. Jealously guarding their bodies
from me, they sent me to possess those they feared or
would punish, or those they would use.'

He sank down and tried to write again, on the hotel
pad and paper. Then he sucked on her breasts, nursed,
shifting slowly from one to the other and back again.
And she slept, and they slept together. When she awoke,
he was taking her, and the orgasms were those long,
dreamlike orgasms that she always felt when she was
almost too exhausted to have them.

At midnight they took off for Frankfurt.

It was the first plane they could get across the
Atlantic.

She was terrified that the stolen passport had been
reported. He told her to rest easy, that human beings
weren't all that smart, that the machinery of international travel moved sluggishly. It wasn't like the world
of the spirits, where things moved at the speed of light
or stood still. He hesitated a long time before putting
on the earphones. 'I am scared of music!' he said. Then
he put them on and surrendered, sliding down in the

seat, and staring forward as if he'd been knocked unconscious. He tapped his fingers with the songs. In fact, the music so entranced him that he didn't want anything else until they landed.

He wouldn't speak to her or answer her, and when she tried to get up to use the rest room, he held her hand in a tight clamp, refusing to cooperate. She won once, and he was watching her as she emerged, standing there in the aisle, earphones locked to his head, arms folded, tapping his foot to some beat she couldn't hear and smiling at her only in passing before they both sat down again, and she slept beneath the blanket.

From Frankfurt they flew to Zurich. He went with her to the bank. She was now weak and dizzy and her breasts were full of milk and ached continuously.

At the bank she was quick and efficient. She hadn't even thought of escape. Protection, subterfuge, those were her only concerns, oh, fool that she had been.

She arranged for enormous transfers of funds, and different accounts in Paris and in London that would give them money, but could not likely be traced.

'Let's go now to Paris,' she said, 'because when they receive these wires they'll be looking for us.'

In Paris, she saw for the first time that a faint bit of hair had grown on his belly, around his navel, curling, and a tiny bit around each of his nipples. The milk was flowing more freely now. It would build up with incredible pleasure. She felt listless and dull-minded as she lay there, letting him suck from her, letting his silky hair tickle her belly, her thighs.

He continued to eat soft food, but the milk from her breasts was all that he really wanted. He ate the food because she thought he should. She believed his body must require the nutrients. And she wondered what the nursing was taking out of her, if it was the reason she felt so weak, so listless. Ordinary mothers felt that, a great slothful ease, or so they had told her. The small aches and the pains had begun.

She asked him to talk of a time *before* the Mayfair Witches, of the most remote and alien things he could recall. He spoke of chaos, darkness, wandering, having no limit. He spoke of having no organized memory. He spoke of his consciousness beginning to organize itself with . . . with . . .

'Suzanne,' she said.

He looked at her blankly. Then he said yes, and he spun off the whole line of the Mayfair Witches in a melody: 'Suzanne, Deborah, Charlotte, Jeanne Louise, Angélique, Marie Claudette, Marguerite, Katherine, Julien, Mary Beth, Stella, Antha, Deirdre, Rowan!'

He accompanied her to the local branch of the Swiss Bank and she arranged for more funds, setting up routes so the money would go through Rome and even in one case through Brazil before it came to her. She found the bank officials very helpful. At a law firm recommended by the bank, he watched and listened patiently as she wrote out instructions, entitling Michael to the First Street house for the rest of his life, and to whatever amount of the legacy he wanted.

'But we will return there, won't we?' he demanded. 'We will live there, someday, you and I. In that house! He will not have it forever.'

'That's impossible now.'

Oh, the folly.

An awe fell over the members of the law firm as they fired up their computers and put the information out on the wire, and soon confirmed for her, yes, Michael Curry in the city of New Orleans, Louisiana, was ill and in intensive care at Mercy Hospital, but definitely living!

He saw as she hung her head and began to cry. One hour after they left the lawyer's office, he told her to sit on the bench in the Tuileries and be still and that he would never be out of sight.

He returned with two new passports. Now they could change hotels and be different people. She felt numb and full of aches. When they reached the second hotel, the glorious George V, she collapsed on the couch in the suite and slept for hours.

How was she to study him? Money wasn't the point; she needed equipment she herself could not operate. She needed a medical staff, electronic programs, brain scan machines, all manner of things.

He went out with her to buy notebooks. He was changing before her very eyes, but it was subtle. A few wrinkles had appeared on his knuckles, and his fingernails now seemed stronger though they were still exactly the color of flesh. His eyelids had the first subtle fold, which really gave his face a little maturity. His mustache and beard were coming in. He let them grow though they were prickly.

In the notebooks, she wrote until she was so tired that she couldn't see, cloaking all her observations in the most dense scientific language. She wrote of his need for air, that he threw open windows everywhere they went, and sometimes gasped, and that his head sweated when he slept and the soft spot was no smaller now than when he'd been born, that he was insatiable for her milk and that she was sick with exhaustion.

The fourth day in Paris, she insisted they go to a large central-city hospital. He did not want to do this. She more or less enticed him, making bets with him as to just how stupid human beings were, and describing the fun of sneaking around and pretending to be regular inmates of the place.

He enjoyed it. 'I get the hang of it,' he said triumphantly, as if that phrase had a special meaning for him. He said lots of such phrases with delight. 'Lo, dear, the coast is clear! Ah, Rowan, bubble bubble, toil and trouble.' And sometimes he just sang rhymes that he had heard that were sort of jokes.

> 'Mother, may I go out to swim,'
> 'Yes, my darling daughter.
> Hang your clothes on a hickory limb,
> But don't go near the water!'

He went into great peals of laughter at such things. Mary Beth had said this one, and Marguerite had said that. And Stella said: 'Peter Piper picked a peck of pickled peppers!' He said it faster and faster until it was a whistling whisper and no more.

She began to try to amuse him, testing him with various little verbal tidbits and such. When she hit him with bizarre English constructions, like 'Throw Mamma from the window a kiss,' he became damned near hysterical. Even alliteration would make him laugh, like the song: 'Bye, Baby Bunting! Mamma's gone a hunting, to get a little rabbit skin, to put her baby bunting in!'

It was as if the shape of her lips amused him. He became obsessed with the rhyme, told to him by her, 'Peter, Peter, pumpkin eater, had a wife and couldn't keep her. Put her in a pumpkin shell, and there he kept

330

her very well!' Sometimes he danced as he sang these songs.

In the realm of the spirits, music had delighted him. He could hear it at times when he could hear no other emanation from humans. Suzanne sang as she worked. A few old phrases came out of him, sounded Gaelic, but he really didn't know what they were! Then he forgot them. Then once he broke into plaintive Latin and sang many verses, but he could not repeat them when he tried.

He woke in the night talking about the Cathedral. About something that had happened. He was all in a sweat. He said they had to go to Scotland.

'That Julien, that clever devil,' he said. 'He wanted to find out all those things. He spoke riddles to me, which I denied.' He lay back and said softly, 'I am Lasher. I am the word made flesh. I am the mystery. I have entered the world and now I must suffer all the consequences of the flesh, and I do not know what they will be. What am I?'

He was by this time conspicuous but not monstrous. His hair was now loose and shoulder length. He wore a black hat, pulled down over his head, and even the most narrow black jackets and pants fitted him loosely as if he were made of sticks, and he actually looked like one of the crazed bohemian young people. An acolyte of the rock music star David Bowie. People everywhere seemed to respond to him, to his mirth, to his innocent questions, to his spontaneous and often exuberant greetings. He struck up conversations with people in shops; he asked questions about everything. His enunciation had taken on a sharpness with a touch of French to it, but could change while he spoke to her, back into her pronunciation.

When she tried to use the phone in the middle of the night, he woke up and tore her hand off the receiver. When she rose and tried to go out the door, he was suddenly standing beside her. The hotel suites, from now on, had bathrooms without windows or he found them unacceptable. He tore out the phones in the baths. He would not let her out of his sight, except during that time when she would lock the bathroom door before he reached it.

She at last tried to argue with him. 'I must call and find out what happened to Michael.' He struck her. The blow was astonishing to her. He knocked her back on the bed, and the entire side of her face was bruised. He was crying. He lay with her, suckling her, and then entering her, and doing both at the same time, the pleasure washing through her. He kissed the bruise on her face and she felt an orgasm moving up through her even though his cock was no longer inside her. Paralyzed with pleasure, she lay with her fingers curling up, her feet to the side, like one who is dead.

At night he talked about being dead, about being lost.

'Tell me the earliest thing you remember.'

That there was no time, he said.

'And what did you feel, was it love for Suzanne?'

He hesitated and said that he thought it was a great burning hatred.

'Hatred? Why was that?'

He honestly didn't know. He looked out the window and said that in general he had no patience with humans. They were clumsy and stupid and could not process data in their brains as he could. He had played the fool for humans. He would not do it again.

'What was the weather on the morning that Suzanne died?' she asked.

'Rainy, cold. It rained so heavily they thought for a while they would have to delay the burning. By noon it had settled. The sky was clear. The village was ready.' He looked baffled.

'Who was King of England then?' she asked. He shook his head. He had no idea. What was the double helix, she wanted to know. Rapidly he described the two twin strands of chromosomes which contain the DNA in the double helix, our genes, he said. She realized he was using the very words she had once memorized from a textbook for an examination in childhood. He spoke them with cadence, as if it was the cadence of them that had impressed them through her into his mind, whatever his mind was ... if you could call it that.

'Who made the world?' she asked.

'I have no idea! What about you? You know who made it?'

'Is there a God?'

'Probably not. Ask the other people. It's too big a secret. When a secret is that big there's nothing to it. No God, no, absolutely not.'

In various clinics, talking authoritatively, and wearing the *de rigueur* white coat, she drew vials and vials of his blood while he complained, and those around her never realized that she did not belong in the large laboratory, was not working on some special assignment. In one place she managed to analyze the blood specimens for hours beneath the microscope, and record her findings. But she did not have the chemicals and equipment she needed.

All this was crude, simplistic. She was frustrated. She wanted to scream. If only she was at the Keplinger Institute! If such a thing were possible, to go back with him to San Francisco, to gain access to that genetic laboratory! Oh, but how could they do it?

One night, she got up thoughtlessly to go down to the lobby and buy a pack of cigarettes. He caught her at the top of the stairs.

'Don't hit me,' she said. She felt rage, a rage as deep and terrible as she had ever known, the kind of rage which in the past had killed others.

'Won't work with me, Mother!'

Nerves frayed, she lost all control and slapped him. It hurt him and he cried. He cried and cried, rocking back and forth in a chair. To comfort him, she sang more songs.

> In Hamlen town, long long ago
> Nobody was happy, no, no, no
> Their pretty little town was full of rats!
> In everything they ate big holes
> And drank their soup from the big soup bowls
> And even made their nests in people's hats!

For a long time she sat beside him on the floor, watching him as he lay there with his eyes open. What a pure marvel he seemed, his hair black and flowing, facial hair thickening and the hands still like baby hands except they were bigger than her own hands, and his thumbs though well-developed were slightly longer than normal thumbs. She felt dizzy. She was confused. She had to eat.

He ordered food for her, and watched her eat. He told her she must eat regularly from now on and then he knelt down before her chair, between her legs, and tore open the silk of her blouse and squeezed her breast so the milk came as out of a fountain into his mouth.

At other medical establishments, she managed to breach the X-ray department, and twice to run a complete brain scan on him, ordering everyone else out of the laboratory. But there were machines she couldn't use and those she didn't know how to. Then she became bolder. She gave orders to people, and they helped her. She was masquerading as herself: 'Dr Rowan Mayfair, neurosurgeon.' Among strangers she took over as though she were a visiting specialist and her needs took priority.

She picked up charts and pencils and phones when she needed them. She was single-minded. Record, test, discover. She studied the X rays of his skull, his hands.

She measured his head, and felt that soft skin again in the very middle of his skull – the fontanel – bigger than that of an infant. Lord God, she could put her fist through that skin, couldn't she?

Sometime in those first few days, he began to have some consistent success with his writing. Especially if he used a fine-pointed pen that nevertheless glided easily. He made a family tree of all the Mayfairs. He scribbled and scribbled. He included in it all sorts of Mayfairs whom she did not know, tracing lines from Jeanne Louise and Pierre of which she'd been unaware, and over and over again, he asked her to tell him what she had read in the Talamasca files. At eight in the morning, his handwriting had been round and childish and slow. By night, it was long, slanted, and at such a speed that she could not actually follow the formation of a letter with her eyes. He also began the strange singing – the humming, the insectile sound.

He wanted her to sing again and again. She sang lots of songs to him, until she was too sleepy to think.

> Along came a fellow slim and tall,
> And said to the man at city hall,
> My dear, I think I have a cure.
> I'll rid your town of every rat
> But you have to pay me well for that,
> And the mayor jumped up and down and cried,
> Why sure.

But more and more, he seemed baffled. He did not remember the rhymes she'd sung to him only days ago. No, no, say it again:

> The man in the wilderness asked of me,
> How many strawberries grew in the sea?
> I answered him, as I thought good,
> As many as red herrings grew in the wood.

She herself was becoming increasingly exhausted. She'd lost weight. The mere sight of herself in a lobby mirror alarmed her.

'I have to find a quiet place, a laboratory, a place where we can work,' she said. 'God help me. I'm tired, I'm seeing things.' In moments of pure fatigue, a dread gripped her. Where was she? What was going to happen to her? He dominated her waking thoughts, and then she sank back into herself and thought, I am lost, I am like a person on a drug trip, an obsession. But she had to study him, see what he was, and in the midst of her worst doubts she realized she was passionately possessive of him, protective, and drawn to him.

What would they do to him if they got hold of him? He had already committed crimes. He had stolen, perhaps he had killed for the passports. She didn't know. She couldn't think straight. Just a quiet place, a laboratory, what if they could go secretly back to San Francisco. If she could get in touch with Mitch Flanagan. But you couldn't simply call the Keplinger Institute.

Their lovemaking had tapered off somewhat. He still drank the milk from her breasts, though less and less often. He discovered the churches of Paris. He became perplexed, hostile, deeply agitated in these churches. He walked up to the stained-glass windows and reached up for them. He stared with hatred and loathing at the statues of the saints, at the tabernacle.

He said it was not the right cathedral.

'Well, if you mean the cathedral in Donnelaith, of course not. We're in Paris.'

He turned on her and in a sharp whisper told her, 'They burnt it.' He wanted to hear a Catholic Mass. He dragged her out of bed before dawn and down to the Church of the Madeleine so that he would witness this ceremony.

It was cold in Paris. She could not complete a thought without his interrupting her. It seemed at times she lost all track of day and night; he'd wake her up, suckling or making love, roughly, yet thrillingly, and then she'd doze again, and he'd wake her to give her food, talking on and on about something he'd seen on the television, on the news, or some other item or thing that he had noticed. It was random and more and more fragmented.

He picked up the hotel menu off the table and sang all the names of the dishes. Then he went back to writing furiously.

'And then Julien brought Evelyn to his house and there conceived Laura Lee, who gave birth to Alicia and Gifford. And from Julien also the illegitimate child, Michael O'Brien, born to the girl in St Margaret's orphanage, who gave it up and went into the convent to become Sister Bridget Marie, and then from that girl, three boys and one girl, and that girl married Alaister Curry, who gave birth to Tim Curry, who . . .'

'Wait a minute, what are you writing?'

'Leave me alone.' Suddenly he stared at it. He tore the paper in little pieces. 'Where are your notebooks, what have you written in them?' he demanded.

They were never too far from the room. She was too weak, too tired. And her breasts no sooner filled with milk than it began to spill under her blouse and he came to drink it. He cradled her in his arms. The swooning pleasure of his nursing from her was so great that nothing else mattered when it happened. All fear left her.

That was his trump card, she figured, the comfort, the pleasure, the high-pitched glamour and joy of just being with him, listening to his rapid, often incoherent speech, watching him react to things.

But what was he? She had lived with the illusion from the very first hour that somehow she had created him, that through her powerful telekinesis she had mutated her own child into him. Now she was beginning to see impossible contradictions. First off, she could remember no distinct scheme of elements being in her mind during that time when he was struggling on the floor to remain alive, the birth fluid all over both of them. She had given some sort of powerful psychic nourishment. She had even given colostrum, she remembered that now, the first spill from her breasts, and there had been a great deal of it.

But this thing, this creature, was highly organized –

338

no Frankenstein's monster, made of parts, no grotesque culmination of witchcraft. He knew his own properties too – that he could run very fast, that he caught scents she did not, that he gave off a scent which others caught without knowing it. That was true. Only now and then did the scent intrude on her, and when it did, she had the eerie feeling it had been engulfing her all along and even controlling her, rather like a pheromone.

More and more she kept her journal in narrative form, so that if something happened to her, if someone found it, that person could understand it.

'We've stayed long enough in Paris,' she said. 'They might come to find us.' Two bank wires had come in. They had a fortune at their disposal and it took her all afternoon, with him at her side, to assign the money to various accounts so they could hide it. She wanted to leave, perhaps only to be warmer.

'Come now, darling dear, we have only been in ten different hotels. Stop worrying, stop checking the locks, you know what it is, it's the serotonin in your brain, it's a fear-flight mechanism gone wrong. You're obsessive-compulsive, you always have been.'

'How do you know that?'

'I told you ... I ...' and then he stopped. He was beginning to be a little less confident, maybe ... 'I knew all that because once you knew. When I was spirit I knew what my witches knew. It was I ...?'

'What's the matter with you, what are you thinking?'

In the night he stood at the window and looked out at the light of Paris. He made love to her over and over, whether she was asleep or awake. His mustache had come in thick and finally soft, and his beard was now covering his entire chin.

339

But the soft spot in his skull was still there.

Indeed, his entire schedule of growth rates seemed programmed and different. She began to make comparisons to other species, listing his various characteristics. For example he possessed the strength of a lower primate in his arms, yet an enhanced ability with his fingers and thumbs. She would like to see what happened if he got access to a piano. His need for air was his great vulnerability. It was conceivable that he could be smothered. But he was so strong. So very strong. What would happen to him in water?

They left Paris for Berlin. He did not like the sound of the German language; it was not ugly to him, but 'pointed', he said, he couldn't shut out the sharp intrusive sounds. He wanted to get out of Germany.

That week she miscarried. Cramps like seizures, and blood all over the bathroom before she'd realized what was happening. He stared at the blood in utter puzzlement.

I have to rest, she said again. If only she could rest, some quiet place, where there was no singing and no poems and nothing, just peace. But she scraped up the tiny gelatinous mass at the core of her hemorrhage. An embryo at that stage of pregnancy would have been microscopic. There was something here, and it had limbs! It repulsed her and fascinated her. She insisted that they go to a laboratory where she could study it further.

She managed three hours there before people began to question them. She had made copious notes.

'There are two kinds of mutation,' she told him, 'those which can be passed on and those which cannot. This is not a singular occurrence, your birth, it's conceivable that you are . . . a species. But how could this be? How could this happen? How could one combination of telekinesis . . .' She broke off, resorting again to scientific terms. From the clinic she had stolen blood equipment and now she drew some of her own and properly sealed the vials.

He smiled at her in a grim way. 'You don't really love me,' he said coldly.

'Of course I do.'

'Can you love the truth more than mystery?'

'What is the truth?' She approached him, put her hands on his face and looked into his eyes. 'What do you remember way back, from the very beginning, from the time before humans came on the earth? You remember you talked of such things, of the world of the spirits and how the spirits had learned from humans. You spoke . . .'

'I don't remember anything,' he said blankly.

He sat at the table reading over what he had written. He stretched out his long legs, crossed his ankles, cradled his head on his wrists against the back of the chair and listened to his own tape recordings. His hair now reached his shoulders. He asked her questions as if testing her, 'Who was Mary Beth? Who was her mother?'

Over and over she recounted the family history as she knew it. She repeated the stories from the Talamasca files and random things she had heard from the others. She described – at his request – all the living Mayfairs she knew. He had begun to be quiet, listening to her, forcing her to speak, for hours.

This was agony.

'I am by nature quiet,' she said. 'I cannot . . . I cannot . . .'

'Who were Julien's brothers, name them and their children.'

At last, so exhausted she couldn't move, the cramps coming again as if she had been impregnated again and was in fact already aborting, she said, 'I can do this no longer.'

'Donnelaith,' he said. 'I want to go there.'

He'd been standing by the window, crying. 'You do love me, don't you? You aren't afraid of me?'

She thought a long time before she said, 'Yes, I do love you. You are all alone . . . and I love you. I do. But I'm frightened. This is frenzy. This is not organization and work. This is mania. I am afraid . . . of you.'

When he bent over her, she clasped his head in her hands and guided it to her nipple; then came the trance as he sucked up the milk. Would he never tire of it? Would he nurse forever? The thought made her laugh and laugh. He would be an infant forever – an infant who walks and talks and makes love.

'Yes, and sings, don't forget that!' he said when she told him.

He finally began to watch television in long unbroken periods. She could use the bathroom without his hovering about. She could bathe slowly. She did not bleed anymore. Oh, for the Keplinger Institute, she thought. Think of the things the Mayfair money could do, if only she dared. Surely they were looking for her, looking for them both.

She had gone about this all wrong! She should have hidden him in New Orleans and pretended that he had never been there! Blundering, mad, but she hadn't been able to think on that day, that awful Christmas morning! God, an eternity had come and gone since then!

He was glaring at her. He looked vicious and afraid.

'What's the matter with you?' he said.

'Tell their names,' she said.

'No, you tell me . . .'

He picked up one of the pages he'd so carefully written out, in narrow cluttered scrawl, and then he laid it down. 'How long have we been here?'

'Don't you know?'

He wept for a while. She slept, and when she awoke, he was composed and dressed. The bags were packed. He told her they were going to England.

They drove north from London to Donnelaith. She drove most of the time, but then he learned, and was able on the lonely stretches of country road to manage the vehicle acceptably. They had all their possessions in the car. She felt safer here than in Paris.

'But why? Won't they look for us here?' he asked.

'I don't know. I don't know that they expect us to go to Scotland. I don't know that they expect you to remember things . . .'

He laughed bitterly. 'Well, sometimes I don't.'

'What do you remember now?'

He looked hateful and solemn. His beard and the mustache were ominous on his face. Signs of obvious sexual maturity. The miscarriage. The fontanel. This was the mature animal, or was it merely adolescent?

Donnelaith.

It wasn't a town at all. It was no more than the inn, and the nearby headquarters of the archaeological project, where a small contingent of archaeological students slept and ate. Tours were offered of the ruined castle above the loch, and of the ruined town down in

343

the glen, with its Cathedral – which could not be seen from the inn – and farther out the ancient primal circle of stones, which was quite a walk but worth it. But you could go only in the designated areas. If you roamed alone, you must obey all signs. The tours would be tomorrow in the morning.

It chilled her to look down from the window of the inn and actually see it in the dim distorting distance, the place where it had all begun, where Suzanne, the cunning woman of the village, had called up a spirit named Lasher and that spirit had attached itself forever to Suzanne's female descendants. It chilled her. And the great awesome glen was gray and melancholy and softly beautiful, beautiful as damp and green and northern places can be, like the remote high counties of Northern California. The twilight was coming, thick and shining in the damp gloom, and the entire world below appeared mysterious, something of fairy tales.

It was possible to see any car approaching the town, from any direction. There was only one road, and you could see for miles north and south. And the majority of the tourists came from nearby cities and in busloads.

Only a few die-hards stayed at the inn, a girl from America writing a paper on the lost cathedrals of Scotland. An old gentleman, researching his clan in these remote parts, convinced that it led back to Robert the Bruce. A young couple in love who cared about no one.

And Lasher and Rowan. At supper he tried some of the hard food. He hated it. He wanted to nurse. He stared at her hungrily.

They had the best and most spacious room, very prim and proper with a ruffled bed beneath the low white-painted beams, a thick carpet and a little fire to take

344

away the chill, and a sweeping view of the glen below them. He told the innkeeper they must not have a phone in the room, they must have privacy, and what meals he wanted prepared for them and when, and then he took her wrist in his terrible, painful grip and said, 'We are going out into the valley.'

He pulled her down the stairs into the front room of the inn. The couple sat glowering at them from a small distant table.

'It's dark,' she said. She was tired from the drive and faintly sick again. 'Why don't we wait until morning?'

'No,' he said. 'Put on your walking shoes.' He turned and bent down and started to pull off her shoes. People were staring at him. It occurred to her that it wasn't at all unusual for him to behave like this. It was typical. He had a madman's judgment; a madman's naïveté.

'I'll do it,' she said. They went back upstairs. He watched as she dressed for the cold outdoors. She came out fit for a long night of exploration, walking shoes laced over wool socks.

It seemed they walked an endless time down the slope and then along the banks of the loch.

The half-moon illuminated the jagged and broken walls of the castle.

The cliffs were perilous, but there were well-worn paths. He climbed the path, pulling her along with him. The archaeologists had set up barriers, signs, warnings, but there was no one around. They went where they chose to go. New wooden staircases had been built in the high half-ruined towers, and down into dungeons. He crept ahead of her, very surefooted, and almost frenzied.

It occurred to her that this might be the best time for

escape. That if she only had the nerve she could push him off the top of one of these fragile staircases, and down he would go and splat, he'd have to suffer like any human! His bones weren't brittle, they were mostly cartilage still, but he would die, surely he would. Even as she considered it, she began to cry. She felt she could not do it. She could not dispatch him like that. Kill him? She couldn't do it.

It was a cowardly and rash thing to imagine, far more rash than leaving with him had been. But that had been rash also. She realized it now. She was mad to think she could manage or control or study him on her own; what a fool, what a fool, what a fool. To leave that house alone with this wild and domineering demon, to be so obsessed in pride and hubris with her own creation!

But would he have let it happen any other way? When she looked back on it, had he not rushed her, had he not pushed her, had he not said Hurry to her countless times? What did he fear? Michael, yes, Michael had been something to fear.

But it was my error. I could have contained the whole situation! I could have had this thing under control.

And in the pool of moonlight falling on the grassy floor of the castle's gutted main hall, she found it easier to blame herself, to castigate herself, to hate herself, than to hurt him.

It was doubtful she could have done it anyway. The one time she accelerated her step behind him on the stairs, he turned and grabbed hold of her and put her up in front of him. He was ever vigilant. He could lift her effortlessly with one of his long gibbonlike arms, and deposit her on her feet wherever he wished. He had no fear of falling.

But something in the castle made him afraid.

He was trembling and crying as they left the castle. He said he wanted to see the Cathedral. The moon had drifted behind the clouds, but the glen was still washed in an even pale light, and he knew the way, ignoring the preordained path and cutting down through the slopes from the base of the castle.

At last they came to the town itself, to the excavated foundations of its walls, its battlements, its gates, its little main street, all roped off and marked, and there, there loomed the immense ruin of the Cathedral, dwarfing every other structure, with its four standing walls and their broken arches reaching like arms to enclose the lowering heavens.

He went down on his knees in the grass, staring into the long roofless nave. One could see half the circle of what had once been the lofty rose window. But no glass survived among these stones, many of which had been newly put in place and plastered to re-create walls that apparently had tumbled down. Great quarries of stones lay to the left and to the right, obviously brought from other places to reassemble the building.

He rose, grabbed her and dragged her with him, past the barrier and the signs, until they stood in the church itself, gazing up and up past the arches on either side, at the cloudy sky and the moon giving just a teasing light through the clouds that had no shape to it. The Cathedral had been Gothic, vast, overreaching perhaps for such a place, unless in those times there had been hordes of the faithful.

He was trembling all over. He had his hands to his lips, and then he began to give off that humming, that singing, and rock on his feet.

He walked doggedly, against his own mood, along the wall and then pointed up at one high narrow empty window. 'There, there!' he cried. And it seemed he spoke other words, or tried to and was then weary and agitated again. He sank down, drawing up his knees, and hugged her close to him, his head on her shoulder, and then nuzzling down onto her breasts. Rudely he pushed up the sweater and began to suckle. She lay back, all will leaving her. Staring up at the clouds. Begging for stars but there were no stars, only the dissolving light of the moon, and the lovely illusion that it was not the clouds which moved but the high walls and the empty arched windows.

In the morning, when she awoke, he was not in the room! But neither was there a phone anymore, and when she opened the window, she saw it was a straight drop some twenty feet or more to the grass below. And what would she do if she did manage to get down there? He had the keys to the car. He always carried them. Would she run to others for help, explain she was being kept prisoner? Then what would he do?

She could think it through, all the possibilities. They went round like horses on a carousel in her mind until she gave up.

She washed, dressed, and wrote in her diary. Once again, she listed all the little things she had observed: that his skin was maturing, that his jaw was now firm, but not the top of his head, but mostly she recounted what had happened since they had come to Donnelaith, his curious reactions to the ruins.

In the great room of the inn downstairs, she found him at the table with the old innkeeper in fast conversation. The man stood for her, respectfully, and pulled out her chair.

'Sit down,' Lasher said to her. Her breakfast was being prepared now, he had heard her tread above when she stepped out of bed.

'I'm sure,' she said grimly.

'Go on,' he said to the old man.

The old man was champing at the bit and picked up apparently where he'd left off, that the archaeological project had been funded for ninety years, through both wars, by American money. Some family in the States interested in the Clan of Donnelaith.

But only in recent years had real progress been made. When they'd realized the Cathedral dated back to 1228, they'd asked the family in the States for more money. To their amazement the old trust was beefed up, and a whole gang from Edinburgh was now here, had been for twenty years, gathering stones that had been scattered and finding the entire foundations of not only the church itself but a monastery and an older village, possibly from the 700s. The time of the Venerable Bede, he explained, some sort of cult place. He didn't know the details.

'We always knew there was Donnelaith, you see,' said the old man. 'But the Earls had died out in the great fire of 1689, and after that there wasn't much of a town at all, and by the turn of the century nothing. When the archaeological project began, my father came to build this inn. Nice gentleman from the United States leased him this property.'

'Who was this?' he asked in utter bafflement.

'Julien Mayfair, it's the Julien Mayfair Trust,' said the old man. 'But you really ought to talk to the young chaps from the project. They are a well-behaved and serious lot, these students, they stop the tourists from picking up stones and whatnot and wandering off with them.

'And speaking of stones, there is the old circle, you know, and for a long time that was the place where they did most of their work. They say it's as old as Stonehenge, but the Cathedral is the real discovery. Talk to the chaps.'

'Julien Mayfair,' he repeated, staring at the old man. He looked helpless, bewildered, on guard. And as if the words meant nothing. 'Julien . . .'

By afternoon, they had wined and dined several of the students, and the entire picture emerged, as well as packets of old pamphlets printed from time to time to sell to the public to raise money.

The present Mayfair Trust was handled out of New York, and the founding family was most generous.

The eldest on the project, a blond Englishwoman, with bobbed hair and a cheerful face, rather chunky in her tweed coat and leather boots, didn't mind at all answering their questions. She'd been working here since 1970. She'd applied twice for more funds and found the family entirely cooperative.

Yes, one of the family had come to visit once. A Lauren Mayfair, rather stiff. 'You would have never known she was American.' The old woman thought that was hilarious. 'But she didn't care for it here, you know. She took some pictures from the family and was off at once to London. I remember her saying she was going on to Rome. She loved Italy. I don't suppose most people love both climes – the damp Highlands and sunny Italy.'

'Italy,' he whispered. 'Sunny Italy.' His eyes were filling with tears. Hastily he wiped them on his napkin.

The woman had never noticed. She was talking on and on.

'But what do you know about the Cathedral?' he asked. For the first time in all his brief life, as Rowan had known it, he looked tired to her. He looked almost frail. He'd wiped his eyes several times more with a handkerchief, saying it was an 'allergy' and not tears, but she could see he was cracking.

'That's just it, we've been wrong about it before, we don't put forth many theories. Definitely the grand Gothic structure was built around 1228, same time as Elgin, but it incorporated an earlier church, one possibly which contained stained-glass windows. And the monastery was Cistercian, at least for a while. Then it became Franciscan.'

He was staring at her.

'There seems to have been a cathedral school, perhaps even a library. Oh, God only knows what we are going to find. Yesterday we found a new graveyard. You have to realize people have been carrying off stones from this place for centuries. We've only just unearthed the ruins of the thirteenth-century south transept and a chapel we didn't know was there, containing a burial chamber. This definitely involves a saint, but we cannot identify him. His effigy is carved on top of the tomb. We're debating. Dare we open it? Dare we seek to find something in there?'

He said nothing. The stillness around them was suddenly unnerving; Rowan was afraid he would cry out, do something utterly wild, draw attention to them. She tried to remind herself that it would be perfectly fine if this happened. She felt sleepy, heavy with milk. The old woman talked on and on about the castle, about the warring of the clans in these parts, the endless battles and slaughter.

'What destroyed the Cathedral?' Rowan asked. The lack of chronology was disturbing to her. She wanted a chart in her mind.

He glared at her angrily, as if she'd no right to speak.

'I'm not sure,' said the old woman. 'But I have a hunch. There was some sort of clan war.'

'Wrong,' he said softly. 'Look deeper. It was the Protestants, the iconoclasts.'

She clapped her hands almost with glee. 'Oh, you must tell me what makes you think so.' She went on a tirade about the Protestant Reformation in Scotland, the burning of witches that had gone on for a century or more right to the very end of the history of Donnelaith, cruel cruel burnings.

He sat dazed.

'I'll bet you're absolutely right. It was John Knox and his reformers! Donnelaith had remained, right up to the bloody fire, a powerful Catholic stronghold. Not even wicked Henry the Eighth could suppress Donnelaith.'

The woman was now repeating herself, and going on at length about how she hated the political and religious forces which destroyed art and buildings. 'All of that magnificent stained glass, imagine!'

'Yes, beautiful glass.'

But he had received all she had to give.

As evening fell they went out again. He had been silent, not hungry, not disposed for love, and not letting her out of his sight. He walked ahead of her, all the way across the grassy plain until they came again to the Cathedral. Much of the excavations of the south transept was sheltered by a great makeshift wooden roof, and locked doors. He broke the glass on a window, and unlocked a door and went inside. They were standing in the ruins of a chapel. The students had been rebuilding the wall. Much earth had been dug away from one central tomb, with the figure of a man carved on the top of it – almost ghostly now that it was so worn away. He stood staring down at it, and then up at what they had restored of the windows. In a rage he began to beat on the wooden walls.

'Stop, they'll come,' she cried. But then she lapsed back, thinking, Let them come. Let them put him in jail for a madman. He saw the cunning in her eyes, the hate which for a moment she could not disguise.

When they got back to the inn, he started listening to his own tapes, then turning them off, rummaging through his pages. 'Julien, Julien, Julien Mayfair,' he said.

'You don't remember him, do you?'

'What?'

'You don't remember any of it – who Julien was or Mary Beth or Deborah, or Suzanne. You've been forgetting all along. Do you remember Suzanne?'

He stared at her, blanched and in a silent fury.

'You don't remember,' she taunted again. 'You started to forget in Paris. Now you don't know who they *were*.'

He approached her, and sank down on his knees in front of her. He seemed wildly excited, the rage going into some rampant and acceptable enthusiasm.

'I don't know who *they* were,' he said. 'I'm not too sure who *you* are! But *I know now who I am!*'

*

Past midnight, he'd wakened her in the act of rape, and when it was done, he wanted to go, to get away before anyone came to look for them. 'These Mayfairs, they must be very clever people.'

She laughed bitterly.

'And what sort of monster are you?' she asked. 'You're nothing I made. I know that now. I'm not Mary Shelley!'

He stopped the car and dragged her out into the high grass and struck her again and again. He struck her so hard he almost broke the bones of her jaw. She shouted a warning to him, that the damage would be irreparable. He stopped his blows and stood over her with his fists clenched.

'I love you,' he said, crying, 'and I hate you.'

'I know just what you mean,' she answered dully. There was so much pain in her face she thought perhaps he had broken her nose and her jaw. But it wasn't so. Finally she sat up.

He had flopped down beside her, all knees and elbows, and with his large warm hands began to caress her. In pure confusion, she sobbed against his chest.

'Oh, my God, my God, what shall we do?' she asked. He was stroking her, covering her with kisses, suckling her again, all of his old tricks, his evil tricks, the Devil slipping into the cell of the nun, get away from me! But she didn't have the courage to do anything. Or was it the physical strength she lacked? It had been so long since she had felt normal, healthy, vital.

The next time he became angry, it was when they'd stopped for gas and she'd wandered near the phone booth. He caught her, and she began to say very fast an old rhyme that her mother had taught her:

Alas! Alas! for Miss Mackay!
Her knives and forks have run away;
And when the cups and spoons are going,
She's sure there is no way of knowing!

Just as she hoped, it made him weak with laughter. He actually fell to his knees. Such big feet he had. She stood there over him chanting:

Tom, Tom, the piper's son,
Stole a pig and away he run,
The pig was eat, and Tom was beat
And Tom went crying down the street.

He begged her to stop, half laughing, half crying. 'I have one for you,' he cried, and he leapt up and sang as he danced, slamming his feet on the ground, and slapping his thighs:

The sow came in with the saddle.
The little pig rocked the cradle.
The dish jumped over the table
To see the pot swallow the ladle.
The spit that stood behind the door
Threw the pudding-stick on the floor.
'Odsplut!' said the gridiron,
'Can't you agree?
I'm the head constable,
Bring them to me!'

And then he grabbed her roughly, teeth clenched, and dragged her back to the car.

When they reached London, her face was entirely swollen. Anyone who caught a glimpse of her was alarmed. He put them up in a fine hotel, though where it was she had no idea, and he fed her hot tea and sweets and sang to her.

He said that he was sorry for all he'd done, that he had been reborn, did she not realize this, what it meant? That in him resided a miracle. Then came the predictable kissing and suckling and a coarse rough-and-tumble sex that was as good as any. This time, out of sheer desperation, she pushed him to do it again. Maybe she did this because it was the only way she could exert her will. She discovered that after the fourth time even he was spent, and he lay sleeping. She didn't dare move. When she sighed, he opened his eyes.

He was now truly beautiful. The mustache and beard were of biblical length and shape and each morning he clipped them appropriately. His hair was very long. His shoulders were too big but it didn't matter. His entire appearance was regal, majestic. Are those words for the same thing? He bowed to people when he spoke, he tipped his soft shapeless gray hat. People loved to look at him.

They went to Westminster Abbey and he walked through the entire place studying every detail of it. He watched the faithful moving about. He said at last: 'I have only one simple mission. Old as the earth itself.'

'What is that?' she asked.

He did not answer her.

When they reached the hotel he said:

'I want your study to begin in earnest. We shall get a secure place . . . not here in Europe . . . in the States, so close to them that they won't suspect. We need everything. Cost must be no obstacle. We will not go to Zurich! They'll be looking for you there. Can you arrange for large amounts of money?'

'I already have,' she reminded him. It was clear from this and other remarks that he did not remember simple things well in sequence. 'The bank trail is well laid. We can go back to the States if you wish.'

In fact, her heart silently leapt at the thought of it.

'There is a neurological institute in Geneva,' she said. 'That's where we should go. It's famous worldwide. It's vast. We can do some work there. And complete all the arrangements directly with the Swiss Bank. And we can plan there. It's best, believe me.'

'Yes,' he said. 'And from there, we must return to the States. They are going to be looking for you. And for me. We must return. I am thinking of the place.'

She fell asleep, dreaming only of the lab, the slides, the tests, the microscope, of knowledge as though it were exorcism. She knew of course she could not do it on her own. The best she could do was get computer equipment and record her findings. She needed a city full of laboratories, a city where hospitals grew as if on trees, where she could go to one large center and then another . . .

He sat at the table reading the Mayfair History over and over. His lips moved so fast, it was the humming again. He laughed at things in the history as if they were entirely new to him. He knelt by her and looked into her face.

He said, 'The milk's drying up, isn't it?'

'I don't know. There is so much aching.'

He began to kiss her. He took some milk between his fingers and put it on her lips; she sighed. She said it tasted like water.

In Geneva, everything was planned, down to the last detail.

The most obvious choice for their final destination was the city of Houston, Texas. Reason? There were, very simply, hospitals and medical centers everywhere. Every form of medical research went on in Houston. She would find a building perhaps for them, some medical space now vacant due to the oil depression. Houston was overbuilt. It had three downtowns, they said. No one could find them there.

Money was no obstacle. Her large transfers were safe in the giant Swiss Bank. She had only to set up some sort of dummy accounts in California and in Houston.

She lay in bed, his fingers tight around her wrist, thinking Houston, Texas, only one hour by air from home. 'Only one hour.'

'Yes, they'll never guess,' he said. 'You might as well have taken us to the South Pole, you couldn't have thought of a more clever hiding place.'

Her heart sank. She slept. She was sick. When she woke she was bleeding. Miscarriage again, this time the viscid core was perhaps two inches long, maybe even longer, before it had begun to disintegrate.

In the morning after she had rested, she took a stand. She was going to the institute, to test this thing, and to run what tests she could on him. She screamed and screamed. And finally in terror, and misery, he consented.

'You're frightened to be without me, aren't you?' she asked.

'What if you were the last man on earth?' he asked. 'And I were the last woman?'

She didn't know what that meant. But he seemed to know. He took her to the institute. All the normal motions of life were now nothing to him – hailing cabs,

358

tipping, reading, walking, running, going up in an elevator. He had bought himself a cheap little wooden flute in a store, and he played it on the street, very dissatisfied with it, and with his own ability to make melodies with it. He didn't dare buy a radio. It would get its hands around his throat.

Again, at the institute, she managed a white coat, a chart, a pencil, the things she needed, forms from a raft of desktop pockets, yellow, pink, blue slips for various tests, and began to fill out the bogus orders.

She was at one minute his doctor, at another the technician, and whenever questioned, he rattled away like a celebrity in hiding.

In the midst of it all, she managed to fill out a long note on one of the triplicate forms, addressed to the concierge at the hotel, instructing him to arrange for a medical shipment. The address Samuel Larkin, MD, University Hospital, San Francisco, California. She would make available the material as soon as she could. The concierge was to charge her account for overnight delivery, heat-sensitive medical material.

When they returned to the hotel room, she picked up a lamp and struck him. He reeled and then fell down, blood spattering from his face, into his eyes, but he came back, that wonderfully plastic skin and bones, like an infant surviving a fall from a ridiculously high window. He grabbed her and beat her again, until she lost consciousness.

In the night she woke. Her face was swollen, but the bones were not broken. One of her eyes was almost shut. That would mean days in this room. Days. She did not know if she could endure it.

The next morning he tied her to the bed for the first

time. He used bits and pieces of sheet and made powerful knots, and had it half done when she awoke and discovered the gag in her mouth. He was gone for hours. No one came to the room. Surely some warning or instructions had been issued. She kicked, screamed, to no avail. She could not make a sound that was loud enough.

When he returned, he took the phone out of hiding and ordered a feast for her and once again begged her forgiveness. He played his small flute.

As she ate, he watched her every move. His eyes were thoughtful, speculating.

The next day she did not fight when he tied her up, and this time it was with the masking tape he'd brought back the day before, and quite impossible to break. He was going to tape her mouth when she advised him calmly that she might smother. He settled on a less painful and efficient gag. She went mad struggling after he left. It did no good. Nothing did any good. The milk leaked from her breasts. She was sick, and the room spun.

The following afternoon, after they had made love, he lay on top of her, heavy, sweet, his soft black hair between her breasts, his left hand on her right hand, dreaming, humming. She was not tied. He had cut the tape cuffs and let them dangle. He would make new ones when he wanted them.

She looked at the top of his head, at the shining black mane, she breathed in the scent of him, and pressed her body against his weight, and then lapsed back half into sleep for an hour.

Still he had not waked up. He was breathing deeply.

She reached over with her left hand and picked up

the phone. Nothing else in her stirred. She managed to hold the earpiece and punch the button for the desk, and she spoke so low they could barely hear her.

It was night in California. Lark listened to what she had to say. Lark had been her boss. Lark was her friend. Lark was the only person who might believe her, the only person who would vow to take these specimens to Keplinger. Whatever happened to her, these specimens had to be taken to Keplinger. Mitch Flanagan was the man there she trusted, though he might not remember her.

Somebody had to know.

Lark tried to ask her all sorts of questions. He could not hear her, he said, speak up. She told him she was in danger. And might be interrupted at any moment. She wanted to blurt out the name of the hotel, but she was divided. If he came to look for her while she was still helpless, possibly she could not get the specimens out of here. Her mind was overwrought. She couldn't reason. She was babbling something to Lark about the miscarriages. Then Lasher looked up, snatched the phone from her hand, ripped the entire apparatus out of the wall and started to hit her.

He stopped because she reminded him that the marks would show. They had to go to America. They should leave tomorrow. And when he tied her up she wanted him to make everything looser. If he kept tying her up so tight she would lose the use of her limbs. There was an art to keeping a prisoner.

He wept in a dry quiet way. 'I love you,' he said. 'If only I could trust you. If only you could be my helpmate, if you give me your love and trust. But I made you what you are, a calculating witch. You look at me and you try to kill me.'

'You're right,' she said. 'But we should go to America now, unless you want them to find us.'

She thought if she did not get out of this room she would go completely mad and be useless. She tried to make a plan. Cross the sea, get closer to home. Get closer. Houston is closer.

A dull hopelessness covered everything. She knew now what she had to do. She had to die before she conceived by this being again. She could not give birth to another, could not. But he was breeding with her; he had impregnated her twice already. Her mind went blank with fear. For the first time in her life, she understood why some human beings cannot act when they are frightened, why some freeze and stare in a meek fashion.

What had become of her notes?

In the morning, they packed the suitcases together. Everything medical was in one bag, and in this she placed the copies of all the various tags and slips she had used to order various information at the clinics. She placed on top the written instructions for the concierge which included Lark's address. He did not seem to notice.

She had taken considerable amounts of packing from the lab, but now she shoved towels in around the material. She shoved in her old bloodstained clothes.

'Why don't you throw that away?' he demanded, 'that horrid smell.'

'I don't smell anything,' she said coldly. 'And I need the packing, I told you. But I can't find my notebooks. I had all these notebooks.'

'Yes, I read them,' he said quietly. '*I threw them away*.'

She stared at him.

No record now but these specimens. No communication to anyone that this thing lived and breathed and wanted to breed.

At the doors of the hotel, as he arranged for the car to take them to the airport, she gave the bag of medical specimens to the doorman, with a bundle of Swiss francs, and said in German hurriedly that the bag must go at once to Dr Samuel Larkin. Turning her back on the man immediately, she walked towards the waiting car as Lasher turned and smiled at her and put out his hand.

'My wife, how tired she looks,' he said softly with a little smile. 'How sick she has been.'

'Yes, very,' she said, wondering what the bellhop saw when he looked at her, her bruised and thin face.

'Let me hold you, darling dear.' He put his arms around her in the backseat. He kissed her as they drove away. She did not bother to look to see if the doorman had gone inside with the medical bag. She did not dare. The concierge would find the address inside. He had to.

When they reached New York, he realized the medical bag and all the test results were gone. He threatened to kill her.

She lay on the bed, refusing to speak. He tied her up gently, carefully, giving her room to move her limbs but not to get free, the twined tape making the strongest rope in the world. He covered her carefully so she wouldn't be cold. He turned on the fan vent in the bathroom and then the television at a high but not unreasonable volume, and went out.

It was a full twenty-four hours before he returned. She had been unable to hold the urine. She hated him.

She wished for his death. She wished she knew charms with which to kill him.

He sat by her as she made all the arrangements in Houston – yes, two floors in a fifty-story building where they would have complete privacy. It was small in Houston terms, such a complex as this, and right downtown, and Houston had quite a few empty ones. This had been the headquarters of a cancer research program until it had gone broke. There were presently no other tenants.

All kinds of equipment was still on these three floors. It had all been repossessed by the owners of the property. But they could warrant nothing about it. Fine with her. She leased the entire space, complete with living quarters, offices, reception rooms, examining rooms, and laboratories. She arranged for utilities, rental cars, everything they would need to begin their serious study.

His eyes were very cold as he watched her. He watched her fingers when she pressed the buttons. He listened to every syllable that passed her lips.

'This city is very near to New Orleans,' she said, 'you realize that.' She did not want him to discover it later and rail at her. Her wrists ached from his dragging her about. She was hungry.

'Oh yes, the Mayfairs,' he said, gesturing to the printed history, which lay in its folder. Not a day passed that he did not study this or his notes or his tapes. 'But they would never think to look for you only one hour away by air, would they?'

'No,' she said. 'If you hurt Michael Curry, I will take my own life. I will not be of further use to you.'

'I'm not sure you're of use to me now,' he said. 'The

364

world is filled with more amiable and agreeable people than you, people who sing better.'

'So why don't you kill me?' she said. As he reflected, she did her level best with every invisible power at her command to kill him. It was useless.

She wanted now to die, or to sleep forever. Possibly they were the same thing.

'I thought you were something immense, something innocent,' she said. 'Something wholly unknown and new.'

'I know you did!' he answered sharply, infuriated, and dangerous, blue eyes flashing.

'I don't think you are now.'

'Your job is to find out what I am.'

'I'm trying,' she said.

'You know you find me beautiful.'

'So what?' she said. 'I hate you.'

'Yes, it was plain in your notebooks, "this new species", "this creature", "this being" – how clinically you spoke of me, and you know? You are wrong. I am not new, my darling dear, I am old, older by far than you can imagine. But my time is coming again. I could not have chosen a better moment for my childlike loving progeny. Don't you want to know what I am?'

'You're monstrous, you're unnatural, you're cruel and impulsive. You cannot think straight or concentrate. You're mad.'

He was so angry that he couldn't answer her for a moment. He wanted to hit her. She could see his hand opening and closing.

'Imagine,' he said, 'if all mankind died out, my darling dear, and all the genes for mankind rode in the blood of one miserable apelike creature, and he passed it down and down, and finally, to the apes was born again a man!'

She said nothing.

'Do you think that man would be very merciful to the lower apes? Especially if he secured a mate? An ape woman who could breed with him to form a new dynasty of superior beings –'

'You're not superior to us,' she said coldly.

'The hell I'm not!' he said wrathfully.

'I don't know for sure how it happened, but I know it will never happen again.'

He shook his head, smiling at her. 'What a fool you are. What an egotist. You make me think of all the scientists whose words I read now and listen to on the television. It's happened before, and before and before ... and this time is the right time, this time is the moment, this time there shall be no sacrifice, this time we will strive as never in the past!'

'I'll die before I help you.'

He shook his head wanly. He looked away. He seemed to be dreaming. 'Do you think we will be merciful when we rule? Has any superior being ever been merciful to the weaker? Were the Spaniards when they came to the New World merciful to the savages they found there? No, it's never happened in history, has it, that the higher species, the species with the advantages, has been kind to those who were lower. On the contrary, the higher species wipes out the lower. Isn't that so? It's your world, tell me about it! As if I didn't know.'

The tears rose in his eyes. He laid his head on his arm and wept, and when he finished, he dried his eyes with a towel from the bath. 'Oh, what might have been between us!'

'What's that?' she asked.

He started to kiss her again, to stroke her, and to open his clothes.

'Stop this. I've miscarried twice. I'm sick. Look at me. Look at my face and my hands. Look at my arms. A third miscarriage will kill me, don't you realize it? I'm dying now. You're killing me. Where will you turn when I'm gone? Who will help you? Who knows about you?'

He mused. Then, suddenly, he slapped her. He hesitated, but it seemed to have satisfied him. She was staring at him.

He laid her on the bed, and he began stroking her hair. There was very little milk now. He drank it. He massaged her shoulders and her arms, and her feet. He kissed her all over. She lost consciousness. When she came round, it was late at night, and her thighs were sore and wet from him, and from her own desire.

When they reached Houston, she realized she had arranged for a prison. The building was deserted. And she had leased two floors very high up. He indulged her for two days, as they acquired various things for their comfort in this high fairy-tale tower amid the neon and sparkling lights. She watched, she waited, she struggled to seize the slightest opportunity, but he was too wakeful, too fast.

And then he tied her up. There was to be no study, no project. 'I know what I need to know.'

The first time he left it was for a day. The second time for an entire night and most of the morning. The third time had been this time – four days perhaps.

And now look what he had done to this cold modern bedroom of white walls and glass windows, and laminated furniture.

*

367

Her legs hurt so much. She limped out of the bathroom and into the bedroom. He had cleaned up the bed; it was draped in rose-colored sheets, and he had surrounded it with flowers. This brought a strange image to her mind, of a woman who had committed suicide in California. She had ordered lots of flowers for herself first, then put them all around the bed, and taken poison. Or was she simply remembering Deirdre's funeral, with all those flowers and the woman in the coffin like a big doll?

This looked like a place to die. Flowers in big bouquets, and in vases everywhere she looked. And if she died, perhaps he'd blunder. He was so foolish. She had to be calm. She had to think, to live and be clever.

'Such lilies. Such roses. Did you bring them up yourself?' she asked.

He shook his head. 'They were all delivered and outside the door before I ever put the key in the lock.'

'You thought you'd find me dead in here, didn't you?'

'I'm not that sentimental, except when it comes to music,' he said with a bright smile. 'The food is in the other room. I'll bring it to you. What can I do to make you love me? Is there something I can tell you? Is there any news that will bring you to your senses?'

'I hate you totally and completely,' she said. She sat down on the bed, because there were no chairs in the room, and she could not stand any longer. Her ankles ached. Her arms ached. She was starving. 'Why do you keep me alive?'

He went out and came back with a large tray full of delicatessen salads, packs of cold meat, portable processed garbage.

She ate it ravenously. Then she shoved the tray away. There was a quart of orange juice there and she drank all of it. She rose and staggered into the bathroom, nearly falling. She remained in that small room for a long time, crouched on the toilet, her head against the wall. She feared she would vomit. Slowly she made an inventory of the room. There was nothing with which to kill herself.

She wasn't going to try it yet anyway. She had fight in her, plenty of it. If necessary, the two of them would go up in flames. That she could arrange surely. But how?

Wearily, she opened the door. He was there, with arms folded. He picked her up and carried her to the bed. He had littered it with white daisies from one of the bouquets and when she sank down on the stiff stems and fragrant blossoms, she laughed. It felt so good she let herself go, laughing and laughing, until it rippled out of her just like a song.

He bent to kiss her.

'Don't do it again. If I miscarry again, I'll die. There are easier, quicker ways to kill me. You can't have a child by me, don't you understand? What makes you think you can have a child by anyone?'

'Ah, but you won't miscarry this time,' he said. He lay beside her. He placed his hand on her belly. He smiled. He uttered a string of rapid syllables in a hum, his mouth grotesque for one moment as he did it – it was a language!

'Yes, my darling, my love, the child's alive and the child can hear me. The child is female. The child is there.'

She screamed.

She turned her fury on the unborn thing, kill it, kill it, kill it, and then – as she lay back, drenched in sweat, stinking again, the taste of vomit in her mouth – she heard a sound that was like someone crying.

He made that strange humming song.

Then came the crying.

She shut her eyes, trying to break it down into something coherent.

She could not. But she could hear a new voice now and the new voice was inside her and it was speaking to her in a tongue she could understand, without words. It sought her love, her consolation.

I won't hurt you anymore, she thought. Without words, in gratitude and with love, it answered her.

Good God, it was alive, he was right. It was alive and it could hear her. It was in pain.

'It won't take very long,' he said. 'I'll care for you with all my heart. You are my Eve, yet you are sinless. And once it's born, then if you wish, you can die.'

She didn't answer him. Why should she? For the first time in two months, there was someone else there to talk to. She turned her head away.

THIRTEEN

Anne Marie Mayfair sat stiffly on the smooth beige plastic couch in the hospital lobby. Mona saw her as soon as she came in. Anne Marie wore her funeral suit, still, of navy blue, and her usual prim blouse with its score of ruffles. She was reading a magazine, her legs crossed, her black glasses down on her nose, and there was something cute about her as always, with her black hair drawn back in a twist, and her small nose and mouth, and the big glasses made her look both stupid and intelligent.

She looked up as Mona approached. Mona pecked her on the cheek and then flopped down beside her.

'Did Ryan call you?' asked Anne Marie, her voice hushed and private though there were very few other people moving in the brightly lighted lobby. Elevator doors opened and closed in an alcove far away. The reception desk with its high impersonal counter was empty.

'You mean about Mother?' Mona said. She hated this place. It occurred to her that when she was very rich and a huge Mayfair Mogul with mutual funds in every sector of the economy, she would spend some time on interior design, trying to liven up places as sterile and cold as this. Then she thought of Mayfair Medical! Of course that plan had to go forward! She had to help Ryan. They couldn't shut her out. She'd talk to Pierce about it tomorrow. She'd speak to Michael, soon as he felt a little better.

She looked at Anne Marie. 'Ryan said Mother was in here.'

'Yes, well, she is, and according to the nurses she thinks we're trying to permanently commit her. That's what she told them this morning when they brought her in. She's been asleep ever since they stuck a needle in her arm. The nurse is supposed to call me if she wakes up. What I meant was – did Ryan call you about Edith?'

'No, what happened to Edith?' Mona barely knew Edith. Edith was Lauren's granddaughter, a timid belligerent recluse who lived on Esplanade Avenue and spent all her time with her cats, a predictable and boring woman, never went anywhere ever, not even to funerals apparently. Edith. What did she look like? Mona wasn't sure.

Anne Marie sat up, slapped the magazine on the table, and pushed her glasses up against her pretty eyes. 'Edith died this afternoon. Hemorrhage same as Gifford. Ryan says for none of the women in the family to be alone. It might be something genetic. We're to be around people all the time. That way if something happens, we can call for help. Edith had been all alone, like Gifford.'

'You're kidding me. You mean Edith Mayfair is dead? This really actually happened?'

'Yeah, I know. Believe me. Think how Lauren feels. Lauren went over there to scold her for not showing up at Gifford's funeral. And there was Edith lying on the bathroom floor. Bled to death. And her cats were all around her licking up the blood.'

Mona didn't say anything for a moment. She had to

372

reflect, not only upon what she knew, but upon how much of it she could tell anybody else, and to what purpose. Partly she was simply shocked.

'You're saying this was a uterine hemorrhage too.'

'Yeah, possible miscarriage, they said. I would say impossible on that, myself, knowing Edith. Same with Gifford. Neither could have been pregnant. They're doing an autopsy this time. So at least the family is doing something other than burning candles and saying prayers and giving each other the evil eye.'

'That's good,' Mona said in a dull voice, drawing back into herself, hoping her cousin would keep quiet for a moment. No such luck.

'Look, everybody is very upset,' said Anne Marie. 'But we have to follow the directive. A person can have a hemorrhage without it being a miscarriage, obviously. So don't go off by yourself. If you feel faint, or any unusual physical symptoms, you need to be able to get help immediately.'

Mona nodded, staring off at the blank walls of this place, at its sparse signs and its large sand-filled cylindrical ashtrays. One half hour ago, Mona had been sound asleep when something waked her as surely as a hand touching her – a smell, a song coming from a Victrola. She pictured that open window again, the sash all the way up, the night outside bending in with its dark yews and oaks. She tried to remember *the smell*.

'Talk to me, kid,' said Anne Marie. 'I'm worried about you.'

'Yeah, well, I'm fine. OK. Everybody better follow that advice, don't be alone, whether they think they could be pregnant or not. You're right. Doesn't matter. I'm going upstairs to see Mother.'

'Don't wake her up.'

'You said she's been sleeping since morning? Maybe she's in a coma. Maybe she's dead.'

Anne Marie smiled and shook her head. She picked up her magazine and started reading again. 'Don't get in an argument with her, Mona,' she said, just as Mona turned away.

The elevator doors opened quietly on the seventh floor. This was where they always put Mayfairs, unless there was some pressing reason to be in a special department. Mayfairs had rooms with parlors here, and little kitchens where they could make their own microwave coffee, or store their ice cream. Alicia had been in here before, four times as a matter of fact – dehydrated, malnourished, broken ankle, suicidal – and vowed never to be brought back. They'd probably had to restrain her.

Mona padded softly down the corridor, catching a glimpse of herself in the dark glass of an observation room, and hating what she saw – the chunky white cotton dress, shapeless on a person who wasn't a little girl. Well, that was the least of her problems.

She caught the fragrance as soon as she reached the doors to Seventh Floor West. That was it. The exact same smell.

She stopped, took a deep breath and realized that for the first time in her life she felt really afraid of something. It made her disgusted. She stood, head cocked to the side, thinking it over. There was an exit to the stairs. There were the doors ahead. There was an exit on the other side of the ward. There were people right inside at the desk.

If only she had Michael here, she'd push open that

exit door, see if someone was standing in the stairwell, someone who gave off this odor.

But the smell was already weak. It was going away. And as she stood there, considering this, getting quietly furious that she didn't have the guts to just open that damned door, someone else opened it, and let it swing shut as he went down the corridor. A young doctor with a stethoscope over his shoulder. The landing had been empty.

But that didn't mean somebody wasn't hiding above or below. Either the smell was going away, however, or Mona was simply getting used to it. She took a deep slow breath; it was so rich, so sensuous, so delicious. But what was it?

She pushed through the double doors into the ward. The smell grew stronger. But there were the three nurses, sitting, writing away, in an island of light surrounded by high wooden counters, one of them whispering on a phone as she wrote, the others seemingly in deep concentration.

No one noticed as Mona walked past the station and passed into the narrow corridor. The smell was very strong here.

'Jesus Christ, don't tell me this,' Mona whispered. She glanced at the doors to her left and her right. But the smell told her before she even saw the chart that said 'Alicia (CeeCee) Mayfair'.

The door was ajar, and the room was dark; its one window opened upon an airwell. Blank wall stared in through the glass at the still woman, lying with her head to the wall, beneath the white covers. A small digital machine recorded the progress of the IV – a plastic sack of glucose, clear as glass, feeding down through a tiny tube into the woman's right hand, beneath a mass of tape, the hand itself flat on the white blanket.

Mona stood very still, then pushed open the door. She pushed it all the way back, so that she could see into the open bathroom to the right. Porcelain toilet. Empty shower stall. Quickly, she examined the rest of the room, and then turned back to the bed, confident that she and her mother were alone.

Her mother's profile bore a remarkable resemblance to that of her sister, Gifford, in the coffin. All points and angles, the emaciated face sunk into the large, softly yielding pillow.

The covers made a mound over the body. All white except for a small irregular blotch of red in the very center of the covers, very near to where the hand lay with its tape and its tubing and needle.

Mona drew closer, clamped her left hand on the chrome bar of the bed, and touched the red spot. Very wet. Even as she stared at it the blotch grew bigger. Something seeping up through the covers from below. Roughly Mona pulled the blanket down from under Alicia's limp arm. Her mother didn't stir. Her mother was dead. The blood was everywhere. The bed was soaked with it.

There was a sound behind Mona; and then a female voice spoke in a rasping, unfriendly whisper.

'Don't wake her up, dear. We had a hell of a time with her this morning.'

'Check her vital signs lately?' Mona asked, turning to the nurse. But the nurse had already seen the blood. 'I don't think there's much chance of waking her up. Why don't you call my cousin Anne Marie? She's down in the lobby. Tell her to come up here immediately.'

The nurse was an old woman; she picked up the dead woman's hand. At once she set it down, and then she backed away from the bed, and out of the room.

'Wait a minute,' said Mona. 'Did you see anybody come in here?'

But in an instant she knew the question was pointless. This woman was too afraid of being blamed for this to even respond. Mona followed her, and watched her rush down to the station, walking about as fast as a person can walk without running. Then Mona went back to the bed.

She felt the hand. Not ice-cold. She gave a long sigh; she could hear footsteps in the corridor, the muffled sound of rubber-soled shoes. She leaned over the bed, and brushed her mother's hair back from her face, and kissed her. The cheek held only a tiny bit of fading warmth. Her forehead was already cold.

She thought sure her mother would turn her head and look up at her and shout out: 'Be careful what you wish for. Didn't I tell you? It might come true.'

Within minutes the room was filled with staff. Anne Marie was in the hallway, wiping her eyes with a paper handkerchief. Mona backed off.

For a long time she stood at the nurses' station just listening to everything. An intern had to be called to say that Alicia was legally dead. They had to wait for him, and that would take twenty minutes. It was past eight o'clock. Meantime the family doctor had been summoned. And Ryan, of course. Poor Ryan. Oh, God help Ryan. The phone was ringing now continuously. And Lauren? What shape was she in?

Mona walked off down the hall. When the elevator door opened, it was the young intern who came out –

kid who didn't look old enough to know if somebody was dead. He passed her without even looking at her.

In a daze Mona rode down to the lobby and walked out the doors. The hospital was on Prytania Street, only one block from Amelia and St Charles, where Mona lived. She walked slowly along the pavement, under the lunar light of the street lamps, thinking quietly to herself.

'I don't think I want to wear dresses like this anymore.' She said it out loud when she stood on the corner. 'Nope, it's time to dump this dress and this ribbon.' Across the street, her home was brightly lighted for once. There were people climbing out of cars. All the crisp excitement already begun.

Several Mayfairs had seen her; one was pointing to her. Someone was walking to the corner to reach out towards her as if that might mean she might not be run down as she crossed the street.

'Well, I don't think I like these clothes anymore,' she said under her breath as she walked fast before the distant oncoming traffic. 'Nope, sick of it. Won't do it anymore.'

'Mona, darling!' said her cousin Gerald.

'Yeah, well, it was just a matter of time,' said Mona. 'But I sure didn't count on both of them dying. No, didn't see that coming at all.' She walked past Gerald, and past the Mayfairs assembled around the gate and the path to the steps.

'Yeah, OK,' she said to those who tried to speak to her. 'I've got to get out of these ridiculous clothes.'

FOURTEEN

JULIEN'S STORY

It is not the story of my life which you require, but let me explain how I came upon my various secrets. As you know I was born in the year 1828, but I wonder if you realize what this means. Those were the very last days of an ancient way of life – the last decades in which the rich landowners of the world lived pretty much as they had for centuries.

We not only knew nothing of railroads, telephones, Victrolas, or horseless carriages. We didn't even dream of such things!

And Riverbend – with its vast main house crammed with fine furniture and books, and all its many outbuildings sheltering uncles and aunts and cousins, and its fields stretching as far as the eye could see from the riverbank, south, and east and west – truly was Paradise.

Into this world I slipped almost without notice. I was a boy child, and this was a family that wanted female witches. I was a mere Prince of the Blood, and the court was a loving and friendly place, but no one observed that a little boy had been born who possessed probably greater witches' gifts than any man or woman ever in the family.

In fact, my grandmother Marie Claudette was so disappointed that I was not a girl child that she stopped speaking to my mother, Marguerite. Marguerite had already given birth to one male, my older brother, Rémy, and now, having had the audacity to bring another into the world, she crashed down completely from favor.

Of course Marguerite rectified this mistake as soon as possible, giving birth in 1830 to Katherine, who was to become her heiress and designee of the legacy – my darling little sister. But a coldness by then existed between mother and daughter, and was never healed in Marie Claudette's lifetime.

Also I personally suspect that Marie Claudette took one look at Katherine and thought, 'What an idiot,' for that is just what Katherine turned out to be. But a female witch was needed, and Marie Claudette would lay eyes upon a granddaughter before she died, so on to this little witless baby who was bawling in the cradle Marie Claudette passed the great emerald.

Now as you know, by the time Katherine was a young woman I had come into my own as a family influence, was much valued as a carrier of witches' gifts, and it was I who fathered, by Katherine, Mary Beth Mayfair, who was the last in fact of the great Mayfair Witches.

I fathered Mary Beth's daughter Stella, as I am sure you also know, and fathered by Stella her daughter, Antha.

But let me return to the perilous times of my early childhood, when men and women both warned me in hushed voices to be well-behaved, ask no questions, defer to the family customs in every regard, and pay no attention to anything strange that I might see pertaining to the realm of ghosts and spirits.

It was made known to me in no uncertain terms that strong Mayfair males did not do well; early death, madness, exile – those were the fates of the troublemakers.

When I look back on it, I think it is absolutely impossible that I could have become one of the great Passive Well-Behaved, along with my Oncle Maurice and Lestan and countless other goody-two-shoes cousins.

First of all, I saw ghosts all the time; heard spirits; could see life leaving a body when the body died; could read people's minds, and sometimes even move or hurt matter without even really getting angry or meaning to do it. I was a natural little witch or warlock or whatever the word might be.

And I can't remember a time when I couldn't see Lasher. He was standing by my mother's chair many a morning when I went in to greet her. I saw him by Katherine's cradle. But he never cast his eyes on me, and I'd been warned very early on that I must never speak to him, nor seek to know who or what he was, or say his name, or make him look at me.

My uncles, all very happy men, said, 'Remember this, a Mayfair male can have everything he desires – wine, women, and wealth beyond imagining. But he cannot seek to know the family secrets. Leave it in the hands of the great witch, for she sees all and directs all, and upon that principle our vast power has been founded.'

Well, I wanted to know what this was about. I had no intention of merely accepting the situation. And my grandmother, never someone not to catch the eye, became for me an extreme magnet of curiosity.

Meantime, my mother, Marguerite, grew rather

distant. She snatched me up and kissed me whenever we chanced to meet but that wasn't often. She was always going into the city to shop, to see the opera, to dance, to drink, to do God knows what, or locking herself in her study screaming if anyone dared to disturb her.

I found her most fascinating of course. But my grandmother Marie Claudette was more a constant figure. And she became for me in my idle moments – which were few – a great irresistible attraction.

First let me explain about my other learning. The books. They were everywhere. That wasn't so common in the Old South, believe me. It has never been common among the very rich to read; it is more a middle-class obsession. But we had all been lovers of books; and I cannot remember a time when I couldn't read French, English and Latin.

German? Yes, I had to teach myself that, as well as Spanish and Italian.

But I cannot recall a point in childhood where I had not read some of every book we possessed, and in this case that meant a library of such glory you cannot envision it. Most of those volumes have over the years simply rotted away; some have been stolen; some I entrusted many decades later to those who would cherish them. But then I had all I wanted of Aristotle, Plato, Plautus and Terence, Virgil and Horace. And I read the night away with Chapman's Homer, and Golding's *Metamorphoses*, a mammoth and charming translation of Ovid. Then there was Shakespeare, whom I adored, naturally enough, and lots of very funny English novels. *Tristram Shandy* and *Tom Jones* and *Robinson Crusoe*.

I read it all. I read it when I didn't know what it meant until I did. I dragged my books with me about the house, pulling on skirts and jackets and asking, 'What does this mean?' and even asking uncles, aunts, cousins or slaves to read various puzzling passages aloud to me.

When I wasn't reading I was adventuring about with the older boys, both white and black, jumping onto horses bareback, or trekking into the swamps to find snakes, or climbing the swamp cypress and the oaks to watch out for pirates invading from the south. At two and a half, I was lost in the swamps during a storm. I almost died, I suppose. But I shall never forget it. And after I was found, I never again suffered any fear of lightning. I think I had my little wits nearly blown out of my head by thunder and lightning that night. I screamed and screamed and nothing happened. The thunder and lightning went on; I didn't die; and in the morning I was sitting at the table with my tearful mother, having breakfast.

Ah, the point is this: I learned from everything, and there was plenty to learn from.

My principal tutor in those first three years of life was in fact my mother's coachman, Octavius, a free man of color and a Mayfair by five different lines of descent from the early ones through their various black mistresses. Octavius was then only eighteen or so, and more fun than anyone else on the plantation. My witch powers did not so much frighten him, and when he wasn't telling me to hide them from everybody else, he was telling me how to use them.

I learnt from him for example how to reach people's thoughts even when they meant to keep them inside, and how to give them suggestions without words, which they invariably obeyed! And how even to force my will with subtle words and gestures on another. I learnt also from him how to cast spells, making the entire world around appear to change for myself and for others who were with me. I also learnt many erotic tricks, for as many children are, I was erotically mad at age three and then four, and would attempt things then which made me blush by the time I was twelve – at least for a year or two.

But to return to the witches and how I came to be known to them.

My grandmother Marie Claudette was always there amongst us. She sat out in the garden, with a small orchestra of black musicians to play for her. There were two fine fiddlers, both slaves, and several who played the pipes, as we called them, but which were wooden flutes known as recorders. There was one who played a big bass fiddle of a homemade sort, and another who played two drums, caressing them with his soft fingers. Marie Claudette had taught these musicians their songs, and soon told me that many such songs came from Scotland.

More and more I gravitated to her. The noise I did not like, but I found that if I could get her to take me in her arms she was sweet and loving and had things to say as interesting as the things I read in the library.

She was stately, blue-eyed, white-haired, and picturesque as she lay on a couch of wicker and fancy pillows, beneath a canopy that blew just a little in the breeze, sometimes singing to herself in Gaelic. Or letting loose long strings of curses on Lasher.

For what had happened you see was that Lasher had tired of her! He had gone on to serve Marguerite and to hover about Katherine, the new baby. And for Marie

Claudette he had only an occasional kiss or word or two of poetry.

Perhaps every few days or so, he came to beg Marie Claudette's forgiveness for giving all his attentions to Marguerite, and to say in a very pure and beautiful voice, which I could hear, that Marguerite would not have it otherwise. Sometimes when he came to kiss and court Marie Claudette, he was dressed as a man in frock coat and pants, which were then a novelty you understand, we are only a few decades past tricorne and breeches, and sometimes he had a more rustic look to him, in rawhide garments of a very rough cut; but always his hair was brown and his eyes brown, and he was most beautiful.

And guess who came along, all ringlets and smiles, and hopped up into her lap, and said, 'Grandmère, tell me why you are so sad? Tell me everything.'

'Can you see that man who comes to me?' she asked.

'Of course,' I said, 'but everybody says I should lie to you about it, though why I don't know because he seems to like to be seen, and will even frighten the slaves by appearing to them, for no good reason, it seems to me, except vanity.'

She fell in love with me at that moment. She smiled approvingly at my observations. She also said she'd never encountered a two-year-old child who was so bright. I was two and a half but I didn't bother to point this out. Within a day or two of our first real conversation about 'the man', she began to tell me everything.

She told me all about her old home in Saint-Domingue and how she missed it, about voodoo charms and devil worship in the islands and how she'd mastered every slave trick for her own purposes.

'I am a great witch,' she said, 'far greater than your mother will ever be, for your mother is slightly mad and laughs at everything. As for the baby Katherine, who knows. Something tells me you had best look out for her. I myself laugh at very little.'

Every day I jumped in her lap and started asking her questions. The hideous little orchestra played on and on – she would never tell them to stop – but very soon she began to expect me to come, and if I did not she sent Octavius to find me, wash me and deliver me. I was happy. Only the music sometimes sounded to me like cats howling. I asked her once if she wouldn't like to listen instead to the song of the birds, but she only shook her head and said that it helped her think to have this background.

Meantime, over the din, her tales became more and more involved and filled with colorful pictures and violence.

Until the end of her life, she talked to me. In the last days, she brought the orchestra into the bedroom, and while they played, she and I whispered together on the pillow.

Basically, she told me how Suzanne, the cunning woman, had called up the spirit Lasher, 'in error', in Donnelaith, and then been burnt; how her daughter, Deborah, was taken away by sorcerers from Amsterdam; how the beautiful Deborah was followed by Lasher, and courted by him, and made powerful and rich, only to suffer a horrible death in a French town on the day they tried to burn her as they had burnt her mother. Then came Charlotte into the picture, daughter of Deborah by one of the sorcerers from Amsterdam, and the strongest of the first three, who used the spirit

Lasher as never before to acquire great wealth and influence and unlimited power.

And Charlotte – by her own father, Petyr van Abel, one of these daring and mysterious Amsterdam wizards, who had for her own good followed her to the New World to warn her of the evil of intercourse with spirits – then conceived Jeanne Louise and her twin brother, Peter, and from Jeanne Louise and her brother was born Angélique, who had been Marie Claudette's mother.

Gold, jewels, coin of every realm, and every luxury, this family had acquired. Not even the revolution on Saint-Domingue had destroyed its immense wealth, very little of which rode upon the success of the crops, but was piled up now in a string of safe places.

'Your mother does not even know what she possesses,' said Marie Claudette, 'and the more I think of it, the more important it is that I tell you.'

I naturally agreed. All this power and wealth, said Grandmère, had come to us through the machinations of this spirit, Lasher, who could kill those whom the witch marked for death, torment those whom she marked for madness, reveal to her secrets which other mortals strove to keep, and even acquire jewels and gold by transporting these things magically, though for this the spirit required great energy.

A loving thing was this spirit, she said, but it took some craft to manage. Look how it had abandoned her of late, and spent all its time hovering about Katherine's crib.

'That's because Katherine can't see it,' I said. 'It's trying very hard. It won't give up, but it's useless.'

'Ah, is that so? I don't believe it, a granddaughter of mine can't see that thing?'

'Go see for yourself. The child's eyes don't move. It cannot see the creature even when it comes in its strongest form, which anyone might touch and feel as solid.'

'Ah, so you know it does that.'

'I hear its footsteps on the stairs,' I said. 'I know its tricks. It can go from vapor to a solid being, and then in a gust of warm wind vanish.'

'Oh, you're very observant,' she said. 'I love you.'

I was very thrilled to the heart by this and I told her I loved her too, which I did. She was precious to me. Also, I had come to realize, while sitting on her knee, that I found old people more beautiful in the main than young ones.

This was to prove true of me all my life. I love young people too, of course, especially when they are very careless and brave, as my Stella was, or my Mary Beth. But people in the very middle of life? I can hardly tolerate them.

Allow me to say, Michael, you are an exception. No, don't speak. Don't break the trance. I won't tell you you are a child at heart, but you do have some childlike faith and goodness in you, and this has been both intriguing to me and somewhat maddening. You have challenged me. Like many a man with Irish blood, you know all sorts of supernatural things are possible. Yet you don't care. You go about talking to wooden joists and beams and plaster!

Enough. Everything depends on you now. Let me return to Marie Claudette and the particular things she told me about our family ghost.

'It has two kinds of voices,' she declared, 'a voice one can hear only in one's head, and the voice you heard, which can be heard by anyone with the right ears to hear it. And sometimes even a voice so loud and clear that it can be heard by everyone. But that isn't often, you see, for that wears it out, and where does it get its strength? From us – from me, from your mother, and possibly even from you, for I have seen it near me when you were here, and I have seen you look at it.

'As for the inner voice, it can devil you with it anytime, as it has done many an enemy, unless of course you are defended against it.'

'And how do you defend yourself?' I asked.

'Can't you guess?' she said. 'Let me see how smart you are. You see it with me, which means it appears, no? It summons its strength, it comes together, it becomes as a man for a few cherished moments. Then it is gone and exhausted. Why do you think it gives so much of itself to me, instead of merely whispering inside my head, "Poor old soul, I shall never forget you"?'

'To be seen,' I said with a shrug. 'It's vain.'

She laughed with delight. 'Ah, yes, and no. It has to take form to come to me for a simple reason. I surround myself night and day with music. It cannot get through unless it gathers all its strength, and concentrates most fiercely in the manifestation of a human form and a human voice. It must drown out the rhythm which at every moment enchants it and distracts it.

'Understand it likes music of course, but music is a thing with a sway over it, as music sometimes is with wild beasts or mythical persons in stories. And as long as I command my band to play, it cannot plague my mind alone, but must come and tap me on the shoulder.'

I remember that it was my turn to laugh with delight. The spirit was no worse than me in a way. I had had to learn to concentrate on my grandmother's stories when the music seemed to make it all but impossible. But for Lasher, to concentrate was to exist. When spirits dream, they don't know themselves.

I could digress on that. But I have too much to tell, and I'm too . . . tired now.

Let me go on. Where was I? Ah, yes, she told me about the power of music over the thing, and how she kept the music near her so that it would be forced to come and pay court, for otherwise it wouldn't have bothered.

'Does it know this?' I asked.

'Yes, and no,' she said. 'It begs me to shut out the din, but I cry and say I cannot, and it then comes to me and kisses my hand, and I look at it. You are right that it is vain. It would be seen again and again, just to be reassured that I have not drifted out of its realm, but it no longer loves or needs me. It has a place in its heart for me. That's all, and that is nothing.'

'You mean it has a heart?' I asked.

'Oh, yes, it loves us all, and we great witches above all things, for we have brought it into knowing itself, and have greatly aided it to increase its power.'

'I see,' I said. 'But what if you didn't want it around anymore? If you . . .'

'Shhhh . . . never say such a thing!' she said, 'not even with trumpets or bells pealing all about you.'

'All right,' I said, feeling strongly already that I must never be given the same advice more than once, and I said no more about that. 'But can you tell me what it is?' I asked.

'A devil,' she said, 'a great devil.'

I told her, 'I don't think so.'

She was amazed. 'Why do you say that? Who else but the Devil would serve a witch?'

I told her all I knew of the Devil, from prayers and hymns and Mass and the quick-witted slaves all around me. 'The Devil is just plain bad,' I said. 'And he treats badly all who trust him. This thing is too damned good to us.'

She agreed, but it was like the Devil, she said, in that it would not submit to God's laws, but would come through as flesh and be a man.

'Why?' I said. 'Isn't it a hell of a lot stronger the way it is? Why would it want to catch yellow fever or lockjaw?'

She laughed and laughed. 'It would be flesh to feel all that flesh can feel, to see what men can see, and hear what they can hear, and not have forever to be collecting itself out of a dream and fear the losing of itself. It would be flesh to be real; to be in the world and of the world, and to defy God, who gave it no body.'

'Hmmm, sounds like it has overrated the whole experience,' I said. Or in words that a three-year-old might choose for pretty much the same thing, for by that age, like many a country child of the times, I'd seen plenty of death and suffering.

Once again, she laughed, and she said that it would have what it would have, and lavished everything upon us because we served its purpose.

'It wants strength; every hour and every day in our presence, we give it strength; and it pushes for one thing: that is the birth of a witch so strong that she can make it once and for all material.'

'Well, that isn't going to be my baby sister, Katherine,' I said.

She smiled and nodded her head. 'I fear you're right, but the strength comes and goes. You have it. Your brother has none.'

'Don't be so sure,' I said. 'He's more easily frightened. He's seen it and it has made an ugly face at him to keep him from Katherine's cradle. I don't require ugly faces, nor do I flee from them. And I have too much sense to overturn Katherine's cradle. But tell me, how is a witch going to make it flesh forever? Even with Mother, I see it solid for no more than two, three minutes at most. What does it mean to do?'

'I don't know,' she said. 'Truly I don't know the secret. But let me tell you this while the music plays on, and listen to me carefully. I've never even expressed this in thought to myself but I confide it to you. When it has what it wants, it shall destroy the entire family.'

'Why?' I said.

'I don't know,' she said again very gravely. 'It's just what I fear. For I think and I feel in my bones, that though it loves us and needs us – it also hates us.'

I thought about this in quiet.

'Of course it doesn't know this, perhaps,' she said, 'or does not wish for me to know. The more I think on it the more I wonder if you weren't sent here to pass on what I have to say to that baby in the cradle. God knows Marguerite will not listen now. She thinks she rules the world. And I fear hell in my old age and crave the company of a cherubic three-year-old.'

'Flesh, the thing wants to be flesh,' I pressed, for I remember I was almost carried off course by being called cherubic, which I liked very much, and wanted her to digress on my charms. But I went back to the evil thing. 'How can it be flesh? Human flesh? What? Would it be born into the world again, or take a body that is dead, or one that is . . .'

'No,' she said. 'It says it knows its destiny. It says it carries the sketch within itself of what it would be again, and that someday a witch and a man shall make the magical egg from which its form will be made, and into which it will come again, knowing its own form, and the infant soul shall not knock it loose, and all the world will come to understand it.'

'All the world, hmmm.' I thought. 'And you said, "again". By that you mean the thing has been flesh before?'

'It was something before which it is not now, but what it was, I can't rightly tell you. I think it was a creature fallen, damned to suffer intelligence and loneliness in a vaporish form! And it would end the sentence. Through us it wants a strong witch, who can be as the Virgin Mary was to Christ, the vessel of an Incarnation.'

I pondered all this. 'It's no devil,' I said.

'And why do you say that?' she asked again, as if we hadn't discussed this before.

'Because,' I said, 'the Devil has more important things to do if he exists at all, and on the point of his existence at all I am not certain.'

'Where did you get an idea there was no Devil?'

'Rousseau,' I said. 'His philosophy argues that the worst evil is in man.'

'Well,' she said, 'read some more before you make up your mind.'

And that was the end of that part of it.

But before she died, which was not so long after that at all, she told me many things about this spirit. It killed through fright mostly. In the form of a man, it startled coachmen and riders at night, causing them to veer off the road and into the swamps; and sometimes it even frighted the horses as well as the men, which was proof that it was indeed material.

It could be sent to stalk a mortal man or woman, and tell in its own childish way what that person had done all the livelong day, but one had to interpret its peculiar expressions carefully.

It could steal, of course, small things mostly, though sometimes whole banknotes for considerable amounts. And it could come into mortals for a bit of time, to see through their eyes and feel through their hands, but this was never long-lasting. Indeed the battle left it fatigued and often more tormented than it had been before, and it oftentimes killed whom it had possessed out of sheer rage and envy. This meant one had to be very careful in helping it with such tricks, for the innocent body used for such purposes might very well be destroyed after.

Such had happened to one of Marie Claudette's nephews, she told me – one of my very own cousins – before she had learnt to control the thing and make it obey or starve it with silence and covering her eyes and pretending not to hear it. 'It is not so hard to torture at times,' she said. 'It feels, and it forgets, and it weeps. I don't envy it.'

'Me neither,' I said aloud and she said:

'Never scorn it. It will hate you for that. Look away always when you see it.'

Like hell, I thought, but I didn't confess it.

It wasn't more than a month after that that she died.

I was out in the swamps with Octavius. We had run away to live in the wild like Robinson Crusoe. We had docked our little flat-bottomed boat and had made a camp, and while he gathered wood I tried to make fire with what we already had, and was having no success at it.

When suddenly, the kindling in my hand leapt into flames, and I looked up and what should I see but Marie Claudette, my beloved grandmother, only looking more splendid and vigorous than she ever had in old age, with full, rosy cheeks and a beautiful soft mouth. She picked me up off the ground, kissed me and then set me down, and she was gone. Like that. And the little fire was blazing.

I knew what it meant. Farewell. She was dead. I insisted we go back to Riverbend immediately. And as we drew closer and closer to the house, we came into a heavy storm, and had, at last, to run through the water, against a fierce wind filled with leaves and debris and even sharp stones, until we came to the gates, and the slaves ran to shelter us with blankets.

Marie Claudette was indeed dead, and when I sobbed and told my mother how I knew, I think for the very first time in her life, she actually *saw* me. I had been a cuddly thing, of course, but in that moment, she spoke to me not as one does to a dog or a child, but as to a human being.

'You saw her and she gave you her kiss,' she said.

And then right there in the sickroom, with everyone sobbing and the shutters banging in the wind, and the priest in a state of terror, the damned fiend appeared over my mother's shoulder, and our eyes met, and his were soft with a plea, and filled with tears for me to see, and then of course, like that, he vanished.

That's the way my own tale will end, don't you think?

You will tell the final words. 'Then Julien vanished.' And where will I be? Where will I go? Was I in heaven before you called me here, or in hell? I am so weary I don't care anymore and that is perhaps a blessing.

But to return to that long-ago noisy moment when the rain was blowing in, and my grandmother lay neat and small on the bed beneath layers of pretty lace and my mother, gaunt and dark-haired, stared at me, and the fiend behind took the form of a handsome man, and little Katherine cried in the cradle – it was the beginning of my true life as my mother's cohort.

First, after the funeral and the burial in the parish cemetery – we Catholics never had cemeteries on our own land, but only in consecrated ground – my mother went mad. And I was the only witness.

Halfway up the stairs, coming home from the graveyard, she began to scream, and I rushed behind her into her room before she bolted the doors to the gallery. Then she gave one aching cry after another. All this was grief for her mother, and what she had not done, and had not said, but then it passed from grief into great wild anger.

Why could this spirit not prevent death? 'Lasher, Lasher, Lasher.' She caught up the feather pillows from the bed and ripped the cloth and strewed the feathers everywhere. If you've never seen such a spectacle, you might rip up such a pillow and give it a try. There isn't anything quite like it, and she tore up three pillows in her rage, and soon the entire air was full of feathers and in the midst of them she screamed, and looked more miserable and forlorn than any being I have ever beheld in all my little life, and soon I began to weep helplessly.

She held tight to me; she begged my forgiveness that

she'd shown me such a sight. We lay down together and finally she cried herself to sleep, and the night descended upon the plantation, which, in those days of precious few oil lamps and candles, brought everything to an early halt, and finally only silence.

It must have been past midnight when I awoke. I don't recall the face of the clock; only the feeling of deep night, and that it was spring and that I wanted to push through the netting which surrounded our bed and walk outside and talk to the moon and stars for a while.

Well, I managed to sit up and there before me was the thing itself, sitting on the side of the bed, and it reached out its white hand for me. I did not scream. There was no time. For all at once I felt the stroke of its fingers on my cheek and it felt good to me. Then it seemed the air around me made a caress, and the thing, having dissolved, was kissing me with invisible lips and touching me and filling my body with whatever pleasure it could feel at so young an age, which, as you probably remember, was something!

After it was finished with me, and I lay there, a little puddle of baby juice beside my mother's sleeping body, I saw it material again, this being, standing by the window. I climbed out of bed, weak and confused by the pleasure I'd felt, and went towards it. I reached out to take its hand, which dangled at its side like a man's hand, and then it looked down at me and gave me its most tearful gaze and together we pushed the window netting aside and went out on the gallery.

It seemed to me that it trembled in the light, that it vanished some three or four times only to reappear, and then it died away, leaving the air very warm behind it. I stood in the warmth and I heard its voice for the first time in my head, its private confiding voice:

'I have broken my vow to Deborah.'

'Which was what?' I asked.

'You do not even know who Deborah was, you miserable child of flesh and blood,' it said, and went on with some hysterically funny pronouncement upon me that seemed made up of all the worst doggerel in the library. Mind you, I was nearly four by this time, and I couldn't claim to know poetry as anything more than song, but I knew when the words were downright preposterous. And the cunning laughter of the slaves had taught me this too. I knew pomposity.

'I know who Deborah was,' I said, and I told it then the story of Deborah as told to me by Marie Claudette, of how she had risen high, and then been accused of witchcraft.

'Betrayed by her husband and sons, she was, and before that, by her father. Aye, her father. And I took my vengeance upon him,' it said. 'I took my vengeance on him for what he and his ilk had done to her *and to me!*'

The voice broke off. I had the distinct feeling in my little three-year-old mind that it had been about to launch on another long song of rotten poetry but had changed its mind at the last minute.

'You understand what I say?' it asked. 'I vowed to Deborah that I would never smile upon a male child, nor favor a male over a female.'

'Yes, I know what you are saying,' I said, 'and also my Grandmamma told me. Deborah was born in the Highlands, a merry-begot, bastard child of the May revels, and her father was most likely the lord of the land himself, and did not raise a finger when her mother, Suzanne, was burnt at the stake, a poor persecuted witch who knew almost nothing.'

'Aye,' he said. 'So it was. So it was! My poor Suzanne, who called me from the depths like a child who pulls a snake from a deep pond without knowing. Stringing syllables in the air, she called my name, and I heard her.

'And it was indeed the lord of the land, the chief of the Clan of Donnelaith, who got her with child and then shivered in fear when they burnt her! Donnelaith. Can you see that word? Can you make it in letters? Go there and see the ruins of the castle I laid waste. See the graves of the last of that clan, stricken from the earth, until such time as . . .'

'Until such time as what?'

And then it said nothing more, but went back again to caressing me.

I was musing. 'And you?' I asked. 'Are you male or female, or simply a neuter thing?'

'Don't you know?' it asked.

'I wouldn't ask if I did,' I answered.

'Male!' it said. 'Male, male, male, male!'

I stifled my own giggles at its pride and ranting.

But I must confess that from then on, it was in my mind both an 'it' and a 'he' as you can hear from my story. At some times it seemed so devoid of common sense that I could only perceive it as a monstrous thing, and at other times, it took on a distinct character. So bear with my vacillation if you will. When calling it by name, I often thought of it as 'he'. And in my angry moments, stripped it of its sex, and cursed it as too childish to be anything but neuter.

You will see from this tale that the witches saw it variously as 'he' and 'it'. And there were reasons.

But let me return to the moment. The porch, the being caressing me.

When I grew tired of its embrace, and I turned around, there was my mother in the doorway, watching all of this, and she reached out and clutched me to herself, and said to it: 'You shall never hurt him. He is a harmless boy!'

And I think then it answered her in her head because she grew quiet. It was gone. That was all I knew for certain.

The next morning I went at once to the nursery where I still slept with Rémy and Katherine and some other sweet cousins best forgotten. I could not write very well. And understand now on this point, many people in those years could read, but couldn't write.

In fact, to read but not to write was common. I could read anything, as I've said, and words like *transubstantiation* rolled off my tongue both in English and in Latin. But I had only just begun to form written letters with agility and speed, and I had a hell of a time recording what the fiend had said, but finally, asking, 'How do you spell –?' of everybody who chanced to pass through the room, I got it down, exactly. And if you want to know, those words are still scratched deep in the little desk, a thing handmade of cypress which is in the far back attic now and which you, Michael, have touched with your own hands once as you repaired the rafters there.

'Until such time as . . .' Those were the words the fiend had spoken. Which struck me as powerfully significant.

I determined then and there to learn to write, and did so within six months, though my handwriting did not

400

assume its truly polished form till I was near twelve. My early writing was fast and clumsy.

I told my mother all the fiend had told me. She was filled with fear. 'It knows our thoughts,' she said at once in a whisper.

'Well, these are not secrets,' I said, 'but even if they were, let us play music if we want to talk of them.'

'What do you mean?' asked she.

'Didn't your own mother tell you?'

No, she confessed, her mother had not. So I did. And she began to laugh as wildly as she had cried the night before, clapping her hands and even sinking down upon the floor and drawing up her knees. At once she sent for the very musicians who had played for her mother.

And under cover of the wild band, which sounded like drunken gypsies fighting musical war with Cajuns of the Bayou over matters of life and death, I told her everything Marie Claudette had told me.

Meantime the spirit appeared in the room, behind the band, where his manly form could not be seen by them but only by us, and began to dance madly. Finally the shaky apparition fell to rocking back and forth, and then vanished. But we could still feel its presence in the room, and that it had fallen into the band's repetitive and distinctly African rhythm.

We spoke under this cover.

Marguerite had not cared for 'ancient history'. She had never heard the word *Donnelaith*. She did not remember much about Suzanne. She was glad I had taken note of this. And there were history books which she would give to me.

Magic was her passion, she explained, and told me in detail how her mother had never appreciated her talents.

Early on she, Marguerite, had befriended the powerful voodooiennes of New Orleans. She'd learned from them, and she would now heal, spellbind, and cast curses with good effect, and in all this Lasher was her slave and devotee and lover.

There began a conversation between my mother and me which was to last all her life, in which she gave me everything she knew without compromise and I gave to her all that I knew, as well, and I was close to her at last, and in her arms, and she was my mother.

But it was soon clear to me that my mother was mad; or shall we say she was maniacally focused upon her magical experiments. It seemed a certainty in her mind that Lasher was the Devil; and that anything else he might have said was lies; indeed, the only truth I'd given her was the trick of shutting him out by music. Her real passions lay in hunting the swamps for magical plants, talking to the old black women of bizarre cures, and attempting to transform things through the use of chemicals and telekinetic power.

Of course we did not use that word then. We didn't know it. She was certain of Lasher's love. She had had the girl child, and would try to have another, stronger girl, if that was what he wanted. But with every passing year, she became less interested in men, more addicted to the fiend's embraces, and altogether less coherent.

Meantime, I was growing fast, and just as I had been a miracle of a three-year-old, I became a miracle at every age, continuing my reading, and my adventures, and my intercourse with the daemon.

The slaves knew now that I had it in my power. They came to me for aid; they begged a cure from me when they were ill, and very soon I had supplanted my mother as the object of mystery.

Now, here, Michael, I face a clear choice. I can tell you all that Marguerite and I learnt and how; or I can go on ahead with those things which are most important. Let me choose a compromise and make a swift summary of our experiments.

But before I do, let me say that my sister, Katherine, was coming along, utterly lacking in guile, but beautiful as she was innocent, a flower I adored and wished to protect, and knowing it pleased the fiend when I shepherded her about, I did it all the more willingly. But I conceived a great love for her in my own right, and I came to realize that she did in fact see 'the man' but that he frightened her. She seemed shy of all that was unwholesome or otherworldly. Of our mother she was terrified, and with reason.

Marguerite's experiments were becoming ever more reckless. If a baby was born dead on our land, she wanted it. The slaves tried to hide from her their lost children, lest these poor beings end up in jars in Marguerite's study. And one of my keenest memories of those times is of Marguerite dashing into the house with a bundle in her hands, and then flashing at me her eager smile, and throwing back the cloth to reveal a tiny dead black baby form, and then covering it up again in jubilation as she went to lock herself in her study.

Meantime the spirit was ever attentive. It put gold coins in my pockets every day. It warned me when amongst my cousins I had some petty enemy. It stood guard over my room, and once struck down a thieving runaway who sought to steal the few jewels I possessed.

And when I was alone, it often came to me and caressed me and gave me a pleasure more keening than any I could achieve with others.

And this it did too with Marguerite faithfully. And all the while it tried its blandishments on Katherine but seemed to get nowhere with her.

She had it in her head that such evil pleasures as were offered to her in the dark of night were mortal sin. I think she was perhaps the first of the witches to actually believe this, and how the Catholic conception took root in her so strong and so soon – before the fiend could carry her off into erotic dreams – I can't honestly say. If you believe in God, you might say God was with her. I don't think so.

Whatever, my mother and I, tiring of my grandmother's awful band, soon hired a piano player and a fiddler to play for us. The spirit seemed at first to delight in this as it had in the cacophonous band. In dazzling male form, it would appear in the room, spellbound and happy to reveal it.

But it came to realize we whispered to each other under the notes of the song, and it couldn't hear or know what we thought or planned, it became fiercely angry. We needed louder music to shut it out and brought back the others to create their din, and then we saw that what was most effective was melody and rhythm. Noise alone was not sufficient to do it.

Meantime, as we prospered, as the plantation was flush, and our money seemed to breed upon itself in foreign banks, and our cousins married far and wide, the name Mayfair became greater and greater along the River Coast, and we reigned supreme on our own land. No one could bother us or touch us.

I was nine years old when I demanded of the fiend:

'What is it you really want of us, of my mother and me?'

'What I want of you all,' he said. 'That you make me flesh!' and, imitating the band, it began to sing these words over and over, and shake the objects in the room to the rhythm as it were of a drum, until I put my hands over my ears and begged for mercy.

'Laughter,' he said. 'Laughter.'

'Which means what?' I asked.

'I am laughing at you because I too can make music to make you rock.'

I laughed. 'You're right,' I said. 'And you say this word, because you cannot actually laugh.'

'Just so,' he said, petulantly. 'When I am flesh I shall laugh again.'

'Again?' said I.

He said nothing.

Ah, this moment is so clear in my memory. I stood out on the upper gallery of the house, shielded somewhat by the banana leaves that stroked the wooden banisters. And out on the river, ships made their way north to the port through the channels. All the fields lay in warm spring sunlight, and below on the grass my cousins played, some forty or fifty of them, all below the age of twelve, and around them in rocking chairs sat the uncles and aunts, fanning themselves and chatting.

And here I stood with this thing, my hands on the rail, my face very grave most likely for the age of nine, trying to get to the heart of it.

'All this I have given you,' he said, as if he had read my emotions more clearly than I had myself. 'Your family is my family; I will bring blessing upon blessing. You do not know what wealth can give. You are too young. You will come to see that you are a prince in a great kingdom. No crowned head in Europe enjoys such power as you have.'

'I love you,' I said mechanically to it, and sought to believe this for an instant, as if I were seducing a mortal adult.

'I shall continue,' he said. 'Protect Katherine until she can bear a girl child. Carry on the line; Katherine is weak, strong ones will come, it must happen.'

I pondered.

'This is all I can do?' I asked.

'For now,' he said. 'But you are very strong, Julien. Things will come into your mind, and when you see what is to be done I shall see it.'

Again I pondered. I studied the happy throng on the lawn. My brother was calling for me to come down and play; they would be taking a boat out soon to the Bayou. Did I want to come with them?

I saw, then, two founts of enterprise at work now in this family – one was the witches' fount, to use the spirit to acquire wealth and advantage; and the other was the natural or normal fount, already bubbling with a great strong flow that might not be stopped were the spirit destroyed.

Once again, it answered me.

'War on me and I destroy all this! You are living now because Katherine needs you.'

I didn't answer. I went inside, took my diary, went down to the parlor, and urged the musicians to play loud and strong, and then I wrote my thoughts in my diary.

Meantime, my gifts and those of my mother were growing stronger. We healed, as I have said, we cast spells, we sent Lasher to spy upon those about whom we would know the truth, and sometimes to gauge the financial change of the future.

This was no easy thing, and the older I became, the more I realized my mother was slowly becoming too mad to do much of anything practical. Indeed, our cousin Augustin, manager of the plantation, was pretty much doing what he wanted with its profits.

By the time I was fifteen, I knew seven languages, and could write very well in any one, and was now the unofficial overseer and manager of the entire plantation. My cousin Augustin grew jealous of me, and so in a fit of rage I shot him.

This was an awful moment.

I had not meant to kill him. Indeed, he was the one who had produced the gun and threatened me; and I in my rage had snatched it from his hand and fired the ball into his forehead. My plan had been 'short-range', that is, to knock him about, and *voilà!* he was totally and finally dead forever! No one could have been more surprised than I was. Not even him, wherever he went, for I did see his soul rise, befuddled and staring through a vague human form as it disintegrated.

The whole family went into chaos. The cousins fled to their cottages, the city cousins to their town houses in New Orleans; indeed the plantation shut down in mourning for Augustin, and the priest came, and the funeral preparations commenced.

I sat in my room weeping. I imagined that I would be punished for my crime, but very soon, I realized that nothing of the sort was going to happen!

No one was going to touch me. Everyone was frightened. Even Augustin's wife and children were frightened. They had come to tell me they knew it was 'an accident' and did not want to risk my disfavor.

My mother watched this with astonished eyes, barely

interested at all, and said, 'Now you can run things as you like.'

And the spirit came, nudging me playfully, delighted it could knock the quill pen out of my hand, and give me a start with a smile in the mirror.

'Julien,' it said, 'I could have done this thing stealthily for you! Put away your gun. You do not need it.'

'Can you so easily kill?'

'Laughter.'

I told it then of two enemies I had made, one a tutor who had insulted my beloved Katherine, and another a merchant who had crassly cheated us. 'Kill them,' I said.

The fiend did. Within the week both had met a bad end – one beneath the wheels of a carriage, the other thrown from his horse.

'It was simple,' said the fiend.

'So I see,' said I. I think I was fairly drunk with my power. And remember I was only fifteen, and this was the time before the war when we were still isolated from all the world beyond us.

As it turned out, Augustin's descendants left our land. They went deep into the Bayou country and built the beautiful plantation of Fontevrault. But that is another story. Someday you must journey up the river road and over the Sunshine Bridge and into that land, and see the ruins of Fontevrault, for many many things happened there.

But let me only say now, that with Tobias, the eldest son of Augustin, I was never reconciled. He had been a toddler on the night of the killing, and in later years his hate for me remained great, though his line was prosperous and they kept to the name Mayfair and their progeny married with our progeny. This was one of many branches of the family tree. But it was one of the strongest. And as you know Mona comes from this line, and from my later entanglement with it.

Now, to return to our day-to-day life, as Katherine became more and more beautiful, Marguerite began to fade, as if some vital energy were drawn from her by her daughter. But nothing of the sort really happened.

Marguerite was only mad with her experiments, of trying to bring the dead infants back to life, of inviting Lasher to plunge into their flesh, and make the limbs move, but he could never restore the soul itself. The idea was preposterous.

Nevertheless, she delved deep and drew me with her into magic. We sent for books from all over the world. The slaves came to us for medicines for every illness. And we grew stronger and stronger so that soon we could cure many common aches with the simple laying on of hands. And Lasher was always our ally in this, and if the daemon knew some secret that would cure the sick one – that he had been accidentally poisoned perhaps – it would make these secrets known to us.

When I was not at my experiments, I was with Katherine, taking her into New Orleans to see the opera, the ballet, whatever dramas we could, showing her the fine restaurants, and taking her for walks so that she might see the world itself, which a woman could not really do without an escort. She was as always innocent and full of love, slight of build, dark, and perhaps a little feebleminded.

It began to penetrate to me that in our inbreeding we had encouraged certain weaknesses. In fact, now amongst my cousins I began to study these things, and feeblemindedness of a certain charming sort was definitely part of it. There were also among us many with witches' gifts, and some even with witches' marks – a black mole or birth pattern of peculiar shape; a sixth finger. Indeed the sixth finger was a common thing, and could take various forms. It might be a tiny digit projecting from the outside edge of the hand, an adjunct to the little finger. Or it could be near the thumb, and sometimes a second thumb. But wherever it appeared, you can be sure someone was ashamed of it.

Meantime I had read the history of Scotland, under the fiend's nose, most likely without his being aware of it. For if I had a fiddler standing by, playing a dreary melody as I read, the fiend hardly noticed anything. Indeed, he often tired of being invaded by the music as it were and went off to court my mother.

Well and good. Donnelaith was not a town of importance. But there were some old stories that told it once had been, and that a great cathedral had stood there. Indeed there had been a school and a great saint in those parts, and Catholics had journeyed for miles and miles to worship at his shrine.

I kept this information for future use. I would go there. I would find the history of these people of Donnelaith.

Meanwhile my mother laughed at all this. And under the cover of music, said, 'Ask him questions. You will soon discover he is no one or anything and comes from hell. It's that simple.'

I took up the theme with it.

And sure enough, what she had said was true. I would say, 'Who made the world?' and on it would go about mist and land and spirits always being there, and then I would say, 'And Jesus Christ, did you witness His birth?' and it would say that there was no time where it lived and it saw only witches.

I spoke of Scotland, and it wept for Suzanne, and told me that she had died in fear and pain, and Deborah had watched with solemn eyes before the evil wizards of Amsterdam came to fetch her.

'And who were these wizards?' I asked, and the fiend said: 'You will know soon enough. They watch you. Beware of them, for they know all and can bring harm to you.'

'Why don't you kill them?' I said.

'Because I would know what they know,' he said, 'and there is no real reason. Beware of them. They are alchemists and liars.'

'How old are you?'

'Ageless!'

'Why were you in Donnelaith?'

Silence.

'How did you come to be there?'

'Suzanne called me, I told you.'

'But you were there before Suzanne.'

'There is no there before Suzanne.'

And so on it went, intriguing but never really advancing the story very far or revealing a practical secret.

'It is time for you to come and help your mother. Your strength is necessary.'

This meant, of course, help Marguerite with her experiments. All right, I thought, though if she keeps burning those stinking candles and mumbling Latin words of which she doesn't know the meaning, I am leaving!

I followed Lasher into her rooms. She had just come in with an infant, feeble but alive, which had been left at the church door by its slave mother. The infant cried, a tiny brown creature with curling brown hair, and a little pink mouth that could break your heart. It seemed too small to survive very long. She was delighted with it. She put me in mind at once of a little boy playing with a bug in a jar, so savage was her interest, and so disconnected was she from the fact that this fragile wailing thing was human.

She shut the doors, lighted the candles, and then knelt beside the child and invited Lasher to go inside it.

With a great chant she egged the daemon on: 'Into its limbs; see through its eyes; speak through its mouth; live in its breath and in its heartbeat.'

The room seemed to swell and to contract, though of course it did not, and all that could rattle was moved, and the noise became a subtle murmuring – bottles jiggling, bells tinkling, shutters fluttering in the wind – and then this tiny baby before my eyes began to change. It coordinated its tiny limbs and the expression of its little face became malevolent or merely adultlike.

It was no longer an infant at all but a hideous mannequin of sorts, for though it had not changed physically, a grown man was inside it and manipulating it, and spoke now, in a gurgling voice. 'I am Lasher. See me here.'

'Grow, grow strong!' declared Marguerite, holding up both her fists. 'Julien, command it to grow. Stare at its arms and legs. Command them to grow.'

I did, and against all I believed I saw that its little legs and arms were lengthening. Indeed, the eyes of the infant, pale blue at birth, were now suddenly dark brown, and its hair slowly darkened as well as though absorbing a dark liquid.

Its skin on the other hand began to pale; color pulsed in its cheeks. Its legs for one instant were stretched like tentacles. And then the little thing died. Just died. Let out a cry, and died.

And Marguerite grabbed it off the bed, and threw it at the dresser mirror. The little one splashed with blood and gore on the glass but didn't break it and down it tumbled, one nameless dead child among her perfumes, potions and hair combs.

The room was trembling again. He was near, and then gone, and the cold was all around us. It was as if Lasher had taken the balmy heat with him.

She sat down and wept. 'It's always so. We get that far, and the vessel is too weak to contain him. He destroys what he changes. How will he ever be flesh? And now he is so tired from what he has done that he cannot come to us. We must wait and let him drift and recollect, there is nothing to be done for it.'

I was spellbound by what I'd seen. I wanted to go out and write it down. She stopped me.

'What can we do to make him flesh?' she said.

'Well, don't try with an infant, for one thing. Try with the body of a man. Find someone disabled in mind and body too, perhaps, who is already near to death, someone who cannot resist any more than an infant could. And see if Lasher can go into it.'

'Ah, but he said that from a little child he must grow. A little child like the infant in the manger.'

'Lasher said this? When?' I asked, and took note of this along with all its other little slips.

'From a little child, he will be born, from the most powerful witch, but the baby shall start out small as the Christ Child, but ah, if only we could bring him into the flesh now, think what we would have done, and then, and then, we could bring back the dead in the very same fashion.'

'You think so?'

'Come here,' she said. She took me by the hand, and dropped to her knees and pulled a small trunk from beneath the bed, and in it lay dolls, dolls of bone and hair and carefully stitched clothes. And mark, Michael, they weren't rotted as they were when you saw them. They were swaddled in lace and surrounded in some cases with beautiful jewels, and strands of pearls, and they peered at us with their tiny specks for eyes.

'These are the dead,' she said. 'See? This is Marie Claudette.' She lifted a tiny doll with gray hair, clothed in red taffeta, and made from a stocking it seemed and filled with things that felt like pebbles. 'Parings of her nails, one bone from her hand, taken by me from her grave, and her hair, lots of her hair, that is what makes up this doll, and within the hour of her death, I had taken the spittle from her mouth and soaked its face, and the blood she had vomited, and smeared that as well on the doll beneath its clothing. Now hold it and you will see that she is here.'

She put the doll in my hands, and in a flash I saw the living Marie Claudette! I was knocked backwards by the shock. I stared down at this thing of cloth. I squeezed it again and there she stood, motionless for an instant, staring at me. I called out to her. I did this over and over again, summoning her, seeing her, calling to her, and then losing her.

'This is nothing,' I said. 'She is not there.'

'No, no, but she is and she speaks to me.'

'I don't believe it.'

I squeezed the doll once more and said, 'Grandmère, tell me the truth,' and then I heard a tiny voice in my head which said, 'I love you, Julien.' Of course I knew it was not Marie Claudette speaking to me. It was Lasher, but how was I to prove this?

I did a daring thing. So that my mother could hear, I said, 'Marie Claudette, Marie Claudette, beloved Grandmère, do you remember the day that as the band played, we buried my little wooden toy horse in the garden? Do you remember how I cried and the poem which you told to me?'

'Yes, yes, my child,' said the secret voice and the image, which both my mother and I could see, held fast for the longest time yet, a graceful vision of Marie Claudette as she had been the last time I ever glimpsed her.

'The poem,' I said, 'help me to recall it.'

'Think back, my child, you will remember,' said the ghost.

And then I said, 'Ah, yes, "Toy horse, toy horse, ride on into the fields of heaven!"'

Ah yes, she said, and repeated this line with me.

I threw down the doll! 'This is nonsense,' I declared. 'I never owned a toy wooden horse. I never had an interest in such things. I never buried it in the yard, and I never wrote any stupid poem to it.'

The fiend went into a frenzy. My mother threw her hands over me to protect me. Everything was flying about ... furniture, bottles, jars, books. It was worse than all those feathers had been, and things were raining down upon us.

'Stop!' my mother declared. 'Who will protect Katherine?'

The room grew quiet.

'Do not become my enemy, Julien,' said the thing.

I was at this point scared to death. I'd proved my point. This thing was a liar. This thing was not the repository of any sanctified wisdom. And this thing could kill me all right, as surely as it had my enemies, and I had made it very angry.

I was wily. 'All right, you would be flesh?'

'I would be flesh, I would be flesh, I would be flesh!'

'Then we shall proceed with our experiments in earnest.'

Michael, you yourself have seen the fruits of those years. When you came to this house, you saw the human heads rotted in their jars of fluid. You saw the infants swimming there in darkness. You saw the sum total of our accomplishments.

So let me be brief about these dark disasters and what we did, and I did, out of fear of the thing, and seeing myself sinking into deeper and deeper evil.

It was the year 1847 by this time. Katherine was a lithe thing of seventeen, courted by cousins and strangers alike, but showed no desire to marry. The poor girl's most wicked pleasure in fact was to let me dress her as a boy and take her with me to the quadroon balls and to the riverfront drinking places where no true white woman could ever enter. All this was fun and sport for her, and I loved it too, seeing this seamy rotten world through her pretty eyes . . .

But! As all that went on, as the city grew rich and yearly full of more diversions, I carried out with Marguerite in the privacy of the study our worst sacrifices to the daemon.

Our first victim of any note was a voodoo doctor, a

mulatto with yellow hair, very old, but still strong, whom we stole from his front steps, and took to Riverbend, plying him with fancy words and wine and heaps of gold, and assuring him we would know what he knew of God and the Devil.

He had been possessed by many a spirit, he averred. Fine, we have a nice one for you. We talked voodoo and we talked trash and lies. We had him ripe to welcome this powerful god, Lasher.

In Marguerite's rooms with the doors bolted once more, we called Lasher down into this man, who of his own free will surrendered to the possession.

At first, the creature lay still, a small-boned old man, skin very pale, hair very yellow, and then as he opened his eyes, we saw another life was inside him! The eyes fixed upon us, and the mouth moved, and a voice deeper than that of the man himself, yet from the same throat, said:

'Ah, my beloveds, I see you.' The voice was flat and horrid. Indeed it roared from the mouth, and the eyes of the creature were wild and without intelligent expression.

'Sit up!' declared Marguerite. 'Be strong! Take possession!' And she urged me to say these words with her, and we repeated them again, our eyes fixed on the thing.

The man rose up, arms outstretched, and then these were let to flop at his sides, and he almost toppled over. He struggled to his feet, and then he did fall, but we rushed to catch him. His fingers wriggled in the air, and then he managed to close one hand on my neck, which I didn't particularly like, but I knew he was too weak to do me any harm, and it said again in that awful voice:

'My beloved Julien.'

'Take possession of the being forever,' cried Marguerite. 'Take this body as if it were your right.'

And then the whole body began to tremble; and before my eyes once more, as had happened with the infant, the hair of the creature began somewhat to darken. And it seemed the face was wildly contorted.

And then the poor old body fell dead, in our arms, and if the old man was there again even for an instant, we never knew it.

But as we laid him down upon the bed, Marguerite made a careful study. She showed me patches of his skin which had been rendered white, and the parts of the hair which were distinctly dark as if some energy had erupted from within and changed these things. I noted it was only the new and short hair which had changed, and the skin was already fading back to its yellowish hue.

'What do we do with all this, Mother? We must keep it secret from the family.'

'Well, of course,' she said. 'But first we take off the head here to save it.'

I collapsed in exhaustion, sitting against the wall, crossing my ankles and watching in silence as she slowly severed the man's head, using a hatchet for the purpose. And then I saw this thing immersed in the chemicals she had so lately bought for the purpose and the jar sealed, and the man's eyes staring out at me.

By then Lasher had gathered his wits, if that's what they were. And he was there, a human-looking male, strong, beside her. And I remember that moment as perfectly as any other – the fiend standing there in the form of an innocent man, wide-eyed and almost sweet, and Marguerite, clamping the top on that jar and holding it up to the light and talking baby talk to the head inside. 'You've done well, little head, you've done well.'

Then back she went to scribbling about future experiments.

Michael, when you came to this house and saw the jars, you saw all that ever resulted from this magic. There was nothing more. But how were we to know that?

With each new victim we grew more cunning and bold; and more hopeful; we learnt that the body must be strong, not old, and that a youngster with no family or home was our best prospect.

I lived in dread Katherine would find out. Katherine was my joy. I sat sometimes looking at Katherine and thinking, If only you knew, yet I could not draw myself away from my mother or from the thing, from any of it. Katherine was my innocent self, perhaps, the child I had never been, the good one I had never cared to be. I loved her.

As for my machinations with the fiend, I enjoyed them. I took a secret pleasure even in catching the victims and bringing them home, leading them up the steps, and inducing them to make themselves proper vessels. Each experiment brought me to a powerful level of excitement. The flickering candles, the victim on the bed, the possession itself – it was all hypnotic.

Lasher too began to express his preferences. Bring those of light complexion and hair so that he could change them more easily to what he wanted; and for longer periods of time, he walked and talked in their bodies.

Some superficial mutation was always accomplished.

419

But that's all it ever was! It was skin and it was hair and no more.

And the victim inevitably died as the result.

But the spirit loved it; the spirit soon lived for it.

'I would see the moon tonight with human eyes,' Lasher said, 'bring a child to me. I would dance to the music tonight with human feet. Have the fiddlers outside the door and bring me legs that know dancing.'

And to reward us, the thing brought us gold and jewels beyond imagining. I was always finding money in my pockets. And ever more prosperous we grew, the thing warning us when to take our investments out of this or that place, and never failing in this.

Something else happened as well. The thing began to imitate me. I saw it.

This stemmed from a few careless remarks of mine. 'Why must you look like that when you appear? So prim, so dusty?'

'Suzanne thought this was a handsome man. What would you have me look like?'

And in a few carefully chosen words I designed its clothes for it. Thereafter it appeared exactly like me to frighten me and amuse me. And we soon discovered that it could fool others on this score completely. I could leave it at my desk pretending to be me and run away, and people thought I had never left the house at all.

It was marvelous. Of course it could be nothing solid for very long. But it was getting stronger and stronger.

And something else had come clear to me. The thing, though it gave me pleasure whenever I desired it, had no jealousy of others where I was concerned. Indeed the thing liked to watch such goings-on – with lovers, whores, mistresses. The thing often hovered about my armoires, causing my coats to stir in the wind as he touched them. The thing was taking me as some sort of interesting model.

Whereas Marguerite now kept to her mad laboratory night and day, I went forth into the city. And with me the fiend went, observing everything. And I felt great power to have it at my side, my secret confidant, my supernatural eye, my guardian.

And now when Marguerite and I did hide from it beneath music, it appeared and danced, as it had once appeared to Marie Claudette. That is, our shutting it out made it show its strength, and in dandified clothes, it put on a show, distracting us as we distracted it, flinging itself into the melody.

If there was anyone at Riverbend who had not seen this fiend in material form for at least thirty seconds, that person was either blind or crazy.

Michael, I could tell you so much! But it is not the story of my life that matters. Suffice it to say I lived as few men ever have, learning what I wanted, and doing what I wanted, and enjoying all manner of pleasure. And the fiend was my best lover, of course, always. No man or woman kept me from it for long.

'Laughter, Julien. Am I not better?'

'You are, I must confess,' I said, flinging myself back on the bed, and letting it go to work pulling at my clothes and caressing me.

'Why do you love so to do it?' I asked.

'You become warm; you become close; I am close; we are nearly together. You are beautiful, Julien. We are men, you and I.'

Makes sense, I thought, and, drunk on erotic pleasure,

I gave myself to it for days on end, emerging finally to go to the city again and amuse myself in some other way, lest I go as mad as my mother.

Of course I now knew the experiments would never get us anywhere. Lasher's addiction to possession was all that kept us going.

Marguerite meantime was now officially mad. But no one cared. Why should they? We were a family of hundreds! My brother, Rémy, had married and had numerous children, both by his wife, and by his quadroon mistress. There were Mayfairs to the left and Mayfairs to the right, and many of our ilk went into town and built fine houses throughout the city.

If the head witch kept to her rooms during the lavish picnics we gave, or the balls we held, who cared? No one missed her. I was there, dancing with Katherine of course, who broke the hearts of all the young men who chased after her – Katherine now past twenty-five years of age, an old maid in the South of those times, but so beautiful no one dared even think such a thing, and so wealthy, of course, that she need never marry.

In fact, it soon came clear to me that she was afraid to marry. Of course my mother and I had told her what we could. And she had been horrified. She didn't want to have a child, for fear the evil seed would be carried on. 'I shall die a virgin,' she said, 'and that will be the end. There will be no more witches.'

'Any comments?' I asked Lasher.

'Laughter' was his solitary reply. 'She is human. Humans crave each other's company; humans crave little ones. There are many cousins to choose from. Look at those who have the marks. Look at those who *see*.'

I did. I pushed every Mayfair with a witch's gift into Katherine's face for all the good it did. She was a dreamy sweet sort. She never argued.

But then the unthinkable occurred.

It began innocently enough. She wanted a house in the city. I should hire the Irish architect Darcy Monahan to build it for her, in the Faubourg uptown where all the Americans had settled.

'You must be mad,' I said. My father had been Irish, true, but I had never known him. I was a Creole, and spoke only French. 'Why would we want to live up there with those splashy Americans? With merchants and trash such as that?'

I bought from Darcy a town house in the Rue Dumaine which he had already completed for a man who'd gone bankrupt and blown his brains out. I could see the ghost of this man from time to time, but it didn't bother me. It was like that ghost of Marie Claudette, something lifeless and unable to communicate.

I moved into this flat, and made lavish rooms for Katherine. Not good enough. And so I said, 'All right, we shall buy the square of land at Chestnut Street and First, and we will build some grand horror of a Greek temple to suit your tastes, go ahead. Go wild. What do I care?'

Darcy commenced at once to design and build the house in which I am now standing. I was disdainful, but Lasher came to me, leaning over my shoulder, duplicating me, and then fading back into that brown-haired man he preferred to be, and said:

'Make it full of pattern; make it full of ornament and design: make it beautiful.'

'Tell Katherine these things,' I urged, and the daemon

obeyed, putting these thoughts in her head and guiding the plans, and she as guileless as ever.

'This shall be a great house,' the fiend said to me when we rode uptown together, the thing materializing to step out of the very carriage and stand at the gate. 'In this house miracles will happen.'

'How do you know?' I said.

'I see now. I see the way. You are my beloved Julien.'

What does that mean, I wondered, but I was in too thick to think about it much, that was certain. I threw myself into my business dealings, the acquiring of land, my investments abroad, and in general tried to keep my mind off Katherine's plan for this American house, this Greek Revival house, this uptown house, and to lure her back to the Quarter to sup with me whenever possible.

As you know, she fell in love with Darcy! Indeed it was Lasher who revealed the plot to me. I was headed uptown, for Katherine had not come home, and I did not like it that she stayed late after the builders had gone, roaming around the half-built house alone with that wicked Irishman.

Lasher sought to divert me. First he would talk. Then he would have a victim to possess.

'Not now,' says I. 'I must find Katherine.'

And finally, in manly form, he did his worst trick, affrighting my coachman and driving us off the Nyades Road, where we broke a wheel, and I was soon sitting on the curb as the repairs went on, perfectly furious. But I could see now that the daemon did not want me to go uptown.

So the next night, I sought to deflect it. I sent it upon a mission to find for me some rare coins which I would have, and then off I went alone on my mare, singing the entire time, lest it come near enough to read my thoughts and intentions.

It was twilight when I reached this house. Like a great castle it stood, its brick plastered over to imitate stone, its columns in place, its windows ready for the glass to be installed. And it was dark and deserted.

I came inside, and on the floor of the parlor found my blessed sister and her man. I almost killed him. Indeed, I had him by the neck and was pounding him with my fist, when Katherine, to my horror, cried out:

'Come now, my Lasher. Be my avenger. Stop him from destroying the one I love.'

Shrieking and sobbing, she fell to the floor in a faint. But Lasher was there. I felt him surrounding me in the darkness, as if he were a great creature of the sea and I a helpless victim. Darkness wrapped itself around me in the shell of the double parlor below, and then I felt the thing stretch out and stroke the walls, and come together again.

'Hold back, Julien,' Lasher said. 'The witch loves this mortal man. Be careful. She has used ancient and sanctified words to call me.'

Darcy Monahan rose to his feet and came to assault me. Lasher stayed his hand. He was superstitious as anyone with Irish blood, and he looked around sensing the presence in the dark, and then he saw his lovely Katherine in a heap, moaning, and he went to revive her.

I stalked out in a rage. I went back to my flat in the Rue Dumaine and brought several quadroon ladies of the night to my house, and there coupled with them one after another, in an abandon of grief. Katherine and that Irish beast; uptown in the land of the Americans.

I see when I look back upon the story that I had kept too much knowledge from her. She thought the man was a ghost or a simple thing. She had no knowledge of what Lasher could do when she called upon him.

'Well,' I told her, 'if you want to kill me, just call on him again like that, and he will try to do your bidding.'

I wasn't sure this was true, but I didn't want her flinging curses at me. First she had betrayed me with Darcy and then with Lasher himself, and she was the witch, and all my life I had shielded her. 'You don't know what you command,' I said, 'I've saved you from it.'

She was horrified and tearful and sad, but she was also resolved to marry Darcy Monahan. 'You don't need to save me anymore,' she said. 'I shall marry with the emerald around my neck as our family laws require, but I marry in God's house before His altar, and my children shall be baptized at His font, and they shall turn their back on evil.'

I shrugged. We had always married at a Catholic altar, had we not? We were all baptized. What was this? But I said nothing to her.

My mother and I set out to turn her away from Darcy. But there was no doing it. Indeed, she was ready to renounce the legacy for this Irish fool, or so she told everyone. The cousins came to me *en masse*. What will happen? What is the law? Will we lose our good fortune? And then it was clear how much they knew of the dark secret furnace of evil which fueled the entire enterprise and how willing they were to go along with it.

But it was Lasher who gave the bride away.

'Let her marry the Celt,' he said. 'Your father had the Irish blood, and in it rode the witches' gifts which have ridden in such blood for centuries. The Irish, the Scots, they are gifted with second sight. Your father's blood made you strong. Let us see what this Irishman can do with your sister.'

But you know the story. Katherine lost two babies, both boys; then had by Darcy two sons. Then despite her prayers, her Masses, her rosaries and her priests, she lost one baby after another.

As the Civil War raged, as the city fell, as fortunes were destroyed overnight, as Yankee troops went through our streets, she reared her boys in the First Street house, among American friends and traitors. Katherine thought she had left the family curse behind. Indeed, she had given back the emerald on her wedding day.

The family was frantic. The witch was gone. For the first time I heard many of them whispering the word. 'But she is the witch!' they would say. 'How can she desert us?'

And the emerald. It lay on Mother's dresser among all her voodoo trash, like a hideous trinket. I picked it up, finally, and hung it round the neck of the nearby plaster Virgin.

This for me was a dark time, a time of great freedom and also great learning. Katherine was gone, and nothing else much mattered to me. If I had ever doubted it, I knew it now – my family was my world. I could have gone to Europe then; I could have gone to China. I could have gone beyond war and pestilence and poverty. I could have lived as a potentate. But this small part of the earth was my home, and without my loved ones around me, nothing had any flavor.

Pathetic, I thought. But it was true. And I learned

what only a powerful and rich man can ever know – what it was I truly wanted.

Meantime, the fiend was ever urging me to new lovers; and watching what went on as eagerly as ever. He imitated me more and more. Even when he visited Mother now, he came in a guise so like me that others thought it was I. He seemed to have lost any sense of himself, if he had ever had any.

'What do you really look like?' I asked.

'Laughter. Why ask me such a question?'

'When you are flesh what will you be?'

'Like you, Julien.'

'And why not like you were at first – brown-haired and brown-eyed?'

'That was only for Suzanne, that was what Suzanne would see, and so I took that shape and grew in that shape, a Scotsman of her village. I would be you. You are beautiful.'

I pondered much. I gambled, drank, danced until dawn, fought and argued with Confederate patriots and Yankee enemies, made and lost fortunes in various realms, fell in love a couple of times, and in general came to realize I grieved night and day for my Katherine. Perhaps I needed a purpose to my life, something beyond the making of money and the lavishing of it upon cousins far and wide, something besides the building of new bungalows on our lands, and the acquisition of more and more property. Katherine had been a purpose of sorts. I had never had any other.

Except for the fiend, of course. To play with him, to mutate flesh, to court and use him. Ah, I began to see through everything!

Then came the year 1871. Summer, and yellow fever,

as it always struck, running rampant among the newest of the immigrants.

Darcy and Katherine and their boys had lately been abroad. In fact, for six months, they had been in Europe, and no sooner had the handsome Irishman set foot on shore than he came down with the fever.

He'd lost his immunity to it in foreign lands, I suppose, or whatever, I don't honestly know, except that the Irish were always dying of this disease, and we were never affected by it. Katherine went mad. She sent letters to me in the Rue Dumaine; please come and cure him.

I said to Lasher, 'Will he die?'

Lasher appeared at the foot of my bed, collected, arms folded, dressed as I had been dressed the day before, all illusion of course.

'I think he will die,' he said. 'And perhaps it's time. Don't fret. There is nothing even a witch can do against this fever.'

I wasn't so sure. But when I called upon Marguerite she began to cackle and dance: 'Let the bastard die and all his spawn with him.'

This disgusted me. What had little Clay and Vincent done, those innocent children, except be born boys as I had been with my brother, Rémy?

I went back to the city, pondering what to do, consulting doctors and nurses, and of course the fever raged as it always did in hot weather, and the bodies piled high at the cemeteries. The city stank of death. Great fires were burned to drive away the evil effluvia.

The rich cotton factors and merchandising giants who had come south to make a buck after the war went down to the Grim Reaper as easily as the Irish peasants off the ships.

Then Darcy died. He died. And there was Katherine's coachman at my door.

'He's dead, Monsieur. Your sister begs you to come!'

What could I do? I had never set foot in that First Street house since it had been completed. I did not even know poor little Clay or Vincent by sight! I had not seen my sister in a year, except to argue with her once in a public street. Suddenly all my riches and my pleasures seemed nothing to me. My sister was begging me to come.

I had to go and I had to forgive her.

'Lasher, what do I do?'

'You will see,' he said.

'But there is no female to carry on the line! She will wither as a widow behind closed doors. You know it. I know it.'

'You will see,' he said again. 'Go to her.'

The whole family held its breath. What will happen?

I went to the First Street house. It was a rainy night, very hot and simmering, and in the Irish slums only blocks away, the bodies of fever victims were stacked in the gutters.

A stench wafted on the breeze from the river. But there stood this house as it always has, majestic among its oaks and magnolia trees, a narrow and high-flung castle complete with battlements and walls that appear indestructible. A deep secretive house, full of graceful designs yet somehow ominous.

I saw the window of the master bedroom to the north. I saw a sight which many have seen since, and which you have seen, the flicker of candles against the shutters.

I came into the house, forcing the door, with Lasher's

help or my own strength I do not know, only that it yielded to me, and the lock broke and was thereafter useless.

I took off my rain-drenched coat and went up the stairs. The door to the master bedroom lay open.

Of course I expected to see the dead Irish architect lying there putrefying on summer schedule. But I soon realized he had been taken away on account of the contagion. The superstitious Irish maids came to tell me this, that Darcy, poor soul, was already buried, and with the bells of St Alphonsus tolling night and day, there had been no time for a Requiem.

Within the room, all had been scrubbed down and cleaned, and it was Katherine who lay on the bed, a giant four-poster with black carved lions' heads in its posts, crying softly into the embroidered pillow.

She looked so small and so frail; she looked like my little sister. Indeed, I called her that. I sat by her and comforted her. She sobbed on my shoulder. Her long black hair was still thick and soft, and her face held its beauty. All those babies lost had not taken away her charms or her innocence, or the radiant faith in her eyes when she looked at me.

'Julien, take me home to Riverbend,' she said. 'Take me home. Make Mother forgive me. I cannot live here alone. Everywhere I look I see Darcy, only Darcy.'

'I will try, Katherine,' I said. But there was no doubt in my mind, I could not make a reconciliation with Mother. Mother was so crazy now, she might not even know who Katherine was, or where she'd been. Things were that out of hand there. Last I saw Mother, she and Lasher had been making flowers spring early from their seeds. And Lasher had told Mother secrets of plants which could make a brew to make her see visions. That was Mother's life of late. I might tell her Katherine had died and come back to earth and we had to be good to her. And who knows? She might have bought it.

'Don't worry, my beautiful girl,' I said. 'I'll take you home if you want to go, and your little babies with you. All the family is there as always.'

She nodded her head, and gestured in a helpless graceful way as if to say it was in my hands.

I kissed her and held her in my arms, and then laid her down to rest, assuring her that I would sit with her until morning.

The door was closed. The nurse was gone. The little boys were quiet, wherever they were. I went out of the room to have a smoke.

I saw Lasher.

He stood at the foot of the staircase looking up at me. He said in his silent voice, Study this house. Study its doors, its rooms, its patterns. Riverbend will perish as did the citadel we built in far-off Saint-Domingue, but this house will last to serve its purpose.

A dreamy feeling came over me. I went down the stairs, and began to do what you have done, Michael, a thousand times. Walk about this house slowly, in and around, laying my hands upon its doorframes and its brass knobs and musing at the paintings in the dining room and the lovely plaster ornament that everywhere decorated its ceilings.

Yes, a beautiful house, I thought. Poor Darcy. No wonder his designs had been so much the fashion. But he had had no witch's blood I supposed. I suspected my nephews Clay and Vincent were as innocent as my brother, Rémy. I went out into the gardens. I perceived what had been done, a great octagon of a lawn, with an octagon carved in the stone posts that ended the lime-stone balustrades. And everywhere flagstones at angles, so that one was beset in the moonlight with lines and designs and patterns.

'Behold the roses in the iron,' said Lasher to me. By this he meant the cast-iron railings. And I saw what he pointed out, lines at angles, echoing the angles of the flags, as well as the roses.

He walked with his arm around me now, and I felt a thrill in this, this closeness with him. I had half a mind to invite him into the trees, and give myself over to him. I was addicted as I said. But I had to remember my beloved sister. She might wake and cry and think that I had left her.

'Remember all these things,' he said again. 'For this house will last.'

As I came into the hallway, I saw him in the high dining room door with his hands on the frame. How it soared above him with its tapered keyhole shape, more narrow above, and thereby looking higher.

I turned to note that the front door, through which I'd just come, which I had left wide open, was of the same design, and there he stood, as if he had never been in the other place at all, a man like me with his hands on the frame, peering back at me.

'Would you live after death, Julien? Of all my witches you ask me so little about that final darkness.'

'You don't know anything about it, Lasher,' I commented. 'You said so yourself.'

'Don't be cruel with me, Julien. Not tonight of all nights. I am glad to be here. Would you live after death? Would you hover and stay, that is what I am asking you?'

'I don't know. If the Devil was trying to take me into hell I might hover and stay, if that's what you mean, a purgatorial soul wandering about, appearing to voodoo queens and spiritualists. I suppose I could do it.' I crushed out my cigar in the ashtray on the marble table, which is there now, this very day, in the lower hallway.

'Is that what you've done, Lasher? Are you some vile human being become a ghost, hovering forever, and seeking to wrap yourself in an undeserved mystery?'

I saw something in the face of the fiend change. One moment he was my twin and then he had smiled. Indeed, he was imitating my very smile and to perfection. I had not seen him do this trick before very often. And as he slumped against the doorframe, he folded his arms as I might, and he made a little sound of cloth brushing the wood, to let me know how strong he was.

'Julien,' he said, actually shaping his mouth with the words, he was so strong, 'maybe all mysteries are nothing at the core. Maybe the world is made from waste.'

'And you were there when it happened?'

'I don't know,' he said, imitating my own sarcastic tone exactly. He raised his eyebrows as I raise mine. I had never seen him so strong.

'Shut the door, Lasher,' I said, 'if you are so very mighty.'

And to my astonishment, he reached for the knob and stepped aside, and made the door close exactly as if he were a man doing it. That was the limit for him, for it had been an astonishing feat. He was gone. The air held the heat as it always did.

'Admirable,' I whispered.

'Remember this place if you would linger or come back; remember its patterns. In the dim world beyond they will shine in your eyes, they will guide you home. This is a house for centuries to come. This is a house worthy of the spirits of the dead; this is a house in which you may safely remain. War or revolution or fire, or the river's current, will not trouble you. I was held once . . . by two patterns. Two simple patterns. A circle, and stones in the form of a cross . . . two patterns.'

I memorized this. More proof that he was not the great Devil himself.

I went up the stairs. I had gotten just a little more out of him than I usually did, but nothing much really. And then there was Katherine.

This time I found her awake, and standing by the window.

'Where did you go?' she asked me breathlessly. And then she threw her arms around me again and leant against me. It seemed I felt Lasher stirring near us. I told him through the mind, Do not come here now, you'll scare her. I lifted her chin as men do to women, though how the little things stand it, I don't know, and I kissed her.

At that very second, something caught me by surprise. It was the pressure of her breasts against me. She wore nothing but a soft white dressing gown, and I felt her nipples, her heat, and then a stream of heat it seemed from her lips. But when I drew back and looked at her I saw only innocence.

I also saw a woman. A beautiful woman. A woman whom I had loved, who had risen up against me and cast me aside for another, a body loved by me as a brother should love his sister, with nothing about it unfamiliar to me from all our childhood romps and swims, and yet it was a woman's body, and it was in my arms, and in a moment of daring, I kissed her again, and then again, and then even once more, and I felt her begin to burn against me.

I was repelled. This was my baby sister, Katherine. I took her to the bed and laid her down; she seemed confused, looking at me. Dare I say spellbound? Did she think it was Darcy come back?

'No,' she whispered. 'I know it is you. I have always loved you. I'm sorry. You must forgive my little sins, but when I was a little girl I used to dream we would marry. We would walk down the aisle. It was only when Darcy came that I gave up that silly incestuous dream. God forgive me.'

She made the Sign of the Cross, and drew up her knees, and reached for the covers.

I don't know what came over me. Fury? I looked down at this little feminine thing, this creature with her outstretched hand and ragged veil of black hair, and pale shivering face, and I saw her make the Sign of the Cross, and I became enraged.

'How dare you play with me in this way!' I said, and I threw her back on the bed. Her dressing gown opened and there were her breasts, a luscious enticement.

Within seconds, I was ripping open my own clothes. She had begun to scream. She was terrified.

'No, no Julien, don't!' she cried.

But I was on top of her, and spreading her legs, and ripping what cloth was left out of my way.

'Oh Julien, please, please, don't,' she cried in the most heartbreaking voice. 'It's me, it's Katherine.'

But it was done. I had raped her and I took my time in finishing it and then climbed off the bed and went to the window. I thought my heart would burst. And I could not believe what I had done.

Meantime, she had gone from a little curl of a sobbing woman in the bed, to rushing to me, and suddenly flinging her arms around me and crying again my name, 'Julien, Julien!'

What did this mean? That she wanted me to protect her from myself?

'Oh, darling child,' I said. And I broke down utterly, kissing her.

And then we did it again, and again, and again.

And Mary Beth was born to us nine months after.

By then we had been at Riverbend all that time, and I could scarcely stand the sight of Katherine.

I had not dared to trouble her under our own roof, and I doubt she would have received me anyway. She had blotted the truth from her mind. She thought the thing in her belly was Darcy's baby. She said her rosary all the time, for Darcy's unborn child.

And everyone, everyone knew what I had done to her. Julien the evil one. Julien had got his sister with child. The cousins stared at me as if I were anathema. Out of Fontevrault, Augustin's son Tobias came especially to curse me and tell me I was the Devil. Far and wide people knew who did not dare to show their displeasure.

And then there were all my gambling, whoring friends, who thought it strange and unmanly, but when I did not falter a step in my usual dance, they merely gave a shrug and accepted it. That's one thing I found out, you can carry off most any sin, if you just do nothing.

Ah, but the baby was coming. Once again, the whole family held its breath.

And Lasher? When I saw him at all, he was as

impassive as he had ever been. He hovered near Katherine all the time, unseen by her.

'It was his doing,' my mother said. 'He pushed you into her arms. Stop fretting. She has to have more babies, everyone knows, she has to have a daughter. Why not you for the father, a powerful witch? I think it's a fine idea.'

I didn't bother to talk about it again with her.

And I didn't know if it had been his doing. I don't know now. All I knew was it was the most expensive pleasure I'd ever bought, this rape, and that I, Julien, who could kill men at any time without a qualm, felt filthy and acquainted with cruelty and with evil.

Katherine really lost her mind before Mary Beth was born. But nobody knew it.

From the time of the rape, really, she was never anything any more than a mumbling woman saying her beads, and talking about angels and saints, good for playing with little children.

But then came the night of Mary Beth's birth; Katherine was huge with the child, and screaming in agony. I was in the room, with the black midwives and the white doctor, and with Marguerite and all those who were to attend and help. You never saw such a committee assembled.

And finally with her last and most wrenching scream, Katherine pushed Mary Beth forth into the world, and here it came, this beautiful and perfect child, resembling more a small female than an infant. By that I mean that though its head was a baby's head, it had rich black curls already, and one shining tooth flashed beneath the baby's upper lip, and its arms and legs were exquisite. It writhed with life and gave forth the most soft and beautiful and lustful cries.

They put it into my arms.

'*Eh bien*, Monsieur, this is your niece,' said the old doctor with great ceremony.

And I looked down at this daughter of mine, and then in the corner of my eye saw the devil come in vapor form, my Lasher, not in the solid way so that others in this room might see, but merely an apparition, soft as silk brushing my shoulder. And the child's eyes had seen it too! The child was making its tiny precocious mouth into a smile for it.

Her cries grew quiet; her tiny hands opened and closed. I planted my kiss on her forehead. A witch, a witch through and through; the scent of power rose from her like perfume.

And then came the most ominous words I had ever heard, confidential from the fiend to me:

'Well done, Julien. *You have served your purpose!*'

I was thunderstruck. Every silent and deafening syllable sank in slowly.

I let my right hand slip up and around the baby's throat, beneath its covers of white linen and lace, and closed my thumb and my forefinger tightly against the pale flesh, though no one in the room took notice

'Julien, no!' came his whisper in my head.

'Oh, come now,' I asked in my secret voice, 'you need me to protect it for a little while longer, don't you? Look around you, spirit. Look with a human's cunning, for once, and not the addled brains of an angel. What do you see? An old hag and a mumbling madwoman, and a baby girl. Who will teach it what it needs to know? Who will be there to protect it when it begins to show its gifts?'

'Julien, I never meant that I would harm you.'

I laughed and everyone thought I was laughing at the wriggling child, which did certainly seem to have its little eyes focused tight upon something which no one else could now see, just over my shoulder, and now I gave it over to the nurses, and they bathed it again to make it ready for its mother.

I withdrew from the room. I was steaming with rage. *You have served your purpose!* Indeed, had that been it from the very first? More than likely. And all the rest was games and I knew it.

But I knew this too. Around me in all directions, there thrived an immense and prosperous family, a family of people I loved, who had once loved me before this abominable act, and stood to love me still if I could earn their forgiveness. And in that room behind me was a darling child who touched my heart as all children always have – and this child was mine, my firstborn!

All the good things, I thought, the good things which are life itself! And damn this demon to hell that I cannot get rid of it!

But what right had I to complain? What right had I to regret? What right had I to be ashamed? I'd let the thing enslave me from my earliest years, when I knew it was treacherous and fanciful and pompous and selfish. I'd known. I'd played into its hands as all the witches had, as the whole family had.

And now, if it was to let me live, I had to be of some clear use to it. I had to think of something. Teaching Mary Beth wouldn't be enough. No, not nearly enough. After all the thing itself was a damned good teacher. No, I had to think of something quick, and it was going to take all my witches' gifts to do it.

Even as I brooded, the family gathered. Cousins

440

came running, shouting and waving and clapping their hands.

'It's a girl, it's a girl! At last, Katherine has given birth to a girl!'

And suddenly I was surrounded by loving hands, and loving kisses. It was perfectly fine that I'd raped my sister; or I'd done penance enough; whatever, I didn't know. But Riverbend was filled with cheering voices. Champagne corks popped; musicians played. The baby was held aloft from the gallery. Ships on the river began to blow their whistles to honor our visible and obvious festivity.

Oh God in heaven! What will you do now, I thought, you evil evil man? What will you do merely to keep yourself alive and to save that tiny baby from utter destruction?

FIFTEEN

The world shook with Father's song and Father's laughter. Father said, in his fast high-pitched voice, 'Emaleth, be strong; take what you must; Mother may try to harm you. Fight, Emaleth, fight to be with me. Think of the glen and the sunshine and of all our children.'

Emaleth saw children – thousands and thousands of people like Father, and like Emaleth herself, for she did see herself now, her own long fingers, and long limbs, and hair swimming in the water of the world that was Mother. The world that was already too small for her.

How Father laughed. She saw him dance; she saw him dance as Mother saw him. His song to her was long and beautiful.

Flowers were in the room. Lots and lots of flowers. The scent was everywhere mingled with the scent of Father. Mother cried and cried and Father tied her hands to the bed. Mother kicked him and Father cursed; and there was thunder in heaven.

Father, please, please, be kind to Mother.

'I will. I'm going now, child.' He gave her the secret message. 'And I'll come back with food for your mother, food that will make you grow strong; and when the time comes, Emaleth, fight to be born, fight anything which tries to oppose you.'

It made her sad to think of fighting. Whom was she

to fight? Surely not Mother! Emaleth was Mother. Emaleth's heart was tied to Mother's heart. When Mother felt pain, Emaleth felt it, as if someone had pushed her through the wall of the world that was Mother.

Only a moment ago Emaleth could have sworn that Mother knew she was there! That for one instant Mother understood that she had Emaleth inside her, but then the quarreling had come again, between Father and Mother.

And now as the door shut, and Father's scent was gone away, and the flowers shifted and nodded and pulsed in the twilight room, Emaleth heard Mother crying.

Don't cry, Mother, please. You make me sad when you cry. All the world is nothing but sadness.

Can you really hear me, my darling?

Mother *did* know she was there! Emaleth turned and twisted in her tiny constricted world, and pushed at the roof, and heard Mother sigh: *Yes, Mother, say my name as Father says it. Emaleth. Call my name!*

Emaleth.

Then Mother began to talk to her in earnest. *Listen to me, baby girl, I'm in trouble. I am weak and sick. I'm starved. You are inside of me, and thank God, you take what you must have from my teeth, from my bones, from my blood. But I'm weak. He's tied me up again. You must begin to help me. What am I to do to save both of us?*

Mother, he loves us. He loves you and he loves me. He wants to fill the world with our children.

Mother moaned in the silence. 'Emaleth, be still,' she said. 'I am sick.'

And Mother twisted in pain on the bed, her ankles bound apart, her wrists bound apart, the scent of the flowers sickening her.

Emaleth wept. The sadness of Mother was too terrible for her to bear. She saw Mother as Father had seen her, so wan and worn with the dark circles around her eyes, like an owl in the bed, an owl; and Emaleth saw in the deep dark woods an owl.

Darling, listen to me, you will not be inside me forever. Soon you'll be born and at that time, Emaleth, I may die. It may be at the very moment of my death that you come.

No, Mother! That was too terrible to think of, Mother dead! Emaleth knew dead. She could smell dead. She saw the owl shot with an arrow and falling to the floor of the forest. Leaves stirred. She knew Death as she knew up and down and all around, and water, and her own skin and her hair which she caught in her fingers, and rubbed to her own lips. Dead was not alive! And the long stories of Father drifted through her head, of the glen, and how they must come together and grow strong.

'Remember,' Father had said to her once, 'they show no mercy to those who are not their kind. And you must be just as merciless. You, my daughter, my wife, my little mother.'

Don't die, Mother. You cannot do this. Do not die.

'I'm trying, my darling, but listen to me. Father is mad. He dreams dreams which are bad, and when you are born you must get away from here. You must get clear of me and of him, and you must seek those who can help you.' Then Mother began to cry again, woebegone and crushed and shaking her head.

Father was coming back. The key in the lock. The smell of Father and food.

'Here, precious darling,' he said, 'I have orange juice for you, and milk, and good things.'

He sank down beside Mother on the bed.

'Ah, it won't be long!' he said. 'See how she struggles! And your breasts, they are filling with milk again!'

Mother screamed. He covered Mother's mouth with his hand, and she tried to bite his fingers!

Emaleth wept. This was terrible, terrible, this darkness and clangor over the entire horizon. What was the world when one suffered so? It was nothing. She wanted to put things in their mouths to stop their mouths so they could not speak hate to each other. She pushed at the roof of the world. She saw herself a woman born running from one to the other, and stuffing their mouths with leaves from the forest floor so they could not say hurtful words to each other.

'You will drink the orange juice, you will drink the milk,' said Father in fury.

'Only if you untie me again, and let me up. Then I'll eat. If I can sit on the side of the bed, I'll eat.'

Please, Father, be kind to Mother. Mother's heart is full of sorrow. Mother must have the food. Mother has been starved. Mother is weak.

Very well, my darling dear. Father was afraid. He could not again leave Mother without food and water.

He cut loose the tape that was tied around Mother's arms, and around her legs.

At once Mother drew all her limbs together, and turned her feet to the side, and they were walking, she and Mother, back and forth and back and forth. Into the bathroom they went, full of bright light and shining things, and the smell of water, and the chemicals of water.

Mother closed the door, and lifted a large slab of white porcelain from the back of the toilet. These things Emaleth understood because Mother understood, but not entirely. Porcelain was hard and heavy; Mother was afraid. Mother held the porcelain slab up high. It was like a tombstone.

Father pushed open the door, and Mother turned and brought down the big slab of porcelain on Father's head and Father cried out.

Anguish for Emaleth. *Mother, don't do it.*

But Father sank down silent in peace, with no complaint, on the floor, and dreamed, and again Mother struck him with the porcelain slab. The blood ran out of his ears onto the floor. He shut his eyes. He dreamed. Mother drew back, sobbing, and dropped the porcelain slab.

But Mother was filled with excitement, filled with hope. Mother almost fell down too, but she climbed over Father, and ran out into the room, and snatched her clothes and purse from the closet floor, her purse, yes, her purse, she had to have her purse, and off she ran down the hallway in her bare feet, Emaleth tossed and thrown and reaching out for the world to make it steady.

They were in the tiny elevator going down, down, down! It felt so good to Emaleth! They were in the world outside the room. Mother lay against the back of the elevator, putting on her clothes, mumbling aloud to herself, crying, wiping at her face. She pulled the red sweater over her head. Pulled on the skirt, but she could not button it. She pulled the sweater down over it.

Where were they going?

Mother, what happened to Father? Where are we going?

Father wants us to go. We have to go, be quiet and be patient.

Mother wasn't telling the truth. Far off, Emaleth heard Father whisper her name.

Mother stopped in the elevator door. The pain was too much for her. More and more there was pain. Emaleth sighed and tried to make herself very small, no pain for Mother. But the world grew tight and small and then Mother gasped, and put her hand over her eyes, and leaned to the side.

Mother, don't fall.

Then Mother fitted her shoes to her feet and began to run, her purse dangling from her shoulder, banging the glass doors as she ran out. But she could not run far. She was too heavy. With her arms around Emaleth she stopped, hugging Emaleth and steadying her.

Mother, I love you.

I love you too, my dear. I do. But I must get to Michael.

Mother thought of Michael, pictured him, the man with the dark hair and the smile, burly and kind, and not at all like Father. Angel, Mother said, to save us. Mother was calm for a moment and her hope and her joy flooded through Emaleth. Emaleth felt joy.

Emaleth felt for the first time in all her life Mother's happiness. *Michael.*

But in the midst of this lovely calm, when Emaleth laid her head against Mother and Mother's hands held Emaleth's world, Emaleth heard Father calling.

Mother, Father has waked up. I can hear him. He's calling.

Mother stepped into the street. The cars and trucks roared by. Mother rushed towards a big noisy truck that rose up before her like a wall of shining steel, looking just like a big face with a mean mouth and nose above her.

Yes, darling dear, that about covers it.

With all her might, Mother managed to make the high step and pull open the door.

'Please, sir, take me with you, wherever you are going! I have to go!' Mother slammed the door of the truck. 'Drive, for the love of God, I'm only a woman alone. I can't hurt you!'

Emaleth, where are you?

'Lady, you need to get to a hospital. You're sick,' said the man but he obeyed.

The big truck took off, the motor filling the world with noise. Mother was sick with the rattle and bounce of the truck, with pain. Circular pain. Mother's head fell back on the seat.

Emaleth, your mother has hurt me!

Mother, he is calling to us.

Darling, if you love me, don't answer him.

'Lady, I'm taking you to Houston General.'

Mother wanted to say, No, please, don't do this. Take me away. She could not catch her breath. She tasted of sickness, even of blood. She was in pain. The pain hurt Emaleth too.

Father's voice was very far away, making no words, only cries.

'New Orleans,' she said. 'That's my home. I have to get back there. I have to get to the Mayfair house, on First and Chestnut.'

Emaleth knew what Mother knew. That is where Michael was. She wished she could speak to the truck driver. She wished she could. Mother was so sick.

Mother would soon vomit, and that smell would come. *Be calm, Mother. I don't hear Father anymore.*

'Michael Curry, in New Orleans, I have to reach him there. He'll pay you. He'll pay you plenty. I will pay you. Call him. Look – We'll stop at a phone, later, when we're out of town, but look –'

And now from her purse she brought out the money, lots and lots of money, and the man stared at Mother with his round human eyes, very amazed but wanting to make her not sick, wanting to help her, wanting to do as she said, thinking she was soft and young and pretty.

'Are we headed south?' Mother asked, sick again, almost unable to speak. The pain wrapped around her, and wrapped around Emaleth too. OOOOOh . . . this was the worst Emaleth had ever felt. She kicked at the world. But she did not mean to kick at Mother.

Father's voice had long ago died out in the rumble of cars, in the glare of lights. The world was huge all around them.

'We are going south now, lady,' he said. 'We're going south, now, all right, but I wish you'd let me take you to a hospital.'

Mother closed her eyes. The light went out of her mind. Her head fell to the side. She slept; she dreamed. The money lay on her lap, on the floor of the truck, all over the pedals. The man reached down and picked up one bill at a time, trying not to take his eyes off the cars that zoomed along the road in front of him. Cars, road, signs, freeway; New Orleans, south.

'Michael,' Mother said. 'Michael Curry. New Orleans. But you know, you know when I think about it, I think the phone is listed under Mayfair. Mayfair and Mayfair. Call Mayfair and Mayfair.'

SIXTEEN

They figured that Alicia CeeCee Mayfair had miscarried at about 4 p.m. She'd been dead for over three hours when Mona came to see her. They had checked on her, of course. They had shone the light on her, and the nurse said that she hadn't wanted to wake her up. And Anne Marie had been in and out, both before and after the time of death.

Nobody had seen anyone else go to that room. It was strictly private.

Leslie Ann Mayfair was making calls to all the women in the family. Ryan was making calls from downtown. His secretary, Carla, was making calls.

Mona, when she finally got free of their hugs and kisses, bolted the door of her room against them. Then she tore off the white dress and the ribbon in a fury.

Of course she couldn't call Michael and tell him, ask him to come. The phone was all tied up, naturally.

In her slip and bra, she pyrooted through the closet for better clothes. There were none. She unlocked the door, and crossed the hall to Mom's room. No one even noticed her. All the conversation came up the stairwell like a roar. Car doors were slamming outside. Ancient Evelyn was crying somewhere loudly and terribly.

CeeCee's closet. CeeCee had been only five foot one,

and Mona was almost that now. She pyrooted through
the dresses and coats and suits until she found a little
skirt, too short, Mom had said. Well, that's just fine,
and then one of those frilly blouses CeeCee wore between about nine and eleven each morning before drinking lunch and putting on her nightgown to watch the
afternoon soaps in the living room.

Well, CeeCee wasn't going to do that anymore, was
she? Mona's head was spinning. These clothes smelled
like Mother. She thought of that smell in the hospital.
No, it wasn't here, nowhere here. Or she would have
caught it.

She looked in the mirror. She looked like a little
woman now, well, sort of. She picked up CeeCee's
brush and caught up her hair in back, the way CeeCee
used to do, and put a barrette in it.

And just for an instant, no more than that, like the
blink of an eye, she thought she saw Mother. She
groaned. She wanted so badly for it to be true. But
there was no one in the mirror but Mona, with her hair
clipped back, looking very grown-up. There was
CeeCee's lipstick, the soft pink kind, 'cause she wasn't
sober enough anymore to do anything fancy with bright
red unless she wanted to look like a clown, she said.

Mona put it on.

OK, now back across the hall, slam the door, and
boot the computer.

The WordStar Directory came up, big and bright and
green and full of the classic menu. Mona punched R for
Run a Program and commanded the program to make
subdirectory \WS\MONA\HELP.

At once she changed to that new directory and hit D
to make a file named Help, and then she was in it.

'This is Mona Mayfair, writing on March 3rd. And this is for those who come after me and may never understand what happened. Something is preying upon the women in our family. They are being warned, but they think it is a disease. It is not, it is something worse, something that will deceive everyone.

'I am going to help warn the women.'

She hit the KD for save. And the file vanished into the machine, silently. She was left in the dark room before the computer as before the glow of a fire, and the noise from the Avenue slowly overcame the stolid silence. A traffic jam outside. Someone knocking on her door.

She went to the door and slid back the bolt. Paint flaked off, settling on her fingers. She opened the door.

'I was looking for Mona. Oh, Mona! I didn't recognize you.' It was Aunt Bea. 'Good God, child, you found your mother?'

'Yeah, I'm fine,' said Mona. 'But you have to call everyone.'

'We're doing that, darling, come down with me. Let me hold you.'

'No one can be alone, not even the way I was just alone, no one.'

Mona walked past her, down the hall to the head of the stairs. 'No one can be alone!' Mona cried.

Mayfairs packed the long lower hall, cigarette smoke rose in layers below the light. Crying, sobbing, the smell of coffee.

'Mona, honey, are there any cookies I can put out?'

'Mona, did you find her?'

'It's Mona, Mona, honey!'

'Well, they were almost like twins, CeeCee and Gifford.'

'No, I tell you, it wasn't like that.'

'It's not an illness,' Mona said.

Bea was puzzled and sad, holding Mona's shoulder.

'Well, I know, that's what Aaron said. They are even calling the women in New York and California.'

'Yes, everywhere.'

'Oh, God,' said Bea. 'Carlotta was right. We should have burnt that house. We should have. It came out of that house, didn't it?'

'It ain't over yet, Beatrice dear,' said Mona. She went down the stairs.

When she got into the lower bathroom alone, and once again locked a door against the world, she began to cry.

'Goddamnit, Mom, goddamnit, goddamnit, goddamnit.'

But this didn't last long. There wasn't time. There had been another death. She could hear it – the pitch of the voices rising, a door slamming. Someone actually gave a little scream. Had to be another death.

Ryan had come and was calling Mona's name. She could hear their muffled voices through the heavy cypress door. Lindsay Mayfair had been found dead in Houston, Texas, at noon today. The family had only just contacted them.

Mona came out into the hallway. Someone put a glass of water in her hand, and for a moment she merely stared at it, not even knowing what it could be. Then she drank it.

'Thank you,' she said.

Pierce was there, red-eyed and staring at her.

'You heard about Lindsay.'

'Listen to me,' she said. 'It's not a disease. It's just a

person. A person who killed them all. This is what they must do. In every city they must all gather in one house, and keep company and stay together. No one must leave that house. And this will not last long, because we will stop it. We are very strong, all of us . . .'

She stopped; the relatives had fallen silent around her. The silence was spreading through the hall.

'It's just a lone thing,' she said quietly.

Only Aunt Evelyn still cried, softly, and far away. 'My darlings, my darlings, my darlings . . .'

And then Bea began to cry. And so did Mona. And Pierce said, 'Get a hold of yourself. I need you.'

And the others went on crying but Mona quietly stopped.

SEVENTEEN

JULIEN'S STORY CONTINUES

The days after Mary Beth's birth were the darkest of my life. If I ever possessed a moral vision it was in those moments. The cause of it precisely I am not certain, and as it isn't the subject of the narrative I shall try to pass over it quickly.

Let me just say that as a precocious child I had become accustomed to murder, to witchcraft, to evil in general before I had time to evaluate it. The war, the loss of my sister, her subsequent rape – all these had further illuminated for me what I'd already come to suspect, that I required something deep and of value to make me happy. Wealth wasn't enough; the flesh wasn't enough. If my family could not prosper I could not draw breath! And I wanted to draw breath. I was no more ready to let go of life – of health, of pleasure, of prosperity – than a newborn baby screaming as loudly as Mary Beth had screamed.

Also I wanted to know and love my daughter. Above all else I wanted this, and I knew for the first time why so many legends and so many fairy tales have at their core the simple treasure – a child, an heir, a little infant in one's arm, made up of oneself and another.

Enough. You get the picture. My life hung by a thread, and I knew I didn't want to lose it.

What could I do?

The answer came within days. I saw the fiend perpetually hovering by Mary Beth's cradle. Everyone else saw it too. 'The man' gave his blessings to Mary Beth; Mary Beth's little baby eyes could make him solid and strong; he guarded the child; he fawned upon her already. And the thing appeared as me! He wore my styles, he affected my manners, he exuded, if you will, my charm!

Calling the band together to play, a din I had begun to resent as much as an aching tooth that would never be pulled, I tried to speak with Marguerite about Lasher, and what he was, and what everyone had ever known of him.

She made little sense, speaking only of her power to make plants grow, wounds to heal, and to make potions that might give her longevity. 'The fiend will someday be flesh, and if it can come through, so can we. The dead can come back through the same doorway.'

'That's a perfectly dreadful idea,' I said.

'You think so because you're not dead. Just wait!'

'Mother, do you want the earth peopled with the dead? Where are we going to put them?'

In a fit of rage, she said, 'Why do you ask all these questions! You put yourself in danger. You think Lasher can't do away with you? Of course he can. Be quiet and do what you were born to do. You have life all around you. What more do you want?'

I went into the city, to my flat in the Rue Dumaine. It was again raining as it had been on the night I went to the First Street house, and the rain has always soothed my nerves and made me happy. I opened the doors to the porch. I let the rain splash in, noisy and beautiful, drenching the iron railings and splattering on the silk curtains. What did I care? I could have hung the windows with gold, if I'd wanted.

I lay on the bed, hands cradled beneath my head, one boot against the footboard, and I listed my various sins in my head ... not sins of passion, for I counted them not at all ... but sins of viciousness and cruelty.

Well, I thought, you have given this damned fiend your soul. What more can you give him? You can promise to protect and strengthen the babe, but again, the babe sees him already. He can teach the babe, he must know that.

Then as the rain died away, and the moon came out, flooding down into the Rue Dumaine, I saw the answer.

I would give him my human form. He already had my soul. Why not give him the form he was always imitating? I would offer him my body for possession.

Of course he might try to mutate me and kill me. But it seemed that in all past ventures, he had required the help of me and my mother to mutate flesh. Even to mutate plants or make them spring open. If he had been good at that by himself, he would never have needed any of us.

So, it was a safe enough risk, as I would let him live in me and walk about and dance and see, but not mutate me.

Now, not knowing whether he would or could hear me over the miles, I called to him.

Within seconds I saw him materialize near the oval mirror which stood in the corner. And I saw his reflection in the mirror! That I had never spied before. How strange that I had not even thought of it. He vanished soon enough. But he had smiled and showed me he was dressed in fine clothes such as I wore.

'You want to be in the flesh?' I asked. 'You want to see with my eyes? Why don't you come into me? Why don't I welcome you and lie quiet while you are inside, and let you make of me what you will for as long as you have the power to do it?'

'You would do this?'

'Well, surely my ancestors gave you this invitation. Surely Deborah invited you in or Charlotte.'

'Do not mock me, Julien,' he said in a cold secret soundless voice. 'You know I would not go into the body of a woman.'

'A body is a body,' I said.

'I am no woman.'

'Well, now you have a male witch to command. I make the offer. Perhaps it was my destiny. Come into me, I invite you. I lay myself open to you. You have certainly been close enough to me.'

'Don't mock me,' he said again. 'When I make love to you it is men with men as always.'

I smiled. I didn't say anything. But I was powerfully amused by this show of male pride, and it fitted with my entire picture of the childish nature of the thing. I thought to myself how I hated it, and how I had to bury that thought in my soul. So I dreamed of it soothing me with kisses and caresses. 'You can reward me after as you always have,' I said.

'This will be hard for you to bear.'

'For you, I'll do it. You've done much for me.'

'Aye, and now you fear me.'

'Yes, somewhat. I want to live. I want to educate Mary Beth. She is my child.'

Silence. 'Come into you . . .' it said.

'Yes, do it.'

'And you will not roust me with all your power.'

'I'll do my best to behave like a perfect gentleman.'

'Oh, you are so different from a woman.'

'Really, how so?' asked I.

'You never really love me as they do.'

'Hmmm, I could digress on all this,' I said, 'but be assured that you and I can further each other's aims. If women are too squeamish to say such things, then let us trust they have other ways of gaining their ends.'

'Laughter.'

'You can laugh when you're in me. You know you can.'

The room grew perfectly still. The curtains seemed to die on their rods. The rain was gone. The gallery shone in the light of the moon. It seemed I felt an emptiness. The hair tingled all over my body. I sat up, struggling to prepare myself, though for what I couldn't imagine, and then *whoom*, the thing had descended upon me, surrounding me and enclosing me, and I felt a great drunken swoon, and all sounds outside were melted in one single roar.

I was standing, I was walking, but I was falling. It was shadowy and vague and nightmarish, the stairs appearing before me, the shining street, and people even waving their hands, and through a great rolling ocean of water, voices echoing. '*Eh bien*, Julien!'

I knew I was walking because I had to be. But I could feel no ground beneath my feet, no balance, no up, no down, and I began to sicken with terror. I held back. I did not fight, I tried with all my might to relax into this thing, to fall into it, even as it seemed I was losing consciousness.

What followed was an eternity of such confusion.

It was two of the clock when next I had a coherent thought. I was sitting in the Rue Dumaine, still, but in a café, at a small marble-top table. I was smoking a cigarette, and my body was exhausted and full of aches, and I realized I was staring at the bartender, who stooped over me to ask again, perhaps for the sixth time:

'Monsieur, another before we close?'

'Absinthe.' My own voice came in a hoarse whisper out of my throat. There was no part of me that didn't hurt.

'You damned son of a bitch,' I said in my secret voice, 'what the hell have you been doing with me?'

But there came no answer. It was too damned exhausted to answer. It had possessed me for hours and run about in my form. Good God, there was mud on my clothes; look at my shoes. And my pants had been taken off and put back on and badly fastened. Oh, so we'd had some woman or man, had we? And what else did we catch, I'd like to know?

I took the fresh glass of absinthe and drank it down, and stood up and nearly fell over. My ankle was sore. I had blood on my knuckles. 'We've been fighting?'

I managed to make it to my rooms in the Rue Dumaine. My servant, Christian, was there, a man of color, a Mayfair by blood, very well-paid, very smart, and often very sarcastic. I asked if my bed was ready, and he said in his usual way, 'What do you think?'

I fell into it. I let him pull off my clothes and take them away. I asked for a bottle of wine.

'You've had enough.'

'Get me the wine,' I said, 'or I will climb up off this bed and strangle you till you die.'

He got the wine. 'Get out,' I said. He did. I lay in the dark drinking and trying to remember what I had done ... the street, the drunken whoozy feeling, voices coming at me through water. And then clear memories began to emerge, oh yes, of course, with only the familiarity that one's own memories can have, that I had gone down into the glen and drawn all the people together, and then the entire procession had come into the Cathedral. The Cathedral was more beautiful than I had ever beheld it in my life, hung with bows for the season, greenery everywhere, and I held the Christ Child. The singing was euphoric, and the tears were sliding down my face. I am home, I am here. I looked up at the great stained window of the saint. Yes. In the hands of God and the saint, I thought.

I woke with a start. What memory was this? I knew that the place was Scotland. I knew it was Donnelaith. And I knew that it had to be centuries ago. And yet the memory had been mine, fresh and clear, and immediate as only memory can be.

I rushed to my desk and scribbled it all down. Up came the fiend, weak and vague and without a form, his voice only a suggestion. 'What are you doing, Julien?'

'I might ask you the same thing!' I said. 'Did you enjoy your romp?'

'Yes, Julien. I want to do it again, Julien. Now. But I am too weak.'

'Small wonder. Go off and make like smoke. I'm exhausted too. We'll do it . . .'

'. . . as soon as we can.'

'All right, all right, you devil.'

I shoved the pages into the desk. I lay in a dead sleep, and when I woke it was sunlight and I knew I'd been again in the Cathedral. I remembered the rose window. I remembered the carving of the saint on top of its tomb. And the people singing . . .

What could this mean, I thought? This demon is in fact a saint? No, no. A bad angel fallen into hell. What? I don't know. Or did he serve some saint, venerate him, and then . . . what?

But the point is there could be no doubt these were mortal memories. The thing remembered being flesh; it had those memories in itself, and they had been left with me, who was perhaps the only one who could examine them. No doubt the fiend knew the memory of its fleshly self was there, but the fiend couldn't really think! The fiend used us to think! The fiend would only know what it had been if I told it.

The idea was born in my mind. Each time, remember more. Be the fiend, and know the fiend, and ultimately you will possess the truth about it. If the truth can't help, what can? 'You tawdry, evil ghost!' I thought, 'you are only someone who wants to be reborn. You have no right, you greedy greedy fiend. You have been alive. You are no wise or eternal thing. Go to hell and be gone.'

I slept again, the livelong day, I was so tired.

That night I rode to Riverbend. I called up the band, told them to play 'Dixie', for the love of God, and then I sat with Mother. I told her. She would have none of it.

'First of all, he is all-powerful and from time immemorial.'

'The hell.'

'And next, he will know it if you pit your soul against his. He'll kill you.'

'Likely.'

I never confided in her again. I don't believe I ever really spoke to her again. I don't think she much noticed.

I went into the nursery. The fiend was hanging about the cradle. I saw him in a flash, dressed as me, all full of mud, the way he'd been before. Idiot thing. I smiled.

'You want to come into me now?'

'Time to be with her, my baby,' he said. 'See how beautiful she is. Your witches' gifts are in her, yours and those from her mother's mother, and her mother's mother. And to think I might have wasted you.'

'You never know, do you? What do you learn when you are in me?'

He didn't answer for a long while. Then he appeared in an even more brilliant flash, my spitting image as they say, and he glared at me, and smiled, and then he tried to laugh, but nothing came from his mouth, and he vanished. But what I'd caught was his improved mimicry; his greater love for my form.

I walked out. I now saw what I had to do. Study the problem when the thing was occupied with the baby. And keep it coming into me when it would, for as long as I could endure it.

The months passed. Mary Beth's first-birthday party was a great fete. The city was booming again; the shadows of the war were gone; money was to be had everywhere. Mansions were rising uptown.

The fiend took possession of me on the average once a week.

That is all either of us could take of it. It lasted some four or five hours, then *whoom!* I was back. I might be anywhere when it left me. Sometimes in bed, and even with a man. So it had tastes as broad as my own, when we came right down to it.

But this was the twist. It wasn't Dr Jekyll and Mr Hyde, no, by no means. The fiend, inside me, was unfailingly charming to people. Almost angelic. 'My darling, last night you were so sweet,' said my mistress, 'to give me those pearls!'

'What!'

That sort of thing. It was also clear that people thought me staggering drunk when he was inside. My reputation became even more lurid and controversial. I wasn't much of a drunk on the natch. I hated to be befuddled. But it couldn't do any better than that in me. And so I lived with the recriminations and the smiles and the teasing. 'Boy, were you in your cups last night.' 'No kidding? I don't remember.'

Meantime, night and day the vision of the Cathedral haunted me. I saw the grassy hills, sometimes I saw a castle as if I were looking through a clear piece of a stained-glass window. I saw the glen, and the mist. And some vast and unsupportable horror would overtake the memory. It would blot out all sense. And I could get no further with it. Pain. I knew pain when I tried. I knew pain unthinkable.

I did not attempt to discuss this with the villain. And as for what he learnt while he was I . . . this seemed a matter of pure sensuality. He guzzled, he danced, he laid waste, he fought. But there were times when he despaired afterwards. *I must be flesh myself*, he would lament.

There is also some evidence that when he walked in my shoes, he accumulated information. But as always, he did not seem to be able to do anything with this information. But this information would come out of him in great enthusiastic volleys.

We spoke of the changing times, for instance, of the railroads and how they had eroded the river trade; we spoke of changing fashions. We spoke of photography, with which the villain had a strong fascination. He went often to have himself photographed when he was in my body, though drunk and clumsy as he was, he had difficulty holding still for the camera. He often left these pictures in my pockets.

But this whole endeavor proved a great task for him. He would have flesh of his own, not lumber about in mine. And his adoration for Mary Beth knew no bounds.

Indeed, sometimes weeks went by when he did not have the fortitude to come into me. Just as well, as it took me two days to recover. And as Mary Beth grew, Lasher used Mary Beth very often as his excuse. Fine with me, I thought. My reputation's bad enough, and I'm growing older.

Also as Mary Beth gained in beauty with every passing day, my soul became more and more troubled. I detested the charade that she was my niece and not my daughter. I wanted my own children, indeed, I wanted sons. My values came down to such a pitiful and powerful few that I was appalled by the simplicity of it.

But my life ran on an even keel. I remained sane, in spite of the demon's assaults. I never even approached true madness. I made money in all the new postwar enterprises – building, merchandising, cotton factoring, whatever opportunity there was, and I perceived also that to keep my family rich, I had to extend its interests far beyond New Orleans. New Orleans went through waves of boom and bust; but as a port we were losing our preeminence.

I made my first trips to New York in the postwar years. With the fiend happily occupied at home, I lived as a free man in Manhattan.

I began in earnest the real building of an enduring fortune.

My brother, Rémy, went to live in the First Street house. I visited often.

And in time, convincing myself that there was no reason I could not have everything a good man should have, I fell in love with my young cousin Suzette, who reminded me of Katherine in her innocence. I prepared to occupy the First Street house as master, with my brother and his family living there agreeably as part of the household.

Now, something else was coming across to me, in bright flashes, about the villain and his memories. As I continued to 'recall' the Cathedral and the glen, the town of Donnelaith, images became more vivid to me. I did not move back and forth in time very much, but I saw more detail. And I came to realize that the euphoria I felt in my dream of the Cathedral was the love of God.

I learnt this for sure one weekday morning. I was outside the St Louis Cathedral on Jackson Square, and I heard a lovely singing. I went inside. Little quadroon girls, very beautiful all, 'colored children' as we would have called them then, were making their First Communion. They were dressed in gorgeous white, and the ceremony was breath-taking, like so many child brides of Christ filing up the aisle, each with her rosary and white prayer book.

The love of God. That is what I felt in the St Louis Cathedral right in my own little city. And I knew it was what I knew in the glen in the ancient Cathedral. I was stricken. I wandered about all day, evoking the feeling and then doing my best to dispel it.

In flashes I saw Donnelaith. I saw its stone houses. I saw its little square. I saw the Cathedral itself in the distance – oh, great great Gothic church. Olden times!

I sank down finally in a café, as always, drank a cold glass of beer and rolled my head on the wall behind me.

The demon was there, invisible.

'What are you thinking?'

Cautiously and deliberately I told him.

He was silent and confused.

Then in a timid voice, he said: 'I will be flesh.'

'Yes, I'm sure you will,' I said, 'and Mary Beth and I have vowed to help you.'

'Good, for I can show you then how to remain, and come back yourself, it can be done, and others have done it.'

'Why has it taken so long for you?'

'There is no time where I am,' he said. 'It is an idea. It will be realized. Only when I am in your body is there a sort of time, measured by noise and movement. But I am out of time. I wait. I see far. I see myself come again, and then everyone will suffer.'

'Everyone.'

'Everyone but our clan, yours and mine. The Clan of Donnelaith, for you are of that clan and so am I.'

'Is that so? Are you telling me then that all our cousins, all our ilk, all our descendants . . .'

'Yes, all blessed, the most powerful in the earth. Blessed. Look what I have done in your time. I can do more, much more, and when I am come into the flesh again, for true, I will be one of you!'

'Promise me this,' I said. 'Vow it.'

'You shall all be upheld. All of you.'

I closed my eyes. I saw the glen, the Cathedral, the candles, the villagers in procession, the Christ Child. The fiend screamed in pain.

Not a sound anywhere. Only the dull street, the café, the door open, the breeze, but the demon was shrieking in pain and only I, Julien Mayfair, could hear it.

Could the child Mary Beth hear it?

The fiend was gone. All around me the flat natural world lay undisturbed anymore and beautifully ordinary. I got up, put on my hat, picked up my stick, walked across Canal Street into the American District and on to a nearby rectory. I don't even know the church. It was some new church, a neighborhood filled with Irish and German immigrants.

Out came an Irish priest, for Irish priests were everywhere in those days. We were a missionary country for the Irish, who were out to convert the world as surely then as they had been in the time of St Brendan.

'Listen to me,' I said, 'if I wanted to exorcise a devil, would it help to know exactly who he was? To know his name if he had one?'

'Yes,' said he. 'But you should trust such things to priests. Knowing his name could be a great great advantage.'

'I thought so,' said I.

I looked up. We stood at the rectory door at the curb of the street but to the right lay a walled garden. And now I saw the trees begin to thrash and move and throw down their leaves. Indeed so strong came the wind that it stirred the little bell in the small church steeple.

'I'll learn its name,' I said.

The more the trees thrashed, the more the leaves were whipped into a storm, the more distinctly I repeated it.

'I'll learn its name.'

'To be sure,' said the priest, 'do that. For there are many many demons. The fallen angels, all of them, and the old gods of the pagans who became demons when Christ was born, and the little people even are from hell, you know.'

'The old gods of the pagans?' asked I. For I had never come across this wrinkle in theology. 'I thought the old gods were false gods and didn't exist. That our God was the One True God.'

'Oh, the gods existed, but they were demons. They are the spooks and spirits that trouble us by night, deposed, vicious, vengeful. Same with the fairy people. The little people. I have seen the little people. I saw them in Ireland and I saw them here.'

'Right,' I said. 'May I walk in your garden?' I gave him a handful of American dollars. He was pleased. He went round inside to open the gate in the brick wall.

'Seems it's going to storm,' he said. 'That tree is going to break.' His cassock was blowing every which way.

'You go inside,' I said. 'I like the storm and I'll close the gate behind me.'

I stood alone among the trees in the crowded little place where the Morning Glory grew wild, and there were a few scattered vibrant pink lilies. A little untended garden by and large, and in a grotto, covered over with green moss, the Virgin standing. The trees were now whipped to a fury. The lilies were torn and trampled as if the wind had big boots. I had to place my hand on the trunk of the tree to steady myself. I was smiling.

'Well? What can you do to me?' I asked. 'Shower me with leaves? Make it rain if you will. I shall change my clothes when I go home. Do your damnedest!'

I waited. The trees grew still. A few vagrant raindrops fell on the brick path. I reached down and picked up one of the lilies, crushed and broken.

I heard the great faint and undeniable sound of weeping. Not audible you understand, not through the ear. Only through my soul, a heartbroken weeping.

There was more than sorrow in it. There was a dignity. There was a great depth, more terrible than any smile or expression of face it had ever made to fright me. And the sorrow mingled in my soul with that remembered euphoria.

Latin words came to my mind, but I didn't really know them. They sprang from me as if I were a priest and I were saying a litany. I heard the sound of pipes; I heard the bells ring.

'It's the Devil's Knell,' someone said. 'All Christmas Eve the bells will ring to drive the devils from the glen, to fright the little people!'

And then the sky was quiet. I was alone. The garden was still, it was simply New Orleans again, and the warm southern sun was shining down upon me. The priest peeped out from the door.

'*Merci, Mon Père*,' I said, tipped my hat and left.

The streets were soft with sunshine and breeze. I walked home through the Garden District to the First

Street house, and there was my beautiful Mary Beth sitting on the steps, and he was with her, a shadow, a thing of air, and both seemed glad to see me.

EIGHTEEN

The bright fluorescent lights of the station made an island in the dark swampland. The little phone booth was no more than a fold of plastic around a single chrome phone. The tiny square numbers were now a blur. She could no longer make them out, no matter what she did.

Again came the busy signal. 'Please try to cut in again,' she asked the operator. 'I have to reach Mayfair and Mayfair. There is more than one line. Please try for me. Say it is an emergency call from Rowan Mayfair.'

'Ma'am, they will not accept the interrupt. They are getting requests for interrupts from all over.'

The driver had climbed back up in his cab. She heard the engine start. She made a motion for him to wait, and hastily gave the operator the house number. 'This is my home, punch it in for me, please. I can't . . . can't read the numbers.'

The pain came again, the tight wire of wraparound pain, so like a menstrual cramp, yet far worse than any she'd ever experienced.

'Michael, please answer. Michael, please . . .'

On and on it rang.

'Ma'am, we've rung twenty times.'

'Listen, I have to reach somebody. Do this for me. Keep calling. Tell them . . .'

Some official objection was coming back. But the huge jarring noise of the truck's diesel engines obliterated everything. Smoke came out of the little pipe at the front of the cab.

When she turned around, the receiver slipped out of her fingers and banged against the plastic enclosure. The driver appeared to be beckoning for her to come.

Mother, help me. Where is Father?

We are all right, Emaleth. Be still, be quiet. Be patient with me.

She stepped forward, one moment sure of the ground and the distance, and all points of reference, and the next minute plunging to the asphalt. Her knees struck with a fierce pain, and she felt herself going over.

Mother, I am frightened.

'Hang on, baby girl,' she said. 'Hang on.' She had her hands out on the ground to steady herself. Only her knees had been hurt. Two men were running towards her from the office of the filling station, and the truck driver had come down and around to help her.

'Are you OK, lady?' he said.

'Yes, let's go,' she said. She looked up in the man's face. 'We have to hurry!' The truth was – if they hadn't been pulling her up, she couldn't have risen. She leant on the truck driver's arm. The sky beyond the swamps was purple.

'Couldn't get them?'

'No,' she said, 'but we have to push on.'

'Lady, I have to make my stop in St Martinville. No way around it, I have to pick up . . .'

'I understand. I'll call from there again. Just drive, please. Go. Take us away from here.'

Here. The isolated gas station on the swamp's edge,

the sky purple overhead, the stars peeping through and a great bright moon rising.

He lifted her with considerable ease and set her down on the seat, then came around, released the emergency brake and let the big truck creak and wheeze before he slammed the door and pressed on the accelerator. They were turning back to the marginless road.

'We still in Texas?'

'No, ma'am. Louisiana. I sure wish you'd let me take you to the doctor.'

'I'll be all right.'

Just as she said it the pain again clamped tight, and made her nearly cry out. She felt the sharp jab from within.

Emaleth, for the love of God and Mother.

But Mother, it gets smaller and smaller. Mother. I'm frightened. Where is Father? Can I be born into the world without Father?

Not yet, Emaleth. She sighed. She turned her head to the road. The big truck was racing along now at ninety on the narrow road with its battered shoulders and ditches, and the purple sky darkened above as the trees closed in and grew higher. The headlamps made a bright path ahead. The driver whistled to himself.

'Mind if I play the radio, ma'am?'

'Please do,' she said.

There came another jab. The smooth dark voices of the Judds came out of the little grill. She smiled. Devil's music. Another jab, and she pitched forward, steadying herself on the dashboard. Then she realized she had never put on the seat belt. Terrible, and she a mother carrying a child.

Mother . . .

I'm here, Emaleth.

The time is coming.

That can't be yet. Stay quiet. Wait until we are both certain.

But another circle of pain wrapped tight around her middle. It pressed white-hot against the small of her back. And there came another jab and a soundless sense of something breaking. Fluid leaked between her legs. She felt the wetness and at the same time the blood seemed to drain from her face. That awful lightheaded feeling – you're going to pass out.

'Stop the truck now here,' she said.

At first he didn't understand.

'You need help, lady?'

'No. Stop the truck. See those lights? Stop there. That's where I'm going. Stop the truck!' She flashed her eyes on him. She saw the intimidation, the fear, yet he eased into the stop.

'Do you know who lives back up in there?'

'Course I do.' She opened the door, and got out, stumbling over the step. Her dress was soaked. No doubt the seat behind her was wet, and now in the glare of oncoming lights he could see it. Poor man. How disgusting it must all seem to him. That she had lost control of her bladder, when that wasn't it at all.

'Go on, now, thanks.' She slammed the cab door. But she heard him hollering from inside.

'Ma'am, your purse. Here. No, no, that's OK, you already give me plenty money.'

The truck wouldn't move on. She cut across the ditch, hurriedly, and climbed up into the high grass on the other side, and passed into the dense bank of trees, into the soft relentless chorus of the tree frogs. Up ahead she saw light, and she moved towards it, at last hearing the sound of the truck drive away and vanish within seconds in the silence.

'I'm finding a place, Emaleth, a soft dry place. Be quiet, and be patient.'

Mother, I cannot. I must come out.

She had come through the trees into a clearing. The lights she'd seen lay way far away to the right. She did not care about them. It was the great grassy place that lay ahead, and a beautiful oak, immense in size and leaning tragically on its long arms as if reaching out to the woods beyond in a futile effort to join with it.

The oak broke her heart suddenly, its giant knuckled branches, its great sweeps of dark moss, and in the soft glowing starry night, the sky was so bright behind it.

It's beautiful, please, Emaleth. Emaleth, if I die, go to Michael. Once again, she registered the vision of Michael's face, the numbers of the house, numbers of the phone – data for the tiny mind inside her, which knew what she knew.

Mother, I cannot be born if you die. Mother, I need you. I need Father.

The tree was so distinct, massive and graceful. Some lovely vision came to her of the forests of olden times when trees like this must have been the temples. She saw a green field, hills covered with forest.

Donnelaith, Mother. Father said I was to go to Donnelaith, that we were to meet there.

'No, darling,' she said aloud, reaching out for the trunk of the tree and then falling against its dark, good-smelling rough surface. Like stone it felt, no hint that it was alive, not here at the craggy base where the roots were like rocks, only up and out there where the small branches moved in the wind. 'Go to Michael, Emaleth. Tell him everything. Go to Michael.'

It hurts, Mother, it hurts.

'Remember, Emaleth, go to Michael.'

Mother, do not die. You must help me be born. You must give me your eyes and the milk, lest I be small and useless.

She wandered out from the trunk, to where the grass was soft and silken under her feet, between a pair of the great sprawling elbow branches.

Dark and sweet here.

I'm going to die, darling.

No, Mother. I'm coming now. Help me!

It was dark and sweet here, with heaps of leaves and moss like a bower. She lay on her back, her body pulsing with one shock of pain after another. Moss above, soft moss hanging down, and the moon snagged up there, and so beautiful.

She felt the fluid gush, warm against her thighs, and then the worst of the pain, and something soft and wet stroking her. She lifted her own hand, unable to coordinate, unable to reach down.

Dear God, was the child reaching out from the womb? Was the child's hand against her thigh? The darkness above closed in as if the branches had closed, and then the moon shone bright again, making the moss gray for an instant. She let her head roll to the side. Stars falling down in the purple sky. This is heaven.

'I made an error, a terrible terrible error,' she said. 'The sin was vanity. Tell Michael this.'

The pain widened; she knew the causes of this, the mouth of the womb wrenched open. She screamed, she couldn't help it, and she felt nothing but the pain grow worse and worse and then suddenly it stopped. Slipping back into ache and sickness, she struggled to see the branches again, struggled to lift her hands to help Emaleth, but she could not do it.

A great warm heaviness lay on her thighs. It lay on her belly. She felt the warm wet touch on her breast.

'Mother, help me!'

In the vague sweet darkness, she saw the small head rising above her, like the head of a nun, its long wet hair so sleek, like a nun's veil, the head rising and rising.

'Mother, see me. Help me! Lest I be small and useless!'

The face loomed above hers, the great blue eyes peering down into her own, and the wet hand suddenly closing on her breast, making the milk squirt from the nipple.

'Are you my baby girl?' she cried. 'Ah, the scent of Father. Are you my baby girl?'

There was the burning smell, the smell of the night he was born, the smell of something heated and dangerous and chemical, but nothing glowed in the dark. She felt the arms encircling her, the wet hair on her stomach, the mouth on her breast and then that delicious suckling, that wondrous suckling, sending the pleasure all through her.

The pain was gone. So beautifully and wholly gone. The darkness of the night seemed to enfold her, and lock her down to the fallen leaves, to the bed of moss, beneath the delicious weight of the woman who lay on top of her.

'Emaleth!'

Yes, Mother. The milk is good. The milk is fine. I am born, Mother.

I want to die. I want you to die. Both of us now. Die.

But there was no longer much to worry about. She was floating and Emaleth drank the milk in deep hearty gulps and there wasn't anything now that she could do. She could not even feel her own arms and legs. She could feel nothing but this suckling and then when she tried to say ... it was gone, whatever it had been; I want to open my eyes. I want to see the stars again.

'They are so beautiful, Mother. They could guide me to Donnelaith if the great sea didn't lie between us.'

She wanted to say, No, not Donnelaith, and to say Michael's name again, but then she couldn't quite follow it, couldn't quite remember who Michael was, or why she had wanted to say that.

'Mother, don't leave me!'

Her eyes opened for one precious second, yes, see, and there was the purple sky and a tall willowy figure standing over her. It could not have been her child, no, not this, not this woman rising out of the dark like some grotesque growth from the warm, verdant earth, something monstrous and ...

'No, Mother. No. I am beautiful. Mother, please, please, don't leave me.'

NINETEEN

The position wasn't embarrassing. It was flat-out crazy. He had been on the phone for forty-five minutes to the Keplinger people.

'Look,' said the young doctor on the other end. 'It says you came yourself, you took the files, you said that it was top secret.'

'Damn it, I'm in New Orleans, Louisiana, you fool. I was here all day yesterday. I'm at the Pontchartrain Hotel. I'm with the Mayfair and Mayfair people now! I didn't pick up anything! What you're saying is, the material is gone.'

'Absolutely, Dr Larkin. Gone. Unless there's a copy somewhere filed in such a way that I can't access it. And I don't think there is. I can keep . . .'

'About Mitch. How is he?'

'Oh, he's not going to make it, Dr Larkin. If you could see him, you wouldn't want him to. Don't pray for that now. Look, his wife's on the other line. I'll call you back.'

'No, you won't. You'll run for cover. You know what's happened. Somebody's walked out of there with all the material Rowan Mayfair entrusted to me, everything Flanagan was working on. You guys slipped up! And Flanagan is critically hurt and unable to communicate.'

There was a pause on the other end of the line. Then the same young, brittle voice again:

'Correction. Dr Flanagan's dead. Died twenty minutes ago. I'll *have* to call you *back*, Doctor.'

'You better find the records, you better find the complete and entire computer record of every experiment made by Mitch Flanagan on behalf of Dr Samuel Larkin for Dr Rowan Mayfair.'

'You have a record of sending us these things?'

'I brought them.'

'And that was you, the real you, who brought the stuff – not somebody apparently pretending to be you? Like this doctor yesterday who wasn't you. But said that he was? Oh, yeah, OK. Now, I'm looking at a videotape of this man. Yesterday 4 p.m. Pacific Standard Time. He's tall, dark-haired, smiling, and he's holding up to the camera his identification, a California driver's license: Dr Samuel Larkin. And you say you are Samuel Larkin and that you are in New Orleans?'

Lark was speechless. He cleared his throat.

He realized he was staring at Ryan Mayfair, who had been watching from the shadows of the office for some time now. The others still waited in the conference room – a distant and solemn ring of faces around the mahogany table.

'OK, Dr Barry whoever-you-are,' Lark said. 'I'm going to have my lawyer send you a full description of me and copies of my passport, driver's license, and ID card from University. You'll see I'm not this man on your tape. Please hold on to the tape. Don't surrender it to somebody who comes in and smiles and tells you he is the reincarnation of J. Edgar Hoover. And indeed, yes, I am Samuel Larkin, and when you speak to

Martha Flanagan, please convey my sympathies to her. Don't bother to call the San Francisco police about this. I will call.'

'You're wasting your time, Doctor. If there's been a misunderstanding, there was no way we could know that this man was not who he said he was. Just forget about the police because you know as well as I do . . .'

'Better find those records, Doctor. There have to be copies.'

He hung up before the young jerk could answer.

He was steaming. But he was also stunned. Flanagan was dead. Flanagan struck by a car crossing California Street. He couldn't remember if he'd ever heard of anybody being killed downtown on that corner, unless it was an out-of-state driver on a rainy day who tried to race a cable car.

He looked at Ryan, but he volunteered nothing for the moment. Then he punched in the 415 area code again. And a number he knew by heart.

'Darlene,' he said, 'this is Samuel Larkin. I need you to send flowers to Martha Flanagan. Right. Right. Nearly instantaneous. Not quite. That would be fine. Just sign it "Lark." Thank you.'

Ryan moved out of the shadows, turned his back on Larkin and walked into the conference room.

Lark waited for a moment. His face was wet and he was tired, and he could not think what he meant to do. There were so many conflicting thoughts in his head, so much outrage, so much impatience, so much . . . so much pure astonishment. He and Mitch had made that dash together so many times, heading up to Grant Avenue to find their favorite little Gooey Louie's for egg rolls and cheap fried rice, the kind they'd loved since the New York days and med school.

He stood up. He didn't know what he was going to say. He didn't know how to explain all this.

He heard the door behind him open, and he saw with relief that it was Lightner, and Lightner had a manila folder in his hand. He looked drawn and tired, about as out of sorts as he'd been in the car this afternoon on the way down here.

That seemed like centuries ago. Flanagan had died in the interim.

They went into the conference room together. How calm these people looked, how incredibly calm, both men and women red-eyed from crying, and all in their lawyerly tropical wool and oxford cloth.

'Well, this is ... this is very disturbing news,' Lark said. He could feel the blood rushing to his face now. He laid his hands on the back of the leather chair. He didn't want to sit down. He caught a disconcerting reflection of himself in the distant windows. The lights of the city were a smear beyond. What he saw was mainly all this – the floor lamps, the ring of high-backed leather chairs, the figure of Ryan standing in the corner.

'All the material is gone,' said Ryan, quietly and without recrimination.

'I'm afraid so. Dr Flanagan is ... is dead, and they can't find the records. Also someone ... and I can't for the life of me ...'

'We understand,' said Ryan. 'The same thing happened in New York yesterday afternoon. All the genetic records were removed. Same thing at the Genetic Institute in Paris.'

'Well, then I am in a very very embarrassing position,'

said Lark. 'You have only my word that this creature exists, that the blood and tissues sampled revealed this mysterious genome . . .'

'We understand,' said Ryan.

'I wouldn't blame you if you told me to get the hell out of this office and never come south of the Mason-Dixon Line again,' said Lark. 'I wouldn't blame you if . . .'

'We understand,' said Ryan and for the first time he forced an icy smile. He gestured for calm. 'The superficial and immediate autopsy results on Edith Mayfair and Alicia Mayfair indicate they miscarried. The tissue is abnormal. There is every indication, even at this early stage, that it corroborates what you've told us about the material you received. I thank you for all your help.'

Lark was flabbergasted.

'That's it?'

'We will of course pay you for your time, and all your expenses . . .'

'No, I mean, wait a minute, what are you going to do?'

'Well, what would you suggest we do?' Ryan asked. 'Should we call a news conference and tell the national media that there is a genetic mutant male with ninety-two chromosomes preying on the women in our family, attempting to impregnate them and apparently killing them?'

'I won't let this go,' said Lark.

'I don't like people impersonating me! I'm going to find out who this was, who . . .'

'You won't find out,' said Aaron.

'You mean it was one of your people?'

'If it was, you will never prove it. And we all know that it had to be one of my people, didn't it? No one else knew this work was being carried on at Keplinger. No one but you and the deceased Dr Flanagan. And Mayfair and Mayfair after you told them. There isn't much more to it. I think we need to see you back safely to your hotel. I think I have to help the family now. This is really a family matter.'

'You're out of your mind.'

'No, I am not, Dr Larkin,' said Lightner, 'and I want you to stay at the hotel, with Gerald and Carl Mayfair. They're outside waiting to take you back. Don't leave the hotel, please. Just stay in the suite until you hear from me.'

'Are you implying that someone is going to try to harm *me*?'

Ryan made a quiet, polite little gesture for attention. He was still standing in the corner of the room.

'Dr Larkin, we have a lot of work to do. This is a big family. Just reaching everyone is quite a chore. And since five o'clock, we've had another death in the Houston area.'

'Who was this?' asked Aaron.

'Clytee Mayfair,' said Ryan. 'She didn't live that far from Lindsay. She died at nearly the same time, as a matter of fact. We suspect that she opened her front door to a visitor probably an hour or so after Lindsay had done the same thing in Sherman Oaks. At least that seems to be the picture. Please, Dr Larkin, go back to the hotel.'

'In other words, you *believe* everything I've told you! You believe this creature is . . .'

'We know it is,' said Ryan. 'Now please do go. Settle

in at the Pontchartrain, and make yourself comfortable, and don't go out. Gerald and Carl will be with you.'

Aaron had taken Lark's arm before he could answer. Aaron escorted Lark into the outer office and then into the corridor of the building. Lark saw the two young men, more cookie-cutter Mayfairs in pale wool suits with lemon or pink silk ties.

'Look, I . . . er . . . I have to sit down a minute,' he said.

'At the hotel,' said Lightner.

'Your people did this? Your people went into Keplinger and took that information?'

'That's my guess,' said Lightner. Obviously the man was miserable.

'Then that means they ran down Flanagan? They killed him?'

'No, it doesn't necessarily mean that. No, I can't say that it means that. I don't believe it means that. I believe that they . . . took advantage of a sudden opportunity. I can't believe anything else at this moment. But until I can reach the Elders in Amsterdam, until I can find out who sent whom where, I have no real answers.'

'I see,' said Lark.

'Go back to the hotel and rest.'

'But the women –'

'Everyone's being contacted. There are calls being made to every Mayfair connection known to the family. I'll call you as soon as I have word. Try to get your mind off it.'

'Get my mind off it!'

'What else can you do, Dr Larkin?'

Lark was about to speak, but there were no words. Nothing came out. He looked up and saw that the young man named Gerald held the door open for him, and that the other man was eager to go, and in the act of turning. This meant something, meant he had to move. He didn't consciously decide.

Suddenly he was in the corridor, and they were moving towards the elevator together. There were two uniformed policemen by the elevator. The young men passed them without a word.

Once they were inside and on the way down, the younger one spoke.

'It's all my fault,' he said. This was the one they called Gerald. He couldn't have been more than twenty-five. The other, older, thinner, and a little tougher-looking all around, asked:

'Why?'

'I should have burnt the house the way Carlotta wanted.'

'What house?' demanded Lark.

Neither man answered him. He asked the question again, but he realized they were not even listening to him. He said nothing more.

The lobby of the building was lined with uniformed security officers, policemen, other seemingly official personnel, some of whom looked at them impassively. Lark saw the big limo hovering out there in the putrid glare of the mercury lights.

'What about Rowan!' he said. 'Is anybody still looking for Rowan!'

He stopped in his tracks. But again, neither man answered. Neither man seemed even to hear. There was nothing to be done but get into the leather-lined car. Icebox pie. The Pontchartrain had just about the best icebox pie he had ever tasted. He didn't think he wanted anything else. Just coffee and chicory and icebox pie . . .

'That's what I want when we get back. Icebox pie and coffee.'

'Sure thing,' said Gerald, as if this were the first time Lark had said anything that made sense.

Lark just laughed to himself. He wondered if Martha had family around to go with her to Flanagan's funeral.

TWENTY

JULIEN'S STORY CONTINUES

Let me pass quickly to the point. I did not lay eyes
upon the bleak dreamy landscape of Donnelaith until
the year 1888. My 'memories' continued much in the
same vein, though there was increasingly confusing
material mixed up with them.

By that time, Mary Beth had grown into a powerful
witch, more quick-witted, cunning and philosophically
interesting than Katherine, Marguerite and even Marie
Claudette insofar as I could judge such things. But then
Mary Beth was of a new age – postwar, post-crinoline,
as they said.

She worked by my side in my three endeavors: care of
family; pursuit of pleasure; making money. She became
my confidante, and my only friend.

I had many lovers during these years – men and
women. I was married. My darling wife, Suzette, whom
I loved very much in my own selfish way, gave me four
children. I wish I could tell you the story of all this,
because in a way, everything a man does is part of the
moral fabric of who he is, and what he is. And this was
never more true than with me.

But there isn't time. So let me only explain that no
matter how close I was to wife, lovers, and children, it
was Mary Beth who was my friend, who shared the

secret of the knowledge of Lasher and all its burdens and dangers.

New Orleans was, throughout that period, vice-ridden, and a great place for whoring, gambling, and merely watching the spectacle of life in all its seediness and violence. I adored it, felt fearless in its midst and pursued my passions. And Mary Beth, disguised as a boy, went with me everywhere. While I protected my sons somewhat, sending them off to Eastern schools and preparing them for the world at large, I nurtured Mary Beth with much stronger ingredients.

Mary Beth was the single most intelligent human being I have ever known. There was nothing in business or politics or any realm which she could not grasp. She was cool, relentless, logical, but above all imaginatively brilliant. She saw the larger scheme of things.

And she perceived early on that the demon did not.

Let me give an example. There came to New Orleans in the early 1880s a musician called Blind Henry. Blind Henry was an idiot savant. There was nothing he could not play on the piano. He played Mozart, Beethoven, Gottschalk, but Blind Henry was otherwise just what the title implies, an utter idiot.

When Mary Beth and I attended this concert, she wrote on her program a note to me, right under the nose of the demon, so to speak, who was totally taken by the music. 'Blind Henry and Lasher – same form of intellect.'

This was exactly right. It is a far more mysterious question than we can examine here. And today you know more in the modern world about idiot savants, autistic children and the like. But in her simple way, she was trying to communicate to me: Lasher cannot put either learning or perception into any real context. We, the living, have a context for what we know and feel. This dead thing does not.

And having understood this from an early age, Mary Beth did not mythologize the spirit. When I suggested it was a vengeful ghost, she shrugged and considered the possibility.

But – and this is key – she didn't despise Lasher as I did, either.

On the contrary, she bore him love; and he forged with her a close emotional link, drawing from her a sympathy which I did not feel for the being.

And as I saw this happening, as I saw her nodding to my ironic statements, and carefully veiled warnings, as I saw her understanding me perfectly, yet nevertheless loving *him*, I understood better why he had always preferred women to men, for I think he played to a part of women which is more dormant in men. They were more likely to fall in love with, to feel pity for, to be enamored of, that which gives them erotic pleasure.

Of course this is a bias on my part. A bias. I presented it to her, and she sneered. 'It's like the old argument from the witch judges,' she said, 'that women are more susceptible to the Devil's blandishments because they are more stupid. Shame on you, Julien. Maybe the simple fact is I am more capable of love than you are.'

We argued about this all of our lives. All of our lives.

I once suggested in rapid debate that most women were morally flawed and could be led to anything. She

491

quietly pointed out to me that she felt a deep honor-bound responsibility to Lasher, which I, the pragmatist and diplomat, did not feel. I was the one morally flawed, she said. And perhaps she was right.

Whatever the case, I always felt an abhorrence for the thing. And she didn't feel it.

'When you are gone someday,' she said 'there will be only I and that thing. It will be my love, my solace, my witness. I do not really care what it is or whence it comes. I do not care what I am or whence I come. The idea that I can think of myself in those terms is an illusion.'

She was then fifteen, tall, black-haired, very sturdy of build and very pretty in a dark strong way which some men would not have found appealing. Her manner was quiet, and highly persuasive. All admired her, and anyone not afraid of her unflinching gaze and mannish poise usually was smitten by her.

I was impressed, of course. All the more because after saying such a thing, she could smile and do this trick which never failed to delight me: to take the thick braid of her black hair and untangle it so that the whole veil spilled over her shoulders in sharp little waves, and then shake it out and laugh, as if transforming herself at once in that gesture from my intellectual companion to a budding woman.

But understand, I was the only male ever to have power with Lasher. And I still maintain that I had a male's immunity to the thing's blandishments. And mark, I've been frank with you about my male amours. I am not prejudiced against that love that dares not say its name, and so forth. Love to me . . . is love. In my heart of hearts I loathed the creature! I loathed its reckless mistakes! I loathed its sense of humor.

Alors. Sharing my ambition in every regard, Mary Beth became familiar with our business dealings from early childhood. By the time she was twelve she had participated with me in decisions which so diversified and extended our fortune that an unstoppable money-making machine had been created from the Mayfair capital.

We were as active in Boston and New York and London as in the South. Money was in place where it could only make more money, and that money automatically made more money, and so forth and so on, and so it has been really since those days.

Mary Beth was a genius at it. And she learnt to use the spirit very skillfully, as her spy, her informant, her observer, her idiot savant adviser. It was quite startling to watch her at work with the being.

Meantime we had made the First Street house ours. My brother, Rémy, was quiet, retiring, his children sweet and good-natured. My boys were off at school. My poor daughter Jeannette, feebleminded as Katherine had been, died young. That is another tale – all that. My sweet Jeannette, my beloved wife, Suzette. I cannot tell it.

After the death of those two, which came much later on, and the death of my mother, Marguerite, Mary Beth and I were quite isolated from all the world in our shared knowledge and passion, and our relentless pursuit of pleasure. But this isolation had already begun.

We were also mad for the modern world. We journeyed to New York frequently merely to be in the thriving capital. We adored the railroads; we kept abreast of new inventions; indeed we invested in progress, *per se.* We had a passion for change, while

493

many in our family and in our home had nothing of the sort. Rather they clung to a sleepy, glamorous Old World past, receding behind closed shutters. Not so with us.

We had ... as they say in your time ... we had our hands into everything.

And let me note that until we went to Europe in the year 1887, Mary Beth had maintained her status as a Virgin Warrior, so to speak, never allowing any man in any sort of way to really touch her. That is, she had fun in a thousand ways, but she ran no risk of mothering a witch until such a time as she could pick the father. That is why she preferred the boy disguise when we went cavorting on the town. And beautiful dark-eyed boy that she was, she never let anyone too close to her.

Finally the time came when we could break away for a long European trip, a Grand Tour, an exercise of our wealth on a large scale, a marvelous and long-overdue education. Overdue for me, that is, and perhaps even for her. If I have one regret it is that I did not travel more in life; and that I did not encourage others in my family to travel. But that is of small import now.

The spirit was very loath for us to go; over and over he warned against the dangers of wandering; he told us we possessed Paradise where we were. But we would not be deterred; Mary Beth was desperate to see the world, and the spirit would keep her happy; and within an hour of our departure it was clear that he was journeying with us.

Throughout our tour, he could be summoned with a silent wish, and frequently when I saw Mary Beth at a distance I saw him beside her.

In the city of Rome, he went into me for many hours,

but the effort exhausted him. Indeed it seemed to madden him. He begged to go home, that we cross the sea, that we return to the house he so loved. He said that he detested this place; indeed he could not endure it. I told him we had to take this trip, that it was folly to think the Mayfairs would never journey afar, and to be quiet, there was nothing to be done for it.

When we journeyed north of Rome towards Florence, he became disconsolate, and turbulent, and actually left us. Mary Beth was afraid. She could not summon him, no matter what she did.

'So we are on our own in the mortal world,' I said with a shrug. 'What can happen to us?'

She was leery and sad, and wandered the streets of Siena and Assisi by herself, scarce speaking to me. She missed the daemon. She said that we had caused it pain.

I was indifferent.

But oh, to my regret! When we reached Venice, and lodged in a gorgeous palazzo on the Grand Canal, the monster came to me. It was one of his most vicious and contrived and strong gestures.

I had left at home in New Orleans my beloved secretary and young quadroon lover Victor Gregoire, who was running my office for me in my absence as no one else could have ever done, I supposed.

When I reached Venice, I expected the usual communications from Victor to be waiting for me – some letters, contracts to be notarized, signed, that sort of thing. But mainly I anticipated his written assurance that all was well in New Orleans.

What greeted me was this: as I sat at my desk, above the canal, in a great vast drearily painted room in the Italian style, hung with velvet and very damp, with a

495

cold marble floor, in walked Victor. Or so it seemed. For I knew in an instant this was not my Victor but someone who made himself look identical to him. He stood before me, smiling almost coyly – the young man I knew with pale golden skin, blue eyes, black hair, and a tall powerful body dressed to perfection. And then vanished.

Of course it had been the monster pretending to be Victor; making this vision to torment me. But why? I knew. I laid my head down on the desk and wept. Within an hour Mary Beth came in with the news from America. Victor had been killed two weeks ago in an accident. He had stepped off the curb at Prytania and Philip and been run down, right outside the apothecary. Two days later he had died, calling for me.

'We had better go home,' she said.

'I will not!' I declared. 'Lasher has done this.'

'He would not.'

'Oh, hell yes he would and he did.' I was in a rage. I locked myself in my bedroom on the third floor of the palazzo. I had only a view of the narrow *calle* below. I paced in a fury.

'Come to me,' I said. 'Come!'

And finally he did, once again tricked out as a brittle, shiny smiling cutout of my Victor.

'Laughter, Julien. I would go home now.'

I turned my back on the vision. He made the draperies blow, the floors rattle. It seemed he made the deep stone walls rumble.

At last I opened my eyes.

'I would not be here!' he declared. 'I would be home.'

'Ah, and to walk the streets of Venice means nothing to you?'

'I loathe this place. I do not want to hear hymns. I hate you. I hate Italy.'

'Ah, but what of Donnelaith, what of that? Were we to go north to Scotland?' For that had been one of my most important goals on this trip, to see the town for myself where Suzanne had called up the thing.

He passed into a tantrum. Papers flew from my table, the bedcovers were snatched up and twirled into a great shape, which knocked me flat on my back before I realized what was happening. Never had I seen the thing so strong. All my life, its strength had been increasing. And now it had struck me.

I shot up from the floor, snatched the fabric and cast it down and cursed the thing. 'Be gone from me, Devil! Feast no more on my soul, Devil. My family shall cast you out, Devil!' And I tried with all my might and main to see *it*, spirit that it was – and I did, a great dark collecting force in the room, and with my entire will and a great roar I drove it out of the windows, out over the *calle*, and above the rooftops, where it seemed to unfurl like a monstrous fabric without end.

Mary Beth came rushing to me. Back it came to the window. Again I shot it my most heated and venomous curses!

'I shall return to Eden,' it roared. 'I shall slay all who bear the name Mayfair.'

'Ah,' said Mary Beth, opening her arms. 'And then you will never be flesh, and we will never return, and all our dreams shall be laid waste and those who love you and know you best will be gone. You will be alone again.'

I got out of the way. I saw what was coming. She reached out to it again, and in the softest voice wooed it. 'You have built this family. You have made the Eden in which it lives. Grant us this little time. All the good that has come to us has been through you. Will you begrudge us this little journey, you who have always given us our way, and what would make us happy?'

The spirit was weeping. I could hear that peculiar soundless sound. It was a wonder it didn't plunk down the syllables: *Weeping!* the way it plunked down the syllables: *Laughter*. But it did not. It took the more eloquent and heartrending path.

Mary Beth stood at the window. Like many an Italian girl, she had matured young in our own southern heat; she was a luscious flower in her red dress, the small-waisted, big-skirted fashion of the times making her full breasts and hips all the more gorgeous. I saw her bow her head and rest her lips on her hands, and then give this kiss in offering to the being.

It wrapped itself slowly around her, lifting and caressing her hair, and twisting it, and letting it fall again. She let her head turn on her shoulders. She gave herself to it.

I turned my back. I brooded and waited in silence.

At last it came to me. 'I love you, Julien.'

'Would you be flesh? Would you continue to shower all blessings upon us – your children, your helpers, your witches?'

'Yes, Julien.'

'Let us go to Donnelaith,' I said, choosing my words carefully. 'Let me see the glen where our family was born. Let me lay a wreath of flowers on the glen floor where our Suzanne was burnt alive. Let me do this.'

This was the most shameful lying! I no more wanted to do that than to go play the bagpipes and wear the tartan! But I was determined to see Donnelaith, to know it, to penetrate to the core of this mystery!

'Very well,' Lasher said, buying the lie, for after all, who could lie to him better than I could, by this time?

'Take my hand when we are there,' I said. 'Tell me what I should know.'

'I will,' he said in a resigned voice. 'Only leave this accursed popish country. Leave these Italians and their crumbling church. Get away from here. Go north, yes, and I go with you, your servant, your lover – Lasher.'

'Very well, spirit,' I said. And then trying to mean it with all my heart, and finding some meaning in it, I said, 'I love you, spirit, as well as you love me!' And then the tears sprang to my eyes.

'We will know each other in the darkness someday, Julien,' he said. 'We will know each other as ghosts when we roam the halls of First Street. I must be flesh. The witches must prosper.'

I found this thought so terrifying that I said nothing. But be assured, Michael, it hasn't been so. I am in no realm that is shared by any other soul.

These things cannot be explained; even now my understanding is too dim for words. I know only that you and I are here, that I see you, and you see me. Maybe that is all creatures are ever meant to know in any realm.

But I didn't know that then. Any more than any other living being, I couldn't grasp the immense loneliness of earthbound spirits. I was in the flesh as you are now. I knew nothing else, nothing unbounded and purgatorial as what I have since suffered. Mine was the naïveté of the living; now it is the confusion and longing of the dead.

Pray when I am finished this tale, I will go on to something greater. Punishment even would have its shape, its purpose, some conviction of meaning. I cannot imagine eternal flames. But I can imagine eternal meaning.

We left Italy immediately as the daemon had asked us to do. We journeyed north, stopping again in Paris for only two days before we made the crossing, and drove north to Edinburgh.

The daemon seemed quiet. When I tried to engage it in conversation, it would say only, 'I remember Suzanne,' and there was something utterly without hope in its manner.

Now in Edinburgh a remarkable thing happened. Mary Beth, in my presence, begged that the daemon come with her and protect her. She, who had gone out with me disguised, would now wander on her own, with only her familiar to protect her. In sum, she lured Lasher away, whistling to herself as she went out, walking in a man's tweed coat and breeches, her hair swept up beneath a small shapeless cap, her steps big and easy as any boy's steps might be.

And I, alone, went at once to the University of Edinburgh, on the trail of the finest professor of history in those parts, and soon cornered the man, and, plying him with drink and money, was soon closeted away with him in his study.

His was a charming house in the Old Town, which many of the rich had long deserted but which he still preferred, for he knew the whole history of the building. The rooms were filled with books, even to the narrow hallways, and the stairway landing.

He was an ingratiating, volatile little creature – with a shiny bald head, silver spectacles and rather showy flaring white whiskers, which were then the style – who spoke with a thick Scots accent to his English, and he was passionately in love with the folklore of his country. His rooms were crammed with dreary pictures of Robert Burns, and Mary Queen of Scots, and Robert the Bruce, and even Bonnie Prince Charlie.

I thought it all rather amusing, but I was too excited to keep still when he admitted that indeed he was, as his students had told me, an expert on the ancient folklore of the Highlands.

'Donnelaith,' says I. 'I may have the spelling wrong. Here. But this is the word.'

'No, you've got it right,' he said. 'But wherever did you hear of it? The only folks who go up there now are the students interested in the old stones, and the fishermen and the hunters. That glen is a haunted place, very beautiful of course, and well worth the trek, but only if you have some purpose. There are terrible legends in those parts, as terrible as the legends of Loch Ness, or Glamis Castle.'

'I have a purpose. Tell me about it, everything that you know,' said I, frightened that any moment I would feel the spirit's presence. I wondered if Mary Beth had gone into some dangerous pub where women are in the main not allowed, just to keep Lasher on his toes.

'Well, it all goes back to the Romans,' said the professor. 'Pagan worship in those parts, but the name Donnelaith refers to an ancient clan stronghold. The Clan Donnelaith were Irish and Scots, descendants of the missionaries who went up there from Ireland to spread the word of God in the time of St Brendan. And of course the Picts were up there, before the Romans. Rumor was they built their castle in Donnelaith because it was a place blessed by the pagan spirits. We are talking now of the Picts when we speak of pagans. That was their part of Scotland up there, and the Donnelaith clan probably descended from them as well. You know how it went, pagans and Catholics.'

'Catholics built upon pagan shrines to appease and include the local superstitions.'

'Exactly,' said he. 'And even the Roman documents mention terrible things about that glen and the things that lurked in it. They mention a sinister childlike breed, which could overrun the world if ever allowed to stray from the valley. And a particularly vicious species of the "little people". Of course you are familiar with the little people. Don't laugh at them, I warn you.' Yet he smiled as he said this. 'But you can't find the original material on any of that anymore. Whatever, even before the Venerable Bede those tribes up there had become the Clan of Donnelaith, and Bede even mentions a cult center, a Christian church there.'

'What was its name?' I asked.

'Don't know,' says he. 'The Venerable Bede never said, at least not that I remember, but it had to do with a great saint who was, as you can probably guess, a converted pagan. You know, one of those legendary kings of great potency who suddenly fell upon his knees and allowed himself to be baptized, and then worked a score of miracles. Just the sort of things the Celts and the Picts of those times required of their God if they were going to go over to him.

'The Romans never really tamed the Highlands, you know. And neither really did the Irish missionaries. The

Romans actually forbade their soldiers from going into the glen, or to the nearby islands. Something to do with the licentiousness of the women. The Highlanders were Catholic later on, yes, fiercely so, ready to fight to the death, but they were Catholic in their own strange way. And that was their downfall.'

'Explain,' said I, pouring him another glass of port, and peering over the parchment map which he spread out before us. This was a facsimile, he explained, that he'd made himself from the real thing under glass in the British Museum.

'The town reached its height in the fourteen hundreds. There is some evidence it was a market town. The loch was a true port in those times. Rumor was, the Cathedral was magnificent. Not the church Bede mentions, you understand, but a Cathedral which had taken centuries to build, and all the time under the wing of the Clan of Donnelaith, who were devoted to this saint, and regarded him as the guardian of all Scots, and the one someday to save the nation.

'You have to go to travel accounts for descriptions of the shrine, and there isn't very much there, and nobody has ever bothered to compile it.'

'I'll compile it,' I said.

'If you have a century to stay here, you might,' said he, 'but you ought to go up to the glen and see how little remains of all that. A castle, a pagan circle of stones, the foundations of the town, now totally overgrown, and then those terrible ruins of the Cathedral.'

'But what did happen to it? What did you mean its Catholicism was its ruin?'

'Those Highland Catholics would yield to no one,' he said. 'Not to Henry the Eighth when he tried to convert

503

them to his new church in the name of Anne Boleyn, and not to the great reformer John Knox, either. But it was John Knox – or his followers – who destroyed them.'

I closed my eyes; I was seeing the Cathedral. I was seeing the flames, and the stained glass exploding in all directions. I opened my eyes with a shudder.

'You're a strange man,' he said. 'You've got the Irish blood, don't you?'

I nodded. Told him my father's name. He was flabbergasted. Of course he remembered Tyrone McNamara, the great singer. But he didn't think anyone else did. 'And you are his son?'

'Aye,' I said. 'But go on. How did the followers of Knox destroy Donnelaith? Oh, and the stained glass. There was stained glass, wasn't there, where would that have come from?'

'Made right there,' said he, 'all through the twelve hundreds and thirteen hundreds by the Franciscan monks from Italy.'

'Franciscans from Italy. You mean the Order of St Francis of Assisi was there.'

'Most definitely so. The Order of St Francis was popular right up to the time of Anne Boleyn,' he said. 'The Observant Friars were the refuge of Queen Catherine, when Henry divorced her, of course. But I don't think Observant Friars built or maintained the Cathedral at Donnelaith; it was far too elaborate, too rich, too full of ritual for simple Franciscans. No, it was probably the Conventuals; they were the Franciscans who kept the property, I believe. Whatever the case, when King Henry broke with the pope, and went to looting the monasteries all around, the Clan of Donnelaith drove out his soldiers without a moment's hesitation. Terrible, terrible bloody battles in the glen. And even the bravest British soldiers were loath to go up there.'

'The name of the saint.'

'I don't know. I told you. Probably some meaningless Gaelic collection of syllables and when we break it down we'll find it's descriptive like Veronica or Christopher.'

I sighed. 'And John Knox.'

'Well, Henry died, as you know, and his Catholic daughter, Mary, took the throne, and another bloodbath ensued and this time it was Protestants who were burnt or hanged or whatever. But next, we had Elizabeth the First! The Great Queen, and once again Great Britain was Protestant.

'The Highlands were prepared to ignore the whole thing, but then came John Knox, the great reformer, and preached his famous sermon against the idolatry of the papists, at Perth in 1559, and it was war in the glen as the Presbyterians descended upon the Cathedral. Burnt it, smashed the glass to pieces, laid ruin the Cathedral school, burnt the books, all of it gone. Horrible horrible story. Of course they claimed the people were witches in the glen, that they worshiped a devil who looked like a man; that they had it all mixed up with the saints; but it was Protestant against Catholic finally.

'The town never recovered. It hung on till the late sixteen hundreds, when the last of the clan was killed in a fire in the castle. Then there was no more Donnelaith. Just nothing.'

'And no more saint.'

'Oh, the saint was gone in 1559, whoever he was, God bless him. His cult disappeared with the Cathedral. You have only a little Presbyterian town after that, with the "abominable" pagan circle of stones outside it.'

'What do we know about the pagan legends in particular?' I asked.

'Only that there are those who still believe them. Now and then, someone will come from as far away as Italy. They will ask about the stones. They seek the road to Donnelaith. They even ask about the Cathedral. Yes, I'm telling you the truth; they'll come asking for the Glen of Donnelaith and they'll journey up there to look about in search of something. And then you are here, asking the very same questions, really, in your own way. The last person was a scholar from Amsterdam.'

'Amsterdam.'

'Yes, there is an order of scholars there. Indeed, they have a Motherhouse in London also. They are organized like religious but they have no beliefs. Over my lifetime they have come some six times to explore the glen. They have a very strange name. Luckier than the saint, I suppose. Their name is unforgettable.'

'What is it?' asked I.

'Talamasca,' he said. 'They are really very well-educated men, with a great respect for books. Here, see this little Book of the Hours? It's a gem! They gave it to me. They always bring me something. See this? This is one of the first King James Bibles ever printed. They brought that last time they visited. They go camp in that glen, really, they do. They stay for weeks and then they go away, invariably disappointed.'

I was overcome with excitement. All I could think of

for a moment was Marie Claudette's strange tale to me when I was only three of how a scholar from Amsterdam had come to Scotland and rescued poor Deborah, daughter of Suzanne. For a moment all manner of images came back to me, from the daemon's memories, and I almost lost consciousness. But time was too precious to indulge in any trances now. I had this kindly little doctor of history and had to get everything I could from him.

'Witchcraft,' I said. 'Witchcraft up there. The burnings in the seventeenth century. What do you know of them?'

'Oh, ghastly tale. Suzanne, the Milkmaid of Donnelaith. On that I happen to have an invaluable piece of material, one of the original pamphlets circulated in those days by the witch judges.'

He went to his press and took out of it a small, crumbling quarto of pages. I could see a coarse engraving of a woman surrounded by flames that resembled more huge leaves or tongues of fire. And in thick English letters was written:

THE TALE OF THE WITCH OF DONNELAITH

'I will buy this from you,' I said.

'Not on your life,' says he. 'But I'll have it copied in detail for you.'

'Good enough.' I took out my wallet and laid down a wad of American dollars.

'That will do, that will do. Don't get carried away! What a passionate fellow you are. Must be the Irish blood. The French are by nature so much more reticent.

It's my granddaughter who does the copying and it won't take her that long. She'll give you a lovely transcript in facsimile form on parchment.'

'Good, now tell me what it says.'

'Oh, same old foolishness. These pamphlets were circulated all over Europe. This one was printed in Edinburgh in 1670. Tells how Suzanne, the cunning woman, came under the sway of Satan, and gave him her soul, and how she was tried and burnt, but her daughter the merry-begot was spared, for the child had been conceived on the first of May, and was sacred to God, and no one dared touch her.

'The daughter was at last entrusted to the care of a Calvinist minister who took her to Switzerland, I believe, for the salvation of her soul. Name Petyr van Abel.'

'Petyr van Abel, you are certain of that name? It says it there?' I could scarcely contain myself. This was the only written word I had ever beheld to confirm the tale which Marie Claudette had told me. I did not dare say this was my ancestor as well. Having Tyrone McNamara seemed gauche enough. I merely fell silent, overwhelmed, and even contemplated stealing the pamphlet.

'Yes, indeed, Petyr van Abel, right here,' said he. 'All written by a minister here in Edinburgh and printed here too and sold for quite a profit. These things were popular, you know, just like the magazines of today. Imagine people sitting around the fire and looking at this horrid picture of the poor girl burning.

'You know they were burning witches, right here in Edinburgh – at the Witches' Well, on the Esplanade, right up till the seventeen hundreds.'

I made some murmur of total sympathy. But I was too stunned by this little confirmation to think clearly. Again I might have yielded to a load of Lasher's memories if I had allowed myself to do so. Hurriedly, I put my questions:

'But by the time of the witch, the Cathedral was long burnt,' said I, trying to get my bearings.

'Yes, everything was pretty much gone. Only sheep-herders up there. But do understand, some historians do believe that the witchcraft persecutions were a last bit of Protestant-Catholic feuding. There may be some truth to it. What they say specifically is this – life became very dull under John Knox, what with stained glass and statues gone, and all the old Latin hymns banned; and colorful Highland customs abandoned; and the people went back to some of their pagan ceremonies just to put some fancy in their lives, you know, some color.'

'Do you think that was the case in Donnelaith?'

'No. It was a typical trial. The Earl of Donnelaith was a poor man, living in a dreary castle. We hear nothing of him in that century, except that he later died in the fire that killed his son and grandson. The witch was a poor cunning woman from the village, called to account for bewitching some other humble person. We hear of no Sabbats. But God knows, they were held in other places up there. And this woman had been known to go to the pagan circle of stones, and that was used against her.'

'The stones themselves. What do you know of them?'

'Big controversy. Some say they are as old as Stone-henge, maybe older. I think they have something to do with the Picts, that at one time there were carvings on

509

them. They're very rough, those stones, and all of different sizes. They are remnants of what was once there, and I think at one time, they were deliberately defaced – all the inscriptions chipped off or worn off, and then the rest of the work was done by the weather.'

He opened a small book of drawings. 'This is the art of the Picts,' he said.

I felt a terrible moment of disorientation. I don't know what it meant. I shall never forget it. I looked at these warriors, rows and rows of crude little profile figures with shields and swords. I didn't know what to make of it.

'I think the stones were their worshiping place. To hell with Stonehenge. But who will ever know? Perhaps the stones belonged to one of these strange tribes, or even the little people.'

'Who owns this valley?' said I.

The man wasn't sure. All the land had been cleared up there by the government, the last starving settlers driven out for their own good. Pitiful. Just pitiful. Many had gone to America. Did I know of the Highland clearances?

'I've told you all I know,' he said. 'I wish I knew more.'

'You will,' I said. 'I will leave you the means to make a study.'

Then I begged him to join me on my trek to Donnelaith, but he swore he wasn't up to it. 'I love that glen,' he said. 'I did go there many years ago with a man from the Amsterdam order. Alexander Cunningham was his name, a brilliant fellow. He paid for everything, and what a picnic we took with us. We stayed in the glen for a full week. I tell you I was glad to get back to civilization. But he said the strangest thing when he left me here, after our final dinner.

'"You didn't really find what you wanted up there, did you?" I asked him.

'"No, indeed, I didn't, and thank God for that, if there is one." He went out of the house and then he came back. "Let me tell you something, old friend. Never make light of the legends of those glens," he said. "And never laugh at the story of Castle Glamis. The little people are still to be found, and they'd bring the witches to the Sabbat if they could for the old purpose."

'Naturally I said to the man, "What purpose?" But he wouldn't answer on that, and seemed to be sincere in his silence.'

'But what is the Glamis Castle story?' asked I.

'Oh, that there is some curse in that family, you see, and when they tell the new heir he never smiles again. Many have written of that. I've been to Glamis Castle. Who knows? But this man from the Talamasca, he was a studious and passionate sort. We had a splendid time up there, in the glen, looking at the moon.'

'But you didn't see the little people.'

He fell silent, then: 'I did see something. But it wasn't fairies, I don't think. It was just a smallish man and woman, rather misshapen, same unfortunates you see begging in the streets. I did see those two once very early in the morning, and when I told my Talamasca friend he was in a perfect fury that he himself had not seen them. They didn't come again.'

'With your own eyes, you saw them. Were they frightening?'

'Oh, they gave me the shivers!' He shook his head. 'I

don't like to tell that tale,' he said. 'Remember, to us, my friend, fairies aren't merely humorous little beings. They are demons of the wild; they are powerful and dangerous and can be vengeful. I'll tell you this, there are fairy lights in that glen. Fairy lights, those flames that rise up in the night on the distant horizon without explanation. I wish you luck in going there. I really wish I could go. We'll begin collecting these research materials for you immediately.'

I went home to our fine lodgings in New Town.

Mary Beth had still not come back. I sat alone in our suite, a comfortable pair of bedrooms and a sitting room in between, and I drank my sherry and wrote down all that I could remember of what the man had told me. It was cold in these rooms. It would be cold in the glen. But I had to go there. The saint, the fairies, it's all mixed up, I thought.

Then, in the silence, a feeling stole over me. Lasher was near. Lasher was in the room, and he knew my thoughts, and was close to me.

'Are you there, beloved?' I asked casually as I jotted down the last few words.

'So they gave you his name,' he said in his secret voice.

'Petyr van Abel, yes, but not the name of the saint.'

'Aye, Petyr,' he said softly. 'I remember Petyr van Abel. Petyr van Abel saw Lasher.' His entire demeanor seemed tame and thoughtful. His secret voice was at its most resonant and beautiful.

'Tell me,' I coaxed.

'In the great circle,' he said. 'We will go there. I have always been there. I mean that you will go there.'

'Can you be there and with us at the same time?'

'Yes,' he said with a sigh. But there seemed some doubt in his mind. It was, again, the limits of his thinking.

'Be clever, spirit, who are you?' I asked.

'Lasher, called by Suzanne, in the glen,' said he. 'You know me. I have done so well for you, Julien.'

'Tell me where my daughter Mary Beth is, then, spirit. I hope you did not leave her somewhere in this dark city to her own devices.'

'Her devices are very good, Julien, allow me to remind you. But I left her to her own vices rather than devices.'

'Which means what?'

'She found a Scot who would be the father of her witch.'

I shot out of the chair in a protective rage! 'Where is Mary Beth?'

But even then I heard her singing as she came down the corridor. She opened the door. She was very red-cheeked and beautiful from the cold, indeed, sort of glistening, and her hair was loose. 'Well, I have done it at last,' she said. She danced into the room, and then put a kiss on my cheek. 'Don't look so stricken.'

'But who is the man?'

'Don't give it another of your precious thoughts, Julien,' she said. 'I shall never again lay eyes on him. Lord Mayfair is a good name, don't you think?'

And so that was the lie that was written home, just as soon as we knew she had conceived. Lord Mayfair of Donnelaith had fathered her child. Indeed her 'marriage' had been held in that 'town' – though of course there was no town at all.

But I jump ahead of my story. I had the keen feeling at that moment that she had mated with success, and as she described this man to me, pure Scots, and black-haired and wicked and charming and very rich, I thought, Well, perhaps this is as good a way to choose a father for one's child as any.

Any pain I felt, jealousy, shame, fear, whatever, I buried it inside me. We were committed libertines, she and I. I would not have her laughing at me. Besides, I was too eager to go to Donnelaith.

As I told her what I knew, our beloved spirit did nothing to come between us. Indeed, he was quiet that night. We were all quiet. Though down the street there was quite a bit of talk. Seems one of the local lords had been murdered.

I didn't learn till later who it was. And even then the name didn't mean anything. But I think I know now that it was the father of Mary Beth's baby.

Let's go on to Donnelaith now. And let me tell you what I discovered there.

We set out the very next day, with two big carriages, one for ourselves and our luggage, the other for several servants needed to assist us. We went north to Darkirk, to the inn there, and from Darkirk on together on horseback, with two pack animals, and two of the local Scotsmen also on horseback to guide us.

We were both great lovers of horses, you understand, and riding in this treacherous hilly terrain was rather a treat for us. We had fine horses for the trip and provisions to stay the night, though not long after we set out, I became aware of my age, and aware of many aches and pains that I had been able to ignore before this time. Our guides were young. Mary Beth was young. I was pretty much on my own, bringing up the rear, but the beauty of the surrounding hills, of the rich forests, and the sky itself drugged me and made me very happy.

There was a chilly haunted glory to all this, however. Scotland! But I had to go all the way to the glen. When I felt the urge to turn round, I kept my counsel and went on. We had a hasty lunch, then rode until almost sunset.

It was just then that we came to the glen, or rather a slope descending upon it. And from a high promontory, just out of the deep forest of Scots pine and alder and oak, we saw the distant castle across the gulf, a hollow overgrown monstrous thing above the beautiful glowing waters. And in the valley itself the high straggled arches of the Cathedral, and the circle of stones, remote, and austere but plainly visible.

Darkness or no darkness, we decided to press on. We lighted our lanterns and went down through the scattered groves of trees, and into the grassy glen, and did not pitch camp till we had reached the remnants of the town, or more visibly, the village which had lingered on after it.

Mary Beth was for pitching camp in the pagan stones. But the two Scotsmen refused. Indeed, they seemed outraged. 'That's a fairy circle, madam,' said one of them. 'You wouldn't dare to do such a thing as camp there. The little people would take it very ill, believe me.'

'These Scots are as crazy as the Irish,' said Mary Beth. 'Why didn't we go on to Dublin if we wanted to hear about leprechauns?'

Her words gave me a little thrill of fear. We were now deep in the broad glen. The village did not include one single stone left standing. Our tents, our lanterns must have been visible for miles around. And suddenly, I felt strangely naked and undefended.

We should have gone up to the ruins of the castle, I thought. And then I realized it. We had not heard from our spirit all day. We had not felt his touch, his nudge, his breath.

The thrill of fear deepened. 'Lasher, come to me,' I whispered. I feared suddenly that he had gone off to do some terrible thing to those we loved, that he was angry.

But he was quick to respond. As I walked out alone with my unlighted lantern in the tall grass, each step an ordeal since I was so sore from the ride, he came with a great cooling breeze, and made the grass bow to me in a huge circle.

'I am not angry with you, Julien,' he said. But his voice was thick with suffering. 'We are in our land, the land of Donnelaith. I see what you see, and I weep for what I see, for I remember what there was once in this valley.'

'Tell me, spirit,' I said.

'Ah, the great church which you know, and processions of the penitent and the ill come for miles through the hills and down to worship at the shrine. And the thriving town full of shops and tradesmen, selling images . . . images . . .'

'Images of what?' asked I.

'What is it to me? I would be born again, and never waste my flesh this next time as I did in those years. I am not the slave of history but rather the slave of ambition. Do you understand the difference, Julien?'

'Enlighten me,' I said. 'There are few times when you make me genuinely curious.'

'You are too frank, Julien,' it said. 'What I mean to say is this. There is no past. Absolutely none. There is only the future. And the more we learn the more we know – reverence for the past is simply superstition. You do what you must do to make the clan strong. So do I. I dream of the witch who will see me and make me flesh. You dream of wealth and power for your children.'

'I do,' said I.

'There is nothing else. And you have brought me back to this place, which I have never left, that I might know it.'

I was standing there idle under the darkling sky, the valley huge, the ruins of the Cathedral just ahead of me. These words sank into my soul. I memorized them.

'Who taught you these things?' I asked.

'You did,' Lasher said. 'It was you and your kind who taught me to want, to aim, to reach, rather than to lament. And now I remind you, for the past calls to you under false pretenses.'

'You think so,' I said.

'Yes,' he said. 'These stones, what are they? They are nothing.'

'May I see the church, spirit?'

'Oh yes,' said he. 'Light your lantern if you will. But you will never see it as I saw it.'

'You're wrong, spirit. When you come into me, you leave something of yourself behind. I have seen it. I have seen it with the faithful crowded to the doors, and the candles and the Christmas green –'

'Silence!' he declared and I felt him like the wind wrapping me so roughly suddenly he might knock me over. I went down on my knees. The wind ceased.

'Thank you, spirit,' said I. I struck a match, shielding it carefully, and lighted the wick of the lantern. 'Won't you tell me of those times?'

'I'd tell you what I see from here. I see my children.'

'Do you speak of us now?'

But that was all he would say, though he followed me as I made a path through the high grass, over rocky and uneven ground, and came at last to the ruins themselves and stood in the giant nave looking at the broken arches.

Dear God, what a grand cathedral it must have been. I had seen its like all over Europe. It was not in the Roman style, with rounded arches and paintings galore; no doubt it was cold stone, and lofty and graceful as the Cathedral of Chartres or Canterbury.

'But the glass, does anything remain of the glorious glass?' I whispered.

And in mournful answer the wind swept broadly and serenely across the entire darkening glen and passed through the nave, once again, making the wild grass bend to and fro, and ruffling around me as if to embrace me. The moon had risen a bit, and the stars were shining through.

And suddenly beyond the very end of the nave, where the rose window had once been, where the arch stood at its height, I saw the spirit himself, immense, and huge and dark and translucent, spread across the sky like a great storm rolling in, only silent, and collecting and re-collecting and then in one sudden burst dispersing into nothingness.

Clear sky, the moon, the distant mountain, the wood. All that was plain and still and the air felt cold and empty. My lantern burnt on bright. I stood alone. The

Cathedral seemed to grow taller around me, and I to be dwarfed and vain and petty and desperate. I sank down to the ground. I drew up my knee, and rested my hand and my chin upon it. I peered through the dark. I wished for Lasher's memories to come to me.

But nothing came but my loneliness, and my sense of the absolute wonder of my life, and how much I loved my family, and how they flourished beneath the wing of this terrible evil.

Maybe it was so with all families, I thought. At the heart a curse, a devil's bargain. A terrible sin. For how else can one attain such riches and freedom? But I didn't really believe this. I believed, on the contrary, in virtue.

I saw my definition of virtue. To be good, to love, to father, to mother, to nurture, to heal. I saw it in its shining simplicity. 'What can you do, you fool?' I asked of myself. 'Except keep your family safe, give them the means to live on their own, strong and healthy and good. Give them conscience and protect them from evil.'

Then a solemn thought came to me. I was sitting there still, with the warm light of the lantern about me, and the high church on both sides, and the grass flattened like a bed before me. I looked up again, and saw that the moon had moved right into the great circle of the rose window. The glass of course was all gone. I knew it had been a rose window because I knew what they were. And I knew the meaning as well, the great hierarchy of all things which had prevailed in the Catholic Church and how the rose was the highest of flowers and therefore the symbol of the highest of women, the Virgin Mary.

I thought on that, and on nothing. And I prayed. Not to the Virgin. No, just to the air of this place, just to time, perhaps to the earth. I said: God, as if all this had that name, can we make this bargain? I will go to hell if you will save my family. Mary Beth will go to hell, perhaps, and each witch after her. *But save my family. Keep them strong, keep them happy, keep them blessed.*

No answer came to my prayers. I sat there a long time. The moon was veiled by clouds, then free again and brilliant and beautiful. Of course I did not expect to hear any answer to my prayers. But my bargain gave me hope. We, the witches, shall suffer the evil; and the others shall prosper. That was my vow.

I climbed to my feet, I lifted the lantern and I started to walk back.

Mary Beth had already gone to sleep in her tent. The two guides were smoking their pipes, and invited me to join them. I told them I was weary. I'd sleep and wake early.

'You weren't praying up there, were you, sir?' asked one of the men. ''Tis a dangerous thing to pray in the ruins of that church.'

'Oh, and why is that?' asked I.

''Tis St Ashlar's church, and St Ashlar is likely to answer your prayer and who knows what will happen!'

Both men roared with laughter, slapping their thighs and nodding to one another.

'St Ashlar!' I said. 'You said Ashlar!'

'Yes, sir,' said the other, who had not spoken till now. 'Was his shrine in olden times, the most powerful saint of Scotland, and the Presbyterians made it a sin to speak his name. A sin! But the witches always knew it!'

Time and space were naught. In the quiet haunted night of the glen, I was remembering: a boy of three, the old witch, the plantation, her tales to me in French. 'Called up by accident in the glen ...' I whispered to myself, 'Come now my Lasher. Come now my Ashlar. Come now, my Lasher! Come now, my Ashlar!'

I began to murmur it, and then to say it aloud, the two men not understanding at all of course, and then out of the heart of the glen came the roaring wind, so fierce and huge it wailed against the mountains.

The tents flapped and whipped in the wind. The men ran to steady them. The lanterns went out. The wind became a gale, and as Mary Beth crept to my side, and held tight to my arm, a storm came down on Donnelaith, a storm of rain and thunder so fierce that we were all cowering before it.

All save I. I righted myself soon enough, realizing it was pointless to cower, and I stared back into it. I stared up into the heavens as the rain pelted and stung my face.

'Damn you, St Ashlar, that's who you are! Go to hell with you!' I cried. 'A saint, a deposed saint, a saint knocked from his throne! Go back to hell with you. You are no saint. You are a daemon!'

One tent was torn loose and carried away. The guides ran to stop the other. Mary Beth tried to quiet me. The wind and the rain gave their full breath, strong perhaps as a hurricane.

To a peak of anger it came, so we saw a ghastly funnel of black cloud rising suddenly from the grass and spinning and spinning and darkening the whole sky, and suddenly – as swiftly as it had come – it vanished.

I stood stock-still. I was dripping wet. My shirt was half torn from my shoulder. Mary Beth uncovered her hair and walked round in the damp, staring upwards, bravely and curiously.

One of the guides came back to me.

'Goddamnit, man,' said he. 'I told you not to pray to him. Whatever in hell did you pray for!'

I laughed softly to myself. 'Oh, God, help me,' I sighed. 'Is that the proof, Almighty God, that you are not there, that your saints could be such petty demons?'

The air was warming slightly. The men had the lanterns lighted. The water had vanished from the earth as if it had never come at all. We were still battered and wet but the moon was clear again, and flooding the glen with light. We went to right the tents, to dry the bedding.

I lay awake the whole night. As the sun came up, I went to the guides. 'I have to know the story of this saint,' said I.

'Well, don't say his name for god's sakes,' said the other. 'I wish I hadn't said it last night, I'll tell you. And I don't know his story and you won't hear it from anyone else I know either. It's an old legend, man, perhaps a joke,' he said, 'though we'll be talking about that storm last night for many a night to come, I can tell you.'

'Tell me all,' I said.

'I don't know. My grandmother said his name when she wished for an impossible thing, and said always to take care, and never wish for something from him unless you really wanted it. I've heard his name once or twice up there in the hills. There's an old song they sing. But that's all I know of it. I'm no Catholic. I don't know saints. No one hereabouts knows saints.'

The other man nodded. 'I myself did not know that much. I've heard my daughter call on him, though, to make the young men turn their heads to notice her.'

I pounded them with questions. They gave me nothing more. It was time for us to survey the ruins proper, the circle, the castle. The spirit lay back. I neither heard his voice nor saw any evidence of him.

Only once did fear come on me when searching the castle.

It was treacherous there. But he played no tricks.

We took our time. It was sunset before we made camp again. I had seen all that I had the strength to see. Many feet of dirt covered the original Cathedral floor, and who knew what lay below it? What tombs? What caches of books or documents? Or perhaps nothing.

And where had my precious Suzanne died, I wondered. No trace was left of roads or marketplaces. I could not tell. I did not dare to challenge Lasher or say any words to make him angry. I remembered everything.

In Darkirk, a small, clean Presbyterian town of white buildings, I could find no one who knew a thing of Catholic saints. They would talk of the circle, the witches, the old days, Sabbats in the glen, and the evil little people who sometimes stole babies. But it was all remote to them. They were more interested in taking the train to Edinburgh or Glasgow. They had no love of the woods or the glen. They wanted an iron smelting factory to come. Cut down the trees. It was all bread and butter.

I was a week in Edinburgh, with the bankers, buying the land. But at last I had title to all of it. And I had set up a trust for its study with my little professor of history, who welcomed me back from my journey with a fine dinner of roast duck and claret.

Mary Beth went off on her own, another escapade, and took with her the demon. He and I had not exchanged one silent or audible word since that terrible night, but he had hovered close to her, and spoken with her. And I had told her nothing of what I had done or learnt or said, and she had asked me nothing.

I was afraid to utter the name Ashlar. That was the truth. I was afraid. I kept seeing that storm around me. And those frightened men, and Mary Beth peering so curiously into the rainy darkness. I was frightened, though why I wasn't sure. I had won, had I not? I had the thing's name. Was I ready to wager my life in a battle with it?

At last I sat down with my little bald-headed bespectacled teacher in Edinburgh and said, 'I've been through all the lives of the saints in the library, all the histories of Scotland, and I can find no mention of St Ashlar.'

He gave me a cheerful laugh as he poured the wine. He was in great form tonight, as I had just laid upon him thousands and thousands of American dollars to do nothing but study Donnelaith, and his security was assured and that of his children.

'"By St Ashlar,"' said he. 'That's an expression the schoolchildren use. Saint of the impossible, I believe, rather like Jude in other parts. But there is no tale to it, none I know, but remember, this is a Presbyterian land now. The Catholics are very few, and the past is wrapped in mystery.'

Nevertheless he promised we would search through

his books when the meal was over. And in the meantime, we discussed the trust for the excavation and preservation of Donnelaith. The ruins would be fully explored, mapped, described, and then made an object of ongoing study.

Finally, we retired to the library together, and he sought, among his books, some old Catholic texts dating back to the days before King Henry, one in particular, *A Secret Historie of the Highland Clans*, which carried no author's name on it. It was a very old book, of black leather, and rather large, and many of the leaves had come unbound, so it was more like a folio of damaged pages. When he laid it down in the light, I saw they were covered with writing.

There was a family tree of sorts described, and he followed it down with his finger.

'Ah, here, can you read this? Well, of course you can't. It's Gaelic. But it's Ashlar, son of Olaf and husband of Janet, founders of the clan of Drummard and Donnelaith, yes, there it is. The word *Donnelaith*, and to think all these years I had never spotted it here. Though Ashlar I have seen in countless places. Yes, St Ashlar.'

He paged through the sloppy fragile text until he came to another page. 'Ashlar,' he said, reading the crabbed hand. 'Yes, King of Drummard – Ashlar.'

He carefully read the text, translating it for me, and jotting notes on a pad with his pencil.

'King Ashlar of the pagans, beloved by his people, husband of Queen Janet, rulers of High Dearmach far north of the Great Glen in the Highland forests. Converted in the year 566 by St Columba of Ireland. Yes, here it is, the legend of St Ashlar. Died at Drummard, where a great cathedral was raised in his name. Drummard later became Donnelaith, you see. Relics ... cures ... ah, but his wife, Janet, refused to give up the pagan faith and was burnt at the stake for her stubborn pride. "And when the great saint mourned her loss, a spring gushed forth from the burnt ground in which thousands were baptized." '

The image virtually paralyzed me. Janet burnt at the stake. The saint, the magic spring. I was too overcome to speak.

The scholar was tantalized. He quickly promised me that all this would be copied out and sent to me.

And now to his other books he went, finding in the history of the Picts the same Ashlar and Janet, and the dreadful story of how Janet refused to accept the faith of Christ, and indeed offered to die by fire, cursing her kinsmen and husband, and preferring to be delivered by fire to the gods than live with cowardly Christians.

'Now this is all legend, you understand. Nobody really knows about the Picts, you see. And it's confusing. Doesn't even really say for sure that they were Picts. Here, see these words in Gaelic, this means "tall men and women of the glen". And this here, it can be roughly translated to mean "the big children".

'Ah, here, King Ashlar, defeated the Danes in the year 567, waving the fiery cross before their fleeing armies. Janet, daughter of Ranald, burnt at the stake by Ashlar's clan in 567, though the saint himself was innocent, and begged his newly converted followers to show mercy.'

He took down yet another book.

LEGENDS OF THE HIGHLANDS

'Ah, here we are. St Ashlar, still venerated in some parts of Scotland as late as the sixteen hundreds, principally by young girls who would have their most secret wishes granted. Not a true canonical saint.'

He closed the book. 'Well, that doesn't surprise me. Not a true canonical saint. All of this is too early for us to call it history. That means he was never canonized by Rome, you understand. We're dealing with another St Christopher.'

'I know,' said I, but I was mainly quiet, swept up again in the memories. I saw the Cathedral so distinctly. For the first time I truly saw its windows – narrow, high, with bits of colored glass, not pictures, but mostly glass mosaics of gold, red and blue – and the rose window, ah, the rose window! Suddenly I saw the flames. I saw the glass shattering. I heard the cries of the mob. I felt myself so much in the midst of it that I knew for an instant my height as I faced the oncoming crowd, I saw my own hands outstretched against them!

I shook it off. The old professor was peering curiously at me.

'You do have a great passion for these things, don't you?'

'Almost an unholy passion,' I said. 'A cathedral of the twelve hundreds. That's not too early to be called history.'

'No, indeed not,' he said, and now he went to another shelf, to a whole series of books on the churches and ruins of Scotland. 'So much has been lost, you see, so much. Why, if it weren't for the present scholarly interest in all these things, every trace of those Catholic edifices would have been ... here, "Highland Cathedrals".

'Donnelaith Cathedral, under the patronage of the Clan of Donnelaith, greatly expanded and enhanced from 1205 to 1266, by their chieftains. A special Christmas Devotion fostered by the Franciscan friars drew thousands from the surrounding area. No records remain today, but the principal patrons were always members of the Donnelaith clan. Some records believed to be . . . in Italy.'

I gave a long sigh. I didn't want to be dislodged from the present by the memories again. What had the memories taught me?

He turned several pages. 'Ah, see here, a crude family tree of the Donnelaith clan. King Ashlar, then look here, the great-grandson, Ashlar the Venerable, and here another descendant, Ashlar the Blessed, married to the Norman queen Mora. My, but there are any number of Ashlars.'

'I see.'

'And here an Ashlar, and an Ashlar, but you can trace the progress of the name, that is, if you believe all these chieftains existed! You know these clans reveled so in all this, and their mossback descendants write up these fanciful accounts. I don't know.'

'It's quite enough to satisfy my lust for the moment,' I said.

'Ah, lust, yes, that's the word, isn't it?' He shut the book. 'There must be more. I'll find it for you. But to tell you the truth, it's going to be pretty much like this, in these old privately published texts, and the best you can say of it is it's folklore.'

'But the fifteen hundreds, the time of John Knox, surely there were records of that time; there must have been.'

'Up in smoke,' said the old man. 'We're talking about an ecclesiastical revolution. You cannot imagine the number of monasteries destroyed by Henry the Eighth. Statues and paintings were sold off, burnt. Sacred books lost forever. And when they finally broke the defenses of Donnelaith, everything was reduced to cinders.'

He sat down and began to pile these books in a semblance of order. 'I'll find everything for you,' he said. 'If there is any indication anywhere of records from Donnelaith being taken somewhere else I'll find it. But I can tell you my guess. It's lost. A land of monasteries and cathedrals lost its treasures then. And Henry, the scoundrel, it was all for money. All for money and that he would marry Anne Boleyn! Ah, despair, that one man should so turn the tide. Ah, here, look, "St Ashlar, the special saint of young girls who would have their secret wishes granted." I know I'll find a dozen more mentions such as this.'

At last I left the man in peace.

I had what I wanted. I knew now *the thing had once lived; it was full of vengeance! It was a ghost.*

And I felt I had the proof of it in all this, and all that I had ever known, and as I walked home alone up the hill from the old man's house, I kept repeating these details to myself, and thinking, What does it mean that this devil has attached himself to us! That he would be flesh. What does it mean? But above all how can I use this name to destroy him?

When I came into my rooms, Mary Beth was already home and asleep on the couch there, and Lasher was standing beside her. He was in his very old garb of rawhide clothing, hair longish, which I had not seen in years, and he was smiling at me.

For one moment, I was so struck by his vivid quality and his beauty that I did nothing but stare at him. And this he loved; it was as if I were giving him water to drink, you see. And he grew brighter and more distinct.

'You think you know, but you know nothing,' he said, moving his lips. 'And I remind you again that the future is everything.'

'You are no great spirit,' I said. 'You are no great mystery. That is what I must teach my family.'

'Then you teach them a lie. Their future is in my hands. And my future is theirs. That is your strongest suit. Be quick-witted for once, with all your learning.'

I didn't answer. I was amazed that the thing would hold a visible form so long.

'A saint turned against God?' I asked.

'Don't mock me with that foolish folklore, that nonsense. Do you think I was ever one of you? You are mad to suppose it. When I come again, I ...' and he broke off, clearly on the verge of threats. Then he said with childish quickness, 'Julien, I need you. The child in Mary Beth's womb, it is no witch, but a feebleminded girl, suffering the same defect as Katherine, your sister, and even Marguerite, your mother. You must make the witch with your daughter.'

'So I have *that* to bargain with,' I said with a sigh, 'and you want me to couple with my own daughter.'

But he had exhausted himself. He was fading. Mary Beth lay sleeping, lush and quiet on the couch, covered in blankets, her dark hair sleek and glowing in the light of the little fire.

'Will she give birth to this child?'

'Yes, bide your time, and wait. You shall make a great witch with her.'

'And she herself?'

'The greatest of all,' he said with an audible voice and sigh. 'Unless one counts Julien.'

Michael, that was my greatest triumph. I learnt what I have told you now, its name, its history, that it was of our blood, but more than that I never discovered!

Ashlar, it was all connected with that name. But was the daemon Ashlar, and if so which of the Ashlars in the pages of the old man's books? The first or one who came after?

The following morning, I left Edinburgh, leaving only a note for Mary Beth, and I traveled north to Donnelaith, going from Darkirk again on horseback. I was too old to make this journey on my own, but I was crazed with my discoveries.

Once again I searched the Cathedral, under the cool Highlands sun coming down in beautiful rays through the clouds, and then I walked out to the circle of stones, and stood there.

I called upon it. I cursed it. I said, 'I want you to go back to hell, St Ashlar! That is your name, that is who you are, a two-legged man, who would have been worshiped, and in pride you have survived, an evil daemon to torment us.'

My voice rang out in the glen. But I was alone. It had not even deigned to answer me. But then as I stood in the circle, I suddenly felt that awful woozy feeling, as if I'd been dealt a blow, which meant the thing was coming into me.

'No, back into hell!' I screamed, but I was falling to the grass. The world had become the wind itself, roaring in my ears, and carrying all distinct shapes and points of reference away with it.

It was night when I awoke. I was bruised. My clothes were torn. The thing had run rampant in me, and here of all places.

I was for a moment in fear for my life, sitting there in the dark, not knowing what had become of my horse, or which way to walk to leave this awful haunted glen. Finally I staggered to my feet, and realized a man held me by the shoulders.

It was *he*, strong again, material again, guiding me, his face very near to mine, in the dark. We were walking towards the castle. He was so real I could smell the leather of his jerkin, and I could smell the grass clinging to him, and the fragrance of the woods hanging about him. He vanished and I staggered on alone, only to have him reappear again and help me.

At last we entered a broken doorway to the floor of the great hall, and there I fell down to sleep, too exhausted to go further. He was sitting there in the dark, a vapor, and now and then solid, and sometimes merely there, wrapped around me.

In my sheer exhaustion and despair, I said, 'Lasher, what do I do? What is it you will do finally?'

'To live, Julien, that is all I want. To live, to come back out into the light. I am not what you think. I am not what you imagine. Look at your memories. The saint is in the glass, is he not? How could I be the saint if I could see him in the window? I never knew the saint; the saint was my downfall!'

I had never seen the saint in the window. I had seen only the colors, but now as I lay on the ground I remembered the church again, I was there, in a former time, and I was intimately recalling how I had, in that time, gone into the transept and entered the chapel of the saint, and yes, there he was emblazoned in the gorgeous glass, with the sun pouring through his image, the warrior priest, long-haired, bearded. St Ashlar, crushing the monsters beneath his foot: St Ashlar.

I found myself saying, in this former time, desperately from my soul: *St Ashlar, how can I be this thing? Help me. God help me.* They were taking me away. What choice had I been given?

Such longing, such pain!

I blacked out. All consciousness left me. I was never to know the fiend again so vividly as I had in that moment, when I stood in its flesh in the Cathedral. *St Ashlar!* I even heard *his voice,* my voice, echoing beneath the lofty stone roof. *How can I be this thing, St Ashlar!* And the brittle shining glass gave no reply. It did what pictures always do – remain constant, remain dominant.

Blackness.

When I awoke that morning, in the ruins of the castle, guides from Darkirk had come to find me. They brought food and drink and blankets and a fresh horse. They had feared for me. My mount had gone all the way home without me.

In the splendor of the morning, the valley looked innocent, lovely. I wanted to lie down and sleep, but alas, I could not until I was in the inn at Darkirk, and there I slept on and off for two days, suffering a bit of fever, but in general merely resting.

When I returned to Edinburgh Mary Beth was in a panic. She had thought me gone forever. She had accused Lasher of doing me harm. He had wept.

I told her to come and sit by the fire, and I told her everything. I told her the history and what it meant. I told her again the memories.

'You must be stronger than this thing to the last of your days,' I said. 'You must never let it get the better of you. It can kill; it can dominate! It can destroy; it wants to be alive, yes, and it is a bitter thing, a thing not of transcendent wisdom but under God, you see, something of blackness and utter despair, something that has been defeated!'

'Aye, suffered,' she said, '*that's* the word. But Julien, you are past all patience. You cannot go on with this opposition to it. You must from now on leave this thing entirely to me.'

She rose to her feet and began to declaim in her calm voice, with few gestures, as was her manner.

'I shall use this thing to make our family richer than your wildest imaginings. I shall build a clan so great that no revolution, no war, no uprising could ever destroy it. I shall unite our cousins when I can, encourage marriage within the clan, and see to it that the family name is borne by all who would be part of us. I shall triumph in the family, Julien, and this it understands. This it knows. This is what it wants. There is no battle between us.'

'Is that so?' I asked. 'Has it told you what I would do for it next? That I should father a witch by you?' I was trembling with apprehension and rage.

She smiled at me in a soft appeasing and calm way, and then, stroking my face, said: 'Now, really, when the time comes, will that be so very hard, my darling?'

That night I dreamed of witches in the glen. I dreamed of orgies. I dreamed of all manner of things I would forget but never did. From Edinburgh we went to London. There we remained until Mary Beth gave birth to Belle in 1888, and from the beginning we knew the radiant child was not normal only because Lasher had told us.

In London, I procured a large book with a leather cover and fine-quality parchment paper, and I wrote down everything I knew of Lasher in it. I wrote down everything I knew of our family. I had much such writing at home, other books started, stopped, forgotten. But now, from memory I collected everything.

I recorded any and all details about Riverbend, Donnelaith, the legends, the saint. All of it. I wrote fast and in a fury. For I didn't know but that, at any moment, the monster might stop me.

But the monster did nothing.

Letters came to me daily from the old scholar, but mostly they were stories of St Ashlar, that St Ashlar would grant a miracle to a young girl, for he was their special protector. And the rest was repetitive of what we had discovered. Some excavations were begun at Donnelaith but that work would take a century. And what would we find that I did not now know?

Yet I wrote enthusiastically to my professor and his friends, increased the endowments and gave in to their wishes in any project to further the study of Donnelaith and its complex of ruins.

Each letter I copied out into my book.

Then I took up another book and began to write my own life story in it. This book too was chosen for its strong binding and good paper. I never dreamt that both books would perish before I did.

Lasher meantime did not trouble me while I did this, but spent his time with Mary Beth, who almost up to the hour of giving birth went traipsing all about London and down to Canterbury and off to Stonehenge. She was ever in the company of young men. I believe there were two of them with her, Oxford scholars both, deeply in love, when she gave birth to baby Belle in the hospital.

I have never felt so separate from her as during this time. She was in love with the city and all the ancient sites and the newfangled things, rushing to see factories and theaters and all sorts of new inventions. She went to the Tower of London, of course, and the wax museum, which was all the rage. Her pregnancy was nothing to her. She was so tall, so strong, so hearty; the impersonation of a man was more than natural to her. And yet she was a woman, through and through, beautiful and eager for the child, though she had been told by now that it would not be the witch.

'It is mine,' she would say. 'It is mine. Its name is Mayfair, as is my name. That is what matters.'

I was locked up in my rooms with the past, desperate to make a record which might invite a later interpretation. And the more I was left alone to it, and the more I realized I had written everything I knew, the more helpless and hopeless I felt.

Finally Lasher appeared.

He was as he had been that day we walked to the castle. A friend to me, a comfort. I let him stroke my brow; I let him soothe me with kisses. But secretly I lamented. I had found the thing I needed to know, and it would not help me. I could do no more. Mary Beth loved him, and did not see his power any more than any other witch who had ever dabbled with him, or commanded him or been kissed by him.

Finally, I asked him politely and kindly to go away, to go back to the witch and see to her. He consented.

Mary Beth, who had only the day before given birth, was still with the blessed baby girl in the hospital, resting comfortably, surrounded by nurses.

I went walking by myself through London.

I came to an old church, perhaps from those times, I don't know. I don't even know what it was, only I went into it, and sat in a rear pew, and bowed my head and gave myself over to almost praying.

'God help me,' I said. 'I have never in my life really prayed to you, except when I felt I was in the memory of that creature in the old Cathedral, standing in his flesh before the window of St Ashlar. I have learnt how to pray from that one single moment of possession, when I was in him, and he prayed. Now I am trying. I am praying now. What do I do? If I destroy this thing, do I destroy my family?'

I was deep in this prayer when someone tapped me on the shoulder. I looked up to see a young man standing there, dressed neatly in black, with a black silk tie, and looking a little too well-dressed and well-bred to be ordinary. He had beautifully groomed dark hair, and startling eyes, small but very gray and bright.

'Come with me,' he said.

'Why, are you the answer to my prayer?'

'No, but I would know what you know. I am from the Talamasca. Do you know who we are?'

Of course I knew these were the Amsterdam scholars. These were the men the old professor had described to me. My ancestor Petyr van Abel had more than likely been one of these.

'Ah, that is true, Julien, you know more than I thought,' said the man. 'Now come, I would talk with you.'

'I'm not so certain,' said I. 'Why should I?'

At once I felt the air around me stir, grow warm, and suddenly a gust of wind swept through the church, banging the doors, and startling this man so that he looked about him frightened.

'I thought you wanted to know what I know,' said I. 'You seem afraid now.'

'Julien Mayfair, you don't know what you do,' he said.

'But you know, I am to suppose?'

The wind grew stronger and banged the doors open, letting in a flood of ugly daylight among the dusty statues and carved wood, the sanctified shadows of the place.

The man backed away. He stared at the faraway altar. I felt the air collecting itself, I felt the wind growing strong, and rolling towards this man. I knew it would strike him one fine blow and then it did. He went sprawling on the marble floor, scrambling quickly to his feet and backing away from me. Blood ran from his nose, down his lips and his chin, and with a fancy handkerchief, he went to blot it.

But the wind wasn't finished. The church was now giving off a low rumble as if the earth beneath it were moving.

The man rushed from the church. He was gone. The wind died down. The air was still, as if nothing had ever happened here. The shadows closed upon the nave. The dusty sun came only through the windows.

I sat down again, and peered once more at the altar.

'Well, spirit?' I said.

Lasher's secret voice spoke to me out of the emptiness and the silence.

'I would not have those scholars near you. I would not have them near my witches.'

'But they know you, do they not? They have been to the glen. They know you. My ancestor Petyr van Abel . . .'

'Yes, yes and yes. I have told you the past is nothing.'

'There is no power in knowing it? Then why did you drive the scholar away? Spirit, I must tell you, all this is most suspicious to me.'

'For the future, Julien. For the future.'

'Ah, and this means that what I have learnt may stop what you see in the future.'

'You are old, Julien, you have served me well. You will serve me again. I love you. But I would not have you speak to the men of the Talamasca ever, at any time, nor would I have them trouble Mary Beth or any of my witches.'

'But what do they want? What is their interest? The old professor in Edinburgh told me they were antiquarians.'

'They are liars. They tell you they are scholars and scholars only. But they harbor a horrid secret, and I know what it is. I would not have them come close to you.'

'You know them then as they know you?'

'Yes. They feel an irresistible attraction to mysteries. But they lie. They would use their knowledge for their own ends. Tell them nothing. Remember what I say. They lie. Protect the clan from them.'

I nodded. I went out. I went up to my rooms and opened my big book, the book of the clan and of Lasher.

'Spirit, I know not whether you can read these words, whether you are here or not, or whether you have gone to protect your witch. I know none of these things. But this I wonder. *If you really feared those scholars, as you say, if you would really shut them out, why in the name of God did you make such a show of power for them?*

'*Why did you show your undeniable presence and force to that man, as you have seldom ever shown it to others? And he, a scholar who has gone to the Glen of Donnelaith, who knows something of you? Oh, vain childish spirit, I would be rid of you.*'

I closed the book.

Later in the week, as Mary Beth came back to our rooms in triumphant motherhood, and commenced to buy out every baby shop in London for its lace and trinkets and trash, I went to make my own historical study of this mysterious order.

The Talamasca.

Indeed, this was no easy task. Mentions were fewer than of St Ashlar, and inquiries among the professors at Cambridge gave me only vague suggestions: antiquarians, collectors, historians.

I knew this could not be the entire picture. I remembered too vividly that gray-eyed young man, and his manner. I remembered too vividly his fear when the wind knocked him down.

At last I discovered the Motherhouse of the place, but it was impossible for me to draw close to it. I came to the entrance to the park. I saw the high windows and chimneys. But the daemon stood between me and it, and said: 'Julien, go back, these men are evil. These men will destroy your family. Julien, go back. Julien, you must make a witch with Mary Beth. You have your purpose. I see far and I see ever more clearly.'

The battle was simply too much for me. I realized

Lasher had let me acquire what little knowledge of the Talamasca I had acquired because it was meaningless. Anything further he would prevent.

All this I wrote in my book. But I was highly suspicious now of this order.

And now let me conclude my tale, let me tell you briefly of those last years, and of one last small bit of knowledge I acquired with which you must be armed now. It is nothing much, only what I think you have come to suspect, that you must trust in no one, no one but your own self, to destroy this being, and destroy Lasher you must. Now it is in the flesh. It *can* be killed; it can be driven out; and where it shall then go, and whence return, who knows but God? But you can put an end to its tyranny here; an end to its horror.

After I returned home, I urged Mary Beth into marriage with Daniel McIntyre, one of my own lovers and a man of great charm, of whom she was fond, yet Lasher egged me on to couple with her. Her first child by Daniel became a willful and grim young girl, Carlotta by name, who was of a strict Catholic mind from the beginning. It was as if the angels claimed Carlotta at birth. I wish they'd taken her straight to heaven. Lasher was ever at me to father a new daughter.

But we were in a new age. The modern age. You cannot imagine the impact of the changes around us. And Mary Beth had been so powerful in her resolve, and so successful, that the great concrete reality of the family seemed everything.

The knowledge of Lasher she kept to herself, and ordered me not to show my books to anyone. Lasher she would make a ghost and legend, and thereby inisignificant even among our own, who were shut out now, far and wide, from all secrets.

At last – when she had given birth by Daniel to two children, neither of whom could serve her purposes, for the second, Lionel, was a boy and more unsuitable even than Carlotta – I did what she wanted me to do and what Lasher wanted me to do, and from that union – of an old man and his daughter – was born my beautiful Stella.

Stella was the witch; she saw Lasher. Her gifts were great, yes, but from early girlhood she had a love of fun which outstripped any other passion. She was carefree, wanton, gay, loving to sing and dance. And there were times in my old age when I wondered how in the world she would ever bear the burden of the secrets at all, and whether or not she had been created merely to give me happiness.

Stella, my beautiful Stella. She wore the secrets as if they were light veils she could tear off at will. But she showed no signs of madness, and that was enough for Mary Beth. This was her heiress, this was Lasher's link to the witch who would someday bring him into the world again.

I was so old by the turn of the century!

I still rode my horse up the neutral ground of St Charles Avenue. At Audubon Park, I would dismount and I would walk with my horse along the lagoon there, and I would look back at the great façades of the universities. All changed, all changed. The whole world changed. No more the pastoral paradise of Riverbend, no more those who would work sorcery with evil spells and candles and chants, no more.

Only a great and rich family, a family that could be

challenged by none, in which the history had been relegated to fireside tales to tantalize the children.

Of course I enjoyed these years. I did. No one in this long line of Mayfairs has ever prospered any more than I did. I never worked as hard as Mary Beth, I never personally cared for so many.

I did found the firm of Mayfair and Mayfair with my sons, Cortland, Barclay and Garland. Mary Beth and I worked together on this, as the legacy took even greater and greater legal form. But I reveled in pleasure.

When not chatting happily with my sons and their wives, or playing with my grandchildren, or laughing at Stella, I was off to Storyville, the remarkable red-light district of those times, to sleep with the best of women. And though Mary Beth, now the dutiful mother of three, would not go with me on my romps anymore, I took my young lovers with me, and had the double pleasure of the women and my young men with them.

Ah, Storyville, that is another wondrous tale, an experiment gone awry so to speak, a part of our great history. But we must pass over that too.

I lied to my sons in those years. I lied to them about my sins, my debauchery, my powers, about Mary Beth, and about her Stella. I tried to turn their eyes to the world, to the practical, to truths in nature and in books, which I had learnt when I was so little. I did not dare to pass my secrets to them, and also, as they grew to manhood, I knew that none of them was a proper recipient of this knowledge. They were all so solid, my boys, so good. So keen on the making of money and the fostering of the family. I had made three engines of my good self in them. I dared not trust them with the bad self.

543

And every time I tried to tell Stella anything, she either fell asleep or started laughing. 'You needn't scare me with all that,' she said once. 'Mother's told me your fantasies and dreams. Lasher is my dearest spirit and will do as I say. That's all that matters. You know, Julien, it's quite a thing to have one's own family ghost.'

I was stupefied. This was a girl of modern times. She didn't know what she was saying! Ah, to have lived so long to see the truth come down to this – Carlotta, the elder, a vicious clerical-minded monster; and this sparkling child, who thought the whole thing quaint though she could see the spirit with her own eyes! I am going mad, I thought.

Even as I lived on in comfort and luxury, even as I spent my days tasting the pleasures of the new age, driving my automobile and listening to my Victrola, even as I read, I dreaded the future.

I *knew* the daemon was evil. I *knew* it lied. I *knew* it was a lethal mystery. And I feared those scholars in Amsterdam. I feared that man who had spoken to me so briefly in the church.

And when my professor wrote to me from Edinburgh, saying that the Talamasca had pestered him to see his letters to me, I at once admonished him that he was to reveal nothing. I doubled his income on that account. He gave me his assurances. And I never doubted him.

It did not make sense, you see, the conduct of those scholars. Or the conduct of the spirit in front of them. Why had the man been so sinister with me? And why had the spirit deliberately made such a show of itself? I sensed something political in all this. And wondered if the spirit did not enjoy teasing those men, but was it just childishness?

Finally in my last years, I retired to the attic room, and took with me one of the most splendid of all the new inventions, the portable windup Victrola. I can't tell you what a delight these things were to us, to be able to listen to music from those old records. To go out onto the lawn with the thing, and play a song from an opera.

I adored it. And of course when the music played, Lasher could not come into my head, though he did this less and less anyhow.

He had both Mary Beth and little Stella to content him. And both of them he adored in different ways, drawing strength from each and passing back and forth between the two of them. Indeed, his happiest moments were when he had mother and daughter together.

I had no need of Lasher by this time. No need at all. I wrote in my books, storing them under my bed; I had my lover Richard Llewellyn, a charming young man who worshiped the ground I walked on and was ever congenial company to me, and in whom I never dared to confide, for his own safety's sake.

My life was rich in other ways. My nephew Clay lived with us then, Rémy's daughter Millie, and my sons were growing hale and fine, and steps were being taken to strengthen the law firm of Mayfair and Mayfair, or the beginnings of it in any event – which would control our family enterprises.

At last, when Carlotta was twelve, I sought to confide in her. I tried to tell her the whole story. I showed her the books. I tried to warn her. I told her that Stella would inherit the emerald, and she would be the darling of the daemon, and how tricky the daemon was, and that it was a ghost, it had lived before, and that to live again was its only objective.

I shall never forget her reaction, the names she heaped upon me, the curses. 'Devil, witch, sorcerer. Always I have known this evil lived in the shadows here. Now you give it a name and history.'

She would turn to the Catholic Church to destroy the thing, she said, 'to the power of Christ, and His Holy Mother, and the saints.'

We fought a terrible battle of words. I cried out: 'Don't you see that that is nothing but another form of witchcraft?'

'And what do you teach me, you evil old man, that I must have intercourse with devils? To defeat it, I must know it? I shall stamp it out. I shall stamp out the line itself!' she cried. 'You wait and you shall see. I shall leave the legacy without an heir. I shall see an end to it.'

I was in despair. I begged her to listen, to refine her concepts, to accept counsel and not to believe such a thing was possible. We were now an immense family! But she had taken all these mysteries, put them under her Catholic foot, and relied upon her rosary and her Masses to save her.

Later Mary Beth told me to put no store in her words whatsoever. 'She is a sad child,' she said. 'I do not love her. I tried to love her, but I do not. I love Stella. And Carlotta knows this, and knows she will not inherit the emerald. She has always known, and she is shaped in hate and jealousy.'

'But she is the cunning one, don't you see? Not Stella I love Stella too but Carlotta's the one with the head.'

'It's all done, it was done many a year ago,' said Mary Beth. 'Carlotta's soul is closed to me. It's closed to *him* and he will not abide her here except as something to serve the family case, in the shadows.'

'Ah, but you see how he controls things now. How can Carlotta serve the family case? How do those scholars in Amsterdam serve it? There is something I have to unravel. This thing can kill those it would not suffer to live.'

'You are simply thinking too much for an old man,' she said. 'You don't sleep enough. Scholars in Amsterdam, what is all that? Who cares about people who tell tales of us, and that we are witches? We are, that is our strength. You try to put it all in some kind of order. There is no order.'

'You're wrong,' I said. 'You are miscalculating.'

Every time I looked into Stella's innocent eyes, I realized I could not tell her the full burden of what I knew. And to see her play with the emerald necklace made me shudder.

I showed her where I had hidden my books, beneath my bed; I told her someday she must read all of it. I told her the mystery of the Talamasca, the scholars of Amsterdam who knew of the thing, but these men could be very dangerous to us. They were nothing to play with, these men. I told her how to distract the fiend. I described its vanity. I told her what I could. But not the whole story.

That was the horror. Mary Beth alone knew the whole story. And Mary Beth had changed with the times. Mary Beth was a woman of the twentieth century. Yet Mary Beth taught Stella what Mary Beth felt she should know. Mary Beth gave her the dolls of the witches to play with! Mary Beth gave her a doll made from my mother's skin and nails and bone; and another of Katherine.

One day, I came down the stairs, and I saw Stella

perched on the side of her bed, pink legs crossed, holding these two dolls and making a conversation between them.

'That's rot and stupidity!' I declared, but Mary Beth took me away.

'Come on, Julien, she must know what she is. It's an old custom.'

'It means nothing.'

But I was talking to the air. Mary Beth was in her prime. I was dying.

Ah, that night I lay in bed, unable to shake the vision of the little girl with those worthless dolls, thinking how to separate the real from the unreal and give Stella some warning of how it might go wrong with this devil. What worked against me as well was the dour nature of Carlotta. Carlotta warned and so did I. And Stella listened to neither of us!

Finally I slept, deep and sound, and during the night dreamed again of Donnelaith and the Cathedral.

When I awoke, it was to a dreadful discovery. But I did not make it immediately.

I sat up in bed, drank my chocolate, read for a while, some Shakespeare, I think, for one of my boys had pointed out to me not long before that I had never read one of the plays, ah yes, *The Tempest*. In any account, I read some of it and loved it and found it deep as the tragedies were deep, only with a different rhythm and rules to it. Then came time to write.

I climbed from bed, dropped down to my knees, and reached for my books. They were gone. The space there was empty.

In a hideous instant I knew they were gone from me forever. No one in this house troubled my things. Only one person would have dared in the night to come into my rooms and take those books. Mary Beth. And if Mary Beth had taken them, they were no more.

I rushed down the stairs, nearly falling. Indeed, I was so out of breath by the time I came to the garden windows of the house that I was sick with a pain in my side and in my head, and had to call for the servants to help me.

Then Lasher himself came to wrap himself round me and steady me. 'Be calm, Julien,' he said in his soft voice. 'I have always been good to you.'

But I had already seen through the side windows a raging fire in the far corner of the yard, away from the street, and the figure of Mary Beth hurling one object into it after another.

'Stop her,' I whispered. I could scarce breathe at all. The thing was invisible, yet all around me, sustaining me.

'Julien, I beg you. Do not push this further.'

I stood there, trying not to pass out from weakness, and I saw the stacks of books on the grass, the old pictures, paintings from Saint-Domingue, old portraits of ancestors back to the beginning. I saw the account books and ledgers and sheaves of papers from my mother's old study, the foolishness she'd written. And the letters from Edinburgh, all tied and in bundles! And my books, aye, *one* was left, and this one she threw into the fire as I called out to her!

I reached out with all my power to stop it. She swung round as if caught by a hook, the book still in her fingers, and as she stared at me, dazzled and confused by the power that had stayed her hand, the wind rose and caught the book and sent it flip-flopping and whirling into the flames!

I gasped for breath. My curses had no syllables. The worst kind of curses. All went black.

When I awoke I was in my room.

I was in bed, and Richard, my dear young friend, was with me. And Stella too, holding my hand.

'Mamma had to burn all those old things,' she said.

I said nothing. The fact was, I had suffered a very tiny stroke, and could not for a while speak, though I myself did not know it. I thought my dreamy silence a choice. It was not until the following day when Mary Beth came to me that I realized my words were slurred and I could not find the very ones I chose to use to tell her of my anger.

It was late evening, and when she saw how it was with me she was greatly distressed and called at once for Richard to come, as if it were all his fault. He did come, and together they helped me down the stairs, as if to say, if I could get out of bed and walk, then I could not die that night.

I sat on the living room sofa.

Ah, how I loved that long double parlor. Loved it as you love it, Michael. It was a comfort to me to be there, facing the windows that looked out on the lawn, with all remnants of that brutal fire gone now.

For long hours, Mary Beth spoke. Stella came and went. The gist was that my time and my ways were gone now.

'We are coming into an age,' Mary Beth said, 'when science itself may know the name of this spirit, when science will tell us what it is.' On and on she spoke of spiritualists and mediums and séances and guides, and the scientific study of the occult, and such things as ectoplasm.

I was revolted. Ectoplasm, the thing from which mediums make their spirits material? I didn't even answer. I was sunk into despair. Stella cuddled beside me and held my hand, and said finally:

'Mamma, do shut up. He isn't listening to a word you say and you are boring him.'

I gave no argument one way or the other.

'I see far,' said Mary Beth. 'I see a future in which our thoughts and words do not matter. I see in our clan our immortality. It will not be in our lifetime – any of us – that Lasher will have his final victory. But it will come and no one will prosper from it as greatly as we will. We shall be the mothers of this prosperity.'

'All hope and optimism,' I sighed. 'What of the glen, what of the vengeful spirit? What of the wounds dealt in the olden times, from which its conscience has never healed! This thing was good. I felt its good. But now it is evil!'

And then I was ill again, very ill. They brought my pillows and covers to me there. I could not climb the stairs again until the next day, and I had not quite decided to do it, when something turned my head one last time, with hope, and that was to a final and helpless confidante.

It came about this way.

As I lay on the couch in the heat of the day, feeling the river breeze through the side windows and trying not to smell any taint of that fire in which so much had been burnt, I heard Carlotta arguing – her low sour voice growing ever more fierce as she denounced her mother.

At last she came into the room and glared down at me. She was a thin tall girl of fifteen then, I think.

Though her actual birthday escapes me. I remember that she was not so terribly unattractive then, having rather soft hair and what one calls intelligent eyes.

I said nothing, as it was not my policy to be unkind to children, no matter how unkind those children were to me. I took no notice of her.

'And you fuss over that fire,' said she in a cold righteous way, 'and you let them do what they have done to that child, and you know it is in fear of Mother. Of you and of Mother.'

'What are you talking about? What child?' said I.

But she was gone, angry and despairing, and stalking away. But soon Stella appeared, and I told her all these words.

'Stella, what does all this mean? What is she talking about?'

'She dared to say that to you? She knew you were ill. She knew you and Mother had quarreled.' Tears sprang to Stella's eyes. 'It's nothing to us, it's just those Fontevrault Mayfairs and all their own madness. You know, the Amelia Street gang. Those zombies.'

Of course I knew whom she meant – the Fontevrault Mayfairs being the descendants of my cousin Augustin, whose life I'd taken when I was only fifteen with a pistol shot. His wife and children had founded that line at Fontevrault, as I told you – their own palatial plantation in the Bayou country miles from us, and only now and then at the largest of family get-togethers deigned to pay us a call. We visited their sick. We helped them bury their dead. They did the same with us, but over the years there had been little softening.

Some of them – old Tobias and his son Walker, I believe – had built a fine house on St Charles Avenue, at Amelia Street, only about fifteen blocks away, and I had watched it being built with interest. A whole pack of them lodged there – old women and old men, all of whom personally despised me. Tobias Mayfair was a feeble old fool who had lived too long just as I had, and as vicious a man as I have ever known, who blamed me his whole life for everything.

The others were not so bad. They were of course rich, sharing in the family enterprises with us, though they had no need of us directly. And Mary Beth with her large family fetes had been inviting them into the fold, especially the younger ones. There had always been a few star-crossed cousins marrying cousins across the dividing line, or whatever it was. Tobias in his hatred called the nuptials wedding dances on Augustin's grave, and now it was known that Mary Beth wished all cousins to return to the fold, and Tobias was supposedly uttering curses.

I could tell you many amusing stories about him and all his various attempts to kill me. But it's no matter now. I wanted to know what Stella was talking about, what Carlotta meant. What was all this venom?

'So what have Augustin's children done now?' I asked, for that was all I ever called them, the whole crazy lot of them.

'Rapunzel, Rapunzel,' said Stella. 'That is what it is all about. Let down your long hair, or waste away in the attic forever.'

She positively sang out these words in her merry fashion.

'It's Cousin Evelyn, I mean, my darling dear, and everybody's saying she's Cortland's daughter.'

'I beg your pardon. You are referring to my son

Cortland? You are saying he has got one of their women with child? *Those* Mayfairs?'

'Thirteen years ago, Cortland snuck off to Fontevrault drunk and got Barbara Ann with child, to be exact. You know, Walker's daughter. The child was Evelyn, you know, you remember. Barbara Ann died when Evelyn was born. Well, guess what, darling dear? Evelyn is a witch, as powerful a witch as ever there was, and she can see into the future.'

'Says who?'

'Everyone. She has the sixth finger! She's marked, my darling dear, and positively strange beyond imagining. And Tobias has locked her up for fear that Mother will kill her! Imagine. That you and Mother would harm her. Why, you are the girl's grandfather! Cortland admitted it to me, though he made me swear never to tell you. "You know how Father hates the Fontevrault crowd," he said. "And what good can I do that girl, when everyone in the household loathes me?"'

'Wait a minute, child. Slow down. Do you mean to tell me Cortland took advantage of that addle-brained Barbara Ann, who died giving birth, and he deserted that baby?'

'He never took advantage of her at all,' said Stella. 'She was an attic case too. Doubt she'd ever seen another human being before Cortland went up to meet the poor prisoner for himself. And I don't know what happened. I was barely born then, you know. But don't go getting angry at Cortland. Cortland, of all your boys, adores you. And he'll be angry at me, and round it will go. Forget about it.'

'Forget about it! I have a granddaughter locked in an attic fifteen blocks from here? The hell I will forget about it! Her name is Evelyn? She's the daughter of that poor idiot Barbara Ann! This is what you're telling me? And that monster Tobias has her locked away? No wonder Carlotta is beside herself. She's right. It's atrocious, the whole story!'

Stella leapt up from the chair, clapping her hands. 'Mother, Mother,' she cried. 'Oncle Julien's all recovered. He has no more stroke. He is himself again! We're going to Amelia Street.'

Of course Mary Beth came rushing in. 'Did Carlotta tell you about that girl?' she said. 'Don't mix in it.'

'Don't mix in it!' I was rabid.

'Oh, Mother, really, you are worse than Queen Elizabeth,' cried Stella, 'fearing the power of her poor cousin Mary Queen of Scots. That girl cannot harm us! She is no Mary Queen of Scots.'

'I didn't say that she was, Stella,' said Mary Beth, unruffled and very calm as always. 'I have no fear of the child, no matter how powerful she is. I have only pity for her.' She was towering over me. I sat on the couch, resolved to move but still curious to know more before I did so.

'Carlotta started it all, visiting up there. The girl hides in the attic.'

'Does not. Is locked in!'

'Stella, hush up. Be a witch, not a bitch, for the love of heaven.'

'Mother, she's never been out of the house in her whole life, same story as Barbara Ann! Same reason. There are plenty of witches' gifts in that family, Oncle Julien. Barbara Ann was sort of crazy, they say, but this girl has Cortland's blood too, and she sees the future.'

'No one really sees the future,' Mary Beth declared,

'and no one should want to see it. Julien, the girl is peculiar. She is shy. She hears voices. Sees ghosts. It's nothing new. She is more warped and isolated than most, having been brought up by old people.'

'Cortland, how dare he not tell me this!' I said.

'He *didn't* dare,' said Mary Beth. 'He wouldn't hurt you.'

'He doesn't care,' said I. 'Damn him, to leave a baby daughter with those cousins! And it was Carlotta who went there, to that house, to be under Tobias's roof, Tobias who has always called me a murderer.'

'Oncle Julien, you are a murderer,' said Stella.

'Hush up once and for all,' said Mary Beth.

Stella sulked, which meant at least a temporary victory.

'Carlotta went there to ask the girl what she saw, to ask her to predict, the most dangerous of games. I forbade it, but she went. She'd heard tell of how this girl had more power than anyone ever in our family.'

'That's such an easy claim to make,' I said with a sigh. 'More power than anyone else. There was a time when I made it myself, in a long-ago world of horses and carriages, and slaves and peaceful country. More power.'

'Ah, but you see there's a wrinkle here. This girl has many many Mayfair ancestors. When you mixed Cortland into it, the number became fantastic!'

'Ah, I see,' I said. 'Barbara Ann was the daughter of Walker and Sarah, both Mayfairs. Yes, and Sarah was from Aaron and Melissa Mayfair.'

'Yes, and so on it goes back and back. It's hard to find any ancestor for this child who was not a Mayfair.'

'Now, that is a thought,' said I. And then I wanted

556

my books, I wanted to write this down, to note it and ponder it, and when I remembered with a dull ache that my books were burnt, I felt such bitterness. I grew quiet, and listened to them chatter over me.

'The girl doesn't see the future any more than anyone else,' declared Mary Beth. She sat down beside me. 'Carlotta went there wishing to be upheld, that we were cursed, we were all doomed. It is her song and dance.'

'She sees probabilities as we all do,' said Stella with a melodramatic sigh. 'She has strong presentiments.'

'And what happened?'

'Carlotta went up into the attic, to visit Evelyn. She went more than once. She played to the girl, drew her out, and then the girl, who almost never speaks, or does not for years on end, declared some terrible prediction.'

'Which was what?'

'That we should all perish from the earth,' said Stella, 'afflicted by him who had raised us and upheld us.'

I lifted my head. I looked at Mary Beth.

'Julien, there is nothing in it.'

'Is this why you burned my books? Is that why you destroyed all the knowledge I had gathered?'

'Julien, Julien,' she said. 'You are old and you dream. The girl said what would get her a gift, perhaps, or make Carlotta leave, for all we know. The girl's a mute almost. The girl sits in the window all day and watches the traffic on St Charles Avenue. The girl sings sometimes, or speaks in rhymes. She cannot lace her own shoes or brush her hair.'

'And that wicked Tobias doesn't let her out,' said Stella.

'Damn it all, I've heard enough. Have my car brought round to the front.'

'You can't go driving,' said Mary Beth, 'you're too ill. Do you want to die on the front steps of Amelia Street? Have the courtesy to die in your bed with us.'

'I'm not ready for dying yet, my darling daughter,' I declared, 'and you tell the boys to bring the car around now, or I'll walk up there. Richard, where is Richard! Richard, get me fresh clothes, everything. I will change in the library. I cannot walk upstairs. Hurry.'

'Oh, you are really going to scare them out of their wits,' cried Stella. 'They'll think you've come to kill her.'

'Why would I do that!' I demanded.

'Because she's stronger than us, don't you see? Oncle Julien, look to the legacy, as you are always instructing me. Isn't there a case for her claiming everything?'

'Certainly not,' said I. 'Not so long as Mary Beth has a daughter, and Stella, the daughter of Mary Beth, has a daughter of her own. Not much of a case.'

'Well, they say there are provisions – having to do with power and such, and the witches' gifts, and all. And they hide that girl so we won't kill her.'

Richard had come with my clothes. I hastily dressed, and to the teeth, for this ceremonial visit. I sent him for my riding coat – my Stutz Bearcat was open and the roads were muddy then – for my goggles, and for my gloves, and told him once more to hurry.

'You can't go up there,' Mary Beth said. 'You'll scare him to death and her to death too.'

'If she's my granddaughter I'm going to get her.'

I stormed to the front porch. I was feeling entirely myself, though I alone noticed one tiny deficit. I could not quite control the movement of my left foot. It would not arch and lift properly as I walked, so I had a little to drag it. But they didn't see it, damn them, they didn't know. Death had given a pinch. Death was coming. But I told myself I could live another score of years with this tiny infirmity.

As I went down the front steps, and had the boys help me up into the car, Stella clambered into my lap, nearly castrating and killing me simultaneously. And then out of the shadows beneath the oaks came Carlotta.

'Will you help her?'

'Of course I will,' said I. 'I will take her out of there. Horrible, horrible thing. Why didn't you come to me sooner?'

'I don't know,' Carlotta said, and her face was stricken and her head was bowed. 'The things she said she saw were terrible.'

'You don't listen to the right people. Now, Richard, drive!'

And off we went, with Richard steering wildly up St Charles Avenue, splattering mud and gravel, and finally running right up on the curb in his careless, amateurish way, on the corner of St Charles and Amelia.

'This I have to see for myself, this child in the attic,' I mumbled. I was in a rage. 'And I will throttle Cortland when next he dares to come into my presence.'

Stella helped me down from the car and then started jumping up and down with excitement. This was one of her more endearing or irritating habits, all depending on how one felt at the moment.

'Look, Julien, darling,' she cried. 'Up there in the attic window.'

Now you have no doubt seen this house. It stands today as solid as First Street.

And of course I had seen it too, as I have said, but I never set foot in it. I was not even sure how many Mayfairs lived there. It was, for my money, a pompous Italianate house, very proud yet very beautiful. It was all wood, yet designed to look as if it were stone, like our house. It had columns on the front, Doric down and Corinthian up, and a great alcoved door, and further back octagonal wings jutting out on both sides, and throughout rounded Italian-style windows. It was massive and bulky yet graceful. Not such a bad house, though not pure and old as ours was.

And immediately I spied, as Stella pointed, the attic window.

It was a double dormer, in the very center over the porch, and I swear I could feel the pulse of the girl who peered through the glass at me. A wan bit of face up there, a streak of hair. And then nothing but the sun flashing in the glass.

'Oh, there she is, poor, darling Rapunzel,' Stella cried and waved vigorously though the girl had disappeared. 'Oh Evie, we have come to save you.'

Then out upon the porch came storming Tobias and his son Oliver, the younger brother of Walker, and a blithering fool if ever there was one. It was almost impossible to tell on sight which was which, and which was more feeble.

'Why have you locked that child in the attic?' said I. 'And is this Cortland's girl, or is that some baseless lie you dreamed up to rattle and disconcert my family?'

'You miserable scoundrel,' Tobias declared, stepping forward and nearly losing his balance at the top of the steps. 'Don't you come near my door. Get off my property. You spawn of Satan. Yes, it was Cortland who ruined my Barbara Ann. She died in my arms. And it was Cortland, Cortland who did it. That child is a witch such as you'll never see, and as long as I have breath in my body, she'll make no more witches out of herself and out of you and out of all that went before you.'

That was twice as much as I needed to hear. I went straight up the steps, and both old fools rushed at me.

I stopped and raised my voice:

'Come now, my Lasher,' I cried. 'Make the way for me.'

Both men fell back in terror. Stella gave a gasp of amazement. But the wind did come, as it always had, when I needed it most, when my wounded old soul and pride needed it most, and when I was most unsure of it. It came gusting over the garden and up the porch, forcing back the door with a powerful clatter.

'Thank you, spirit,' I whispered. 'That you have saved face for me.'

I love you, Julien. But it is my wish you leave this house and all those in it.

'That I cannot do,' I said. I entered the house, a long cool dark hallway, lying between rows of doors, with Stella scampering on the boards beside me. The old men came behind, screaming to rouse the women, and out of the long row of doors came numerous Mayfairs – a regular Parliament of Fowls – screeching and screaming. Behind me the wind lashed the oaks. A great scattering of leaves gusted down the hallway before me.

Some of these faces I had seen; all I knew in one fashion or another. As the others peeped out, Tobias sought again to stop me.

'Get out of my way,' I said and planted myself at the

foot of the dark oak stairs and then began to climb them.

It was a huge staircase, to one side of the hall, and turning midway, with a broad landing and grim stained glass which made me pause for a moment. For as the light came through the glass, as it passed through the yellow and red panes, I thought of the Cathedral and 'remembered' it as I had not in years, not since I'd left Scotland.

I could feel the spirit collected around me. I pushed on, out of breath till I reached the upper hall. 'Where is the attic stairs?'

'There, there,' cried Stella, leading me through the double doors to the rear hall, and there was the lesser staircase in a narrow well, and the door at the top of it.

'Evelyn, come down, my child!' I cried. 'Evelyn, come down. I cannot come up this long climb. Come down, my girl, I'm your grandfather come to get you.'

There was silence in the house. All the others crowded in the hallway door, staring, so many white oval faces, mouths agape, eyes large and hollow.

'She will not listen to you,' cried one of the women. 'She has never listened to anyone.'

'She cannot hear,' cried another.

'Or speak!'

'Look, Julien, the door is locked from this side,' cried Stella, 'and the key is in it.'

'Oh, you evil old fools!' I shouted. And I closed my eyes and collected all my strength and was about to command this door to open. I did not know if I could do such a thing, for something like that is never certain. And I could feel Lasher hovering near, and feel his distress and confusion. He did not like this house, these Mayfairs.

Aye, they are not mine, these.

But before I could answer Lasher or persuade him, or make the door move, it opened! The key fell from the lock by some power other than mine, and the door sprang back, letting the sunlight fall into the dusty stairwell.

I knew it was not my power, and so did Lasher! For he collected around me close as if he too were actually fearful.

Calm yourself now, spirit, you are most dangerous when you are afraid. Behave. It is all well and good. The girl herself opened the door. Be silent.

But then he gave me to know the truth. It was the girl who frightened him! Of course. I assured him she was no menace to the likes of us, and please do my bidding.

The sunlight brightened the swirling dust. And then there came a tall thin shadow – a girl of great beauty, with full glossy hair, and still eyes staring down at me. She seemed frightfully tall and thin, even starved perhaps.

'Come down to me, my child,' said I. 'You see yourself you need not be a prisoner of anyone.'

She understood my words and as she came down, silently, step by step with her soft leather shoes, I saw her eyes move above me and to the left and to the right of me, and over Stella, and again as she beheld the invisible thing clustered about us. She saw 'the man', as they say, she saw him invisible and made no secret.

When she reached the foot of the stairs, she turned, beheld the others, and shrank trembling! I have never seen fear so expressed by one without a sound. I snatched up her hand.

'Come with me, darling. You and you alone shall decide whether you wish to live in an attic.'

I pulled her to me; she gave no resistance, and no cooperation either. How strange she seemed, how pale, how accustomed to the darkness. Her neck was long and thin, and she had small ears with no lobes to them, and then I saw on her hand the mark of the witch! She had on her left hand the sixth finger! Just as they had told me. I was amazed.

But they had seen me see it. A great squabble broke out. The girl's uncles had come, Ragnar and Felix Mayfair, young men famous about the town, and known to be suspicious of us. They started to block my way.

But in an instant the wind had gathered. All could feel it stealing along the floor, icy and strong. It whipped those who blocked the way, until they stepped back, and then I took the girl by the hand and led her back into the front hall and down the main staircase. Stella crept at my side.

'Oh, Oncle Julien,' Stella said as breathlessly as some village girl to a great prince. 'I adore you.'

And with us walked this pale swan of a girl, with her shimmering hair and her sticks for arms and sticks for legs, and pitiful dress made from a flowered feed sack. I don't know if you have ever seen such clothing, poorest of the poor. Women used this cloth to line their everyday quilts and she had it for a frock, this cheap flowered cotton. And her shoes, they were scarcely shoes at all, rather leather socks of some sort, laced, like booties of a baby!

I took her through the hall, the wind rattling and swinging the doors, and going before us, stirring the oaks outside, and brushing the many cars and carriages and carts that passed on the Avenue.

No one moved to stop me as I handed her up to

Richard to be placed in the car. And then, sitting close beside her, with Stella again on my knee, I gave the order for Richard to go, and the girl turned round and stared at the house, and at the high window, and at the collection of people on the porch in astonishment.

We had not gone five feet when they all began to scream. 'Murderer, murderer! He's taken Evelyn!' and to cry to one another to do something about it. Young Ragnar ran out and cried that he would proceed against me in a court of law.

'By all means do,' I cried back over the rumbling car, 'ruin yourself in the process. I am father to the finest law firm in the city! Sue! I cannot wait.'

The car made its way awkwardly and noisily up St Charles, yet faster than any horse-drawn carriage. And the girl sat still between Richard and me, under Stella's curious eye, staring at everything as if she had never been out of doors before.

Mary Beth waited on the step.

'And what do you mean to do with her?'

'Richard,' I said, 'I can't walk any farther.'

'I'll fetch the boys, Julien,' he cried, and off he ran, calling and clapping. Stella and the girl climbed down and Stella lifted both her hands to me.

'I've got you, darling. I won't let you fall, my hero.'

The girl stood with her hands at her sides, staring at me, and then at Mary Beth, and then at the house, and at the servant boys who came running.

'What do you mean to do with her?' Mary Beth demanded again.

'Child, will you come into our house?' I said, looking at this lithe and lovely girl with pale shell-pink tender little mouth protruding beautifully on account of her hollow cheeks, and eyes the color of the gray sky in a rainstorm.

'Will you come into our house,' I said again, 'and there safe beneath our roof decide if you want to spend your life a prisoner or not? Stella, if I die on the way upstairs, I charge you to save this girl, you hear me?'

'You won't die,' said Richard, my lover, 'come, I'll help you.' But I could see the apprehension in his face. He was more worried about me than anyone.

Stella led the way. The girl followed, and then Richard came, all but carrying me in his exuberantly manly way, with his arm around me, hoisting me step by step so that I might keep what dignity I had.

At last we entered my room on the third floor of the house.

'Get the girl some food,' I said. 'She looks as if she has never had a square meal.' I sent Stella off with Richard. I collapsed on the side of my bed, too exhausted to think for a moment.

Then I looked up and my soul was filled with despair. This beautiful fresh creature on the brink of life, and I so old, very soon to end it. I was so tired I might have said yes to death now, if this girl, if her case had not demanded my presence here.

'Can you understand me?' I asked. 'Do you know who I am?'

'Yes, Julien,' she said in plain English effortlessly enough. 'I know all about you. This is *your* attic, is it not?' she said in her little treble voice, and as she looked around at the beams, at the books, at the fireplace and the chair, at all my precious things, my Victrola and my piles of songs, she gave a soft trusting smile to me.

'Dear God,' I whispered. 'What shall I do with you?'

TWENTY-ONE

The people who lived in this bright little house were brown people. They had black hair and black eyes; their skin gleamed in the light above the table. They were small with highly visible bones, and they wore clothes in very bright red and blue and white, clothes that were tight around their plump arms. The woman, when she saw Emaleth, got up and came to the transparent door.

'Good heavens, child! Come inside here,' she said, looking up into Emaleth's eyes. 'Jerome, look at this. This child's stalk naked. Look at this girl. Oh, my Lord in heaven.'

'I've washed in the water,' said Emaleth. 'Mother is sick under the tree. Mother can't talk anymore.' Emaleth held out her hands. They were wet. Her hair hung wet on her breasts. She was slightly cold, but the air of the room was warm and still.

'Well, come in here,' said the woman, tugging her hand. She reached for a piece of cloth on a hook and began to wipe Emaleth's long dripping hair. The water made a pool on the shiny floor. How clean things were here. How unnatural. How unlike the fragrant beating night outside, full of wings and racing shadows. This was a shelter against the night, against the insects that stung, and the things that had cut Emaleth's naked feet, and scratched her naked arms.

The man stood still, staring up at Emaleth.

'Get her a towel, Jerome, don't stand there. Get this girl a towel. Get her some clothes. Child, what happened to your clothes? Where are your clothes? Did something bad happen to you?'

Emaleth had never heard voices quite like these, of the brown people. They had a musical note in them that the other people's voices didn't have. They rose and fell in a distinctly different pattern. The whites of their eyes were not purely white, these people. They had a faint yellowish cast to them that went better with their beautiful brown skin. Even Father did not have this kind of soft ringing quality to his words. Father had said, 'You will be born knowing all you need to know. Do not let anything frighten you.'

'Be kind to me,' said Emaleth.

'Jerome, get the clothes!' The woman had taken a big wad of paper off a roll and was blotting Emaleth's shoulders and arms with it. Emaleth took the wad of paper and wiped her face. Hmmmm. This paper felt rough, but it wasn't hurtfully rough, and it smelled good. Paper towels. Everything in the little kitchen smelled good. Bread, milk, cheese. Emaleth smelt the milk and cheese. That was the cheese, wasn't it? Bright orange cheese in a block lying on the table. Emaleth wanted this. But she had not been offered it.

'We are by nature a gentle and polite people,' Father had said. 'This is why they have been so hateful to us in times past.'

'What clothes?' said the man named Jerome, who was taking off his shirt. 'There's nothing in this house that's going to fit her.' He held out the shirt. Emaleth wanted to take it but she also wanted to look at it. It was blue-

and-white-colored. In little squares like the red and white squares on the table.

'Bubby's pants will do it,' said the woman. 'Get a pair of Bubby's pants and give me that shirt.'

The little house was shining. The red and white squares on the table were shining. If she grabbed the edge of the red and white squares she could have pulled them off. It was one sheet, that thing. Shiny white refrigerator with an engine on the back of it. She knew the handle would bend just so, just by looking at it. And inside would be cold milk.

Emaleth was hungry. She had drunk all of Mother's milk as Mother lay staring under the tree. She had cried and cried, and then she had gone to bathe in the water. The water was greenish and not fresh-smelling. But there had been a fountain on the edge of the grass, a fountain with a handle. Emaleth had washed better in that.

The man came rushing back into the room with long pants such as Father wore and he wore. Emaleth put these on, pulling them up over her long thin legs, almost losing her balance. The zipper felt cold against her belly. The button felt cold. But they were all right. Newborn, she was still a little too soft all over.

Father said, 'You will walk but it will be hard.' These pants made a warm heavy covering. 'But remember, you can do everything that you need to do.'

She slipped her arms into the shirt as the woman held it for her. Now, this cloth was nicer. More like the towel with which the woman kept patting her hair. Emaleth's hair was golden yellow. It looked so bright on the woman's fingers, and the inside of the woman's hand was pink, not brown.

Emaleth looked down at the shirt buttons. The woman reached out with nimble fingers and buttoned one button. Very quick. Like that. Emaleth knew this. She buttoned the other buttons very fast. She laughed.

Father said, 'You will be born knowing, as birds know how to build their nests, as giraffes know how to walk, as turtles know to crawl from the land and swim in the open sea, though no one has ever shown them. Remember human beings are not born with this instinctive knowledge. Human beings are born half-formed and helpless but you will be able to run and talk. You will recognize everything.'

Well, not everything, Emaleth thought, but she did know that was a clock on the wall, and that was a radio on the windowsill. If you turned it on, voices came out of it. Or music.

'Where's your mother, child?' asked the woman. 'Where did you say she was sick?'

'How old is this girl?' asked the man of his wife. He stood rigid, hands forming into fists. He had put on his cap, and he glowered at her. 'Where is this woman?'

'How should I know how old she is? She looks like a big tall little girl. Honey, how old are you? Where is your mother?'

'I'm newborn,' said Emaleth. 'That's why my mother is so sick. It wasn't her fault. She doesn't have any more milk. She is sick unto death and she smells like death. But there was enough milk. I am not one of the little people. That is something I no longer need to fear.' She turned and pointed. 'Walk a long way, cross the bridge and under the tree, she's there where the branches touch the ground, but I don't think she'll ever talk anymore. She will dream until she dies.'

Out the door he went, letting it bang loudly after him. With a very determined air he walked across the grass and then he started to run.

The woman was staring at her.

Emaleth put her hands to her ears, but it was too late, the transparent door had banged so loud it made a ringing inside her ears and nothing now would stop it. The ringing had to wear away. Transparent door. Not glass. She knew about glass. The bottle on the table was glass. She remembered glass windows, and glass beads, lots of things of glass. Plastic. The transparent door was screen and plastic.

'It's all encoded inside,' said Father.

She looked at the woman. She wanted to ask the woman for food, but it was more important now to leave here – to find Father or Donnelaith or Michael in New Orleans, whichever proved to be the easier thing to do. She had looked at the stars but they hadn't told her. Father had said you will know from the stars. Now, of that part she wasn't so sure.

She turned and opened the door and stepped outside, careful not to let it bang, holding it for the woman. All the tree frogs sang. All the crickets sang. Things sang of which no one knew the name, not even Father. They rustled and rattled in the dark. All the night was alive. Look at the tiny insects swimming beneath the light bulb! She waved her hand at them. How they scattered, only to come back in a tight little cloud.

She looked at the stars. She would always remember this pattern of the stars, surely enough, the way the stars dipped down to the far trees, and how black the sky seemed at one point and how deep blue at another. Yes, and the moon. Behold the moon. The beautiful radiant moon. *Father, at last I see it.* Yes, but to get to Donnelaith, she had to know how the stars would look when she reached her destination.

The woman took Emaleth's hand. Then the woman looked at her hand and let her go.

'You're so soft!' she said. 'You're as soft and pink as a little baby.'

'Don't tell them you are newborn,' Father had told her. 'Don't tell them that they will soon die. Feel sorry for them. It is their final hour.'

'Thank you,' said Emaleth. 'I'm going now. I'm going to Scotland or New Orleans. Do you know the way?'

'Well, New Orleans is no big problem,' said the woman. 'I don't know about Scotland. But you can't just walk off like this in your bare feet. Let me get Bubby's shoes for you. Lord, yes, Bubby's shoes are the only ones that are going to fit.'

Emaleth looked out over the dark grass to the forest. She saw the darkness close in over the water, beyond the bridge. She wasn't sure she should wait for the shoes.

'They are born hardwired with almost nothing,' Father had said. 'And what is hardwired in them is soon forgotten. They no longer catch scents or see patterns. They no longer know by instinct what to eat. They can be poisoned. They no longer hear sounds the way you do, or hear the full beat of songs. They are not like us. They are fragments. Out of these fragments we will build but it will be their doom. Be merciful.'

Where was Father? If Father had observed the stars over Donnelaith, then she, Emaleth, ought to know them and what they looked like. She caught not the faintest trace of his scent anywhere at all. None had clung anymore to Mother.

The woman had come back. She laid down the shoes. It was hard for Emaleth to get her soft long feet inside them, toes wriggling, the canvas scratching her skin, but she knew that this was best, to have shoes. She ought to wear shoes. Father wore shoes. And so had Mother. Emaleth had cut her foot already on a sharp stone in the grass. This was better. It felt good when the woman tied the laces tight. Little bows, how pretty. She laughed when she saw these bows. But prettier still were the woman's fingers when she tied them.

How big Emaleth's feet looked compared to those small feet of the little woman.

'Good-bye, lady. And thank you,' said Emaleth. 'You've been very kind to me. I'm sorry for everything that is going to happen.'

'And what's that, child?' the woman asked. 'Just exactly what is going to happen? Child, what is that smell? What is on your body? First I thought you were just all wet from the Bayou. But there is another smell.'

'A smell?'

'Yes, it's kind of good, kind of like a good something cooking.'

Ah, so Emaleth had the scent too. Was that why she couldn't smell Father? She was now wrapped in the scent, perhaps. She lifted her fingers to her nose. There it was. The scent came right out of her pores. The smell of Father.

'I don't know,' said Emaleth. 'I think I should know these things. My children will. I have to go now. I should go to New Orleans. That is what Mother said. Mother pleaded and pleaded with me. Go to New Orleans, and Mother said it was on the way to Scotland, that I didn't have to disobey Father. So I'm on my way.'

'Wait a minute, child. Sit down, wait for Jerome to come back. Jerome is looking for your mother.' The woman called out in the dark for Jerome. But Jerome was gone.

'No, lady. I'm going,' said Emaleth, and she bent down and touched her hands lightly to the woman's shoulders and kissed her on the smooth brown forehead. She felt her black hair. She smelled it and smoothed her hand on the lady's cheek. Nice woman.

She could see the woman liked the smell of her.

'Wait, honey.'

This was the first time Emaleth had kissed anyone but Mother and it made the tears come again, and she looked down at the brown woman with the black hair and the big eyes, and she felt sorrow, that they would all die. Kindly people. Kindly people. But the Earth simply wasn't big enough for them, and they had prepared the way for the more gentle, and the more childlike.

'Which way is New Orleans?' she said. Mother hadn't known. Father had never told.

'Well, that way, I reckon,' said the woman. 'I don't know, tell the truth, I think that's east. You can't just . . .'

'Thank you, darling dear,' she said, using Father's favorite phrase. And she started walking.

It felt better with every step. She walked faster and faster on the sodden grass, and then out on the road, and beneath the white electric light, and then on and on, her hair blowing out, her long arms swinging.

She was all dry now underneath the clothes, except for a little water on her back, which she did not like but which would dry soon. And her hair. Her hair was drying quickly, getting lighter and lighter. She saw her shadow on the road and laughed. How tall and thin she was compared to the brown people. How large her head was. And even compared to Mother. Poor little Mother, lying beneath the tree and staring off into the darkness and the greenness. Mother had not even heard Emaleth anymore. Mother could hear nothing. Oh, if only they had not run away from Father.

But she would find him. She had to. They were the only ones in the world. And Michael. Michael was Mother's friend. Michael would help her. Mother had said, 'Go to Michael. Do that first of all.' Those had almost been the last words from Mother. Go to Michael, first of all.

One way or the other, she was obedient to Father, or obedient to Mother.

'And I will be looking for you,' he'd said.

It shouldn't be all that hard, and walking was fun.

TWENTY-TWO

They were gathered by nine o'clock in the office on the top floor of the Mayfair Building – Lightner, Anne Marie, Lauren, Ryan, Randall and Fielding. Fielding really wasn't well enough to be there, anyone could see this. But no one was going to argue.

When Pierce came in, with Mona, there was no complaint and no surprise, though everyone stared at Mona, naturally enough, having never seen her in a blue wool suit, and of course this one – her mother's – was a little too big for her, though not much. She did look years older now, but that was as much on account of the expression on her face as the loss of childish locks and her ribbon. She wore a pair of high heels that did fit all right, and Pierce kept trying not to look at her legs, which were very beautiful.

Pierce had never found it easy to be around his cousin Mona, not even when she was very little. There had been something seductive about her even when she was four and he was eleven. She had tried countless times to lure him into the woods. 'You're just too little' had become lame around five years ago. Now it was really lame. However, Mona was as exhausted as he was.

'Our mothers are dead!' She'd whispered that to him on the way downtown. In fact that was the only thing she'd said between Amelia Street and the office.

What the others would have to understand at some point was that Mona had taken over. Pierce had just gotten to Amelia Street with the news that all the Mayfairs were being called; that cousins as far away as Europe were being contacted. He thought he had things pretty much under control; indeed there was a curious excitement to it all, the excitement that death brings when everything is disrupted. Pierce thought perhaps it was like that at the very beginning of a war, before suffering and death wore everyone into despair.

Whatever, when they'd called to say Mandy Mayfair was dead too, he had not been able to respond. Mona had been at his elbow. 'Give me that phone,' she'd said.

Mandy Mayfair had died about twelve o'clock today. That was midway between Edith's death and Alicia's. Mandy had obviously been dressing for Gifford's funeral. Her prayer book and her rosary had been on the bed. The windows of her French Quarter apartment were wide open to the little courtyard. Anyone could have come over that wall. There was no other sign of foul play, as they said, or forced entry. Mandy had been on the bathroom floor, knees drawn up, arms locked around her waist. There were flowers scattered all around her. Even the police had figured out they came from the courtyard garden. Sprigs of lantana which had bloomed again in the warm months after Christmas. All those little orange and purple blossoms had been broken up on top of her.

Now, no one was going to call this a 'natural death' or the result of some mysterious illness. But Pierce could get no further than that in his reasoning. Because if something came in and killed Edith, and Mandy, and

577

Alicia, and Lindsay in Houston, and the other cousin whose name, shamefully enough, he could not even remember, well, then that something had come in on his mother.

And her last moments had not been tranquil, hand reached out to receive the sea, and all the other mythology he had laid upon it when he saw her dead body, and heard how it had been found, and how the blood was washing away even as they picked her up and put her on the stretcher.

No, that was not the way it was.

He drew the chair back for Mona, adjusted it for her as a gentleman should, and then he sat down. Somehow or other he was facing Randall. But then when Pierce saw the expression on his father's face, he understood. Randall was at the head of the table because Randall was in charge. Ryan was in no condition anymore to do much of anything.

'Well, you know this is not what we thought,' said Mona.

To Pierce's amazement, they all nodded, that is, those who bothered to do anything nodded. Lauren looked exhausted but otherwise calm. Anne Marie was the only one who seemed frankly horrified.

The biggest surprise perhaps was Lightner. Lightner was looking out the window. He was looking at the river down there and the lighted bridges of the Crescent City Connection. He seemed not even to have noticed that Pierce and Mona had come in. He did not look at Pierce now. Or at Mona.

'Aaron,' Pierce said, 'I thought you'd have some help for us, some guidance.' That just popped out of Pierce's mouth before he could stop himself. It was the sort of thing he said which constantly got him into trouble. His father said, 'A lawyer does not speak what is on his mind! A lawyer keeps his own counsel.'

Aaron turned towards the table, and then folded his arms and looked at Mona, and then at Pierce.

'Why would you trust me now?' Aaron asked in a quiet voice.

'The point is this,' said Randall. 'We know this is one individual. We know that he is six and one-half feet tall. That he has black hair; that he is some form of mutant. We know now that Edith and Alicia suffered miscarriages. We know from the superficial autopsy results that this individual was the cause of them. We know that embryonic development in at least two cases was vastly accelerated, and that the mothers went into shock within hours of impregnation. We expect any minute to have Houston confirm similar findings in the cases of Lindsay and Clytee.'

'Ah, that was her name, Clytee,' said Pierce. He realized suddenly that they were all looking at him. He hadn't meant to speak out loud.

'The point is, it is not a disease,' said Randall, 'and it is an individual.'

'And the individual is seeking to mate,' said Lauren coldly. 'The individual is seeking members of this family which may have genetic abnormalities which render them compatible with the individual.'

'And we also know,' said Randall, 'that this individual is seeking his victims among the most inbred lines in the family.'

'OK,' Mona said, 'four deaths here, two in Houston. The Houston deaths were later.'

'Several hours later,' said Randall. 'The individual

could easily have taken a plane to Houston in that time.'

'So there's no supernatural agency involved in that,' said Pierce. 'If it is "the man", the man is flesh like Mother said, and the man has to move like any other man.'

'When did your mother tell you it was the man?'

'Excuse me,' said Ryan quietly. 'Gifford said that some time ago. She didn't really know any more than any of us did. That was her speculation. Let's stick to what we do know. As Randall said, this is an individual.'

'Yes,' said Randall, at once taking command again, 'and if we put our information together with that of Lightner and Dr Larkin from California, we have every reason to believe this individual had a unique genome. He has some ninety-two chromosomes in a double helix exactly like that of a human, but that is, very simply, twice the number of chromosomes in a human being, and we know that the proteins and enzymes in his blood and cells are different.'

Pierce could not stop thinking of his mother, could not escape the image of her lying in the sand, which he himself had not actually seen, and now was doomed to see in various forms forever. Had she been frightened? Had this thing hurt her? How did she get to the water's edge? He stared down at the table.

Randall was talking.

'It is liberating to understand,' said Randall, 'that it is one male, and one which can be stopped, that whatever the history of this being, whatever mysteries shroud its inception, conception or whatever we wish to call it, it is one and can be apprehended.'

'But that's just it,' said Mona. She spoke as she

always did, as if everybody was prepared to listen to her. She looked so different with her red hair pulled back from her face, both younger and older, cheeks so soft, and face so well contoured. 'It clearly is trying to be more than one. And if these embryos develop at an accelerated rate, which I think is putting it mildly by the way, this thing could have a fullborn child any time.'

'That's true,' said Aaron Lightner. 'That's exactly true. And we cannot begin to predict the growth rate of that child. It is conceivable the child will mature as rapidly as the individual did himself, though how that happened is still a mystery. It is conceivable the thing will then breed with the child. Indeed, I would think that would be the first step, since so many lives have been lost in other efforts.'

'Good Lord, you mean that's what it's trying to do?' asked Anne Marie.

'What about Rowan? Anyone hear even one word?' Mona asked.

Negative gestures and noises all around. Only Ryan bothered to mouth the word *no*.

'OK,' said Mona. 'Well, I have this to tell you. The thing nearly got me. This is how it happened.'

She had told Pierce this story at Amelia Street, but as he listened now, he realized she was leaving out certain details – that she'd been with Michael, that she was naked, that she'd been asleep in the library without her clothes, that the Victrola had waked her, not the opening of the window. He wondered why she left those things out. It seemed to him that all his life he had been listening to Mayfairs leave things out. He wanted to say, Tell them that the Victrola played. Tell them. But he didn't.

There seemed some grotesque clash between the mutant individual, as they called him, and the soft legends and miracles which had always hung in a vapor about First Street. The Victrola playing. It belonged to another realm than DNA and RNA and strange fingerprints found by the coroner in Mandy Mayfair's French Quarter apartment.

Mandy's was the first death to be seen as a murder. It was all those flowers sprinkled over her body, a cinch she couldn't have done that herself, and then the bruises on her neck which indicated she had fought the thing. Gifford had not fought. No bruises. His mother must have been taken completely unawares. No fear. No suffering. No bruises.

Mona was explaining about the smell.

'I know what you're saying,' said Ryan, and for the first time he looked even vaguely interesting. 'I know that smell. In Destin, I smelled it there. It's not a bad smell. It's almost . . .'

'It's good, it's sort of delicious. Makes you want to breathe it,' said Mona. 'Well, I can still smell it all over First Street.'

Ryan shook his head. 'It was faint in Destin.'

'Faint to you, and strong to me, but don't you understand, that's probably some marker of genetic compatibility.'

'Mona, what the hell do you know, child,' demanded Randall, 'about genetic compatibility?'

'Don't start in on Mona,' said Ryan quietly. 'There isn't time. We have to do something . . . specific. Find this creature. Figure out where it may appear next. Mona, did you see anything?'

'No, nothing. But I want to try to call Michael again.

I've been calling up there for two hours. I don't get any answer. I'm really worried. I think I'm going to go . . .'

'You're not leaving this room,' said Pierce. 'You're not going anywhere without me.'

'That's fine. You can take me up there.'

Lauren made her characteristic gesture for all to come to attention – the tapping of her pen against the table. Only two taps. Never enough to drive you crazy, Pierce thought.

'Let's go through it again. There are no women who have not been notified.'

'Not that we know,' said Anne Marie, 'and pray God if we don't know who all the Mayfairs are, then the thing doesn't either.'

'There are people about questioning potential witnesses all over New Orleans and Houston,' said Lauren.

'Yes, but no one saw this man leave or enter.'

'Besides, we know what he looks like,' said Mona. 'That Dr Larkin told you. So did the witnesses in Scotland. So did Michael.'

'Lauren, there isn't anything we can do but wait,' said Randall. 'We have done all we can. We must very simply stay together. The thing is not going to give up. It's bound to surface. We simply have to be ready when this happens.'

'How are we going to do that?' asked Mona.

'Aaron,' said Ryan, his voice very soft, 'can't your people in Amsterdam and London help us? I thought this was your field, this sort of thing. I remember Gifford said over and over again, "Aaron knows", "Talk to Aaron".' There was something sad and whimsical in his smile as he said this.

Pierce had never seen his father act or speak in this way.

'That's just it,' said Aaron. 'I don't know. I thought I did. I thought I knew the whole story of the Mayfair Witches. But obviously there are things I do not know. There are people connected with our Order who are investigating this under an authority other than mine. I am getting no clear answer from the London office, except that I am to wait to be contacted. I am at a loss. I really don't know what to tell you to do. I'm ... disillusioned.'

'You can't give up on us,' said Mona. 'Forget about these guys in London. Don't give up on us!'

'You have a point,' said Aaron. 'But I don't know that I have anything new to offer.'

'Oh, hell, come on,' said Mona. 'Look, will somebody go in there and call Michael? I don't understand why we aren't hearing from Michael. Michael was going to change clothes and come up to Amelia Street.'

'Well, maybe he did,' said Anne Marie. She pressed the button on a small box beneath the table. In a subdued voice she said into the speaker, 'Joyce, call Amelia Street. See if Michael Curry is there.' She looked at Mona. 'That's simple enough.'

'Well, if you want me to offer what I have,' said Aaron, 'if you want me to speak up –'

'Yes?' Mona urged him on.

'I'd say the thing is most certainly looking for a mate. And if it does find that mate, if the child is conceived and born while the thing is still there to take the child away, then we have quite literally a monstrous problem.'

'I'd rather stick with catching the thing,' said Randall, 'rather than speculating on –'

'I'm sure you would,' said Aaron. 'But you must think back on everything Dr Larkin said. On what Rowan said to him. This thing has an enormous reproductive advantage! Do you understand what that means? For centuries this family has lived with one simple story: that of the man, and the man wanting to be flesh. Well, we are now dealing with something far worse – the man is not merely flesh, he is a unique and powerful species.'

'Do you think this thing was planned?' Lauren asked. Her voice was cold and small and unhurried – Lauren when she was most unhappy, and most determined. 'Do you think it was planned from the very beginning? That we would not only nourish this thing in our family but provide the women for it?'

'I don't know,' said Aaron, 'but I do know this. Whatever its superiority, it has to have some weaknesses.'

'The scent, it can't hide that,' said Mona.

'No, I'm speaking of physical weaknesses, something of that sort,' Aaron said.

'No. Dr Larkin was specific. So were the people in New York. The thing seems to have a powerful immunity.'

'Increase and multiply and subdue the earth,' said Mona.

'What does that have to do with it?' demanded Randall.

'That's what it will do,' said Aaron quietly. 'If we don't stop it.'

TWENTY-THREE

JULIEN'S STORY CONTINUES

Ah, you cannot imagine the miracle of her voice, and how much I loved her, loved her completely whether she was Cortland's child or not. It was a love we feel for those who are our own and like unto us, and yet too many years lay between us. I felt desperate and helpless and all alone, and when I sat down on the side of my bed, she sat beside me.

'Tell me, Evelyn, child, you see the future. Carlotta came to you. What did you see?'

'I don't see,' Evelyn said in a voice as small as her round little face, her gray eyes appealing to me to accept and to understand. 'I see the words and I speak the words, but I do not know their meaning. And long ago, I learned to keep quiet and let the words fade away unread, unspoken.'

'No, child. Hold my hand. What do you see? What do you see for me and my family? What do you see for all of us? Are we one clan with one future?'

Even through my tired fingers I felt her pulse, her warmth, the witches' gifts, as we always said, and I saw that small, that evil sixth finger. Oh, I would have had it cut off, painlessly and with skill, if I had been her father. And to think that Cortland was – my own son. I meant to kill Cortland.

First things first. I held tight to her hand.

Something shifted in her perfect little circle of a face; her chin lifted so that her neck seemed all the more long and beautiful. She began to speak the poem, her voice soft and rapid, borne by the rhythm itself:

> One will rise who is too evil.
> One will come who is too good.
> 'Twixt the two, a witch shall falter
> and thereby open wide the door.
>
> Pain and suffering as they stumble
> Blood and fear before they learn.
> Woe betide this Springtime Eden
> Now the vale of those who mourn.
>
> Beware the watchers in that hour
> Bar the doctors from the house
> Scholars will but nourish evil
> Scientists would raise it high.
>
> Let the devil speak his story
> Let him rouse the angel's might
> Make the dead come back to witness
> Put the alchemist to flight.
>
> Slay the flesh that is not human
> Trust to weapons crude and cruel
> For, dying on the verge of wisdom,
> Tortured souls may seek the light.
>
> Crush the babes who are not children
> Show no mercy to the pure
> Else shall Eden have no Springtime.
> Else shall our kind reign no more.

For two nights and two days she stayed in this room with me.

No one dared to break in the door. Her great-grandfather Tobias came and threatened. His son Walker roared at the gate. I do not know how many others came or what they said, or even where all the quarrels took place. Seems I heard my Mary Beth screaming on the landing at her daughter Carlotta. Seems Richard knocked a thousand times, only to be told by me that all was well.

We lay together in the bed, the child and I. I did not want to hurt her. Nor can I blame on her what took place. Let me say we sank into the softest of caresses, and for a long time I cuddled her and sheltered her, and tried to drive away the deep chill of her fear and her loneliness. And fool that I was, I thought that in me, tenderness was now something safe.

But I was too much of a man still for anything so plain and simple. I gave her kisses till she knew she must have them, and opened herself to me.

Through the long night we lay together, musing when all the other voices had died away.

She said that she liked my attic better than her attic, and I knew in my sorrow that I would die in this room, very soon.

I didn't have to tell her. I felt her soft hand on my forehead, trying to cool it. I felt the silken weight of her palm on my eyelids.

And the words of the poem, she said them over and over. And I with her, until I knew every verse.

By dawn, she did not need to correct me any longer. I didn't dare to write it down. My evil Mary Beth will burn it, I told her. Tell the others. Tell Carlotta. Tell Stella. But my heart was so sick. What would it matter?

What would happen? What could the words of the poem mean?

'I've made you sad,' she said gently.

'Child, I was already sad. You have given me hope.'

I think it was late Thursday afternoon that Mary Beth finally took the hinges from the door and opened it.

'Well, they are going to bring the police in here,' Mary Beth said by way of excuse, very practical and nondramatic. Her way of doing things.

'You tell them they can't lock her up again. She's to come and go as she wishes. You call Cortland now in Boston.'

'Cortland is here, Julien.'

I called Cortland to me. Stella was to take the child down to her own room and sit with her, and not let anyone take her away. Carlotta would be with them, just to make sure the girl was safe.

Now this son of mine was my pride and joy, as I've said, my eldest, my brightest, and all these years I had tried to protect him from what I knew. But he was too shrewd to be protected entirely, and now for me he had fallen off his pedestal and I was too angry not to judge him for what had become of this girl.

'Father, I didn't know, I swear it. And even now I don't believe it. It would take me hours to tell you the story of that night. I could swear that Barbara Ann put something in my drink to make me mad. She dragged me out into the swamp with her. We were in the boat together; that is all I remember, and that she was devilish and strange. I swear this, Father. When I woke

I was in the boat. I went up to Fontevrault and they locked me out. Tobias had his shotgun. He said he'd kill me. I walked into St Martinville to call home. I swear this. That's all I remember. If she is my child, I'm sorry. But they never told me. Seems they never wanted me to know. I'll look out for her from now on.'

'That's all well and good for the fifth circuit court of appeals,' said I. 'You knew when she was born. You heard the rumors. Make sure this child is never a prisoner again, you understand? That she has everything she requires, that she goes to school away from here if she wants to, that she has money of her own!'

I turned my back on them. I turned my back on my world. I did not answer when he spoke to me. I thought of Evelyn and how she described her silence, and it seemed an amusing power, to lie there and not to answer, to let them think that I could not.

They came and they went. Evelyn was taken back, with Carlotta and Cortland to speak for her. Or so I was told.

Only Richard's crying broke my heart. I went away from it, deep into myself where I could hear the poem and say the phrases, trying vainly to figure them out.

> Let the devil speak his story,
> Let him rouse the angel's might.

But what did it mean to me? Finally I clung to the last verse of it: 'Else shall Eden have no Springtime.'

We were the Springtime, we Mayfairs, I knew it. Eden was our world. We were the Springtime, and the simple word *Else* meant there was hope. We could be saved somehow. Something could stop the vale of those who mourn!

> Pain and suffering as they stumble
> Blood and fear before they learn . . .

Yes, there was hope in the poem, a purpose to it, a purpose in its telling! But would I ever live to see the words fulfilled? And nothing struck such horror in me as that sentence: 'Slay the flesh that is not human!' for if this thing was not human, what would its powers be? If it was merely St Ashlar – but that did not seem so! Would it become a man when it was born again? Or something worse?

'Slay the flesh that is not human!'

Ah, how I troubled over it. How it obsessed my mind. Sometimes there was nothing in my mind but the words of the poem and feverish images!

I was senseless finally. Days passed. The doctor came. At last I sat up and began to talk so the nincompoop would leave me alone. Science had made great strides since my boyhood, but that didn't prevent this knuckle-head from standing over me and telling my loved ones that I was suffering from 'hardening of the arteries' and 'senile dementia' and couldn't understand anything they said.

It was an absolute delight to rise up and order him out of the room.

Also I wanted to walk around again. I was never one for simply lying there, and this had been my worst hour, and it had ended and I was living still.

Richard helped me dress and I went down all the way to the first floor for supper with my family. I sat at the head of the table and made a great show of polishing off gumbo, roast chicken, and a *boeuf daube* or some other foolishness, just so they would leave me alone. I refused to look at Cortland, who tried again and again to speak to me. I was really making him miserable, my poor fair-haired boy!

The cousins gabbled. Mary Beth spoke of practical things with her drunken husband, Daniel McIntyre, poor old soul, now so sick he was a slovenly ruin of the fine man he'd once been. That's what we did to him, I thought. Richard, my devoted one, kept his eyes on me, and then Stella said – Stella said that we should all go driving, since I was up again, and all right.

Driving, an escapade! The car was all fixed. Oh? I hadn't known it was broken. Well, Cortland took it out ... Shut up, Stella, it's fixed, *mon père*, it's fixed!

'I am worried about that girl!' I declared. 'Evelyn, my granddaughter!'

Cortland hastened to assure me she was taken care of. She'd been taken downtown to buy clothes.

'You Mayfairs think that's the answer to everything, don't you?' asked I. 'Go downtown and buy new clothes.'

'Well, you're the one who taught us, Father,' said Cortland with a little twinkle in his eye.

I was amazed at my cowardice. How I gave in when I saw that affectionate little smile. How I gave in.

'All right, make the car ready, and all of you get out,' I said. 'Stella and Lionel, we'll go, the three of us, an escapade, you can believe it. All of you go. Carlotta, stay.'

She didn't require coaxing. In a moment the vast dining room was still and the murals seemed as always to be closing in on us, ready to transport us out from under the plaster moldings and far away to the verdant fields of Riverbend which they so charmingly rendered. Riverbend, which by this time was gone.

'Did she tell you the poem?' I said to Carlotta.

Carlotta nodded. And very slowly, taking her time, she recited each verse as I remembered it.

'I have told it to Mother,' she said. This shocked me. 'Lot of good that it did. What did you think would happen?' she demanded. 'Did you think you could all dance with the Devil and not pay the price?'

'But I never knew for sure that he was the Devil. There was no God and Devil at Riverbend when I was born. I did the best with what I had.'

'You will burn in hell,' she said.

A bit of terror went through me.

I wanted to answer, to say so much more ... I wanted to tell her all, or all of what there was, but she had risen from the table, thrown down her napkin as if it were a glove, and gone out.

Ah, so she told it to Mary Beth. When Mary Beth came to fetch me, I whispered those dreaded words:

'Slay the flesh that is not human ...'

'Ah, now, darling, don't fuss, please,' she said. 'Go out and have a good time.'

When I came out onto the front gallery, the Stutz Bearcat was cooking and ready, and off we went, I and my little ones, Stella and Lionel. We drove past Amelia Street, but we did not stop to see to Evelyn, for we feared we would do more harm than good.

It was to Storyville, to the houses of my favorite ladies, that we went.

I think it was dawn when we came home. I remember

now that night as distinctly as all else because it was my last in Storyville, listening to the jazz bands, and singing, and taking the children with me right into the fancy parlors of the brothels. Oh, how shocked were my lady friends! But there is nothing in a brothel that cannot be bought.

Stella loved it! This was living, cried Stella, this was life. Stella drank glass after glass of champagne and danced on her tiptoes. Lionel wasn't so certain. But it didn't matter. I was dying! As I sat in the cram-packed parlor of Lulu White's house, listening to the ragtime piano, I thought, I am dying. Dying! And I was as self-centered about it as anyone else. The world shrank and revolved around Julien. Julien knew a storm was coming. And he could not be there to help! Julien knew all pleasure, adventure and triumph were over! Julien was going to be placed in the tomb like everyone else.

That morning when we arrived home, I kissed my Stella. I told her that it had been a grand occasion, and then I retired to the attic, certain that I would never leave it again.

I lay in the dark night after night, thinking. What if somehow I could come back? What if somehow I could stay earthbound as this thing has done?

After all, if it is Ashlar, one of the many Ashlars, a saint, a king, the vengeful ghost, a mere human –! The dark made noises back to me. The bed trembled. I thought of that verse again ... the flesh that isn't human.

'Have you come to trouble me or content me?' I asked.

'Die in peace, Julien,' he said. 'I would have given you my secrets the first day I came with you to this house. I told you then that such a place could draw you out of eternity, that it was as the castles of old. Remember its patterns, Julien, its graceful battlements. And through the mist you will see them, distinct. But you would not have my lessons then. Will you have them now? I know you. You are alive. You didn't want to hear about death.'

'I don't think you know about death,' I said. 'I think you know about wanting, and haunting, and living! But not death.'

I got out of bed. I cranked up the Victrola just to drive the thing away from me. 'Yes, I want to come back,' I whispered. 'I want to come back. I want to remain earthbound, to stay, to be part of this house. But God, I swear it, in my soul of souls, it is not greed to live again, it is that the tale is unfinished, the demon continues, and I die! I would help, I would be an angel of the Lord somehow. Oh, God, I do not believe in you. I do not believe in anything but Lasher and myself.'

I started pacing. I paced and paced and played the waltz of Violetta, a song that seemed utterly oblivious to every kind of sorrow, something so frivolous yet so organized that I found it irresistible.

Then a moment came, so unusual as perhaps to have been unique. In all my long life, I had never been so caught off guard as I was at this moment, and it was by the face of a small girl at my window, a waif of a child crouched upon the high porch roof.

At once I opened the stubborn sash.

'Eve a Lynn,' I said. And perfumed, and soft, and wet from the spring rain, she came into my arms.

'How did you come to me, darling?' I asked her.

'Up the trellis, Oncle Julien, hand over hand. You

have shown me an attic is not a prison. I will come to you as long as I can.'

We made love; we talked together. I lay there with her as the sun came up. She told me they were being kind to her now, letting her go places, that she walked in the evening all the way up the Avenue, and down to Canal Street, that she had ridden in a car again, that she had real shoes. Richard had bought her pretty dresses. Cortland had bought her a coat with fur on the collar. Mary Beth even had given her a silver-backed mirror and a silver-handled comb.

At dawn I sat up and cranked the Victrola. We danced to the waltz. It was a crazy morning, the kind of crazy morning that follows carousing and drunkenness and wandering from dance halls to taverns, yet it had all taken place in this room. She wore only her petticoat then, trimmed in pink lace, and a ribbon in her hair. We danced and danced about the room, giggling, laughing, until finally someone ... ah yes, Mary Beth, opened the door.

I only smiled. I knew my angelic child would visit me again.

In the dark of the night, I talked to the Victrola.

I told it to hold the spell. Of course I did not believe in these things. I had steadfastly refused to believe in them. Yet now I pared my nails and slipped them in between the bottom wood and the side wood. I clipped my hair, and slipped that beneath the turntable. I bit my fingers and drew blood and smeared it into the dark stain. I made the thing like a doll of myself, like the witches' dolls, and I sang the waltz.

I played the waltz and said, 'Come back, come back. Be at hand if they need you. Be at hand if they call you. Come back, come back.'

I was possessed of a terrible vision, that I was dead and rising and the light was coming, and that I turned by back on it, and plummeted with my arms out, digging deep into an air which became thicker and thicker, as dense as it was dark. Earthbound. And it seemed the night was choked with spirits like mine, lost souls, fools, fearing hell, and not believing in Paradise. And the waltz played on.

I saw finally the futility of all these gestures, that witchcraft is but a matter of focus – that one can apply one's fierce and immeasurable energies to an act of choice. I would come back! I would come back. I sang it out to the walls.

Come back.

Beware the watchers in that hour!

Yes, come back in that hour!

> Else shall Eden have no Springtime.
> Else shall our kind reign no more.

Michael, remember now all the verses I've told you.

Remember. See what they say! Michael, I tell you I would not be here if the battle were over. The hour we speak of is yet to come. You have used love, yes, you have done that and it was not enough. But there are other tools you can use. Remember the poem, 'crude and cruel'. Do not hesitate when you see it. Do not let the goodness hold you back.

Why else have I been allowed to come here? Why else have I been allowed once more to hear that waltz beneath this roof? In a moment you must play it for me, Michael, my waltz, my little Victrola. Play it when I am not here.

But let me tell you now of the last few nights I

remember. I'm growing tired. I can see the finish of these words, but not the finish of the story. That is yours to tell. Let me give the few words left. And remember your promise. Play the music for me, Michael. Play it, for whether I go to heaven or hell is not yet known by either of us, and perhaps never will be known.

It was a week after, that I gave the little Victrola to Evelyn. I had taken advantage of an afternoon when no one was about, sending Richard up to fetch her, and tell her to come as soon as she could. I had the boys bring up for me a large Victrola from the dining room, a sizable music box with a fine tone.

And then, when Evie and I were alone, I told her to take the little Victrola up home and keep it and never let it out of her hands till after Mary Beth was gone. I didn't even want Richard to know she'd taken it, for fear he would blab to Mary Beth if she put the screws to him. I told Evie, 'You take it, and sing as you walk out with it, sing and sing.'

That way, I thought, if Lasher were to observe her taking away this mysterious little toy, he would in befuddlement not attach any meaning to what he saw. I had to remember: the monster could read my thoughts.

I was desperate.

No sooner had Evie gone, her high singing voice dying away in the stairwell, than I wound the big new Victrola and called Lasher to me. Perhaps he would not heed her at all.

When he appeared, I appealed to him:

'Lasher, protect always that poor little Evie,' I said. 'Protect her from the others, for my sake, will you protect that child.'

He listened as best he could with the music entrancing him. Invisible, he blundered about the room, knocking things from the mantel, rattling the framed pictures. Fine with me. It was proof that he was there!

'Very well, Julien,' he sang suddenly, appearing in the midst of a jolly dance, feet striking the boards with some semblance of weight and sound. What a smile. What a dazzle. How I wished for an instant that I had loved him.

And by that time, I thought, surely Evie is all the way home.

Weeks passed.

Evie's liberation was now a fact. Richard often took her driving, along with Stella. Tobias took her regularly with him to Mass.

Evie came to me when she wanted, by the front door. But there were still nights when she chose the trellis, seeking me as if she were a fearless little goddess, and whipping my blood, with her courage and her own passion, to an obscene and delirious heat. We lay together for hours, kissing, touching one another. What a wonder that in my dotage I should be a skilled lover for one so young. I told her secrets, but only a few.

The gods had granted me that final pride.

'Julien, I love you,' said the crafty Lasher when he was about, hoping I would play the big Victrola, because he had come to love it so. 'Why would anyone harm Evelyn? What is she to us? I see the future. I see far. We have what we require.'

When Mary Beth came home one afternoon, I sat her down beside me and vowed to her that I had told that little girl nothing of importance and that they must look out for her as the years passed.

Tears came into Mary Beth's eyes, one of the few times I ever saw them.

'Julien, how you misunderstand me and everything that I have done. All these years, I've striven to bring us together, to make us strong in number and in influence. To make us happy! Do you think I would hurt a child that has your blood? Cortland's daughter? Oh, Julien, you break my heart. Trust in me, that I know what I do, that I have done everything right for our family. Trust in me, please. Julien, don't die in agitation and fear. Don't let this happen to you. Don't let the last hours be ugly with fear. I'll sit with you night and day if I have to. Die calm. We are the Mayfair family . . . a million leagues from where we were at Riverbend so long ago. Trust that we shall prevail.'

Nights passed. I lay awake, no longer needing sleep.

I knew by this time that Evelyn carried my child. God gives no quarter to old men! We burn; we father. What a dreadful circumstance! But the girl herself did not seem to know. I did not tell her.

I could only trust to Cortland, whom I called to myself and lectured incessantly. I knew the feathers would fly, as they say, as soon as everyone knew Evelyn was pregnant. I could only trust to the edicts and pronouncements I had issued, *ad nauseam*, that the child must be protected no matter what happened as the years passed.

A night came on, peaceful, warm. It must have been midsummer when I died! Surely it was. The crape myrtles were full of pink blossoms. Surely I have not imagined such a thing.

And I had sent everyone away from me. I knew it was coming. I lay quiet on a heap of pillows looking out at the clouds above the crape myrtle.

I wanted to go back and back to Riverbend, I wanted to sit with Marie Claudette, I wanted to know, honestly, *to know* who had been that young man who kidnapped slaves and brought them to Marguerite's chambers for her wild experiments? Who had been that thoughtless knave?

I lay there, and then a most dreadful truth seized me. A little truth, really. I couldn't move. I couldn't lift myself up. I could not make my arms obey. Death was stealing over me like a winter chill. It was freezing me.

And then, as if there were a God for raconteurs and lechers, there appeared Evelyn above the edge of the roof, her white hands on the green vines.

Up she came and across the porch top and I could hear her voice through the thick glass, 'Open the window, Oncle Julien! It's Evie, open to me.'

I couldn't move. I stared at her, my eyes brimming. 'Oh darling,' I whispered in my heart.

And then Evie called on her witches' gifts, and with her hands and her gifts she sent the window rattling upward. She reached inside and took me by my shoulders, so frail and small I must have been by then. She brought me forward and kissed me.

'Oh darling, yes, yes . . .'

And beyond her, spreading out over the whole sky, the storm gathered. I heard the first raindrops strike the porch roof beneath her. I felt them on my face. I saw the trees begin to move in their fury. And I heard the wind, wailing as if *he* were wailing, lashing the trees and crying in his grief as he had on the death of my mother, and on the death of her mother.

Yes, it was a storm for the death of the witch, and I was the witch. And it was my death and my storm.

TWENTY-FOUR

They stood in the mist, forming a vague circle. What was that low grinding sound? Was it thunder?

They were the most dangerous people he had seen. Ignorance, poverty, that was their heritage, and everywhere he saw the common imperfections of the poor and the untended, the hunchback, the man with the club foot, the child whose arms were too short, and all the others, thin-faced, coarse, misshapen and frightening, in their gray and brown garments, to behold. The grinding noise went on and on, too monotonous for thunder. Could they hear it?

The sky above pressed down upon them, down upon the entire grassy floor of the glen. The stones did have carvings, the old man in Edinburgh had told Julien the truth. The stones were enormous, and they were all together in the circle.

He sat up. He was dizzy. He said, 'I don't belong here. This is a dream. I have to go back where I belong. I can't wake up here. But I don't know how to get back there.' The grinding sound was driving him mad. It was so low, so insistent. Did they hear it? Maybe it was some awful rumble from the earth itself, but probably not. Anything could happen here. Anything could happen. The important thing was to get out.

'We would like to help you,' said one of the men, a

tall man with flowing gray hair. He stepped forward, out of the little circular gathering. He wore black breeches and his mouth was invisible beneath his gray mustache. Only a bit of lip showed as the deep baritone voice came from him. 'But we do not know who you are or what you are doing here. We do not know where you come from. Or how to send you home.'

This was English, modern English. This was all wrong. A dream.

What is that rumbling? That grinding. I know that sound. He wanted to reach out and stop it. I know that sound.

The stone nearest to him must have been some twenty feet high, jagged, like a crude knife rising from the earth, and on it were warriors in rows, with their spears and their shields.

'The Picts,' he said.

They stared at him as if they did not understand him. 'If we leave you here,' said the gray-haired man, 'the little people may come. The little people are full of hatred. The little people will take you away. They'll try to make a giant with you, and reclaim the world. You have the blood in you, you see.'

A sharp ringing sound carried over the blowing grass, suddenly, beneath the great span of boiling gray clouds. It came again, that same familiar peal. It was louder than the low grinding noise that ran on, uninterrupted, beneath it.

'I know what that is!' he said to them. He tried to stand, but then he fell down again into the damp grass. How they stared at his clothes. How different theirs were.

'This is the wrong time! Do you hear that sound? That sound is a telephone. It's trying to bring me back.'

The tall man drew closer. His bare knees were filthy, his long legs streaked with dirt. Rather like a man who has been splashed with dirty water, and has let it dry on his skin. His clothing was matted with dirt.

'I've never seen the little people for myself,' he said. 'But I know they are something to fear. We cannot leave you here.'

'Get away from me,' he said. 'I'm getting out of here. This is a dream and you ought to leave it. Don't wait around. Just go. I have things to do! Important things that must be done!'

And this time he rose full to his feet, and was thrown backwards and felt the floorboards beneath his hands. Again the telephone rang. Again and again. He tried to open his eyes.

Then it stopped. No, I have to wake up, he thought. I have to get up. Don't stop ringing. He brought his knees up close to his chest and managed to get up on all fours. The grinding noise. The Victrola. The heavy arm with its crude little needle caught at the end of the record, grinding, grinding, looking for a new way to begin.

Light in the two windows. His windows. And there the Victrola under Antha's window, the little letters VICTOR printed in gold on the wooden lid, which was propped open.

Someone was coming up the stairs.

'Yes!' He climbed to his feet. His room. The drafting board, his chair. The shelves filled with his books. *Victorian Architecture. The History of the Frame House in America.* My books.

There was a knocking at the door.

'Mr Mike, are you in there? Mr Mike, Mr Ryan is on the phone!'

'Come in, Henri, come in here.' Would Henri hear his fear? Would he know?

The doorknob turned as if it were alive. The light fell in from the landing, Henri's face so dark with the little chandelier behind him that Michael couldn't see it.

'Mr Mike, it's good news and bad news. She's alive, they've found her in St Martinville, Louisiana, but she's sick, real sick, they say she can't move or speak.'

'Christ, they've found her. They know for sure it's Rowan!'

He hurried past Henri and down the stairs. Henri came behind him, talking steadily, hand out to steady Michael when he almost fell.

'Mr Ryan's on his way over here. Coroner called from St Martinville. She had papers in her purse. She fits the description. They say it's Dr Mayfair, for sure.'

Eugenia was standing in his bedroom holding the phone in her hand.

'Yes, sir, we've found him.'

Michael took the receiver.

'Ryan?'

'She's on her way in now,' came the cool voice on the other end. 'The ambulance is taking her straight to Mercy Hospital. She'll be there in about an hour, if they use the siren all the way. Michael, it doesn't look good. They can't get any response from her. They're describing a coma. We're trying to reach her friend Dr Larkin, at the Pontchartrain. But there's no answer.'

'What do I do? Where do I go?' He wanted to get on I-10 and drive north till he saw the oncoming ambulance, then swing around, cutting across the grass, and follow it in. An hour! 'Henri, get me my jacket. Find my wallet. Down in the library. I left my keys and my wallet on the floor.'

'Mercy Hospital,' said Ryan. 'They're ready for her. The Mayfair Floor. We'll meet you there. You haven't seen Dr Larkin, have you?'

Michael had on his jacket within seconds. He drank the glass of orange juice Eugenia pushed at him, as she reminded him in no uncertain terms that he had had no supper, that it was eleven o'clock at night.

'Henri, go bring the car around. Hurry.'

Rowan alive. Rowan would be at Mercy Hospital in less than an hour. Rowan coming home. Goddamnit to hell, I knew it, knew she would come back, but not like this!

He hurried down to the front hall, taking his keys from Eugenia, and his wallet and stuffing it in his pocket. Money clip. Didn't need it. Mayfair Floor. Where he himself had lain after the heart attack, hooked to machines and listening to them, like the grinding of that Victrola. And she was going to be there.

'Listen to me, Eugenia, there's something real important you gotta do,' he said. 'Go upstairs to my room. There's an old Victrola on the floor. Wind it and start the record. OK?'

'Now? At this hour of the night? For what?'

'Just do it. Tell you what. Bring it down to the parlor. That will make it easier. Oh, never mind, you can't carry it. Just go up there, and play that record a few times and then go to bed.'

'Your wife is found, your wife is alive, and you're headed to the hospital to see her, and you don't know whether she's all right or been hit in the head or what, and you're telling me to go play a phonograph record.'

'Right. You got it all exactly right.'

There was the car, a great dark fish sliding beneath

the oaks. He hurried down the steps, turning quickly to Eugenia:

'Do it!' he said, and went out. 'The point is, she is alive.' He climbed into the backseat of the limo. 'Take off.' He slammed the door. 'She is alive, and if she is alive, she'll hear me, I'll talk to her, she'll tell me what happened. Jesus Christ, Julien, she is alive. The hour is not yet come.'

As the car moved onto Magazine Street and headed downtown, the rest of the poem came back to him, all of it, a long string of dark and dreamy words. He heard Julien's voice, with the fancy French accent illuminating the letters, just as surely as the old monks had il-luminated letters when they painted them bright red or gold and decorated them with tiny figures and leaves.

> Beware the watchers in that hour
> Bar the doctors from the house
> Scholars will but nourish evil
> Scientists would raise it high.

'Isn't it the most terrible thing?' Henri was saying. 'All of those poor women. To think of it, all of them dead the same way.'

'What the hell are you talking about?' asked Michael. He wanted a cigarette. He could smell that sweet cheroot of Julien's. The fragrance clung to his clothes. Like a bolt it came back. Julien lighting that cheroot, inhaling and then waving to him. And the deep glint of the brass bed in the room, and Violetta singing to all those men.

'What poor women? What are you talking about? It's like I'm Rip Van Winkle. Give me the time.'

'The time is 11.30 p.m., boss,' said Henri. 'I'm talking about the other Mayfair women, Miss Mona's mother dying uptown, and poor Miss Edith downtown, though best I can remember I never met her, and I don't even remember the name of the other lady, and the lady in Houston and the one after that.'

'You're telling me all these women are dead? These Mayfair women?'

'Yes, boss. All died the same way, Miss Bea said. Mr Aaron called. Everybody was calling. We didn't even know you were home. The lights were out upstairs in that room. How would I know you were asleep on the floor?'

Henri went on, something about looking all over the house for Michael, saying to Eugenia this and that, and going outside to look for him, and on and on. Michael didn't hear it. He was watching the decayed old brick buildings of Magazine Street fly by; he was hearing the poem.

> Pain and suffering as they stumble
> Blood and fear before they learn.

TWENTY-FIVE

So this is Stolov. He knew the moment he stepped off
the plane. They had tracked him all the way. And here
was the big man, waiting for him, a bit overmuscular in
his black raincoat, with large eyes of a pale indistinct
color which nevertheless shone rather bright like clear
glass.

The man had near-invisible blond eyelashes and bushy
brows, and his hair was light. He looked Norwegian to
Yuri. Not Russian. Erich Stolov.

'Stolov,' Yuri said, and, shifting his bag to the left, he
extended his hand.

'Ah, you know me,' said the man. 'I wasn't sure that
you would.' Accent, Scandinavian with a touch of something else. Eastern Europe.

'I always know our people,' said Yuri. 'Why have
you come to New Orleans? Have you been working
with Aaron Lightner? Or are you here simply to meet
me?'

'That is what I've come to explain,' said Stolov,
placing his hand very lightly on Yuri's back as they
followed the carpeted corridor together, passengers
streaming by them, the hollow space itself seeming to
swallow all warm sounds. The man's tone was very
cooperative and open. Yuri didn't quite believe it.

'Yuri,' said the other. 'You shouldn't have left the

Motherhouse, but I understand why you did. But you know we are an authoritarian order. You know obedience is important. And you know why.'

'No, you tell me why. I am excommunicated now. I feel no obligation to talk to you. I came to see Aaron. That's the only reason I am here.'

'I know that, of course I do,' said the other, nodding. 'Here, shall we stop for coffee?'

'No, I want to go to the hotel. I want to meet with Aaron as soon as I can.'

'He couldn't see you now if he wanted to,' said Stolov in a low conciliatory voice. 'The Mayfair family is in a state of crisis. He is with them. Besides, Aaron is an old and loyal member of the Talamasca. He won't be happy that you've come so impulsively. Your show of affection may even embarrass him.'

Yuri was silently infuriated by these words. He didn't like this big blond-haired man.

'So I will find him and find out for myself. Listen, Stolov, I knew when I left I was out. Why are you talking this way to me – so patient, so agreeable? Does Aaron know you are here?'

'Yuri, you are valuable to the Order. Anton is a new Superior General. Perhaps David Talbot would have handled things much better. It's in times of transition that we sometimes lose people whom we come, very much, to miss.'

The man gestured to the empty coffee shop, where china cups shimmered on smooth Formica tables. Smell of weak, American coffee, even here in this town.

'No, I want to go on,' said Yuri. 'I am going to find Aaron. Then the three of us can talk, if you like. I want to tell Aaron I'm here.'

'You can't do that now. Aaron is at the hospital,' said Stolov. 'Rowan Mayfair has been found. Aaron is with the family. Aaron is in danger. That's why it's so important you listen to what I have to say. Don't you see? This misunderstanding amongst us – it came about because we were trying to protect Aaron. And you.'

'Then you can explain it to both of us.'

'Hear me out first,' the man said gently. 'Please.'

Yuri realized the man was virtually blocking his path. The man was larger than he was. He wasn't so much a menace as he was a great obstacle, forceful and stubborn and believing in himself. His face was agreeable and intelligent, and once again he spoke in the same even, patient tone.

'Yuri, we need your cooperation. Otherwise Aaron may be hurt. You might say this is a rescue mission involving Aaron Lightner. Aaron Lightner has been drawn into the Mayfair family. He is no longer using good judgment.'

'Why not?'

But even as he asked this question, Yuri yielded. He turned, allowed himself to be led into the restaurant, and capitulated, taking a chair opposite the tall Norwegian, and watching in silence as the waitress was instructed to bring coffee, and something sweet to eat.

Yuri figured Stolov was perhaps ten years older than he. That meant Stolov was perhaps forty. As the black raincoat fell open, he saw the conventional Talamasca suit, expensive cut, tropical wool, but not ostentatious. The look of this generation. Not the tweed and leather patches of David and Aaron and their ilk.

'You're very suspicious and you have a right to be,' said Stolov. 'But Yuri, we are an order, a family. You

611

shouldn't have gone out of the Motherhouse the way you did.'

'You told me that already. Why did the Elders forbid me to speak to Aaron Lightner?'

'They had no idea that it would have such repercussions. They wanted only silence, an interval, in which to take measures to protect Aaron. They did not imagine those words spoken in a booming voice.'

The waitress filled their china cups with the pale, weak coffee. 'Espresso,' said Yuri. 'I'm sorry.' He pushed the pallid cup away.

The woman laid down rolls for them to eat, sweet-smelling, iced and sticky. Yuri wasn't hungry. He had eaten something wholly unappetizing and very filling on the plane.

'You said they found Rowan Mayfair,' said Yuri, staring at the rolls, and thinking how sticky they would be if he touched them. 'You mentioned a hospital.'

Stolov nodded. He drank his pale amber-colored coffee. He looked up with those peculiar soft light eyes. The absence of any color made them look vacant and then suddenly unaccountably aggressive. Yuri couldn't figure why.

'Aaron is angry with us,' said Stolov. 'He is not being cooperative. On Christmas Day something happened with the Mayfair family. He believes that if he had been present, he could have helped Rowan Mayfair. He blames us that he did not go to Rowan. He's wrong. He would have died. That is what would have happened. Aaron is old. His investigations have seldom if ever involved this sort of direct danger.'

'That wasn't my impression,' said Yuri. 'The Mayfair family tried to kill him once before. Aaron has seen

612

plenty of danger. Aaron has been in danger in other investigations. Aaron is a treasure to the Order because he has seen and done so much.'

'Ah, but you see, it is not the family which is the threat to Aaron now, it is not the Mayfair Witches, it is an individual whom they have aided and abetted, so to speak.'

'Lasher.'

'I see you know the file.'

'I know it.'

'Did you see this individual when you went to Donnelaith?'

'You know I didn't. If you are working on this investigation, you've already seen the reports I copied to the Elders, the reports I made for Aaron. You know I talked to people who had seen this individual, as you put it. But I didn't see him myself. Have you seen him?'

'Why are you so angry, Yuri?' What a lovely, deep, reverent voice.

'I'm not angry, Stolov. I am in the grip of suspicion. All my life I've been devoted to the Talamasca. The Talamasca brought me into adulthood. I might not have been brought that far if it hadn't been for the Order. But something is not right. People are acting in strange ways. Your tone is strange. I want to speak directly with the Elders. I want to speak to them!'

'That never happens, Yuri,' said Stolov quietly. 'No one speaks to the Elders, you know that. Aaron could have told you that. You can communicate with them in the customary fashion . . .'

'Ah, this is an emergency.'

'For the Talamasca? No. For Aaron and for Yuri, yes, definitely. But for the Talamasca, nothing is an emergency. We are like the Church of Rome.'

'Rowan Mayfair, you said they found her. What is this about?'

'She is in Mercy Hospital, but sometime this morning they will take her home. Overnight she was on a respirator. This morning they removed her from it. She continues to breathe on her own. But she will not recover. They confirmed this last night. There has been enormous toxic damage to her brain, the kind of damage produced by shock, drug overdose, an allergic reaction, a sudden rise in insulin; I am quoting her physicians now to you. I'm telling you what they are telling the other members of the family.

'They know she cannot recover. And her own wishes regarding such situations are in writing. As the designee of the legacy she laid down her own medical instructions for such a crisis. That once a negative prognosis had been confirmed, she be removed from life support and taken home.'

Stolov looked at his watch, a rather hideous contraption full of tiny dials and digital letters.

'They are probably taking her home now.' He looked at Yuri. 'Aaron is most surely with them. Give Aaron some time.'

'I'll give *you* exactly twenty minutes. Explain yourself. Then I'm going on.'

'All right. This individual – Lasher – he is very dangerous. He is unique as far as anyone knows. He is trying desperately to propagate. There is some evidence that some members of the Mayfair family might be useful to him in this, that the family carries a genetic peculiarity, an entire set of chromosomes which other humans do not have. There is evidence that Michael Curry carries this same surplus of mysterious chromosomes. That it is a trait peculiar to those of the northern countries, in particular the Celts. When Rowan and Michael mated, they produced this unique creature. Not human. But it might not have been successfully born if there had not been some extraordinary spiritual intervention. The migration, if you will, of a powerful and willful soul. This soul entered the embryo before its own soul had taken control of it, and this soul directed the embryo's development, availing itself of these surplus chromosomes to produce a new and perhaps unprecedented design. It was a meeting if you will of mystery and science, of something spiritual and a genetic irregularity of which that spiritual force took advantage. A sort of physical opportunity for an occult and powerful thing.'

Yuri considered this for a long moment. Lasher, the spirit who would be flesh, who had threatened Petyr van Abel with his grim predictions, who had tried again and again to materialize, had been born to Rowan Mayfair. This much he had deduced before he ever came here. That the creature wanted to mate, to reproduce, that was something he had not considered. But it was logical.

'Oh, very logical,' said Stolov. 'Evolution is about reproduction. This thing is now caught up in the broad scheme of evolution. It has made its grand entry. It would now reproduce and take over. And if it can find the right woman, it will be successful. Rowan Mayfair has been destroyed by its attempts to reproduce. Her body has been ravaged by her brief aborted pregnancies. Other women in the family, lacking the surplus chromosomes, suffered fatal hemorrhages within hours of the creature's visitation. The family knows the creature destroyed Rowan Mayfair, and that it is a menace to other Mayfair females, that it will use up their lives rapidly in an effort to find one who can survive fertilization and successfully give birth. The family will close ranks, protect itself and hide this knowledge, just as it has always done with such occult secrets in the past. It will seek the creature in its own fashion, using its immense resources. It will not allow the world outside to assist or to know.'

'What is the danger to Aaron? I don't see it from what you say.'

'Very obvious. Aaron knows about this creature. He knows what it is. In the first days after Christmas, before the Mayfairs understood what had happened, careless things were done. Forensic evidence was gathered from the site of the creature's birth. It was sent to an impersonal agency. Then Rowan herself contacted a doctor in San Francisco, sending him tissue samples of this creature and of herself. This was a terrible error. The doctor who analyzed these materials in a private institute in San Francisco is now dead. The doctor who delivered the material, who came here to discuss it with the family, has completely disappeared. Last night he left his hotel here without explanation. He has not been seen since. In New York, the genetic tests done in connection with this creature have vanished. Same in a genetic institute in Europe to which the New York institution sent samples of his work. All traces of the being are now gone from official sources.

'But we . . . we the Talamasca know all about this being. We know everything about him. More even than the poor unfortunates who studied his cells beneath the microscope. More even than the family now struggling to protect itself from him. The being will seek to eradicate our knowledge. This was inevitable. Perhaps . . . an error in judgment was made.'

'What do you mean?'

The waitress set down the small cup of black espresso. Yuri tested the porcelain with his fingers. Too hot.

'We watch and we are always here,' said Stolov. 'This is our motto. But sometimes these powerful things we watch, these brooding and unclassifiable forms of energy or evil or whatever they are – these things seek to destroy all witnesses, and we must suffer the consequences of our long vigilance, of our understanding, so to speak. Perhaps if we had been better prepared for the birth of this being. But then . . . I am not sure anyone knew that such a thing was really possible. And now . . . it is too late.

'This thing will surely try to kill Aaron. It will try to kill you. It will try to kill me once it knows that I am involved in this investigation. That is why something has changed with the Talamasca. That is why something, as you said, is not right. The Elders have bolted the doors; the Elders would assist the family, yes, insofar as they can. But the Elders will not allow our members to be placed in jeopardy. They will not stand by idle as this thing seeks to invade our archives, and destroy our priceless records. As I said . . . these things have happened before. We have a mode for such assaults.'

'Yet it isn't an emergency.'

'No, it is merely another way of operating. A tightening of security; a protective concealment of evidence; a demand for blind obedience on the part of those in danger. That you, and that Aaron go back to the Motherhouse at once.'

'Aaron refuses to do this?'

'Adamantly. He will not leave the family. He regrets his obedience on Christmas Day.'

'So what is the official goal of the Order? Merely to protect itself?'

'To do the extreme protective thing.'

'I don't get you.'

'Yes, you do. The extreme protective measure is to destroy the threat. But that is what you must leave to us. To me and to my investigators. For we know how to do this, how to track this being, how to locate it, how to close in upon it, and how to stop it from achieving its goals.'

'And you want me to believe that our Order, our beloved Talamasca, has done this sort of thing in the past.'

'Absolutely. We cannot be passive when our own survival is at stake. We have another mode of operation. In that mode, you and Aaron can play no part.'

'There are pieces missing from this picture.'

'How so? I thought it was very complete.'

'You speak of a threat to the family. You speak of a threat to the Order. What about the threat to others? What is the moral disposition of this entity? If it does mate successfully, what will be the consequences?'

'Ah, but that will not happen. It is unthinkable that that should happen. You do not know what you ask.'

'Oh, I think I do,' said Yuri. 'I spoke, after all, with those who've seen it. Once this creature has secured the proper females, it could propagate at remarkable speed – the sort of speed one sees in the insect world or the world of reptiles, a speed so much greater than that of other mammals that it would soon overrun them, over-power them, conceivably wipe them out.'

'You are very clever. You know too much about this thing. It's unfortunate that you read the file, that you went to Donnelaith. But don't fear, this creature will not succeed. And who knows its life span? Who knows but that its hour, with or without propagation, would not be short?'

Stolov lifted his knife and fork, cut a small wedge-shaped piece from the sweet roll on the plate before him and ate it silently, while Yuri watched. Then he set down the knife and fork and looked at Yuri.

'Persuade Aaron to go back with you. Persuade him to leave the Mayfair family and their problems in our hands.'

'You know, it just doesn't sound right,' said Yuri. 'There is so much involved here. And you don't speak of the big picture. And this is not the style of the Talamasca which I know. This thing, it is so dangerous ... No. This does not fit with what I know of my Order, my brethren, not at all.'

'What in the world can you possibly mean?'

'You're very patient with me. I appreciate it. But our Order is too smooth for all this. The Elders know how to take care of everything without creating suspicion and alarm. There's something crude about the way it all happened. It would have been a simple thing for the Elders to keep me contented in London. To keep Aaron contented. But this is all clumsy, hasty. Impolite. I don't know. This is not the Talamasca to me.'

'Yuri, the Order expected your complete obedience. It had a right to expect it.' For the first time, the man displayed a tiny bit of anger. He laid his napkin down on the table, rudely, beside his fork. Dirty napkin on the table. Napkin smeared with sugar and stained with droplets of coffee. Yuri stared at it.

'Yuri,' said Stolov. 'Women have died in the last forty-eight hours. This doctor, Samuel Larkin, is probably dead too. Rowan Mayfair will die sometime during the next few weeks. The Elders did not expect that you would cause them trouble at this hour. They did not anticipate that you would add to their burdens, any more than they anticipated Aaron's disloyalty.'

'Disloyalty?'

'I told you. He won't leave the family. But he is an old man. There is nothing he can do against Lasher. There never was!' Anger again.

Yuri sat back. He thought for a long moment. He stared at the napkin. The man picked it up, wiped his mouth with it again and laid it back down. Yuri stared at it.

'I want to communicate with the Elders,' said Yuri. 'I want to know these things from them.'

'Of course. Take Aaron with you today. Take him to New York. You're tired. Rest first if you will, but only in a location known to us. Then go. And when you reach New York, you can contact the Elders. You will have time. You can discuss this between you, you and Aaron, and then you must go on back to London. You must go home.'

Yuri stood up. He laid the napkin on the chair. 'Are you coming with me to see Aaron?'

'Yes, maybe it is for the best that you are here. Maybe it is for the best, for on my own I don't know that I could ever have convinced him to leave here. We'll go now. It's time I talked to him myself.'

'You mean you have not done that?'

'Yuri, I have my hands full, as they say. And Aaron is not cooperative now.'

There was a car waiting for them, an egregious American Lincoln limousine. It was lined in gray velvet. Its glass was so dim that the outside world fell under an edict of utter night. Impossible to really see a city through such windows, Yuri thought. He sat very still. He was thinking of something that had happened to him years ago.

He was remembering the long train ride with his mother into Serbia. She had given him something. An ice pick, though he did not know what it was at the time. It was a long rounded and pointed instrument, made of metal, with a wooden handle which had once been painted, and from which the paint had been chipped away.

'Here, you keep this,' she'd said. 'You use it if you have to. You stick it straight in . . . between the ribs.'

How fierce she'd looked in those moments. And he had been so startled. 'But who's going to hurt us?' he had asked. He did not know at this moment whatever became of the ice pick. Perhaps it had been left on the train.

He had failed her, hadn't he? Failed her and himself. And now he realized – as this smooth car went up on the freeway, and gained speed – he had no weapon, no ice pick, no knife. Even the Swiss Army knife he carried he had left at home because he was taking a plane. They don't want such things on a plane.

'You'll feel better once you've communicated with the Elders, once you've reported in and been officially invited to return home.'

Yuri looked at Stolov, who sat there all in priestly black, with only a bit of white collar showing, and his large pale hands opening and closing as they rested on his knees.

Yuri smiled very deliberately. 'You're right,' he said. 'A fax sent to a number in Amsterdam. It is so well calculated to inspire trust.'

'Yuri, please, we need you,' said the man with visible and heartfelt distress.

'I'm sure you do. How far are we from Aaron?'

'Only a few minutes. Everything here is small. Only a few minutes, and we will be there.'

Yuri took the black mouthpiece from the velvet-paneled wall. 'Driver,' he said.

'Yes, sir.'

'I want you to stop at a place that sells weapons, guns. You know such a place? Not far out of the way for us?'

'Yes, sir, South Rampart Street.'

'That will be fine.'

'Why are you doing this?' asked Stolov, pale bushy eyebrows knitted, face almost sad.

'It's the gypsy in me,' said Yuri. 'Don't worry.'

The man on South Rampart Street had an arsenal beneath the glass and on the wall behind him. 'You need a Louisiana driver's license,' he said.

Stolov was watching. This infuriated Yuri, that Stolov stood there, watching, as if he were entitled.

'This is an emergency,' said Yuri. 'I need a gun with a long barrel, there, that's fine. Three fifty-seven Magnum. A box of cartridges. Here.' He took the money out of his pocket, hundred-dollar bills, ten of them, then twenty, slowly counted out. 'Do not worry,' he said. 'I am not a crook. But I need the gun. You understand?'

He loaded it there, in the shadowy little store with Stolov watching. He put the rest of the bullets into his pockets, divided up in little handfuls, heavy, loose.

As they stepped into the sunlight, Stolov said:

'You think it's a simple matter of shooting this thing?'

'No. You are going to stop it, remember? We are going home, Aaron and I. But we are in danger. You said so. Terrible danger. And now I have my gun.' He gestured to the car. 'After you.'

'You must not do anything stupid or foolish,' said the other man. It wasn't anger this time, just apprehension. He laid his hand on Yuri's hand. Yuri looked down. He thought how pale was the skin of this Norwegian, and how dark was his own.

'Like what?'

'Like try to shoot it, that's what.' The man was exasperated. 'The Order has a right,' he said, 'to finer devotion than this.'

'Hmmm. I understand. Don't worry about it. As we say all over the world where English is spoken, no problem! OK?'

He flashed a smile at Stolov and opened the door of the car for him and waited for him to get in. Now it was Stolov who was suspicious, uneasy, even a little frightened.

And I barely know how to pull the trigger, Yuri thought.

TWENTY-SIX

Mona had never thought her first days at Mayfair and Mayfair would be like this. She was at the big desk in Pierce's spacious dark-paneled office, typing furiously on a 386 SX IBM-compatible computer, just a tad slower than the monster she had at home.

Rowan Mayfair was still alive now eighteen hours after surgery, and twelve hours after they'd taken her off the machines. Any minute she might stop breathing. Or she might live for weeks. Nobody really knew.

The investigation was forging ahead. Nothing to do right now but stay with the others, and think, and wait, and write.

She banged away on the white keyboard, faintly annoyed by the noisy click. 'Confidential to File from Mona Mayfair' was her title. It was protected. No one could access this material except Mona herself. When she got home, she'd transfer via modem. But for now, she couldn't leave here. This is where she belonged. She had been here since last night. She was writing down everything she had seen, heard, felt, thought.

Meantime every room in the vast complex of offices was occupied, busy soft voices speaking steadily and in conflict with each other, into different phones, behind partially open doors. Couriers came and went.

It was quiet, without panic. Ryan was behind his

desk in the large office, as they called it, with Randall, and Anne Marie. Lauren was down the hall. Sam Mayfair and two of the Grady Mayfairs from New York were in the conference rooms using all three phones. Somewhere, Liz Mayfair and Cecilia Mayfair made their calls. The family secretaries, Connie, Josephine and Louise Mayfair, were working in another conference room. Faxes kept rolling in on every machine in the place.

Pierce was here with Mona, letting her have the big machine, on his mammoth mahogany desk, and looking rather defenseless at his secretary's smaller, more humble computer, in his tie and shirtsleeves, his coat on the back of the chair. He was not doing much of anything, however. He was simply too sleepy, and too grief-stricken, as Mona herself ought to have been, but was not.

The investigation was entirely private, and it could not have been handled any better by anyone else.

They had begun last night in earnest an hour after Rowan had been found. Several times Pierce and Mona had returned to the hospital. They had been there again at sunrise. And then gone back to work. Ryan, Pierce, Mona and Lauren were the nucleus of the investigation. Randall and several of the others came and went. It was now some eighteen hours since they had commenced their phone calls, their faxes, their communications. It was getting on dusk, and Mona was lightheaded and hungry, but much too excited to think about either thing.

Someone would bring some supper in a little while, wouldn't they? Or maybe they would go uptown. Mona didn't want to leave the office. She figured the next piece of information would be from a Houston emergency room, where the mysterious man, six and a half feet tall, had had to seek some sort of medical help.

The Houston truck driver had been the most important link.

This was the man who had picked up Rowan yesterday afternoon. He had stopped in St Martinville last night to tell the local police about the thin, crazed woman who had struck off on her own into the swamps. On account of him, they had found Rowan. He had been called, questioned further. He had described the place in Houston where she'd run up to his truck. He told all the things she said, how she was desperate to get to New Orleans. He confirmed that as of yesterday evening when he last saw her, Rowan had been right in the head. Crazed perhaps, but talking, walking, thinking. Then she had gone off alone into the swamps.

'That woman was in pain,' he'd told Mona on the phone this morning, recapitulating the entire tale. 'She was hugging herself, you know, like a woman having cramps.'

Gerald Mayfair, still stunned and sick over the fact that Dr Samuel Larkin had slipped away from his care and vanished, had gone with Shelby, Pierce's big sister, and Patrick, Mona's father, off to the swamp near St Martinville to search the spot where Rowan had been found.

Rowan had been hemorrhaging, just like the others, though she was not dead. At twelve last night they had performed an emergency hysterectomy on the unconscious woman, with only Michael there – in tears – to consent. It was either that or she'd never make it till morning. Incomplete miscarriage. Other complications. 'Look, we're lucky she's still breathing.'

And breathing she was.

Who knew what they might discover up there in the grass in that St Martinville swamp park? It was Mona who had suggested this and was all for going herself. Patrick, her dad, was all sobered up now and determined to be of help. Ryan had wanted Mona to remain here with him. Mona couldn't quite figure that one. Was Ryan worried about her?

But then when Ryan started to buzz her over the intercom every few minutes to ask her some minor question, or make some minor suggestion, she knew that he simply wanted her support. OK by her. She was there to give it. In between calls, she typed, she wrote, she recorded, she described.

The Houston office building had been discovered before noon.

It was only walking distance from where Rowan had appeared on the highway. Unoccupied except for the fifteenth floor, which had been leased to a man and a woman. The fifteenth floor was a grim scene. Rowan had been a prisoner. For long periods Rowan had been tied to a bed. The mattress was filthy with urine and feces, yet it had been laid with fresh sheets, and surrounded by flowers, some of which were still fresh. There was fresh food.

It was ghastly, all of it. There had been plenty of blood – not Rowan's – in the bathroom. The man had been hurt there, obviously, maybe even knocked unconscious. Photographs of the bathroom had already come in. But the bloody footprints leading to the elevator, and out the front doors of the building, clearly indicated he had left on his own.

'Looks to me from this like he fell again in the

elevator. See that. That's blood all over the carpet. He's weak, he's hurt.'

Well, he had been *then*, but was he still hurt now?

They were canvassing every emergency room in the entire city. Every hospital, clinic, doctor's office. They would check the suburbs, and then move in concentric circles, checking, until they found where the bleeding man had gone. Within the direct vicinity of the building they were checking door to door. They were checking alleyways, and rooftops, restaurants, buildings that were boarded up. If the man was anywhere nearby, wounded, they would find him.

As it was, the bloody foot tracks had vanished under the wheels of the passing traffic. Whether the man had climbed into a vehicle or simply crossed to the other side could never be known.

The entire investigation was private, the best that money could buy.

One agency after another had been enlisted. Tasks were constantly being assigned, information collated. Private doctors had gathered the blood samples in the Houston bathroom and taken them to private laboratories, the names of which were known only to Lauren and Ryan. The grim prison rooms had been fingerprinted. Every article of clothing, and there had been many, had been packed, labeled and shipped to Mayfair and Mayfair. Things had already started to arrive.

Other leads were being followed. Crumpled stationery and a plastic door key card found in Houston had been traced to a hotel in New York. People were being questioned. Rowan's truck driver was being brought in, at family expense, to give yet another thorough verbal report.

It was a hideous picture, the empty office tower, the filthy prison cell. Dead flowers. The broken porcelain on the bloody floor. Rowan had escaped, but then something dreadful had happened to Rowan. It had happened out in a grass field under a famous tree called Gabriel's Oak. A beautiful spot. Mona knew it. Lots of schoolkids knew it. You went to St Martinville to see it, the Arcadian Museum, and Gabriel's Oak. There was Evangeline Oak in the city of St Martinville, and Gabriel's Oak out there near the old house. Gabriel leaning on his elbows, they said, to wait for Evangeline. Well, Rowan had gone down between the elbows in the grass.

Toxic shock, allergic reaction, immuno-failure. A hundred comparisons had been drawn. But the blood revealed no toxins any longer, not last night, not today. Whatever had happened with the miscarriage was over. Possibly she had simply lost the child and passed out.

Ugly, ugly, all of it.

But could anything have been uglier than the actual sight of Rowan Mayfair, in the white hospital bed, her head straight up on the pillow, her arms by her sides motionless, her eyes staring into space? She had been greatly emaciated, white as paper, but the worst part was the attitude of the arms, parallel, slightly turned in, and the utter blankness of her face. All personality was gone from her expression. She looked faintly idiotic lying there, eyes far too round, and completely unresponsive to movement or to light. Her mouth looked small and strangely round also, as though it had lost whatever character caused it to lengthen into a woman's mouth. Even as Mona sat there watching, Rowan's arms began to pull in closer to the body. The nurses would reach over to stretch them out.

Rowan's hair was thin, as if much of it had fallen out. More evidence of severe malnutrition and the aborted pregnancy. She was so small in the white hospital gown she might as well have been an angel in a Christmas pageant.

And then there was Michael, mussed and shaken, sitting beside her, talking to her, telling her that he was going to take care of her, that everyone was gathered, that she mustn't be afraid. He told her he would put colored pictures up in her room, and he would play music. He had found an old gramophone. He would play that for her. He talked on and on. 'We're going to take care of everything. We're going to . . . going to take care of everything.'

He was scared of saying something like, 'We'll find this bastard thing, this monster.' No, who would want to say that to the innocent, blank creature lying there, the grotesque remnant of a woman who knew how to operate with perfect precision and success upon other people's brains?

Mona knew that Rowan couldn't hear anything. There was nothing in there listening anymore. The brain was still working, a little, causing the lungs to function at a completely mechanical pace, causing the heart to pump with the same frightening regularity, but the outer extremities of the body grew more and more cold.

At any moment the brain might stop giving orders. The body would die. The mind had no concern for itself any longer. The boss of the body had fled. The electroencephalogram was almost flat.

The tiny little blips here and there were no more than you would get if you hooked up the machine to a dead brain in a room on a table. You always got something, they said.

Rowan had been badly physically hurt. That was really ugly. There were bruises on her pale arms and legs. There was evidence of a spontaneous fracture in her left hip. She bore the bruises and marks of rape. The miscarriage had been extremely violent. There was blood and fluid on her thighs.

At six o'clock this morning they had shut off the respirator. She had suffered no complications from the swift and simple surgery. All the tests were completed.

They had rushed to take her home at 10 a.m. for one simple reason. They had not expected her to live out the day. Her instructions had been very explicit. She had written them out when she took possession of the legacy. She was to die in the house on First Street. 'My home.' It was all in her own handwriting, completed in the happy days right before the wedding, beautifully in keeping with the spirit of the legacy. To die in Mary Beth's bed.

Also there was the superstition of the family to consider. People were standing in the corridors of Mercy Hospital and saying, 'She should die in the master bedroom. She should be home.' 'They ought to take her home to First Street.' Old Grandpa Fielding had been adamant. 'She will not die in this hospital. You are torturing her. To release her, you must take her home.'

Mayfair madness in high gear. Even Anne Marie was saying that she ought to be returned to the famous master bedroom. Who knew? Perhaps the spirits of the dead in the house could help her? Even Lauren said bitterly, 'Take the woman home.'

The nuns might have been shocked, if anybody gave a damn, but probably not. Cecilia and Lily had said the rosary aloud in the hospital room all night. Magdalene and Liane and Guy Mayfair had prayed in the chapel with the two Mayfair nuns in the family, the little tiny nuns whose names Mona always mixed up.

Old Sister Michael Marie Mayfair – the oldest of Mayfair Sisters of Mercy – had come down and prayed over Rowan, loudly, chanting Hail Marys and Our Fathers and Glory Bes.

'If that doesn't wake her up,' said Randall, 'nothing will. Go home and get her bedroom ready.'

Beatrice had done it, with a heavy contingent of helpers – Stephanie and Spruce Mayfair, and two young black policemen – reluctant as she was to leave Aaron there.

Now, back at First Street, enshrined beneath the satin-lined half tester and covered with ancient quilts and imported coverlets, Rowan Mayfair continued to breathe, unaided. It was already 6 p.m. and she was not dead.

An hour ago, they had commenced intravenous feeding – fluids, lipids. 'It is not life support,' said Dr Fleming. 'It is nourishment. Otherwise, we would be technically starving her to death.'

Michael apparently hadn't argued. But then there were so many people involved. When he called, he told Mona the room was full of nurses and doctors. He confirmed that the security men were all over, and on the gallery outside the window, and down in the street. People were wondering what was happening.

But the armed guards were not such an unfamiliar sight in a city like New Orleans in this day and age. Everybody hired them for parties, get-togethers. When you went to school for a nighttime function there they were at the gates. The drugstores had guards near the register. Just the way of this banana republic, Gifford had said once.

Mona had answered, 'Yeah, so brilliant. Guys at minimum wage with loaded thirty-eights.'

However crude, these measures had been relentless and effective for the family.

No further assaults had been made on Mayfair women. All the women were gathered in at various houses. There was no group smaller than six or seven. There was no group without men.

A separate fleet of detectives brought in from Dallas combed the city of Houston, fanning out from the building, asking anyone and everyone if he or she had seen this tall black-haired man. They had made drawings of him, based on Aaron's verbal description, which had come to him through the Talamasca.

They were also searching for Dr Samuel Larkin. They could not understand why he had left the Pontchartrain Hotel without telling anyone – until they found the message at the desk which had been called up to his room.

'Meet Rowan. Come alone.'

The message had everyone worried. It was a cinch Rowan had not called Dr Larkin. Rowan was already on a hospital gurney in St Martinville by the time the call had come in.

Samuel Larkin had been last seen walking fast up St Charles Avenue, towards Jackson. 'You be careful now,' a cabdriver had said, begrudgingly perhaps because the doctor wouldn't hire the taxi. What did it matter? It had definitely been Dr Larkin. And by the time Gerald hit the pavement, there was no sign of him in sight.

In a way, Beatrice Mayfair had been the biggest

nuisance and the biggest consolation the entire time. Beatrice was the one who kept insisting on normal procedures, who kept refusing to believe that anything 'horrible' had really happened, that they should send for specialists and take more tests.

Beatrice had always taken that position. She was the one who went to call on poor crazy Deirdre and take her candy, which she could not eat, and silk negligees she never wore. She was the one who came three or four times a year to visit Ancient Evelyn, even during periods when Ancient Evelyn had not talked for six months.

'Well, sweetheart, it's just the most dreadful shame they closed the Holmes lunch counter. Do you remember all the times we went down there to lunch at D. H. Holmes, you and me and Millie and Belle?'

And there she was at the house now fussing in the bedroom, most likely. And gone back up to Amelia Street to make sure everyone had something to eat. Good thing Michael liked Beatrice. But then everybody liked her. And the most amazing thing about her constant optimism was that she was clearly going to marry Aaron Lightner, and if anybody knew something horrible had happened it was Lightner, beyond doubt.

Aaron Lightner had taken one long look at Rowan and then walked out of the room. The expression on his face had been so wrathful, so dark. He had stared at Mona for a moment, and then he had gone off fast down the corridor to find a phone he could use in private, to call Dr Larkin, and that is when they discovered that Dr Larkin had left the suite.

What in the world did Beatrice and Aaron talk about with each other? She would say one minute, 'Well, we ought to inject her with something, you know, to give her energy!' And all but clap her hands. And he would just stand there in the dim corridor, refusing to answer the questions put to him by the others, staring fixedly at Mona, and then at nothing, and then at Mona, and then at nothing, until the others simply started talking to one another and forgot he was there.

Nobody reported a strange fragrance in the rooms in Houston. But as soon as the first package had come, containing clothing and pillow slips, Mona had smelled the fragrance.

'Yeah, that's it, that's the smell of this being,' she had said. Randall had raised his eyebrows. 'Well, I sure as hell don't know what that's got to do with it.'

Mona had defeated him cold by answering simply, 'Neither do I.'

Two hours later he had wandered in and said, 'You ought to go home and be with Ancient Evelyn.'

'There are seventeen different women in that house now, and six different men. What makes you think I ought to go there? I don't want to be there now. I don't want to see my mother's stuff, and her things and all. I don't want to. It's illogical to go up there. It makes no sense for the daughter of the dead woman to go up there. Which I am. Why don't you lie down and take a nap?'

One of the agencies had called directly after, but only to report that no one, absolutely no one, had seen the mysterious man leave the Houston building. Every single reported death in the entire Houston area was being investigated. None fitted the pattern of the deceased Mayfair women. Each had its own context, precluding the involvement of the mysterious man.

The net was huge; the net was fine-spun; the net was strong.

Then at five had come the first reports from the airlines. Yes, a person with long black flowing hair, beard and mustache had taken the three o'clock flight Ash Wednesday from New Orleans to Houston. First Class aisle seat. Exceptionally tall and soft-spoken. Beautiful manner, beautiful eyes.

Had he taken a taxi from the airport – a limo? A bus? Houston's airport was enormous. But there were hundreds of people asking questions, proceeding quietly to one potential witness after another. 'If he walked, we'll find somebody who saw him.'

'What about planes from Houston to here? Last night? Yesterday?' Checking, checking, checking.

Finally Mona thought, I'm going up there. I'm going to go see my cousin Rowan Mayfair. I'm going to make my call. It made her choke up. She couldn't speak or think for a minute. But she had to go.

It was now dark.

A fax had just come in, a copy of the boarding ticket issued to the mysterious man by the airlines when he had flown back to Houston on Ash Wednesday. He had used the name Samuel Newton. He had paid for the ticket with cash. Samuel Newton. If there was such a person in any public record anywhere in the continental United States, he would surely be found.

But then he might have made up the name on the spur of the moment. He had drunk milk on the plane, glass after glass of milk. They had had to go back to coach to get him more milk. Not much happens on a flight between New Orleans and Houston. It isn't long enough. But they had given him his milk.

Mona stared at the computer screen.

'We do not have a clue as to the man's whereabouts.

But all the women are protected. If another death is discovered, it will be an old death.'

Then she hit the key to save and close the file. She waited as the tiny lights flashed. Then she hit the off button. The low drone of the fan died away.

She stood up, groping for a purse, on instinct, her hand always going back at such a moment right to where she had dropped the purse, though she herself did not know where that was.

She slipped the strap over her shoulder. Her feet hurt just a little in her mother's smooth grown-up leather shoes. The suit wasn't all that bad. The blouse was pretty. But the shoes? Forget it. That part of being a woman held not the slightest charm.

A little memory came back to her. She was drifting. Aunt Gifford was telling her about buying the first pair of heels. 'They would only let us have French heels. We went to Maison Blanche. Ancient Evelyn and I. And I wanted the high high heels, but she said no.'

Pierce gave a start. He had been almost asleep when he saw her standing behind the desk.

'I'm going uptown,' she said.

'Not by yourself, you're not. You're not even riding down in the elevator alone.'

'I know that. There are guards everywhere. I'm riding the streetcar. I have to think.'

Naturally he came with her.

He had not rested for one hour since his mother's funeral and certainly not before that. Poor handsome Pierce, standing desolate and anxious on the corner of Carondolet and Canal, amid the common crowd, waiting for a streetcar. He'd probably never ridden it in his life.

'You should have called Clancy before you left,' she said to him. 'Clancy called earlier. Did they tell you?'

He nodded. 'Clancy's all right. She's with Claire and Jenn. Jenn is crying. She wanted you to be with her.'

'I can't do that now.' Jenn. Jenn was still a little kid. You couldn't tell any of this to Jenn. And protecting Jenn would be too much hard work.

The streetcar was jammed with tourists. Very few of the real people at all. The tourists wore bright, neatly pressed clothes because the weather was still cool. When the humid summer came on, they would be as disheveled and half-naked as everyone else. Mona and Pierce sat quiet together on a wooden seat as the car screeched and roared through lower St Charles Avenue, the small Manhattan-style canyon of office buildings, then around Lee Circle and on uptown.

It was almost magical what happened at the corner of Jackson and St Charles. The oaks sprang up, huge, dark and hovering over the Avenue. The shabby stucco buildings fell away. The world of the columns and the magnolias began. The Garden District. You could almost feel the quiet surround you, press against you, lift you out of yourself.

Mona got off the car in front of Pierce and crossed quickly over to the river side, cut across Jackson and started up St Charles. It was not so cold right now. Not here. It was mild and windless. The cicadas were singing. It seemed early in the year for them, but she was glad, she loved the sound. She had never figured out if there was a season for cicadas. Seems they sang at all different times of the year. Maybe every time it got warm enough, they woke up. She had loved them all her life. Couldn't live in a place that didn't purr like this now and then, she thought, walking back the broken pavements of First Street.

Pierce walked along saying nothing, looking vaguely astonished whenever she glanced at him, as though he were falling asleep on his feet.

As they reached Prytania they could see people outside the big house, see the cars parked. See the guards. Some of the guards wore khaki and were from a private agency. Others were off-duty New Orleans policemen in their customary blue.

Mona couldn't stand the high heels any longer. She took them off and walked in her stocking feet.

'If you step on one of those big roaches, you're going to hate it,' Pierce said.

'Boy, you're sure right about that.'

'Oh, that's your new technique, Mona. I heard you use it on Randall. Just flat-out agree. You're going to catch cold in your bare feet. You're going to tear your stockings.'

'Pierce, the roaches don't come out this time of year. But what's the point of my telling you this? Are you going to listen? You realize our mothers are dead, Pierce? Our mothers? Both dead. Have I said this to you before?'

'I don't remember,' he said. 'It's hard to remember that they're dead, as a matter of fact. I keep thinking, my mother will know what to do about all this, she'll be here any minute. Did you know that my father was not faithful to my mother?'

'You're crazy.'

'No, there was another woman. I saw him with her this morning, down in the coffee shop in the building. He was holding her hand. She's a Mayfair. Her name's Clemence. He kissed her.'

'She's a worried cousin. She works in the building. I used to see her all the time down there at lunch.'

'No, she's a woman for my father. I'll bet my mother knew all about it. I hope she didn't care.'

'I'm not going to believe that about Uncle Ryan,' said Mona, instantly realizing that she did believe it. She did. Uncle Ryan was such a handsome man, so accomplished, so successful, and he'd been married so long to Gifford.

Best not to think of those things. Gifford in the vault, cleanly dead and buried before the slaughter. Mourned while there was still time to mourn. Of Alicia, what could you say, 'Would she had died hereafter?' Mona realized she didn't even know where her mother's body had been taken. Was it at the hospital? At the morgue? She didn't want to think it was in the morgue. Well, she can sleep now forever. Passed out for all time. Mona started to choke up again, and swallowed hard.

They crossed Chestnut Street, pushing through the small informal gathering of guards and cousins – Eulalee, and Tony, and Betsy Mayfair. Garvey Mayfair on the porch with Danny and Jim. Several voices rose at once to tell the guards that Mona and Pierce could come in.

Guards in the hallway. Guard in the double parlor. A guard in the door to the dining room, a dark hulking figure, with broad hips.

And only that faint old lingering smell. Nothing fresh, nothing new. Just faint, the way it had clung to the clothing from Houston. The way it had clung to Rowan when they brought her in.

Guards at the top of the stairs. Guard at the bedroom door. Guard inside at the long window to the gallery.

Nurse in slick cheap nylon white with her arms raised, adjusting the IV. Rowan under the lace coverlet, small insignificant expressionless face against the big ruffled pillow. Michael sitting there, smoking a cigarette.

'There isn't any oxygen in here, is there?'

'No, dear, they got on my case already about that.' He took another drag defiantly, and then crushed it out in the glass ashtray on the bedside table. His voice was beautifully low and soft, rubbed smooth by the tragedy.

In the corner opposite sat young Magdalene Mayfair, and old Aunt Lily, both very still in straight-backed chairs. Magdalene was saying her rosary, and the amber beads glinted just a little as she slipped one bead more through her hand. Lily's eyes were closed.

Others in the shadows. The beam of the bedside lamp fell directly on the face of Rowan Mayfair. As if it were a keylight for a camera. The unconscious woman seemed smaller than a small child. Urchin or angelic. Her hair was all swept back.

Mona tried to find the old expression in her, the stamp of her personality. All gone.

'I was playing music,' Michael said, speaking in the same low thoughtful voice as before. He looked up at Mona. 'I was playing the Victrola. Julien's Victrola. And then the nurse said, perhaps she didn't like that sound. It's scratchy, it's . . . special. You would have to like it, wouldn't you?'

'The nurse probably didn't like it,' said Mona. 'You want me to put on a record? If you want, I can get your radio from the library downstairs. I saw it, yesterday, in there, by your chair.'

'No, that's all right. Can you come here and sit for a little while? I'm glad to see you. You know I saw Julien.'

Pierce stiffened. In the corner, another Mayfair, was his name Hamilton, glanced suddenly at Michael and then away. Lily's eyes opened and veered to the left to fix upon Michael. Magdalene went on with her rosary, eyes taking in all of them slowly, and then returning to Michael as he went on.

It was as if Michael had forgotten they were there. Or he didn't give a damn anymore.

'I saw him,' he said in a raw ragged whisper, 'and ah . . . he told me so many things. But he didn't tell me this would happen. He didn't tell me she was coming home.'

Mona took the small velvet chair beside him, facing the bed.

She said in a low voice, resenting the others, 'Julien probably didn't know.'

'Do you mean, *Oncle* Julien?' asked Pierce in a small timid whisper from across the room. Hamilton Mayfair turned and looked directly at Michael as though this was the most fascinating thing in the world.

'Hamilton, what are you doing here?' asked Mona.

'We're all taking turns,' said Magdalene in a little whisper. Then Hamilton said, 'We just want to be here.'

There was something decorous about all of them, yet despairing. Hamilton must have been about twenty-five now. He was good-looking, not beautiful and sparkling like Pierce, but very handsome in his own too narrow way. She couldn't remember the last time she had spoken to him. He looked directly at her as he rested his back against the mantel.

'All the cousins are here,' he said.

Michael looked at her as if he hadn't heard these others speaking. 'What do you mean,' asked Michael, 'that Julien didn't know? He must have known.'

'It's not like that, Michael,' she said, trying to keep it a whisper. 'There's an old Irish saying, "a ghost knows his own business." Besides, it wasn't really him, you know. When the dead come, they aren't there.'

'Oh no,' said Michael in a small, weary but very sincere voice. 'It was Julien. He was there. We talked together for hours.'

'No, Michael. It's like the record. You put the needle in the groove and she sings. But she's not in the room.'

'No, he was there,' Michael said softly, though not argumentatively. He reached over almost absently and picked up Rowan's hand. Rowan's arm resisted him slightly, the hand wanted to be close to the body. He gripped it gently and then he leaned over and kissed it.

Mona wanted to kiss him, to touch him, to say something, to apologize, to confess, to say she was sorry, to say don't worry, but she couldn't think of the right words. She had a deep terrible fear that he hadn't seen Oncle Julien, that he was simply losing his mind. She thought about the Victrola, about the moment when she and Ancient Evelyn had sat on the library floor with the Victrola between them, and Mona had wanted to crank it, and Ancient Evelyn said, 'We cannot play music while Gifford is waiting. We cannot play radios or pianos while Gifford is laid out.'

'What did Oncle Julien actually tell you?' asked Pierce, in his baffled innocent fashion. Not making fun. Truly wanting to know what Michael would say.

'Don't worry,' said Michael. 'There'll be a time. Soon, I think. And I'll know what to do.'

'You sound so sure of yourself,' said Hamilton Mayfair in a low voice. 'I wish I had an inkling of what was going on.'

643

'Forget about it,' said Mona.

'Now we should all be quiet,' said the nurse. 'Remember Dr Mayfair might be listening.' She nodded vigorously to them, a silent signal that they must pay attention. 'You don't want to say anything . . . disruptive, you know.'

The other nurse sat at a small mahogany table, writing, her white stockings stretched tight over her chubby legs.

'You hungry, Michael?' asked Pierce.

'No, son. Thank you.'

'I am,' said Mona. 'We'll be back. We're going downstairs to get something to eat.'

'You will come back, won't you?' asked Michael. 'Lord, you must be so tired, Mona. Mona, I'm sorry about your mother. I didn't know until afterwards.'

'That's OK,' said Mona. She wanted to kiss him. She wanted to say I stayed away all day because of what we did. I couldn't bring myself to come under her roof with her like this and me doing it with you, and I wouldn't have done it with you if I'd known she was coming home so soon and like this. I thought . . . I thought . . .

'I know, baby doll,' he said, smiling at her brightly. 'She doesn't care about that now. It's OK.'

Mona nodded, threw him her own secret passing smile.

Just before she went out the door, Michael lit another cigarette. Snap, flash, and both the nurses turned and glared at him.

'Shut up,' said Hamilton Mayfair.

'Let him smoke!' said Magdalene.

The nurses looked at each other, obdurate, cold. Why don't we get some other nurses? thought Mona.

'Yes,' said Magdalene softly, 'we'll see to that right away.'

Right on, thought Mona. She went out with Pierce and down the steps.

In the dining room sat a very elderly priest who must have been Timothy Mayfair from Washington. Clean and old-fashioned in his unmistakable suit, black shirt-front and gleaming white Roman collar. As Mona and Pierce passed, the elderly priest said in a loud echoing whisper to the woman next to him:

'You realize when she dies . . . there won't be a storm! For the first time, there won't be a storm.'

TWENTY-SEVEN

Aaron wasn't buying it either. They stood together, the three men, out on the lawn. Yuri wondered if later this would rank as one of the worst days of his life. Searching for Aaron, finding him at last in the evening, at this big pink house on this avenue, with the noisy streetcars passing, and with all those people weeping inside. And Stolov with him, every moment, an overbearing and confusing presence, uttering formal and soft words constantly as they had gone from the hotel to the Mayfair house on First Street and finally uptown to 'Amelia', as this sprawling mansion was apparently called.

Inside dozens of people wept, the way gypsies weep and wail at a funeral. There was much drinking. Clusters of persons stood outside smoking and talking. It was convivial yet tense. Everyone was waiting for something.

But no bodies were coming here. One was in the vault already, Yuri had learnt, and the others were in the freezer of the hospital very nearby. This was not a gathering to mourn; it was a defensive coming together, as if all the serfs had fled to the shelter of the castle, only these people had never been serfs.

Aaron didn't seem tense. He looked good, all things considered, as robust as Yuri had ever seen him, of good color, and with a sharpening to his face which came from his cold suspicion of Stolov as Stolov talked on and on. It seemed as if Aaron had become younger here, less his aging bookish self and more the energetic gentleman of years before. His white curly hair was longish and fuller around his face, and his eyes had their characteristic brightness. Whatever had happened here had not weakened him, or aged him. There was that deep tone of discouragement in him but it was now turning to anger.

Yuri knew because he knew Aaron so well. If Stolov knew he didn't show it. Stolov was too busy talking, trying to persuade them to his point of view.

They stood far away on the close-clipped grass, beneath what Aaron called a magnolia. It had no blossoms, this tree. Too early. But it had the largest shiniest green leaves.

On and on Stolov talked, in his quiet persuasive entirely sympathetic manner. And Aaron's eyes were two pieces of cold gray stone. Reflecting nothing. Revealing nothing except the anger. Aaron looked at Yuri. What did he see? Yuri shot a meaningful glance towards Stolov, but this was as narrow and quick as a splinter of light, a spark.

Aaron's eyes moved back to Stolov. Stolov had not glanced at Yuri. Stolov's attentions were entirely fixed upon Aaron, as if this was a victory he must have.

'If you won't leave tonight, then surely tomorrow,' said Stolov.

Aaron said nothing.

Stolov had poured out everything now, at least two complete times. A beautiful elderly woman with dark smooth gray hair stood at the end of the wooden porch and called to Aaron. He waved and gestured that he would be coming. He looked at Stolov.

'Good God, man, say something,' said Stolov. 'We know how hard this has been for you. Go on home to London. Take a well-deserved rest.'

Just wrong. Everything the man was saying, his manner, his words.

'Right you are,' said Aaron softly.

'What?' said Stolov.

'I'm not leaving, Erich. It's been a pleasure to finally make your acquaintance, and I know better than to try to deter you from obeying your orders. You're here to do something. You will try to do it. But I'm not leaving. Yuri, will you stay with me?'

'Now, Aaron,' said Stolov, 'that is very simply out of the question for Yuri. He is already . . .'

'Of course I will stay,' said Yuri. 'It was for you that I came.'

'Where are your lodgings, Erich? Are you at the Pontchartrain with the rest of us?' Aaron asked.

'Downtown,' said Stolov. He was getting impatient again, flustered. 'Aaron, you are no help to the Talamasca now.'

'I'm sorry,' said Aaron. 'But I must confess, Erich, that the Talamasca – at this moment – is no help to me. These are my people now, Erich. Glad to have met you.'

This was dismissal. Aaron extended his hand. The tall blond one looked for one moment as if he would lose his temper, then he cooled, and drew himself up. 'I'll contact you in the morning. Where will you be?'

'I don't know,' said Aaron. 'Probably here . . . with all these people,' he said. 'My people. I think it's the safest place for us now, don't you?'

'I don't know how you could take this attitude,

Aaron. We need your cooperation. As soon as possible, I want to make contact, speak with Michael Curry . . .'

'No. That is not going to happen, Erich. You do what the Elders told you to do, as I'm sure you will. But you will not bother this family, at least not with my permission or with my introduction.'

'Aaron, we want to help! That's why I am here.'

'Good-night, Erich.'

In sheer consternation, the blond one stood there silently, and then he turned on his heel and walked away. The big black car was waiting for him as it had been for two hours, during which this act had been played and replayed.

'He's lying,' said Aaron.

'He's not Talamasca,' said Yuri, though it was more a suggestion than a statement.

'Oh, yes, he is. He's one of us, and he's lying. Don't turn your back on him for an instant.'

'No, I wouldn't. But Aaron, how can this be? How can such a thing . . .'

'I don't know. I've heard of him. He's been with us for three years. I've heard of his work in Italy and in Russia. He's very much respected. David Talbot thought highly of him. If only we hadn't lost David. But Stolov's not so very clever. He can't read minds that well. He could perhaps if he himself weren't putting on such an act. But the façade requires all his cunning. And so he's not very good.'

The black car had silently slithered away from the curb.

'God, Yuri,' Aaron suddenly whispered. 'I'm glad you're here.'

'I am too, Aaron. I don't understand it. I want to

contact the Elders. I want to speak directly to someone, to hear a voice.'

'That will never happen, my boy,' said Aaron.

'Aaron, in the years before the computer, what did you do?'

'It was always typewritten. All communications went to the Motherhouse in Amsterdam, and the replies came by mail. Communication took greater time; less was said, I suspect. But there was never a voice attached to it, Yuri, or a face. In the days before the typewriter, a scribe wrote the letters for the Elders. No one knew who this was.'

'Aaron, let me tell you something.'

'I know what you're going to say,' said Aaron calmly, thoughtfully. 'You knew the Amsterdam Motherhouse well before you ever left it – every nook and cranny. You cannot imagine where the Elders came together, where they received their communications. Nobody knows.'

'Aaron, you have been in the Order for decades. You can appeal to the Elders. Surely there is some way under such circumstances . . .'

Aaron smiled in a cold, knowing way. 'Your expectations are higher than mine, Yuri,' he said.

The pretty gray-haired woman had left the porch and was coming towards them. Small-boned, with delicate wrists, she wore her simple flaring silk dress with grace. Her ankles were as slender and well-shaped as those of a girl.

'Aaron,' she said in a soft scolding whisper. Her hands flew out, youthful, dainty, covered with rings, and clasped Aaron by the shoulders, and then she gently kissed his cheek. Aaron nodded to her in quiet understanding.

'Come inside with us,' said Aaron to Yuri. 'They need us now. We'll talk later on.' His face had changed dramatically. Now that Stolov was gone, he appeared more serene, more like himself.

The house was filled with good rich cooking smells, and a high tempestuous mingle of voices. The laughter was loud, bursting, the merry ecstatic kind of laughter of people at a wake. One could hear others crying. Women and men crying. An old man sat with his arms folded before him on a table, crying. A young girl with soft brown hair patted his shoulder over and over, her own face evincing only fear.

Upstairs, Yuri was shown to a rear bedroom, small, faded, but quite appealing to him, with a narrow single four-poster bed, and a dark golden satin bedspread that had seen better days. There were dusty curtains on the windows. But he liked the warmth, the coziness, even the faded flowers on the wall. He glimpsed himself in the mirrored door of the chifforobe – dark hair, dark skin, too thin.

'I am grateful,' he said to the gray-haired woman, Beatrice, 'but don't you think I should go to the hotel, that I should look out for myself?'

'No,' said Aaron. 'Don't go anywhere. I want you here with me.'

Yuri was prepared to protest further. The house was needed for the family. But he could see simply that Aaron meant for him to stay here.

'Oh, now, don't start being sad again,' said the woman. 'I won't have it. Come on, now, we're going to have something to eat and some wine. Aaron, I want you to sit down and drink a nice cool glass of wine. You too, Yuri. Now, both of you come.'

They went down the rear stairs, into the warmer air, and the misty white layers of cigarette smoke. Around a breakfast table, near a bright fire, sat several people crying and laughing simultaneously. And one solemn man who merely stared morosely into the flames. Yuri could not actually see the fire. He stood behind the chimney, but he saw the flicker and he heard the crackle and he felt the warmth.

He was distracted suddenly by a wraith of a female creature in a small back room, looking out the rear window into the night. She was very old, fragile; she wore gabardine and withered lace, and a heavy golden pin that was a hand with diamonds for nails. Her fine-spun white hair was soft around her face, nested in the old-fashioned way, with pins against the back of her head. Another woman, younger yet still impossibly old, held the hand of this very old one as if she would protect her from something, though how, one could not tell.

'Come on, Ancient Evelyn, come with us,' said Beatrice. 'Come on, darling Viv. Let's go near the fire.'

The very old woman, Ancient Evelyn, whispered something softly under her breath. She pointed to the window, her finger dropping as if she hadn't strength to keep it aloft. Again she pointed; again the finger dropped.

'Come on, now, dear, you're doing it again,' said the woman addressed as Darling Viv. She was kind. 'I can't hear you. Now, Ancient Evelyn, you can talk.' She sounded as if she were coaxing a baby. 'You know you can. You were talking words all day yesterday. Talk, dear, talk so I can hear.'

The ancient one murmured again indistinctly. She

continued to point. All Yuri saw was the dark street, the neighboring houses, the lights, the dark heavy soaring trees.

Aaron took his arm.

A young woman with jet-black hair and beautiful gold earrings approached them. She wore a red wool dress, and a fancy belt. She stood near to the fire for a moment, warming her hands; then she drew closer, gathering the attention of Aaron and Beatrice, and even Darling Viv. There was a cool authority to her.

'Everyone's together,' she said to Aaron meaningfully. 'Everyone is all right. They are patrolling this block and the one across the street, and two blocks uptown and two blocks down.'

'It will be peaceful for a while, I think,' said Aaron. 'He blundered, like a child. He could have caused more death, more suffering . . .'

'Oh, darlings, please,' said Beatrice. 'Must we speak of this? Polly Mayfair, Sweetheart, go back downtown to the office. They need you there.'

Polly Mayfair, Sweetheart, ignored Beatrice completely.

'We're ready for him,' said Aaron. 'We are many and he is one. He'll come.'

'Come?' Polly Mayfair, Sweetheart, was puzzled. 'Why do you say he'll come? Why would he come? Shouldn't he be running away as fast as he can?'

'What if he's dead?' said Beatrice, 'assuming there is such a personage! What if he wandered from that building in Houston and simply . . . you know . . . expired on the street?' She shuddered.

'That would be too much to hope for,' said Aaron. 'But if it's happened, they'll find him and then we'll know.'

'Oh, God, I hope so,' said Polly Mayfair, Sweetheart. 'I hope she killed him when she hit him. I hope he staggered out and died.'

'I don't,' said Aaron. 'I don't want him to hurt anyone else. That must not happen. He must not harm anyone. That he brought harm is unspeakable. But I want to see him; I want to talk to him; I want to hear what he has to say. I should have confronted him a long time ago. I was a fool, a fool for others, as they say. But I cannot miss this opportunity now. I want to talk to him. Ask him what he thinks, where the hell he comes from, what he truly wants?'

'Aaron, let's not go into the ghost stories,' pleaded Beatrice. 'Come, all of you –'

'You think it will be like that? He'll speak?' asked Polly Mayfair, Sweetheart. 'I never thought of it. I thought we'd find him and we'd, you know . . . take care of this . . . destroy him. We would put an end to something that should never have been allowed to begin. No one would ever know. I never thought of *speaking* to him.'

Aaron gave a little shrug. He looked at Yuri as he spoke.

'I'm only undecided on one point,' Aaron said. 'Will he go to First Street? Will he go to Mayfair and Mayfair? Will he go out to Metairie to those gathered at Ryan's house? Or will he come here? Whom will he seek out – to speak with, to trust, to lure to his side of it? I haven't figured it all out.'

'But you believe he will do that!'

'Darling, he has to,' said Aaron. 'This is his family. They are all under lock and key. What else can he do? Where else can he go?'

TWENTY-EIGHT

The music came from electric mouths high up on the white walls. The people danced in the center of the room, awkwardly, rocking back and forth, but right with the music, as though they too loved it. The musicians were many, and they had crude instruments, nothing as beautiful as the bagpipes or the clarsach. It was as if she could hear that old music in this music, but the two were twined, and she could not think again. Just music. She saw the glen. She saw all the brothers and sisters dancing, and singing. And then someone pointed. The soldiers had come!

The band stopped. The silence clattered in on her. When the door opened, she jumped. People laughing inside, someone staring at her, a woman in a baggy sad dress.

She ought to go on to New Orleans. She had miles and miles to walk. She was hungry. She wanted some milk. They had food there but they didn't have milk. She would have smelled it if they had it. But there were cows in the fields. She'd seen them, and she knew how to take the milk. She should have done it before now. How long had she been here listening to this music? It had all started so long ago, and she couldn't remember, but this was just the first real day of her life.

When the sun had risen, she had opened the door of

a small kitchen, and taken the milk from the refrigerator and drunk the whole container. That had been morning, the delicious taste of cold milk, and the warm yellow sun coming down in long slender dusty rays through the thin, dead-looking trees, and over the grass. Someone from the house had found her. She had said thank you for the milk. She was sorry it was all gone, but she had to have it.

In the long run, these things weren't important. These people wouldn't hurt her. They didn't know what she was. In the old days, if you had stolen milk like that they would have run after you, chasing you deep deep into the mountains, maybe even . . .

'But all that is no longer important,' said Father. 'This is our time to rule.'

Go now, to New Orleans. Find Michael for Mother. Yes, that is what Mother wanted with all her heart. Stop in the field where the cows stand in sleep, waiting for you. Drink the warm milk from the udder. Drink and drink and drink.

She turned, but the band started. Once more, the music. Warming it up with three or four notes and then pounding up through her shoes, and through her throat, as if she were breathing it in through the mouth. She closed her eyes, just loving it. Oh, the world is wondrous. She began to rock.

Someone touched her, and she turned and looked at a man who was almost as tall as she. Wrinkled and tan and smelling of smoke all over, an old being, in a dark blue shirt and pants stained with grease. He spoke to her but she could only hear the music, beating and beating. She rocked her head back and forth. This was lovely.

He leant over and said right in her ear:

'You been watching a long time, honey. Why don't you come in and dance?'

She stepped back. It was so hard for her to keep her balance with this music. She saw him take her hand, felt his harsh dry fingers. All the tiny lines in his hands were full of grease. He smelled like the highway and the cars that shot by. He smelled like cigarettes.

She let him tug her gently through the door, into the warm enfolding light, where the people were dancing. Now the vibration passed all through her. She might have gone slack all over, and fallen down in a heap on the floor. There she could have lain forever listening and singing with it, seeing the glen. The glen was as beautiful as the island ever had been.

It was either that or pull herself together with it, dance and dance and dance.

That's what they were doing; the man had begun to dance with her, had placed his arm around her waist and had come close to her. He said something. She couldn't hear it. She thought it was 'You smell good!'

She shut her eyes, and turned round and round, leaning on his arm, holding tight to him, tilting from side to side. The man was laughing. In a flash she saw his face, saw his mouth moving with words again. The music was thunderous. When she closed her eyes, she was back with the others, dancing in the circles, round and round, out from the stone circle, so many circles that those in the first could not see all the way to those in the last. Hundreds and hundreds dancing to the pipes and the harp.

Oh, but those were the first days, before the soldiers came.

In the glen, later, everyone danced together, tall and little and poor and rich, human and nonhuman. They had come together to make the Taltos. Many would die, but if the Taltos were made . . . If somehow there were two . . . She stopped, her hands to her ears. She had to go. Father. I'm coming. I'll find Michael for Mother. Mother, I did not forget. I am not childish. *All of you are simpletons, children!* Help me.

The man pulled her off balance, but then she realized he was just trying to make her dance some more. Turning her, twisting her. She began again, sliding into it, loving it, rocking back and forth ever more violently, letting her hair swing.

Yes, love it. In a blur, she saw the real music makers. Scrawny and fat and wearing glasses over their eyes, they scratched at their fiddles, and sang in high voices, through their noses, rapidly, unintelligibly, and they played a little bellows organ of which she did not know the name. That was something not inside her, that word. Or the word for the mouth instrument, like the Jew's harp, which wasn't quite the same. But she loved this music, she loved the insistent pulse of it, the divine monotony, the buzz all through her limbs. It seemed to tap on her eardrums, to tap on her heart, to freeze her and consume her.

As in the glen, these humans here danced – old women, young women, boys and men. Even little children. Look at them. But these people couldn't make the Taltos. Get to Father. Get to . . .

'Come on, honeybabe!'

Something . . . a purpose. Leave here. But she couldn't think while the music went on, and it didn't matter.

Yes, let him make her twirl. Dance. She laughed delightedly. How good it felt. Now was the time for dancing. Whoa! Dance. Father would understand.

TWENTY-NINE

It was 4 a.m. They were gathered in the double parlors – Mona, Lauren, Lily and Fielding. Randall was also there. Soon Paige Mayfair from New York would come. Her plane had arrived on schedule. Ryan had gone to get her from the airport.

They sat quietly and waited. Nobody believes in it, thought Mona. But we have to try it. What are we if we don't give it a try?

Earlier, Aunt Bea had come from Amelia Street, to lay a midnight buffet out on the table. And she had put thick votive candles in the two fireplaces. They were only half melted away and the hearths still gave a warm and dancing light.

Upstairs, the nurses on standby talked in low voices – having made a station, so to speak, with their coffee and their charts in Aunt Vivian's room. Aunt Vivian had graciously gone up to stay at Amelia Street, yielding to the firm attachment of Ancient Evelyn, who had gestured and murmured all evening to Vivian, though no one was sure that Evelyn really knew who Vivian was.

'Two old ladies meant for each other,' said Aunt Bea. 'Let's call them Tweedledee and Tweedledum. Ancient Evelyn isn't speaking again. It's a cinch, she's Tweedledum.'

Throughout the house, in other rooms, even up on the third floor, in makeshift beds, cousins slept. Pierce and Ryan and Mandrake and Shelby were all here, somewhere. Jenn and Clancy were in the front bedroom upstairs. Other Mayfairs were out in the guest house beyond Deirdre's oak.

They heard the car stop in front of the gate.

They did not move. Henri opened the door, admitting the woman whom none of them had ever seen in their lives. Paige Mayfair, great-granddaughter of Cortland and his wife, Amanda Grady Mayfair, who had left Cortland years before and gone north.

Paige was a lithe little woman, not unlike Gifford and Alicia in face and form, and only a little more birdlike, with long thin legs and wrists. That type of Mayfair, thought Mona. The woman's hair was sharply bobbed, and she wore those huge dazzling clip-on earrings which a woman must remove before answering a phone.

She was matter-of-fact in her entrance. All but Fielding rose to greet her, to bestow the kisses that were customary even with a cousin whom no one had ever seen before.

'Cousin Paige. Cousin Randall. Cousin Mona. Cousin Fielding.'

Paige sat down finally in the gold French chair with her back to the piano. Her little black skirt rode up on her thighs, revealing that they were almost as slender as her calves. Her legs looked painfully naked compared to the rest of her, swaddled in wool, even to a cashmere scarf which she unwound now from around her neck. It was very cold in New York.

She stared at the long mirror at the far end of the room. Of course it reflected the mirror behind her, and the illusion of endless chambers, each fitted with its own crystal chandeliers.

'You didn't come from the airport alone, did you?' demanded Fielding, startling the woman as usual with his youthful and vigorous voice. Mona realized she didn't know who was older – Fielding or Lily – but Fielding looked so old with his translucent yellow skin and the spots on the backs of his thin hands that you had to wonder what was keeping him alive.

Lily had vigor to her, though her body seemed all ropes and tendons beneath her severe silk suit.

'I told you, Great-granddaddy,' said Mona, 'we had two policemen with her. They're outside. Everybody in New York is together. They've been told. There isn't a single member of this family anywhere who is alone now. Everyone has been told.'

'And nothing further has happened,' said Paige politely, 'isn't that so?'

'Correct,' said Lauren. She had managed to remain her well-groomed corporate-style self even through the long day and night. Not a single silver hair out of place. 'We haven't found him,' she said as if trying to soothe a hysterical client. 'But there has been no further trouble of any sort. There are people working on this investigation as we speak.'

Paige nodded. Her eyes veered to Mona. 'And you're the legend, Mona,' she said. She gave the indulgent smile one gives to pretty children. 'I've heard so much about you. Beatrice is always talking about you in her letters. And you are the designee if we cannot get Rowan to come back.'

Shock.

No one had said such a thing to Mona. She had not

picked up the slightest vibe of it from any of them, either here, or downtown, or anywhere. She couldn't stop herself from glancing at Lauren.

Lauren didn't meet her gaze.

You mean this has already been decided?

No one would look at her. Closed minds. She realized suddenly that only Fielding was staring at her. And she also realized none of them had been shocked by Paige's words, except for her. It had been decided, but not in her presence, and no one wanted to explain or amplify or clarify now. It was too much to discuss just now. Yet it was enormous, the designee of the legacy. And some very sarcastic little phrase went through Mona's mind suddenly, 'You mean crazy little Mona in her sash and bow, drunken Alicia's vagabond kid?'

She didn't say it. Inside, she felt the tightest most strangling pain. *Rowan, don't die. Rowan, I'm sorry.* Some vicious and perfectly luscious memory came back to her of Michael Curry's chest looming over her, and his cock slipping out of her so that she saw it for an instant, the shaft descending out of the nest of hair. She shut her eyes tight.

'Let's believe we can help Rowan,' said Lauren, though the voice sounded so low and so hopeless that it contradicted its own words. 'The legacy is a vast question. There are three lawyers going over the papers now. But Rowan is still alive. Rowan is upstairs. She has survived the surgery. It was the least of her worries. The doctors have done their magic. Now it's time for us to try.'

'You know what we want to do?' asked Lily, whose eyes were glazed still from crying. Lily had assumed a defensive posture, arms over her breasts, one hand

663

resting right below her throat. For the first time ever, thought Mona, Lily's voice sounded shaky, old.

'Yes, I know,' said Paige. 'My uncle told me everything. I understand. All these years. I've heard so much about you, all of you, and now I am here. I'm in this house. But let me say this: I don't know that I'll be of any help to you. It's a power others feel. I myself do not feel it. I don't really know how to use it. But I am always willing to try.'

'You're one of the strongest,' said Mona. 'That is what matters. We are the strongest here. None of us know how to use these gifts.'

'Then let's go. Let's see what we can do,' said Paige.

'I don't want there to be any mumbo jumbo,' said Randall. 'If anybody starts saying crazy words –'

'Certainly not,' said Fielding, eyes sunken, hands folded on his cane. 'I have to go up in the elevator. Mona, you take me. Randall, you should ride in the elevator too.'

'If you don't want to come with us,' remarked Lauren in a steel-cold voice, 'you do not have to, either of you. We will do this ourselves.'

'I'm coming,' said Randall grumpily. 'I want it noted for the record that this family is now following the advice of a thirteen-year-old girl!'

'That's not true,' said Lily. 'We all want to do it. Randall, please help us. Please don't be trouble at this time.'

They went out *en masse*, moving through the shadowy hall. Mona had never liked this elevator. It was too small, too dusty, too old and too powerful and it went too fast. She followed the two old men inside, helping Fielding to the one chair in the corner, a small wooden antique chair with a cane seat. Then she pulled shut the door, clanged the gate and pressed the button. She put her hand on Fielding's shoulder. 'Remember, it stops with a jolt.'

There came the slamming halt as predicted.

'Damn thing,' muttered Fielding. 'Typical of Stella, to get an elevator strong enough to take people to the top of the American Bank.'

'There is no more American Bank,' said Randall.

'Well, you know what I mean,' said Fielding. 'Don't be short-tempered with me. This isn't my idea. I think it's ridiculous. Why don't we go out to Metairie and try to raise Gifford from the dead?'

Mona helped Fielding to stand and position his cane. 'The American Bank used to be the tallest building in New Orleans,' he said to Mona.

'I know,' she answered. She hadn't known, but that was the best way to stop that line of conversation cold.

When they came into the master bedroom, the others were already assembled. Michael was with them, standing with arms folded in the far corner looking down at Rowan's unchanged face.

The blessed candles were burning on the bedside table nearest the door. The Virgin was there. Probably Aunt Bea did this, thought Mona – these candles, this Virgin with her bowed head, white veil, tiny plaster hands outstretched. Gifford certainly would have done it, if she had been around.

No one said a word. Finally Mona spoke.

'I think the nurses need to go out.'

'Well, just what are you going to do in here,' said the younger nurse crossly, a sallow woman with blond hair parted in the middle beneath her stiff starched cap. She was nunlike in her sterility and cleanliness. She glanced at the older nurse, a dark-faced black woman who spoke not a word.

'We're going to lay hands on her and try to heal her,' said Paige Mayfair. 'It probably won't do any good, but we all have this gift. We are going to try.'

'I don't know if you should do this!' said the young nurse distrustfully.

But then the older black woman shook her head negatively, and gestured to let it all go by.

'Go on out, both of you,' said Michael in a quiet commanding voice.

The nurses left.

Mona closed the door.

'It's so strange,' said Lily. 'This is like being from a family of great musicians, yet not knowing how to read music, not even knowing how to carry a tune.'

Only Paige Mayfair seemed unembarrassed, the one from away, the one who hadn't grown up in the shadow of First Street, hearing people answer each other's thoughts as easily as each other's words.

Paige laid her small leather pocketbook on the floor, and came to the bed. 'Turn out the lights, except for the candles.'

'That's nonsense,' said Fielding.

'I prefer it that way,' said Paige. 'I prefer that there will be no distractions.' Then she looked down at Rowan, studying her slowly from her smooth forehead down to the feet poking straight up beneath the sheet. Paige's face looked sad, deliberately sad and thoughtful.

'This is useless,' said Fielding. He was obviously finding it difficult to remain standing.

Mona tugged him over closer to the bed. 'Here, lean

on the mattress,' she said, trying not to be impatient. 'I've got your arm. Lay your hand on her. One hand will do it.'

'No, both hands, please,' said Paige.

'Absolute idiocy!' said Fielding.

The others closed in around the bed. Michael stepped back but then Lily gestured that he must join them too. They all laid their hands on Rowan, Fielding tilting forward at a precarious angle, his labored breathing audible, a little cough collecting in his wattled throat.

Mona felt Rowan's soft pale arm. She had laid her fingers right on the bruises. What had caused them? Had he grabbed Rowan and shaken her? You could almost see the marks of the fingers. Mona laid her own fingers on top of the marks.

Rowan, heal! She hadn't waited for the others, and now she saw that all had made the same silent unceremonious decision. She heard the communal prayer rising; she saw that Paige and Lily had closed their eyes. 'Heal,' whispered Paige. 'Heal,' whispered Mona.

'Heal, Rowan,' said Randall in a deep decisive voice.

Finally the disgruntled murmur came from Fielding. 'Heal, child, if the power is within you. Heal. Heal. Heal.'

When Mona opened her eyes again she saw that Michael was crying. He was holding Rowan's right hand tight in both of his. He was whispering the word along with all of them. Mona closed her eyes and said it again.

'Come on, Rowan! Heal!'

Moments passed as they remained there. Moments passed in which this or that one whispered, or stirred, or clasped the flesh more tightly or patted it. Lily laid

667

her hand on Rowan's forehead. Michael bent to kiss Rowan's head.

It was Paige finally who said that they had done what they could do.

'Has she had the Last Sacraments?' asked Fielding.

'Yes, at the hospital, before the surgery,' said Lauren. 'But she is not going to die. She is holding steady. She is in a deep coma. And she could go on like that for days.'

Michael had turned his back on the assembly. Silently, they slipped out of the room.

In the living room, Lauren and Lily poured the coffee. Mona set out the sugar and the cream. It was still pitch-dark outside, wintry, still.

The great clock chimed five. Paige looked at it, as if startled. And then dropped her eyes.

'What do you think?' asked Randall.

'She's not dying,' said Paige. 'But there is absolutely no response. At least none that I could feel.'

'None,' said Lily.

'Well, we tried it,' said Mona. 'That's the important thing. We tried.'

She went out of the double parlor into the hallway. For a moment she thought she saw Michael at the top of the stairs. But it was just the nurse passing. The house creaked and rustled as it always did. She hurried up, deliberately on tiptoe, trying not to play the stairs like musical keys.

The bedside lamp had been lighted again. The candle flames were lost in the brash yellow illumination.

Mona wiped her eyes and took Rowan's hand. Her own hand was shaking. 'Heal, Rowan!' she said. 'Heal, Rowan! Heal! You're not dying, Rowan! Heal!'

Michael put his arms around her, kissed her cheek.

She didn't turn away. 'Heal, Rowan,' she said. I'm sorry I did it with him. I'm sorry. 'Heal, please,' she whispered, 'what good is it all ... the heritage, the money, any of it ... if we can't ... if we can't heal?'

It must have been six-thirty when Mona made the resolve. There would be a Mayfair Medical. It would happen just as Rowan had planned.

Mona had taken a wool blanket with her out under the oak tree, before the guest house, and she was sitting there on the dry blanket, watching the morning shimmer in the wetness around her, the fresh light green leaves of the bananas, the crinkled elephant ears, the ginger lilies, the green moss on the bricks. The sky was violet now just as it might be at sunset, something she witnessed far more often than dawn.

A guard slept in a straight-backed chair at the garden gate. Another walked back and forth on the other side of the picket gates along the flagstones beside the pool.

The house seemed to grow brighter, more distant against the deepening violet. A deep blood-red aurora began to rise slowly to the far right. You never really knew east from west in New Orleans, until the sun came, or the sun went. Well, here it was coming, glorious and not altogether silent. It seemed the birds heard it; the birds were incited; and all the thick shaggy leaves around her were rattling and alive.

It made her happy to see it, incompletely and impatiently happy. It made her feel alone. *Designee of the legacy*. Lauren had said in a low whisper, 'This shouldn't come as much of a surprise to you. It's a matter of lineage. You traced it yourself in your computer. We'll explain it all. I cannot talk about it while Rowan lives and breathes.'

669

There will be a Mayfair Medical, Rowan. That will be your legacy, and we will take our secrets with us into our own private and ultimately dispensable history, but the stones of Mayfair Medical will stand firm for all to see.

She felt dizzy suddenly. Kind of sick. She really hated being awake at this time of morning. Always had. And when Mona was little, Alicia had always wanted to go to Mass. Drunk or sober the night before, didn't matter. Alicia had to get up and go to Mass. They went uptown to Holy Name on the streetcar. Mona always felt bad like this, headachy with a bad taste in her mouth. That had only stopped in the last few years when Alicia was drinking in the morning, finally, and was already with a beer in her hand, sitting on the back steps, when Mona came down.

But it wasn't so bad being awake now, seeing this deep red color rising miraculously, seeing it turn to gold. The sheer excitement of the last few days rendered things so precious, so clear. Look at this garden, never forget to look at it. The legacy. *Christ, Mona, this is your garden! Or soon will be!*

No wonder she couldn't sleep. She had tried. Best to use this time for thinking, for planning, for laying out in orderly fashion the thing that had begun to obsess her, the location and the structure of Mayfair Medical, where the word *Heal* would be written. In stone? In stained glass?

Pierce would be her strongest ally; he was of the same conservative ilk as Ryan, but the idea was dear to him; he wanted it to work. The last two months, he had kept the plan alive. With a little pushing, he could be made to formulate, imagine, envision. It would all work out, the conservatives in the firm holding them back a little, and their insistence to be bold, to think big, to dream.

Pierce lay asleep not very far away in one of the many scattered lounge chairs, his jacket over his shoulder. He had wanted the bracing air, he said. He was near the pool. He couldn't take the stuffiness of indoors. He had looked like a baby when she passed him.

We'll do it, thought Mona. It's more than a childish resolve to go around the world before I am twenty, or dig a tunnel to China, or start the most successful mutual fund in the international stock market. *Designee of the legacy*. All things are possible, that is the key thing to remember.

Not Alicia's view as she sat with her beer on the step. 'I'm too tired to do anything anymore.' Don't think about her in a freezer drawer. They don't really freeze people in the morgue, do they? Don't they just keep them cold?

All those books on hospitals, where had Mona seen them? In Rowan's room, when Mona had been plotting to seduce Michael. Those books were in the nightstand by the bed. Mona would read them later, study the entire project. That was important – have an advanced scheme before you bring them to the table; run the meeting like an ad for new computers, with all those shiny laser printouts of floor plans, and spreadsheets and lists.

Finally she closed her eyes. She could feel the sun now. Didn't have to see it.

She would play a little trick on herself that always made her sleep. Her mind was going a mile a second, and so she made it do something: decorate the lobbies and offices of Mayfair Medical – made it pick colors, made it hang drapes, made it choose paintings for the interior, paintings that would make waiting patients happy, paintings that would give overworked doctors and nurses a moment of illumination when they stepped into a corridor or into a stairwell, or came in the front doors.

Representations of healing, something like that beautiful painting by Rembrandt of the Anatomy Lesson. She opened her eyes with a start. No, they wouldn't want to see that, nothing that terrible. Think of other things, the passive and beautiful faces of Piero della Francesca, the soft sweet eyes of Botticelli's women, soothing fancies. Things that were better than real.

She was so sleepy. She was trying to remember all the people in that big Medici painting in Florence, the one with Lorenzo looking out of the corner of his eye. She'd been five when Gifford took her to Europe the first time.

'Mothers and babies!' she'd said as they went through the Palazzo Vecchio. She'd so loved to skip and twirl on the stone floors. She had never seen so many pictures of that one grand theme. Gifford had whispered sternly, 'Madonna with Child'.

Gifford bent down to kiss her. *Go to sleep for a while.*

Yes, think I will. I didn't mean to, I mean with Michael, I never meant to . . .

They know that. It doesn't matter now. It's small. You are so like a Mayfair, to want to be fierce and reckless, and then be guilt-ridden! Don't you know that's how it is with us? Nobody gets off light.

Are you certain she wouldn't hate me for it? That it was so small? I didn't think you would think it was small. That's the whole trick of it, deciding what is small and large.

It's small.

Finally, her head against the rough bark of the oak, she slept.

THIRTY

He liked the house. It stood on the street, that is Esplanade Avenue, rather like a palazzo in Rome or a town house in Amsterdam, and though it was brick stuccoed over, it had the appearance of stone. It was painted in Roman colors, the dark Pompeian red, with a deep ocher trim.

Esplanade Avenue had seen better days. But it was architecturally fascinating to Yuri, all these marvelous vintage buildings, amid the other commercial makeshift trash. He'd enjoyed his long walk through the Quarter, meandering, and then coming upon this house just as he reached the border of the district, the grand avenue which had once been the high street of the French and Spanish, and was now still full of mansions such as this. Of course two men were following him. But so what?

He felt the big heavy gun in his pocket. Wooden handle, long barrel. All right.

Beatrice let him in.

'Oh, thank God, darling, Aaron is on tenterhooks. What can I get for you?' She glanced past him. She saw the man under the tree across the street.

'Nothing, madam, thank you,' said Yuri. 'I like my coffee very black and strong, and I stopped for a nice quick shot of it in one of the little cafés.'

They stood in a massive center hall, with a grand

stairway flowing up beyond them, branched at its landing, sending narrow stairs up the right wall and the left. The floor was mosaic tile and the walls were like those outside, a deep terra-cotta red.

'That's exactly the kind of coffee I make,' said Beatrice, taking his raincoat from him, virtually helping him out of it. The gun was in his jacket, thank God. 'Brewed regular but from espresso roast. Now go into the parlor. Aaron will be so relieved.'

'Ah, then I will accept, thank you,' said Yuri.

Parlors lay to the left of him and to the right. But he could feel the warmth coming from the one just before him, and then he saw Aaron in one of his worn gray wool cardigans, pipe in hand, standing by the fire. Again, he was impressed with the vigor in Aaron and how it seemed mingled with his anger, and his suspicion. There was a hard line to Aaron's mouth but it made him look more the conventional man.

'We have a communication from the Elders,' said Aaron without preamble. 'It came in on the fax line at the Pontchartrain Hotel.'

'The Elders used such a means?'

'It's written entirely in Latin. It's addressed to us both. There are two copies, one for each of us.'

'How considerate of them.'

Deep oxblood leather couches faced each other before the fireplace, revealing only the center of a dark blue Chinese rug. The table was glass, littered with papers. There were large rich modern paintings, abstracts mostly, in gilt frames. Marble-top tables; armchairs of tufted velvet, a little worn. Fresh flowers, such as one usually sees only in public lobbies. Big gorgeous blooms arranged in porcelain vases before various mirrors, here and there, and above the mantel with its solemn marble lion's head beneath it. All very beautiful and comfortable to behold. Communications from the Elders, dear God.

'Sit down, I'll translate it for you.'

Yuri sat down. 'You don't have to translate it for me, Aaron. I read Latin.' He gave a little laugh. 'I sometimes write to the Elders in Latin, just to keep sharp.'

'Ah, of course you do,' said Aaron. 'How could I not know that? That was stupid of me.' He gestured to the two shiny fax copies on the table, strewn, as it were, over the magazines – those large expensive compendiums of furnishings and architecture full of designer names and famous faces and advertisements for the sort of fine items which were everywhere in this very room.

'You don't remember Cambridge?' asked Yuri. 'Those afternoons when I read Virgil to you? You don't remember my translation of Marcus Aurelius that I made for you?'

'Remember it.' Aaron pressed his lips together. 'I carry it with me. I'm going soft in the head. I'm so used to those of your generation not reading Latin. Just a slipup. The day I first laid eyes on you, how many languages did you speak?'

'I don't know. I know what I *don't* know. Let me read it.'

'Yes, but tell me first what you found out.'

'Stolov is at the Windsor Court, very fancy, very expensive. He has two other men with him, possibly three. There are others from the Order. They were following me when I came back down Chartres Street to come here. There is a man across the street. All of them same age, same style – young Anglo-Saxon or

Scandinavian, dark suits, same thing. I would say there are six of them I know now by face. They took no pains to conceal themselves. Indeed, I think it is their motive to frighten, or to compel, if you know what I mean.'

Beatrice came sweeping into the room, her high heels clicking glamorously on the tile floor. She set down the tray with small cups of steaming espresso. 'There's a potful,' she said. 'Now I'm going to call Cecilia.'

'Is there any more family news?' asked Yuri.

'Rowan's doing well. There's no change. There is brain activity, but it's minimal. Yet she's breathing on her own.'

'Persistent vegetative state,' said Aaron softly.

'Oooh, why do you have to say those words again?' Beatrice scolded gently.

'You know why. Rowan is not – at this *time* – recovering. One must keep that in mind.'

'But the mysterious man himself,' asked Yuri.

'No sight of him anywhere,' said Beatrice. 'They are saying he couldn't be in Houston. You can't imagine how many people are searching the city of Houston. He may have cut his hair, of course, but there's nothing he can do about being six and a half feet in height. God only knows where he is. I'm going to leave you with Aaron. I don't want to think about it. I am cooking dinner with an armed guard in my kitchen.'

'He won't eat very much,' said Aaron with a little smile.

'Oh, hush up.' She seemed on the verge of something, then simply went to Aaron and kissed him brusquely and affectionately, and dashed out in a flurry of silk and clicking heels as she had come.

Yuri loved the coffee. A pot of it. His hands would

soon be trembling and he would have indigestion, but he didn't care. When you love coffee you abandon everything to that love.

He picked up the fax. He knew Latin so well he did not have to translate in his mind. It was as clear to him as any tongue he spoke:

From the Elders
to
Aaron Lightner
Yuri Stefano

Gentlemen:

Seldom have we been faced with such a dilemma: the defection of two members of the Order who are not only dear to us all, but invaluable, seasoned investigators who have both become models for the incoming novices and postulants. We are hard put to understand how this situation came about.

We fault ourselves. Aaron, we did not inform you of all that was involved in the Case of the Mayfair Witches. Wishing to focus your attentions upon the Mayfair family, we withheld certain relevant information concerning the legends of Donnelaith in Scotland, indeed, concerning the Celts in that area of north Britain and in Ireland. We realize now we should have been more explicit and open from the start.

Please understand it was never the intention of the Order to manipulate you or exploit you. In the spirit of good investigation, we were reluctant to present presumptions or suspicions, lest we control the answers to the very questions we asked.

We know now that we have in a very practical sense made an error in judgment. You have abandoned us. And we know also that this is not something you would have ever done lightly. Once again the burden for this tragedy lies with us.

Let us now come to the point. You are no longer members of the Talamasca. You are excommunicated without prejudice, which means simply that you are honorably separated from the Order, from its privileges, its obligations, its records and its support.

You have no further permission from us to make any use of records compiled by you while you were under our wing. You cannot reproduce, discuss, circulate any knowledge you have now or may come to have on the subject of the Mayfair Witches. We wish to be very explicit on this point.

The investigation of the Mayfair Witches is now in the hands of Erich Stolov and Clement Norgan, as well as several other men who have worked with these two in other parts of the world. They will proceed to make contact with the family – without your assistance and with full disclosure that you are no longer connected with us and that they are not connected with you.

We are asking you only this: do not interfere with what must be done. We release you from all obligation. But you must not become an obstacle to what we have to do.

It is a great and pressing concern to us that the being called Lasher be found. Our members have their orders. Please understand that henceforth you will not be given any special consideration by them.

At some point in the future, we invite you both to return to the Motherhouse, to discuss with us in detail (through written communication) your defection and the possibility of your rededication and renewal of your vows.

At this time, we must say farewell on behalf of your brothers and sisters in the Talamasca, on behalf of Anton Marcus, the new Superior General, on behalf of all of us who love you and value you and are saddened that you are no longer in the fold.

Please take note at the appropriate time and through the

appropriate channels that ample funds have been deposited in your accounts to cover severance expenses. This is the last material support you will receive from . . .

The Talamasca

Yuri folded the slick pages, and slipped his copy into his jacket pocket right alongside of the gun.

He looked up at Aaron, who seemed calm, unconcerned, deep in thought.

'Is this my fault?' asked Yuri. 'That you are excommunicated so quickly? Should I not have come?'

'No, don't let the word chill your heart. I was excommunicated because I refused to leave here. I was excommunicated because I would not stop sending queries to Amsterdam as to what was actually going on. I was excommunicated because I ceased to "watch and be always here". I'm glad you're here, because now I feel anxiety for all my fellow members. I don't know how to tell them. But you, you who were the dearest to me, besides David, you are here and you know what I know.'

'How do you mean that you are frightened for the other members?'

'I am not an Elder,' said Aaron. 'I am seventy-nine years old but I am not an Elder.' He looked at Yuri.

Of course this simple admission was a flagrant violation of the rules.

Aaron went on: 'David Talbot was never an Elder. He told me so before he . . . left the Order. He told me that he had never spoken with anyone who was an Elder, indeed, he had obtained many a surreptitious and frequent denial from the older ones – they weren't Elders. They didn't know who the Elders were.'

Yuri didn't answer. All his life, since the age of twelve, he had lived with the idea that the Elders were his brethren, a jury, so to speak, of his peers.

'Precisely,' said Aaron. 'And now I don't know who they are or what their motives are. I think they killed a doctor in San Francisco. I believe they killed Dr Samuel Larkin. I believe that they have used people like me all our lives – to gather information for some occult purpose that was never understood or appreciated by those of my generation. That is the only thing I can believe.'

Yuri again didn't reply. But this was a full and eloquent expression of his own suspicion – the deep sinister feelings which had come over him not long after his return to the Motherhouse from Donnelaith.

'If I try now to access the main files, I'll be denied,' he said, sort of thinking aloud.

'Possibly,' said Aaron. 'Not everyone in the Order knows computers as you know them, Yuri. If you know the access code of any other member.'

'I know several,' he said. 'I should go at once to some place where I can make the calls. I should find out anything else that is there – cross-referenced in any conceivable way. It will take me two days or more to do this. I can go into the Latin which has been scanned and collated. I can use search words. There is much perhaps I could find out.'

'They might have thought of all that. They must have. But it's worth a try. My mind is too old for it, and so are my fingers. But there is a computer modem with a phone in the house on Amelia Street. It belongs to Mona Mayfair. She's given permission for you to use it. She says you'll figure it out. It's DOS. You understand this? DOS?'

Yuri laughed softly. 'You make it sound like a Druidic god. It means the operating system of the computer, that it is IBM-compatible. Yes.'

'She said she left some instructions for you on the contents of the hard drive but you could boot a directory and see it all for yourself. She said her own files are locked.'

'I know of Mona and her computer,' said Yuri softly. 'I would not go into her files.'

'It was her meaning that you could access anything else.'

'I see.'

'There are dozens of computer modem systems at Mayfair and Mayfair. I believe Mona's is the best, however – the state of the art.'

Yuri nodded. 'I'm going to do that immediately.' He drank another stiff cup of the smooth rich coffee. He remembered Mona with uncommon warmth. 'And then we can talk.'

'Yes, talk.'

But what would they say? They were too crestfallen to say much of anything. In fact, a terrible gloom hovered near Yuri ready to descend in full force, rather like the gloom when the gypsies had taken him from his dead mother. Strangers. A world full of strangers. Except for Aaron, and these kindly people, this Mona whom he liked already very much.

At Amelia Street, Yuri had met Mona today, sometime around noon. He'd been eating American dry cereal with milk at the breakfast table. She had talked to him nonstop, questioning him, chatting with him, all to one purpose or another as she gnawed on an apple till there was perhaps one seed left.

The entire family was electric with the news that she would be the next designee of the legacy. They had come up to her continuously, paying court to her, doing everything but asking to kiss her ring. But then she did not have a ring.

Finally Mona had said, 'How can we carry on this way when Rowan is still alive?'

And Randall, the huge, soft old man with the many chins, had said: 'Darling, that's got nothing to do with it. Whether she lives or dies, Rowan is now incapable of ever bearing another child.'

Mona had looked stunned, then only nodded, and whispered, 'Of course.'

'Don't you want the legacy?' asked Yuri under his breath, because she sat there so silent, and so close to him, looking into his eyes.

She laughed and laughed. Nothing mean and ugly in it. It was light and pretty.

'Ryan will explain it all, Mona,' one of the young men had said. Was it Gerald? 'But you can hit those legal documents yourself any time you want.'

A dreadful dark look had come over Mona's face. 'What was that saying?' she had asked. 'St Francis said it? Oncle Julien used to say it. Ancient Evelyn told me. Mom said it. "Be careful what you wish for ... your wish might come true."'

'Sounds like Oncle Julien, Ancient Evelyn *and* St Francis,' said Gerald.

Then Mona had departed with the swift and amazing American drawl of: 'I gotta hit the computer. Out of my way.'

The computer.

When Yuri had gone to get his valise, he had heard

the keys clicking. Front room. He had not dared to walk down the hall and meddle in the open door.

'I like Mona Mayfair,' he said now to Aaron. 'That is a clever one. I like them all.'

He felt a sudden unwelcome flush in his cheeks. He did more than like her. Hmm. But she was too young. Wasn't she too young?

He stood to go. Such a lovely house. He was aware, perhaps for the first time, of the fragrances coming from the kitchen.

'Not so quickly,' said Aaron.

'Aaron, they will lock everything!'

Beatrice had just come in. She held a tweed jacket over her arm, one of Aaron's, worn and loved. And the raincoat for Yuri.

'We want you to stay for supper,' said Beatrice. 'It will be ready in half an hour. It's a very special supper to us. Aaron will be brokenhearted if you go away. I will be brokenhearted if you go away. Here, put this on.'

'We are having supper here but we are leaving?' asked Yuri, as he took the black raincoat from her hand.

'We're going to the Cathedral,' said Aaron. He slipped on the tweed coat and straightened the thick lapels. He checked for his linen handkerchief. How many times had Yuri watched this procedure? Now Aaron checked his pockets for his keys, and his passport and another piece of paper, which he unfolded as he looked at Beatrice and smiled.

'Come with us and witness the marriage,' said Beatrice. 'Magdalene and Lily will meet us there.'

'Ah, you are really to be married!'

'Yes, darling,' said Beatrice. 'Let's be off. The supper will be ruined if we keep it waiting too long. This is a Mayfair recipe, Yuri. You appreciate spicy food, I hope? This is crawfish *étouffée*.'

'Thank you, Yuri,' said Aaron softly.

She slipped into her own dark jacket, which made the shirtwaist silk dress look suddenly very formal and sedate.

'Ah, this is a privilege,' said Yuri. For this he would wait for Mona's computer, hard as that would be.

'You know,' said Beatrice, leading the way, 'it's a shame to forgo the big wedding. When all this is over maybe we'll have a banquet, Aaron, what do you think? When everyone is happy and it's all over, we'll have the most splendid party! But the fact is, I will not wait.' She shook her head. Then she said again with just a hint of panic, 'I will not wait.'

THIRTY-ONE

He chose his moments for bathroom breaks. Made
sure the nurse was standing right there. Then he walked
the four steps into the bathroom, shut the door, did
what he had to do and came back again.

His worst fear was that while he was taking a piss,
she would die. While he was washing his hands, she
would die. While he was talking on the phone, she
would die.

His hands were still wet now; he hadn't taken time to
dry them. He sat down in the wing chair and looked
across the room, at the old wallpaper above the fireplace, an oriental pattern of a willow and a stream.
They had so reverently left it when they refurbished.
Just that one old panel, the chimney panel. All the rest
of the room was fresh and new, surrounding the high
antique bed with swaddling comfort.

She lay as before, light glinting in her motionless
eyes.

This evening around eight, they had run all the grams
again, as he called them. Electroencephalo and electro-
cardio and so forth and so on. Her heartbeat was no
stronger than it had been when she was first found. Her
brain was as dead as a brain can get and still have life in
it. Her soft, delicate face with its beautiful cheekbones
was a bit more ruddy. She didn't have the dried-out

look anymore. He could see the result of the fluids, especially around her eyes, and in her normal-looking hands. Mona said it didn't look like Rowan. It was Rowan.

Pray you are in some soft and beautiful valley, safe from knowing. Pray our thoughts can't touch you. Only our comforting hands.

They had put a big rose-colored wing chair in the corner for him, between the bed and the bathroom door. There was the chest of drawers there to the right with his cigarettes and with his ashtray and also with the gun Mona had given him, a big heavy .357 Magnum that had belonged to Gifford. Ryan had brought it home from Destin two days before.

'You keep this. That way if the son of a bitch comes into this room, you can pop him,' Mona had said.

'Yes, I got it,' he said. He had wanted just such a weapon, 'a simple tool' to use the phrase of Julien, to use the phrase of his many revelations. Just a simple tool to blow away the face of the being who had done this to her.

At moments, his time spent with Julien in the attic was more real than anything else. He had not tried to tell anyone else but Mona. He really wanted to tell Aaron. But the maddening thing was, he couldn't get a moment alone with Aaron. Aaron was so angry about the suspect involvement of the Talamasca that he was spending every hour elsewhere, checking on things, verifying, whatever. Except of course for the brief wedding in the sacristy of the Cathedral, which Michael had been compelled to miss.

'Downtown Mayfairs marry at the Cathedral,' Mona had explained.

Mona was asleep now in the front bedroom, on the

bed which had been his and Rowan's. It must be exhausting to go from being a fairly poor relation to the Queen in the Castle, he thought.

But the family was losing no time in designating Mona. It was a matter of expediency. Never had the family known such turmoil and jeopardy. There had been more 'change' in the last six months than ever in the family's history, including the revolution in the 1700s in Saint-Domingue. The family intended to lock up the matter of the designee before any of the cousins could challenge it, before any internecine war began among divisions of descendants. And Mona was a child, a child whom they knew and loved and felt that they could ultimately control.

Michael had smiled at that bit of frank explanation which had dropped so naively from Pierce's lips.

'The family's going to control Mona?' Michael had murmured.

But they were in the hall, right outside Rowan's door, and he hadn't wanted to talk about all this. He had his eye on Rowan. He could see the rise and fall of her breath. A person on a respirator could not have been so regular.

'This is what's important,' said Pierce. 'Mona is the right person. Everyone knows this for various different reasons. She'll have a few crazy schemes, it's bound to happen, but Mona is basically very smart and mentally sound.'

Interesting, those words, mentally sound. Were there many people in the family who were flat-out crazy? Probably.

'What Dad wants you to know,' Pierce had continued, 'is that this is your house till the day you die. It's

Rowan's house. If there should be some kind of miracle, I mean if . . .'

'I know . . .'

'Then everything reverts to Rowan, with Mona designated as the heir. Even if Rowan could speak now, this would have to be decided, who would be the heir. All those years when Deirdre was in her famous rocker, we knew that Rowan Mayfair in California was the heir. Also those were the days of Carlotta. We couldn't make her cooperate. This time we will do things immediately and smoothly and efficiently. I know to you it must seem very strange . . .'

'Not so strange,' he'd said. 'I want to go back in. It makes me edgy to leave her.'

'Sometime or other you'll have to sleep.'

'I sleep, son, I sleep right there in the chair. I'm fine. I sleep better than I did when I was on all that medicine. It's kind of deep and natural. I sleep holding her hand.'

And I try not to think, Rowan, why the hell did you leave me? Why did you drive me out on Christmas Eve? Why didn't you trust me? And Aaron, why the hell didn't you break the laws of the Talamasca and come here? But that wasn't fair. Aaron himself had explained that situation – how they had given him his orders to stay away, and how guilty, how spineless, he had felt.

'I sat there at Oak Haven giving you all those excuses. I let you return to the house alone. I should have trusted my own conscience. Dear God, it's the old dilemma.' Aaron's entire loyalty to the Talamasca was now in question. Thank God that he loved Beatrice, that she loved him. What would become of a man like that, cast out of the Talamasca? Hell, the handsome gypsy with the jet-black eyes and the golden skin was young.

He closed his eyes.

He knew the nurse was fiddling with the IV again. He could hear her, and hear the little beeps which came from the electronic control. How he hated these machines, machines which had surrounded him in the cardiac unit for so long.

And now she lay there at their mercy, she who had taken so many people through the techno-medical vale of tears.

Whatever happened, she had suffered for it unspeakably, and he had made his vow. When that thing was found, he would kill it. Nobody would stop him. He would kill it. He would not hesitate for the sake of any legal or religious authority, or any family pressure or any moral qualm. He would kill it. That had been Julien's message. You will have one more chance.

And as soon as he could leave this bedside without worrying, as soon as he really knew that Rowan was stable, he'd go looking for it himself.

It had failed to couple with its daughters ... the Mayfair Witches. It had chosen those who did possess the extra chromosomes, but the births had failed. How had he known his brides – by scent, perhaps, or something visible which others didn't see? For massive irregularities had been found in Gifford and in Alicia, and in Edith, and in the two cousins in Houston.

Would he now seek a mate at random? Who could know.

Michael was in terror of the news – another rash of inexplicable deaths. An unknown disease surfacing suddenly in the headlines. Women on slabs in Dallas or Oklahoma City, or New York. Imagine it, this tall blue-eyed creature, bringing death with his embrace. For without exception, his deadly semen had caused them to ovulate instantly, for the egg then to be fertilized and for the embryo to grow out of control.

All that was known now from the analysis of the doctors. It was also known that he, Michael, had the chromosomes, though they were inactive. And so did Mona, in whom they were also inactive, and so did Paige Mayfair from New York, and so did Ancient Evelyn and Gerald and Ryan himself.

The family was handling it fairly well, as far as he was concerned, though there was much discussion now as to whether Clancy and Pierce should marry, for both of them had the extra complement, too.

And what was he to do with Mona? Did he dare touch Mona again? They both had the abnormality. How significant was it? How much of Lasher's birth had been chromosomal, and how much his soul sliding in there and taking over? What right had Michael to be touching Mona anyway? That was all past. It was past the minute he saw Rowan lying on the stretcher. Past, past, past. He'd had enough fun in life. He could sit in that chair forever. Just be with her.

However, there were good arguments for ignoring the genetic analysis, said the doctors, at least for Clancy and Pierce to trust to 'nature', whatever that might truly be. Pierce's sisters did not have the extra-long double helix. They had extra genes, but it simply wasn't the same. Ryan and Gifford, both with extra genes, had failed to produce a monster. Michael had had lovers. Yes, and if years ago his girlfriend hadn't chosen an abortion against his heartfelt wishes, he might have had a normal child.

Forensic analysis of Deirdre's genetic blueprint had

also indicated she did not possess the extra chromosomes, yet she had given birth to a child who did. Still, should those who carried the extra package court disaster?

'Look, that thing came through on Christmas. Rowan and I didn't make it. We just created a fetus, and the thing took it out of God's hands. It didn't grow out of control in Rowan's body. It didn't make her abort. Not until that thing went into it.'

God's hands. How odd of him to have used the word *God*. But the longer he stayed in this house, the longer he stayed in New Orleans, and there was no reason to presume he wouldn't forever, the more normal the concept of God seemed.

Whatever, the genetic material had only been discovered. A small core of family-managed doctors were working right round the clock to solve the mystery, working even now . . .

Nothing was going to happen to these doctors either. Only Ryan and Lauren knew their actual location, their names, the laboratory in which they worked. The Talamasca would not be told this time, the Talamasca whom Aaron no longer trusted, and whom he suspected of the worst, most unspeakable wrongs.

'Aaron, take it easy,' Michael had said earlier this afternoon. 'Lasher could have killed those doctors, it's just that simple. He could have killed anyone who had any evidence.'

'He is one being, Michael. He cannot be in two places at once. Please believe me, a man of my ilk doesn't make rash statements, especially not about an organization to which he has given his undivided loyalty for an entire life.'

Michael hadn't pressed him. But he hadn't liked the idea, not at all. On the other hand, there was something he should have told Aaron! If only they'd been alone, but that never seemed to happen. When Aaron had stopped this morning, Yuri, the gypsy kid, had been with him, and the indefatigable Ryan and his clone, son Pierce.

Michael looked at his watch. It was ten-thirty. And it was Aaron's wedding night. He sat back, wondering when it would be proper to call. Of course there would be no honeymoon for Aaron or Beatrice. How could there be? But they were married now, lawfully under the same roof, and the entire family was happy. Michael had heard enough to be sure of it from the cousins who had come to visit all day long.

Well, he had to get a message to Aaron. He had to not forget this. He had to remember everything, and be ready, and his weariness couldn't get to him, or fuddle him. Not this time.

He turned and opened the top drawer of the chest very quietly. The big gun was a beauty. He'd love to take that down to a shooting gallery and fire away. Funny thing was, Mona said she liked to do that. And he'd gotten a kick out of it. Mona and Gifford had gone target practicing together in a funny place in Gretna where you wore ear covers and eye covers and fired at paper targets in long concrete carrels.

Ah, the gun, yes, and also here was the notepad he had put there himself some weeks before. And a fine-point black pen, perfect.

He took the pad and pen, and shut the drawer.

Dear Aaron,

Somebody's going to take this note to you. Because I will not have a chance to tell you this for some time. I still think you're all wrong about the T. They couldn't have done those things. They just couldn't. But there is another corroborating opinion. This you need to know.

This is the poem Julien recited to me, the poem Ancient Evelyn recited to him over seventy years ago. I cannot get away to ask Ancient Evelyn if she remembers it. She's no longer talking sense, they tell me. Maybe you can ask her. This is what is written in my mind.

> One will rise who is too evil.
> One will come who is too good.
> 'Twixt the two, a witch shall falter
> and thereby open wide the door.
>
> Pain and suffering as they stumble
> Blood and fear before they learn.
> Woe betide this Springtime Eden
> Now the vale of those who mourn.
>
> Beware the watchers in that hour
> Bar the doctors from the house
> Scholars will but nourish evil
> Scientists would raise it high.
>
> Let the devil speak his story
> Let him rouse the angel's might
> Make the dead come back to witness
> Put the alchemist to flight.
>
> Slay the flesh that is not human
> Trust to weapons crude and cruel
> For, dying on the verge of wisdom,
> Tortured souls may seek the light.

Crush the babes who are not children
Show no mercy to the pure
Else shall Eden have no Springtime.
Else shall our kind reign no more.

He read it over. Dreadful handwriting. You've let it go to pot, buddy. But it was readable, and now he circled the words *Scholars*, *Scientists*, *alchemist*.

He wrote: 'Julien was suspicious too. Incident in a church in London. Not in your files.'

He folded the paper, and put it in his pocket. He'd entrust this to Pierce or Gerald only, and one of them would be along before midnight. Or maybe even Hamilton, who was out taking a nap. Hamilton wasn't a bad guy at all.

He slipped the pen in his pocket and reached out with his left hand to clasp Rowan's fingers. There was a sudden jerk. He rose up with a start.

'Just a reflex, Mr Curry,' said the nurse from the shadows. 'It happens now and then. If she was hooked to one of the machines, it would drive the needle crazy, but it doesn't mean a damned thing.'

He sat back, holding tight to her hand, refusing to admit it was as cool and lifeless as before. He looked at her profile. It seemed to have slipped a little to the left. But maybe that was a mistake. Or they had lifted her head for some reason, or he was just dreaming.

Then he felt the fingers tighten again.

'There, it happened,' he said. He stood up. 'Turn on that lamp.'

'It's nothing, you're torturing yourself,' said the nurse. She came softly to the side of the bed, and she laid her fingers on Rowan's right wrist. Then, removing a small flashlight from her pocket, she bent over and directed the tiny beam right into Rowan's eye.

She stepped back, shaking her head.

Michael sat down again. *OK, honey. OK. I'm going to get him. I'm going to kill him. I'm going to destroy him. I'm going to see that his brief fleshly life comes to a swift end. I am going to do it. Nothing this time will stop me. Nothing.* He kissed her open palm. No movement in the fingers. He kissed it again, and then he folded the hand closed and put it at her side.

How terrible to think she might not want him to be touching her, might not like the light or the candles, might not want anyone near her, and yet she was locked inside, unable to utter a single word.

'Love you, darling dear,' he said to her. 'I love you. I love you.'

The clock struck eleven. How strange it was. The hours dragged and then they flew. Only Rowan's breathing had the constant rhythm.

He lay back in the chair, and closed his eyes.

It was past midnight when he looked up again. He studied his watch, and then cautiously he looked at Rowan. Was she exactly the same? The nurse was at the little mahogany table, writing as always. Hamilton was in a chair in the far corner, reading by a small high-beam light.

Her eyes somehow ... But the nurse would scoff at him. Still ...

The guard stood outside, on the gallery, his back to the window which he had shut.

Another figure stood in the room. It was Yuri, the gypsy with the slanted eyes and the black hair. He was smiling at Michael and just for a moment Michael was uncomfortably startled, off base. But the face was kind. Almost beatific like that of Aaron.

He stood up, and motioned for the man to move out into the hall.

'I came from Aaron,' said Yuri. 'He says to tell you he is happily married. He says he wants you to remember what he said. You are not to let anyone from the Talamasca in here. Not anyone. You must tell them. It was a snap for me to get in. Won't you tell them all, now?'

'Yes, yes, I'll do that.' He turned and made a little motion to the nurse. She knew what it meant. Take Rowan's vital signs. I have to go out for three minutes. I won't do it unless you take her pulse.

The nurse went about it quickly and made the sign to him. 'No change.'

'Are you sure?'

The nurse sighed coldly. 'Yes, Mr Curry.'

They went down the stairs, Michael going first, a little lightheaded and thinking maybe he ought to eat. Had to remember to eat. Then he remembered. Someone had given him a big plate of dinner. So he should be perfectly all right.

He went out on the porch and called the guards from the gate. In a moment there were five uniformed security men around him. Yuri told them. No one from the Talamasca. Only Yuri. Aaron Lightner. Yuri showed them his passport. 'You know Aaron,' he said.

They nodded; they understood.

'Well, we're not letting anybody in here, unless we know that person, you know. We've got the nurses' names on a list.'

Michael walked Yuri back out to the gate. The fresh air felt good. It was waking him up.

'I talked my way past them,' said Yuri. 'I don't want to get them in trouble, but stay on them. Remind them. I never gave them my name.'

'I got you,' said Michael. He turned and looked up at the window of the master bedroom. On the first night that he had ever seen it candles had been flickering behind the closed blinds. He looked at the window below it, which led to the library, the window through which that thing had almost come.

'I hope you're close. I hope you're coming,' he said in a bitter whisper meant only for Lasher, his secret and old friend.

'You have the gun Mona gave you?' Yuri asked.

'Upstairs. How did you know about that?'

'She told me,' he said. 'Put it in your pocket. Carry it always. You have other reasons.' He gestured to a figure in the shadows across Chestnut Street, against the stone wall.

'That is one of the Talamasca,' he said.

'Yuri, surely you and Aaron don't really believe these men to be dangerous. They're being devious, I see that. They aren't helping. But dangerous? You're angry, something's happened. But you don't think men from the Talamasca would take human life. Yuri, I did my own investigating of the Talamasca. So did Ryan Mayfair before I married Rowan. The Talamasca is made up of bibliophiles and linguists, medievalists and clerks.'

'Nice description. Your words?'

'I don't know. I think so. Seems I said it crossly to Aaron once. But seriously. Lasher is the thing to fear. Lasher is the thing to catch –' He reached into his pocket. 'Almost forgot. Take this to Aaron. You can read it if you like. It's a poem. I didn't write it. Make sure he gets this. Not tonight, tomorrow – whenever you see him – will be soon enough. It contradicts what I'm saying, actually, but that's not the point. I just want him to see it, all of it. Maybe some of it will mean something to him. I don't know.'

'All right. I will see him in an hour. I am going back there. But keep the gun near you. See that man? His name is Clement Norgan. Don't speak to him. Don't let him come in.'

'You mean don't ask him what the hell he's doing there?'

'Exactly. Don't let him goad you into engaging him in conversation. Just keep an eye.'

'All this sounds so Catholic, so Talamasca,' said Michael. 'Don't engage the Devil in conversation; do not converse with the evil spirit.'

Yuri shrugged, with a small bit of a smile. He looked off into the dark. His eyes fixed on the distant figure of Clement Norgan. Michael could scarcely make it out. There was a time when he could have seen it clearly, but now his night vision wasn't so good. He knew it was a man there. And it crossed his mind that somewhere out here in this soft, gentle darkness, somewhere Lasher could be standing, watching, waiting.

But for what?

'What will you do now, Yuri?' asked Michael. 'Aaron says they've kicked you both out.'

'Hmmm, I don't know,' said Yuri. The smile broadened. 'It's nice to realize that. I can do things. I can . . . do something completely new. I hadn't thought of it before.' Then his face darkened. 'But I have a destiny,' he said softly.

'What is it?'

'To discover why all this happened with the Talamasca. To discover ... who made what decision when.
Don't tell me. It sounds very governmental. Central
Intelligence, that sort of thing. Tonight I was at the
house of Mona Mayfair, using her computer. I tried to
reach the Motherhouse archives. Every code was
blocked. Imagine changing so many codes, just to defeat
me. Maybe it is always done. But never did anyone
change a code while I was there. No, it's crazy.'

Michael nodded. For him, things were really simple.
He was going to kill the thing. But why explain? 'Tell
Aaron I'm sorry I couldn't be there for the wedding. I
wanted to be.'

'Yes, he knows. Be careful. Watch. And listen. Two
enemies, remember?'

And with that Yuri stepped back and then darted
away. He was across Chestnut Street with a few large
strides, and then gone down First, without so much as a
sideways glance at Norgan.

Michael went back up the steps. He summoned the
guard nearest the door.

'That man over there, keep an eye on him,' said Michael.

'Oh, he's OK. He's a private detective hired by the
family.'

'Are you sure?'

'Absolutely. Showed us his identification earlier.'

'I don't think so,' said Michael. 'Yuri knew him. He's
not a private detective. Did any of the family tell you
they had hired him to be here?'

The guard was flustered. 'No. He showed me his
identification. You're right. It should have come from
Ryan or Pierce Mayfair.'

'You better believe it.'

Michael was about to say, 'Call him.' He was about to walk down the steps and go over to the man himself. Then he remembered that strange religious admonition, 'Do not engage him in conversation.'

'You know the next shift?' asked Michael. 'Their names, their faces?'

'Yes, all of them. And the guys out back. I know who's coming at three tomorrow afternoon and at midnight tomorrow night. Got all those names. I should have questioned this guy. Look, let me run that bastard out of here. He said he was working for the Mayfair family.'

'No, just watch him. Maybe Ryan did hire him. Maybe Ryan forgot to tell you and me. Just watch him, watch him and anybody like him, and don't let anyone in without talking to me.'

'Yes, sir.'

Michael went back inside, shutting the big door behind him. For a moment he stood against it, looking down the narrow hallway, at the old familiar sight of the high keyhole door to the dining room, and the bit of colored mural beyond.

'What's going to happen, Julien? How is it going to work itself out?'

Tomorrow the family would convene in the dining room to discuss this very question. If the man had not surfaced, what should they do? What was their obligation to others? How should it be handled?

'We will deal with the specifics,' Ryan had said, 'with what we know, as corporate lawyers are bound to do. This man abducted and abused Rowan. That is all the various law enforcement agencies need to be told.'

Michael smiled. He started the slow climb up the long flight of stairs. Don't count them, don't think about it, don't think about a twinge in your chest, or a swimming feeling in your head.

It was going to be fun working with 'law enforcement agencies', trying to keep all this secret. Ah, Lord, would the papers have a field day. He suspected the simplest angle would be some cheap statement as to the man's being a 'Satanist', a member of a violent and dangerous 'cult'.

And then he thought of that shining spirit, 'the man' whom he had once seen behind the crib at Christmas, and staring at him in the garden below. He thought of that radiant countenance.

What's it like, Lasher, to be lost in the flesh and to have the whole world looking for you? Like being a needle in a haystack, instead of such a powerful ghost? In this day and age, they find needles in haystacks. And you are a bit more like the family emerald, lost in a box of jewels. Not so hard to see you, snatch you, snare you, keep you, the way no one could have ever done when you were Julien's daemon or fiend.

He stopped at the door of the bedroom. All was as he had left it. Hamilton reading. The nurse with her chart. The candles giving off the sweet good odor of expensive wax, and the shadow of the Virgin's statue dancing behind them, the shiver of the shadow thrown across Rowan's face and giving it a false life.

He was about to resume his old position when he spied a movement in the bedroom at the end of the hall. Must be the other nurse, he thought, but he didn't like it, and he went down the hall to check.

For one moment, he couldn't make out what he was

seeing – a tall gray-haired woman in a flannel gown. Sunken cheeks, bright eyes, a high forehead. Her white hair was loose over her shoulders. Her gown hung to her bare feet. The twinge in his chest became a pain.

'It's Cecilia,' she said mercifully, patiently. 'I know. Some of us Mayfairs were born looking like ghosts. I'll come in and sit with her if you like. I've just slept a good eight hours. Why don't you lie down here for a little while?'

He shook his head. He felt so foolish and so badly shaken. And he hoped to God he hadn't hurt her feelings!

He went back in to take up the vigil as before. Rowan, my Rowan.

'What's that spot on her gown?' he asked the nurse.

'Oh, must be a little water,' said the nurse, pressing a dry washcloth to Rowan's breast. 'I was wiping her face and moistening her lips. Do you want me to massage her now, just move her arms, keep them flexible?'

'Yes, do it. Do anything and everything. Do it whenever you get bored. If she shows the slightest . . .'

'Of course.'

He sat down and closed his eyes. He was drifting. Julien said something to him, but he was just remembering, the long story, the image of Marie Claudette with her six fingers. Six fingers on the left hand. Rowan had had beautiful and perfect hands. Hands of a surgeon.

What if she had done what Carlotta Mayfair wanted? What her mother had wanted? What if she had never come home?

He awoke with a start. The nurse was lifting Rowan's right leg, carefully, gently, smoothing the lotion over the skin. Look how thin, how worn. 'This will keep her from getting drop foot. We have to do it regularly. You want to remind the others. I'll write it on the chart. But you remember.'

'I will,' he said.

'She must have been a beautiful woman,' said the nurse, shaking her head.

'She *is* a beautiful woman,' said Michael, but there was no anger in it, no resentment. Just setting the record straight.

THIRTY-TWO

He wanted to do it again. Emaleth didn't want to stop dancing. The building was empty; no one else came this evening. And she wasn't dancing, except in her sleep. She opened her eyes. There he was. The music was playing, she'd been hearing it in her dreams, and now he was so insistent. Do it. He wanted to take off her long pants again and be inside her. She didn't mind it, but she had to be going to New Orleans. She really did. Look, it was dark again, positively late-night dark. The stars would be hanging low over the field outside, over the swampland, over the smooth highway with its silver wires, and its dreamy white lights. Got to start walking.

'Come on, honey.'

'I told you, we can't make a baby,' she said. 'It just won't work.'

'That's just fine, darlin'. I don't mind at all about not making a baby. Come on, now, you're my sweet little thing. What if I turned off the music? And here, I got you some milk? Some fresh milk. Said you wanted some more milk, remember? Look, I got you ice cream too.'

'Hmmmm, that's good,' she said. 'Turn down the dial on the music.'

Only then could she move. The music was little and tiny and thumping on her brain, kind of like a fish splashing in a tiny pool, trying to get bigger. It was grating, but it didn't engulf her.

She tore open the plastic top of the big bottle and began to drink and drink. Ah, good milk. Not Mother's milk, but it was milk. Not fresh and warm. But it was good. If only there had been more milk in Mother. She was so hungry for Mother. So hungry to lie in Mother's arms and drink. This feeling became worse instead of better. When she thought of Mother she wanted to cry.

But she had taken every drop she could get from Mother, and it had been enough. She had grown tall, and only left Mother when she knew she had to.

Pray the brown people had found Mother and taken Mother to a proper grave. Pray they had sung and dropped the red ocher and the flowers. Mother would never wake again. Mother would never speak. There wouldn't be any more milk ever in Mother. Mother had made every drop that she would ever make.

Was Mother dead? She ought to go to Michael, tell Michael what Mother said. A feeling of love and tenderness came over her when she thought of Michael, and Mother's love for him. Then go on to Donnelaith. What if Father was waiting there for her now?

On and on she drank. He was laughing. He had turned up the music again. Boom, boom, boom. She let the bottle drop, and wiped her lips. She should be walking. 'Got to leave you.'

'Not yet, darlin'.' He sat down beside her, took the milk bottle and laid it carefully out of the way. 'Want some ice cream? People who like milk always like ice cream.'

'I never had any before,' she said.

'Honey, you'll love ice cream.' He opened the package. He began to feed her with a small white spoon. Oh, this tasted even more like Mother's breast, sweeter and delicious. It made a shiver pass through her. She took the carton and began to eat. She was humming with the music. Suddenly the music and the taste were all she knew. She tried to shake herself back into the moment. The little building in the woods; he and she alone on the floor. All the dancers gone. His wanting to do it with her. And the spot of blood after, when she had reached down. 'It just died like that.'

'What was that, darlin'?'

'The baby. I can't make them with men, only with Father.'

'Ho, ho, honey! Keep that secret to yourself.'

She didn't know what he meant. But he was happy. He was gentle. He thought she was beautiful. He didn't have to say so. She saw it in his eyes. Music or no music, she saw his adoring eyes. And he loved the smell of her. It made him feel young.

He was pulling her up to her feet. The ice cream rolled on the floor. It felt good to be in his arms, swaying back and forth and back and forth. Like a bell swinging, calling all the people down into the glen. Hear the bell, that's the Devil's Knell? Hear the bell?

He held her close, and she felt her breasts ache against his chest. Strange, prickly feeling.

'Oh, you've made milk in me,' she whispered. She backed up, trying to clear her head of the music. 'Look at it.' She reached in her shirt, tearing loose the buttons, and pinched her own nipple.

Droplets of thin milk. It would not do her any good to drink her own milk. She ached for Mother, ached to nurse. And look, because he'd made the tiny baby die in her, he'd made her have milk. Well, it would go away, especially if he would stop doing it to her. But what if it didn't? It was all right. When she came together with Father at the Beginning, she would need milk, breasts heavy with milk. Out of her loins would come all the children, hungry, beautiful children, until the glen was filled once again, as it had been, after they were driven from the island.

She turned around and went down on her knees and lifted the milk bottle. The music almost knocked her over. Almost made her not know up from down.

She drank and drank until there was no more.

'Gee, honey, you sure do like your milk.'

'Oh yes, very much,' she said. Then she could not remember what he had just said. The music. Turn down the music.

He was pushing her down on the floor. 'Let's do it again, honey.'

'OK,' she said, 'but I will just bleed some more.' Her breasts hurt just a little. But it was probably all right. 'Can't make a baby, remember.'

'Promise me that, sweetheart, why you're the most precious little gal, the most precious little thing I've ever ... ever ... known.'

THIRTY-THREE

The meeting in the dining room began at one o'clock. The nurses had promised to call Michael if there was the slightest change.

The dining room required no artificial light at this time of day. A flood of sun came through the south-facing windows, and even the north window on the street. The murals of Riverbend showed infinitely more detail than ever they did by the light of the chandelier. A sterling-silver coffee urn gleamed on the buffet. Extra chairs, of which there were many, were pushed back to the white-painted rail.

As the family sat around the oval table, in somewhat uneasy silence, the doctor spoke first.

'Rowan is stable. She is taking the liquid diet well. Her blood work is better. Her fluid output is good. Her heart is strong. We cannot expect recovery. But it is Michael's wish that we conduct this case as if Rowan were indeed going to recover; that we do everything to stimulate Rowan and to make her as comfortable as we can. This means music in the room, or perhaps films, or television, or radio, and certainly conversation on sensible subjects in a calm way. Rowan's limbs will be exercised daily; her hair will be groomed and maintained in a fashionable style. Her nails will be manicured. She will be cared for as lovingly as if she were conscious.

She has the means for the best, and the best she shall have.'

'But she *could* wake up,' said Michael. 'It could happen –!'

'Yes,' said the doctor. 'It's always possible. But it's not probable at all.'

Nevertheless, everyone was in agreement. Everything must be done. Indeed, Cecilia and Lily expressed their relief at these ideas, as they themselves had felt rather hopeless after their long night sitting by the bed. Beatrice said Rowan could undoubtedly feel this love and this care. Michael mentioned that he didn't know what kind of music Rowan really liked. Did any of them know?

The doctor had more to say.

'We will continue intravenous feeding for as long as the body can successfully metabolize the food. Now there may come a time when the body cannot do this; when we have problems with the liver and kidneys; but that is down the road a bit. For now Rowan is receiving a balanced diet. This morning the nurse swore Rowan sucked a tiny bit of fluid from a straw. We will continue to offer this. But unless there is some real ability to take nourishment in this way – which I doubt – we will continue to feed through the vein.'

Everyone nodded.

'It was only a drop or two,' said Lily. 'Just like a baby's reflex, sucking up the fluid.'

'This can be rewarded and strengthened!' said Mona. 'Christ, maybe she likes the taste of the food!'

'Yes, surely that would make a difference to her,' said Pierce. 'We can try periodically to . . .'

The doctor nodded placatingly and gestured for attention:

'At any time,' he said, 'that Rowan's heart does stop, she will not be resuscitated by artificial means. No one will give her any injections, or pump oxygen into her. There is no respirator here. She will be allowed to die as God wills. Now, because you ask me, I must tell you. This could go on indefinitely. It could stop at any time. Patients like this have been known to survive for years. A few have come back, true. Others die within days. All we can say now is that Rowan's body is restoring itself – from her injuries, from the malnutrition she suffered. But the brain . . . the brain cannot be restored in the same way.'

'But she could live into another era,' said Pierce eagerly, 'into a time of some momentous new discovery.'

'Absolutely,' said the doctor. 'And every conceivable medical possibility will be explored. Neurological consultations will begin tomorrow. It is easily within our means to bring every neurologist of note to this house to see Rowan. We will do it. We will meet periodically to discuss treatments. We will always be open to the possibility of a surgical procedure or some other experiment which could restore Rowan's mentation. But let me remind you, my friends, this is not very likely. There are patients throughout the world in this condition. The electroencephalogram confirms that there is almost no brain activity in Rowan at all.'

'Can't they transplant a piece of somebody's brain into her?' asked Gerald.

'I volunteer,' said Mona dryly. 'Take as many cells as you want. I've always had more than everybody else here.'

'You don't have to get nasty, Mona,' said Gerald, 'I was just asking a simple –'

'I'm not getting nasty,' said Mona, 'what I'm suggesting is that we need to read up on this and not make inane statements. Brain transplants aren't done. Not the kind she needs, anyway. Rowan is a vegetable! Don't you get it?'

'That's unfortunately the truth,' said the doctor softly. '"Persistent vegetative state" is only a little kinder, perhaps. But that is the case. We can and should pray for miracles. And a time will come when perhaps the collective decision will be made to withhold fluids and lipids. But at this juncture such a decision would be murder. It cannot be done.'

With a few handshakes and thank-yous, the doctor now made his way to the front door.

Ryan took the chair at the head of the table. He was a little more rested than yesterday, and seemed eager to make his report.

There was still no news whatsoever of Rowan's kidnapper or captor. There had been no further assaults on Mayfair women. The decision had been made to notify the authorities about 'the man' in a limited way.

'We have made a sketch, which Michael has approved. We have added the hair and the mustache and beard described by witnesses. We are requesting an interstate search. But no one, and I mean no one, in this room is to speak of this matter outside the family. No one is to give any more information than is necessary to the agencies who will cooperate with us.'

'You'll only hurt the investigation,' said Randall, 'if you go talking devils and spirits.'

'We are dealing with a man,' said Ryan. 'A man who walks and talks and wears clothes like other men. We have considerable circumstantial evidence to indicate he kidnapped and imprisoned Rowan. There is no need to bring in any chemical evidence right now.'

'In other words keep the blood samples under wraps,' said Mona.

'Exactly,' Ryan said. 'When this man is caught, then we can come forward with more details of the story. And the man himself will be living proof of what is alleged. Now Aaron has some things to say.'

Michael could see this was no pleasure for Aaron. He had been sitting silent throughout the meeting, beside Beatrice, who kept her fingers wrapped protectively about his arm. He was dressed somberly in dark blue, more like the rest of the family, as though he had put his old tweed style away. He looked not like an Englishman now but a southerner, Michael thought. Aaron shook his head as if to express some silent appreciation of what lay before them all. Then he spoke.

'What I have to say won't come as a surprise to you. I have severed my connection with the Talamasca. Things have been done by members of our Order – apparently – which have violated the trust of the family. I ask that all of you now regard the Talamasca as a hostile agency, and do not give any cooperation to anyone claiming connection with it from now on.'

'This wasn't Aaron's fault,' said Beatrice.

'How interesting that you would say this,' said Fielding dourly. He had been all this time as quiet as Aaron, and his voice now commanded immediate attention, as it usually did. His brown suit with its pinstripe of pink seemed as old as he was. He seemed bound to exercise the privilege of the very old – to say exactly what he thought.

'You realize,' he said to Aaron, 'that all this began with you, don't you?'

713

'That's not true,' Aaron said, calmly.

'Ah, but it is true,' said Fielding. 'You were in contact with Deirdre Mayfair when she became pregnant with Rowan. You have . . .'

'This is inappropriate, and badly timed,' said Ryan. His voice was steady but uncompromising. 'This family investigates everyone who becomes involved with it by way of marriage or even sometimes in casual social affairs. This man was, as much as I dislike to admit it, thoroughly investigated by us when he first came here. He is not connected with what happened. He is what he says he is – a scholar, who has been observing this family because of his access to certain historical documents regarding it, about which he has been painfully and fully candid from the start.'

'You're sure of that?' asked Randall. 'The history of the family as we know it – is the history which this man had given us, this Talamasca File on the Mayfair Witches as it is so audaciously called, and now we find ourselves embroiled in events which make sense in terms of this file.'

'Oh, so you two are in this together,' said Beatrice in a cold small voice, very unlike herself.

'This is preposterous,' said Lauren softly. 'Are you trying to imply that Aaron Lightner was responsible for the events he documented? Good heavens, have you no memory of the things that you yourself have seen and heard?'

Ryan interrupted: 'The Talamasca was thoroughly investigated in the nineteen-fifties by Carlotta,' he said. 'Her investigation was hardly sympathetic. She was looking for legal grounds to attack the organization. She found none. There has been no grim conspiracy originating with the Talamasca against us.'

Lauren spoke up again, decisively, drowning out at once the other voices which struggled to be heard.

'There is absolutely nothing to be gained from pursuing this question,' she said. 'Our tasks are simple. We take care of Rowan. And we find this man.' She looked at the others, one by one, first those to her right, then those to her left, then those across the table from her, and finally at Aaron. She went on:

'The historical records of the Talamasca have been of invaluable help to us in tracing the history of our family. Anything which can be verified *has* been verified without a single contradiction or flaw.'

'What the hell does that mean?' demanded Randall. 'How do you verify nonsense like –?'

'All the historical facts,' said Lauren, 'which have been mentioned in the narrative have been checked. The painting by Rembrandt of Deborah has been authenticated. Records regarding the Dutchman Petyr van Abel, still extant in Amsterdam, have been copied for our private family files. But I will not get drawn off into a long defense of the documents or of the Talamasca. Suffice it to say they have been helpful to us throughout the time of Rowan's disappearance. They are the ones who investigated the visit of Rowan and Lasher to Donnelaith. They are the ones who have placed in our hands the most detailed physical descriptions of this person, which our detectives have only confirmed. It is very doubtful any other agency of any kind, secular, religious or legal, would have given us this kind of assistance. But . . . Aaron has asked us to break off formal contact with the Talamasca, and with reason, and that we will do.'

'You can't sweep it all under the table,' said Fielding. 'What about that Dr Larkin?'

'No one knows what has happened to Dr Larkin,' said Ryan. 'That we all have to accept. But Lauren is correct. We have no material evidence of any wrong-doing on the part of the Talamasca. However, our contact has been exclusively through Aaron. Aaron is our friend. Aaron is now a member of the family through his marriage to Beatrice . . .'

'Yes, very convenient,' said Randall.

'You're a fool,' said Beatrice before she could stop herself.

'Amen to that,' said Mona.

To which Ryan immediately said, 'Pipe down.'

He seemed to realize it was more than a little inappro-priate, or at least Mona did everything in her power to freeze him into humiliation with her brilliant green eyes slitted like those of a basilisk. But he only patted the back of her hand by way of apology and went on.

'Aaron has advised us . . . as our friend, and as our kinsman, to have nothing further to do with the Tala-masca. And we shall do as he asks.'

Once again, several of them began to speak at the same time. Lily wanted to know more about why Aaron had turned on the Order. Cecilia wanted to remind everyone that there was a man from the Talamasca asking questions around the neighborhood, the neigh-bors had told her, and Anne Marie wanted 'just a little more clarification on a point or two'.

Lauren brought them all to silence. 'The Talamasca has confiscated medical information. It has refused to share its present knowledge of this case with us. It has cut itself off, as Aaron would explain to you if we gave him the opportunity! But you will not. We are moving forward. It's that simple. Report any mention of the

Order to the office; answer no questions; continue to preserve all security measures.' She leant forward, lowering her voice for emphasis: 'Maintain closed ranks!'

There was an uneasy silence.

'Michael, what do you have to say?' asked Lauren.

The question surprised him. He had been watching it all in a detached way as if it were baseball or football, or even chess. He had been drifting in and out of memories of Julien, Julien's words. Now he had to conceal his thoughts. To speak them frankly and openly, that wouldn't help anybody. Yet somehow the words came quietly out of his mouth.

'I will put an end to this man, whenever and wherever he's found. No one will keep him safe from me.'

Randall began to speak. So did Fielding. But Michael put up his hand.

'I want to go back upstairs and be with my wife. I want my wife to recover. I want to be with her now.'

'Other business quickly and finally,' said Ryan. He opened his large leather folder and removed several sheets of paper covered with typewritten words. 'Ah, no blood or tissue of any sort was found in St Martinville in the area where Rowan's unconscious body was discovered. If she did suffer a miscarriage there as the doctors believe, the evidence is long gone.

'The area is public. And there had been at least two rainstorms during the day, while Rowan lay there, and another after she was found. We have sent two skilled detectives back to the site. But as of now, we have no clues from there as to what really happened to Rowan. We are combing the surrounding area thoroughly for anyone who might have seen Rowan, or heard or seen anything that can be of help.'

There were a few resigned nods.

'Now, Michael, we are prepared to take the rest of this meeting downtown. It concerns the legacy, it concerns Mona. We'll leave you here now, with Aaron, and we'll be back later this evening, if you will allow.'

'Yes, of course,' said Michael. 'We're fine here. We have settled into a routine. Hamilton is upstairs with the nurses. Things are going as smoothly as one could expect.'

'Michael,' said Lauren. 'I know this is a difficult question. But I must ask it. Do you know the whereabouts of the Mayfair emerald?'

'Oh, for god's sakes!' said Bea, 'that cursed thing.'

'It's a legal matter,' said Lauren frostily. 'Legal. We must seek the emerald and place it around the neck of the designee.'

'Well, if it was up to me,' said Fielding, 'I'd go get a piece of green glass at Woolworth's. But I'm too old to go downtown.'

'Wasn't there a fake made of that thing by Stella?' asked Randall coldly, 'so she could fling it from a Mardi Gras float?'

'If there was,' said Lauren, 'she threw it from the float.'

'I don't know where it is,' said Michael. 'I think you asked me that when I was still sick, when I was in the hospital. I haven't seen it. I think you searched this house.'

'Yes, we did,' said Ryan. 'We thought perhaps we had overlooked something.'

'*He* probably has it,' said Mona softly.

No one responded.

'That could be,' said Michael. He gave a little smile.

'He probably has it. Probably considered it his very own. But you never know . . .' He tried not to look like a lunatic, but it was suddenly very funny to him. The emerald! Did Lasher have it in his pocket? Would he try to sell it? That would be a hoot.

The meeting had clearly come to an end. Bea would go up to Amelia Street. The others would go downtown.

Mona threw her arms around Michael and kissed him and then ducked out as if she didn't want to see his anxious or reproving look. He was a bit stunned; it was like all her sweetness was clinging to him, and then there was this emptiness where she had just been.

Beatrice gave Michael an urgent kiss, then took leave of her new husband, swearing to collect him later for supper and to make Michael eat something as well.

'So many people are trying to make me eat something,' Michael murmured at the sheer wonder of it. 'Ever since Rowan left. Eat, Michael, eat.'

Within moments they were gone. The big door had shut for the final time. There had been that faint vibration throughout the house that always sounded damaging, Michael thought, but probably wasn't.

Aaron remained at the far end of the table, across from Michael, leaning on his elbows, his back to the windows.

'I'm happy for you and Bea,' Michael said. 'You get the poem I sent to you with Yuri? The note?'

'Yes, he gave it to me. You must tell me about Julien. Tell me what happened, not as some snoop from across the Atlantic, but as your friend, please.'

Michael smiled. 'I want to tell you. I want to relive every second of it. I've been sort of jotting it down up

719

there, you know, so I won't forget. But the truth is, Julien had one purpose. It was to tell me to kill this thing, to stop it. That I was the one who was counted upon for that.'

Aaron appeared to be intrigued.

'Where's your friend Yuri?' asked Michael. 'He's still on good terms with us, isn't he?'

'Absolutely,' said Aaron. 'He's up at the Amelia Street house again. He's trying again, through Mona's computer. Mona said he could use her computer to contact the Elders, but the Elders are not acknowledging his pleas for clarification. It's all rather terrible for him, I think.'

'But not for you.'

Aaron was thoughtful for a moment, then he said, 'No . . . Not as much . . .'

'Good,' said Michael. 'Julien was suspicious of the Talamasca, I guess you got that from my note. Julien had more to say on it . . . but it all came down to the same thing – this creature is treacherous and deceitful; and it has to be destroyed. I'll kill it as soon as I can.'

Aaron seemed fascinated by this.

'But what if you had it in your power? What if you had it contained where it couldn't . . .'

'No. That's the mistake. Read the poem again. I'm to kill it. Go upstairs and look at my wife again, if you have any doubts. Go hold her hand. I'll kill it. And I will have a chance to do it. Evelyn's poem and Julien's visit have promised me that.'

'You're like a man who's experienced religious conversion,' said Aaron. 'A week ago you were philosophical, almost despairing. You were actually physically sick.'

'Well, I thought my wife had abandoned me. I was

grieving for my wife and for my own courage, both of which had been lost. Now I know she didn't mean to abandon me.

'And why wouldn't I be like St Paul after his vision on the road to Damascus? You realize I'm the only one living who has seen and spoken to this thing?' He gave a little laugh. 'Gifford, Edith, Alicia ... I don't even remember their names. All dead. And Rowan mute now, just like Deirdre. But I'm not dead. I'm not mute. I know what it looks like. I know the sound of its voice. And I'm the one to whom Julien came. I guess I do have the conviction of a convert. Or maybe just the conviction of a saint.'

He reached into his jacket pocket, drew out the medal that Ryan had returned to him, the medal which Gifford had found Christmas Day by the pool. 'You gave this to me, remember?' he said to Aaron. 'What's it like when St Michael sinks his trident into a demon? Does the demon wriggle and scream for its mother? Must be difficult to be St Michael. This time, I will find out.'

'Julien was its enemy then? Of this you're sure.'

Michael sighed. Ought to go upstairs. 'What would the nurses do if I got in bed with her? What would they do if I just snuggled up to her and held her in my arms?'

'It's your house,' said Aaron. 'Lie beside her if you wish. Tell them to sit outside the door.'

Michael shook his head. 'If only I knew she wanted me near her. If only I knew she wanted anything at all.'

He thought for a long moment.

'Aaron,' he said. 'If you were he – Lasher – where would you be right now? What would you be doing?'

Aaron shook his head. 'I don't know. Michael, tell

me why Julien was so sure Lasher was evil? Tell me what Julien knew.'

'Julien went after its origins. He went to Donnelaith to investigate the ruins. It wasn't the famous circle of stones that mattered to him. It was the Cathedral. A saint named Ashlar. An early Highlands saint. The thing had something to do with the Christian times in that glen. Something to do with the saint.'

'Ashlar, I've heard the story of St Ashlar,' said Aaron quietly. 'It's in the Latin files in the archives. I remember reading it, but not in connection with this case. Oh, if only they hadn't locked Yuri out of the computers. What has Lasher to do with this saint?'

'Julien never quite figured it out. He thought at first the thing was the saint – a vengeful ghost. But it wasn't that simple. Yet the thing did originate there, in that place. It didn't come from heaven or hell or all time or whatever lies it always tells the witches. It started its dark destiny in the Glen of Donnelaith.' He paused. 'What do you know about Ashlar?'

'It's an old Scottish legend. Very pagan actually,' said Aaron. 'Michael, why didn't you tell me these things?'

'I am telling you, Aaron, but it doesn't matter. I'm going to kill it. We can find out all about its past after it's dead. So what do you know about Ashlar, the Scottish saint?'

'Ah . . . something about the saint returning every so many hundred years. It's in books here and there. But I never realized it had to do with Donnelaith. There's another mystery for you. Why wasn't it in the files? We cross-reference. We are so careful. But I never saw a mention of any legends connected with Donnelaith. I assumed there was no relevant material.'

'But what story did you hear?'

'The saint had special physical characteristics. From time to time someone would be born having those characteristics. And he would be declared the reincarnation of the saint. The new saint. All very pagan. Not Catholic at all. In the Catholic Church if you are a saint, it's because you are in heaven, not migrating into new flesh.'

Michael nodded. Gave a little laugh.

'Write it down for me,' said Aaron. 'Everything Julien told you. You must.'

'I will, but remember what I said. Julien only had one message. It was to kill the thing. Not to be "interested in it", but to wipe it out.' Michael sighed. 'Should have done it at Christmas. Should have killed it. I could have, probably, but naturally Rowan didn't want me to. How could she? This newborn thing, this mystery. That's what always happens. It seduces people. And now it's flesh, and what is the old prayer, "And the word was made flesh and dwelt amongst us."'

Aaron nodded. 'Let me say it once aloud to you,' he said in a low voice, 'so I don't say it over and over forever in my heart and soul. I should have come here with you on Christmas Eve. I should not have let you come up against it alone, come up against it and her.'

'Don't condemn her.'

'I don't. I don't mean that. I mean I should have been here. That's all I mean. If it matters, I don't intend to desert you now.'

'It matters,' said Michael, with a shrug. 'But you know, I have this curious feeling. It's going to be easy now that I've made up my mind. Kill it.' He snapped his fingers. 'That's my problem. I was afraid to do that from the start.'

*

It was eight o'clock. Dark, cold. You could feel the cold if you put your hands on the panes.

Aaron had just come back for supper with Yuri. Yuri was returning to the Amelia Street house to talk to Mona. Yuri had blushed when he said he was going. Michael had realized the reason why. Yuri was taken with Mona. Then Yuri had stammered, 'She reminds me of myself at her age. She is unusual. She said she would show me all her computer tricks. We will . . . talk.'

Flustered, stammering, blushing. Ah, the power of Mona, thought Michael. And now she had the legacy to contend with, as well as everything else.

But there was something pure about Yuri, pure and loyal and good.

'He can be trusted,' Aaron had said quietly. 'He is a gentleman, and he is honorable. Mona will be quite safe in his company. Never fear.'

'No one has to fear for Mona,' said Michael, a little ashamed, and getting just a wisp again of those sensual moments, when he'd held her and knew it was wrong and that it was going to happen and so what?

There were so few times when Michael had done bad things and said, So what?

Aaron was asleep in the upstairs bedroom.

'Men of my age nap after meals,' he had said apologetically. He had gone to lie down. He was utterly exhausted, and Michael wouldn't talk anymore about Julien just now, and maybe that was best because Aaron needed the rest.

Just you and me now, Julien, Michael thought.

It was quiet in the house.

Hamilton had gone home to pay some bills. Bea

would return later. Only one nurse was on duty because all the money in the world could not procure another, such was the shortage. A nurse's aide, very capable, was upstairs in Aunt Vivian's room going into her third quarter hour on the phone.

He could hear the rise and fall of the woman's voice.

He stood in the living room, looking out into the side yard. Darkness. Cold. Remembering. Drums of Comus. A man smiling in the darkness. Suddenly Michael was a small child again, and would never know what it meant to be strong or to be safe. Fear had kicked in the door of childhood. Fear had laid waste the safety that had been Mother.

Drums and torches on Mardi Gras Night struck terror. We die when we get old. We are no more. No more. He tried to imagine himself dead. A skull in the earth. This thought had come to him often in his life. I will be that way someday, absolutely. It is a certainty, one of the few in my life. I will be dead. I may be a skull in the earth. I may be a skull in a coffin. I don't know. But I will die.

It seemed the nurse's aide was crying. Not possible. There was the soft vibration of steps. The front door closed. That was all so far away from him, people coming, going. If she took a turn for the worse, they'd shout his name.

And he'd run upstairs, but why? To be there when the breath left her. To hold her cold hand. To lay his head on her breast and feel the last of the warmth in her. How did he know it would be like that? Had anyone ever told him? Or was it just that her hands were getting colder and colder and stiffer and stiffer, and when he looked at her nails, her pretty clean nails, they were faintly blue.

'We will not manicure them,' the nurse had said. 'You can scrap that part of the plan. We have to be able to see their color. It has to do with oxygen. She was a beautiful woman.'

Yes, you said that before. But *she* hadn't. It had been the *other* nurse who had said it. How many other insensitive things had they said?

The movement of the dark trees outside chilled him. Chilled him to look at it. He didn't want to be here, staring out the window in the cold empty side yard. He wanted to be warm and be with her.

He turned around and walked slowly back across the double parlor, beneath the cypress arch, a beautiful ornamental thing. Maybe he should read to her, softly, so that she could tune it out if she hated it. Maybe play the radio for a while. Maybe play Julien's Victrola. That mean nurse who didn't like the Victrola was no longer here.

He could send the nurses out of the room, couldn't he? Gradually it had been penetrating to him. Do we need these nurses?

He saw her dead. He saw her gray and cold and finished. He saw her buried, more or less. Not the whole detailed picture, step by step, and strewn over time. Just the concept, in a flashing light – a coffin sliding into a vault. Like Gifford. Only it was here, their cemetery on the edge of the Garden District, and he could walk over there any day, and lay his hand on the slab of marble that was only four or five inches from her soft dark blond hair. Rowan, Rowan.

Remember, mon fils.

He turned. Who had said this? The great long hall was hollow and empty and slightly cold. The dining room was altogether dark. He listened, not for real sounds, but for supernatural ones, for the voice again. Remember, yes, I will.

'Yes, I will,' he said.

Silence. All around him silence, wrapping up his spoken words and making them loud. Making them sharp in the stillness, like a movement, like a drop in temperature. Silence.

There was absolutely no one about. No one in the dining room. No one visible at the top of the stairs. He could see Aunt Vivian's room was no longer lighted. No one talking on the phone. Empty. Darkness.

And then it penetrated to him. He was alone.

No, couldn't be. He walked to the front door and opened it. For one moment, he could not take it in. No one at the black iron gate. No one on the porch. No one across the street. Just the solemn empty silence of the Garden District, deserted as a ruined city beneath the motionless street light, the soft clumps of oak leaves. The house as still and undisturbed as it had ever been the first time he saw it.

'Where are they?' He felt the sudden thrust of panic. 'Christ, what's going on?'

'Michael Curry?'

The man was standing to his left. In the shadows, almost invisible, except for his blond hair. He came forward. He must have been two inches taller than Michael. Michael looked into his pale eyes.

'You sent for me?' the man asked softly, respectfully. He extended his hand. 'I'm sorry, Mr Curry.'

'Sent for you? What do you mean?'

'You had the priest call the hotel for me, you asked that I come. I'm sorry it is over.'

'I don't know what you're talking about. Where are the guards who were here? Where is the watchman who was at the gate? What happened to everybody?'

'The priest sent them away,' said the man gently. 'As soon as she died. He told me on the phone that he was sending them away. That I was to come and wait here, by the door, for you. I'm sorry she's dead. I hope she knew no pain or fear.'

'Oh no, I'm dreaming. She's not dead! She's upstairs. What priest? There's no priest here! Aaron!'

He turned, staring into the deep darkness of the hallway, for a moment unable to make out the red carpet of the stairs. Then he bolted, taking the flight in one bound after another, and rushing to her closed door.

'Goddamnit, she didn't die. She didn't. They would have told me.'

When he felt the knob, and realized he couldn't open it, he was about to ram it with his shoulder.

'Aaron!' he shouted again.

A click inside. The little lock turning. The door popping back, just a little as if of its own accord. Doors all have their own pace and rhythm, their own way of opening or closing. Doors in New Orleans are never neat or efficient about it. In summer this door would swell up and scarcely close. Now it danced open.

He stared at it, at the white wooden panels. Inside the candles gleamed as before. Flicker on the silk of the tester, on the marble fireplace.

Aaron was speaking to him. Aaron said a name behind him. It sounded Russian. And the blond man said softly:

'But he asked for me, Aaron. He called me. The priest told me. He asked that I come.'

He walked into the room. The candles were the only light. They were blazing on the little altar, and the Virgin's shadow rose up the wall, jittering and dancing as before. Rowan lay in the bed; her breasts rose and fell beneath the pink satin of the new gown they'd put on her. Her hands curled inward. Her mouth was open. He could hear her breathing. She was alive. Unchanged.

He fell on his knees next to the bed; he laid his head down on it, and he cried. He took her cold hand and squeezed it, and felt its pliancy, and what tiny bit of human warmth was actually there. She was alive.

'Oh, Rowan, my darling, my darling,' he said. 'I thought . . .' and then he sobbed like a child.

He just let the sobs come out slowly. He knew Aaron was near him. And he knew the other man was there too. And then slowly he looked up and he saw the figure standing at the foot of the bed.

The priest. The thought sprang from him instantly when he saw the old-fashioned cassock of black wool, and the white Roman collar, but it was no priest.

'Hello, Michael.'

Soft voice. Tall as they had said he was. Hair long and black and over his shoulders, beard and mustache beautifully groomed and gleaming, a sort of horrid Christ or Rasputin, with his blanched and tearstained face.

'I too have been weeping for her,' the man said in a whisper. 'She is near death now; she will bear no more; she will love no more; only a little milk was left in her; she is all but gone.'

He was holding to the bedpost with his left hand.

'Lasher!'

Perfectly monstrous suddenly – a man who was taller than an ordinary man. A slight figure, but the perfect incarnation of menace with its blue eyes fixed on him intently, mouth vivid beneath the black gleam of the mustache, white fingers long and bony and almost twined around the bedpost. Monstrous.

Kill it. Now.

He was on his feet in an instant, but Stolov had him around the waist. 'No, Michael, no, don't hurt him. You can't do it!' And then another man, a stranger, was grabbing him around the neck, and Aaron was begging Michael to hold off, to wait.

The figure by the bed remained motionless, secure. It wiped at its tears with a slow languid right hand.

'Hold on, Michael. Hold on,' said Aaron. 'Stolov, I want you to let him go. You too, Norgan. Step back, Michael, we have it surrounded.'

'Only if he will not kill it,' said Stolov. 'He must not kill it.'

'The hell I won't,' said Michael. He arched his back, trying to throw off Stolov, but the other man had his arm too tightly around Michael's neck. Stolov loosened his grip, catching his breath.

The creature looked at him. The tears continued to move, silent, eloquent.

'I'm in your hands, Mr Stolov,' Lasher said. 'I'm all yours.'

Michael jammed his elbow into the gut of the man behind him, then flung him backwards against the wall. He threw Stolov to the side. He was on Lasher in an instant, hands locked around his neck, the creature drawing in his breath in ragged terror, and grasping at Michael's hair. Down they went onto the carpet. But the two other men had Michael, they were pulling him loose, wrenching him with all their strength, and Aaron, even Aaron was pulling his fingers off the creature. Aaron. Dear God.

For a moment Michael almost blacked out. The pain in his chest was sharp and relentless. He felt it in his shoulder and then going down his left arm. They had let him go because he was sitting back against the fireplace, unable now to hurt anybody, and Lasher, still struggling for breath, was climbing slowly, groggily to his feet. A lean figure in the flowing black cassock. The men stood on either side of Michael.

'Wait, Michael!' pleaded Aaron. 'There are four of us against it.'

'Don't hurt it, Michael,' said Stolov, tone as gentle as before.

'You're letting it get away,' said Michael in a hoarse whisper. But when he looked up he saw the tall willowy figure peering down at him, the blue eyes still filled with tears, and the tears running down the smooth white cheeks. If Christ came to you, Michael thought, you would want him to look like this. This was the way painters had rendered him.

'I am not escaping,' said Lasher calmly. 'I will go when they take me, Michael. The men from the Talamasca. I need them now. And they know it. And they will not let you hurt me again.' He turned towards the figure in the bed. 'I came to see my beloved. I had to see her before they took me away.'

Michael tried to get to his feet. He was dizzy and the pain came again. Goddamnit, Julien, give me the strength to do it. Damnation. The gun, the gun is there by the bed. It's right on top of the table, that big gun! He tried to say it out loud to Aaron. Shoot it. Pull the trigger and blow a hole in its head as big as an eye!

Stolov knelt in front of him. Stolov said: 'Be calm, Michael, be calm. Just don't try to hurt him. We will not allow him to leave this place, until we ourselves take him away.'

'I am ready,' said Lasher.

'Michael,' said Stolov. 'Look at him. He is helpless now. He is in our power. Please be calm.'

Aaron stared at the creature as if spellbound.

'I warned you,' said Michael softly.

'Do you really want to kill me?' asked Lasher, tears welling continuously as if he had as many of them as a little child. 'Do you hate me so very much? Just for trying to be alive?'

'You killed her,' Michael whispered. It was such a small, insignificant sound. 'You did that to her. You killed our child.'

'Don't you want to know my side of it, Father?' said the creature.

'I want to kill you,' said Michael.

'Oh, come now. Can you be so cold and unfeeling? Can you not care what was done to me? Can you not care why I am here? Do you think I meant to hurt her?'

Grasping the mantelpiece with one hand and Aaron's hand with the other, Michael finally managed to get to his feet. He was weak all over, almost nauseated. He stood there, breathing slowly, thankful that the pain was gone, and staring at Lasher.

How beautiful the smooth face, how beautiful the soft black mustache and the close-cut beard. The Jesus of Dürer's painting. And the deepest most exquisite blue eyes, mirrors to some unfathomable and seemingly wondrous soul.

'Oh yes, Michael, you want to know. You want to

hear everything. And they will not let you kill me, will you, gentlemen? Not even Aaron will allow it. Not until I've said all I have to say.'

'Lies,' whispered Michael.

The creature swallowed as if struck by the condemnation, and then once again he wiped his eye with the back of his right hand. He did it as a child would, on the playground, and then he pressed his lips together and took a deep breath as if he would give way, as Michael had before – to sobs as well as tears.

Behind him, on the bed, Rowan lay oblivious, eyes staring into space, undisturbed, protected perhaps – unreachable as before.

'No, Michael,' he said. 'No lies. That I promise you. We know better, don't we, than to believe the truth will excuse anything. But lies you will not hear.'

Once again, the dining room. Only this time the light coming through the windows was the dim golden light of the lamps in the yard.

They sat around the table in the shadows. Both the doors were closed. Lasher sat in the place of authority, at the head of the table, one great white hand splayed on the wood before him, staring down at it as if he were dazed.

He raised his head and looked about him. He looked at the murals as though taking up one detail after another and releasing it again to the gloom. He looked at their faces. He looked at Michael, who sat near him just to his right.

The other man, Clement Norgan, was still sore from Michael's jabbing him, still sore from having been cracked against the wall. He sat across the table, red-faced, trying to catch his breath still, drinking sips from a glass of water. His eyes moved from the creature to Michael. Stolov sat to Norgan's left.

Aaron was beside Michael, holding on to his shoulder, holding his hand. Michael could feel the tightness of Aaron's grip.

Lasher.

'Yes, in this house, again,' the creature said, voice tremulous yet deep and confident in its own beauty, its perfect accentless enunciation.

'Let him speak,' said Aaron. 'We are four men. We are resolved he will not leave here. Rowan is resting untroubled. Let him talk.'

'That is correct,' said Stolov. 'We are together. Let him explain himself to us all. You are entitled to such an explanation, Michael. No one contests it.'

'Trickster always,' said Michael. 'You sent her nurses away. You sent the guards away. So clever. They believed you, Father Ashlar, or did you use some other name?'

Lasher gave a long, slow, bitter smile. 'Father Ashlar,' he whispered, running his pink tongue along his lip and then closing his lips quietly. For one instant, Michael saw Rowan in him, saw the resemblance as he had seen on Christmas Day. The fine cheeks, the forehead, even the tender line of the long eyes. But in the depth of the color and in the bright open look to them, they were Michael's eyes.

'She doesn't know she is alone now,' said Lasher solemnly. He spoke the words slowly, eyes moving again around the vast dark room. 'What are nurses anymore to her? She does not know any longer who stands by her, who weeps for her, who loves her, who sheds tears. She has lost the child which was inside her. And there will be no more. All that will happen now will be without her. Her story is told.'

Michael started to rise, but Aaron held him, and the other two glared at him across the table. Lasher remained unafraid.

'And you want to tell us your story,' said Stolov timidly, as if gazing at a monarch or an apparition. 'And we are ready to hear.'

'Yes, I will tell you,' said Lasher with a small, almost brave smile. 'I will tell you what I know now, flesh and blood that I am. I will tell you all of it. And then you can make your judgment.'

Michael uttered a short, mirthless laugh. It startled the others. It startled him. He gazed steadily at Lasher. 'All right, *mon fils*,' he said, pronouncing the French carefully, correctly. 'Remember your promise to me. No lies.'

They looked at one another for a long moment, and then the creature lapsed back into solemnity, only wincing slightly as if he'd been struck.

'Michael,' he said, 'I cannot speak now for what I was in the centuries of darkness; I cannot speak now for a desperate, discarnate thing – without history or memory or reason – that *sought* to reason – rather than suffer, grieve and want.'

Michael's eyes narrowed. He said nothing.

'The story that *I* want to tell is my *own* – who I was before death separated me from the flesh I dreamed of forever after.' He brought his two hands up and crossed them for one moment on his chest.

'In the beginning,' said Michael mockingly.

'In the beginning,' the creature repeated, only without

the irony. He went on, slowly, words heartfelt, imploring. 'In the beginning – long before Suzanne said her prayer in the circle – in the beginning – when I had life, true life in me, as I have it again now.'

Silence.

'Trust us,' said Stolov. It was almost a whisper.

Lasher's eyes remained fixed on Michael.

'You don't know,' he said, 'how eager I am to tell you the truth. I dare you – I dare you to hear me out and not to forgive.'

THIRTY-FOUR

LASHER'S STORY

Let me take you to the first moments, as *I* recall them –
no matter what others said to me after, either in one
life or another, no matter what I came to see in my
dreams.

I remember lying in bed beside my mother; it was a
coffered bed, heavily carven, with bulbous posts and
hung with ocher velvet, and the walls were the same
color though the ceiling of the room, like the ceiling of
the bed, was all of dark wood. My mother was crying.
She was terrified – a wan dark-eyed creature, drawn
and trembling. I was nursing from her, and had her in
my power, in that I was taller than she was, and
stronger, and was holding her as I drank the milk from
her breast.

I knew who she was, that I had been in her, and I
knew that her life was in danger, that when my monstrosity was revealed she would undoubtedly be called a
witch and put to death. She was a Queen. Queens
cannot bear monsters. That the King had not set eyes
on me, that the women were keeping him out of the
chamber, this I also knew. The women were as frightened of me as my mother.

I wanted love from my mother. I wanted the milk.
The men in the castle were beating on the doors. They
were threatening to enter the Queen's chamber if they

were not told immediately why they were being kept out.

My mother was crying continuously and did not want to touch me. She spoke in English, saying that God had cursed her for what she had done, God had cursed her and the King, and now her dreams were ruined; I was the retribution from heaven – my deformity, my size, the obvious fact that I was a monster. That I could not be a human being.

What did I know at that moment? That I was flesh *again*. That I had returned. That I had succeeded in some seemingly endless journey, and had once more found port, safe and sound. I felt happy.

That was all I knew – and that I must take command.

It was I who calmed the women, revealing that I could speak. I said that I had drunk enough milk. I could go out now and find milk and cheese and such on my own. I would have my mother out of danger. I said that for my mother's sake, I must be taken out of the castle, unseen by the rest of the court.

There was of course a shocked silence that I could speak, that I could reason, that I was not merely a giant newborn but possessed a cunning mind. My mother rose up and stared at me through her tears. She held up her left hand. I saw there the mark of the witch, the sixth finger. I knew that I had returned through her because she was a powerful witch, yet she was innocent as all mothers. I knew also that I must leave this place and seek the glen.

My vision of the glen was without contour, color, contrast. This was a concept analogous to an echo. I did not stop to demand of myself, 'What glen?' There was too much danger here in this castle. If there was something more to the vision, it was a circle of stones, and within it a circle of persons, and beyond another circle of persons, and beyond that another, and another, all turning, the circles within circles, and there rose a chanting sound.

This was fleeting.

I said to my mother that I had come from the glen and must go back to it, and she, rising up on her arms, uttered in a whisper the name of my father, Douglas of Donnelaith. She told the women that they must find Douglas, who was, at this very moment, at court, that they must somehow bring him to her at once. She uttered something I could not grasp – something to do with a witch coupling with a witch, and that Douglas had been her terrible error, and that in trying to give the King an heir, she had made a witch's tragic mistake.

She fell back near to unconsciousness.

A message was given through a small window in the doorway to a secret passage. It was the midwife now who calmed the other women and told the men through the door, at last, the tragic news: the Queen's child had been stillborn.

Stillborn! I began to laugh, a soft laughter which seemed a great comfort to me; as wondrous as breathing or milk tasting. But the women only became alarmed. I should have been born in love and in joy and I knew it. This was all wrong.

The voices through the door said the King would see his infant son.

'Please get clothes for me,' I said. 'Hurry. I cannot remain naked and undefended in this place.'

At once they were glad to have this direction. And by the same secret window in the door to the secret passage the message was given for that.

I was uncertain how to dress myself. These weren't clothes I knew. Indeed, the more I looked at these ladies-in-waiting, the midwife, my mother, the more I realized things had greatly changed.

Don't ask, 'Changed from what?' I didn't know. I was dressed quickly in fine green velvet, clothes which in fact were the property of the tallest and most lean attendant of the King. The sleeves were rich and embroidered. There was a trimming of fur to the small sleeveless cape. And a belt for the waist, and a rather long cut to the tunic, and then the leggings were the worst for me, for my legs were so long. I had to bind them where they did not fit. The tunic covered it.

Discovering myself in the mirror, I thought: Yes! And I knew that I was beautiful, otherwise the women would have been even more afraid.

My hair was not yet down to my shoulders, but would be soon. It was brown. My eyes were brown, as were my mother's. I put on the fur-trimmed hat which they gave me.

The midwife then fell on her knees. 'This is the Prince,' she cried. 'This is the heir sought by the King.'

The other women shook their heads in horror, trying to quiet her, telling her it was not possible, such a thing. And my mother turned her head into the pillow, crying for her own mother, for her sister, for those who loved her, averring that no one would stand with her. That were it not a mortal sin in the eyes of God, she would take her own life.

Now how do I escape, I thought. I felt fear for my mother. Yet I hated her that she didn't love me, that she thought me monstrous. I knew what I was. I knew there was a place for me, that I had a destiny. I knew this. I knew that her attitude was irreverent and cruel, but I could not put this into words or defend such a position. I wanted only to protect her.

We stood in this candlelighted chamber, I and these women, beneath this dark wooden ceiling, and the midwife gained possession of herself and forswore her former joy. This monster must be taken out, destroyed.

Destroyed? The same old song. Not *this* time, I thought. I did not intend to be destroyed so easily. No. We must learn more each time, I thought. I will not be destroyed.

Finally to the secret door came my father, Douglas of Donnelaith, a big shaggy man, more crudely dressed but nevertheless noble and decked in fur.

He had been in the castle and in great haste answered the Queen's secret summons. When he was admitted to the birthing room, and beheld me, his face was a puzzle. I did not see in him the pure horror of the women. I saw something else, something vital and partial to me, something almost reverent. And he whispered, 'Ashlar, who comes again and again.'

I saw that his hair and eyes were brown; from him as from the poor sad Queen I had these endowments. But I was Ashlar! I felt this news – and it was news – come into me as if my father had thrown his arms around me and showered me with kisses. I was happy. And when I looked at my mother, in her sadness, I wept.

I said, 'Yes, Father, but this is no place for me. This is a place hostile to me. We must leave here.'

And I realized I knew no more of what I was or what he was than what had been said. It was the strangest kind of knowing, knowing without a tale to it, a knowing that was stable but out of time.

He needed no direction from me. He too was in terror. He knew that we must escape. 'There is no hope now for the Queen,' he said softly, crossing himself and then making the Sign of the Cross on my forehead. We were already following the winding stairs.

We were out of the castle within moments, going down directly to a covered boat which waited for us in the dark waters of the River Thames. It was when we reached the Thames that I realized I had said no farewell to my mother and I was overwhelmed with sorrow, with a sense of horror suddenly that I had been born in this particular dreary and treacherous place and into this inexplicable time. My struggles were to begin all over again. I remember I would have died then if I could; I would have retreated. I stared down at the water, which stank of the filth of London, the filth of thousands, and I wanted to die in this darkness. Indeed, I saw in the mind's mist a dark tunnel down which I had come, and I wanted to go back into it. I began to cry.

My father put his arm around me. 'Don't weep, Ashlar,' he said. 'It is the work of God.'

'How so the work of God? My mother could be burnt at the stake.' I was already thirsting for milk. I wanted hers, and it embittered me that I had not taken more before I left. And the thought that anyone could commit this flesh of my flesh, my mother, to the flames, seemed impious and worth dying to prevent.

This is my birth I'm describing to you. This is a succession of hours, lived by the light of candles and never forgotten as long as I was in the flesh. This is what I now remember vividly, because I am flesh again. But the name Ashlar I didn't know. I do not know now and never will know who Ashlar really was – as you shall see.

Mark me on this. Understand. Understand fully. I know nothing of *the original saint*.

Later I would see things; I would be told tales. I would see St Ashlar in the stained-glass window in the great Highlands Cathedral of Donnelaith. I would be told that I was he, and I had 'come again'.

But what I am telling you now is what I remember. What I knew!

It took us many days and nights to reach Scotland.

It was the dead of winter, it was in fact the first days after Christmas, when the worst fears grip the peasants, and it is thought that spirits walk and witches do their evil work. It was the time when the peasants forsook the teachings of Christ and, dressing in animals' skins, went prowling door to door, demanding tribute of the superstitious inhabitants. Old custom.

We slept only fitfully in small village inns when we came upon them, usually amid the hay and with others, and often sickened and annoyed by the vermin. We stopped again and again so that I might have milk. I drank milk warm from the cow. It was good, but not as sweet as the milk of my mother. I ate the cheese in handfuls. It was pure.

We traveled by horseback, wrapped in heavy woolens and skins, and through most of this journey, I was gazing in quiet astonishment at the falling snow, at the fields through which we rode, the small villages where we sought shelter, with their half-timbered inns and scattered thatched huts. There were revels in the woodland, fires burning, men in the skins of beasts dancing. A fear gripped those who remained indoors.

'Look,' said my father. 'The ruins of the great monastery. See there, on the hill. An abbey built in the time of

St Augustine. Burned by the King. These are days of horror for all Christian men. Everything looted. The nuns driven out. The priests driven out. The statues burned, the windows broken, the cloisters now the shelter of the field rats and the poor. It is all gone, broken. And to think it is the will of one man. One man could destroy so much of the work of others. Ashlar, this is why you have come.'

I was very doubting of this. In fact, it frightened me that my father would think this, that he would express his faith in such simple terms. It was as though I knew something different, and this sense of knowing something different was merely what you call incredulity. I felt an innate doubt, an innate sense that my father was misguided, and dreaming. Yet why I couldn't know.

I saw the vision of the circles again, the many widening circles of figures dancing. I tried to see the stones which were almost at the center, surrounding the first circle of figures inside.

I searched my mind consciously and rigorously for the full extent of the knowledge with which I was endowed. That I had lived before, yes, this was certain, but not that this man knew my purpose or who or what I really was. I trusted that the truth would come to me. But then again, how did I know?

We rode through the ruins of the monastery, our horses' hooves clattering on the stone floors of the roofless cloister. I began to weep. I felt an uncontainable sorrow. The desolation of the place, the loss – it filled me with a crushing sense of hopelessness. I shrank from the pain of being flesh. My father reached out to comfort me. 'Be still, Ashlar, we are going home. This has not happened in our home.'

We entered the dark forest, barely able to see our way. It seemed wolves ran in the darkness; I could smell them near us, smell their fur and their hunger. When we came upon small huts, those within would give no answer, though smoke came from a small hole in the roof.

The deep high forest crept up into the mountains. The roads grew steeper and steeper, and the vantage points more splendid of coast and of sea. At last we had to sleep in the woods without shelter; and we huddled together, my father and I, beneath heavy blankets, with our horses tethered at our feet. I felt defenseless in the darkness, and all the more so for I thought I heard whispers and strange sounds.

It must have been midnight when my father woke and uttered curses, and rose to his feet and swung his sword. He seemed in a fury; but the darkness gave no answer back to him.

'They are helpless, and stupid and eternal,' he muttered.

'But who, Father?'

'The little people. They will not get what they want. Come, we can't sleep here any longer, and we aren't far from home.'

We rode cautiously through the darkness, and then through a forlorn winter day that scarcely gave us any light.

At last we entered the narrow rocky path of the secret pass to the Glen of Donnelaith.

My father told me the story. There were two other known entrances to our precious valley – the main road over which the wagons traveled incessantly, bringing produce to market, and the loch where the ships docked which took the goods to sea. By both routes came the incessant parade of pilgrims to lay gold at the altar of St Ashlar, to seek his healing miracles, to lay hands upon the sarcophagus of the saint.

This story struck terror. What would these people want of me! And I was hungry already for milk, and for cream, and for things that were thick, and white, and pure.

There had been much war in the Highlands, said my father. There had been pitched battles; and our kind, the Clan of Donnelaith, he said, had resisted the King's men and would not burn the monasteries nor sack the churches nor take a vow against the pope in Rome. Only under heavy guard did Scotsmen come into this valley, did the traders come into the small port.

'We are of the Highlands; we are the Christians of St Columba and St Patrick, we are of the old Irish church, and we will not yield to this pompous King in Windsor Castle who shakes his fist in the face of God, or to the Archbishop of Canterbury, his lackey, let both of them be damned. Let all Englishmen be damned. They are burning the priests. So they make martyrs. You will understand all in time.'

These words brought a peace to me, but I could not claim that I knew the name Columba or Patrick, and when I tried again to recollect all I knew it seemed that my inborn knowledge had become smaller even as we had traveled north. Had I known things in my mother's arms which I had forgotten? Had I known things in her womb? I could not chase these receding phantoms with any success. They were gone from me, leaving only a shimmer.

I am born. I am flesh! I was living and breathing

again. The darkness is dispelled and even this soft snow surrounding me is part of the living world, and look! The sky above, a blue no painter could capture, and then the deep glen spreading out before us, as we came out of the mountains – look, the great church.

The snow fell in small soft flakes around us. I was so used to being cold I had forgotten to dislike it. I was charmed by what I saw.

'Wrap the wool around you,' said my father. 'We are going into the castle, that is our home.'

I didn't want to follow the path up to the castle. Rather I wanted to go down into the town. It was a great town then, you cannot imagine. It had nothing to do with the small pathetic village that grew up on its ruins later on. It had its walls, its battlements, and within were its citizens and its merchants, its bankers, and its great Cathedral! And all around lived the farmers, said my father, on rich land which, though it was now covered with snow, gave good harvests, and provided for fat and healthy sheep.

Beyond in the hills, here and there, and there, where he pointed, were other strongholds, in which lesser chieftains loyal to Donnelaith lived under our protection and in peace.

Smoke rose from a hundred chimneys pressed within the battlements and from the towers scattered and barely visible in the high woods. The air was thick with delicious smells of food cooking.

And there rising out of the center of the town stood the massive Cathedral, quite visible beyond the houses and the walls, the snow sliding from its steep Gothic steeples and peaked roof, and light blazing inside it so that its great windows were filled with myriad colors and enchanting designs. I could see, even at this late hour, hundreds moving in and out of the Cathedral doors.

'Father, please let me go there!' I begged. I was drawn to this place as if I knew it, yet I did not. I hungered for the discovery of it.

'No, my son, you come with me.'

We had to go to the castle, high above the loch, which was our home.

Down below, the water was covered with ice, but in the spring, said my father, the merchants would come by the hundreds, and so would the salmon fishermen, and the banks would be full of traders, and men would come to trade linen for the wool and skins and fish which we had to sell.

This castle was a series of round towers, no more beautiful than the ominous heap of stone in which I'd been born. Once inside, I perceived it was less luxurious, but nevertheless filled with a bustling life.

The great hall itself might have been a mountain cave, so crude were its adornments – its few grand arches, its staircase – but it was all decorated for a great banquet, and the fairies of the wood could not have created a scene of greater warmth or charm.

The floor itself was entirely covered in green. And great garlands trimmed the sides of the stairway, and were placed above those arches deep enough to hold them, and placed all about the huge hearth. Indeed green branches of the Scots pine were everywhere laid, fragrant and beautiful, and mistletoe and ivy were likewise used in decorations, and I knew these lovely evergreens. I knew their names.

I saw the splendor with which the woods had been

brought indoors. Candles by the dozens blazed along the walls, and down the length of the banquet table, and benches were being brought up for those who would dine.

'Sit down at the table,' said Father, 'and keep quiet, whatever you do.'

It seemed that we had arrived at the very moment of the banquet, which was only one of the twelve banquets of Christmas, and the entire kindred was gathering for the feast. No sooner were we seated at a bench at the far end, than in came the ladies and men in gorgeous attire.

This attire did not match the clothes given me at the London court, but it was nevertheless very fine, and many of the men wore Highland dress of belted plaid. The ladies had the same fine headdresses as those worn in the King's castle, though their sleeves and skirts were simpler, but nevertheless brightly colored, and there were many who wore jewels.

I was dazzled by the jewels. It seemed to me that in the jewels, all the color and light I beheld around me was concentrated, as if it had been drawn into the bits of glass by magnetism. In sum, were I to drop a ruby in a glass of water, I thought it would sparkle and glow, and that the water would turn bright and red.

My mind was delighting in this sort of mad perceptual error. I beheld that in the fireplace there lay a log so big it seemed an entire tree. Indeed, one could see its various branches still, burnt off at the ends like limbs from which the hands had been cut. It was blazing away furiously and my father gave me to know in a whisper that that was the Yule log, and that his brothers had dragged it out of the woods and into the great hall.

It would burn the full twelve days of Christmas.

And now as dozens of people took their places on either side of the long table, there came the Laird himself down the stairs, my father's father, Douglas the Great Earl of Donnelaith.

He was a white-haired man with close-set very red cheeks, and a full white beard, and he wore his tartan or plaid with a great flourish, and had with him three beautiful women who were his daughters, my aunts.

My father cautioned me again to be quiet. I was attracting some notice. People were wondering, 'Who is the tall young man?' By this time my beard and mustache had grown out full and dark brown, and I could not, on account of my skin, be taken for a tall child. My hair had grown long as well.

I watched with wonder as all the guests were finally seated, and as the great choir of monks took their position upon the stone stairs – all tonsured men, which meant they had only a ring of hair left to them, above the ears, and in white robes. They began their singing, gleeful yet mournful and beautiful. And I would say this music struck me with such force that I was truly intoxicated, that is, shot by the arrow of it, and unable for a long moment to breathe.

I knew what was happening around me. The great roasted boar's head had been brought in, surrounded by greenery and gold and silver decorations and candles, and wooden apples painted to look real.

And the boars for eating were borne in by boys who carried them on the very spits on which they'd been cooked, and now set them down upon side tables and began to cut the steaming meat.

I saw all this, I heard it. But my mind was swept with

the mournful music of the monks. A lovely Gaelic carol rising softly from some twenty or thirty gentle mouths:

> What child is this who laid to rest
> In Mary's arms is sleeping . . .

You know the air, it is as old as Christmas in Ireland or Scotland itself. And if you remember its melody, then you can perhaps grasp a little of what this was to me, this moment, when my heart sang with the monks on the stairs, and the room became subordinated to the song.

It seemed I remembered then the bliss I had known inside my mother. Or was it from some other time? I do not know, except that the feeling was so fully and deeply felt that it could not have been new. It was not frenzied excitement. It was a pure joy. I recalled dancing, my hands outstretched in memory to clasp the hands of others. And yet this moment seemed precious and expensive, as though it had cost me much once long ago.

The music stopped as it had begun. Wine was given to the monks. They left as they had come. The hubbub rose all around me; gay voices.

But now the Laird had risen, raised the toast. The wine was being poured. And all commenced to eat. From the great wheels of cheese, my father chose pieces for me and cautioned me to eat them as if I were a man. He sent for milk for me, and no one among the busy company took notice and there was much talking and laughing, and even some wild wrestling among the younger men.

But I could see that as the time passed, more and more of them took notice of me, enough to glance my way and whisper to the next person, or even to point, or to lean forward and ask my father, 'But who is this you've brought with you to dine with us?'

It seemed that some eruption of chatter or merry laughter always prevented him from having to answer. He ate his meat without enthusiasm. He looked about anxiously, and then suddenly my father sprang to his feet. He raised his cup. I could scarce make out his profile or his eyes, for all his long straggled brown hair and beard, but I heard his voice declare, loud, and ringing, and overriding everything:

'To my beloved father, to my mother, to my elders and to my kindred, I present this boy – Ashlar, my son!'

It seemed a cheer rose from the company, a great awful roar, only to be strangled suddenly into rigid silence beneath a volley of whispers and gasps. All the company went still, eyes fixed upon my father and upon me. He reached down, groping as it were with his right hand, and I rose as he obviously wished me to do, standing taller than he, though he was as tall as the other men.

Again, gasps and whispers came from the company. One of the women gave a scream. The Laird himself peered up from beneath his thick gray eyebrows with sparkling blue eyes that held me in a deadly glance. I looked around me in fear.

Now it seemed the monks, who had only been in the vestibule, once again appeared. One or two came forward to stare at me. They looked remarkable to me, these shining bald creatures all in long dresses like women, but as more and more of them came forward, the entire gathering became ever more alarmed.

'He is my son!' declared my father. 'My son, I tell you! He is Ashlar, come again!'

And this time many women screamed, and some of them fell back as if fainting; the men rose from their benches, and the old Laird rose, bringing down both fists upon the boards so that cups and knives were shaken to the right and to the left. Wine splashed. Plates clattered.

Then, in spite of his age, the old Laird leapt upward onto the bench.

'Taltos!' he said in a low and vicious whisper, leering at me with lowered head.

Taltos. I knew this word. This was the word for me.

I would have run then, instinctively, if my father hadn't held tight to my hand, forcing me to stand firm with him. Others were leaving the hall. A number of the women were ushered out by their anxious attendants, including some of the very old, who were quite confused.

'No!' my father declared. 'St Ashlar. Come again! Speak to them, my son. Tell them it is a sign from heaven.'

'But what shall I say, Father?' I asked. And at the clear sound of my voice, which seemed to me in no way remarkable, the whole company went mad. People were rushing through the various doorways. The Laird now stood on the trestle table, fists clenched, kicking out of his way the laden plates. The servants had surely all taken cover. All the women were gone.

Finally only two of the monks remained. One stood before me, tall but not as tall as I, and red-haired and with soft green eyes. He smiled upon me in that moment, and his smile was like the sound of the music, utterly quieting, and I felt a sinking in my soul.

I knew the others loathed the sight of me! I knew

they had run from me. I knew the panic was the same as I had seen among the women of my mother, and in my mother herself.

I was trying to understand it, to know what it meant. I said, 'Taltos,' as if this would trigger some revelation stored within me, but no more came.

'Taltos,' said the priest – for that is what he was, though I did not then know it, a priest and a Franciscan – and again he gave me this great and gentle smile.

All had fled the hall now but my father, myself, the priest and the Laird, who stood upon the table, and three men crouched by the fireplace, as if in waiting, though for what I couldn't guess.

It frightened me to see them, and the anxious way in which they looked to the Laird and the Laird looked down on me.

'It is Ashlar!' cried my father. 'Do you not see with your own eyes! What must God do to claim your attention? Destroy the tower with lightning? Father, it is he!'

I realized that I had begun to tremble, a most amazing sensation, which I had never felt before. I had not even shivered in the cold of the winter. But I could not control this trembling. Indeed, it must have looked as though I were standing upon a piece of earth that was shaking, so violent was it, though I managed to remain on my feet.

The priest drew close to me; his green eyes very much reminded me of jewels, except that they were obviously made of something soft. He reached out and stroked my hair gently, almost tenderly, and then my cheek and my beard.

'It is Ashlar!' he whispered.

'It is the Taltos, it is the Devil!' declared the Laird. 'Heave him into the fire.'

The three at the hearth came forward, but my father stood in front of me, and so did the priest. Ah, yes, you can imagine it, you can well picture it, can't you? One screaming for my destruction as if he were Michael the Archangel, and the gentler ones not letting such a thing happen.

And I – gazing at the fire in terror, barely aware that it could consume me, that I would suffer unspeakable pain if I were thrown into it, that I would be alive no more. It seemed in my ears I heard the cries of thousands suffering, dying. But as my fear crested, the memory became nothing but the violent quavering of my body, the tensing of my hands.

The priest enfolded me in his arms and went to lead me from the hall. 'You will not destroy what God has done.'

I almost wept at his touch, his warm arms guiding me.

I was then led out of the castle by the priest and by my father, and the Laird, who came with us, eyeing me with great suspicion, and over to the Cathedral we went. The snow still fell lightly, people everywhere passed us, mounded with wool and furs. It was almost impossible to make out who was a man, who was a woman, so covered up were they, and so hunkered over against the cold. Some of them were smallish, rather like children, but I could see their faces were old and gnarled.

The Cathedral was open and filled with lights, and the people were singing, and as we drew close I saw that the same greenery had been strewn all about the great arched doors. The singing was swelling and beautiful beyond belief. The smell of the green pine woods filled the air. Delicious smoke wafted on the wind.

And the noisy song inside was jubilant and merry, something much more festive and discordant and triumphant than the song of the monks had been. There was not a steady rhythm to it which caught me, but rather a general elation. It made the tears come to my eyes.

We fell into line with those entering the church and proceeded slowly, thank God, for I could not keep my balance on account of the song. The Laird, who had thrown his wool cape up over his face, my father, who had never shed his fur garments, and the priest, who had raised his cowl against the cold – these three supported me, astonished by my weakness, yet easily helping me a step at a time.

The informal stream of pilgrims moved sluggishly into the giant nave, and even with the music distracting me I was overcome with wonder at the sheer size and depth of the church. For nothing I had seen so far could equal this structure in grace and in height. Its windows seemed impossibly tall and narrow and its branching arches above to have been made by gods. At the far end, high above the altar, was a window shaped like a flower. It really did occur to my newborn mind that people could not have done it. And then I became overawed and confused.

At last, as we drew closer to the altar, I saw what lay ahead. A great stable full of hay, and there a cow lowing, and an ox, and a sheep. These animals were restless on their tethers and the warm steaming smell of their excrement rose from the floor of hay. Before them stood a man and a woman made entirely from lifeless stone. Indeed, they were symbols only. Their eyes were painted and so was their hair. And between them, in a tiny bed, lay an infant human child, of marble, same as the man and the woman, only the child was chubby and more shiny, with smiling lips and eyes made of shining glass.

This was a marvel to me, for I have already told you how the priest's eyes made me think of jewels, and now I beheld the artificial eyes of this baby, and the connection confused me and held me in thrall.

The music infused these thoughts; indeed it made all thought seem dreamlike and slow, and uncertain, but then in a deep sad moment I knew the truth:

I knew completely that I had never been such a newborn infant as this; that all of these people had been infants; that it was my size and my articulation which had terrified my mother. I was a monster. I felt this completely, perhaps remembering the things the panic-stricken women had cried at my birth. I knew. I knew I was not one of the human race.

The priest told me to go down on my knees and kiss the child, that this was the Christ who had died for our sins. And then he pointed to the bloody crucifix hanging from the high column to the right. I saw the man there, saw the blood streaming from His hands and feet. The crucifix Christ. The God of the Wood. Jack of the Green. These words went through my mind. And I knew the infant and the Christ on the Cross were one. Again, I heard those distant cries in my memory, as if of a massacre.

The music brought it all together. I did truly feel that I would soon faint. Perhaps then the veil came close to falling, and I might have reached through and known the past. Ah, but other, more painful moments would follow, with greater cooperation from me, and nothing much was ever revealed.

Looking at the crucifix, I shuddered all over to think of such a horrible death. It seemed monstrous to me that anyone could have created a beaming child to suffer such a death. And then I realized that all humans were created for death. They were all born as little struggling innocents, learning to live before they knew what it was about. I knelt down and I kissed this hard stone baby all painted to look soft and real. I looked at the stone face of the woman and the man. I looked back at the priest.

The music had died away, leaving only roaring whispers and coughs echoing beneath the arches.

'Come now, Ashlar,' said the priest, and he took me hurriedly through the crowd, obviously not wanting to attract notice, and we entered a chapel off the main nave. There was a steady stream of the faithful coming into this chapel, admitted two by two. Other monks in robes stood guard, and the priest bade them now to close it off and have the others please patiently wait.

The Laird would say his nightly prayer to St Ashlar. It aroused no resentment but seemed a natural thing. Those who must wait fell on their knees and said their beads.

We stood alone in the stone chapel with walls half as high as the nave. Yet how grand it seemed; a narrow holy place. Banks of candles burned beneath its windows. A great sarcophagus with an effigy upon it lay in the middle of the floor. Indeed, it had been around this long rectangular stone box that so many were gathered, praying and kissing their hands and putting kisses to the carved man in the stone.

'Look there, my boy,' said the priest, and pointed not at this stone characterization but up at the window which faced the west. The glass was all black with the night. But I could see easily the figure made into it by the lead seams with which all the pieces of glass were formed. My eye could see a tall man in long robes, with a crown on his head. I could also see that this figure towered over the figures beside him, and that his hair like mine was long and full, and his beard and mustache of similar shape.

Latin words were written into the glass, in three stanzas, which at first I could not understand.

But the priest went to the far wall and, reaching up to point to them – they were well over his head – read them out to me from the Latin into English so their meaning went into me complete and entire:

> St Ashlar Beloved of Christ
> And the Holy Virgin Mary
> Who will come again.
>
> Heal the sick
> Comfort the afflicted
> Ease the pangs
> Of those who must die
>
> Save us
> From everlasting darkness
> Drive out the demons from the glen.
> Be our guide.
> Into the Light.

My soul was filled with reverence. The music began again, distantly, and jubilantly as before. I resisted it, trying not to let it overtake me, but I couldn't prevent it, and the spell of the Latin words was dissipated, and then I was led away.

We were soon gathered in the priest's quarters in the Cathedral sacristy, and he sat with us at the table. The room was small and warm, quite unlike any chamber I had seen so far, except in a country inn perhaps, and very pleasant it seemed to me.

I put my hands to the fire, then remembered that the Laird had wanted to burn me, and drew them back inside my velvet cloak.

'What is this thing, Taltos,' I said, suddenly turning to face the three of them, who were staring at me in silence. 'What is it you called me? And who is Ashlar, the saint who comes again?'

At this last question, my father closed his eyes in grave disappointment and bowed his head. His father looked ferocious with righteous anger, but the priest only continued to gaze at me as though I had come from heaven. He was the one who spoke.

'You are he, my son,' he said. 'You are Ashlar, for it was God's gift to Ashlar that he should be flesh more than once, indeed that he should come again and again into the world for the honor and the glory of his Creator, granted this dispensation from the laws of nature, as was the Virgin when she was assumed into heaven, and as the prophet Elijah who was borne off to heaven, body and soul. God has seen to it that you would find your way into the world more than once through the loins of a woman, and perhaps even through a woman's sin.'

'Aye, that's certain!' said the Laird darkly. 'If it wasn't out of the little ones, by the sin of a witch and a child of our clan it had to be.'

My father was both frightened and ashamed. I looked at the priest. I wanted to tell of my mother, of the extra finger on her left hand, and how she had held it up to me and that she had said it was a witch's finger, but I didn't dare to do this. I knew the old Laird wanted to destroy me. I felt his hatred, and it was worse than the most dreadful bitter cold.

'The mark of God was on the birth, I tell you,' said the great Laird. 'My damned son has done what not all the little people in the hills have been able to do for hundreds of years.'

'Did you see the acorn fall from the oak?' asked the priest. 'How do you know but that this is a changeling and not our spawn? How!'

'She had the sixth finger,' my father said in a whisper.

'And you lay with her!' demanded the Laird.

And my father nodded, yes, that he had; and he whispered that she was a great lady, and he could not name her, but that she was great enough to have made him afraid.

'No one must hear of this,' said the priest. 'No one must know what has taken place. I will take this blessed child in hand and see that he is consecrated to the Virgin, that he never touches the flesh of a woman.'

He then put me into a warm chamber where I might pass the night. He bolted the door on me. There was only a tiny window. The cold air crept in, but I could see a tiny bit of heaven, a few very small and bright stars.

What did all these words mean? I didn't know. When I stood on the bed and peeped out the window, when I saw the dark forest and the jagged cut of the mountains, I felt fear. And I thought I could see the little people coming. I thought I could hear them. I could hear their drums. They would use their drums to freeze the Taltos, to render him helpless, and then they would surround him. *Make a giant for us, make a giantess; make a race that shall punish the people; wipe them from the earth.* One of them would climb the wall, and pry loose the bars, and in they would come –!

I fell back. But when I looked up again, I saw the bars were secure. This had been a fancy. In truth I had spent nights in rustic inns with farting drunkards and belching whores, and in the very woods where even the wolves ran from the little people.

Now I was safe.

It must have been an hour before daylight that the priest called me. For all I knew it was the witching hour, for a bell was tolling, ominously and endlessly, and as I woke, I knew I had heard this bell, like a hammer dropping again and again upon an anvil – in my sleep.

The priest shook me by the shoulder. 'Come with me, Ashlar,' he said.

I saw the battlements of the town. I saw the torches of the watch. I saw the black sky above and the stars. The snow lay still upon the ground. Again and again, the bell rang, and the sound clattered through me, shook me, so that the priest reached out to make me steady and see that I walked at his side.

'That's the Devil's Knell,' said the priest. 'It is ringing to drive the devils and spirits out of the valley, to scatter the Sluagh, and the Ganfers, and whatever evil lurks in the glen. To rout the little people if they have dared to come out. They may know already that you have come. The bell will protect us. The bell will drive them away with all the unseelie court and into the forest, where they can do no harm save to their own kind.'

'But who are such beings?' I whispered. 'I'm afraid of the sound of the bell.'

'No, child, no!' he said. 'It is not to frighten you. This is the voice of God. Take one step after another and follow me into the church.' His arm was warm and strong around me, nudging me forward, and once again he kissed me in a soft, tingling manner on the cheek.

'Yes, Father,' I said. This was like the milk to me, as I have said, this affection.

The Cathedral was deserted; and I could hear the bell more distantly now, for it was high in the tower and made to echo off the mountains and not inside the church.

He kissed my face warmly again and pulled me into the chapel of the saint. It was cold, for there were not thousands of warm bodies within the Cathedral, and the dark winter was right against the glass.

'You are Ashlar, my son. There is no doubt of it. Now tell me what you remember of your birth.'

I didn't want to answer. A horrid shame came over me when I thought of my mother crying in fear, when I thought of her hands pushing at me trying to make me go away from her, and my lips closing on the nipple and drinking the milk.

I didn't answer him.

'Father, tell me who is Ashlar, tell me what I am meant to do.'

'Very well, my son, I will tell you. You are to be sent to Italy, you are to be sent to the house of our Order in the town of Assisi, and there to study to be a priest.'

I considered this but in truth it meant nothing to me.

'Now in this land good priests are persecuted,' he said. 'Outside this valley are rebellious followers of the King and others, the rabid Lutherans and countless other rabble that would destroy us and destroy our great cathedral if they could. You have been sent to save us, but you must be educated and you must be ordained. And above all, you must consecrate yourself to the Virgin. You must never touch the flesh of a woman; you must forgo that pleasure for the glory of God. And mark my word, and never forget it, the sin with women is not for you. Do what you would with other friars. As long as God is served, so what? But never touch the flesh of a woman.

'Now this night, there are men ready to take you away by sea. They will see that you reach Italy. And then – when God gives us a sign that the time is right; or when God reveals His purpose to you directly – then you will come home.'

'And what then shall I do?'

'Lead the people, lead them in prayer, say the Mass for them, lay hands upon them and heal as you did before. Reclaim the people from the Lutheran devils! Be the saint!'

It seemed a lie, an utter lie. Or rather an impossible task. What was Italy? Why should I go?

'Can I do this?' I asked.

'Yes, my son, you can do it.' And then under his breath he said, with a wicked little smile: '*You are the Taltos. The Taltos is a miracle. The Taltos can do miraculous things!*'

'Then both tales are true!' I said. 'I am the saint; I am the monster with the strange name.'

'When you are in Italy,' said the priest, 'when you stand in the Basilica of St Francis, the saint will give you his blessings and all will be in God's hands. The people fear the Taltos – they tell the old tales – but the Taltos comes only once in several centuries, and it is always a good omen! St Ashlar was a Taltos, and that is why we, who know, say that he comes again.'

'Then I am some being other than mortal man,' I said. 'And you are wanting me to declare that I will imitate this saint.'

'Ah, you are very clever for a Taltos,' he said. 'Yet you have the divine simplicity, the goodness. But let me put it this way to your heart which is so pure. It's your choice, don't you see? You can be the evil Taltos or you can be the saint! Would that I had such a choice! Would that I were not this feeble priest in an age when priests are burnt alive by the King of England, or drawn and quartered, or worse. In Germany this very day Luther receives his revelations from God while seated upon a privy and hurls excrement in the Devil's face! Yes, that is religion. That is what it is now. Would you seek the glen and the darkness and a life of beggary and terror? Or would you be our saint?'

Without waiting for me to answer, he said in a low and mournful voice, 'Did you know that Sir Thomas More himself has been executed in London, his head struck off and stuck upon a pike of London Bridge! That was the wish of the King's whore!' said he. 'That is how things stand!'

I wanted to run. I wondered if I could do it. If I could run free and outside where the dawn was coming, where the birds of winter had begun to sing. His words confused me and tormented me, and yet when I thought of the surrounding woods, the valley itself, I was too frightened to move. Some hideous dread rose out of me, causing my heart to beat and my palms to become wet.

'A Taltos is nothing!' he said, leaning close to me. 'Go into the forests if you would be a Taltos. The little people will find you. They will take you prisoner and seek to make by you a legion of giants. It will not happen. It cannot happen. Your progeny will be monstrous or nothing. But a saint! Dear God, you can be a saint!'

Ah, the little people, yes. I gazed at him, trying to understand him.

'You can be a *saint!*'

Several men had come into the Cathedral, heavily armed and covered in furred capes, and to these he gave his instructions in Latin, which at that point I barely understood. I knew I would be taken 'by sea' to Italy. And that I was a prisoner, and in terror I stood there, and then in my desperation I turned to face the window of St Ashlar as if he could save me from all this.

I looked up at the stained-glass window and at this moment a simple miracle occurred. The sun had risen, and though it did not strike this window with its rays, the great swelling light filled it and brought it into vivid and beauteous color. The saint was filled with quiet fire. The saint smiled down upon me, his dark eyes burning in the glass, his lips pink, his robes red. I knew it was the trick of the sunrise, yet I could not take my eyes from it.

An immense peace filled me.

I thought of my mother's horror-stricken face, her screaming, echoing in the little chamber. I saw the great kindred of the Clan of Donnelaith scurrying away from me like so many black rats!

'Be the saint!' said the priest to me in a whisper.

And there in that moment the vow made itself clear to me, though I did not have the courage to speak the words.

I gazed at the window. I took the details of the saint to my heart. I saw that he stood barefoot upon the prone bodies of the little people ... the Ganfers, the Sluagh, the Demons of Hell. And behold, in his hand he held a staff, and the foot of the staff pierced the body of the Devil. I studied the well-drawn bodies of the dwarf people. I heard my heart.

The light had now swelled against the window so that the brighter colors had begun to glow. The saint was made of jewels! A shimmering vision of sparkling gold, and deepest blue and ruby red, and shining white.

'St Ashlar!' I whispered.

The armed men took hold of me.

'Go with God, Ashlar. Give your soul to God and when death comes *again* you will know peace.'

That was my birth, gentlemen. That was my homecoming. Now I shall tell you of what followed, of how high I was to reach.

I was then taken away – I was never to see the old Laird again. For all I knew, I was never to see the glen, the Cathedral, or this priest. A small boat was waiting for me, which had to fight its way through the icy harbor and then south along the coast until I was put aboard a large ship. My chamber was cramped. I was a virtual prisoner. I drank only milk because all other food disgusted me and the boisterous sea made me constantly sick.

No one thought to tell me why I was locked up, or to give me comfort. On the contrary, I had nothing to study, to read, no beads with which to pray. The bearded men who tended me seemed frightened of me, unwilling to answer any question. And at last I fell in a stupor, singing songs, making them up from the words I knew.

Sometimes it seemed to me that I was making songs from words as people might make garlands from flowers, with only a thought as to how pretty was this word or that. I sang for hours. My voice was deep and I liked the sound of it. I lay back in contentment, eyes shut, singing variations of the hymns I'd heard in Donnelaith. I would not stop until awakened, until pulled from this trance, or until I fell asleep.

I do not remember when I realized that the winter had ended, or that we had traveled out of it, that we were along the coast of Italy, and that when I looked out the little barred window I saw the sunlight falling down gracefully on green hills and cliffs of indescribable beauty. At last we docked at a thriving city, the like of which I'd never seen.

Then the most remarkable thing befell me. I was taken by these two men, who still would answer no question from me, and left at the gate of a monastery, after the bell had been rung.

A small parcel was thrust into my hands.

I stood there dazzled by the sun, and then turned to see the monk, who had opened the gate for me, looking me up and down. I wore still the fine clothes from London, but they were very soiled now from the long journey, and my beard and hair had grown very long. I had nothing with me but this parcel, and in confusion I gave it to the monk.

At once he unwrapped it, removing the ragged linen

and leather from it, and then he held it and I saw that it was a large parchment letter which had been folded over in quarto.

'Come in, please,' said this monk in a kindly manner to me. He glanced at the unfolded parchment. Then he rushed away, leaving me in a still and beautiful court-yard filled with golden flowers, and warmed by the midday sun. I could hear singing in the distance, the melancholy mournful sound of men's voices like those of the monks of Donnelaith. I loved the singing. I closed my eyes and breathed the singing, and the per-fume of the flowers.

Then several monks came into the courtyard. Those in Scotland had worn white but these men were in coarse brown and had sandals on their feet. They sur-rounded me and kissed me on both cheeks and embraced me.

'Brother Ashlar!' They all addressed me, more or less in one voice. And their smiles were so warm, so filled with love that I began to cry.

'This is to be your life now. Don't be frightened anymore. You will live and thrive in the love of God.'

I saw then the unfolded quarto which one held in his hand.

'What does it say?' I asked in English.

'That you have dedicated your life to Christ. That you would follow in the steps of our founder, St Francis, that you would be a priest of God.'

Then came more tender words and embraces from these men, who were utterly unafraid of me, and it came to my mind: they don't know anything about me. They don't know how I was born. And inspecting myself – my hands, my legs, my hair – I thought, except for my height and my long locks I might as well be one of them.

This puzzled me.

Throughout the evening meal – and they fed me much better than they fed themselves – I sat silent, not certain of what I should do or say. It was quite obvious to me that I could leave this place if I wanted. I could go over the wall.

But why should I do it? I thought. I went into the chapel with them. I joined in their song. When they heard my voice, they nodded and smiled and touched me with approval, and I was soon lost in the singing, and staring at the crucifix again, the very same symbol, Christ nailed to the Cross. I don't say it like this to sound simple. I say it to make you picture it, as I saw this, this tortured body, afflicted, beaten, crowned with thorns and shedding blood. Jack of the Green, burnt in his wicker; driven through the fields by those with sticks.

A great swimming happiness came over me. I made this bargain with myself. Stay for a while. You can always run away tomorrow. But if you run, then you have lost this place, you have lost St Ashlar.

That night, when they put me in my cell, I said, 'You do not have to lock it.'

They were surprised and confused. They had not intended to do so, they said. Indeed, they showed me – there was no lock.

I lay there, remaining of my own free will, dreaming, in the warm night of Italy, dreaming, and from time to time, I heard them at their chapel song.

In the morning, when they told me it was time to go to Assisi, I said that I was ready. We would walk, they said, for we were Franciscans, and we were of the Observant Franciscans who were true to the spirit of Brother Francis and we would not sit on the back of a horse.

THIRTY-FIVE

LASHER'S STORY CONTINUES

By the time we reached Assisi, I had come to love these friars with whom I was making the journey, and to understand that they knew really nothing about me except that I wanted to be a priest. I was dressed as they were for this journey, in a brown robe, and with sandals, and with only a rope about my waist. I had not cut my hair yet, and I carried my fine clothes in a bundle, but I looked very much like one of them.

As we walked along the roadside, these priests told me the tales of St Francis of Assisi, the founder of their Order – of how Francis, the rich one, had forsworn wealth and become a beggar and a preacher, tending the lepers, of whom he was mortally frightened, and so loving to all living things that the birds of the air came to settle on his arms, and the wolf was tamed by his touch.

Great pictures were made in my mind as they talked; I saw the face of Francis, an amalgam perhaps of the radiant green-eyed Franciscan priest in Scotland, and their own innocent visages; or perhaps it was a mere ideal invented by some part of me which had already developed – to make pictures and dreams.

Whatever it was, I knew Francis.

I knew him. I knew his fear when his father cursed him. I knew the joy when he gave himself to Christ. I

772

knew, above all, his love when he addressed all creatures as his brothers and sisters, and I knew his love for people we saw all around us, the peasants of Italy working in their fields, the townspeople, and those in the monasteries and manor houses which gave us gracious shelter by night.

Indeed, the happier I became, the more I was beginning to wonder if my birth in Britain had not been some sort of nightmare, a thing which could not have happened at all.

I felt I belonged with these Franciscans. I belonged with St Francis. I had been born out of place. And if to be a saint meant to be like Francis, why, I was overjoyed. All this seemed natural to me. And it brought peace to me, as if I were remembering a time when all beings had been gentle, before something terrible had come.

Everywhere that we went we saw children, working in the fields with their parents, playing in the village streets. When we entered the high city of Assisi, it was filled with children of all ages, as is any city, and I understood without being told that these were small human beings, infants on their way to adulthood. They were not the dreaded little people, my enemies who would kill me from envy – that bitter gleam of knowledge which had only served to terrify me with no further understanding of what it meant. Ah, how beautiful were these merely unfolding humans, who grew slowly, taking year after year to attain the height and abilities which I had acquired during and right after my birth.

When I saw the mothers nursing, I wanted the milk. But I knew it was not a witch's milk. It wasn't that strong. It wouldn't help me. But I was grown, was I not? I had become taller even on my journey. And I seemed to all the world a strong and healthy human of some twenty years.

Whatever my thoughts on all this, I resolved to reveal nothing. Rather I stepped out of myself, amongst those around me. I was charmed by the countryside, the vineyards, the greenery, and above, the soft light of the Italian sun.

Assisi itself was at a great elevation, so that from many promontories, one could see the surrounding country in all its soft splendor, so much more inviting than the threatening snow-covered peaks and cliffs which had surrounded Donnelaith.

Indeed, my memory of events in Donnelaith was becoming confused to me. If I had not learnt to write within the next few weeks, and not recorded everything in a secret code, I might have actually erased from my mind my origins. They certainly came to seem vague as time passed.

But let me return to the moment. We entered the gates of Assisi at midday. At once I was taken into the Basilica of St Francis at the opposite end of the town – a grand edifice, though nothing as cold as the Cathedral in Donnelaith. Indeed the place had not pointed arches but rounded ones, and its walls were alive with wondrous paintings of the saint, beneath which was the shrine of the saint, to which the faithful came in droves as they had done for St Ashlar in my home.

Hundreds proceeded to walk round the tomb of the saint, which bore no effigy of him, and was massive, and to lay hands on it, and give their kisses, and to pray loudly to St Francis, to beg him for cures, for solace, for his special intercession with the Good God.

I too laid hands on the sarcophagus and made my prayer to Francis, who had for me now a personality, a figure wrapped in colour and romance. 'Francis,' I whispered to the stone. 'I am here. I am here to become a friar but you know that I have been sent to be a saint.'

There was a surge of pride in me; no one knew the secret. That I would one day return to Scotland with the precepts of Francis, and possibly save my people as the good Father there had told me I must do. I was destined through humility to achieve great things.

But I saw this pride for what it was. 'If you are to become a saint, you must do it truly,' I thought to myself. 'You must imitate Francis, and these friars and the other saints of whom they have told you – you must forget that ambition. For a saint cannot have the ambition to be a saint. A saint is the servant of Christ. Christ may decide that He wants you to be nothing! Be ready for it.'

But though I made this confession or admonition in prayer to myself, I was secretly confident. I am destined to shine like the image of St Ashlar in the coloured glass.

For many hours I remained in the shrine, almost drunk on the devotion of those who passed the big stone tomb. I felt their fervor almost as if it were music. Indeed, it was now clear to me that I was hypersensitive, as you would say today, not merely to music, but in general to all sounds. The shrill of birds; the timbre of people's voices; the rhythms and accidental rhymes of their speech, all this affected me. Indeed, when I encountered a person who spoke naturally with alliteration, I was near paralyzed by it.

But what paralyzed me here in the shrine was the delirium of the faithful and the particular intensity of devotion which Francis himself had inspired.

That very day I was taken up to the Carceri, the hermitage where Francis and his first followers had lived their solitary life. There were the first cells. There was the grand and beautiful view of the countryside. This was the place where Francis had walked, and prayed.

I had no thought now of ever leaving. What worried me was not the vows of poverty, chastity, obedience. What I feared was my secret pride, that this legend of St Ashlar would eat at my soul, while in fact goading me on.

Let me now pause to make a most significant point. I was not to leave Italy, or this life of a Franciscan, for over twenty years. The exact count? I do not know. I never did. It was not thirty-three years, for that I would remember as the age of Christ.

I tell you this so that you will understand two things. That I do not rush to Donnelaith in this tale, for it is not time yet, and that during that time my body remained vigorous and quite limber, quite strong, and quite the same. My skin thickened somewhat, losing its baby softness, and my face gathered expressive lines, but not very many. Otherwise ... well almost ... I remained the same.

I want you to understand how happy I was in this Franciscan life, how natural it was to me, because that is to some extent the heart of the case I wish to make.

Christmas was a great feast in Italy, as it had been back in the Highlands of nightmare which I had so briefly seen. It became to me the most solemn and significant of all Holy Days, and wherever I was in Italy I went home to Assisi at that time.

Even before my first Christmas there, I had read the story of the Christ Child born in the manger and looked at innumerable paintings of it, and I had given myself heart and soul to the little infant in Mary's arms.

I closed my eyes and imagined that I was a tiny baby, which I had never been, that I was helpless and yearning and innocent. And the feeling which came over me was one of rapture. I resolved to see Christ – a pure child – in every man or woman to whom I spoke. If I suffered a moment of anger or annoyance, which was unusual, I thought of the Christ Child. I imagined I was holding Him in my arms. I believed in Him utterly, and that someday when my destiny was fulfilled – whatever and whenever – I would be with Christ. I would kneel in the manger and I would touch the Christ Child's tiny hand.

God, after all, was eternal – Child, Man, Crucified Savior, God the Father, God the Holy Spirit – it was all one. I saw this with perfect clarity almost immediately. I saw it so completely that theological questions made me laugh.

By the time I left Italy, I was a priest of God, a renowned preacher, a singer of canticles, a sometime healer and a man who brought consolation or happiness to all he knew.

But let me now explain with greater care:

From the beginning, my innocent manner and my directness astonished everyone; they never guessed the real reason for it; that I was a child. That I feasted on milk and cheese seemed humorous to people. My speed at learning also drew love from everyone around me. I could write Italian, English and Latin within a short time.

Uncompromising saintliness took me body and soul.

There was no task too low for me to perform. I went with those who tended the lepers outside the gates of the town.

I had no fear of the lepers. I could have had it, I think, but I did not cultivate it, and therein lies a key to my nature. I seemed to be able to cultivate what I wished.

Nothing to date had severely repelled me, except hatred and violence. And this attitude remained constant during all my years on earth. I was either saddened by something or seduced by it. There was seldom a middle ground.

Indeed, I had a fascination with the lepers because other people were so frightened of them; and of course I knew how Francis has fought to overcome this, and I was determined to be as great as he. I gave comfort to the lepers. I bathed and clothed those who were too far gone with the disease to care for themselves. Having heard that St Catherine of Siena once drank the bathwater from a leper, I cheerfully did the same thing.

Very early on, I became known in Assisi – the innocent one, the dazzled one, the fool for God, so to speak. A young monk who is truly on fire with the spirit of Francis, who does naturally what Francis would have us all do.

And because I seemed so completely unsophisticated, so incapable of conniving, so childlike if you will, people tended to open up to me, to tell me things, egged on by my bright curious gaze. I listened to everything. Not a word was wasted. Imagine it – the great infant that I was, learning from people's smallest gestures and slightest confessions all the major truths of life.

That is what was happening inside my mind.

By night I learned to read and finally to write, and I wrote constantly, taking as little sleep as I could. I memorized songs and poems. I studied the paintings of the Basilica, the great murals by Giotto which tell all the significant events of Francis's life, including how the stigmata came to him – the wounds in his hands and feet from God. And I went out among the pilgrims to talk to them, to hear what they had to say of the world.

The first year of which I knew the date was 1536. I went often to Florence, to give to the poor, to visit their hovels and bring bread and something to drink. Florence was still a city of the Medici. Perhaps she was past her great glory, as some have said since, but I don't think at the time that anyone would have said such a thing.

On the contrary, Florence was a magnificent and thriving place. Printed books were sold there by the thousands; the sculptures of Michelangelo were everywhere to be seen. The guilds were powerful, still, though much trade had moved to the New World; and the city was an endless spectacle of processions, such as the great Procession of Corpus Christi, and performances of beautiful tableaux and plays.

The bank of the Medici was then the greatest bank in the world.

Everywhere in Florence men and women were literate

and thoughtful and talkative; this was the city which had produced the poet Dante and the political genius Machiavelli; the city which produced Fra Angelico and Giotto, Leonardo da Vinci and Botticelli, a city of great writers, great painters, great princes and great saints. The city itself was made of solid stone and filled with palaces, churches, wondrous piazzas, gardens and bridges. Perhaps it was a city unique in all the world. It certainly thought that it was, and I did too.

As my duties expanded, I soon knew every inch of Florence, and heard one way or another all the news of the world.

The world of course was on the brink of disaster! People spoke continuously of the final days.

The English King Henry VIII had abandoned the true faith; the great city of Rome was only just recovering from its rape by Protestant troops and Catholic Spaniards alike. Indeed the pope and the cardinals had had to take shelter in the castle of Sant'Angelo, and this had left with people a deep disillusionment and distrust.

The Black Plague was still with us, rising every ten years or so to claim victims. There were wars on the Continent.

The worst tales, however, were of the Protestants abroad – of mad Martin Luther, who had turned the entire German people against the Church, and other rabid heresies – the Anabaptists, and the Calvinists, who made great gains every day in the realm of Christian souls.

The pope was rumored to be powerless against these heresies. Councils were called and called but nothing really was done. The Church was in the midst of reforming itself to answer to the great heretics, John Calvin and Martin Luther. But the world had been rent in half it seemed by the Protestants, who swept an entire culture before them when they broke with the authority of the pope.

Yet our world of Assisi, and Florence and the other cities and towns of Italy, seemed splendid and rich and dedicated to the True Christ. It seemed, when reading Scriptures, impossible to believe that Our Lord had not walked on the Appian Way. Italy filled my soul – with its music, its gardens, its green countryside – it seemed to me the only place that I should ever want to be. Rome was the only city I loved more than Florence, and only perhaps because of its size, because of the splendor of St Peter's. But then Venice too was a great marvel. For me the poor of one city were pretty much as the poor of another. The hungry were the hungry. They were always waiting for me with open arms.

I found it easy and natural to be a true Poverello – to own nothing, to seek shelter wherever I was at nightfall, to let the Holy Spirit come into me when I was asked a complex question, or asked to declare a truth.

I knew joy when I preached my first sermon, in a piazza in Florence, with arms outstretched, eschewing, as was our custom, all squabbling about theology, and talking only of personal dedication to God. 'We must be as the Christ Child – that innocent, that trusting, that good.'

Of course this had been the very wish of Francis, that we be true beggars and vagabonds speaking from the heart. But our Order was much torn by matters of interpretation. What had Francis truly meant? What kind of organization should we have? Who was truly poor? Who was truly pure?

I avoided all decisions and conclusions. I spoke aloud to Francis; I modeled my life upon him. I lost myself utterly in good works, and I cared for the sick with good results.

It was no miracle. A man would not drop his crutches and cry, 'I can walk!' It manifested itself first in a talent for nursing, for bringing the dangerously ill through the fever, back from the brink. It may have been what men call natural. But I began to feel its power in a way; to learn from little things how to enhance it – that if I held the cup myself for the sick one he would fare better from the drink of water than if I let this be done by someone else.

During these early years another form of knowledge came to me: that many of my brothers in the Order did not keep the vow of chastity. Indeed, they had mistresses or went into the legal brothels in Florence, or bedded down with each other under cover of the dark. In fact, I myself was noticing beautiful boys and girls all the time, and feeling desire for them, and waking sometimes in the night with sensuous dreams. I had been fully grown by the time I reached Italy, with dark hair around the genitals and under my arms. I had always been as other men in these respects.

I remembered the words of the Franciscan in Donnelaith. 'You must never touch the flesh of a woman.' I thought about this a great deal. Of course I'd come to realize that coupling led men and women to create children. And I concluded that I had been given this severe warning for one reason: so that I would not father another monster like myself.

But what sort of monster was I? I wasn't sure anymore. My birth and origins became a torture to me in memory, a disgrace that I could not confide to a soul.

At this time too – during those first few years, as my personality formed – I began to think that certain persons were watching me, persons who knew about my imposture and would someday reveal me for what I was.

Often in the streets of Florence I saw Dutchmen, recognizable by their distinctive clothing and hats, and these men seemed always to have their eyes fixed on me. And then once an Englishman came to Assisi and stayed there a long time and came back day after day, simply to hear me preach. This was the beautiful springtime. I was telling the stories or exempla of St Francis; and I remember the cold eyes of this man gazing upon me as I spoke.

Always I confronted these spies. I would stare at them. Sometimes I would even turn and start to walk towards them. Always they fled. Always they returned.

Meantime the question of chastity was torturing me – the question of whether or not I could do it with a woman, and whether or not a monster would be born.

There was no doubt in my mind that I wanted to do what was right in the eyes of God. It seemed a very simple matter to take a mistress, to take a lover. It seemed an immense challenge to enjoy no pleasure of the flesh at all. To live without knowing the answer to the mystery.

I chose the path of the saint.

I allowed no fire to kindle in me, and consequently there was never a blaze.

I became well known for my purity, that I had no eye for women whatsoever, and my healing became more and more accomplished, though still I did not know if it was miraculous and thought it was perhaps a matter of skill.

Another passion meantime swept me up. It was the simple idea current at the time that singing could bring the faithful to Christ, as easily perhaps as evangelical preaching. I began to write my own canticles, simple poetry which I made up, using much rhythm, and to sing these songs at informal gatherings. I much preferred singing to preaching. I was tired of hearing myself promulgate simple truths. But I never got tired of singing.

Soon people knew that when I appeared, there would be music from me – a brief song, sometimes little more than a poem recited to the strumming of a small lute. And I played a little game of which no one else was aware – I tried to see how many days I could go with no speaking, only singing, without irritating anyone or attracting notice to my little sport.

Ten years after my arrival in Italy I was ordained. It would have come sooner if I had wanted it but my study for Holy Orders was deliberately meticulous and slow. I was all the time traveling, walking the roads, and meeting with people and greeting them with the word of God. Time did not seem important. In fact, I had no sense of hurrying towards any destiny at all.

I had become by my ordination utterly fearless of disease. I sang to those who were past all need of physical comfort. I sat in many a room where others feared to step.

But things were not perfect. They were not right. From time to time I remembered my birth with startling effect. I'd wake, sit up, think, Ah, but it's not possible, and then lie back in the darkness, realizing of course it was possible, for I had no other mother, father, sister, brothers! I was not what others believed me to be. I would remember the Queen and the river and the High-lands, as if they were elements of a nightmare.

And sometimes it seemed that after these tumultuous moments, I would see those people following me, spying upon me more than before. Of course I faulted myself for imagining it, but the longer I thought of all this, the more strange my life became.

Then there were times when I betrayed my nature in a particular and spontaneous way. I loved the taste of milk. The Devil was always tempting me with visions of women's breasts. Even during Lent I had to have milk, and I could not endure the fast, and the breaking of the fast for milk was my worst sin. I sometimes grasped handfuls of cheese and ate it. Any soft food was delicious to me, but the craving for cheese and milk was especially bad.

Once I wandered into a field filled with cattle. It was sunrise and no one was about. Or so I thought. I went down on my knees and drank from the udder of a cow, squirting the warm milk out of the udder right into my mouth.

When I had drunk enough I lay in the grass, staring at the sky. I felt bestial and ugly for what I had done. An old farmer came. He was in worn clothing, though neat and well mended, and his face was darkened from working in the sun.

He whispered something to me, full of fear, and ran away. I got up and ran after him, lifting my robes so that I wouldn't trip.

'What did you say to me?' I asked him.

He then whispered something hostile, a curse perhaps, and fled away.

I was overcome with shame. This man knew I wasn't

a human being. And gradually from that day forward my deceit of those around me began to prey on my mind.

I saw the farmer again in the city. He saw me. I could have sworn I saw him with others, and that they were whispering, but this might have been fancy. I let it go. Then one morning I came out of my cell in the cloister to discover a great pitcher of fresh milk there. This froze my soul. For a moment I did not know where I was, or who, or what was happening. I knew only this was an offering, and that it had happened before and before and before. The glen, the little people, and one single giant among them walking down to the edge of the circle, and the offerings of milk. My head swam. For the first time in many many years, I saw the circle of stones, and the circles of figures, so many circles of figures, each wider than the other, and going on so far that I lost count.

I picked up the pitcher and I drank it down greedily the way I always did milk. When I looked up, across the monastery garden, I saw, in the shadows of the cloister, people moving who then darted away.

I think some of the monks saw this. I didn't know what to think of it. I didn't dare tell anyone about it. I dismissed it. I told St Francis, I was his instrument, and I cared only for serving God.

That night for sure a Dutchman was following me. And in the morning I went back to Assisi, to talk to Francis, to renew my vows, to cleanse my soul.

In the days that followed, many people came to me asking to be healed. I laid my hands on them and sometimes with startling results. There was no doubt that the peasants were whispering about me. And offerings of milk began to appear for me in strange places. I might come up a street alone and at the top of it find a pitcher of milk sitting there on the stones.

A certain fact also began to cause me pain. Perhaps I had never been baptized! Unless we can assume the terrified midwife and the ladies-in-waiting had done this. I don't think so. And now as I brooded on this, as I began to try to remember all the details of the northland where I had been born and exiled, I realized that if I had not been baptized, then I could not have received Holy Orders, which meant that when I changed the bread and wine into the Body and Blood of Christ it was nothing of the sort.

Indeed, nothing that I had done could bear fruit. I fell into a state of melancholia. I would talk to no one.

And then it became very plain to me that I must have imagined this birth in England! That nothing of that sort could truly have occurred! Donnelaith. I had never heard mention of a cathedral there, of monks of our Order. But of course for years Henry VIII had persecuted the Catholics. Only recently had Good Queen Mary restored the true church.

If my fancies were true, I had been by my own reckoning alive just over twenty years. Unless my lost childhood was just that – a history lost to the memory, buried experiences, something which I could not call back. But it didn't seem so; and the more I brooded, the more everything about me began to look suspect to me, and the more tormented I became.

Finally I decided I must know a woman. I must know if I was to that extent a man. I was burning to do it, of course. I always had been! And now I knew this was my excuse. Find out.

It was as if in a woman's arms I would know if I was animal enough to have an immortal soul! I laughed at the contradiction, but it was there, and it was true. I wanted to be human, and had to commit a mortal sin to find out if I was.

I went into Florence, to one of the many brothels I knew, where I had in fact brought the sacraments to women when they were dying, and once gave Extreme Unction to a poor merchant who had the misfortune to die in a woman's embrace. I had often visited this brothel in my priestly robes. It was not a shocking thing to do.

So I entered it now on a silent rampage. And the women came to greet me, 'Gentle Father Ashlar!' for they talked to me always as if I were an idiot or a child.

It disgusted me for the first time. I walked out and into the piazza and down to the Arno and across the nearest bridge. It was crowded with shops, very busy, people were coming and going, and when I happened to look I saw a man watching me and knew again that it was a Dutchman just by the look of his clothes. I went towards him, but he fled into the crowd, and I couldn't find him. He was gone in the snap of my fingers. Just gone.

I was then very weary, and finally I threw out my arms and I began to sing. I was on the middle of the bridge, and mad with fear and grief, trying to reconcile my memories with my devotion to Christ, and I began to sing. It wasn't so unusual really, the streets were crowded with all kinds of distractions at such an hour in Florence. One crazed Franciscan swaying and singing was not peculiar at all.

Gradually some people took notice, as they are wont

to do. They stopped their tasks and a little crowd gathered. I was rocking back and forth, holding myself with my arms and singing, and when I looked up, very lost in my song, I saw a beautiful woman staring at me, a woman with green eyes like those of the Franciscan priest in Donnelaith, and long fancy blond hair.

Then the most astonishing thing happened. This woman lowered her veil and walked away! And I realized that the face which had been peering at me was turned to the back of her body, as if her head was put backwards upon her neck. I was fascinated!

My passion was unbearable, but another even more evil excitement leapt in my heart. This is a monster like me.

I let the song die away, and spurned those who would have given me alms. Take them to the church, I said, to those who deserve them. And then I went after the woman, who had waited for me in a side street. Once again, she revealed the face, then walked off. Soon we were in a small alleyway. I was clearly staring at her back when she lifted her veil and revealed her face again.

Finally she spun round in a blur of black garments, silks, satins, velvet and jewels, and rapped hard upon the door. It was opened in the wall and as I rushed up to catch a glimpse of her before she disappeared through it, she grabbed my wrist and pulled me inside.

It was a narrow, crowded garden, like many a courtyard in Florence, with old peeling ocher walls, and bright flowers flourishing in the sheltered sun. Three other women sat there, together on a bench beneath a tree. All wore wide and beautiful skirts, rich sleeves, and had high bosoms which began to drive me mad.

And the one who had brought me in, I saw now she was an ordinary woman! Her face was on the front of her body, like that of anyone else. It had all been some kind of illusion with the veils she pulled from her hair. Some little trick.

She confessed this to me, and this set them all to laughing so much I thought they would never stop.

I was dizzy. Suddenly these women were crowding about me and saying, 'Father, take off your clothes. Come, stay with us in this garden.' And the blond one, who bore the famous name of Lucrezia, said that she had bound me with spells to make me come, but not to fear, they weren't witches, rather their men were gone off to hunt in the country, and they would do as they pleased.

Their men gone off to hunt? This sounded bizarre. But I perceived the truth beneath it. These were whores, but whores free for the day, and I was the object of their desire.

'We are proud to initiate you, virgin child,' said the eldest of the women, who was as beautiful as all the rest. They drew me across the tiles and into the bedchamber. They took off my sandals and removed my robes; then they flung their dresses this way and that, crying out in jubilation, and they danced about me, naked as nymphs, singing some little song. It was all a joke to them! It was all a game. They were shocking the young Franciscan, who though he had a full beard still had the expression of a child.

But I was not shocked. Once more a strange knowing came to me of a time when all the world had done these things; the Garden of Delights it had been, with all romping naked, and playing and singing and dancing; and flowers all about us, and plenty of fruit to eat.

Then fear took hold of me. Gone, all that. Blackness.

I was meantime making like a satyr for these women, which they found very amusing, and which I could not help. At last they tumbled into the bed next to me, covering me with kisses, and I grasped the breasts of the closest woman, and began to suck tenaciously so that I made her cry in pain. The others planted kisses on my naked shoulders, my back, my organ, my chest.

In a twinkling I was back in the birth chamber in England, in the arms of my mother, knowing the fierce pleasure of drawing the milk savagely from her breast. I was drunk with the pleasure, and now it found its worst culmination in the organ, and I soon rode all the women, one after another, crying out in ecstasy, and then beginning with the first to take them all again.

It was now evening. The stars were visible above the courtyard. The roar of the city was dying away.

I slept.

I was with my mother, only she was not hating me and crying in terror, but a long slender creature such as me, much too long to be a real woman, and stroking me with fingers which like mine were too long. Didn't everyone see I was a monster like this woman? How could people be so easily fooled?

I drifted into dreams. I was in a mist, and people were crying, and sobbing, and men were rushing to and fro. It was a massacre. 'Taltos!' Someone shouted it, and then I beheld in my dream the farmer from the field near Florence, and heard him whisper, 'Taltos!' and I saw before me again a pitcher of milk.

Thirsty, I woke, and sat bolt upright as was my custom, and stared around me in the dark.

All the women were still, but with their eyes open.

This struck me as horrid, horrid as the illusion that the woman's face had been on the back of her head. I reached out to shake awake the blond woman, so rigid was her gaze. And I perceived the moment I touched her that she lay dead in a pool of her own blood. Indeed, all of them were dead, one on either side of me, and the three who lay on the floor. They were dead. And the bed was soaked with the blood and it stank of human people.

I rushed out into the courtyard in uncontrollable cowardice, and collapsed near the fountain, on my knees, trembling, unsure of what I had seen. But when I finally rose to my feet and returned, I saw it was true. These women were dead! I laid my hands on them repeatedly but there was no waking them! I couldn't cure them of death!

I gathered up my robes, my sandals, dressed again and ran away.

How could these women have died? I remembered the words the Franciscan had said to me. 'Never touch the flesh of a woman.'

It was the dead of night in Florence, but I managed to return to the monastery, and there I locked myself in my cell. When morning came, news of the deaths was all over Florence. A new form of plague had struck.

I did what I have always done at such trouble. I went home to Assisi, walking the whole way. The mild winter was coming, which is nevertheless a winter, and the journey was not easy. But I did not care. I knew someone was following me, a man on horseback, but I only caught glimpses of him from time to time. I was in despair.

As soon as I reached the monastery I prayed. I

prayed to Francis to guide me and to help me; I prayed to the Blessed Virgin to forgive me for my sins with these women. I lay on the floor of the church, arms outstretched as priests do when they are ordained. I prayed for forgiveness and understanding, and I wept. I didn't want to think my sin had killed these women.

I envisioned the Christ Child, and I became the small helpless baby, and I said, 'Christ, succor me, Holy Mother the Church, succor me. What can I do on my own?'

I went to confession, to one of the oldest priests there.

He was Italian, but had only just come home from England, where many Protestants were now being put to death. We were rebuilding our monasteries in that land, sending priests back to serve the Catholics who had kept the faith during times of persecution.

I chose this priest because I wanted to confess all – my birth, my memories, the strange things said to me! But when I was kneeling in the confessional these things seemed the dreams of a madman! And it really did seem to me that I was a man only, and had had some proper childhood somewhere which had somehow been erased from my mind and heart.

I confessed only that I'd been with the women, that I had brought death to all four but did not know how.

My confessor laughed at me, softly, reassuringly. I had not killed the women. On the contrary, God had preserved me from the plague which had killed them. It was a sign of my special destiny. I should not think of it anymore. Many a priest has stumbled, taken to his bed a whore. The important thing was to be larger than that sin and that guilt, to carry on in the service of God.

'Don't be full of pride, Ashlar. So you finally succumbed like everyone else. Put it behind you. You know now that it is nothing, this pleasure, and God has spared you from the plague for Himself.'

He told me that the time would come perhaps when I was to go to England, that England would need us as never before. 'Queen Mary is dying,' he said. 'If the crown goes to Elizabeth, the daughter of the witch,' he said, 'there shall be terrible persecutions of the Catholics again.'

I left the confessional, said my penance and went out into the wintry windswept fields.

I was unhappy. I did not feel absolved. My eyes were wide and I was walking in a staggering way. I had killed those women, I knew it. I had thought them witches! But they were not! The face on the back of the head, all that had been trickery and illusion! And they had died as the result!

Oh, but what was the larger truth! What was the real story? There was but one way to know! Go to England, go as a missionary to England, to fight the Protestant heresies there, and seek the Glen of Donnelaith. If I found the castle, if I found the Cathedral, if I found the window of St Ashlar, then I would know I had not imagined these things. And I must find the clansmen. I must find the meaning of the words once spoken to me. That I was Ashlar, that I was he who comes again.

I walked alone in the fields, shivering and thinking that even my beautiful Italy could be cold at this time. But was this cold a reminder to me of where I had been born? This was for me a solemn and terrible moment. I had never wanted to leave Italy. And I thought again of the priest's words, spoken in Donnelaith: 'You can choose.'

Could I not choose to stay here in the service of God and St Francis? Could I not forget the past? As for the women, I would never touch them again, never. There would be no more such deaths. And as for St Ashlar, who was this saint who had no feast in the church calendar? Yes, stay here! Stay in sunny Italy, stay in this place which has become your home.

A man was following me. I'd seen him almost as soon as I left the town and now he came riding closer and closer, a man dressed all in black wool and on a black horse.

'Can I offer you my horse, Father?' he asked. It was the accent of the Dutch merchants. I knew it. I had heard it often enough in Florence and in Rome, and everywhere that I had been. I looked up and I saw his reddish-golden hair and blue eyes. Germanic. Dutch. It was all the same to me. A man from a world where heretics thrived.

'You know you cannot,' I said. 'I'm a Franciscan. I won't ride on it. Why have you been following me? I saw you in Florence. I've seen you many times before that.'

'You must talk to me,' he said. 'You must come with me. The others haven't an inkling of your secret nature. But I know what it is.'

I was horrified at these words. It was the dropping of a sword which had been dangling over me forever. My breath went out of me. I bent double as if I'd been struck and I went further out, that way, staggering, into the field. The grass was soft and I lay down, covering my eyes from the glaring sun.

He dismounted and came after, leading his horse. He deliberately stood between me and the sun, so that I

could take my hand away from my eyes. He was powerfully built like many from Northern Europe, and he had
the thick eyebrows those people have, and the pale
cheeks.

'I know who you are, Ashlar,' he said to me in Italian
with a Dutch accent. And then he began to speak Latin.
'I know you were born in the Highlands. I know that
you come from the Clan of Donnelaith. I heard tell of
your birth shortly after it happened. There were those
who caught the scent of it and spread the story – even
to other lands.

'It took me years to find you here, and I have been
watching you. I know you by your height, by your long
fingers, by your power to sing and to rhyme, and by
your craving for milk. I have seen you take the offerings
from the peasants. But do you know what they would
do to you if they could? Your kind would always have
the milk and the cheese, and in the dark woodlands of
the world, the peasants still know this and leave these
offerings for you on the table at night, or at the door.'

'What are you calling me, a devil? A woodland spirit?
Some demon or familiar? I am none of those things.'

My head was aching; what was real to me? This
beautiful grass around me as I rose to my knees, and
then to my feet? This cold blue sky above me? Or those
wretched ghastly memories and the words this man
spoke?

'Nights ago in Florence, you brought death to four
women,' he said. 'That was the final proof.'

'Oh, God, then you know it. It is true.' I began to
weep. 'But how did I kill them? Why did they die? All I
did was what other men have done.'

'You will bring death to any woman whom you

touch! Weren't you told this before you left the glen? Ah, the folly of those who sent you away! And for years and years we have watched and waited for you to come. They should have sent for us. They know who we are, and that we would have paid gold for you, gold, but they are stubborn.'

I was horrified.

'You speak of me as if I were a chattel. I am my father's son, those base-born.'

He went on worrying and wringing his hands, imploring me to understand him:

'They were told again and again by our emissaries, but they were superstitious and blind.'

'Emissaries? From where? The Devil!' Again I stared at him, this man in black with the black horse. 'Who is blind? Dear God in heaven, give me the grace to understand this, to combat the artful lies of the Great Deceiver. You either stop talking in riddles or I will kill you! Tell me why I killed those women, or so help me God, I may break your bones with my bare hands.'

I rose up in a tempest of anger. And it was all I could do to keep from laying my hands on his throat. The anger was as everything else with me, instantaneous and complete. I frightened him as I came towards him. I was so much taller than he was, and when I put my hands out, he fell back.

'Ashlar, listen, for this is not the lies of the Great Deceiver. This is the perfect truth. No ordinary woman can bear your child – only a witch can do it, or a dwarfed monster – the half-breed spawn of your kind and the witches – or a pure female of your own ilk.'

The words dazzled me. A pure one of my own ilk! What did this conjure to my imagination? A tall beauty, pale of skin and fleet of foot, with graceful fingers like my own? Had I not envisioned such a being when I lay with the whores? Or had I dreamed? I was overcome suddenly, as if by incense or singing. But I remembered my mother. She was no pure one. She had held her hand out, and revealed the witch's mark.

'You do not know the danger,' he said, 'if the ignorant peasants of this or any land were to find out. Why do you think the Scots sent you away in such haste?'

'You frighten me, and I want you to stop it. I live a life of love and peace and service to others. They sent me away to become a priest.' At this the calm came over me. I believed these words so completely. I looked up at the sky and its beauty seemed to me the perfect proof of God's grace.

'They sent you away so the peasants would not destroy you as they have always done with the remnants of your breed. The sight of you, the scent of you, the promise of your seed, could pitch them back into their cruel and pagan ways.'

'Breed. What are you saying? Breed.' I could not hear any more. I clenched my fists, unable to lay hands on him, unable to do him harm. In all my life of twenty years or more I had never struck another. I could not do violence. I wept, and I fled.

'You come with me now,' he cried, trying to catch up with me. 'I can make all provisions for the journey. You have no cherished objects, no personal possessions. You carry your breviary with you. You need nothing else. Come. We will go to Amsterdam together and when you are safe, I will tell you the truth.'

'I will not!' I said. 'Amsterdam! A stronghold of the heretics! You are speaking of hell by another name.' I

und. 'What are you saying? That I am not a
...an?'

...n, he was frightened as I leant over him, but he
...owerfully built and he took a stand.

'You have a body which can deceive others,' he said,
'but no one can speak for your soul. In the most ancient
legends, it was said your kind had no souls to be
converted, no souls to be saved. That you could hover
invisible in the darkness forever, between heaven and
earth, because heaven was closed to you, so your only
hope was to return in a likely form.'

I was awestruck, but not only for myself that someone
could believe such a thing of me, but for the sheer
possibility that such creatures could exist! Soulless. In
darkness, with heaven closed to them! I started to weep.

I cleared my vision, and looked at this man, who'd
given words to such a ghastly thought. His words were
like sparks inside of me. Like the snapping and popping
of damp wood. The more I stared at him, I sensed that
he had to be evil, he was from the Devil, he was from
some dark army that would carry my soul to hell.

'And you say that I have no soul? That I have no
soul to be saved? How dare you say this to me! How
dare you tell me that I am without a soul?'

In a fury I did strike him, knocking him with one fine
blow all the way to the ground. I was stupefied by my
own strength and as alarmed by this sin as I had been
by my others.

I ran out of the field and home.

This man followed me, but he didn't come close. He
seemed in a great state of alarm when I entered the
monastery, but he hung back, and I wondered if he was
afraid of the Cross, the church, the sanctified ground.

That night I resolved what I must do. I went down beneath the church and slept on the stones before the tomb of Francis. I prayed to him. 'Francis, how can I not have a soul? Give me guidance, Father. Help me. Mother of God, this is your child. I am bereft and alone.'

I fell into a deep sleep and I saw angels, and I saw the face of the Virgin, and I shrank down into a tiny child in her arms. I lay against her breasts, one with the Christ Child. And Francis said to me that that was my way; not to be one with the crucified Christ, leave that to others, but to be one with that innocent babe. I must go back to Scotland, go back to where it had begun.

I dreaded to leave Assisi so soon before Christmas – not to be here for the great Procession and to help make the crèche with the shepherds and the Holy Family – but I knew that as soon as I obtained permission, I would go.

Travel north and find Donnelaith. See for yourself what is there.

I went to talk to the Guardian, our Father Superior, a wise and kindly man who had served all his life in the place of Francis's birth. He heard me out calmly and then spoke:

'Ashlar, if you go it will be to a martyr's death. Word has just reached Italy. The daughter of the witch Boleyn has been crowned Queen of England. This is Elizabeth, and the burnings of Catholics have once again begun.'

The witch Boleyn. It took me a moment to remember who this was, ah, the mistress of King Henry, the one who had enchanted him and turned him against the Church. Yes, Elizabeth, the daughter. And so Good Queen Mary, who had tried to bring the land back to the faith, was now dead.

'I cannot let this stop me, Father,' I said. 'I cannot.' And then in a rush I told him the whole tale.

I walked back and forth in the chamber. I talked and talked. I told all the words that had been said to me, trying not to fall into a cadence. I told about the strange man from Holland. I told about the old Laird, and my father, and St Ashlar in his window, and the priest who had said to me, 'You are St Ashlar come again. You can be a saint.'

I thought surely he would laugh as had my confessor at the mere statement that I had brought the women death.

He was thunderstruck. He remained quiet for a long time, and then he rang for his assistant. The monk came in. 'You can tell the Scotsman that he might come in now,' he said.

'The Scotsman?' I said. 'Who is this man?'

'This is the man who has come from Scotland to take you away. We have been keeping him from his mission. We did not believe him! But you have confirmed his claim. He is your brother. He comes from your father. Now we know that what he says is true.'

His words caught me utterly unprepared. I realized I had wanted to be proven a liar, to be told this was all devilish fantasy and that I must put such thoughts out of my mind.

'Bring the young Earl's son to me,' said the Father Superior again, to send the baffled attendant on his way.

I was a cornered animal. I found myself looking to the windows as a means of escape.

I was in terror that the man who came into the room would be the Dutchman. This cannot happen to me, I thought, I am in the state of grace. God cannot let the Devil take me to hell. I closed my eyes, and I tried to feel my own soul. Who dares to tell me I have no soul?

There came into the room a tall red-haired man, clearly recognizable as Scots by his wild and rustic attire. He wore the tartan of plaid, and ragged untrimmed fur and crude leather shoes, and seemed a savage of the wood compared to the civilized gentlemen of Italy, who went about in hose and fine sleeves. His hair was streaked with brown and his eyes dark, and when I looked at him I knew him, but I could not remember from where.

Then I saw in memory . . . the men standing by the fireplace. The Yule log burning. The Laird of Donnelaith saying, 'Burn him!' and these men about to obey the command. This was one of the clan, though too young to have been there, then.

'Ashlar!' he said in a whisper. 'Ashlar, we have come for you. We need you. Our father is the Laird now, and would have you come home.'

And then he dropped to his knees and he kissed my hand.

'Don't do this,' I said gently. 'I am only an instrument of the Lord. Please embrace me, man to man, if you will and tell me what you want.'

'I am your brother,' he said, obeying me and caressing me. 'Ashlar, our Cathedral still stands. Our valley still exists by the grace of God. But it may not for long. The heretics have threatened to come down upon us before Christmas; they would destroy our rites; they call us pagans and witches and liars, and it is they who lie. You must help us fight for the true faith. England and Scotland are soaked in blood.'

For a very long moment I looked at him. I looked at the eager excited expression of the Guardian, our Father Superior. I looked at the attendant, who seemed himself carried away by all this as if I were a saint. Of course the heretics did these things – denounced us in those terms which more properly applied to them.

I thought of the Dutchman outside, waiting, watching. Perhaps this was a trick from him. But I knew better. This was my father's son! I saw the resemblance. All the rest was true.

'Come with me,' said my brother. 'Our father is waiting. You have answered our prayers. You are the saint sent by God to lead us. We can't delay any longer. We must go.'

My mind played a strange trick on me. It said, Some of this is true and some is not. But if you take the horror, you must take the illusion. The veracity of one depends upon the other. Yes, the birth happened. And you know that a witch was your mother! And you even suspect who that witch might be. You know. And therefore you are the saint, and your hour has come.

In sum, I knew full well that what lay before me was a likely mixture of fancy and truth – a mixture of legend and puzzling fact – and in my desperation, horrified by what I could not deny, I accepted all in one fell swoop. You might say, I bought the fantasy. I could not be stopped now from going home.

'I will come with you, brother,' I said. And before I could form any thoughts in my mind to the contrary, I submerged myself in the sense of my mission. I let it seduce me and overtake me.

All night, I prayed only for courage, that if there was persecution in England, I would be brave enough to die for the true faith.

That my death would have meaning, I never doubted, and by dawn I think I had convinced myself I was meant to be a martyr, but much adventure and excitement lay ahead before the final flames.

But at early morning, I went to the Guardian of our congregation, and I asked him, to help me in my courage, would he do two things? First, take me into the church, into the baptistry, and there baptize me Ashlar in the name of the Father, and of the Son, and of the Holy Ghost, as if it had never been done before. And then would he lay his hands on me and give me Holy Orders, as if that too were happening for the first time? Would he give the power to me as a priest had given it to him, a priest who had been given it by one before him, who had got it direct from one before that, all the way back to Christ putting His hands on Peter, and saying, 'Upon this Rock, I shall build my church.'

'Yes, my son,' he said, 'my beloved Ashlar. Come, if you want these ceremonies, if they will give you strength, in Francis's name, we shall do them. You have in all these years asked for nothing. Come, we shall do as you wish.'

Then if it is true, I thought, if it is, I am nevertheless a Child of Christ, now born of water and the spirit, and I am an anointed priest of God.

'St Francis, be with me,' I prayed.

It was determined we would travel overland mostly through Catholic France and then over water to England. I was dispensed from my vow not to ride a horse. Expediency demanded it.

And so our long journey began. We were five men, all of us Highlanders, and we traveled as fast and as rough as we could, sometimes making camp in the forest. All the men except for me were heavily armed.

It was in Paris that again I saw the Dutchman! We were in the crowds before Notre Dame on a Sunday morning, going to Mass with thousands of others, in this a Catholic city, and the Dutchman came near to me.

'Ashlar!' he said. 'You are a fool if you go back to the glen.'

'You get away from me!' I cried.

But something in the man's face held me – a coolness, a resignation, almost a sneer. It was as if I was behaving predictably and wildly, and he was prepared for this, and he walked along with me. My brother and his men glared at the Dutchman and were ready at any instant to sink a dagger into him.

'Come to Amsterdam with me,' the Dutchman said. 'Come and hear my story. You go back to the glen and you will die! They are killing priests in England and that is what they think you are. But in the glen you will be an animal of sacrifice to those people! Do not be their fool.'

I drew up close to him. 'Tell me now, here in Paris. Sit down with me and tell me the story now.'

But before I could finish, my brother had drawn the Dutchman back and struck him a blow that sent him backwards into the crowd, creating screams and panic, as he tumbled over others and fell to the ground. 'You've been told before,' he declared to the Dutchman. 'Stay away from our ilk, and from our valley.' He spat in the Dutchman's face.

The Dutchman stared up at me and it seemed I saw hatred in him; pure hatred; or was it merely the thwarted will?

My brother and his men pulled me into the church.

Animal of sacrifice! Death to any ordinary woman . . .

My peace of mind was destroyed. The wonder of the journey was destroyed. I could have sworn that various persons in the Cathedral had seen this little drama and understood it, and that they were staring at me in a wary and cunning way. That they were almost amused. I went to receive Communion.

'Dear God, come into me, find me innocent and pure.'

The crowds of Paris are filled with bizarre figures. It was my imagination, surely, that those on the fringes stared at me, that the gypsies looked, and the deformed ones, those with humps and stunted legs. I closed my eyes and sang my songs in my head.

The next night, we put on plain clothes, and we sailed for England. The mist was thick over the sea. It was now very cold. I was entering the land of winter again, of low skies and dim sunshine, of eternal chill and mystery, the land of secrets, the land of terrible truths.

We made landfall four nights later, in Scotland, surreptitiously, for priests were being hunted by Elizabeth and burnt. We proceeded inland and up into the Highlands, and the winter came down around me like a spider's web which had waited. It was as if the craggy mountains said to me, 'Ah, we have you. You had your chance and now it's gone.'

I could not stop thinking of the man from Amsterdam. But I had one purpose. I would reach Donnelaith and demand the truth from my father, not the legends and the prayers, but the reason for the fear I had seen in my mother and in others – the whole tale.

THIRTY-SIX

LASHER'S STORY CONTINUES

The valley was under siege. The main pass was closed. We came through the secret tunnel, which seemed to have grown smaller and more treacherous in this score of years. There were times when I thought it too steep, too dark, too overgrown, and that we would surely have to go back.

But very suddenly, we had come to the end – and there was the splendor of Donnelaith under its cover of Christmas snow beneath a stalwart and dying winter sun.

Thousands of the faithful had sought shelter in the valley. They had come in to flee the religious wars in the surrounding towns. It was not a multitude such as one would see in Rome or Paris. But for this lonely and beautiful country it was a great population. Haphazard shelters had been built against the walls of the little town, and against the buttresses of the Cathedral, and hovels covered the valley floor. The main pass was barricaded. A thousand fires sent their smoke into the snowy sky. Ornamented tents rose here and there as if for princely war.

The sky was darkening, the sun a flaming orange in the mountainous clouds. Lights in the Cathedral were already burning. The air was wintry, but not freezing, and the splendid windows shone through the early dark in a fierce and beautiful blaze. The waters of the loch held the last of the light jealously and we could see armed Highlanders patrolling the dimming shores.

'I would pray first,' I told my brother.

'No,' he said. 'We must go up to the castle now. Ashlar, that we are not burnt out already is a miracle. This is Christmas Eve. The very night on which they have sworn to attack. There are factions within us who would be Protestant, who think that Calvin and Knox speak for the conscience. There are the old ones, the superstitious ones. Our people could break into their own war on this spot.'

'Very well,' I said, but I ached to see the Cathedral, ached to remember that first Christmas when I had gone to the crib, when I had seen the babe in the manger with the real ox and the real cow and the real donkey tethered there, amid the delicious smell of the hay and the winter greens. Ah, Christmas Eve. That meant that the Child Himself had not yet been laid in the manger. I had come in time to see it, perhaps even to lay the Infant Jesus there with my own hands. And in spite of myself, in spite of the bitter cold and the harsh darkness, I thought, This is my home.

The castle was more or less as I remembered, a great indifferent, cheerless pile of stone, as ugly surely as any edifice built by the Medici, or any I had seen on my progress through wartorn Europe. The mere sight of it filled me suddenly with fear. I turned round as I stood at the drawbridge, looking down into the valley, at the little town which was far smaller and poorer than Assisi. And all of this seemed crude and frightening suddenly – a land of shaggy gruff-spoken light-skinned persons without civilization, without anything that I could understand.

Was this pure cowardice that I felt? I wanted to be in Santa Maria del Fiore in Florence listening to the canticles or the High Mass. I wanted to be in Assisi greeting the Christmas pilgrims. For the first time in over twenty years I was not there!

As darkness fell the crowds about the little city and the church looked all the more ominous, and the woods themselves closer, as though struggling to swallow what few edifices man had made in this place.

For one second, I thought I saw a pair of dwarfish creatures, two little beings, far too ugly and misshapen to be children, and far too quick as they scurried out of the castle yard and across the bridge and beyond.

But so quick had it been, and so dark was it, that I was uncertain I'd seen anything at all.

I took one last look down into the valley. Ah, the beauty of the Cathedral. In its great Gothic ambition, it was more graceful even than the churches of Florence. Its arches challenged heaven. Its windows were visions.

This, this alone, must be saved, I thought. My eyes filled with tears.

Then I went into the castle to learn the truth.

The main hall had its roaring fire, and many in dark woolen garments gathered around the hearth.

My father rose at once from a heavily carved chair. 'Leave the hall,' he told the others.

I recognized him immediately. He was mightily impressive, big-shouldered still, and somewhat resembling his own father, but far more hardy and nothing as old as the old one had been when I came. His hair was streaked with gray but still a deep lustrous brown, and his deep-set eyes were filled with a loving fire.

'Ashlar!' he said. 'Thank God, you have come.' He threw his arms around me. I remembered the first moment I had ever seen him, the same look of love, from one who knew me, and my heart nearly broke. 'Sit down by the fire,' he said, 'and hear me out.'

Elizabeth, wretched daughter of the Boleyn, was on the throne of England, but she herself was not the worst threat to us. John Knox, the rabid Presbyterian, had come back from exile, and he was leading the people in an iconoclastic rebellion throughout the land.

'What is the madness of these people?' demanded my father, 'that they would destroy statues of our Blessed Mother, that they would burn our books? We are not idolaters! Thank God we have our own Ashlar, come back to save us at this time.'

I shuddered.

'Father, we are not idolaters and I am no idol,' I declared. 'I am a priest of God. What can I do in the face of war? All these years in Italy I have heard stories of atrocity. I know only how to do small things!'

'Small things! You are our destiny! We the Catholic Highlanders must have a leader to take a stand for right. At any time the Protestants and the English may build up the courage and the numbers to force the pass. They have told us if we dare to hold Midnight Mass in the Cathedral, they will storm the town. We have sheep; we have grain. If we hold through this night and the twelve days of Christmas, they may see the hand of God in it and be driven away.

'Tonight, you must lead the Procession, Ashlar, you

must lead the Latin hymns. You must place the Infant Jesus in the manger, between the Virgin Mother and good St Joseph. Lead the animals to the manger. Lead them to bow to the Good Child Jesus. Be our priest, Ashlar, what priests were meant to be. Reach to heaven for us, and call down the Mercy of God as only a priest can!'

Of course I knew this was the very concept which the Protestants found archaic, that we of the priesthood were mysterious and elevated, and that we had some communication with God which the ordinary folk did not.

'Father, I can do this as any priest can do it,' said I. 'But what if we do hold through Christmas? Why will they back away then? Why will they not come down upon us at any moment that our sheep and our grain are gone?'

'Christmas is the time of their hate, Ashlar. It is the time of the richest Roman ceremony. It is the time of the finest vestments and incense and candles. It the time of our greatest Latin Mass. And old superstition grips Scotland, Ashlar. Christmas in the pagan years was the time of witches, the time that the restless dead walked. Outside this valley, they say we harbor witches, that indeed, we of Donnelaith have the witches' gifts in our blood. They say our valley is filled with the little people who carry within them the souls of the restless dead! Papists, witchcraft – these denunciations are mixed together by men who fight to the death for the right to say that Christ is not in the bread and wine! That to pray to the Mother of God is a sin!'

'I understand.' Inwardly, I shuddered. *The little people carry within them the souls of the restless dead?*

'They call our saint an idol! They call us Devil worshipers! Our Christ is the Living Christ.'

'And I must strengthen the people . . .' I murmured. 'This does not mean that I myself shall shed blood.'

'Only raise your voice for the Son of God,' said my father. 'Rally the people, and silence the malcontents! For we have them among us, Puritans who would turn the tide, and even those who claim that there are witches in our very midst who must be burnt if we are to prevail. Put a silence to this squabbling. Call the entire people in the name of St Ashlar. Say the Midnight Mass.'

'I see,' I said, 'and you will tell them that I am the saint come from the window.'

'You are!' he declared. 'By the love of God, you are! You know that you are. You are Ashlar who comes again. You are Ashlar who is born knowing. And you know what you are. For twenty-three years you have lived in sanctity in the arms of the Franciscans and you are a true saint. Do not be so humble, my son, that you lack courage. Cowardly priests in this valley we have already, trembling down there in the sacristy, terrified that they will be snatched from the very altar by the town's Puritans and thrown in the Yule fire.'

At these words I remembered that long-ago Christmas. I remembered when my grandfather gave the order that I was to die. The Yule log. Would they bring it in this very night and start it to burning, after the Midnight Mass, when the Light of Christ was born into the world?

I was suddenly brought out of my thoughts. A deep sultry fragrance came to me, a thick and unnameable perfume. I smelled it so strongly that I was confused.

'You are St Ashlar,' my father declared again as if piqued by my silence.

'Father, I don't know,' I uttered softly.

'Ah, but you do know,' cried out a new voice. It was the voice of a woman, and as I turned around I saw a young female, my age, perhaps a little younger, and very fair, with silky long red tresses down her back and a thick and embroidered gown. It was from her that this fragrance emanated, causing a subtle change within my body, a longing and a slow fire.

I was struck by her beauty, by her rippling hair and her eyes so like those of our father, deep-set and bright. My eyes were black. My mother's eyes. I remembered the Dutchman's phrase – a pure female of your own ilk. But she was not this. I knew it. She was a human woman. I could see that she more resembled my father than me. When I saw my like I would know it, just as I have always known certain things.

This woman came towards me. The fragrance was inviting to me. I had no idea what to make of it; I seemed to feel hunger, thirst and passion all at the same time.

'Brother, you are no St Ashlar!' she said. 'You are the Taltos! The curse of this valley since the dark times, the curse that rises without warning in our blood.'

'Silence, bitch,' my father said. 'I mean it! I will kill you and your followers with my own hands.'

'Aye, like the good Protestants of Rome,' she said, mocking him, her voice very clear and ringing as she lifted her chin and pointed her hand. 'What is it they say in Italy, Ashlar? Do you know? "If our own father were a heretic, we would carry the faggots to burn him." Do I quote it right?'

'I think so, Sister,' I said softly, 'but for God's sake, be wise. Speak to me in patience.'

'Patience! Were you born knowing? Or is that a lie too? In the arms of a queen, was it not? And for you, she lost her head.'

'Silence, Emaleth,' cried my father. 'I am not afraid of you.'

'You are the only one then, Father. Brother, look at me, listen to what I say.'

'I don't know what you are saying, I don't understand this. My mother was a great queen. I never knew her name.' I stuttered as I said this, for I had long ago guessed who she might have been, and this was stupid for me to pretend not to know, and this woman knew it. She was clever and she saw past my gentle Franciscan manner and the startled look of innocence on my face.

In an ugly dim flash, I remembered my mother's loathing, the touch of my mouth on her nipple. I brought my hands up to my face. Why had I come back to learn these truths? Why had I not stayed in Italy? Oh, fool! What had I thought an ugly truth could do?

'It was the Boleyn,' said the woman, Emaleth, my sister. 'Queen Anne was your mother, and for witchcraft and for making monsters she was put to death.'

I shook my head. I saw only that poor frightened woman, screaming for me to be taken away. 'The Boleyn,' I whispered. And all the old tales came back to me of the martyrs of those times – the Carthusians and all the priests who would not ratify the evil marriage of the King to the Boleyn.

My sister continued, emboldened when she saw I did not contradict or even speak at all.

'And the Queen of England on the throne now is

your sister,' she said, 'and so frightened is she of the blood from her mother that makes monsters that she will never suffer a man to touch her, and never wed!'

My father tried to interrupt her, but she drove him back with her pointed finger as if it were a weapon that weakened him where he stood.

'Silence, old man. You did it. You coupled with Anne when you knew she had the witch's finger, you knew it – and that, with her deformity and your heritage, the Taltos might come.'

'Who is to prove that such a thing ever happened?' said my father. 'You think any woman or man from those times is alive now? Elizabeth, who was then a baby, that is the only one who is living. And the little princess was not in the castle that night! If she knew she had a living brother, with a claim to the throne of England, he would be dead, monster or no!'

The words struck me as does everything – music, beauty, wonder or fear. I knew. I remembered. I understood. I had only to dwell for a moment in pain on the old story. Queen Anne accused of enchanting His Majesty, and bearing a deformed child in the royal bed. Henry, eager to prove he had not fathered it, had accused her of adultery, and had sent five men – of known laxity and perversity – to pave Anne's way to the block.

'But they were not the father of the bairn,' said my sister. 'It was our father, and I am a witch for it, and you are the Taltos! And the witches of the valley know it. The little people know it – the trivial monsters and outcasts driven into the hills. They dream of a day when I will take a man to my bed who carries the seed in him. And from my loins might spring the Taltos as it did from poor Queen Anne.'

She advanced upon me, looking up into my eyes, her voice harsh and ringing in my ears. I went to cover my ears, but she took my hands.

'And then they would have it again, their soulless demon, their sacrifice. To torment as never a man or a woman was tormented! Ah, yes, you catch this scent that comes from me, and I the scent that comes from you. I am a witch and you are the Evil One. We know each other. On account of this I have taken my vow of chastity as devoutly as Elizabeth. No man will plant a monster in me. But in this valley there are others – witches whether they would be or not – they can smell the scent of the Strong One, the perfume of evil, and it is already in the wind that you have come. Soon the little people will know.'

I thought of those small beings I had seen for an instant at the castle gates. And it seemed at this very minute some sound startled my sister, and she looked about her, and I heard a faint echoing laughter come from the darkness of the stairs.

My father stepped forward.

'Ashlar, for the love of God and His Divine Son, don't listen to your sister. That she is a witch herself is the perfect truth. She hates you, that you are the Taltos, that you were born knowing, and not she. That she was a mewling child like all the rest. She is but a woman – like your mother – who might give birth to such a miracle, or may never. It is unknown. The little people are sad and easily placated; they are old and common monsters, they have always lived in the mountains and the valleys of Ireland and Scotland; they will be here when men are gone. They do not matter.'

'But what is the Taltos, Father!' I demanded. 'Is this

an old and common monster, this Taltos? Whence comes this thing?'

He bowed his head, and gestured that I should listen:

'Against the Romans we protected this valley, when we were warriors of old and gathered the big stones! We protected it against the Danes, the Norsemen and the English as well.'

'Aye,' cried my sister, 'and once we protected it from the Taltos when they fled their island and sought to hide from the armies of the Romans in this glen!'

My father turned his back on her and took me by the shoulders. He shut her out.

'Now we protect Donnelaith from our own Scots people,' he said, 'and in the name of our Catholic Queen, our sovereign, of our faith. Mary Stuart, Queen of Scots, is our only hope. You must put aside these tales of magic and witchcraft. There is a purpose to what you are and why you have come. You will put Mary, Queen of Scots, on the throne of England! You will destroy John Knox and all his ilk. Scotland will never be under the boot of the Puritans or the English again!'

'He has no answer for your question, Brother,' cried Emaleth.

'Sister,' I said quietly. 'What would you have me do?'

'Leave the valley,' she said, 'as you came. Flee for your life and for our sakes before the witches know you are here, before the little people learn! Flee so that they do not bring the Protestants down upon us! You, Brother, are the living proof of their claim. You are the witch's child, deformed, monstrous! If you stir up the old rites, the Protestants will have us with the blood on our hands. You can fool the eyes of the humans around you. But you cannot prevail in a battle for God. You are doomed.'

'Why not!' I cried. 'Why not prevail!'

'These are lies,' said my father. 'The oldest lies in this part of the world. St Ashlar prevailed. St Ashlar was a Taltos, and for God he built the Cathedral! At the very spot where his wife, the pagan Queen, was burnt for the old faith, a blessed spring bubbled up from the ground with which he baptized all those who lived between the loch and the pass. St Ashlar slew the other Taltos! He slew them all so that man made in the image of Christ would rule the earth. Christ's church is built on the Taltos! If that is witchery, then Christ's church is witchery. They are one and the same.'

'Aye, he slew them,' cried Emaleth. 'In the name of one God instead of another! He led the massacre of his own, to save himself from it. He joined in the fear and hatred and the disgust. He slew his clan to save himself! Even his wife he sacrificed. This is your great saint. A monster who deceived those around him so that he might lead and glut himself with glory and not die with his own breed.'

'For the love of God, child,' said my father .o me. 'This is our miracle now. It comes once in so many hundred years.'

My sister turned to glare at me, even as he pulled her back.

And I saw them together, looking at me, and I saw them as humans, and how alike they were.

'Wait,' I said softly, so softly that it might as well have been a wild cry. 'I see clearly,' I said. 'All of us are born with a chance before God. The word *Taltos* means nothing in itself. I am flesh and blood. I am baptized. I have received Holy Orders. I have a soul. Physical monstrosity, that does not keep me out of heaven. It is what I do! We are not predestined as the Lutherans and the Calvinists would have us believe.'

'No one here argues with this, Brother,' said Emaleth.

'Then let me lead the people, Emaleth,' ı said. 'Let me prove by good works that I do indeed have the grace of God in me. I am not an evil thing because I *will not be* an evil thing. When I have done wrong to others it was in error! If I was born as you say, and I know now it is true, then perhaps there was a purposε, that the power of my wretched mother should be broken, and that I should overturn my sister, and put Mary Stuart on the throne.'

'Born knowing. You are born the dupe of those who hold you prisoner. That is what the Taltos has always been. "Find the Taltos, make the Taltos,"' she cried mockingly. '"Breed it for the fire of the gods! that the rain shall fall and the crops grow!"'

'That is old now and does not matter,' said my father. 'Our Lord Jesus Christ is the Jack of the Green. He is our God, and the Taltos is not our sacrifice but our saint. The Blessed Mother is our Holda. When the drunken men of the village don the skins and horns of animals, it is to walk in the Procession to the manger, not to cavort as of old.

'We are one with old spirits and the One True God. We are at peace with all of nature, because we have made the Taltos into St Ashlar! And in this valley we have known safety and prosperity for a thousand years. Think on it, Daughter, a thousand years! The little people fear us! They do not trouble us. We leave out the milk at night in offering, and they dare not take more than what we leave.'

'It's coming to an end,' she said. 'Get out, Ashlar, lest you give the Protestants exactly what they need. The witches of this valley will know you. They will know your scent. Go while there is time and live out your life in Italy where no one knows what you are.'

'I have a soul within me, Sister,' I said. I raised my voice as much as I dared. 'Sister, trust in me. I can rally the people. I can at least keep us safe.'

She shook her head. She turned her back.

'Can *you* do it?' cried my father to her, accusing her. 'Can you, with your magic spells and evil books and sickening incantations? Can you make anything happen in the world at large! Our world is about to perish. What can *you* do? Ashlar, listen to me, we are a small valley, a small glen, only one tiny part of the north country. But we have endured and we would live on. And that is all the world is, finally, small valleys, groups of people who pray and work and love together as we do. Save us, Son. I implore you. Call upon the God you believe in to help you. And what you were – and what your father and mother did – these things do not matter one whit.'

'No Protestant or Catholic can prove anything against me,' I said softly. 'Sister, would you tell them what you know?'

'They will know.'

I walked out of the hall. I was the priest now, not the humble Franciscan but the missionary, and I knew what I had to do.

I went through the castle yard and over the bridge and down the snowy path towards the church. From far around came the people carrying torches, looking at me

820

leerily and then excitedly, and whispering the name 'Ashlar', to which I nodded and gave a great open sign with both hands.

Again I spied one of those tiny twisted creatures, garbed and hooded in black, and running very fast through the field towards me and then away. It seemed the others saw him, and drew together, whispering, but then followed me on down the road.

Out in the fields, I saw men dancing. By the light of torches, and dark against the sky, I saw them with the horns and the skins! They had begun their old pagan Yuletide revelry. I must make the Procession, and take them to the Baby Jesus. There was no doubt.

By the time I reached the gates of the town there was a multitude. I went to the Cathedral and bade them wait. I went into the sacristy, where two elderly priests stood together, looking at me fearfully.

'Give me robes, give me vestments,' said I. 'I would bring the valley together. I must at least have my cassock to begin and a white surplice. Do as I say.'

At once they hurried to help me dress. Several young acolytes appeared, and put on their surplices and their gowns.

'Come on, Fathers,' I said to the frightened priests. 'See, the boys are braver than you are. What is the hour? We must make the Procession. The Mass must be said at the stroke of twelve! Protestant, Catholic, pagan. I cannot save them all, nor bring them together. But I can bring Christ down upon the altar in the Transubstantiation. And Christ will be born tonight in this valley as He has always been!'

I stepped out of the sacristy and to the crowd, I raised my voice.

'Prepare for the Christmas Procession,' I declared. 'Who would be Joseph and who would be our Blessed Mother, and what child have we in this village that I may place in the manger before I step to the Altar of God to say the Mass? Let the Holy Family be flesh and blood tonight, let them be of the valley. And all of you who would take the shape and skins of animals, walk in the Procession to the manger and kneel there as did the ox and the lamb and donkey before the little Christ. Come forward, my faithful ones. It is almost time.'

Everywhere I saw rapt faces; I saw the grace of God in every expression. And only a glimpse of a small deformed woman, peering at me from beneath a heavy wrap of coarse cloth. I saw her bright eye, I saw her toothless smile, and then she had vanished, and the crowd closed around her as if, among the press of the tall ones, she had gone unseen. Only a common thing, I thought. And if there be little people, then they are of the Devil, and the Light of Christ must come and drive them out.

I closed my eyes, folded my hands together so that they would make a small church of their own, very narrow and high, and I began in a soft voice to sing the plaintive beautiful Advent hymn:

> Oh come, Oh come, Emmanuel
> And ransom captive Israel
> That mourns in lonely exile here
> Until the Son of God appear . . .

Voices joined me, voices and the melancholy sound of flutes, and the tapping of tambourines, and even of soft drums:

Rejoice
Rejoice
Emmanuel
Shall come to thee
O Israel!

High in the tower, the bell began its ringing, too rapid for the Devil's Knell, but more the clarion to call all the faithful from mountain and valley and shore.

There were a few cries of 'The Protestants will hear the bell! They will destroy us.' But more and lustier cries of 'Ashlar, St Ashlar, Father Ashlar. It is our saint returned.'

'Let the Devil's Knell be sounded!' I declared. 'Drive the witches and the evil ones from the valley! Drive out the Protestants, for surely they will hear the Devil's Knell too.'

There were cheers of approbation.

And then a thousand voices were raised in the Advent hymn and I retired into the sacristy to put on my full raiment, my Christmas chasuble and vestments of bright green-gold, for the town had them, yes, the town had them as beautiful and embroidered and rich as any I had ever seen in wealthy Florence, and I was soon dressed as a priest should be in the finest linen and gold-threaded robes. The other priests dressed hastily. The acolytes ran to distribute the blessed candles for the Procession, and from all the country round, I was told, the faithful were coming, and the faithful, who had been afraid to do it before, were bringing the Christmas greens.

'Father,' I said my prayer, 'if I die this night, into thy hands I commend my spirit.'

It was nearly midnight, but still too soon to go out, and as I stood there, deep in prayer, seeking to fortify myself, calling on Francis to give me courage, I looked up and saw that my sister had come to the door of the sacristy, in a dark green hood and cloak, and was motioning for me with one thin white hand, to come into the adjacent room.

This was a dark-paneled chamber, with heavy oak furnishings, and shelves of books built into the walls. A place for a priest to hold conferences in quiet, perhaps, or a study. Not a room I had seen before. I saw Latin texts which I knew; I saw the statue of our founder, St Francis, and my heart was filled with happiness, though no plaster or marble Francis had ever been the radiant being I saw in my mind's eye.

My soul was quiet. I didn't want to talk to my sister. I wanted only to pray. The scent made me restless.

She led me inside. Several candles burnt along the wall. Nothing was visible through the tiny diamond-paned windows except the snow falling, and I was stunned to see the Dutchman from Amsterdam seated at the table and motioning for me to sit down. He had taken off his clumsy Dutch hat, and looked at me eagerly as I took the opposite chair.

The strange enticing scent came strongly from my sister, and once again it made me hunger for something, but I did not know for what. If it was an erotic hunger, I did not intend to find out.

I was fully dressed for High Mass. I seated myself carefully and folded my hands on the table.

'What is it you want?' I looked from my sister to the Dutchman. 'Do you come to go to confession so that you can receive the Body and Blood of Christ tonight?'

'Save yourself,' said my sister. 'Leave now.'

'And forsake these good people and this cause? You are mad.'

'Listen to me, Ashlar,' said the man from Amsterdam. 'I'm offering you my protection again. I can take you from the valley tonight, secretly. Let the cowardly priests here gather their courage on their own.'

'Into a Protestant country? For what?'

It was my sister who answered: 'Ashlar, in the dim days of legends before the Romans and the Picts came to this land, your breed lived on an island, naked and mad as apes of the wild – born knowing, yes, but knowing at birth all that they would *ever* know!

'At first the Romans sought to breed with them, as had others. For if they could father sons who grew to manhood within hours, what a powerful people they would become. But they could not breed the Taltos, save once in a thousand times. And as the women died from the seed of the Taltos males, and the Taltos females led the men to endless and fruitless licentiousness, it was decided that they must wipe the Taltos from the earth.

'But in the islands and in the Highlands, the breed survived, for it could multiply like rats. And finally when the Christian faith was brought to this country, when the Irish monks came in the name of St Patrick, it was Ashlar the leader of the Taltos who knelt to the image of the Crucified Christ and declared that all his kind should be murdered, for they had no souls! There was a reason behind it, Ashlar! For he knew that if the Taltos really learnt the ways of civilization, in their childishness, and idiocy, and penchant to breed, they could never be stopped.

'Ashlar was no longer of his people. He was of the Christians. He had been to Rome. He had spoken to Gregory the Great.

'So he condemned his fellow Taltos! He turned on them. The people made it a ritual, an offering, as cruel a pagan slaughter as ever was known.

'But down through the years, in the blood, the seed travels, to throw up these slender giants, born knowing, these strange creatures whom God has given the cleverness of mimicry, and singing, but no true capacity to be serious or firm.'

'Oh, but that is not so,' I said. 'Before God, I am the living proof.'

'No,' said my sister, 'you are a good follower of St Francis, a mendicant and a saint, because you are a simpleton, a fool. That's all St Francis ever was – God's idiot, walking about barefoot preaching goodness, not knowing a word of theology really, and having his followers give away all they possessed. It was the perfect place to send you – the Italy of the Franciscans. You have the addled brain of the Taltos, who would play and sing and dance the livelong day and breed others for playing and singing and dancing . . .'

'I am a celibate,' I said. 'I am consecrated to God. I know nothing of such things.' I was cut so deep it was a miracle the words would come from me. I was wounded. 'I am not such a creature. How dare you?' I whispered, but then I bowed my head in humility. 'Francis, help me now,' I prayed.

'I know this whole story,' declared the Dutchman, as my sister nodded. He went on. 'We are an Order called the Talamasca. We know the Taltos. We always have. Our founder beheld with his own eyes the Taltos of his time. It was his great dream to bring the male Taltos together with the female Taltos, or with the witch whose blood was strong enough to take the male's seed. That has been our purpose for centuries, to watch, to wait, and to rescue the Taltos – to rescue a male and a female in one generation if such a thing does occur! Ashlar, we know where there is a female! Do you understand?'

I could see this startled my sister. She had not known it, and now she looked at the Dutchman with suspicion, but he went on, urgently, as before.

'Have you a soul, Father?' he whispered to me, changing his manner now to a more wily one, 'and a wit to know what it means? A pure female Taltos? And a brood of children born knowing, able to stand and to talk on the first day! Children who can so quickly beget other children?'

'Oh, what a fool you are,' I said. 'You come like the fiend to tempt Christ in the desert. You say to me, "I would make you the ruler of the world."'

'Yes, I say that! And I am prepared to assist you, to bring back your breed in full force and power again.'

'And if you do think me this witless monster! Why would you so generously do this for me?'

'Brother, go with him,' said my sister. 'I don't know if this female exists. I have never beheld a female Taltos. But they are born, that's true. If you don't go, you will die tonight. You have heard tell of the little people. Do you know what they are?'

I didn't answer. I wanted to say, I do not care.

'They are the spawn of the witch that fails to grow into the Taltos. They carry the souls of the damned.'

'The damned are in hell,' I replied.

'You know this isn't so. The damned return in many

forms. The dead can be restless, greedy, filled with vengeance. The little people dance and couple, drawing out the Christian men and women who would be witches, who would dance and fornicate, hoping for the blood to come together, for like to find like, and that the Taltos will be born.

'That is witchcraft, Brother. That is what it has always been – bring together the drunken women, so that they will risk death to make the Taltos. That is the old story of the revels in these dark glens. It is to make a race of giants who will, by sheer numbers, drive other mortals from the earth.'

'God would not let such a thing happen,' I said calmly.

'Neither will the people of the valley!' said the Dutchman. 'Don't you understand? Throughout the centuries they have waited and watched and used the Taltos. It is good luck to them to bring together male and female, but only for their own cruel rituals!'

'I don't know what you are saying. I am not this thing.'

'In my house in Amsterdam there are a thousand books which will tell you of your kind and other miraculous beings; there is all the knowledge we have gathered as we have waited. If you are not the simpleton, then come.'

'And what are you?' I demanded. 'The alchemist who would make a great homunculus?'

My sister put down her head on the table and wept.

'In my childhood I heard the legends,' she said bitterly, wiping at her tears with her long fingers. 'I prayed the Taltos would never come. No man shall ever touch me lest such a creature would be born to me! And if such were to happen, God forbid, I should strangle it before it ever drank the witch's milk from my breasts. But you, Brother, you were allowed to live, you drank your fill of the witch's milk and grew tall. Yet you were sent away to be saved. And now you have come home to fulfill the worst prophecies. Don't you see? The witches may be spreading the word now. The vengeful little people will learn that you are here. The Protestants surround this valley. They are waiting for the chance to come down upon us, waiting for the spark to light their fire.'

'These are lies. Lies to put out the Light of Christ which would come into the world on this night. You hear the bells. I go now to say the Mass. Sister, don't come to the altar with your pagan superstition. I will not put the Body of Christ on your tongue.'

As I rose to go, the Dutchman laid hold of me, and with all my strength I forced him back.

'I am a priest of God,' I said, 'a follower of St Francis of Assisi, I have come to say the Christmas Mass in this valley. I am Ashlar, and I stand on the right hand of God.'

Without stopping I went to the Cathedral doors. Great cheers sounded from the multitude as I opened the church. My head was swimming with their disconnected phrases, threats, suspicions – that it was all demonology, of that, I was sure.

I went out amongst the townspeople, raising my hand in blessing. *In Nomine Patris, et filii, et spiritus sancti, amen.* A beautiful young girl had come forward to be the Blessed Virgin Mary in our pageant, her hair covered by a blue veil, and a rosy-cheeked boy to be Joseph, who had only just got his beard and had to darken it with coal; and then an infant, born only a few days ago, tiny and pink and beautiful, was placed in my arms.

I saw the men in their animal skins gathering, lighted candles in their hands. Indeed the entire valley was ablaze with lighted candles. All the town was filled with lighted candles! And the great beautiful church behind us would soon receive this light.

For a split second again, I did see one of those small beings, hump-backed, heavily clothed, but it seemed no monster – only the common dwarfs one saw in the streets of Florence, or so I told myself again. And it was natural for the people to give it wide berth and to gasp as it fled, for such things frequently frighten the ignorant. They cannot be blamed.

The bell began to chime the hour of midnight. It was Christmas. Christ had come. The bagpipers came into the church, in their full tartan skirts; the little children came in their white, as angels, and all the people, rich, poor, ragged or well dressed, crowded through the doors.

Our voices rose again in the anthem: 'Christ is born. Christ is born.' Once more I heard the tambourines and the pipes playing, and the beat of the drums. The rhythm caught me and made my vision blur, but I walked on, my eyes upon the radiant altar and the manger of hay which had been made to the right of it before the marble Communion rail. The infant in my arms gave strong little cries as if it too would announce the glad tidings, and kicked its sturdy beautiful little legs as I held it high.

I had never been such a child. I had never been such a miracle. I was something ancient and forgotten perhaps and worshiped in the time of darkness. But that did not matter now. Surely God saw me! Surely God knew my love for Him, my love for His people, my love for the Child Jesus born in Bethlehem, and all who would speak His name. Surely St Francis looked down on me, his faithful follower, his child.

At last I had reached the broad sanctuary, and I went down in genuflection and laid the little infant in the bed of hay. Linen had been prepared for it. It cried very hard to be so abandoned, poor little Christ! And my eyes filled with tears to behold its common perfection, its ordinary symmetry, the natural brilliance of its eyes and voice.

I stepped back. The Virgin Mary had knelt beside the little miracle. And to the right of the small crib knelt her young St Joseph, and shepherds came now, our own shepherds of Donnelaith with their warm sheep over their shoulders, and the cow and ox were led to the manger. The singing grew louder and ever more beautiful and blended, with the drums beneath it, and the pipes. I stood there swaying. My eyes misted. I realized in my sadness, as I sank deep into the music, almost irretrievably into it, that I had not seen my saint. I had not thought to glance at the window when I came down the center aisle. But it did not matter. He was nothing but glass and history.

I would now make the Living Christ. My altar boys were ready. I walked to the foot of the steps, and began the ancient words in Latin.

I will go in to the Altar of God.

At the Consecration, as the tiny bells rang out to mark the sacred moment, I held up the Host. This is My Body. I grasped the chalice. This is My Blood. I ate the Body. I drank the Blood.

And finally I turned to give out the Holy Communion, to see them streaming towards me, young and old and feeble and hardy and those with babes who held down the little babies' heads as they themselves opened their mouths to receive the sacred Host.

High above, amid the narrow soaring arches of this vast building, the shadows hovered, but the light rose, blessed and bright, seeking every corner to illuminate it, seeking every bit of cold stone to make it warm.

The Laird himself, my father, came to receive Communion, and with him my fearful sister, Emaleth, who bowed her head at the last second so none would see that I did not give her the Host. And uncles whom I knew from long ago, and kinswomen, yes, and the chieftains of the other strongholds and their clans. And then the farmers of the valley and the shepherds, and the merchants of the town – a never-ending stream.

It seemed an hour or more that we gave Communion, that back and forth we went for cup after cup, until at last all the men and women of the valley had partaken. All had received the Living Christ into their hearts.

Never in any church in Italy had I known such happiness. Never in any open field under God's arching sky, beneath His perfectly painted stars. When I turned to say the final words: 'Go, the Mass is ended!' I saw the courage and happiness and peace on every face.

The bell began to ring faster, indeed madly, with the spirit of rejoicing. The pipes struck up a wild melody, and the drums began to beat.

'To the castle,' cried the people. 'It is time for the Laird's Feast.'

And I found myself raised upon the shoulders of the stout men of the village.

'We will stand against the forces of hell,' cried the people. 'We will fight to the death if we must.' It was a good thing they carried me, for the music had become so merry and so loud that I could not have walked. I was spellbound and crazed as they took me through the nave, and this time I did turn to my right and gaze up at the black glass figure of my saint.

Tomorrow when the sun rises, I thought, I will come to you. Francis, be with me. Tell me if I have done well. Then the music overcame me. It was all I could do to sit upright for those who carried me out of the church and into the darkness where the snow lay gleaming on the ground and the torches of the castle blazed.

The main hall of the castle was strewn with green as I had first seen it, with all its many tapers lighted, and as the villagers set me down before the banquet table, the great Yule tree was dragged into the enormous gaping mouth of the hearth and set alight.

'Burn, burn, burn the twelve nights of Christmas,' sang the villagers. The pipes were shrilling and the drums beating. And in came the servers with platters of meat, and pitchers of wine.

'We will have the Christmas Feast after all,' cried my father. 'We will not live in fear any longer.'

In came the boys with the roasted boar's head on its huge platter, and the roasted animals themselves on their blackened spits, and everywhere I saw about me the ladies in their splendid gowns and the children dancing in groups and in circles, and finally all stood up to make informal rings beneath the great roof and lift one foot and do the tribal dance.

'Ashlar,' said my father. 'You have given the Lord back to us. God bless you.'

I sat at the table astonished, watching all of them, my brain throbbing with the beat of the drums. I saw the bagpipers now dancing as they played, which was no small feat. And I watched the circles break and form into other circles. And the smell of the food was rich and intoxicating. And the fire was a great blinding blaze.

I closed my eyes. I do not know how long I lay with my head against the back of the chair, listening to their laughter and to their songs, and to their music. Someone gave me some wine to drink and I took it. Someone gave me some meat and that I took as well. For it was Christmas and I could have meat if I wanted, and must not be the poor Franciscan on this day of all days.

I heard a change come over the room. I thought it merely a lull. And then I realized the drums had begun to beat more slowly. They had begun to sound more ominous and the pipes were playing an attenuated and dark song.

I opened my eyes. The assembly was wrapped in silence, or the spell of the music. I could not tell which. I felt if I moved I would become dizzy myself. I saw the drummers now; saw their fixed expressions, and the somber drunken faces of those who blew the pipes.

This was not Christmas music. This was something altogether darker and more lustrous and mad. I tried to stand up, but the music overcame me. And it seemed the melody had gone away from it, and it was only one theme repeated over and over, like a person reaching, making the same gesture, again and again, and again.

Then came the scent. Ah, it is only my sister, thought I, and I alone know it and I shall stifle whatever desire it creates.

But then a gasp went up from those scattered about the great room, those gathered on the stairs. Indeed, some turned and hid their faces, and others pushed back against the walls.

'What is it?' I cried out. My father stood staring as if no words could reach him. I saw my sister Emaleth the same, and all of my kin and the other chieftains. The drums beat on and on. The pipes whined and ground.

The scent grew stronger, and as I struggled to remain standing I saw a group of people, clothed only in black and white, come into the hall.

I knew these severe garments. I knew these stiff white collars. These were the Puritans. Had they come to make war?

They concealed something with their number, moving forward in concert, and now it seemed the pipers and the drummers were as wrapped in their music as was I.

I wanted to cry, 'Look, the Protestants!' But my words were far away. The scent grew stronger and stronger.

And at last the gathering of people in black broke open and in the circle stood a small bent and dwarfish female, with a great smiling mouth, and a hump upon her back and burning eyes.

'Taltos, Taltos, Taltos!' she screamed, and came towards me, and I knew the scent was coming from her! I saw my sister plunge towards me but then my father caught her and forced her down to the ground. He held her struggling on her knees.

One of the little people, bitter, fiery of eye.

'Aye, but we shall make giants together, my tall brother, my spouse!' she cried. And opening her arms she opened as well the tatters of her ragged gown. I saw her breasts huge and inviting, hanging down upon her small belly.

The smell was in my nostrils, in my head, and as she stepped up onto the table before me, it seemed she grew tall and beautiful in my eyes, a woman of grace and slender limbs and long white fingers reaching out to caress my face. *Pure female of your own ilk.*

'No, Ashlar!' cried my sister, and I saw the downward movement of my father's fist, and heard her body fall to the stone floor.

The woman before me was beaming; and as I watched, her golden-red hair grew longer and longer, coming down her naked back and down between her breasts. She lifted this veil now and revealed herself to me, cupping her breasts in both hands; and then dropping her hands, she opened the secret lips of the pink wet mouth between her legs.

I knew no reason, only passion, only the music, only the spellbinding beauty. I had been lifted to the table. And she lay down beneath me, and I was lifted over her.

'Taltos, Taltos, Taltos! Make the Taltos!'

The drums beat louder and louder as if there were no limit to the volume. The pipes had become one long drone. And there beneath me, in the golden hair between her legs, was the mouth smiling at me, smiling as though it could speak! It was moist and tender and glowing with the fluid of a woman, and I wanted it, I could smell it, I needed it; I had to have it.

I drew out my organ and drove it into the nether crack and thrust again and again.

It was the ecstasy of nursing from my mother. It was my whores in Florence, the ring of their laughter, the soft squeeze of their plump breasts, it was the hairy secrets beneath their skirts, it was a blaze of flesh tightening on me and drawing out of me cries of ecstasy. But it would not be finished. On and on it went. And to have lived a lifetime with so little of it, I had been a fool, a fool, a fool!

The boards were rattling and booming with our love-making. Cups had fallen to the floor. It seemed the heat of the fire was consuming us; the sweat was pouring out of me.

And beneath me – on the hard slats of wood, in the spilt wine and the scraps of meat and the torn linen – lay not the beautiful woman of shimmering red hair, but the tiny dwarfed hag with her hideous grin.

'Oh, God, I do not care, I do not care! Give it to me!' I all but screamed in my passion. On and on it went until there was no memory anymore of reason or purpose or thought.

In a daze, I realized I had been dragged from the dwarfish woman, and that she was undulating on the boards before me, and that something was coming out of that secret wet place where I had put my seed.

'No, I don't want to see it! Stop it!' I screamed. 'Oh, God, forgive me!' But the whole hall rang with laughter, wild laughter vying with the drums and with the pipes to make a din against which I had to cover my ears. I think I bellowed. Bellowed like a beast. But I could not hear myself.

Out of the loins of the hag came the new Taltos, came its long slithering arms, lengthening as they reached out, thin and groping, and fingers growing longer as they walked upon the boards, and at last its head, its narrow slippery head, as even the mother cried in her agony, and it was born knowing, it was born pushing itself free from the dripping egg within the womb, and looking with knowing eyes at me!

Out of her body it slithered, growing taller and taller, its eyes brilliant, its mouth open, its flawless skin gleaming as perfect as that of any human babe. And it fell upon its mother as I had once done, and began to drink from her, first draining one breast and then the other. And then it stood up, and all around the people cheered and roared.

'Taltos! Taltos! Make another. Make a woman, make Taltos until the sun rises!'

'No, stop this!' I cried, but this newborn horror, this baffled child, this strange wavering giant, had covered the hag of a woman and was now raping her as surely as I had done. And another hag had been brought to me and placed before me, and I was being forced down upon her, and my organ knew her, and knew what it wanted, and knew the smell.

Where were my saints?

It seemed the people in the hall were stamping and singing, chanting now with the drums. All were one voice, monotonous and low and incessant. And when I was pulled back, my eyes rolled and I could not see. The wine was splashed in my face, a child was being born to this new woman who had been given me, and once again the people cried, 'Taltos, Taltos, Taltos!' And finally, 'It is a woman! We have them both!'

The hall went wild with lusty cries. Once more the people were dancing but not in circles, but arm in arm and jumping up onto the boards and onto the chairs and rushing up the steps merely to jump in the air. I saw the Laird's face, full of wrath and horror, his head shaking as he cried out to me, but his words were lost.

'Make them till Christmas morning!' cried the people. 'Make them and burn them!' And as I struggled to my knees, I saw them take the firstborn, the boy who was now as tall as his father, and throw him into the Christmas fire.

'Stop it, stop this in the name of God!' No one could hear me. I could not hear myself. I could not hear him scream though I knew that he did; I saw the anguish in his smooth face. I went down on my knees and bowed my head. 'God help us. It is witchcraft. Stop it, oh, God, help us, they *have* bred us for sacrifice, we *are* the lambs, oh, God, please no more, no more to die!'

The crowd was roaring, swaying, humming in the mighty and endless drone. Then suddenly screams broke the air, more loud and numerous than my own, impossible for them not to hear.

Soldiers had forced the doors! Hundreds streamed into the hall. For every man in armor with a shield and sword, there came a shepherd or a plowman with a pitchfork or a crude plowshare in his hand.

'Witches, witches, witches!' screamed the attackers.

I rose to my feet and cried out for silence. Heads were being lopped from bodies. Those who were stabbed were screaming for mercy. Men fought to protect their women. And not even the little children were being spared.

The assailants laid hold of me. I was carried out of the hall, and with me the other monsters, newborn, and the hags from which they had come. The cold night opened up and it seemed the screams and war cries echoed off the mountains.

'Dear God, help us, help us,' I cried. 'Help us, this is evil, this is wrong, this is not your justice. No. Punish those who are guilty but not all! Dear God!'

My body was flung on the stone floor of the Cathedral and I was dragged up the aisle. All around me I heard the great windows bursting. I saw flames. I began to choke on the black smoke, but my body was being scraped as I was dragged. I saw in the far distance the hay of the manger explode! The tethered animals were bellowing in the fire from which they could not escape.

And finally at the foot of the tomb of St Ashlar I was thrown.

'Through the window, through the window!' they cried.

I struggled to my knees. All the wooden benches and ornaments of the Cathedral were burning. The whole world was smoke and the cries of the massacred, and suddenly my body was lifted by hands that held each foot and each arm, and by these beings I was swung back and forth, back and forth and then flung towards the great window of the saint himself!

I felt my chest and my face slam against the glass. I heard it break, and I thought, Surely now I will die. I will go up into the peace and into the night and into the stars, and God will explain why all this has come about.

It seemed I saw the valley. I saw the town burning. I saw every window a fiery mouth. I saw hovels blazing. I saw the bodies strewn all around me and in a daze I realized that these were not the visions of a rising soul. I still lived.

And then the mob came, and once again laid hands on me in their fury. 'Drag him to the circle,' they said. 'Drag all of them, burn them in the circle, burn the witches and the Taltos.'

All was blackness and panic, a gasp for breath, a desperate attempt for purchase – nothing for one moment that was not wild animal struggle, no, dear God, help us, don't let it be the flames.

As they raised me to my feet I saw the dim ancient circle of stones surrounding us, their crude outlines looming against the sky and against the flames of the town burning behind us, the flames engulfing the great Cathedral, all of its beautiful glass broken and gone.

A stone struck me, and then another, and another. And a third brought the blood pouring from my eye. I heard the flames. I felt the heat. But I was dying beneath the stones. One after another they struck my head, pitching me this way and that way so that I scarce felt the fire when it touched me . . .

'Dear God, into Thy hands, Thy servant Ashlar can do no more. Dear God. Infant Jesus, take me. Blessed Mother, take me. Francis, come to help me up. Holy Mary, Mother of God, now and at the hour . . . into Thy hands!'

And then . . .

And then.

There was no God.

There was no Baby Jesus in my arms.

There was no Blessed Mother, 'now and at the hour of our death.'

There was no Light.

There was no judgment.

There was no heaven.

There was no hell.

. . .

There was darkness.

. . .

And then came Suzanne.

Suzanne calling in the night.

Ashlar, St Ashlar.

A bright fleshly being, scarcely visible in the circle! And look at it, the ring of stones, how round! Hear her voice!

And down the long long years the call came, feeble and tiny, like the faintest spark, and then louder and clearer, and I came together to hear it:

'Come now, my Lasher, hear my voice.'

'Who am I, child?' Was this my voice speaking? Was this my own true voice speaking at last?

No time, no past, no future, no memory . . .

Only a dim vision of warm flesh through the mist, a blurred entity reaching upwards from the circle.

And her childlike answer, her laughter, her love:

'My Lasher, that's who you are, you are my avenger, my Lasher, come!'

THIRTY-SEVEN

Lasher sat silent with his hand flat on the table, his head bowed. Michael said nothing, but cautiously looked up at Clement Norgan, and then at Aaron, and at Erich Stolov. He could see the compassion in Aaron's face. Erich Stolov was amazed.

Lasher's face was very calm, almost serene. The tears were there again, these tears he wears like jewels, Michael thought, and Michael shuddered all over as if trying to break the spell of the being's beauty, of its soft even voice.

'I am yours, gentlemen,' said Lasher in the same gentle manner, gazing at Erich Stolov. 'I have come to you after all these centuries to ask for your help. You offered it to me once; you told me your purpose; I didn't believe you. And now, I find myself hunted and threatened again.'

Stolov glanced uneasily at Aaron and at Michael. Norgan watched Stolov as if for some cue.

'You've done right,' said Stolov. 'You've done wisely. And we're prepared to take you to Amsterdam. That is why we're here.'

'Oh no. You won't do this,' said Michael softly.

'Michael, what do you want of us?' demanded Stolov. 'You think we can stand by and let you destroy this creature?'

'Michael, you have heard my story,' said Lasher sadly, wiping at his tears again so like a child.

'Be assured no harm will come to you,' said Stolov. He turned to Michael. 'We're taking him with us. We're taking him out of your hands and out of any place where he can hurt you or any of your women. It will be as if he was never here . . .'

'No, wait,' said Lasher. 'Michael, you've listened to me,' he said, his voice heartbroken as before. He leant forward; his eyes were glazed and imploring. He looked for all the world like the Christ of Dürer.

'Michael, you cannot hurt me,' he said, his voice unsteady and filled with soft emotion. 'You cannot kill me! Am I to blame for what I am? Look into my eyes, you cannot do it. You know it.'

'You never learn, do you?' Michael whispered.

Aaron quickly tightened his grip on Michael's shoulder.

'There will be no killing,' Aaron said. 'We will take him with us. We'll go to Amsterdam. I shall go with Erich and with Norgan. And with him. I shall make absolutely certain that he is taken directly to the Mother-house and there placed . . .'

'No, you won't,' said Michael.

'Michael,' said Stolov, 'this is too big a mystery to be destroyed in an instant by one man.'

'No, it isn't,' said Michael.

'We have only begun to understand,' said Aaron. 'Dear God. Don't you realize what this means? Michael, come to your senses –'

'Yes, I do realize,' said Michael. 'And so did Rowan. Mystery be damned.' Michael glared at Stolov. 'This was always your goal, wasn't it? Not to watch and wait and collect knowledge, but just what the Dutchman told Lasher, to bring the Taltos together, to unite a male and a female and begin the breed again.'

Erich shook his head. 'We will let no harm come to anyone,' said Stolov, 'and above all, not to him. We want only to study, to learn.'

'Oh, you lie,' said Michael. 'All of you, and now you too, Aaron, are swept up in it. He has at last seduced even you.'

'Michael, look at me,' said Lasher in a half whisper. 'To take a human life requires the greatest will, the greatest vanity. But to take mine? Are you mad, that you would commit me again to the unknown, without examination, that you would undo the miracle! Oh no, you wouldn't do this. You are not so heedless. So cruel.'

'Why must you win me over?' asked Michael. 'Don't you rely on these other men to protect you?'

'Michael, you are my father. Help me. Come with us to Amsterdam.' He turned to Stolov. 'You have the woman, don't you? The female Taltos. In all my attempts, I failed. But you have it.'

Stolov said nothing, but held his gaze evenly.

'No, all that is fancy,' said Aaron. 'We have no female Taltos. We have no such secrets. But we will give you shelter, don't you see? We will provide a sanctuary in which you can be questioned, and write out the tale you've told us, and in which we will aid you in any way that we can.'

Lasher gave a small smile to Aaron, and again he glanced at Stolov. He took another careless swipe at his tears with his long graceful hand. Michael did not take his eyes off the creature.

'Aaron, they killed Dr Larkin,' said Michael. 'They

killed Dr Flanagan in San Francisco. They would destroy any obstacle. They want the Taltos, and it is as the Dutchman told Ashlar five hundred years ago! You've been their dupe and so have I. You knew it when we came into this room.'

'I can't believe it. I can't. Stolov, talk to me,' said Aaron. 'Norgan, go, call Yuri. Yuri is with Mona at the other house. Call there. He must come.'

Norgan didn't move. Slowly Stolov rose to his feet.

'Michael,' said Stolov, 'this will be difficult for you. You want vengeance, you want to destroy.'

'You're not taking him, friend,' Michael answered. 'Don't try it.'

'Be still. Wait for Yuri,' said Aaron.

'Why, so that I'll be further outnumbered? Have you forgotten the poem I gave you?'

'What poem?' asked Lasher, wide-eyed in his curiosity. 'You know a poem? Will you say the poem for me? I love poems. I love to hear them. Rowan said them so well.'

'I know a thousand poems,' said Michael. 'But you listen to this stanza and understand:

> Let the devil speak his story
> Let him rouse the angel's might
> Make the dead come back to witness
> Put the alchemist to flight!

'I don't know the meaning,' said Lasher innocently. 'What is the meaning? I cannot see it. There are not enough rhymes.'

Suddenly Lasher looked to the ceiling. So did Stolov, or rather he cocked his ear and stared off as if putting his sight on hold as he sought to track a sound.

It was that thin music, that old grinding thin music. Julien's gramophone.

Michael laughed. 'As if I needed it, as if I'd forgotten.'

He shot out of the chair, towards Lasher, who slipped back, just escaping his grasp. Lasher backed up behind Stolov and Norgan, who both scrambled to their feet.

'You can't let him kill me!' Lasher whispered. 'Father, you can't do it! No, it will not end for me again like this!'

'The hell it won't,' said Michael.

'Father, you are like the Protestants who would destroy forever the beautiful stained glass.'

'Tough luck!'

The creature bolted to the left and stopped dead, staring at the door to the pantry.

In the blink of an eye Michael had seen it too. The figure of Julien standing in the doorway, vivid, musing, gray-haired and blue-eyed, arms folded, barring the way.

But Lasher was already darting down the hallway as the other men struggled clumsily to follow his fleet and noiseless steps. Michael knocked Aaron backwards, out of his way, and went after them, shoving Stolov hard to one side and dealing a vicious blow to Norgan so that the man buckled and went down.

Lasher had come to a halt. The thing stood frozen, staring towards the front of the house. Again Michael saw it. The very same figure of Julien, framed within the giant keyhole front door. Still, smiling, arms folded as before.

As Michael lunged at Lasher, he danced to the side, and pivoted and ran up the stairs.

Michael was right behind him, chest heaving, his hands out, just missing the hem of Lasher's black cassock, the edge of his black leather shoe. He heard Stolov's shout close behind him; he felt Stolov's hand on his shoulder.

There at the top of the stairs, across the landing blocking the door to the rear of the house, stood Julien once more, and Lasher, seeing him, backed up, almost falling, then ran down the second-floor hall and thundered up the next flight of stairs to the third floor.

'Let me go!' Michael roared, shoving at Stolov.

'No, you are not going to kill him. You will not.'

Michael spun round, left arm rising in the proverbial hook, knuckles connecting with the man's chin and sending him out and over backwards down the entire length of the steep stairs.

For one second, he stared in horrible regret at the figure of Stolov, twisted, smashing to the floor.

But Lasher had reached a haven, the third-floor bedroom, and Michael could hear him sliding the bolt.

Rushing up after him, Michael slammed his fists against the door. He barged into it with his shoulder, once, twice, and then stood back and kicked hard against the wood, splintering it from the lock.

The music was playing thinly from the little gramophone. The window to the porch roof was open.

'No, Michael, for the love of God. No. Don't do this to me,' whispered Lasher. 'What have I done, but try to live?'

'You killed my child, that's what you did,' said Michael. 'You left my wife on the brink of death. You took the living flesh of my child and subjugated it to your will, your dark will, that's what you did. And you killed my wife, you destroyed her, like you destroyed her mother and her mother's mother and all those women, all the way back! Kill you! I will kill you with pleasure! For St Francis I will kill you. For St Michael. For the Blessed Virgin and for the Christ Child you so love!'

Michael's right fist drove into Lasher's face. Lasher caught the blow, staggering to the side and dancing around in a great circle suddenly, the blood pouring from his nose.

'God, no, don't do it. Don't do it.'

'You wanted to be flesh? Well, you are flesh and now you'll know what happens when flesh dies.'

'But I do know, God help me!' Lasher shouted.

As Michael came at him again, Lasher kicked Michael hard in the leg and with his own fist drove Michael back against the wall. The blow astonished Michael, coming as it had from the long slender limb which seemed so powerless, and which was obviously not.

Michael climbed to his feet. Dizzy. Pain again. No. Not yet. 'Damn you,' he said, 'damn you that you have the strength you do, but this time it will not be enough.'

He swung at the creature, but the creature dodged the blow, with another broad graceful bowing step. Again the white fist was clenched and smashing against Michael's jaw before he could duck or raise his right arm in defense.

'Michael, the hammer!' said Julien.

The hammer. On the sill of the open window. The hammer, with which he had searched the house that night, looking for the prowler, and finding only Julien in the dark! He dashed for it, grabbed it by the handle, turned it round, and, holding it with both hands, rushed at the creature and brought the claw end down into the thing's skull.

Through the hair, through the tender skin, through the fontanel, through the opening that had not closed, the iron claw sank. The creature's mouth formed a perfect oval of amazement. The blood exploded upwards as if from a fount. Lasher's hands flew up as if to stop the flood, then drew back as the blood gushed down into his eyes.

Michael wrenched the claw from the wound and brought it down hard again, deeper this time into the creature's brain. A man would have been finished, gone, no reason, but the thing only listed, drifted, staggered, the blood pouring from its head as if from a spout.

'Oh, God, help me!' Lasher cried, the blood flowing down in rivulets past his nostrils into his mouth. 'Oh, God in heaven, why? Why?' he wailed. The blood ran down his chin. Like Christ with the Crown of Thorns he bled.

Michael raised the hammer again.

Norgan appeared suddenly, flustered, red-faced, and then rushed at Michael, coming between him and Lasher. Michael brought the hammer down. The man died instantly as the hammer caved in his forehead and sank three inches through the bone.

Norgan fell forward, hanging from the hammer as Michael jerked it free.

Lasher seemed about to fall. He danced, listed, cried softly, the blood still flowing, mingled now with his sleek black hair. He gazed at the window. The window to the porch roof was open! A frail young woman stood there in the darkness, on the porch roof, the emerald glinting on a golden chain around her neck. She wore a flowered dress, short at her knees, her dark hair close to her face. She beckoned.

'Yes, I'm coming, my darling dear,' said the dazed Lasher, falling forward, and climbing up, and out over the windowsill onto the roof. 'My Antha, wait, don't fall.'

As he rose up to his full height again, he struggled to gain his balance. Michael climbed out on the tarred roof and sprang to his feet. The girl was gone. The night was high and full of the light of the moon. They stood three stories above the flags below. Michael swung the hammer one more time, one last fine blow that caught Lasher on the side of his head and sent him over the edge of the roof.

The body hurtled downward, no scream escaping from it, the head striking the flags with full force.

Michael at once climbed over the small railing. He jabbed the hammer into his belt, and, grabbing hold of the iron trellis with both hands, moved down it, half falling, half tumbling through the vines and the thick banana trees, and letting the stalks cushion him as he hit the earth below.

The thing lay on the garden path, a sprawling body of gangly arms and legs and flowing black hair. It was dead.

Its blue eyes stared up into the night sky, its mouth agape.

Michael went down on his knees beside it, and slammed the hammer down again and again on it, this time the hammer end, shattering and pounding the bones of the forehead, the bones of the cheeks, the bones of the jaw, again and again extricating the weapon from the blood and pulp only to strike once more.

At last there was nothing of the face left. The bones were cartilage, or something perhaps stronger. The thing was collapsed, and twisted and draining like something made from rubber or plastic. Blood seeped out of the battered casing of skin which had once been the face.

Nevertheless Michael hit it again. He brought the claw end down into the throat of the being, tearing it open. He did this again and again until the head was all but severed from the neck.

Finally he fell back against the base of the downstairs porch, sitting there, breathless, the bloody hammer in his hand. He felt the pain in his chest again, but he felt no fear with it. He stared at the dead body; he stared at the dark garden. He stared up at the light coming down from the dark sky. The bananas lay broken and torn under and over the being. Its black hair clung tenaciously to the shapeless bloody pelt of battered nose and broken teeth and bones.

Michael climbed to his feet. The pain in his chest was now large and hot and almost unbearable. He stepped over the body and up onto the soft green grass of the lawn. He walked out into the middle of it, his eyes ranging slowly over the dark façade of the house next door, in which not a single light glimmered, the windows shrouded with yew and banana and magnolia so that nothing could be seen. His eyes moved over the dark shrubbery along the front fence, to glimpse the deserted street beyond.

Nothing stirred in the yard. Nothing stirred in the house. Nothing moved out beyond the fence. There had been no witnesses. In the deep soft silence and shadows of the Garden District, death had been done again and no one had noticed; no one would come. No one would call.

What will you do now? He was shaking all over; his hands were slippery with sweat and with blood. His ankle ached. He'd torn the ligament coming down the trellis, or when he'd fallen the last few feet to the ground. Didn't matter. He could walk, he could move. He could wipe off the hammer. He looked to the back of the dark garden, past the glow of the blue swimming pool, and through the iron gates to the rear yard. He saw the great arms of Deirdre's oak reaching upward, crowding out the pale clouds.

'Under the oak,' he thought. 'When I catch my breath. When I . . . when I . . .' and he went down on the grass, on his knees, and collapsed to the side.

THIRTY-EIGHT

For a long time he lay there. He didn't sleep. The pain
came and went. Finally, he drew in his breath and it
didn't hurt so much. He sat up, and then the pain
started pounding in him, but it seemed small and contained within the chambers or the valves of his heart.
He did not know which. He did not care. He rose to his
feet, and walked to the flags.

The house lay in darkness, quiet, still as before. My
beloved Rowan. Aaron ... But he could not leave this
mangled body here.

It lay as he had left it, only it seemed more flattened
somehow, perhaps merely twisted. He didn't know. He
reached down and gathered up the torso in his arms. The
remains of the head broke loose from it, sticking to the
flagstones, the last bit of flesh tearing like chicken fat.

Well, he would come back for the head. He began to
carry the body, letting its feet drag on the ground, back
along the flagstone path and up and around the pool
and back towards the rear yard.

It was not hard for him after the killing. The body
didn't weigh that much, and he took things very slowly.
He did think once that the proper place to bury it was
really under the crape myrtle tree in front. That was
where he had first seen 'the man' staring at him, smiling,
when, as a boy, he had passed the fence.

But someone might see him from the street. No, the backyard was better. No one could witness the burial under Deirdre's oak. And then there were the other two bodies – Norgan and Stolov. He knew Stolov was dead. He'd known it when he saw him fall backwards. Michael had broken his neck. Norgan was dead. He'd seen that too.

Stolov was what had slowed Norgan, he figured, trying to resuscitate Stolov. Well, there was time to check on all that. Maybe it was really true what everybody said, that in the Mayfair family, you could kill people, and nobody did a thing.

The backyard was dark and damp, the banana trees already grown back from the Christmas freeze, and arching out along the high brick wall. He could scarcely see the roots of the oak for the darkness. He laid the body down and folded its arms over it. Like a big slender doll it looked, with its big feet and huge hands, all white like plastic and cold and still.

He went back to the flagstones beside the porch. He took off his sweater and then his shirt. He put back on the sweater, and then he picked up the head carefully by the hair. He was careful not to get blood on him; he had been spattered enough. He got most of the skin and shattered bone and blood up with the head, but then he had to reach for the remainder in a soft moist bloody handful. And the residue he wiped with his handkerchief and put that in his folded shirt too. A bundle. A bundle of the head.

He wished he had a jar suddenly. He could put it in the jar. But best it was buried. The house was dark and quiet. He couldn't take all night to do this. Rowan needed him. And Aaron, Aaron might even be hurt.

And those other two bodies ... all that to be done People would surely come soon. They always did.

He carried the head back with him to the foot of the oak. Then he closed and locked the iron gates to the rear yard, just in case one of the cousins came wandering about.

The shovel was in the back shed. He had never used it. The gardeners here did that sort of work. And now he was going to bury this body in the pitch dark.

The ground was sodden beneath the tree from all the spring rain, and it wasn't hard for him to dig a fairly deep grave. The roots gave him trouble. He had to go out from the base farther than he intended, but finally he had made a narrow uneven hole, nothing like the rectangular graves of horror films and modern funerals. And he slipped the body down into it. And then the blood-soaked bundle of shirt which contained the head. In the moist heat of the coming summer this thing would rot in no time at all. The rain had already begun.

Blessed rain. He looked down into the dark hole. He really couldn't see anything of the body but one limp white hand. It didn't look like a person's hand. Fingers too long. Knuckles too big. More like something of wax.

He looked up into the dark branches of the trees. The rain was coming all right, but only a few drops had broken through the thick canopy above.

The garden was cold and quiet, and empty. No lights in the back guest house. Not a sound from the neighbors beyond the wall.

Once again, he looked down into the crumbling shape-less grave. The hand was smaller, thinner. It seemed to have become less substantial, fingers tumbling together and fusing so they lost their distinct shape. Hardly a hand at all.

Something else gleamed in the dark – a tiny firefly of green light.

He dropped down to his knees. He slipped forward on the uneven edge of the hole, left hand pitched out to the other side of the grave to steady himself, as with his right, he reached down and groped for that green sparkling thing.

He almost lost his balance, then felt the hard edges of the emerald.

He yanked the chain loose from the bloody, tangled cloth. Up out of the darkness it came, nestled in the palm of his muddy hand.

'Got you!' he whispered, staring at it.

It had been around the creature's neck, inside his clothes.

He held it, turning it, letting the starlight find it, the jewel of jewels. No great emotion came to him. Nothing. Only a sad, grim satisfaction that he had the Mayfair emerald, that he had snatched it from oblivion, from the covert unmarked grave of the one who had finally lost.

Lost.

His vision was blurred. But then it was so divinely dark out here, and so still. He gathered up the gold chain the way you might a rosary, and shoved it – jewel and chain – into the pocket of his pants.

He closed his eyes. Again, he almost lost his balance, almost slipped into the grave. Then the garden appeared to him, glistening and dim. The hand was no longer visible down there at all. Perhaps the tumbling clods of earth had covered it as they must soon cover all the rest.

A sound came from somewhere. A gate closing perhaps. Someone in the house?

But he must hurry, no matter how weary he was and how sluggish and quiet he felt.

Hurry.

Slowly, for a quarter of an hour or more, he shoveled the moist earth into the hole.

Now the rain was whispering around him, lighting up the shiny leaves of the camellias, and the stones of the path.

He stood over the grave, leaning on the shovel. He said aloud the other verse of Julien's poem:

> Slay the flesh that is not human
> Trust to weapons crude and cruel
> For, dying on the verge of wisdom,
> Tortured souls may seek the light.

Then he slumped down beside the oak, and closed his eyes. The pain thudded in him, as if it had waited patiently and now it had its moment. He couldn't breathe for a minute, but then he rested, rested with all his limbs and his heart and his soul, and his breathing became regular, easy again.

He lay there sleeping perhaps, if one can sleep and know everything that one has done. There were dreams ready to come. Indeed it seemed, moment after moment, that he might veer and descend into the blessed darkness where others waited for him, so many others, to question him, to comfort him, to accuse him perhaps. Was the air filled with spirits? Did one but have to sleep to see them face to face, or hear their cries?

He did not know. Old images came back to him, bits and pieces of tales, other dreams. But he would not let himself slip. He would not let himself go all the way down . .

He slept the thin sleep in which he was safe, and in good company with the rain, the sigh of the weightless rain surrounding him but not touching him, in this his garden, beneath the high leafy roof of the mighty tree.

Suddenly he caught a picture of the ruined white body sleeping beneath him, if one could use for the dead a word as gentle as *sleep*.

The living slept as he had been sleeping. What became of the lately dead, or the long dead, or all those inevitably gone from the earth?

Pale, twisted, defeated once again, after centuries, buried without a marker –

He awoke with a start. He had almost cried out.

THIRTY-NINE

When he looked up, he saw through the iron fence that the main house was now full of light.

Lights were on all through the upstairs and downstairs. He thought perhaps he saw someone pass a doorway in the upper hall. Seemed it was Eugenia. Poor old soul. She must have heard it. Maybe she saw the bodies. Just a shadow behind the privacy lattice. He wasn't sure. They were much too far away for him to hear them.

He put the shovel back into the shed, just as the rain came down heavily and with the lovely smell that the rain always brings.

There was a crack of thunder, and one of those jagged rips of white lightning, and then the big drops began to splash on his head, his face, his hands.

He unlocked the gate and went to the faucet by the pool. He slipped off his sweater and washed his arms and his face and his chest. The pain was still there, like something biting him, and he noticed he had little feeling in his left hand. He could close it, however. He could grip. Then he looked back at the dark oak. He could make nothing out of the darkness beneath it, the deep dark of the entire yard now beneath the rainy sky.

The rain washed Lasher's blood from the flags where Lasher had died.

It fell hard and steady, washing them clean until nothing was left to mark the spot at all.

He stood there watching, getting soaked and wishing he could smoke a cigarette but knowing the rain would put it out. Through the dining room window, he could see a hazy image of Aaron still sitting at the table, as if he had never moved, and the tall dark figure of Yuri, standing about, almost idly. And then the figure of someone else he did not know.

All of them in the house. Well, it was bound to happen. Someone was bound to come. Beatrice, Mona, someone . . .

Only after all that blood was washed away did he walk over the spot, and go around to the front door of the house.

There were two police cars parked there, end to end, with their lights flashing, and a gathering of men, including Ryan and young Pierce at the gate. Mona was there in a sweatshirt and jeans. He felt like crying when he saw her.

My God, why don't they arrest me? he wondered. Why didn't they come out into the yard? God, how long have they been here? How long did it take me to dig the grave?

All this seemed vague in his mind.

He noted – there was no ambulance, but that didn't mean anything. Perhaps his wife had died upstairs, and they had already taken her away. Got to go to her, he thought, whatever happens, I'm not being dragged out of here until I kiss her good-bye.

He walked towards the front steps.

Ryan started speaking to him the moment he saw him.

'Michael, thank God you're back. Something really inexcusable happened. It was all a misunderstanding. Happened right after you left. And I promise you, it will not happen again.'

'What is that?' asked Michael.

Mona stared at him, her face impassive and undeniably beautiful in a lovely youthful way. Her eyes were so green. It was amazing to him. He thought about what Lasher had said – about jewels.

'A complete mixup with the guards and the nurses,' said Ryan. 'Everybody, unaccountably, went home. Even Henri was told to go home. Aaron was the only one here and he was asleep.'

Mona made a little negative gesture to him, and lifted one of her soft, babyfied little hands. Pretty Mona.

'Rowan is all right?' Michael asked. He could not now remember what Ryan had been saying, only that he'd known, by Ryan's manner, that Rowan wasn't dead.

'Yes, she's fine,' said Ryan. 'She was apparently alone in the house for a while, however, and the door was unlocked. Someone apparently told the guards they weren't needed anymore. Apparently it was a priest from the parish church, but we haven't been able to find the man. We will. Whatever, the nurses were actually told that Rowan was . . . was . . .'

'But Rowan's OK.'

'The point is nothing was disturbed. Eugenia was in her room the whole time too, lot of good it did. But nothing happened. Mona and Yuri came and they found the place deserted. They woke up Aaron. They called me.'

'I see,' said Michael.

'We didn't know where you were. Then Aaron remembered that you'd gone off for a long walk. I got here as soon as I could. No harm done as far as I can tell. Of course those people have been fired. These are all new people.'

'Yeah, I understand,' said Michael with a little nod.

They went up the steps and into the front hall. Everything looked as it should, the red carpet going up the stairway. The oriental rug before the door. A few natural scuff marks here and there as always on the waxed wood.

He looked at Mona, who was standing back away from her uncle. The jeans could not have been any tighter. In fact, the whole history of fashion might have been different in the twentieth century, Michael thought, if denim hadn't been such a tough fabric, if it hadn't had such a capacity to stretch to a woman's little hips like that.

'Nothing was disturbed,' said Ryan. 'Nothing was missing. We haven't searched the whole house yet but . . .'

'I'll do it,' said Michael. 'It's OK.'

'I've doubled the guards,' said Ryan, 'and doubled the shift of nurses. No one leaves this property without express permission of a member of the family. You have to be able to know you can take a walk and come back and Rowan is all right.'

'Yeah,' said Michael. 'I should go up and see Rowan.'

Rowan wore a fresh gown of white silk. It had long sleeves and narrow cuffs. She was as she had been when he left her – same gentle wondering expression, hands folded before her, on a fresh cover of embroidered linen with a lovely trimming of blue ribbon at the edge. The room smelled clean, and full of the scent of the blessed candles, and a huge vase of yellow flowers that stood on the table where the nurses were accustomed to write.

'Pretty flowers,' said Michael.

'Yes, Bea got them,' said Pierce. 'Whenever anything happens, Bea just gets flowers. But I don't think Rowan had the slightest inkling ever that anything was amiss.'

'No, no inkling,' said Michael.

Ryan continued to apologize, continued to aver that this would never happen again. Hamilton Mayfair stepped out of the shadows and gave a little nod of greeting and then vanished as softly and soundlessly as he had appeared.

Beatrice came into the room with a soft jingling noise, perhaps of bracelets, Michael didn't know. Michael felt her kiss before he saw her, and caught her jasmine perfume. It made him think of the garden in summer. Summer. That wasn't so very far away. The bedroom was shadowy as always with the candles and only one small lamp. Beatrice put her arms around him and held him tight.

'Oh, darling,' she said, 'you're soaking wet.'

Michael nodded. 'That's true.'

'Now don't be upset,' said Bea, scoldingly, 'everything turned out just fine. Mona and Yuri took care of everything. We were determined to have everything straightened out before you came back.'

'That was kind of you,' said Michael.

'You're exhausted,' said Mona. 'You need to rest.'

'Now, come, you must get out of these wet clothes,' said Beatrice. 'You're going to be chilled. Are your things in the front room?'

He nodded.

'I'll help you,' said Mona.

'Aaron. Where is Aaron?' asked Michael.

'Oh, he's just fine,' said Beatrice. She turned and flashed a brilliant smile at him. 'Don't you worry about Aaron. He's in the dining room having his tea. He snapped right into action when Mona and Yuri woke him up. He's fine. Just fine. Now I'm going downstairs to get you something hot to drink. Please let Mona help you. Get out of those clothes now.'

She cast a long look up and down at him, and he looked down and saw the dark splatters all over his sweater and pants. The clothes were so wet and so dark you couldn't tell the difference between the blood and the water. But when the clothes dried, you could.

Mona opened the door of the front bedroom and he followed her inside. There was the wedding bed with its white canopy. More flowers. Yellow roses. The draperies of the front windows were opened, and the street light shone in the wandering branches of the oaks. Like a treehouse, this bedroom, Michael thought.

Mona started to help him with his sweater. 'You know what? These clothes are so old, I'm going to do you a real favor. I'm going to burn them. Does this fireplace work?'

He nodded.

'What did you do with the bodies of the two men?'

'Shhh. Don't talk so loud,' she said with an immediate sense of immense drama. 'Yuri and I took care of that. Don't ask again.'

She pulled down his zipper.

'You know I killed it,' he said.

She nodded. 'Right. I wish I could have seen it. Just one time! You know, had a really good look at him!'

No, you didn't want to see it, and don't ever go looking for it, don't ever ask me where I disposed of it, or . . .'

She didn't answer him. Her face seemed still, determined, beyond his influence, beyond his tenderness or his concern. Her own unique mixture of innocence and knowledge baffled him as surely now as it had ever done. She seemed unmarked in her freshness, her beauty, yet deep within some dangerous chamber of her own thoughts.

'You feel cheated?' he whispered.

Still she didn't answer. She'd never looked so mature – so knowing, so much the woman. And so much the mystery – the simple mystery of another being, alien to us by simple nature and separateness – one among many whom we will never fully possess or know or comprehend.

He reached into his pocket. He held out the muddy emerald, and he heard her gasp before he looked up again and saw the amazement in her face.

'Take this away with you,' he said under his breath. 'This is yours now. Take it. And don't ever, ever turn around and look over your shoulder. Don't ever try to understand.'

Again, she was grave and silent, absorbing his words, but giving no hint of her own true response. Perhaps her expression was respectful; perhaps it was merely remote.

She closed her hand over the emerald as though to conceal it utterly. She pressed her closed hand into the bundle of his soiled clothes.

'Go bathe now,' she said calmly. 'Go rest. But first – the pants, and the socks and shoes. Let me get rid of them too.'

FORTY

The morning light woke him up. He was sitting in her room, by the bed, and she was staring at the light just as if she could see it. He didn't remember falling asleep.

Sometime during the night he had told her the whole story. Everything. He had told Lasher's story and how he'd killed Lasher and how he'd slammed the hammer right into the soft spot in the top of Lasher's head. He didn't even know if he'd been talking loud enough for her to hear. He thought so. He had told it in a monotone. He had thought, She would want to know. She would want to know that it's finished and what happened. She had told the man in the truck that she was coming home.

Then he'd fallen quiet. When he closed his eyes he heard Lasher's soft voice in his memory, talking of Italy and the beautiful sunshine, and the Baby Jesus; he wondered how much Rowan had known.

He wondered if Lasher's soul was up there, if it was true that St Ashlar would come again. Where would it be next time? At Donnelaith? Or here in this house? Impossible to know.

'I'll be dead and gone by then, that's for certain,' he said softly. 'It took him a century to come to Suzanne. But I don't think he's here any longer. I think he found the light. I think Julien found it. Maybe Julien helped him find it. Maybe Evelyn's words were true.'

He said the poem over to her softly, stopping before the last verse. Then he said it:

> Crush the babes who are not children
> Show no mercy to the pure
> Else shall Eden have no Springtime.
> Else shall our kind reign no more.

He waited a moment, then he said, 'I felt sorry for him. I felt the horror. I felt it. But I had to do what I did. I did it for the small reasons, if the love of one's wife and child can be called small. But there were the great reasons, and I knew the others wouldn't do it; I knew he would seduce and overcome all of them; he had to. That was the horror of it. He was pure.'

After that he'd fallen asleep. He thought he had dreamed of England, of snowy valleys and great cathedrals. He figured he would dream these dreams for some time. Maybe for always. It was raining right through the sunshine. Good thing.

'Honey, do you want me to sing to you?' he asked softly. Then he laughed. 'I only know about twenty-five old Irish songs.' But then he lost his nerve. Or maybe he thought about Lasher's face when Lasher had told about singing to the people, the big innocent blue eyes. He thought of the smooth black beard and the hair on the upper lip, and the great childlike vivacity in him, and the way he had sung *sotto voce* to show them what the melody had been.

Dead, I killed it. He shuddered all over! Morning. Don't worry. Get up.

Hamilton Mayfair had come into the room.

'Want some coffee? I'll sit with her for a while. She looks so . . . pretty this morning.'

'She always looks pretty,' said Michael. 'Thanks, I will go down for a while.'

He went out and down the steps.

The house was full of light, and the rain sparkled on the clear panes of the windows.

He could still smell the fire in the house, which Mona had made last night in the bedroom fireplace when she burnt his clothes.

It made him want to make a real big fire in the living room and drink his coffee there, with the sun and the fire to make him warm.

He crossed the parlor to the first fireplace, his favorite of the two, with its flowers carved in marble, and he sat down, folded his legs Indian style and leaned back against the stone. He hadn't the energy to make a cup of coffee, or to get the kindling and the wood. He didn't know who was in the house. He didn't know what he would do.

He closed his eyes. Dead, it's dead, you killed it. It's finished.

He heard the front door open and close, and Aaron came into the room. He didn't see Michael at first, and then when he did he gave a little start.

Aaron was freshly shaved, and wore a pale gray wool Norfolk jacket and a clean white shirt and tie. His thick white hair was beautifully combed, and his eyes were rested and clear.

'I know you'll never forgive me,' said Michael. 'But I had to do it. I had to. That's the only reason I was ever here.'

'Oh, there's no question of my forgiving you,' said Aaron in a deliberately comforting voice. 'Don't think

869

of this, not even for a moment. Put it out of your mind as though it were something harmful to you to think about. Put it away. It's just – I couldn't help you. I couldn't have done it myself.'

'Why? Was it the mystery of the thing or did you feel sorry for it, or was it love?'

Aaron pondered. He glanced about, to make certain perhaps that no one else was near. He came forward slowly, then sank down on the edge of the needlepoint chair.

'I honestly don't know,' he said, looking gravely at Michael. 'I couldn't have killed it.' His voice dropped so low Michael could scarcely hear him as he went on. 'I couldn't have done it.'

'And the Order? What about them?'

'I have no answers when it comes to the Order. I have messages – to call Amsterdam, to call London. To come back. I won't go. Yuri will find the answer. Yuri left this morning. It took wild horses to drag him from Mona, but he had to go. He has promised to call us both every night. He is so smitten with Mona that only this mission could distract him. But he has to seek an audience with the Elders. He is determined to discover what really happened, if Stolov and Norgan were sent to bring it back, and if so, were the Elders the ones who directed them in what they did.'

'And you? What do you think, or should I say suspect?'

'I honestly don't know. Sometimes I think I've spent my life being the dupe of others. I think they will come soon and I will die, just the way the two doctors did. And you mustn't do anything if that should happen. There is nothing you can do. At other times I don't believe the Order is anything but a group of old scholars, gathering information that others would destroy. I cannot believe it had an occult purpose! I cannot. I believe we will discover that Stolov and Norgan made the decision to breed the being. That when the medical information fell into their hands, they saw something they couldn't resist. Must have been rather like it was for Rowan. Seeing this medical miracle. Must have been what she felt when she took the being out of this house. "Scholars will but nourish evil. Scientists would raise it high."'

'Yes, perhaps so. They happened upon a dangerous and useful discovery. They broke faith with the others. They lied to the Elders. I don't know. I'm not part of it anymore. I'm outside. Whatever is discovered, it won't be made known to me.'

'But Yuri? Could they hurt him?'

Aaron gave a discouraged sigh.

'They've taken him back. Or so they say. He isn't afraid of them, that's certain. He has gone back to London to face them. I think he thinks he can care for himself.'

Michael thought of Yuri – of their brief acquaintance – not in terms of one picture, but many, and an overall impression of innocence and shrewdness and strength.

'I am not so worried,' said Aaron. 'Mainly because of Mona. He wants to come back to Mona. Therefore he'll be more careful. For her sake.'

Michael smiled and nodded. 'Makes sense.'

'I hope he finds the answer. It's his obsession now, the Order, the mystery of the Elders, the purpose. But then maybe Mona will save him. As Beatrice saved me. Strange, isn't it, the power of this family? The power that they possess that has nothing whatsoever to do with . . . him.'

'And Stolov and Norgan? Will someone come looking for them?'

'No. Put that out of your mind too. Yuri will take care of it. There is no evidence here of either man. No one will come looking, asking. You'll see.'

'You seem very resigned but you're not happy,' said Michael.

'Well, I think it's a bit early to be happy,' said Aaron softly. 'But I'm a damned sight happier than I was before.' He thought for a moment. 'I am not ready to sweep away all the beliefs of a lifetime because two men did evil things.'

'Lasher told you,' said Michael. 'He told you it was the purpose of the Order.'

'Ah, he did. But that was long long ago. That was in another time when men believed in things that they do not believe in now.'

'Yes, I suppose it was.'

Aaron sighed and gave a graceful shrug.

'Yuri will find out. Yuri will come back.'

'But you're not really afraid they'll hurt you, if they are the bad guys, I mean.'

'No,' said Aaron. 'I don't think they will bother. I do know them . . . somewhat . . . after all these years.'

Michael made no answer.

'And I know I am no longer a part of them,' Aaron continued, 'in any conceivable way. I know that this is my home. I know I am married and I will stay with Bea and this is my family. And perhaps . . . perhaps . . . as for the rest of it . . . the Talamasca, its secrets, its purposes . . . perhaps . . . I don't care. Perhaps I stopped caring on Christmas when Rowan lost the first round of her battle. Perhaps I ceased to care altogether and for certain when I saw Rowan on the stretcher, and her face blank, her mind gone. I don't care. And when I don't care about something, in an odd way, I can be as determined about it as about anything else.'

'Why didn't you call the police about Stolov and Norgan?'

Aaron seemed surprised. 'You know the answer,' he said. 'I owed you that much, don't you think? Let me give you some of my serenity. Besides, Mona and Yuri made the decision, really. I was a bit too dazed to take credit. We did the simpler thing. As a rule of thumb, always do the simpler thing.'

'The simpler thing.'

'Yes, what you did to Lasher. The simpler thing.'

Michael didn't answer.

'There is so much to be done,' said Aaron. 'The family doesn't realize that it is safe, but it soon will. There will be many subtle changes as people come to realize that it's finished. That the blinds are really open and the sun can really come in.'

'Yes.'

'We will get doctors for Rowan. We will get the best. Ah, I meant to bring a tape with me, the Canon by Pachelbel. Bea said Rowan loved it, that one day they had played it when Rowan was at Bea's. Bea's. I'm speaking of my own home.'

'Did you believe all he said – about the Taltos, about the legends and the little people?'

'Yes. And no.'

Aaron thought for a long moment, then he added:

'I want no more mysteries or puzzles.' He seemed

amazed at his own calm. 'I want only to be with my family. I want for Deirdre Mayfair to forgive me for not helping her; for Rowan Mayfair to forgive me for letting this happen to her. I want you to forgive me for letting you be hurt, for letting the burden of the killing fall upon you. And then I want, as they say, to forget.'

'The family won,' said Michael. 'Julien won.'

'You won,' said Aaron. 'And Mona has just begun her victories,' he said with a little smile. 'Quite a daughter you have in Mona. I think I'll walk uptown to see Mona. She says she is so in love with Yuri that if he doesn't call by midnight, she may go mad! Mad as Ophelia went mad. I have to see Vivian and visit with Ancient Evelyn. Would you like to come? It's a beautiful walk up the Avenue, just the right length, about ten blocks.'

'Not now. A little later perhaps. You go on.'

There was a pause.

'They want you up at Amelia Street,' said Aaron. 'Mona is hoping you will guide the restorations. The place hasn't been tampered with in many a year.'

'It's beautiful. I've seen it.'

'It needs you.'

'Sounds like something I can handle. You go on.'

The rain came again the next morning. Michael was sitting under the oak outside, near the freshly turned earth, merely looking at it, looking at the torn-up grass.

Ryan came out to talk to him, staying carefully to the path not to get mud on his shoes. Michael could see it was nothing urgent. Ryan looked rested. It was as if Ryan could sense that things were over. Ryan ought to know.

Ryan didn't even glance at the big patch of earth above the grave. It all looked like the moist and sparse earth around the roots of a big tree where grass would not grow.

'I have to tell you something,' said Michael.

He saw Ryan stop – a sudden revelation of weariness and fear – then catch up with himself and very slowly nod.

'There's no danger anymore,' Michael said. 'From anyone now. You can pull off the guards. One nurse in the evenings. That is all we require. Get rid of Henri too, if you would. Pension him off or something. Or send him up to Mona's place.'

Ryan said nothing, then he nodded again.

'I leave it to you, how you tell the others,' said Michael. 'But they should know. The danger's past. No more women will suffer. No more doctors will die. Not in connection with this. You may hear again from the Talamasca. If you do, you can send them to me. I don't want the women to go on being frightened. Nothing will happen. They are safe. As for those doctors who died, I know nothing that would help. Absolutely nothing at all.'

Ryan seemed about to ask a question, but then he thought better of it, obviously, and he nodded again.

'I'll take care of it,' Ryan said. 'You needn't worry about any of those things. I'll take care of the question of the doctors. And that is a very good suggestion, regarding Henri. I will send him uptown. Patrick will just have to put up with it. He's in no condition to argue, I suppose. I came out to see how you were. Now I know that you are all right.'

It was Michael's turn to nod. He gave a little smile.

*

After lunch, he sat again by Rowan's bed. He had sent the nurse away. He couldn't stand her presence any longer. He wanted to be here alone. And she had hinted heavily that she needed to visit her own sick mother at Touro Infirmary, and he said, 'Things are just fine around here. You go on. Come back at six o'clock.'

She'd been so grateful. He stood by the window watching her walk away. She lit a cigarette before she reached the corner, then hurried off to catch the car.

There was a tall young woman standing out there, gazing at the house, her hands on the fence. Reddish-golden hair, very long, kind of pretty. But she was like so many women now, bone-thin. Maybe one of the cousins, come to pay her respects. He hoped not. He moved away from the window. If she rang the bell, he wouldn't answer. It felt too good to be alone at last.

He went back to the chair and sat down.

The gun lay on the marble-top table, big and sort of ugly or beautiful, depending on how one feels about guns. They were no enemy to him. But he didn't like it there, because he had a vision of taking it and shooting himself with it, and then he stared at Rowan, and thought: 'No, not as long as you need me, honey, I won't. Not before something happens . . .' He stopped.

He wondered if she could sense anything, anything at all.

The doctor had said this morning she was stronger; but the vegetative state was unchanged.

They had given her the lipids. They had worked her arms and legs. They had put the lipstick on her. Yes, look at it, very pink, and they had brushed her hair.

And then there's Mona, he thought. 'Yuri or no Yuri, she needs me too. Oh, it's not really that she does,' he said aloud to the silence. 'It's that anything more would hurt her. It would hurt them all. I have to be here on St Patrick's Day, don't I? To greet them at the door. To shake their hands. I am the keeper of the house until such time as . . .'

He lay back against the chair thinking of Mona, whose kisses had been so chaste since Rowan came home. Beautiful little Mona. And that dark, clever Yuri. In love.

Maybe Mona was already working out the scheme for Mayfair Medical. Maybe she and Pierce were working on it now uptown.

'Now, we are not handing the family fortune over to this juvenile delinquent!' Randall had said in a booming voice last night, when arguing with Bea outside Rowan's door.

'Oh, do be quiet,' Bea had answered. 'That's ridiculous. It's like royalty, you old idiot. She is a symbol. That's all.'

He sat back, legs outstretched under the bedskirt, hands clasped on his chest, staring at the gun – staring at its silver-gray trigger, so inviting, and its fat gray cylinder full of cartridges, and the sheath of black synthetic closed over the barrel, oddly like a hangman's noose.

No, sometime later, perhaps, he thought. Although he didn't think he would ever do it that way. Maybe just drink something strong, something that crept through you and poisoned you slowly, and then crawl in bed beside her and hold onto her, and go to sleep with her in his arms.

When she dies, he thought. Yes. That's exactly what I'll do.

He had to remember to take the gun away and put it someplace safe. With all the children, you never knew what would happen. They had brought children to see Rowan this morning – and St Patrick's Day would draw the children, as well. Big parade on Magazine Street only two blocks away. Floats. People throwing potatoes and cabbages – all the makings of an Irish stew. The family loved it; they'd told him. He would love it too.

But move the gun. Do that. One of the children might see it.

Silence.

The rain falling. The house creaking as if it were populated when it was not. A door slamming somewhere as if in the wind. Maybe a door of a car outside, or the door of another house. Sound could play tricks on you like that.

Rain tapping on the granite windowsills, a sound peculiar to this octagonal and ornate room.

'I wish . . . I wish there was someone to whom I could . . . confess,' he said softly. 'The main thing for you to know is that you never have to worry anymore. It's finished, the way I think you wanted it finished. I just wish there was some kind of final absolution. It's strange. It was so bad when I failed at Christmas. And now somehow it's harder, that I've won. There are some battles you don't want to fight. And winning costs too much.'

Rowan's face remained unchanged.

'You want some music, darling?' he asked. 'You want to hear that old gramophone? I frankly find it a comforting sound. I don't think anybody else is listening to it now but you, and me. But I'd like to play it. Let me go get it.'

He stood up and bent down to kiss her. Her soft mouth gave no resistance. Taste of lipstick. High school. He smiled. Maybe the nurse had put on the lipstick. He could barely see it. She looked past him. She looked pale and beautiful and plain.

In the attic room, he found the gramophone. He gathered it up, along with the records of *La Traviata*. He stood still, holding this light burden, once again entranced by the simple combination of rain and sun.

The window was closed.

The floor was clean.

He thought of Julien again, the instantaneous Julien standing in the front doorway, blocking Lasher's path. 'And I haven't even thought of you since that moment,' he said. 'I guess I hope and pray you've gone on.'

The moments ticked by. He wondered if he could ever use this room again. He stared at the window, at the edge of the porch roof. He remembered that flashing glimmer of Antha gesturing for Lasher to come. 'Make the dead come back to witness,' he whispered. 'That you did.'

He walked down the steps slowly, stopping quite suddenly, in alarm, before he knew exactly why. What was this sound? He was holding the gramophone and the records, and now he set them carefully down and out of the way.

A woman was crying, or was it a child? It was a soft heartbroken crying. And it wasn't the nurse. She wouldn't be back for hours. No. And the crying came from Rowan's room.

He didn't dare to hope it was Rowan! He didn't dare, and he knew as well as he knew anything else that it wasn't Rowan's voice.

'Oh, darling dear,' said the crying voice. 'Darling dear, I love you so much. Yes, drink it, drink the milk, take it, oh, poor Mother, poor darling dear.'

His mind could find no explanation; it was empty and consumed with silent fear. He went down the steps, careful not to make a sound, and, turning, peered through the bedroom door.

A great tall girl sat on the side of the bed, a long willowy white thing, tall and thin as Lasher had been, with reddish-golden locks falling down her long graceful back. It was the girl he had glimpsed below in the street! In her arms the girl held Rowan, Rowan, who was sitting up and clinging to her, actually clinging to her, and nursing from the girl's bare right breast.

'That's it, dear Mother, drink it, yes,' said the girl, and the tears splattered right out of her big green eyes and down her cheeks. 'Yes, Mother, drink, oh, it hurts but drink it! It's our milk. Our strong milk.' And then the giant girl drew back and tossed her hair, and gave Rowan the left breast. Frantically, Rowan drank from it, her left hand rising, groping, as if to catch hold of the girl's head.

The girl saw him. Her tear-filled eyes opened wide. Just like Lasher's eyes, so big and wide! Her face was a perfect oval. Her mouth a cherub's mouth.

A muted sound came from Rowan, and then suddenly Rowan's back straightened, and her left hand caught the girl's hair tight. She drew back away from the breast and out of her mouth came a loud and terrible scream:

'Michael, Michael, Michael!'

Rowan shrank back against the headboard, drawing up her knees, and staring and pointing to the girl, who had leapt up and put her hands over her ears.

'Michael!'

The tall thin girl wept. Her face crumpled like that of a baby, her big green eyes squeezing shut. 'No, Mother, no.' Her long white spidery fingers covered her white forehead and her wet trembling mouth. 'Mother, no.'

'Michael, kill it!' screamed Rowan. 'Kill it. Michael, stop it.'

The girl fell back against the wall sobbing, 'Mother, Mother, no . . .'

'Kill it!' Rowan roared.

'I can't,' cried Michael. 'I can't kill it. For the love of God.'

'Then I will,' cried Rowan, and she reached out and picked up the gun from the night table, and, holding it in both her trembling hands, and blinking as she pulled the trigger, she shot three bullets into the girl's face. The room stank of smoke and burning.

The girl's face went to pieces. The blood welled from within as if through broken bits of china, a bleeding and shattered oval mask.

The long thin body slumped and fell heavily and noisily to the floor, the hair spreading out on the rug.

Rowan dropped the gun. She was sobbing now, sobbing as the girl had been, and her left hand was up to gag her sobs as she slipped from the bed, and stood shakily, reaching out for the post.

'Close the door,' she said in a rough, choking voice, her shoulders heaving. She seemed about to collapse.

Yet she stumbled forward, her entire body trembling with the effort, and then, beside the girl's body, she sank down on her knees.

'Oh, Emaleth, oh, baby, oh, little Emaleth,' she sobbed.

The girl lay dead, her arms out, her shirt open, face a soft mass of blood. Once again, the hair was all tangled in it, fine and beautiful, as Lasher's hair had been, and there was no face left. The long thin hands lay open like the thin delicate branches of a tree in winter, and the blood oozed down upon the floor.

'Oh, my baby, my poor darling,' said Rowan.

And then she closed her mouth again on the girl's breast.

The room was still. No sound but the sound of suckling. Rowan drank from the left breast and then moved to the other, sucking as ravenously as before.

Michael stared, speechless.

At last she sat back, wiping her mouth, and a low sad groan came from her, and another deep sob.

Michael knelt down beside her. Rowan was staring at the dead girl. Then she deliberately blinked her eyes as if trying to clear her vision. A tiny bit of milk remained on the girl's right nipple. She reached out and took it on her fingertip and put it to her lips.

The tears came down from her eyes, but then she looked deliberately at Michael, deliberately as if she wanted him to know that she knew. She knew everything that had happened, she was here now. She was Rowan. She was healed.

And suddenly, the tears spilling down ner face, she took his hands to try to comfort him, though her own hands were trembling and cold.

'Don't worry anymore, Michael,' she said. 'Don't worry. I'll take her out there under the tree. No one will ever think of it. I will do it. I'll put her with him. You've done enough, you leave my daughter to me.'

She sat back crying in a soft, raw muffled way. Her

eyes closed and her head slipped to the side. Fiercely she patted Michael's hands. 'Don't worry,' she said again. 'My darling, my baby, my Emaleth. I'll take her down. I'll put her in the earth myself.'

10 p.m.
August 5, 1992

Memnoch the Devil

Anne Rice

'Startling, fiendish, compelling'
New York Daily News

The Vampire Lestat – monster, outsider, hero-wanderer – is
snatched from this world to face his most extraordinary adver-
sary ever in Anne Rice's darkest and most daring novel to date.
His guide – Memnoch, the Devil, who takes him on a tour of
Creation and leads him into the mythical worlds we must all one
day confront – the very realms of Heaven and Hell.

'Lavish description, rapid narrative, gorgeous costume, and
larger-than-life heroes, al against the biggest concept of them
all: immortality'
Guardian

'Rice's most passionate and inventive work since *Interview with
the Vampire*, Memnoch has a half-maddened, fever-pitch
intensity and tells a tale as old as Scripture's legends and as
modern as today's religious strife'
Mikal Gilmore, *Rolling Stone*

'A modern Paradise Lost . . . an ambitious close to the series,
as well as a classy exit for a classic horror character'
Washington Post

arrow books

The Mummy

Anne Rice

Ramses the Great has reawakened in opulent Edwardian London. Having drunk the elixir of life, he is now Ramses the Damned, doomed forever to wander the earth, desperate to quell hungers that can never be satisfied. He becomes the close companion of a voluptuous heiress, Julie Stratford, but his cursed past again propels him towards disaster. He is tormented by searing memories of his last reawakening, at the behest of Cleopatra, his beloved queen of Egypt. And his intense longing for her, undiminished over the centuries, will force him to commit an act that will place everyone around him in the gravest danger . . .

'Rice succeeds masterfully in blending horror and romance . . . Ramses is a fascinating character, heroic, yet tragically flawed by his human desires'
Atlanta Journal

'Vintage Anne Rice: quickly paced, elegantly erotic and full of enchanting terror'
Detroit Free Press

'The reader is held captive, and, ultimately, seduced'
San Francisco Chronicle

arrow books

The Witching Hour

Anne Rice

On the verandah of a great New Orleans house, now faded, a mute and fragile woman sits rocking. And the witching hour begins . . .

Demonstrating once again her gift for spellbinding storytelling and the creation of legend, Anne Rice makes real for us a great dynasty of witches in this engrossing and hypnotic tale of the occult spanning four centuries – a family given to poetry and incest, to murder and philosophy, a family that over the ages is itself haunted by a powerful, dangerous, and seductive being.

'Compelling . . . Sensuous . . . Engrossing . . . Rich'
The Wall Street Journal

'Rice goes for the jugular with morbid delights, sexually charged passages and wicked, wild tragedy'
Publishers Weekly

'Vintage Rice . . . lush prose, dense atmosphere, steamy sex, gothic tension'
San Francisco Chronicle

arrow books